SYLVIANNA

KERYL RAIST

SYLVIANNA

Published by Keryl Raist
Copyright © Keryl Raist 2010
Cover art by Keryl Raist
Cover design by Keryl Raist

ISBN-13: 978-1456489021
ISBN-10: 145648902X

Printed in the United States of America

This is a work of fiction. Names, characters, places, incidents are products of the author's imagination or used fictitiously.

For more information visit: www.kerylraist.com

For Gail Giewont

A truly lovely friend who got me writing, read everything I asked her to, answered my grammar questions, and made suggestions that made this book immensely better.

Thank you.

Acknowledgements:

There is a group of people who very kindly offered their time and attention to this book: my beta readers. I'd like to thank Nick, Amy, Jill, Elise, and Karen for taking the time to read and give me commentary. The book is vastly better because of them.

A year before this book was published my computer died, taking with it fifty pages of the story. Fortunately my friends Joe and Jolauna were able to save it.

Dan, seeing my cover art needed a bit of refining, offered his time and Photoshop skills. He not only made my cover printable, he did it in less than half an hour!

When writing acknowledgement there is a tricky area, people who have added to your project and inspired it, but who probably don't want their names splashed about on it. If you're one of them, you know who you are.

To all of you, thank you so much for adding to my book.

I'd also like to thank my husband and children who have graciously tolerated, and intend to continue graciously tolerating, a woman who spends vastly too much time with imaginary people.

The Cast:

Chris Mettinger/Cellin Ath Dath Wa "Cell"
Former High Priest of Hidiri. Battle Mage.

Sarah Metz/Althiira Ut Cell Wa
Cell's wife. Healer.

Pat Calumn/Ahni Al Ath Gyr Bui
Cell's bodyguard. Battle Wizard.

Chuck Cuthart/Anthur Sud Dath Wa
Cell's half-brother. Telepath.

Dave Boyle/Dia Qul Cell Wa
Althiira's brother. Wizard.

Mike Tamont/Burq Ath Ben Burq
Cell's bodyguard. Sword Mage.

Autumn Rennier/Illynanthananthus "Illyn"
Fairy.

Allan Reeter
Sarah's landlord. Mage.

Eric Morrell
Sarah's Arabic Professor. Mage

Claire Morrell
Eric's wife. Witch.

Ben Metz
Sarah's oldest brother. Allan's friend. Mage.

The Presence
The God of Hidiri

Mildred/Mjur
Highest Angel of The Presence

Minions
Generic term for all of the lower angels of the Presence.

Prologue

1988

Allan Reeter critically eyed the edge of the black obsidian blade he was making. It was almost ready. Three, maybe four more flakes knapped off and it would be perfect. Seven months of painstaking work and three pounds of ruined obsidian had gotten him to this point.

He placed the deer antler against the blade and gave it a quick, sharp tap. A tiny flake of razor sharp stone hit the floor with a slight tink. He spent another moment looking at the blade, thinking of the balance it should have. Allan held it in his right hand and gave it an experimental swing. Not quite right yet.

He knapped off two more flakes and swung it again. It was right and perfect in his hands. He almost took his protective leather gloves off, but memories of the cuts from previous ungloved clean-ups convinced him that was a bad idea. He put the blade carefully on his desk and swept the shards from the floor. He straightened up and stretched. Allan took a moment to enjoy the peace in being finished.

His fingers ran lightly over the spine of the blade. Tomorrow, he'd start looking for a good piece of wood for the handle. Soon his athame would be finished.

Without warning, icy cold fear wrapped around his body while the sluggish, sick heat of magic settled in the pit of his stomach. His heart pounded, and his fingers clenched around the blade. He cast quickly, charging the blade with as much energy as he could pull on the fly. Turning to face whatever had invaded his home, he knew it had to be bad; nothing had gotten past his shields before.

The shock of seeing it left his hands limp at his sides. It was beautiful beyond anything he had ever imagined. It looked like a fantasy elf but with dragon-like wings. Compared to what was standing in his room a typical elf was gross and coarse. It was taller than the room should have been able to hold, with skin of the lightest milky blue he had ever seen. Its hair and wings were the color of the dawn before the thunderclouds blotted it from the sky. It faced him, and the sorrow it projected knocked Allan to his knees.

Allan watched, unable to move or make a sound, as it slid through the wall into his sister's room.

Her screams jerked him off the floor. He ran into her room and saw April on the floor, eyes closed, fingers clutching at her head, screaming. The winged elf, *an angel* he knew with a sudden flash of insight, stood in the middle of the room, wings spread, head thrown back, arms wide, sorrow and pain radiating off of it palpably. Allan felt sick. He knew he was fighting way out of his weight class.

Allan stood over his sister, trying to protect her. He swung at the angel with his blade. It whispered through without making contact. Allan tried to force it to leave, calling the magic, forming it into a wall, and trying to push the angel out of April's room. The wall went through it. The angel didn't even seem to notice he was in the room. It finished whatever it was doing to April and looked down at him, filling him with such horrendous sorrow that it was all he could do to keep standing. Then it vanished.

He knelt beside April, trying to calm her, doing anything he could think of to stop the screaming. He called for Ben with his mind. In a few minutes Ben was there with him, holding April, touching her face, speaking to her soothingly, bending the magic around him, forcing the energies to calm her, but it wasn't helping. Her screaming didn't stop.

Ben looked up at him, panic in his dark brown eyes. "Call 9-1-1. I can't fix this."

Allan ran to the phone in the living room and dialed the numbers.

The Student Union coffee shop was dim and quiet. Five minutes earlier Jennifer had hustled the last of the kids out, flipped the sign from "Open" to "Closed," and turned off most of the lights. Unlike her normal closing shift, she wasn't counting out the register. Tonight she made another pot of coffee, waiting for her friends to join her. She didn't hear them enter, John could open any door without making a sound, but she did feel the energy in the room change.

"I'll have this ready in a minute. Grab some munchies and get settled," she called over her shoulder to the five others.

They did. Very quietly. That didn't bode well. They usually chattered like magpies when together. If they were that silent, the visit to April must have been very bad. Ben came over, wrapped his arms around her, and kissed her on the neck. For a moment Ben just held her, his face pressed against her shoulder, taking comfort from her presence.

He whispered quietly, "You're so lucky you didn't have to go."

Jennifer wrapped her hand around the back of his neck, gave him a gentle squeeze, and a little boost of comfort. "Is she still screaming?"

"No, she's burned out her voice. She just lays there writhing, mouth open, no sound. It's..." He closed his eyes, and she felt his defeat. "It's nothing I ever want to see again," he said very quietly without looking at her.

"Can you help her?" Jennifer turned and cupped his face in her hand; the tips of her fingers just brushed his short black hair.

For a long time Ben didn't answer. Then he quietly said, "No, I can't help her. I'm not even sure she's still there to help." Jennifer gave him a look that said she knew he wasn't telling her everything, but she wasn't going to push it. He kissed her: quiet thanks for the reprieve.

"How's Allan?" Jennifer looked at the young man with the long brown hair, untidy brown beard, and soft brown eyes. He was fiddling with a muffin but not eating it. The black circles under his eyes told the world he hadn't slept in a long time, and the way his clothing fit said he had lost a good deal of weight recently.

"If they can't do something for her soon, I think he's going to break."

"Have they tried sedating her?"

"Yes, so far the dosage hasn't been high enough. They're talking about Thorazine soon. If that doesn't work, they're going to put her in a coma." The last drop of coffee plunked into the pot. Jennifer picked it up. She and Ben slid into the booth the four others had claimed. They helped themselves to coffee.

With all six of them settled, Robert said, "If we can figure out a way to stop those things from coming here, and if we can destroy the ones that are here, then Allan's sister might get better.

"So, here's what we know: They come here from some place in the ravine. The eyeless things just sort of sit there and watch the kids who went loopy last semester. We know they're watching Hank especially closely these last few days. They probably send the information back to the Angel. Then the Angel does something and causes immense pain. So, we know who the targets are. We know where the Angel comes from. What's the plan for taking care of it?"

"The total absence of plan is the problem," Allan said grimly.

Cindy reached for her coffee and sipped it. "I'd been thinking about that. From what we can tell there's a doorway. Things from the other side keep jumping out. So, we can either find a way to close the door, stitch it shut like a hole in a pair of jeans maybe, or we can shut off the magic that's powering it and hope it collapses. Once that's done, we can deal with whatever's still on this side of the door. It's easier to clean up a mess once you've stopped making it." Cindy set down her coffee cup and began to weave strands of her long red hair between her fingers.

Allan looked down at his fist, peering into the depths of the small obsidian bear he always carried with him. "We need to figure out how to deal with the door before we go in guns blazing and end up dead."

No one said anything. Of course, dead was a concept they had all bandied about before. Among other things they were all convinced thirty wasn't ever going to be an age they'd face, but, with the visit to April fresh in their minds, this was the first time death meant more than a vaguely romantic end to young adult drama.

Cindy laid her hand on Allan's. An outsider would have just seen an affectionate caress. The others at the table felt the quick energy boost she gave him. "No one's going to end up dead, Allan. We'll shut it. And we'll kill those things. And your sister will get better. The plan will work."

"Other than we don't have a plan yet," Ben added.

John usually didn't say much. Usually he listened and slowly nursed a cup of coffee, so when he spoke, everyone listened carefully. John put his cup down and pushed his shaggy blonde hair back from his forehead. "We don't know how to seal it, and the last time we went to visit it we were attacked. I say two of us go back. Allan and Jen, you've got the best cloaking, so you'll go and do recon. See if you can figure out a way to close the door. Cindy, you're our best fighter, so I'm thinking you need to go and take out one of the eyeless things. Figure out a way to hurt it or at least make it go away. Once you three have done that, we'll get back together and start on a plan."

Three days later Jennifer, John, Cindy, and Robert stood in the parking lot at the base of the ravine where the eyeless things and the Angel had emerged. The last minute prep was done. Their magical tools were bright. Their shields were in place. All they had to do now was walk into the ravine.

They stood there, silent and tense, until Jennifer said, "The last stand of the Knights of the Naugahyde Table." She tried to laugh, but it was too close to what they were secretly dreading to work as a joke. They'd been feeling uneasy about this for two days now. When it came down to it, the plan really wasn't all that great, but yesterday Hank started screaming. That spurred them into moving faster than they would have otherwise.

"Let's hope not." Cindy stepped into the ravine, toward the oozing rip in the universe they had so euphemistically named "the Doorway." She looked over her shoulder at the other three. "Come on. Let's get this done before the Angel hops out again and drives someone else insane."

Robert exhaled quickly, flicked his cigarette to the ground, and joined the two girls. John took a deep breath and focused on the ley line that ran closest to the ravine. "I'm ready."

If all went according to plan, John would reverse the flow of that line for as long as he could hold it, two or three minutes at most. Jennifer would wait until she felt the flow change and then block all magical energy from the area. The idea was that a dead zone in the local magic would cause the Doorway to collapse.

Allan and Jennifer scouted the Doorway three times in the last two days. All three times they had been attacked. Dealing with attackers was Cindy and Robert's job. They had to keep Jennifer safe long enough to let her kill the magic.

That everything would go according to plan and work was beyond a long shot. But yesterday, Hank started screaming. Within hours of that the eyeless things started following a girl named Katherine. Maybe, if they pulled this off now, Katherine wouldn't end up screaming.

Six hours later Ben had had enough. His coffee was cold. He had been reading the same page of the same textbook for the last hour. If it had worked, they should have felt it. If it had worked, the others would have been back hours ago. Even if it had failed horribly, they should have been back hours ago.

"Let's go." Ben slammed his textbook shut.

"John told us to stay here. They'd come back to us," Allan said between shaky drags on his eighth cigarette of the hour.

"I don't care. This late? They're in trouble. Either they need us to get them out or come up with a Plan B for dealing with this. We won't know which until we get there."

"One more hour."

"You're afraid."

"Of course I'm afraid!" Allan was jittery, pacing around the room, his voice and panic rising with each word. "I saw it. None of the rest of you did. None of you felt—"

"I know Allan," Ben cut in. One of Ben's skills was the ability to calm with his voice. He used it here. "But it's not going to get better in an hour. They need us. I can feel it."

"Fuck." Allan sounded wearier than any human possibly could. "I can, too." He ground out his cigarette. "Give me a minute to gear up. Do you have your stuff with you?"

"My rod and my staff shall comfort me." Ben caressed the Star of David his father had given him and the ring that matched the one he had given Jennifer. He wore them on a leather thong around his neck. "I'm ready. What do you want to get?"

"The blade."

"That thing gives me the creeps."

"It should. It's not your flavor of magic. I'll be back in a minute." Allan left. While waiting for Allan, Ben prayed. He had been doing it on and off all night. This time he changed it from "Keep my friends safe." to "Protect me."

Allan returned. Ben thought he looked scarier, harder, and more sharply edged when he carried the blade. When he asked about it, Allan told him he was taking on the qualities of the obsidian he carried. For all Ben knew that could be true, or it could be with the blade Allan was harder and more dangerous. What Ben did know was since April started screaming Allan had spent hours, days probably, making sure that blade carried enough magic to destroy anything it attacked. Allan wasn't usually a fighter, but if he had to fight again, he'd hurt whatever he went up against.

The ravine was a tense six-minute walk. Ben's heart stopped when he saw John crumpled in a heap at the foot of it. He knelt beside John, relief washing over him when he felt John breathe. A quick check showed him John was very cold, his heart was beating too fast, and his skin looked cadaverous.

"Leave him here and look for the others?" Allan asked the question Ben had been debating in his own mind.

"Yes." Ben laid his hands on John and worked his magic. John's breathing and heart rate slowed to normal; he began to warm up. "Can you make him invisible?"

"No, but I can make sure nothing looks in this direction."

"Good enough." Ben stood up. "I don't want to leave him here too long. Let's find the others and get out of here."

They stood in front of the ravine for another minute. The night was fairly bright. Between the moon and the streetlights it wasn't hard to see, but the ravine with its high rocky walls and large trees was inky black. Ben had the silly notion that even the light was afraid to go in.

"What if something happens to us in there?" Ben asked.

"The spell will break, and someone will find him eventually. If John's really sharp, he'll say he drank too much and passed out on the way home."

Ben took the first step. Allan followed. Seven minutes of stumbling through the rocks and underbrush brought them to where the Doorway should have been.

"Fuck," Allan said reverently.

"Yeah," Ben agreed.

The Doorway was gone.

So was everything else. Cindy, Jennifer, and Robert were gone. The plants were gone. Under their feet was a circle about twenty feet wide with nothing alive. Even the trees, some of which had been twenty feet tall and more than eight inches around, were gone. The magic was gone, and it had taken every trace of life with it.

Allan and Ben looked at each other, turned around, and went back to John.

The big news story that summer was the hunt for three missing college students who vanished without a trace right before finals. They were never found.

1.

August 23, 2008 Sylvianna College

My new landlord, Allan, opened the door to my apartment and handed me the keys. I looked around. It was precisely what I was expecting from the pictures he had sent me. Three rooms: a kitchen-living room hybrid, bedroom, and bathroom, all painted a bland beige. The apartment was boring, but right on campus, and had plenty of space for one person. Best of all, it had a washing machine and a dishwasher. Everything I wanted in an apartment for the price I was willing to pay.

I looked around for a moment. Nothing jumped out as being a problem. "Can I paint?"

"Sure. As long as it's this color or something similar when you leave."

"No problem."

"If you need anything, Sarah, I'm usually around." He watched me like he expected something. It made me slightly uncomfortable. For a moment I was thinking that possibly sharing a house with my landlord, let alone signing up for all four years, may leave something to be desired. But the price really was too good to pass up, and he looked so meek and almost beaten down it was hard to imagine he'd be any sort of a problem beyond creepy stalker guy. When it came down to it, I had ways of dealing with creepy stalker guys.

"Okay." Allan turned and left when I said that. I headed down the stairs to my motorcycle and grabbed my backpack and saddle bags. Unpacking took a minute. Nothing more to do until my furniture showed up tomorrow.

I rolled my towel into a pillow and lay down on the floor. I'd had a low-grade headache since I stepped into the house and some rest would help. I love my bike, but eight hours on it left me feeling a little tight and sore. After an hour of rest took the edge off the headache, it was time for a grocery run.

A full night of sleep left me feeling ready to explore. Morning meant jogging time. I'm not a huge fan of jogging. I am a huge fan of eating pretty much anything I want and not turning into a pudgy mess. So I run, for at least an hour, every morning but Saturday. It was good jogging weather, cool and not very bright yet. The sun hadn't made it past the tree line.

I grabbed my camera before heading out; my brothers want shots of my new world. They've seen it before since Ben went to school here twenty years ago, but, they want pictures, so I will take pictures and send them on.

An hour of running introduced me to a place that could have been called Generic College Town, USA. It was old and a little shabby. Most of the houses were Victorian looking rentals for students that hadn't been kept up all that well. I was on my way back down the hill, looking forward to a shower when I saw something… someone, who caught my eye.

I found myself staring at the red house two doors up from mine. A car, stuffed with boxes, was in the driveway. Through the open front door, I caught a glimpse of a guy about my age with impossibly red hair carrying something up the stairs.

He saw me as well and smiled. I waved. Something about him tugged at my mind, but I couldn't place it. He probably just looked like someone I knew. But I didn't think I'd ever seen that shade of red hair before. It probably looked black if the light was bad, but in the morning sun it was polished rosewood or charred brick. *Charred brick.* I liked that. Blackened with cracks of red showing through. *Are you done yet? It's just hair. Really nice hair—Stop it!*

Up my stairs. It was time to grab a quick shower and scrounge up some breakfast. That done, all I needed was something to fill the hours between now and when my furniture was supposed to show up.

Checking out the sculpture garden across the street sounded like a good plan. One hundred and fifty years of art projects called the four acres of rolling lawn across the street from my apartment home. Some of the statues were old, classically styled humans carved in exquisite detail out of marble or granite. Some were so modern I couldn't begin to guess what they were supposed to be. One called to me. It was directly across the street from my house. I saw it yesterday, but it hadn't caught my attention as anything more than a piece of the background then.

Now I stared at it. I couldn't tell if it was deliberately made the way it was, or if time and weather were wearing away at it. It was vaguely human, kneeling on one knee. The rough, tan clay of its body was melting away from its frame of wooden bones. A sharp stick jutted out where its shoulder should have been. One elbow sat on its bent knee, and its head rested against a melted mass of clay with five sticks where fingers would have been. A small plaque at the base said it was called "Secrets" and had been made by John Chalmers in 1987.

I felt compelled to touch it. I rested my hand on its arm and quickly jerked away. It was cold. Much too cold for something that had been sitting in direct sunlight all summer long. I touched it again, not believing it could have been that cold. It was. I looked around, trying to find why it would be so cold. Nothing logical jumped out at me. I didn't want to think too hard about the illogical answer I had. I touched one of the sculptures near it. It was just as warm as I thought it should be.

I looked back at "Secrets." It was made of clay. Everything else here was stone or metal. Maybe clay holds cold longer? Ceramic is supposed to have a really high melting point; it's used for heat insulation. Maybe that was it. It just doesn't warm up as fast as stone does. It must be holding the cool of the night longer than everything else. I didn't really like that answer, but it was the best I was going to come up with. The best of what I was willing to let myself believe.

I studied it further and decided it had been made the way it was. The one shoulder and the fingers were the only parts of the skeleton exposed. That wouldn't happen if weather was the culprit. My fingers were inches from the skeleton when I decided not to touch it. I didn't want to know if the wood was impossibly cold, too.

From the front I could see it had no face. Some extra clay about where a nose should go could have been a nose—or it could have been a bit of extra clay. It was the most accidental-looking human form I had ever seen.

I laid my hand on it again and once more marveled at how cold it was.

I bet you could move. I shook my head. Where did that come from? Statues don't move. This one would break if it tried. This one would break if anyone tried to move it.

I walked away to look at more of the other sculptures, but every few minutes I'd find myself looking back at "Secrets." More and more the idea that it could move kept nagging at me. Then I laughed. It was a golem, the man made of clay by the rabbis for the protection of the village. *That's why you think it can move. That's why it keeps attracting your attention. Silly subconscious.*

Once more I looked at it, and once again it seemed as if it could move. I snorted with laughter. The stories we're told as children don't let go of us, even as adults. Still, I liked the idea of a protector right outside my door. I went back to my house. My furniture would be here soon.

The moving truck pulled up, blocking my view of the redhead in the sculpture garden. He'd wandered out there while I was taking pictures of my apartment. I snapped a shot of him and my golem. He had been hovering around it. I wondered if he felt the same sense of attraction when he looked at it. I was ready to go over and introduce myself when the truck pulled up.

I could hear the delivery guy knock on Allan's door.

"Sarah Metz?"

"Her stairs are on the right."

"Great."

I opened the door and poked my head out. "Hello." It didn't take them too long to lug my stuff up the steps. I don't have a lot of furniture. I also don't have a lot of apartment, so it works pretty well.

By the time the hour was over they had everything up the stairs. I signed the papers, and off they went. Two hours later, I had my bed back together, clothing actually in my dresser, and my desk in the corner of my bedroom. That was enough for one bit of unpacking. I took a few more photos and decided to go in search of some WiFi. I wasn't precisely counting the hours until I could get set up with Sylvianna's network, but I was looking forward to it.

There are very few feelings in this world as good as stomping on the accelerator of a motorcycle and taking off in a rush of sound and air. Unfortunately that was not what I was doing at this moment. I was tooling slowly and gently down Alden Street. It's steep and made of brick. I wasn't about to go tearing off on it until I had a better feel for riding on it. No need to start my college experience with a broken arm or leg and a tour of Reevesville's hospital.

Half a mile of brick got me to Main Street. Once my tires touched the blacktop, I hit the throttle and took off. There's a Zen state that goes with the air, speed, and vibrations of a well-tuned motor. I love it.

Sylvianna whizzed by in a blur of trees, grass, and red brick buildings. At slower speeds it was a graceful old campus filled with colonial red brick buildings covered in ivy and rolling green lawns, nestled amid the forests it was named for.

Two minutes got me into Reevesville proper. It had seen better days. Like 1910—that had probably been a good year for Reevesville. This year hadn't been a great one. In better times, the downtown could have come right out of a Norman Rockwell painting. Now about a fifth of the buildings were empty, and many of the ones that still had businesses in them looked like they were hanging on by their fingernails.

Further down the street, I found one sort of business in Reevesville was thriving: junk food. Here the search for WiFi ended. Starbucks or McDonalds? Coffee I didn't like, or food I wouldn't eat? *Ahh, the choices.* Starbucks won out. At least it's kosher, or close enough I'm willing to let it slip. I ordered whatever it is they call a chocolate milkshake and got online.

I uploaded my photos and looked through them. My eyes lingered on the photo of the redhead standing next to the Golem, his hand on its shoulder. Familiarity tugged at my mind again, but I couldn't place him.

I checked my email: one from Ben, my oldest brother, one from Ari, my man. I'd read them after I got done writing.

Hello Loves,

Sorry about the mass email here. I've only got an hour online. I'll write more on Sunday when I get set up at school.

So, I am here! My furniture came today. The incredible den of beigeness in the first two photos is my apartment. I will probably paint.

The next shot is across the street. Yes, I live across from the Nelson Art Building; those statues are 150 years of art projects. I don't know who the guy is in the photo, but I've dubbed the statue he's standing next to "The Golem." See Ari, I've already got a protector in place!

The shots after that are various campus photos. The huge horribly out of place building of glass and concrete is where I'll be spending a whole lot of my time. That's Jones, the Applied Science Building. They built it in '91. Just after you graduated, right Ben?

The huge granite castle-looking thing is actually the gym. Supposedly they have fencing as a class. I'm thinking that'll be fun.

The gray Victorian house in the last shot is mine. It's in better shape than a lot of the other houses around here. Allan, my landlord, lives below me, so maybe he likes a house that looks good. Go up those stairs on the right and you'll be in the den of all that is beige. I really need to paint!

I am off in search of real food now. So far I have found no meat! Please, Ben, send me some goodies from home. Vegetarianism doesn't agree with me.

Sam, David, kiss the kiddies for me.

Ari, I can stay up late tomorrow if you've got time for a call.

Love you all,

Real letters soon,

Sarah

I hit send and read the emails from Ben and Ari. Ben's was mostly just stuff about the farm and wanting to know if I had gotten settled yet. He's a little apprehensive about me being here. Which is weird because he was more relaxed about me enlisting in the Israeli Defense Force than he was about me coming here, but he won't tell me why. He just says be careful. So, I'll be careful. But really, compared to the Negev, I'm not expecting any trouble here.

Ari's letter was a sweet little thing. About two thirds what was going on in Tel Aviv and another third telling me about how much he wanted to see me. *I miss you, too.* I really hoped he'd be able to swing a call tomorrow night. Emails are fine, but I want his voice. Moments like this make me think maybe coming back to the US wasn't a great idea. There are universities in Israel. It's not like I had to come back here. *You wanted to be independent, remember?*

Enough of that. I logged out before they kicked me off. Time to go see if I could find some kosher meat. I'd been to Walmart yesterday. They didn't have what I wanted. Maybe the local grocery store would bear fruit, but I wasn't wildly hopeful. A three-minute ride past more fast food joints and Victorian looking homes ranging from decrepit to nearly well kept got me there.

Hurford's: old sign, small parking lot, and an air of pervasive shabbiness. There was nothing encouraging about the place. My skin broke out in goose bumps as I walked in, and between shivers my head started to ache. The AC had to be set at fifty-five. It was ridiculously cold in there. The lights washed the color out of everything, a layer of subtle grime covered the shelves, and the people shuffled around like the cast of a zombie movie. I left without buying anything. *The Grocery Store of the Damned.* I wasn't going back there, not if I had any choice about it.

Back to Walmart for more food.

I was halfway home, saddlebags full of groceries, when a building made electric fear course through me. I stopped and stared at it. It may have been someone's idea of what a

Georgian building should look like, on a distortedly large scale. If a building could loom, it loomed with menace. It should have been pretty. The red brick walls, white granite steps, and gracious trees in front were all lovely by themselves. But combined they looked grim.

My eyes kept darting to the roof. Nothing was there, but the little voice I spent two years honing kept calling danger. The last time I felt like this I was crouching with way too little cover bandaging up one of my girls while a sniper I couldn't see took shots at us. I scanned the building. Finally, my eyes found a tiny sign on the front. Reevesville Junior High School, 1893. I shuddered again. Junior high was bad enough. Junior high here would be pure torment.

I gunned the cycle and returned home. I wanted to get away from that building.

Home meant more unpacking, and unpacking made me very happy I'd signed up for all four years with this apartment. Not having to do this again anytime soon was a pleasure. By dinnertime, I had my home set up. The apartment looked more like a home and less like the Den of Beige. I still needed some more pillows before the window seat in the living room/kitchen space would be properly comfortable, and a few more blankets would probably come in handy.

I flopped onto my sofa with a book and looked around. I was home. In a few days it would be time to start my new life as Sarah Metz, Sylvianna student.

2.

Chris Mettinger hated moving. The fact he hadn't been able to avoid it bothered him even more than moving did. Apparently there are some things magic, personal charm, and reason cannot shift, one of which was the policy stating students had to move all of their property off campus within twenty-four hours of their last final. So, even though he was living in the same room of the same house as he had last spring, he was once again lugging his stuff up the narrow stairs of the Writers' House.

On the upside, magic made the boxes easier to lift and gave him enough energy to get up and down the stairs very quickly. Personal charm allowed him to talk other people into helping him move those boxes; his brother, Tom, was putting one in his room that instant. Reason won him the use of his mom's car though she preferred he take the bus and ship his things to him.

Magic had other values. He had just stepped into the house when he felt her energy coming near him. Joy and fear raced through him. *She's back! No. Can't be her. It just feels like her. Another healer. That has to be it.* He felt her getting closer and wanted to see who she was. A smallish girl with short black hair and light skin jogged past him. She saw him, smiled, and waved. In and out of his view in less than three seconds.

Chris hurried up the stairs. He wanted to get done unpacking so he could send his message to the others unseen. Tom would want to know what was so urgent he had to text about it right that second, and that was one thing, among many, Tom didn't need to know about.

He and Tom got the car unpacked in record time. He was, yet again, setting up his room when he saw her through the window. She wandered about the sculpture garden across the street. Tom saw him gazing out the window and looked out as well.

"She's cute."

"Yes."

"Going to go talk to her?"

"Not today."

"It would be a shame if you lost her because you didn't move now."

"Tom, there's less than two thousand students here. I'll find her again." Tom looked remarkably unimpressed by his lack of action. But Tom would go out of his way to flirt with anything that moved and probably a few things that didn't.

"If you say so. We get everything out of the car?"

"Yes."

"Then I need to get going." They hugged briefly. "I'll see you at Thanksgiving?" Tom asked.

"Don't see any reason why not."

He walked his brother back to the car and waved as Tom pulled out. Chris texted as he went back into the house. In less than a minute he told Autumn, Mike, and Dave, his housemates, he had found a healer. He looked out the window at her again. She was doing something with one of the statues. She touched it and moved away but kept looking back at it. Obviously something about it attracted her attention.

You could go and say 'Hi.' You could ask her what she sees. You could see if she feels as much like Althiira up close as she did far away. Then it was too late. While he had been thinking about it, she walked out of his view.

He got back to getting his room in order. A minute into that, his cell phone buzzed. He read the text quickly.

??? From Autumn.

She was walking around the statues a minute ago. He texted back to her.

Are you sure? Came from Mike a minute later.

Yes.

His phone buzzed again. Did the shields hold? Dave asked. Trust Dave to ask the practical question. Granted, Dave's talent for invisibility meant he had the least use for a healer of anyone in their group.

Working on them. He wrote back. They had held as well as anyone could have hoped with all of them away for three months. Which meant they were ghosts of their former selves. Chuck had been up a few times over the summer to make sure they didn't falter completely, and more importantly, to make sure there were no nasty surprises waiting for them upon their return.

Chris focused on what was left of his shields and started fixing them. He redirected the magic, bent it to his will, forcing it to protect his home, and to let him know if anyone who shouldn't be there entered.

Got mine back up. Wards are up, too. He sent back to Dave.

Good. Mine?

Can't feel them.

Several minutes passed. Chris felt the magic shift around him again.

Now?

Yes.

Good. See you day after tomorrow.

Chuck would be coming over soon. He puttered about the house for a few more minutes. The sculptures across the street caught his attention again.

What had she seen? He crossed the street to the sculpture garden and looked around. He'd never spent much time here though he had lived across the street from it for a year and a half.

He studied the statue carefully. It perpetually knelt, head on its hand, facing east. Something about it had attracted her attention. Whatever it was he didn't see it. He touched it, the way she had, but felt nothing unusual. He let his mind wander about the campus, feeling for her energy. Nothing. *Odd.* That level of energy shouldn't have just vanished.

He felt another very familiar presence and looked up, past the moving van that had just pulled up across the street. Chuck headed toward him. He noticed Chuck still had a slight limp left over from the fight at Hurford's. Chris had hoped three months without having to walk up to campus would have given him enough rest for it to get better.

Maybe she'd be able to help.

"Hey." Chuck smiled at him.

"Hello."

"Good trip?"

"Yeah. Tom drove. We may have set the land speed record."

"Amazingly enough not a single cop noticed you."

"Yeah." Chris gave him a half smile. "Amazing. Dave's trick works wonders when you want to get somewhere fast."

"When did you become an art lover?" Chuck gestured to the sculptures.

"I found our healer."

"Great. Still doesn't explain you being here."

"I'm getting to it. She was here, looking at this," he patted the statue, "and touched it a few times. Something about it really had her attention. I figured I'd take a look."

"You mean now, after she's gone, instead of using it as a way to strike up a conversation and get to know her."

"Tom was still here."

"I doubt he would have minded heading across the street to go say 'Hi' to a pretty girl."

"I didn't say she was pretty."

"You didn't need to. You would have said 'Hi' if she hadn't been."

Chris focused on the image of the healer: her short hair, dark eyes, wide mouth, and pale skin. She wasn't pretty. Her face was too strong and square for pretty. Striking maybe, but not pretty. He held the image in his mind for Chuck to see.

"I'm not sure I'd call her pretty."

"I see what you mean. Still, she's attractive and nicely shaped. That's enough to make you skittish."

Chris didn't roll his eyes. He wanted to. They'd been having this conversation on and off since they found each other. No need to give Chuck the satisfaction of getting into it again. "Anyway, she's here. I think this is going to be the year."

"Good." They walked back to the Writers' House. Chris slowed his pace to match Chuck's without having to think about it.

"Think she's a transfer student?" Chuck asked as they walked up the porch.

"No idea. You're right, though. She's a bit old for a freshman. She's got to be our age."

Chuck sat across the sofa, taking up all three cushions and rubbing his damaged ankle. Chris took one of the chairs across from him. "When are the others due?"

"I've got the place to myself today. Autumn and Mike will be in tomorrow. They're meeting up at the airport. She's renting a car and driving them up. Dave should be here the next day. How's your leg doing?"

"As well as can be expected. Doc says it needs to be broken and reset to heal up properly."

"Maybe she'll be able to fix it." Chris pushed his glasses back up his nose.

"I doubt it. If she had gotten to it right away, sure. But now? No one's that good."

"I felt her more than fifty feet away from the house. She's got some serious power to her."

"Good. We can get Autumn looking as well if that's the case. We can break into two groups and double our search radius."

"That would be good. If she's here, I bet Ahni Al is, too. I can't imagine all the rest of us would be here and he doesn't show up."

"Can you feel him?"

"Not yet, but if he's a freshman, he's still three days off."

"I still think he's dead. He should be the same age we are. He should have been here two years ago."

Chris shook his head. "If he had died, we would have felt it. *I* would have felt it. I'm sure of that. He might not have found a body as quickly as we did. You know him. He would have been picky."

Chuck nodded and changed the topic. "So, what's the great epiphany you didn't want to tell me about yesterday?"

Chris stood up. "Let me get a drink first. You want anything?"

"I'm good. Do you even have anything in the fridge?"

Chris turned back around. "Forgot about that. Feel like a grocery run?"

"Sure. As long as you talk and walk at the same time."

"I can do that." Chris waited for Chuck to get up. They headed down the hill toward Hurford's.

"So, tell me...," Chuck prompted.

"I was thinking about how much easier the Minions were to kill back home. A few quick pulses of magic, and that was the end of it."

"For you, maybe. Not quite that easy for the rest of us."

"Well, for me, then. Last night I was thinking about what was different now. And really, the answer was so obvious I can't believe I didn't think of it before. They don't have bodies here. If there was a way to make them have bodies, they'd be easier to kill. If I could get to the point where killing them takes me a few seconds, and you guys no more than a minute, we'd be a lot better off. And, if I can recorporealize them, I'll probably be able to do it to Mildred."

Chuck thought about that for minute. "How?"

"Not sure yet. There's got to be a way to do it. There's a link between energy and matter, so maybe a chat or two with one of the physics professors would be a good idea."

"Assuming you get a physics professor to answer you, could you even follow the answer, Mr. English Major?"

Chris rolled his eyes. He had four semesters of statistics to keep up with his econ classes. How much different than stats could physics be? "If it's the difference between surviving this year or not, I'll learn enough to follow the answer. I just need to know how the link works, and then I can use it."

"Okay. On a practical level, what are you thinking?"

"I'm thinking we start looking for ghosts. See if any of them can be made solid."

"That I can do."

They walked into Hurford's. Chris winced. The building reeked of stale summoning magic and madness. "Happy to see how long your fix lasted?"

"Fucking thrilled. This was so worth breaking an ankle and dislocating my knee for." Chuck answered quietly as Chris grabbed a basket. "As I told Mr. Hurford when I was here last spring, the problem isn't the magic: it's the idiot who keeps using it. Until he gets rid of whoever's using this place as his own personal summoning center, the problem can't be more than temporarily fixed."

"Wonderful."

"On the upside, I'll probably get called back in the spring to clean this place out again. It'll be good money."

"I'm coming with you this time."

"Of course."

3.

Pat Calumn wasn't paying attention to the speaker. The President of Sylvianna College stood in front of the class of 2012, all gathered together in Mellon Chapel, and blathered away through the matriculation ceremony, saying nothing even remotely interesting.

Pat was paying attention to the nasty critter he could feel looming in the space behind the choir loft. He took a racket-ball-sized sphere of black granite out of his duster, held it in his hand, and told the critter to back off. It wasn't happy to see him. He wasn't thrilled to see it but wasn't surprised, either. Pretty much anywhere with this many young adults was likely to have some sort of nasty summoned critter roaming around. As long as it stayed away from him, he'd leave it in peace.

Its interest moved away from him; he went back to watching the students around him. Pat noticed a few in the crowd looked particularly uncomfortable. One caught his attention.

He felt his breath hold. *What is she doing here? She's home!* But she wasn't home. She was sitting twenty feet away, looking like only immense force of will was holding her in her seat. Her control finally broke. She bolted from the chapel. He waited a few minutes, not wanting to attract too much attention, then followed her.

Pat stood outside the chapel and set his magic to find her. It was a simple spell. He could do it in his sleep. After a frustrating minute that provided no insight as to where she might be, he admitted that it didn't work. He looked around for a better place to cast. The stone bridge across a little ravine behind the chapel would do. It was limestone—Pat preferred granite—but it would work. He tried the spell again, pulling energy off the stones to increase his sensitivity. Once again he came up with nothing.

She hadn't any shields or cloaking when she was in the chapel, and now she was gone. So it must be wherever she'd gone to was hiding her. He let his mind wander around the campus, looking for places that were especially well-shielded and found one close enough to hide her. Across Main Street, up Alden Street, past the library, past Nelson, there was a small red house with a sign on it that read 'The Writers' House.' It might as well be Fort Knox or NORAD. Pat walked past it, looking for a good place to study it discretely.

He felt a whiff of familiar work about it. Pat walked another block up Alden street and turned into the gym. There was a stairwell off the entrance with a good view of the house. *Perfect.*

He closed his eyes, rested his hand on the sphere, and let himself really feel the red house across the street. It was more than a whiff; the magic was mostly Cell's work, with layers of Dia and Illyn, and a faint hint of Anthur. He looked for Burq; if the others were there, Burq had to be around somewhere, but Pat couldn't feel him. Of course, looking for Burq by his magic wasn't a good way to find him, like trying to find a match by its glow in full sunlight. If he wanted to find Burq, he needed to go looking for swords.

There was no hint of Althiira there, though. That made even less sense. Until he remembered she, like him, was a freshman. She wouldn't have found the others yet.

Why was she here? Where did she go? Pat spent a moment thinking about that before letting it go. No way for him to answer those questions now.

So, how about some questions he could answer? They were all in one place again. *Did they call me here?* He thought he would have felt it if that had been in play. Had something else called him here? Obviously, but he hadn't felt that, either. Pulling him out of New York would have been up to the letter of the agreement he had made six years ago, if not the spirit. Of course, the creatures he had dealt with back then had no interest in the spirit of any agreement.

He spent an hour pondering how they had all ended up here until his time sense told him he had to get going. He stood up, found his map of the campus in the pocket of his duster, and located the Heston Theatre. Time for his freshman orientation activity of choice: Improv.

Pat set his shields on high and made sure he was well-cloaked before leaving the gym. He'd see them again. That couldn't be avoided, but he'd do it on his terms. Right now he didn't feel like saying "Hi" until he had a better idea of what was going on. He crossed a large grassy courtyard, walked past the Student Union, across Main Street again, and headed north for five minutes until he found a large brick rectangle of a building with the name Heston on it.

The theater was in the basement. Pat smiled as he surveyed the other students in the Improv group, mostly girls. There were some perks to this world over his last one, one of which was the girls here didn't wear much clothing in the summertime. Most of the sweet young things sitting on the stage had on tiny shorts, tank tops, and sandals. He leaned against the wall and let his eyes linger on them. Yes, he did like the scenery here much better than home.

The group leader was getting ready to start when she walked in. So much for having to find her, she'd just fallen into his lap.

The leader asked them all to get up on stage and introduce themselves. He watched her intently as the others gave their names and where they came from. She noticed him watching and smiled. Pat grinned back at her but was troubled to see she didn't recognize him. That was the sort of friendly smile you give someone who's checking you out to let them know the attention isn't unwelcome. It wasn't the look you gave a man you've known and loved for fifty years.

Her look intrigued him. An oversized t-shirt, cargo pants, boots with a knife tucked into one of them, a knife and multi-pliers on her belt. He wasn't certain, but he thought she might have dog tags under her shirt as well as something that glowed. *A star? Is she Jewish?* That was bewildering. Why would she have a new religion here? *People convert... but that's just weird.*

Her hair was black. Her eyes were brown. He knew his own hair wouldn't hold another color. It looked like a new penny, and there was nothing he could do to change it. He was willing to bet the others had red hair, too. *Why wasn't her hair white?*

The introductions got to her. Her voice was clear and low. "I'm Sarah Metz, from Plemmesy, New York. I'm here to study bio, and this looked like more fun than the other options on the list."

He grinned at her when she said that. A minute later it was his turn. "Pat Calumn, New York, New York. I'm here to show you all how it's done." His grin softened the cockiness of his statement. He wanted to appear confident but not like an ass.

After a few more of the tank-top-wearing girls introduced themselves, the group leader asked them to pair up. Pat looked immediately at Sarah, which she caught because he was the first person she looked at, too. His look asked permission. Her nod granted it. They met halfway across the stage.

"So, you ever do this before?" He looked for any glimmer of recognition in her eyes; they were stubbornly blank.

"To slightly redo Drew Carey's famous comment on the show, 'only at parties with no boys or booze.'"

He was pleased to see she was familiar with the Improv show this game was based on. "You watched *Whose Line Is It Anyway*?" Pat asked, looking for something to keep the conversation going.

"Yeah, my brothers considered it appropriate viewing for the whole family. We'd tape it and watch it in the evenings."

"How about the British version?"

"Every now and again when it was on Comedy Central."

"We'll do just fine." He smiled again. They spent the next hour mostly watching the other groups improvise. If it hadn't been for the immense weirdness of sitting next to a woman he had loved for half a century and knowing with absolute certainty she had no clue who he was, Pat would have enjoyed it immensely.

They had just sat down after a quick round of Scenes from a Hat where he had come up with "CSI Mayberry" as a TV show that didn't make it when she quietly said, "'CSI Mayberry.' What does that look like?"

"Barney Fife dusting his own gun for fingerprints. But he messes up, gets black powder all over the place, and shoots himself," he answered just as quietly.

"Of course." She smiled at him again. He remembered her less than complimentary line about Harry Potter during round one and decided it would do for a conversation starter.

"I take it you weren't impressed with *Deathly Hallows*?"

"You could say that."

"I just did."

"Clever."

"Thanks. Want to get some coffee after this? Maybe talk where we don't have to whisper?" If he was going to have to rebuild his entire relationship with her, might as well start soon.

"Sure." Pat felt relieved she'd said yes. Then he felt massively relieved. Sarah didn't know him. He checked her hand, no ring. She was a freshman. There was no chance she'd remember Cell if she had forgotten him. Pat couldn't stop the grin; the glow of knowing she wasn't married here dominated his mind.

Pat and Sarah walked across the campus in a comfortable quiet. They were halfway to the Student Union when he started to talk.

"You know, it's a dumb name for a building."

"Student Union?"

"Yeah."

"Why?"

"Because this isn't Russia in the 1930s. Students here don't actually unionize."

"That's a point." Sarah patted down her pockets and found her map. "It does have another name: Alden Campus Center."

"Much better. I'll have to remember that." Pat paused for a moment and popped his back. Part of it was for show. He wanted to see how she'd react. Part of it was his back bothered him. Sarah tried not to wince visibly as he did it, but he saw her nonetheless. Exactly the right reaction. He figured if he did it a few more times she'd offer to fix his back. Even if she didn't know him, she was still a healer.

They continued their walk and entered the student-run coffee shop. It was half of the top floor of the Student Union. A space littered with Salvation Army furniture dressed up with bright hand-sewn pillows. The walls were covered in student artwork. Some good, some interesting, some… She pointed to one of the pieces, "Is that an abstract portrait of Barney with a huge vagina in his head?"

Pat stared at it and moved closer. He took a deep breath and let it out quickly. "You know, I really hope that wasn't the effect the artist was going for. But now you've said it, I can't see anything else. How about we sit where we can't see it?"

"Suits me. The corner table is free."

"Great, I'll go claim it. Back in a sec." He draped his duster over one booth and joined her in the line.

They ordered and paid. Pat looked at her cup with something like amazement. A half-caff mocha latte with extra whipped cream and cinnamon was frillier than he was expecting, especially given her clothing. Sarah caught him looking at it in wonder.

"I like girly drinks."

"I didn't say anything."

His plain cappuccino was more in character. They settled into the booth across from each other.

"So what's your story?" Pat stirred his drink, hoping he'd get a hint of what happened from her tale.

"You know, the regular. Graduated high school, joined the IDF…"

He raised an eyebrow. IDF didn't mean anything to him.

"The Israeli Defense Force. I went to Tel Aviv, joined up, became a medic, got stationed in the Negev. Not too much going on most of the time. Lots of dull with little bits of very not dull. Came back to New York, worked on my brothers' farm for a few months, applied to college, and came here. Once I'm done here, it's off to med school and then back to Israel."

"Regular, huh? What's unusual in your world?"

"Graduating high school. Going straight to college. It seems exotic to me."

"Then call me Mr. Exotic."

"Hello, Mr. Exotic."

"Did you say your brothers' farm?" *Where were her parents?*

"Yeah, our family raises kosher beef and lamb. It used to be my dad's farm, but he passed on four years ago."

"Oh. I'm sorry."

"Me too. I still miss him. But it wasn't a huge shock when it happened. I'm the youngest by quite a bit in my family. Dad was seventy-six when I was seventeen."

"I'm feeling more and more exotic by the moment."

"Yeah, nothing but boring and common where I come from. My oldest brother is twenty years older than I am. My dad never said anything, but I get the sense I'm an oops. Ben is forty-one, Sam is thirty-seven, and David is thirty-five. I'm twenty-one. Anyway, when Dad died he left nine-tenths of the farm to my brothers and one-tenth to me. When I went abroad, they bought me out."

Pat realized he had a good opening to find out what happened to her mother. "He left the farm to you and your brothers. Does that mean your mom is dead, too?"

"Yes. I don't much remember her. She died when I was three: bad car accident. It's funny how your experiences flavor your perceptions. I went to Israel, joined the army, and people actually shot at me. I was a block away when a bomb went off once, but it's when I get behind the wheel of a car my brothers worry. Car accidents are real to them, bullets, not so much."

"Or you're a really bad driver." He smiled to soften those words.

"Well, that could be true. You know what they say, eighty-nine percent of drivers report they're better than average. So, tell me about you."

It's me Althiira, Ahni! "Let's see, I battled my way through the wonders and horrors of high school in Manhattan. Then after a triumphant moment, when it became clear I would indeed pass my Regents, I applied to half a dozen colleges, all pretty much indistinguishable from this one. Sylvianna gave me the best deal, so here I am." Pat cracked his back again. She winced again.

"Parents? Siblings?" Sarah asked as she licked the last remnant of whipped cream off her cup.

"Mom and Dad are still married, poster children for domestic bliss. One little sister, she's twelve. And three Persian cats. My mom breeds the things. So, at any given time, there's a pregnant cat or two and a whole mess of kittens at our house."

"I like kittens." Sarah smiled.

"I do too, but eight or ten of them produces a lot of fur! Like keeping clean, fur-free clothing at school so you don't show up covered in it, lot of fur." Pat drank deeply and sighed.

"That's a lot of fur. Not so much fur when it comes to cows. The sheep have fleeces, but the shearers show up in the spring and take care of it for us. We've got one hippy lady who lives down the street who always buys six or seven of them. She dyes them and makes yarn. Actually Ben tells me he's thinking of seeing if she knows anyone else who would want to buy the things. He's pretty sharp. If there's a way for our farm to make more money, he's on it."

"Like what?"

"Well, we sell kosher meat. It's a good market; lots of nice little delis and stuff in New York buy our meat and feed it to the locals. Then Ben noticed 'organic, grass fed' meat is selling for big bucks in the high-end restaurants. So he's selling the bits of the cow you can't use for kosher meat to them. Everyone's happy, we've got less waste, more money, and my nieces and nephews will inherit a farm. Most of our neighbors are losing theirs."

"I bet I've eaten your meat."

"You probably have."

"Ellen's?"

"We sell to them."

"Huh. Small world. I've sat there eating pastrami on rye, and you and your brothers raised the cows I was eating. Cool."

"I like to think so. Besides cats what do your parents do?"

"Dad's a banker. Mom does some accounting for the family and a few friends, but mostly she does cats. Breeding them, showing them, raising them, and selling them. Come tax season my sister and I ended up with most of the cat work, but the rest of the year she's all kittens all the time. Dad's with Goldman Sachs." Pat cracked his back yet again.

"Look, I don't want to be too forward, but I can't stand seeing you do that. Please, let me work on your back."

"Work on it how?" He didn't let the grin hit his face.

"I give the best back rubs ever." That wasn't precisely the answer he was expecting, but if Sarah was being cagey it was a good cover. She should be able to feel his magic. She should know she didn't need to pretend to just give back rubs.

"No false modesty for you," Pat answered her.

"Nope, I've been at it since I was thirteen, and I'm really good. I hate seeing you crack and pop. I may not fix it, but I promise I'll make it better."

"Well, never let it be said I turned down a back rub. But it's pretty bad, and I've had other people work on it without any luck." Which was something of an understatement. He'd had numerous massages that did nothing. Five healers of different stripes had taken a whack at it with no luck.

"Well, what's the worst thing to happen? You get a back rub."

"I can think of worse ways to spend an afternoon. My place?"

"Sure." Pat stood up and twisted again. Sarah winced once more for effect and then spent the next minute watching him stand and walk more carefully than she had before. He could sense Sarah trying to get a feel for what was wrong. It'd be interesting to see if she could figure it out.

They walked across the campus. "I live in the Ravine Dorm."

Sarah grimaced. "No wonder you're hurting. I jog by every morning, just the sight of all those stairs looks daunting. How many trips did it take to get all your stuff up?"

"Not too bad. Five trips."

They walked down the stairs on the west side of the ravine, across the parking lot, and back up the east side. "Who thought this was a good idea?" Sarah asked.

"You've got to wonder what the plan was. This is the ass end of nowhere."

"I guess it's quiet."

"It's a freshman men's dorm. I think it's out here to allow the rest of the campus to get some quiet."

She stopped at the top of the steps and looked back toward the ravine. "Pretty view."

"Yeah, pretty." Pat was slightly out of breath. He hated the fact his back problem messed with his lung capacity. He had to quit smoking to cope, which didn't make him happy.

"Do you hear thumping?"

Pat didn't, and he had exceptional hearing. Sarah was feeling something, but it wasn't on his radar. He shook his head. "Only my heart."

"Nope, probably someone's music. Odd choice of music, though. It lacks anything I'd call rhythm." She turned from the ravine as he led her into his dorm.

They walked through a series of eggshell corridors. Although the freshmen had only been there for two days it already reeked of young man: a sweaty, funky, colongy musk too many boys in too small a space with too few showers created. Pat noticed her wrinkling her nose. It wouldn't break his heart to spend less time here; her place had to smell better.

He opened the door marked 239. The room was tiny, a claustrophobic's hell. Two bunk bed-desk combinations took up close to seventy-five percent of the space. A young man looked up from one of the desks.

"This is Stuart." Pat gestured to his roommate.

"Hello, I'm Sarah."

Stuart stood up ruler straight and offered her his hand.

"You're ROTC aren't you?" Sarah asked him.

"Yes. How'd you know?"

"I can always spot one of us. Army?" Stuart looked scornful.

"Marines," he said while looking her over carefully. She moved out of slouch mode and into what Pat thought of as military posture. "I can tell you've been in, but I'm not coming up with where. Navy?"

"IDF."

"Cool."

"Thanks. What are you planning on studying?"

"History. I'm working on planning my schedule now. You?"

"Pre-med. Not too much choice for me this semester. Bio I, Calc II, Organic Chemistry. My one free class will hopefully be Arabic. I'll probably take fencing and get my gym credit out of the way while I'm at it." Pat and Stuart looked interested in fencing.

"They've got fencing this semester?" Pat asked.

"Yep. Eight a.m. Monday, Wednesday, Friday," Sarah answered.

"Cool beans! I've got to sign up for that." That's how he'd find Burq. If there were swords, Burq was sure to be nearby.

Stuart looked crestfallen. "It's the same time Introduction to European History is, which I have to take because it's the pre-req for pretty much everything else I want to take."

"Sorry to hear it. Maybe next semester?" Sarah's eyes scanned the room.

"Yeah, maybe." Stuart went back to hunting for classes.

Pat saw her notice the stones on the top of his dresser. Pat felt the start of a satisfied grin and stopped it before it got to his face. At the very least, she could feel the magic of his stones. He had brought his eight favorites along with him. They sat in a small semi-circle around the stand he had for the granite sphere. He put the sphere back in its place.

Sarah watched him do it and asked, "Can I touch it?"

"You wanna touch my rocks?" He leered jokingly when he said it.

"Oh, yes. Nothing would make me happier than to stroke your hard, heavy rocks." Pat could just about hear Stuart's eyes roll.

"Well, in that case, stroke away."

She picked it up and almost dropped it. Sarah put it back on its stand very quickly. He wondered what she felt when she picked it up.

"Do you keep it in the freezer when it's not on your shelf?" Sarah asked.

"No. It just sits there. Sometimes I carry it with me when I go out."

"It's really cold." *Cold? Why would she feel it as cold?*

"Always feels a little too warm to me. Here." Pat held her hand, checking to see if her hands were warmer than his. They were slightly warmer but not enough for the rock to feel cold to her.

Stuart came over. "It's a rock, guys." He picked it up and gave it a quick toss. Pat grimaced and noticed Sarah watching his reaction with interest. "It feels cool, not cold, just like any other room temperature piece of stone should," Stuart said and handed it back to Sarah.

Sarah cupped the stone in her hand. Goose bumps rose on her arm while the beds of her fingernails turned blue. Apparently here she felt magic as cold. At least she felt it. It didn't look like Sarah knew what she was feeling, though. She looked puzzled, like she wanted to find an answer, and didn't like what she was coming up with. Sarah put the stone carefully back on its stand and let her other hand hover over the rest of his collection.

"You like rocks, huh?"

"Yeah, you should see my collection at home. These are just my favorites. You said something about a back rub?" Pat popped his back once again to remind her why they were there.

Sarah shuddered. "Yeah, every time you crack your back, I want to wince. Lie down, and let me fix it."

"My back's been bothering me for years."

"Don't worry. I'm really good at this." She pointed toward the floor. He shucked off his shirt and lay down. Pat could feel her eyes on him. He thought she liked what she saw but cast a quick glamour just in case. It wouldn't make him look different. He'd still be a tall, wiry redhead with too many freckles and more body hair than was typically fashionable. She would just find tall, wiry, somewhat furry redheads more appealing.

Sarah's fingers ghosted along his back. "What did you do to yourself? This is a mess." Her fingers slid along his back as she talked about it. "You've got what, three ribs out of place? And your hip's not right; it's pulling on the *quadratus lumborum* and yanking at least two vertebrae out of place. I can feel it's old, but I can't think of what would mess up your back this way."

"When I was thirteen, I was in an accident with some of my friends. My back never quite healed up."

"To say the least. This is just..." Sarah focused on what she was doing, slowly manipulating the layers of muscle to let those ribs go back where they wanted to be. "You have a hard time breathing deeply?"

"Yes. It put a crimp in my MMA career."

"MMA?"

"Mixed Martial Arts."

"What's your specialty?" Sarah leaned into his back.

"A little bit of everything. I'm not bound by any particular discipline. I just go for whatever works given the situation."

"Okay. Sounds like an intelligent way to fight."

"I like to think so." She rested her hands on Pat's shoulders and got to work in earnest. It was a moment of confusing bliss for him. Bliss, she was back in his life and touching him; confusion, it was just a massage. A good massage. Sarah was right; she knew what she was doing. But there was no magic in her touch. Healing, what she had done as naturally as breathing before, was gone. She should have been wrapping his energy around hers and straightening it out; instead, she was slowly easing muscles apart, forcing them to relax. She kept returning to one spot, and each time she hit it he'd twitch.

"Is it tender?"

"No, it's... electric. You hit it, and I feel a shock through my entire chest."

"Hmmm. It feels stuck to me. Do you mind if I keep poking at it?"

"Not at all."

After a few minutes, she laid her hands on that spot. Then Pat felt her magic. He dropped his shields so she could work more easily. Her magic was sloppy and wild, burning way more energy than necessary. Sarah was healing him on sheer instinct alone. Pat wasn't even sure she knew she was doing anything beyond giving him a back rub. It wasn't just him she didn't know: her whole self, including her magic, had vanished from her. But it was coming back. Her technique got better as she moved from problem to problem. Sarah might not remember Althiira. She might have lost her technique. But she still had the power. And she still had the touch. *It would come back.*

Eventually Sarah pulled back from him. She looked weak and shaky and collapsed in a limp heap on the floor. Pat stood up, stretched, and five audible pops followed. He let out a happy sigh. "Marry me! I can give you all the Persian cats you want."

Sarah didn't open her eyes. "I told you I was good at this."

"You're fantastic, and you look beat."

"I am."

"Lay there. I'll be back in a few minutes." Pat laid his blanket on her and headed out to the vending machine in the hallway to get her some snacks. It had been a long time since he'd dealt with a mage; however, he remembered feeding them after they worked was a good thing.

I had just about drifted off to sleep when the door opened again.

"I brought you sugar. I've got Coke, a Snickers bar, and some peanut butter crackers. A little food should help you perk back up."

"Let me rest a bit more. Then I'll eat."

"You want my bed?"

"Nope, don't want to move." Then I slept.

I knew he was a man. If man was the correct word. Elf might have been better. He was a little too broad and muscular for a typical fantasy elf. His lapis lazuli colored skin wasn't typical for an elf, either. He was taller than I was, with long pointed ears, and a long angular face. His hair was the color of bright new copper, his eyes the color of glacial ice under stormy skies.

I saw a hand reaching to the blue elf: light milky blue skin with exceptionally long fingers. I knew it was mine. In it was a cup filled with something spicy and warm, but nothing I had ever drunk before. As I noticed the cup was warm, I also noticed the air was cold.

I handed him the cup. He smiled and nodded at me. I turned and walked toward a large wooden door in what looked like a castle from a fantasy novel.

Once again I was awake.

"Good nap?" Pat lounged on his bed, book in hand.

"Weird dream. How long was I out?"

"Almost an hour. Hungry?"

"Yes!" I was absolutely ravenous. I scarfed down the food he got me in two minutes flat. I looked around the room and found a clock. A little before five. "I've got to get dinner."

"Want me to go with you?"

"Sure, but I eat at my place, not the cafeteria." He looked confused. "I'm fine getting drinks and the occasional munchies there, but they don't do kosher food."

"I should have figured that out. How about I keep you company at your place, and then you join me?"

"Sounds good."

As I stood up to leave, I noticed Pat looked taller. "Can I see your back again?"

"Sure." He'd been in the middle of putting his black duster on when I asked. He took it off, laid it over his chair, and then pulled his gray t-shirt off. I spent a less-than-professional moment enjoying his tightly muscled self. I had the feeling he didn't mind if I spent a little while admiring him. I like men who look like men, not those little, androgynous, girly things they keep putting on magazine covers. Pat, with his just-got-out-of-a-hurricane copper-colored hair, raggedy cutoff jeans, somewhat fuzzy exterior, and light gray eyes, looked like a man. *Stop it! He's noticing you ogling him!* I made myself focus on what I had asked to see.

"Wow," I said as I looked over his ribs, low back, and hips.

"Wow?"

"Yeah." I touched his skin. "That looks way better than I expected."

"What do you mean?"

"I mean, I never even got to your hips, but they're even now. And your ribs slid back into place. You look better than you did when I took my nap."

"I'm feeling better. I spent a few minutes stretching out. I did feel my ribs move. It hurt but hurt good."

"Wonderful." My stomach growled. "Dinner then?"

"Yes."

We headed to my house. While I cooked, he puttered about my place, looking at my photos. I pointed out who was who in the family shots.

"Who's your friend?" He picked up the shot of Ari and me.

"That's Ari. He's my man."

"You have a man?"

"Lover sounds dumb, and boyfriend is worse. So, he's my man."

I thought he said something like 'damn.' He didn't say it loudly enough for me to hear clearly, so I didn't ask.

"He's old."

"Twenty-eight. He's not exactly ancient."

"Well, no. He's still a lot older than we are. Where are you in that shot?"

"A beach near Tel Aviv. It is nice. People forget Israel is on the Mediterranean. It's got some lovely beaches."

"And is Mr. Ari still in Tel Aviv?"

"Yes. He's Israeli."

"I didn't know there were black Israelis."

"His mom is Ethiopian. His dad is Russian. Hence, my lovely cocoa-colored Ari."

"Are you two serious?"

I flashed him my naked left hand. "We aren't engaged"—I had the feeling he was thinking of asking before I told him I was heading back to the States for school, but I didn't see any reason to mention that to Pat—"but, yes, we're serious. Is there a girlfriend at home for you?"

"There was." He sounded tired and bitter. "We didn't have a fantastic relationship to begin with, and just before I left she tried to fake a pregnancy to get me to stay."

"That's nasty."

"Yes. But, that is done, and judging by the smell, I think your dinner is getting close, too."

"Oh. Yes." I hustled to the stove to grab the Mac & Cheese I had made. "Have I told you how much I'm looking forward to my brothers sending me some meat? I'm not a vegetarian by choice; I'm starting to get bored with veg, veg, and a side of veg."

"You know, some vegetarians eat rice, pasta, and beans."

"Yep. I have that with my vegetables. I'm sure I'm doing better on my vitamins than usual. Thanks to the miracle that is protein bars, I'm good on that front. Still, I miss meat."

"So, what would you be eating if you could have whatever you want?"

"Hmm… steak, roasted sweet potatoes, and green beans. What about you?"

"Cheesecake. I have a feeling there isn't any decent cheesecake to be had 'round here."

"You might be right about that. Maybe one day we'll head down to Pittsburgh. See if we can find some."

"You have a car?"

"Motorcycle."

"I like motorcycles."

"I am less than shocked."

We sat at my table. He drank a pop while I ate my Mac & Cheese. I told him about my pre-med aspirations. He told me about his goals of being a playwright and his love of fiction.

He was here to become a better writer and thought studying history would help give him things to write about. We found we were both fans of Terry Pratchett and had a perverse love of the *Twilight* series even though we loathed the main characters. Then we headed to the cafeteria and rounded out his dinner with more conversation on sci-fi/fantasy and how many of the recent offerings in the field had been disappointing.

When the conversation wound down, we fiddled with the remains of our drinks for a minute. "So, want to go to the sexual harassment lecture tomorrow with me?" I asked him. It was about time to break off for the night, and I wanted to make sure I saw him again.

"Only if you don't mind me mocking it viciously."

"You know, I think we're going to get along famously," I said, a smile creeping across my face.

"Yes, I think we are." He had a matching smile on his face.

"Good. I'll meet you outside the theater; say ten minutes before it starts."

"That works for me." He stood up, and I followed him. "Time for me to go home and set up my computer."

"That's pretty much my plan for tonight, too." We split up, and I headed home. Getting the computer online was surprisingly simple. Usually when I try to do something like that I end up banging my head against the wall while cursing as it keeps telling me it can't find the network. This time I booted up, used the instructions in the packet, and yay! I was online!

I spent the rest of the night sending emails and enjoying being in touch with the real world again. There were three emails from Ari. I read each one twice before writing him back. Finally, having gotten caught back up with the world outside Reevesville, I went to sleep.

4.

There was a box waiting on the porch for Chris when they got back from dinner. He took it up to his room and slit it open. Inside, among his textbooks, was some non-school reading he had decided to order. If he could get one of the physics professors to talk with him, he wanted to follow the answer. He took the book down to the living room and began thumbing through it.

Autumn looked up from her book and asked, "*Physics for Dummies*?" He glanced at the small blonde sitting on the sofa next to the front door. He thought she might have changed her glamour slightly from last spring. Her eyes were green now. He thought they had been dark blue before. She was also a little plumper this year. Not fat but round and curvy. Still short, she couldn't be much past 4'10". He wasn't sure if she did that as a remembrance of the fairy she used to be or if she just preferred being small.

"Yeah."

"Why?"

"Research." Dave and Mike came out of the kitchen with drinks. Mike slid *Call of Duty* into the Playstation. Dave shot. Mike spotted for him. They had gotten pretty good at working together at all sorts of games. This was just the newest one. Mike was already studying the terrain. His limestone green eyes scanned quickly over the TV, searching out Nazis in dull gray.

Dave looked over at Chris, saw the book, raised an eyebrow, and asked, "How bad did the textbook run hurt this year?"

"On your left, behind the burned tank," Mike alerted him. Dave turned back to the screen.

"Got it." He shot a Nazi in gray.

"It hurt. Three hundred and eighty dollars," Chris replied. Mike winced and turned his attention back to the screen.

"Ouch," Autumn said.

"How can two Econ classes and two English classes cost you three hundred and eighty dollars?" Dave asked.

"Even on Amazon, the Econ texts were sixty a piece: two for Global Macro Economics, and two for Advanced Forecasting."

"I'm going to be in the same boat tomorrow. I swear they write new Comp Sci books every six months just to screw us out of more money."

"On the right, see it?" Mike asked. The sound of rifle fire filled the room.

"Not too bad for me this semester. One independent study and my senior thesis means only two classes with books I've got to pay through the nose for," Autumn told them.

"Lucky you." Dave blew another Nazi to bits.

"Yeah. Lucky me. Feel like trading your junior seminar for my senior thesis?"

"No thanks. I'm actually looking forward to Comparative Fascism. Your thesis is about what? Great diplomats of history?"

"Close enough. It's a study of the diplomatic techniques of the pre-World War II era compared to the pre-Iraqi Freedom era. I'm thinking of calling it, 'With the Best of All Intentions…'"

"Sounds like a fascinating read," Mike commented, his voice only mildly sarcastic.

"Oh, it will be." She gave them a hard smile. "My thesis committee will be riveted, unable to put it down."

"And how much of that will have to do with the content of the piece?" Dave questioned.

"Very little. But they'll remember it as being a very insightful, well-written work." Autumn smiled serenely at them.

"You're going to glamour your senior thesis?" Chris guessed he shouldn't be surprised. They all used magic on occasion to deal with sticky assignments. Though glamouring a thesis was way beyond the somewhat traditional date fixing that was their most common use of magic when dealing with professors.

"If I can."

"Why not take the time to just write it well?" Chris asked.

"What would be the challenge in that?" She smiled prettily and twisted her long blonde hair between her fingers. "I already know how to write a decent report. I've known how to do that for literally millennia. I don't know how to charm an electronic document to make the person who reads it think it was wonderful. If I pull this off, it'll hold even after the document is printed. After all, this is supposed to be about learning a useful skill. Trust me, that will be much more useful than creating a perfect report about idiots blathering about appeasement."

Dave paused the game. "If you can do it, will you teach me?"

"What'll you trade me for it?"

"Depends on how well it works."

"We'll talk once I've got it figured."

He unpaused the game. "Good."

For a few minutes the room was quiet, save for the sound of gunfire and attacking Nazis. Autumn went off to get a drink and resettled herself on the couch Chris was sitting on, her feet inches from his thigh. She read for a few minutes and put down her book.

"So, Tuesday nights for Golem?"

"Works for me," Chris said. Golem, the creative writing group their house hosted, usually met on Tuesdays.

"I'll get the email out tomorrow," Dave added.

"And the real meeting, we'll do that after?" Mike brushed his jaw-length auburn hair out of his eyes.

"Like always," Autumn said. "Will you tell us more about the healer, now we're all here and settled?"

"Not much more to tell. I saw her jogging past the house and walking around the sculpture garden when I was moving in. I haven't seen her since, and I can't find her by magic. She was here, and then she vanished. I'm actually thinking of getting up at the unseemly hour of seven to see if she jogs by. It'd be nice to know I didn't imagine her."

Mike looked away from the TV towards the group. "What about Ahni? Anyone got a feel for him?"

The other three denied it. "If he's a freshman he won't be here until tomorrow anyway," Chris said.

"Then tomorrow we'll look for him. He went through, right?" Mike added.

"Yes, he did. Whether or not he's still here is open for discussion. But he stepped through the circle, so as of twenty-one years ago, he was here," Autumn answered.

"He'll be here. He was probably just very picky when he went body hunting. You know him. He would have taken the time to find exactly the right body, with exactly the right family," Chris responded.

"Yeah, he would have," Mike agreed. "And if he's here, then this is it."

"I hope so." Chris put the book down. "I can't think of any other reason we'd all be in the same place at the same time. Speaking of which…" He got up and headed to his room. He opened the top drawer to his desk and took out a manila folder. He brought it downstairs with him, walked carefully past Mike and Dave so as not to disturb their game, to the Formica table on the far end of the room. It was supposed to be a kitchen table, but the kitchen was so small the table was in their living room. He opened the quarter of the map he needed.

It was the only map of its kind. Mike had made it freshman year, using Google Earth, the biggest printer in the computer lab, and a lot of tape. It was a ten foot by ten foot map of

Reevesville. Over the years they had searched almost half of it. After each search, they listed anything magical.

"I saw Chuck two days ago. He's thinking S18 and T18 might be of interest to us."

"The doorway?" Autumn asked, walking over to the map, right across Dave and Mike's line of view. They made annoyed noises. Dave's soldier grunted when he got shot. She stood next to Chris, her shoulder against his arm, as she looked at the map. He didn't grit his teeth. He wanted to. It wasn't like she needed to stand that close to him. It wasn't like she needed to look at the map; she knew where S18 and T18 were. By now they all did. The only reason he got it out was he liked looking at it while he planned. It was like a crystal ball or a flame, something for him to stare at while his brain worked.

"Yeah. He noticed there's a small bit of ravine between those two fields." He tapped the map with a pencil. S18 and T18 were in the middle of someone's farm. "It's rocky, it's got trees, and we haven't checked there yet."

"Sounds good. Thursday night?" Autumn leaned closer to the map. The strap of her tank top slipped off of her shoulder, and her hair lightly brushed his arm. He took a step to the right, away from her.

"Thursday works," Mike said.

"I've got plans," Chris added quickly.

"I can go, too," Dave responded.

Thanks, Chris thought at Dave.

No problem, Dave thought back at him.

"Good. Then you three will go. It's probably nothing. I don't remember a farm…"

"But it's worth checking. Yeah, we know." Dave looked away from the game to him. "So, why are you reading *Physics for Dummies*?"

"I need to know more about the relationship between energy and matter."

"Of course," Mike said. "The guy who spent four solid semesters complaining bitterly about the math involved in his econ classes is feeling a burning need for advanced physics."

"I'd prefer reading just about anything else. But I've got something I want to play with. I'll need this to try doing it."

"Want to tell us more than that wonderfully vague description?" Autumn smiled up at him.

"Not now. No use getting anyone's hopes up if I can't work it." He continued to stare at the map, willing it to tell him something it hadn't already. Like every other time he stood there looking at it, nothing jumped out at him. He folded it up and took it back to his room.

When he got downstairs again, Autumn had taken the sofa next to the door again. He settled himself on the one in front of the TV, this time lying across it. He felt a bit bad; Mike or Dave couldn't sit on it if they wanted to, but neither could Autumn. He figured they would forgive him for it. He picked up *Physics for Dummies* and tried to focus. There was a trick to doing this; all he had to do was find it.

5.

Faster than I had thought possible, it was Monday morning and time for classes to begin. As I headed past the Writers' House on the tail end of my jog, I had the feeling of someone watching me. The left window on second floor kept attracting my attention, but I couldn't see anyone. *Odd.* I wondered if that was the redhead's room.

Fencing was my first class of the day. Pat was in the class as well. He looked like he was having second thoughts about the desirability of an eight a.m. class. I couldn't tell if the t-shirt and sweat pants he wore were his fencing clothes, or he had just rolled out of bed and was still in his jammies. Either way it didn't much matter. The first class was all about safety, gear, how matches go, and what we would need to do in class. Coach Junt told us on Wednesday we'd start fencing.

I was starting to think eight a.m. Fencing might not have been the greatest idea. Nine a.m. Chemistry was on the other side of the campus in Jones. Biology was at ten followed by Calculus at eleven. When I set up my schedule, I thought it was brilliant. All my classes were on Monday, Wednesday, and Friday. I had Bio lab Monday afternoon and Chemistry lab at eight on Tuesday. It turned out my Arabic lessons had to be done as an independent study. Professor Scott, my advisor, was still tracking down someone to work with me on them, but when he found a professor for them, I'd have plenty of free time.

While hoofing it across the campus, it occurred to me I was liable to be tired and sweaty after fencing, and I hadn't scheduled time for a shower or change of clothing. No way to fix it now. I'd just have to hope I wasn't too funky smelling in class.

Chemistry and Biology followed much the same format as Fencing. For Calculus, Professor Myrton had us start the second we got in. There was a syllabus on each desk, and the board was already covered in equations. As soon as the bell rang, Myrton started to lecture. He didn't finish until a minute after the closing bell rang. Apparently, there would be no wasted time in his class.

Bio lab might as well have been Fencing. We got a tour of the lab, checked out the equipment, inspected the syllabus, and went home. Prof. Scott told us he preferred to have labs on a day other than the first day of class because he hated wasting the time but this year it couldn't be helped.

I returned home to my computer and problem sets. Pat joined me later that afternoon. He had a notebook and a pile of books under his arm.

"So, the good news is all I have to do is read."

"And the bad news?"

He dropped at least a thousand pages of text in front of me. "This is all due by next week."

"Ouch."

"Mind if I hang out here and work 'til dinner?"

"Not at all; some company with work would be nice."

"Good. I have a feeling your couch would be a really good place for reading."

"It is."

Tuesday morning went well. Chemistry Lab was fun. We had the get to know the lab and how to use the equipment speech. Then, because that only took one of the three hours, we went on to do an "identify that element" game. I didn't win. I didn't embarrass myself, either. Some elements, like raw lead versus raw silver, were hard. Some elements, like mercury, were easy. I thought it was a good exercise. We're expected to have the periodic table and all of the values memorized by next Monday. Having an image to go with about a third of the table made it easier to keep things straight.

Home again and more work. Once more Pat showed up in the late afternoon, keeping me company while we both trudged through our homework. I had the feeling a pattern was starting, and I liked it.

Fencing class again, this time we got our blades out. Well, foils out. They don't exactly have blades. It looked like the class would be mostly a matter of us facing off with each other while Coach Junt hovered around telling us how to do better. Pat and I paired up, suited up, plugged in, and got busy.

We faced off properly. With a quick salute the match began. I'm not bad with a foil. I may not be an expert by any stretch of the imagination, but I know which end to point at the other guy. Also, I'm familiar enough with general combat to read other people's moves and anticipate what's about to happen.

Pat, on the other hand, is brilliant. His body just shifted gently while his arm moved in a blur. He had five points on me before I even deflected one of his blows. Our match to fifteen ended in less than a minute with me feeling like an eight-year-old who'd never handled any sort of weapon before.

He took off his face mask; he wasn't even sweating. Then he grinned at me. I began to feel a little better.

"Maybe I need to pair up with someone closer to my own skill level?" I gave him a quick salute.

"That depends: It looks like I'm better at this than anyone else here. If you want to get really good, you'll stay with me. If you want to pound someone else, we'll switch."

I growled at him gently. "I'll stick with you. Not worth doing if I'm not going to get as good as possible."

"Exactly." We retreated to the side of the gym, allowing others to fence. Our turn would come up again in a few minutes.

"So, you wear two knives, you like fencing, and you were in the IDF. If you ever want to try any other sparring, I'm game," he said while we watched two other freshmen flail around with their foils.

"Like what?"

"Hand to hand?"

I looked him up and down. He had at least ten inches and seventy pounds on me. I was certain I'd get my ass handed to me. On the other hand, it had been a very long time since I had had a chance to play with someone like that.

"Sure." I smiled at him. "I think this space is free tonight."

"That suits. Just remember: be gentle with me."

I laughed at him. "Yeah, I'm sure gentle is what you need." Our space opened up, and back to fencing we went. This second match went better. He moved slower, giving me more time to see what he was doing. He beat me soundly again, but I didn't look quite so much like a dork while he did it.

By the end of the class I was tired. The crouched fencing stance had my quads quivering and begging for respite. Sinking into my seat for Chemistry felt so good I wasn't self-conscious about my disheveled post workout look.

At the end of my second Biology class, Professor Scott waved me over.

"I've found your Arabic teacher. Are you free this afternoon?"

"Yes."

"Then meet me in Howard in front of Professor Morrell's office at three-thirty. I'll make the introductions and get you set up."

"Wonderful."

Professor Scott led me into a cluttered office in the history building. "I'd like you to meet your new best friend. Sarah Metz, this is Professor Morrell. He *is* the Classics department here at Sylvianna, and, in addition to Latin, Greek, French, German, and English, he also speaks Hebrew and Arabic." A man with light olive skin and black curly hair stood in front of me. He was either amazingly youthful or not much past twenty-seven years old. He smiled at me, and I smiled back.

"Hello." I offered him my hand. He shook it with a good firm touch, not bone crushing and not the 'I don't know what to do with a woman's hand' fragile shake some men come up with. Professor Scott and Professor Morrell exchanged pleasantries. Then Scott left. Morrell gestured to the chairs in his office. We both sat.

"Arabic is not a common choice for an independent study," he said to me.

I grinned. "I'm not a common sort of person." He smiled back. I had a feeling we'd get along well. "I'm not just looking for Arabic lessons. I was told when I applied someone could accommodate me on a second major. Call it Middle Eastern Languages or whatever. Hebrew and Arabic. I'll need to have them mastered by the time I get out of medical school. I don't anticipate a lot of time during med school for studying them, so now looks like the time."

Morrell nodded. "I understand you already speak Hebrew."

"And write it, but not as well as I would like. I speak a little street Arabic."

"Well, I read both, write both, but do not actually speak either. We'll be working on speaking them together. Why Hebrew and Arabic?"

"I hope to be a trauma surgeon in Israel. I lived there for two years, so I already speak Hebrew well, but I don't write it as well as a doctor should. As for Arabic, I've got to learn it for the same reason you'd learn Spanish if you intend to be a doctor in southern Texas."

"Makes sense. Is this your *Aliyah*?"

His question pleased me. "It's nice to meet someone here who has a clue as to why I'd want to do this."

"I did my undergrad at Brandeis. I had a pretty good taste of American Jewish culture there."

"Ah. So, how do we go about doing this?"

"Well, what's your highest priority?"

"Mastering written Hebrew. Then spoken Arabic. Lastly written Arabic."

"And you're also majoring in biology?"

"Yes."

He thought for a moment, fingers steepled together in front of his face, before continuing. "Here's what I'd suggest. As you spend your four years here, the biology course work will get harder and harder. It's progressive. Because of what we're going to do here, there's not as much need for that. We can start with the hardest, learning a new language practically from scratch. In three years when biology is monopolizing your time, we can switch to polishing up your written Hebrew skills."

"Beautiful."

"Here's what I'm thinking on the language front: we'll get copies of the Arabic version of Rosetta Stone. Since spoken is more of what you want, that's a better tool than the regular textbook route. We can meet twice a week for class work; by the time the semester is over, we'll both be speaking it."

"I can do that. When do you want to meet?"

"Do you have a copy of your schedule?"

I handed it to him. He swiveled toward his computer. After comparing his schedule to mine, he turned to me. "We both have two to four on Tuesday and Thursday free. Does that work for you?"

"It does."

"Excellent. I'll see you Thursday. We can plan our classes."

Pat met Sarah after dinner in the gym. They decided the center circle in the basketball court made a good fight boundary. She slipped off her shoes while he bounced around to get warmed up.

When they faced off, he gave her a quick bow, and she shot a fast salute to him. Pat stood there, waiting for her to move. He wanted to see what sort of skills she had picked up. More than that, Pat didn't want to just charge in and tackle Sarah. If she was going to do this again, he had to keep his fight reined in enough so she had a chance to enjoy it as well. He could feel her tension building, muscles waiting for that first twitch, first blink, first anything. Then, the second she decided to aim a kick at him, he swept into a low roundhouse to take her legs out from under her.

Sarah jumped it but couldn't get away from the follow-up. Pat caught her squarely in the thigh with his other knee. She surprised him. As she fell, she managed to hit him in the arm with her elbow. It was a good shot, too: a nerve strike. The first three fingers on his left hand were tingling and moving sluggishly.

They broke apart and moved to the opposite sides of the ring. Pat shook his arm.

"Nerve strike?" Sarah asked him.

"Yeah, my hand's numb."

"Good, I'd hate to think I was totally useless in that last pass. Want to wait until you've got feeling back?"

"If you don't mind."

"Not at all. I have a feeling I won't want to see my leg tomorrow."

"I didn't hit you *that* hard." He hadn't really. He had the power to shatter a leg with his kick if he put a little magic into it. However, Pat decided it might be a good idea pull back a little further just in case. He didn't want to leave her covered in bruises.

"I'd hate to see what 'that hard' looks like."

His fingers moved quickly now. "I'm ready when you are."

"Fine." This time she went straight berserker, rushing him before he had the chance to get his balance. He smiled to himself and let her think he was going to fall back. Then he grabbed Sarah around the waist and took her down as well.

Pat rolled in a tidy ball and was up again in a second. She was still down on her back. He felt for what she would do next. She was hoping he'd get close enough for her to trip him, so he stayed just out of reach.

He watched her think through her next move. Pretty much what he had just done, curl into a ball and roll into a standing position. Pat figured there was no reason to attack her while she was getting up. Sarah added a little twist and kick once she was on her feet.

He blocked it easily and took another lazy roundhouse kick toward her. She dodged that one. He wanted to see how well she read body language, so he tensed like he was going to punch. Pat saw her notice it. He leapt into a surprise high kick that caught her in the shoulder and knocked her to the floor.

"You're amazing," Sarah said from the floor.

He picked his response carefully. "Thank you. I've worked hard to become so." He offered her a hand and pulled her up.

"If you tell me you're not left-handed, I'll have to drop you." Pat grinned, happy she caught the reference.

"Well, I'm not, but it doesn't matter nearly as much with this. Want another round?"

"Sure, I'm not a walking bruise yet."

This time he let her defend. She was better when she was reacting than when she was attacking. She landed a few solid hits before he flipped her over his shoulder. She looked up from the floor and said, "I'm done."

"Want to do this again sometime?"

"After I heal up? Sure. Once upon a time, I was considered good at this."

"You are good at this. I'm better." He grinned at her. She really was good, but she hadn't been fighting for over one hundred years.

"Yes, you are better. You're fucking amazing."

He decided to go for the modest approach. "No, I'm just really good. Some of the guys I did MMA with really are fucking amazing."

She stood up slowly. "Maybe next week?"

"Sounds good. What's on for the rest of your night?"

"About a thousand pounds of homework. You?"

"Seven hundred pages down. Three hundred to go."

"Want to come to my place to read?"

"Sure. I'll be over in a bit. Got to get my books and a shower."

"See you then."

6.

I spent a few minutes milling around the outside of the Activities Fair. It was packed with small folding tables covered in posters. Students wandered about slowly looking at them.

"Want to split up? I'll get the right; you get the left. Then we can regroup and report back?" Pat asked.

"Sure. See you in an hour or so?"

"Sounds good." I entered the fray. It was hard to see everything because of the crush of students in my way. So, like all the rest of them, I got in line and began shuffling from one table to another. I picked up fliers for the Role Playing Group, the Improv Group, and the Organic Gardeners.

"Golem." The word caught my eye. It was printed at the top of a bright orange poster with a sketch of the statue I had given that name. Obviously I wasn't the only one to make that connection. I had to go see it. I fought my way across two lines of tables and roaming students. Sitting at the table next to the Golem poster were three students. They all looked about my age or a little older, upperclassmen. The girl was a tiny, plump, smiling, cherubic blonde. A non-descript, dark-haired boy faded into the background next to her. On the far side was the thin redhead from the Writers' House. He watched me as I walked up to the table. I couldn't make myself look away from him for more than a second. I felt like I had known him longer and better than a few quick glances. He didn't look away from me, either. I wondered if he felt this insane sense of familiarity.

I got to the table and saw the motto under the picture of the Golem. 'Words Make Life.' Next to the poster was a small pile of cheaply printed magazines.

"Hi. We're Golem. We meet at the Writers' House on Tuesdays at seven and help each other become better writers," the blonde chirped. She beamed a smile at me. Instead of thinking, 'Oh, what a nice friendly girl,' I found myself feeling cold and focusing on her teeth. Small, perfect, white teeth that looked almost unreal, too sharp.

"I'm not much of a writer. I like to read, though."

"You can't be a good writer if you can't make readers happy. If you come check us out, you can read other people's things and tell them how to make it better. Really, it's fun." Her high-beam smile was still aimed at me, making me feel uncomfortable and shivery.

"Ummm…"

The redhead handed me a piece of paper about Golem while saying, "Really, come. It'll be worth your while. Being a reader for us is fun." His fingers brushed mine when he slid the paper into my hand. I found myself thinking reading for them would be a blast.

"Sure. Tuesday at seven, you said?"

"Yes." He smiled at me. Suddenly everything was fine; the world was a better place because his smile was in it. I smiled back at him. For a moment the rest of the room faded away. There was only him and me and a feeling of intense contentment. Like this was the place I was supposed to be, and the person I was meant to be with.

Then I was back in my own head. I turned away from the table quickly, feeling ridiculous. I wasn't some dopy teen cooing over the boy with the wonderful, thick, wavy red hair and the big, gray eyes. Big, gray eyes with impossibly long lashes behind small round glasses. I shook my head again and turned to look back at the redhead. He was still watching me. I knew he felt that contentment as intensely as I had.

"I don't think it's her," Autumn said yet again. They'd been arguing about it for almost an hour. Chris and Dave were convinced. Autumn didn't agree.

"Look, Autumn. It's her. She feels like a healer. Like one of our Healers at least. She's got to be magic. Otherwise, we'd be able to find her," Dave said while sipping a beer.

"Are you sure? She had no shields, no magic of any sort. I don't see any reason why you can't find her."

"She had on a pendant of some sort," Dave answered. "And you're welcome to find her if it's just incompetence on my part, Chris' part, and Chuck's part that we can't find her."

"Let me restate. I don't see anything she's doing that's keeping you from finding her. There's, what, half a dozen places within half a mile of here where she could be living and we wouldn't be able to locate her?"

"Something like that," Chris replied grudgingly. "I've broken the shields and searched four of them, watched the other two for hours, and I still can't find her. It's like she disappears after she jogs by here. If we hadn't seen her today, I would have gotten up tomorrow and gone jogging just to see where she goes."

"There's an image. Do you even own sneakers?" Autumn looked pointedly at the loafers he was wearing.

Chris looked mildly exasperated. "Yes, I own sneakers. I just don't need them all that often."

"There's an understatement," Dave added.

"And when was the last time you went out and did anything even remotely like exercise?" Chris shot back at Dave.

"I very rarely do anything 'out.' Inside is an entirely different story, and I don't need shoes if I'm inside. But that's beside the point. We've found her. When she comes to Golem, we can study her further and go from there."

Chris stood up. Dave was right; there was no point in arguing about it further. "Bedtime for me." He headed up the stairs to his room. It was a good-sized room for a college student: ten by ten. He'd decorated it in muted grays and blues with black and white still-life photographs on the walls. The entire room radiated an adult tidiness more consistent with a forty-year-old than a college student. He kicked off his shoes, took his toothbrush and toothpaste out of the plastic caddy in his closet, and headed into the bathroom.

A few minutes later he was back in his room. He locked the door, stripped out of his clothing, and put on his pajamas. Green boxers would do for tonight. He lay on his bed; it was much too warm for getting under the light blue blanket and gray sheets.

Chris clasped his hands behind his head and stared at the ceiling. The image of the healer filled his mind.

I've missed you, he said to the girl in his fantsy, his fingers stroking her neck.

And I you, my love, she said back. Her eyes warm with pleasure at finding him again. He sighed. She didn't miss him because it wasn't the same woman. He let the image go and willed himself to sleep.

All I could see was green fabric rubbing against my nose. Voices murmured around me while a hand on my arm led me somewhere. Gentle pressure let me know it was time to stop. The hand released me.

A voice spoke to me. I answered in words that held no meaning. The first voice spoke again; another responded. Once more the first voice spoke.

Trembling hands lifted the veil carefully from my face. In front of me stood another of the blue-skinned elves. This one was a very young man, barely out of adolescence. His skin was robin's egg blue and his hair a dark, inky red. The color of a ripe black cherry. I couldn't see his eyes. He was looking down at the hands he had held out, palms up, toward me.

I knew what I needed to do. I placed my palms against his. My fingers rested on his wrists, his on mine. His eyes, stony gray with metallic flashes, darted up to meet mine, and I felt myself blush. I looked down at our hands. A tattoo decorated his left arm, a tangle of ivy vines. My left arm was bare. As the first voice continued speaking, a matching mark crept up my arm.

The first voice continued to speak. I turned and saw an older man with sky blue skin and graying red hair. He appeared quite happy. I felt myself smile at him.

I turned my attention back to the boy in front of me. I could feel his pulse under my fingers. It was fast. He was as nervous as I was. That felt good. He gave my wrist a quick stroke with his index finger.

I looked up at him briefly. He was still looking down at our hands. My thumbs were under his hands, out of view. I stroked the back of his hand with my thumb. He looked up at me, his granite-colored eyes meeting mine. I felt him smile though his lips didn't move.

Then I was in bed. I slid out of the dream as quickly as I had gone into it. No warning. One second I was there with the blue boy, the next the sun was streaming in over me, saying it was time to go jogging. By the time I was out of the house and half a block up the street, the dream had faded, leaving me with a sense I had dreamed something interesting, but I couldn't remember what.

7.

Pat could feel the traces of the magic before he saw Burq. He stood next to Sarah, looking quiet and relaxed, supposedly paying attention to Coach Junt's lecture about the system for ranking fencers. In reality he was debating if he wanted to out himself yet. Pat knew his own shields were good enough the others hadn't noticed him. He watched Cell, Dia, and Illyn call Sarah over last night. Obviously, he wasn't the only one who recognized her. Pat decided to steer clear of them. He knew he was just putting off the inevitable; for the time being Pat didn't mind.

Another man entered the room. *Burq.* There was no mistaking the presence of that magic. Burq had chin-length, dark auburn hair, eyes the color of old limestone, traces of Dia's and Anthur's magic, and the confident, easy moves of a man who knows he's the best fighter in the room. Pat took a breath. Time to hide or declare himself.

Fuck. Not worth hiding. Pat dropped the cloaking spell. Burq's eyes met Pat's, and he looked surprised. Pat smiled at him. Coach Junt continued to talk and then pointed at Burq. "This is Mike Tamon. He's the highest-rated fencer in the state of Pennsylvania. He's here to work with anyone who wants to."

Pat bounced up almost before Coach Junt had finished speaking. "I'm game for a match if you are."

Burq… Mike nodded. They moved into position and saluted each other. Mike asked, "All out?"

"Sure. You'll probably win, but it'll be interesting," Pat responded before sliding the mask over his face.

Pat had forgotten what it felt like to really fight someone. Even with the rules of fencing keeping them from digging deeply into their respective bags of tricks, this was much better than anything he'd done since leaving Hidiri. The two of them definitely had to do this again, maybe with real blades if Mike would let him borrow one.

Pat figured it hadn't been too long in real time, maybe eight minutes—almost an eternity in fencing time—before Mike landed his fifteenth point. Mike pulled off his helmet, and Pat did likewise, happy to salute an old friend.

Pat walked back over to Sarah while Mike caught his breath. Coach Junt stopped looking stunned long enough to tell everyone to pair up and start fencing.

"That was incredible," she said to him.

He grinned at her. "It was nice to really work for once."

"That's one way of putting it. Think he'd be willing to join us to fight?"

"I certainly hope so. Most fencers I know don't have much desire to try hand to hand, though."

"You might have something there. Still…"

"Yeah."

Mike didn't run to the Writers' House after fencing class. He managed to walk sedately. *Ahni Al Ath Gyr Bui!* He was back. They said he would be here. That he had to be here this year, and, of course, he was. Ahni had to have known it was him when he volunteered to fight. They sparred like that before. Mike always won with a blade. Ahni would always win with bare hands.

He got into the house. Autumn was still in her room getting ready to leave. He could feel Chris in the kitchen and assumed Dave was up in his room.

"I found him," he announced. All three of his housemates appeared in an instant.

"Ahni?" Chris asked eagerly.

"Yes, he's here. Just like you said he would be."

"Did you talk to him?" Autumn's face was hard to read, but she sounded excited.

"No chance. He's got a friend. She was with him the whole time."

"Short, dark hair, tight body?" Chris questioned.

"Yes."

"I think he's found our healer," Chris said.

"Well, let's hope that's the only pattern that repeats this time," Autumn answered bitterly.

"So, what do you want to do on Friday?" Pat asked Sarah when he put down his homework.

"Same thing I do every Friday: cook a good meal, light some candles, and celebrate the Sabbath."

"Oh." He had been hoping to get her out to do something on Friday: hit a party, go dancing maybe.

"Wanna come?" She smiled at him.

"Is that okay?" It wasn't his first choice, but it was still time with her.

"Yes. It's not just okay; it's encouraged."

"Really?"

"Yep, really. I light the candles eighteen minutes before sunset, so you want to be here by seven. Then we'll eat, hang out, and enjoy ourselves. No work. If you want to read, bring a fun book."

"I can do that. Do I need a hat or something?"

"If you've got one, that would be good."

"I've got a Yankees cap."

"Well, it's profane but better than nothing." Pat looked blankly at Sarah and saw her realize he didn't get her joke. "My family is filled with lifelong Mets fans."

"Heathens! You aren't a Mets fan, too?"

"I couldn't care less about baseball. But you should have seen my nephews in their tiny, little Mets uniforms when they were babies. That was awfully cute."

Pat shook his head. *Mets fans.*

Friday afternoon Pat headed downtown to the state store. Yet another reason why he wasn't going to settle in Pennsylvania: no decent wine shops here. He cruised around the store, looking at a barely adequate collection of overpriced bottles until he found a nice pinot noir. Pat paid and left with no problems. He didn't have to whip out any magic; the clerk didn't ask for ID.

He got home, showered, and looked around for something appropriate to wear. After badgering from his mom, Pat brought one suit with him, but he thought that would be overkill. He settled on a dark blue button down and jeans that weren't threadbare and battered. He put on the cap and set a spell to keep himself cool. Then he headed to her place.

Sarah opened the door, looking pleased at how he was dressed. She was in her usual cargo pants and t-shirt. He hoped he wasn't horribly overdressed.

Sarah smiled, gestured at the bottle, and asked Pat, "Do I want to know how you got that?" as he walked in.

"Let's just say no one has ever checked my ID when I wanted to buy alcohol." Which was true though, on occasion, he had to make them not check.

"Cool. They always check mine."

"Curse of your sweet baby face."

"Yep."

"So, what happens now?" Pat asked.

"I change..." *Good.* He wasn't horribly overdressed, just early. "light the candles, say the blessing, and then we eat."

"It smells good. What are we eating?"

"Lasagna. Alas, I am still awaiting meat from my brothers. Next week, with any luck, we'll have some roast beef."

"You plan on feeding me regularly?"

"I certainly hoped to. Assuming you're okay with joining me for Sabbath."

Pat smiled widely. "Yes."

"Let me go get changed. I'll be back shortly." He puttered around her place and heard the water turn on in Sarah's shower. Her computer was on the table. It took him a few minutes to find her Rhapsody subscription, several more to set up a playlist. Pat wasn't sure what was appropriate for Sabbath dinner, so he stayed with classic rock.

Tom Petty was working his way through "Free Falling" when she emerged. Pat smiled softly. Sarah had on a rosy pink sundress and some sort of white cardigan-looking thing. It was just so light, pretty, and feminine Pat didn't know quite what to do with himself. He did know what he wanted to do—walk over, wrap his arms around her, and kiss her until she forgot dinner—wasn't appropriate.

"You own a dress?" *Oh, that was really smooth.*

She smiled at him. "I own several dresses. If we were going out, I'd put on sandals, too." Sarah wiggled her bare toes at him, then went around the room lighting candles. When she finished, she waved him over to join her at the table.

Pat didn't ask many questions. He watched her say the blessings and go through the motions. The language was wrong and the motions different, but her prayers felt like home. It reminded him of the observance of the moon in Hidiri. *How could she not remember them?*

"You seem very serious tonight," Sarah said to him as she took a bite of the salad.

"This isn't a serious occasion?" That was as good an answer as any.

"Yes, but not solemn. It's the weekend, the start of the day of rest. It's about joy and relaxation, good food, and good friends." She lifted her glass to Pat. He lifted his in return and smiled.

They spent the rest of dinner talking about the different groups they checked out at the Activities Fair and which ones looked like they were worth visiting. She wanted to join Golem. He couldn't think of any good reason why he wouldn't. It was a writing group. He was a writer. Trying to explain why he didn't want to take her into the Writers' House was more trouble than it was worth. Mike obviously didn't recognize her, and if Illyn started trouble, he could handle it. He agreed to go. They talked about starting up a MMA group as they wrapped up dinner.

He left her home an hour later, walking around campus aimlessly. It was too early to go to bed, and Pat wasn't in a party mood. He wondered how long would be appropriate to wait before he tried to kiss Sarah. He wondered how much she really loved Ari if she was willing to move across the world to go to school. Most of all, Pat wondered how she got here without her memory. Had she died? Did she come on purpose? Had she followed them? What happened to her boys? Wandering around the campus gave him no answers.

8.

"You think she'll come?" Autumn asked.

"Yes. She'll come. I made sure of that," Chris told the others while he set chairs around the perimeter of their living room. The Writers' House always got cramped at Golem time. The thirty-ish members could just be squeezed into the long narrow living room.

"Then let's set up a test," Autumn said.

"I like that idea." Chuck smiled and rested his hand on Chris' right shoulder.

Chris jumped back. "Son of a bitch! That hurt! You can set up the rest of the damn chairs yourself." He shook his hand; the last two fingers moved sluggishly. "What did you do? I can't feel my fingers."

"Nothing I can't fix if she doesn't." Chuck's smile reminded Chris of when they'd played as children and Chuck would hit him for the fun of it.

"Great." He rubbed his hand. "How did I end up the guinea pig? You've actually got a hurt leg she could work on."

"I want to observe. You're already convinced. Besides, she gets bonus points if she can figure out what actually happened to you."

A young man with dark brown hair poked his head through the door. "Hey, can I come in?"

"Harold!" Autumn went over and hugged him. "How was your summer?"

Pat and I entered the small red house a few minutes before seven the next Tuesday. About thirty people sat around a long rectangular living room, chatting away. Most of them were in groups of twos and threes, like Pat and me. One very pretty girl with black hair and big blue eyes, who looked like she had come alone, scooted over on a sofa and motioned for us to join her. We did.

"Hi, I'm Emily."

"Hello, I'm Pat; that's Sarah. This your first meeting?"

"Yep, I like to write poetry, so it sounded like a good idea. What about you guys?"

I shrugged and pointed at Pat, "He's the writer. I'm a reader, and they said they needed readers, so here we are." I felt the muscles at the back of my skull tighten as a low ache settled there. I twisted my head trying to relieve the tension while listening to the others. It was oddly cold in there, too. I didn't see any AC, but it had been sweltering outside.

"What do you write?" A boy sitting in the chair on the other side of us asked Pat.

"Short stories, plays, the occasional attempt at a novel."

"No poems?"

Pat laughed. "I write bad poetry. I wouldn't want to inflict it on anyone else."

"How bad?"

"Well, it's not 'Ode to a Small Lump of Green Putty…' but it's pretty bad." Emily laughed; the boy looked blankly at Pat. Then the group hushed because the tall redhead with the amazing gray eyes stood up and spoke to us.

I'll admit I didn't really listen to what he had to say. Most of it was about submission guidelines, how to become a member, and what was expected of members. The blonde girl passed out papers with all that information on it anyway. What I was listening to was the sound of his voice. It wasn't particularly deep or forceful, but if whiskey and silk could mate and produce a sound, it would be his voice.

I gazed at him intently. I'd never have a better excuse to stare. He wasn't handsome. He was too tall, too thin, too pale, and too sharply edged for handsome. But he was arresting. Those gray eyes, granite flecked with steel: they grabbed a hold of me and wouldn't let go. His red hair: thick and wavy, the color of charred brick, a color I had never seen on a person before. I found myself wanting to run my fingers through it, wishing it was just a little bit longer so I could get a good grip on it. I wanted to see if it smelled as good as it looked.

I suddenly knew he had caught me day dreaming while I was studying him. He appeared to find it amusing. I felt like he grinned at me, but I didn't see a grin.

I smiled back at him. Once again I knew his reaction—surprise—without actually seeing the reaction on his face. *Odd.* Why would my smile surprise him? Maybe I was supposed to blush and look away? *Fat chance!* The daydreams would have to be a lot more interesting than petting his hair before I started blushing.

He finished his 'Get To Know Golem' speech and sat down. The blonde who handed out the papers took over.

"Let's all introduce ourselves. I'm Autumn, a senior political science major. I write mostly poetry with the occasional short story…"

They went around the circle. I tried to listen but really couldn't muster much attention. "Hi, I'm [insert name here]. I write poetry…" That pretty much summed up the group. I wanted to know the redhead's name, which meant sitting through everyone else.

"Hi, I'm Pat. I write stories, and I try to write plays."

My turn. "I'm Sarah. I don't write, but I like to read. They," I said, waving at Autumn and the redhead, "told me you needed readers."

The girl next to me: "Hello, I'm Emily, I also write poetry. Seems like we've got a lot of poets in this group." I sighed quietly. How would Indiana Jones say it? 'Poets? Why does it have to be poets?' Something like that. I love to read. I like sci-fi. I love fantasy. I like mysteries and satires and historical fiction. Most poetry leaves me cold, though. I had a feeling this might very well be my first and last Golem meeting if all I would have to read was reams and reams of poetry.

The introductions continued to circle around the group. I noticed Mike from our fencing class was there. "Hello, I'm Mike. I write plays." Thank the Lord! Not poetry! Maybe this would be a good way to get to know him better. Invite him to our sparring sessions if we got along.

I went back to watching the redhead while the introductions flowed around me. He'd watch me intently and then switch to Pat. After a while, I noticed he wasn't looking back at me. I could feel disappointment build. I really, really hoped he wasn't gay. It's silly; I know, but for some reason, even if I'm fully aware of the fact nothing will ever happen, I prefer the men I find interesting to be straight.

"Hello, I'm Chuck. I write short stories, long stories, and one never-ending novel." Yay! Another non-poet. Things were looking up. And yet another redhead. Five of the thirty or so Golemites were redheads. Maybe I could use that for my senior thesis: are red hair and creativity genetically linked traits? I snapped away from gene sequencing to the introductions. My redhead—*The redhead. Not mine. Never mine.*—was about to speak.

"Hello, I'm Chris. I write the occasional poem as well, but most of the time I just read." Finally, he had a name. And he was a reader. Perhaps one day we'd have a chat about the fine art of reading for writers. That could be interesting. Like he heard me think it, he caught my eye and smiled. This time the smile actually made it to his lips. I felt like we had just made a date without speaking a word.

After introductions, Autumn passed us two short poems. We were told to read them; then we'd work on how to make them better. Since this was the first meeting, the poems had been picked from works submitted in previous years, so the authors weren't present. We were supposed to be honest but kind, remembering the coming works would have authors present.

The first wasn't terrible. But like with most poems, I read through and thought, 'Yep, it's a poem.' While the others were talking about word choice, meter, and imagery, I didn't have much to add.

The second piece was better. It was a short little funny bit about an alarm clock. I kind of dug it, but I wouldn't have bought a book filled with poems like it.

Then we were done. Autumn told us we were welcome to hang out and mingle; there were copies of next week's submissions on the table as well as drinks and cookies. I watched the group, feeling a little silly about not knowing anyone's name. Chris talked quietly with the never-ending novelist, Chuck, I thought. Chris kept flexing his wrist and rubbing the last two fingers. I looked closer. They had a faint tinge of blue. Well, if there was ever a better icebreaker than, 'Hey, let me show you how to not hurt anymore,' I didn't know what it was. And, I thought with a little spark of wicked joy, it'd be nice to get my hands on him.

I walked over to them, glancing around to see what Pat was up to. He was busy chatting up Emily. Having him vouch for my pure intentions might be a good thing. Granted in this case my intentions were only about ninety-three percent pure.

I got within a step of them when they both turned to look at me.

"I know this is going to sound stupid, but I can show you how to make your wrist feel better." I had been expecting them to look surprised or puzzled, but I got the feeling both of them had expected me to come over. The neverending novelist looked at me like he had just eaten something rancid. Chris looked smugly pleased, like he had just won a bet.

"Why do you think it hurts?" Chris asked. That's not the usual question when faced with someone offering to fix you. Most people ask, 'How?'

"You're rubbing your pinky and ring finger like they're numb. When you flex and twist your wrist, I can see it catch and grind. It should move smoothly."

"And you can help?" The other redhead sounded skeptical.

"I think so. No guarantees. A few spots cause that kind of problem, and I'm fairly certain which one is bothering you based on your posture."

"I'm game." Chris smiled at me.

"Good." I pointed to the chair he was sitting in. "Can you turn around and straddle that chair?" He complied. "I want you to pull your arm across your chest. That'll move your shoulder blade out of the way." He did as told. "Now, there's only three places that cause what's happening with your wrist and hand. This is the most common one." I gently leaned my elbow into a tight bundle of muscles that had been hiding under his scapula.

He tensed, hissed softly, and said, "I can feel that all the way to my fingers."

"Exactly." I leaned into it then pulled back, rubbing gently, repeating the action a few times. And, by doing so, I attracted some attention.

"Are we doing back rubs? I love back rubs. I've always wanted to get really good at giving them," another girl, whose name I couldn't remember, said while edging me away from Chris as she babbled a stream of inane words about massage. I stepped aside, and she hopped into my place, her hands clenching into his shoulders.

"Hello, Brooke," Chris said while she mauled his *trapezius*.

"Hi, Brooke." I began trying to show her how to do a better job. "Here, you want to be firm but not that hard. Use your whole hand, not just the tips of your fingers." She wasn't getting my verbal instructions, or she was trying to hurt him on purpose.

I moved behind her and shifted her hair out of the way. It was beautiful hair: thick, wavy, the color of polished walnut in sunlight, and mid-back length. It was the prettiest thing about her. Her body was short and squat, not fat so much as thick. Her face probably would have been pleasant, were it not for her rudeness. In spite of that, I was going to try to show her what a decent massage should feel like, if for no other reason than to prevent Chris from getting hurt. I started to work on her shoulder while telling her what I was doing and how. "Here. Feel the way I'm touching you? I've got my whole hand on your *trapezius*, not just my fingers. So you're getting a rub, not a poke." Then I took her hand and held it to show her what to do with Chris.

She was getting better. Chris stopped wincing, so I moved off. It wasn't too hard to see she didn't want me near him; I had no desire to fight her. Chris could find me if he wanted to continue the massage.

I wandered to the other side of the room and grabbed a soda. Next to the snacks was the stack of next week's submissions. I grabbed them, found a comfy seat, and began to read.

Which lasted all of nine seconds. It was poetry. Bad poetry. Lame, whiny, angst-filled, 'I'd rather be shot in the head than have to spend another minute on this Earth, but instead of doing the honorable thing and killing myself, I'll put it on paper and inflict it on you,' poetry. I flipped to the next submission; someone was way, way too interested in his coffee addiction, spending close to three pages singing about it in excruciating detail. The third one was a fantastic short story about the day cows began falling from the sky. That one had me laughing out loud. "Falling Cows" won me over. If there were chances to read things like that by being a member, I'd become a member.

Having finished the submissions for next week I went back to watching Chris. Brooke was still fondling his shoulders. Autumn swooped over, glaring daggers at her.

Either Brooke was the worst observer of body language ever, or she was carefully ignoring it. It looked like only extreme force of will, and the fact Brooke was eight inches taller and probably thirty pounds heavier kept Autumn from physically removing her from Chris' shoulders.

Pat plopped down next to me. "So, do you think the catfight actually breaks out?" he asked after studying the scene for a moment.

"I'm thinking no."

"Damn. The big one's got the size advantage, but the little one looks mean."

"Not just her…" I thought for a second and came up with a name. "Chuck?" Pat nodded at me. I had the name right. "Looks like he doesn't want Brooke around, either."

"No, he doesn't. She, however, looks like she never wants to leave."

"And Chris looks like he's trying to get her off of him." That made me think about Chris checking Pat out at the meeting. "Did you see Chris checking you out?"

"I saw no such thing. Even if I did, it would be a direct violation of my intensely heterosexual orientation to admit it. I did however notice him watching you, as well."

"As well?" I smiled at him.

He winked at me and answered in a sing-song voice. "Well, maybe I'm not perfectly straight."

We both laughed. "Just straight enough then?" I asked him.

"Just straight enough." We laughed again. "If I had to guess, that's the camp I'd put Chris in, too. Though he is a tidy dresser, and, unless I'm mistaken, that's gel in his hair. I did see him watching me. Autumn and Chuck were watching, too. I don't know why I'm so fascinating today. Whatever they were looking for, it didn't feel sexy."

"Yeah, there is a feel to that kind of look. That's not how he was watching me, either. I didn't pay much attention to Autumn and Chuck. Were they watching me as well?"

"Chuck, yes. Autumn, no. Or if she did, I didn't catch her at it. Finally." Chris put his hand on Brooke's, told her he was feeling much better, and stood up.

"She's just standing there beaming at him."

"This is like watching a train wreck. It's horrible, but you can't look away. Do you really think she has no idea they're all scowling at her?"

"It doesn't look like it." I gently shook my head.

"I mean, I've seen determined women before, but this girl looks one step away from scary stalker chick that boils your bunny."

"Oh, look, he's moving away, and yes, she's following him."

Emily sat down next to us on the couch. "What are we watching so intently?"

"See the redhead and the girl with the long, brown hair following him?" Pat asked.

"Yeah. Chris and Brooke."

"Yep. Anyway, he's been trying to get rid of her for fifteen minutes now, and she's not taking the hint. And by 'hint' I mean he's done everything but specifically tell her to back off," Pat filled her in.

Emily looked over at them and back at me. "Oh. Hey, weren't you giving him a back rub? Did she muscle you out?"

"Yes, I was giving him a back rub. And yes, she literally edged me out. She just kept talking inanely about massage and moving closer and closer. It was either let go of Chris or get hip checked. As soon as I let go, she pounced."

"Think she's his girlfriend?" Emily wanted to know.

"Doesn't look like it," Pat answered. "Just keep watching; the body language is all wrong."

We watched as Chris got a drink, Brooke following a step behind him. He didn't offer her one, so she grabbed her own. He said something to her and went upstairs without her following. A minute later she left.

"Yeah, not his girlfriend." Emily turned to me. "So, why were you rubbing his back? A not so subtle come-on?"

I grinned. "He's lovely, but no. He was rubbing his fingers and twisting his wrist. Looked like his arm hurt, and if I was right, I knew how to make it better. When I poked him in the shoulder, I found out I was right. Then Brooke pounced before I could really fix it."

We talked about massage for a bit, and then Pat and Emily started talking about *Hitchhiker's Guide To the Galaxy*. Emily went off to get the two of them drinks.

When she left, Chuck drifted over to us. "Sarah, right?"

"Yes."

"He's upstairs pretending to do some school work. If you went up and finished what you started, he'd appreciate it."

"He could come down and tell me himself."

Chuck's voice dropped lower. "And risk Brooke and Autumn again? No, he'll be up there all night. But you'd be welcome to go up."

"And you'd know why?"

"I'm his best friend. I know."

"Uh huh. I live two doors down. Second floor of the gray house, stairs are on the right. I'll be heading off in a minute. He's welcome if he wants me to finish working on him."

Chuck didn't look happy about what I said. He wandered off, chatted with a dark-haired boy I knew I had seen before but couldn't place, and headed upstairs.

"You sure you want him in your house?" Pat asked me.

"More than I want to go wandering up and invade his territory. It's weird. There's nothing he's done, but I just don't want to do anything on Chuck's say-so. He just... rubs me wrong. Besides, if I'm going to be touching strange guys I've not spoken more than fifty words to, I'd rather do it at my place."

"You want me to come with you?" I was touched by how concerned he was.

"Nah, stay here. Keep chatting up Emily. I think she likes you."

"I think she does, too. You're sure?"

"How many knives am I wearing?"

"Two."

"Think I've got something even better at home in case a guy gets frisky and I don't want it?"

He smiled slowly at me and nodded. "Yeah."

"Good. Go have fun." I smiled at him and passed Emily returning with their drinks. I gave her a smile as well and headed off into the night.

9.

Chris closed his door harder than necessary. *Fucking Brooke!* He had almost told her to piss off and die. She had been touching him, and Brooke came over and ruined it.

Sarah. Her name is Sarah. She was interested in him. He felt that very strongly when she was watching him. That she had a clue as to what he was thinking was even better. He hadn't expected that. He usually knew when someone was reading him but hadn't felt her do it. She just knew.

He would have to remember to talk to Dave about that. He didn't feel her use any magic to do it. He hadn't felt her use any magic period. Dave might have some extra insight into that. During the meeting Chuck had been echoing in his head about how it was a bust; Sarah couldn't be a healer. Then the beautiful 'I told you so' moment when she walked over and offered to fix his shoulder.

Then Chuck's 'I told you so' back. There had been no magic in her touch. But she had known what to do, how to do it, and seen it across the room. There had to be something there. *Maybe she doesn't know how to use it?* It was possible she'd been coasting on natural talent without ever really working on it. It wasn't impossible she was a latent talent.

He heard footsteps on his stairs and was disappointed they weren't Sarah's. Those steps were Chuck's. Chuck didn't knock; he knew he was welcome.

"She says if you want to finish up, go to her house."

"She doesn't want to come up here?"

Chuck shook his head. "Apparently not. She lives in the gray house, two doors down."

"That's where she's been hiding?" He stood up and slipped on shoes. "You coming?"

"She didn't invite me."

"Come anyway. I want you to see this, too."

"Watching you get a back rub isn't my idea of fun."

"Seeing Dave and I are right and she's our healer is worth your time. Besides, it'll give you a chance to see what's in her place that's keeping her hidden."

I had two something betters at home: a .45 Glock and a tiny Baretta .22. I put the Baretta in my top right leg pocket. One of the great things about cargo pants: they've got pockets for everything. That done, I settled down on my couch to do some chemistry problems.

Through my open window I heard two muted male voices and footsteps. Chris and Chuck. Looks like I'm not the only cautious one. I was at the door by the time they got to the top of my stairs but waited for them to knock to answer.

"Come in. Welcome to my home."

"Hello." Chris smiled at me.

"Hey." Chuck didn't smile. Once again there wasn't anything impolite or particularly wrong about Chuck; his existence just bothered me. The tension in my neck that started at the beginning of Golem intensified. *Of all the times to develop a headache! Why is it I can fix other people, but I can't make these stupid headaches go away?*

They hadn't moved off my porch. I gestured to welcome them into my apartment and asked, "So, want me to fix your arm?"

"Yes, that'd be great," Chris said while walking in, Chuck half a step behind him.

"Then take off your shirt and straddle that chair." Chris looked a little uncomfortable but untucked his t-shirt, anyway. Perhaps he had been looking for some more conversation before I got working on him. Perhaps he was just shy. When I caught a glimpse of his deliciously flat tummy with a line of dark red hair below his navel, I stopped wondering and turned to face Chuck. "Can I get either of you something to drink or eat?" Chris shook his head at me before sliding his t-shirt over his head.

"I could use a drink. What do you have?" Chuck asked.

"Water, soda, hot tea if you want to toss some water in the microwave, iced tea if you want to do that and then pour it over ice." I watched as Chris carefully folded his shirt and placed it on my kitchen table. Then he took off his glasses and put them on the shirt.

"Nothing harder?"

"I'm not much of a drinker. I usually have wine in the house, just not right now." Pat and I kicked the bottle he brought for Sabbath, and I hadn't gotten a new one yet.

"I'll take some soda then." I took out a glass and grabbed the bottle of Pepsi.

"Ice?"

"Yes." I used pouring the drink as an excuse to think more about how Chris looked without looking like I was ogling him. The back of my stove is shiny black. I could see him clearly reflected in it. His outer appearance was tidy and preppy. His jeans were in pristine shape, worn with a conservative leather belt and loafers. The t-shirt had a collar and looked more like golf wear than hanging out at school clothing. Hiding under the shirt were three necklaces and a tattoo that looked like a Celtic knot done in black and green vines around his arm just below his left deltoid. The soda stopped fizzing. Time to face them again. I gave Chuck his drink and went into my bedroom, returning a few seconds later with my pillow.

"Here." I handed it to Chris. "Put it between you and the back of the chair. It'll be more comfortable to lean against."

He put the pillow against the back of the chair and rested his head on it. I spent another moment just looking at him while I rubbed my hands together to warm them. Like Pat, and probably just about every other natural redhead on Earth, his skin was pale, almost milky. Unlike Pat he was unfreckled and, other than sparse hair on his chest and the trail below his navel that I really, really needed to stop fantasizing about, smooth. And, unlike Pat, there was nothing visibly wrong with him.

"What happened to your arm?" I lay my hands on the top of his shoulder and began to get a feel for what was going on. The quick poke I got in before only told me he had trigger point issues. Now that I had the time to really see what was going on, I wasn't about to skimp on him. Placing my hands on his shoulders felt right and strangely familiar. The tactile equivalent of that moment during the Activities Fair when the world faded away. *Stop it.* I pulled myself back to something nearing professional.

"I think I slept on it wrong. I woke up with it under me and numb. Fourteen hours later and it's still not right."

"Your ring finger and pinky are numb, right?" I jiggled his shoulder gently to get the muscles to loosen up.

"Yes. You got that just by watching me rub my hand?"

I let go of his shoulder and picked up his hand, tracing my fingers down his last two fingers. He watched me so intensely it made me wonder if he too felt this insane rightness of my skin on his. *He asked you a question. Answer it!* "That and the color on those two fingers doesn't quite match the other three. You have to know to look for it to see it. Do you mind taking off your rings?"

"No." He slid the class ring he had on his ring finger and the gold Celtic knot on his middle finger off and put them on his left middle finger. He watched me stroke his fingers for a few seconds before asking, "How did you know to look for it?"

I knelt in front of him and started to seriously work on his hand. Stretching the fingers apart and rubbing my knuckles into the base of his palm. "I see someone in pain. I look to see if there's anything I can do about it. You were obviously dealing with some sort of wrist/hand issue, so I looked close to see if it was something I could help. Lucky for you, it looked right up my alley."

"So you're what, the massage fairy? Bringing back rubs to all the good little boys and girls?" Chuck quipped.

I gave him a wry half-smile while flexing Chris' wrist. "I suppose you could say that. Ever heard the term *mitzvah*?"

"As in Bar Mitzvah?" Chris asked.

"Yes, it's part of the same concept. It literally means 'commandment.' But in general terms a *mitzvah* is a good deed, an act of human kindness. These are my good deeds. I think your wrist is slightly out of alignment. Do you mind if I pop it back into place?"

"Will it hurt?"

"Probably not. It will make a loud pop."

"Sounds fine to me." I held his forearm in one hand, his hand in the other, and twisted them quickly in opposite directions. There was a loud, satisfying pop. Chris ran his hand through its range of motion, flexing his fingers. The catching, grinding motion he had before was gone.

"Better?"

"Much."

"Good. We aren't done yet. Let me get a hold of your shoulder and neck again. By the time we're done you'll think you've got a new arm." I went to work, sliding my fingers along his neck, squeezing and kneading tight flesh, stroking his cream colored skin just a bit more than was strictly necessary. Chuck watched me work with hard eyes. Like he knew I wasn't being totally professional. I couldn't tell if he was being jealous or protective, though.

"Let me know if I do anything too hard or you feel it somewhere other than where I'm touching you."

"Everything feels good so far."

The area in need of the most work was directly under his necklaces. He didn't really look like the kind of guy to wear jewelry. Yet here he was, wearing three necklaces, two of which I couldn't really see because they were between his chest and the pillow. They were loose enough to not be a problem. The third was a snug band of hemp with bone beads. I slid the hemp necklace up his neck, out of the way. It felt oddly cold, but I lost that thought when I noticed he tensed when I moved the necklace.

"Sorry, is it scratchy?"

"Yeah, a little."

"That's why I don't wear hemp, always feels itchy to me."

"It was a gift from a good friend."

"Ah, I can see that. I've worn things from friends I wouldn't have otherwise." I worked my fingers into the tight muscles at the junction of his neck and his shoulder. "Anyway, how's this feeling?"

He was flexing his hand again. "I can feel that all the way down my arm."

"The nerve that lets you move your hand has to go through the muscles here. If they get too tight, they press on that nerve and things get numb."

"Good to know."

"Yeah, it is. You can work on this yourself; just use your left hand." I spent a few more minutes rubbing his neck while Chuck wandered around my rooms. Then he put his soda down on the table and went to the bathroom. I heard the door close and figured this was the only time I'd get alone with Chris tonight.

"My friend Pat, the guy you were really checking out, isn't gay."

"What?!?" He sat straight up and twisted to face me. I felt all the good work I had done on relaxing those muscles vanish as they all tightened back up again.

"We noticed you checking him out at the meeting. He's not gay."

"Neither am I!"

"Okay…" I held up a palm in a gesture of peace. "I don't want to offend you. But I didn't want you to get burned if that's how you lean."

"It's not." He turned back to face the pillow and slumped into it.

"Fine." I put my hands back on his shoulders and started to work on him again. After a few seconds, he sat right back up again and twisted to look at me again.

"I was looking at you, too."

"Yeah, but you were looking at him more."

"I was looking at you a lot more than I was looking at him!" He seemed really indignant. Well, some guys are sensitive about that. The question: Was he protesting too much because he actually was gay but not out yet? Or just annoyed at the idea anyone would mistake him for gay? Or was he annoyed that I missed him checking me out because I was watching him check my guy friend out? I could speculate on that later. If he had been checking me out, it was time to shoot that down, too.

"Okay… well, see that picture on my mantel of me and the black guy?"

"No, I can't see that far away without my glasses on."

"Oh. Anyway, that's a picture of me and my man."

"You have a boyfriend?"

"Yeah."

We heard the toilet flush and knew it was time to drop that subject. Chris rested his head against the chair again. I went back to working on his shoulder. A few seconds later I heard the door to my bathroom opening.

"I need you to pull your arm across your chest like you did before." He did so without saying anything. Once more I eased the point of my elbow into that stubborn knot. "You've had this one for a long time."

"Yes. Years. Car accident when I was younger caused the scar on my arm." He gestured to the star-shaped white splotch on his bicep, "After six weeks with that arm in a cast and sling, my shoulder was never quite right again."

I knew what that sort of scar meant. His *humerus* had poked through his arm. I shuddered at the thought of that sort of pain. "That's why I hate broken bones: the bone heals up fine but weeks of not moving the muscles around it can cause real problems."

"Have you done a lot of post-broken bone work?" Chuck asked me.

"Some. I mean, I'm not a pro, so it's not like I've worked on hundreds of people. I was working on Pat last week. He had some back problem left over from a car accident, and I got that sorted. Back with my unit I had a few girls who got hurt, came back a few months later, and I'd help them get back to full strength.

"My brother Sam broke a wrist when one of the cows kicked him. I spent some time trying to get his hand working properly again after he was out of the cast. That's actually how I got into doing this. His hand just wasn't healing up properly. I knew I wanted to be a doctor and looked at it like my first real patient. I did lots of research and found massage. I could do it. I did do it. Turned out I was good at it. I've been at it ever since."

Chris turned his head toward Chuck. "You should let her see your ankle." Chuck didn't glare at Chris, but I got the idea he wasn't thrilled at the idea.

"What happened to your ankle?" I wanted to know..

"Stupid accident. You know Hurford's Grocery?"

"Grocery Store of the Damned?" Chris burst out laughing. Chuck looked mildly amused.

"That's not a bad description. It does feel pretty bad there. The cheapest fluorescent lights on Earth don't help, either. Anyway, I used to work there. They had me stocking the high shelves one night after it closed. I was the only one there. The ladder broke while I was doing it. Down I went, tangled in it. Then I had to drag myself to the phone so I could call for an ambulance. Since Reevesville only has one ambulance, and I had the immense good luck to call while someone else was having a heart attack, I got to spend the next hour waiting for them to come. Eventually I got to the hospital. My ankle was broken in three spots, my knee dislocated, and I got to enjoy a whole mess of shots because the damn ladder was so old and rusty. It was a great night."

I nodded at him. "Sounds fabulous. If you want me to, I'll take a look at your ankle." I smoothed my hands over Chris' shoulder and arm. "And I think I'm done with you. How are you feeling?"

"Really good. Better than I was before I went to sleep last night and messed it up in the first place."

"Wonderful." I picked up his hand one last time, holding his palm against mine, and ran the fingers of my left hand down his ring finger and pinky. "Yeah, that looks better. Those fingers are the right color again."

"And I can feel them again." Chris turned around in the chair. I could see the necklaces clearly now. Seeing them I felt even more like his clothing was some sort of armor, something to keep others from knowing the man underneath. A black leather cord with a silver seven pointed star and a silver chain with a silver capped moonstone rested against his chest. Neither the necklaces, nor the tattoo, went with the clothing he was wearing.

Chris flexed his fingers one more time and asked, "You game, Chuck? You keep telling me your ankle isn't right."

I pointed to my couch. "You sit on one side, and I'll sit on the other. We can try to make it better."

He gave me a half-smile. I was sure he was humoring Chris. "Sure."

We settled onto the couch. Chris poured himself a soda and sat across from us on the window seat. He hadn't put his shirt back on, so I guessed the hesitation I noticed before wasn't shyness. Or he wasn't shy now. Or, just possibly, he decided with it in the mid-eighties and fairly humid outside, no shirt was just more comfortable.

I took a moment to really look at Chuck. He also had dark red hair, unlike Chris it was on the dark end of the copper spectrum. He wasn't as tall as Chris but bigger, more muscular, with a prettier face. Not feminine but, less sharply angled. Realistically, I should have thought Chuck was the better looking of the two. I just didn't.

Chuck wore shorts and Birkenstocks. Getting to his ankle required very little work. Realizing this injury was way out of my league took about a second more.

"I might be able to make it feel better for a while, but I can't fix this."

"You haven't even touched it yet."

"Yeah, but I know what an ankle is supposed to look like, and that's not it. You snapped it on both the lateral and medial sides when you went down. From the looks of it the medial side didn't heal right."

"That's the same thing the doctor said. He's telling me they'll have to re-break and reset it."

"So, what are you waiting for?"

I felt the bitterness before I heard it in his voice. "Let's see: a job with insurance, time when I don't need to hike up the hill every day to go to class—which is what did it in the first time—and...oh... the magic money fairy to show up so I can afford to take the time off work to heal up as well."

"Oh. I'm sorry."

"It's not your fault. Workman's Comp paid for the first round of bills. The settlement from the bad ladder is paying for school. But until I've managed to swing a job I can sit down for, I'm not going back."

"Does your knee hurt, too?"

"Yes, and my hip." I nodded and traced my fingers over his leg. "You still intend to work on it?" Chuck sounded surprised.

"No reason not to make you feel better. If I'm lucky, I might be able to help your knee and hip some. It won't hold long term because I can't fix your ankle, but..."

"I'll take some time feeling better over none." Chuck nodded at me. I probed the muscles of his calf. They may as well have been made of stone. I slid my hands up and down his leg, fingers slipping over freckled skin and crisp reddish orange hairs, trying to get his muscles to relax, but they held. I had never felt a muscle that didn't respond to me at least a bit. To make matters worse, I was having a hard time concentrating because the headache that had begun shortly after they came over got worse with each passing minute.

This was stupid. I'm good at massage. I make muscles get soft and happy. I stopped for a few minutes and pushed the pain out of my head and focused on his leg. Then I knew what to do. I let go of his calf and started to dig my fingers into the muscles and tendons around his kneecap.

I found it. He hissed when I hit the spot just above and to the left of his kneecap. I pressed deeply into it and ignored everything but that spot. He cursed quietly. From far away I could feel the part of me that usually did this saying, 'Back off.' But on a deeper level, I knew this was what he needed. If he could hold on for just a little bit longer...

The muscle gave. It twitched under my fingers, flexing and rippling. Chuck was still cursing but in amazement now. That spot started a chain reaction, and the muscles from his knee on down relaxed.

I let go of him and slumped back onto my side of the couch. The headache slammed back into me full force.

"Well, that was interesting," I said between the throbs in my head.

"Yeah. What happened? It hurt like hell. Then suddenly everything twitched, and my leg wasn't hurting anymore."

"I've read about it but never done it before. You find the main trigger point, press on it until it gives up, and then like a chain reaction all the satellite triggers deactivate. So, moral of the story: when your leg acts up, poke that spot on your knee."

"Shouldn't be too hard to find. I think I've got a permanent dent from your fingers there."

"Sorry. Let me get you some ice." The spot was an angry red and would probably bruise. I filled a bag with ice. "I don't usually just power through a spot like that. It just seemed like what your leg needed."

"I'm not sure I needed another bruise, but my calf and ankle are feeling a lot better."

I put the ice on his knee and then gently began to work on the rest of his leg. Muscles that had been fighting me earlier were now softening nicely under my hands. After a few more minutes, I could move his ankle through almost three quarters of a normal range of motion. About as good as I thought it could get until it was reset.

"Does that make up for me torturing your knee?"

He flexed his foot. "Yes."

"Want more ice?"

"Nah. I'm good with what I've got."

I got up, snagged a drink for myself, discretely took two Tylenol, and offered refills to the guys. They both accepted, so I figured they intended to stay a while.

Chuck looked at my chemistry homework. "I didn't catch what you're studying."

"I didn't say. I'm pre-med. How about you two?"

"English with a minor in economics. On the off chance poetry doesn't make me fabulously wealthy, I think it might be good to have something that might get me a job at some point," Chris replied.

"I'm not really sure yet," Chuck began. "I can usually swing about two classes a semester, so technically I'm a first-semester sophomore. Right now I'm getting the basic classes out of the way. Probably I'll end up with a degree in business. Maybe statistics. I like writing and English classes, but I also like the idea of a good job when I'm done with this. Unfortunately that doesn't go with an English major."

"You could teach," I said to him.

"And I could poke my eyeballs out with hot skewers. I didn't like high school or junior high the first time. I'm not about to go back."

"I can understand that. They weren't my favorite years, either."

"I loved high school. It was the best time of my life." For a second I believed Chris. Then I saw Chuck smirk.

"So, not on your top ten either?"

"Noooooo… not on my top ten. More like my bottom ten. Bottom five? It's not the worst thing that ever happened to me, but it was pretty close."

"So, we're all in agreement. High school sucks. Onto the next topic. How did you two meet? I'm guessing you're local, Chuck. Chris, you're not, are you?"

"No, I'm from over the line in beautiful Winesburg, Ohio."

"Never heard of it."

"You and everyone else from more than five minutes away. Little town in the middle of nowhere."

"Suburban paradise?"

"Down to the strip malls."

"Which doesn't tell her how we met," Chuck interjected.

"Well, how we met isn't fascinating. We were both in the same English 101, Introduction to Literature, class. We got paired up on a project and hit it off."

"Started eating lunch together and decided, like you, to go check Golem out."

"How about you and the guy you were with? Pat, right?" Chris asked.

"Yeah. We were in the same Intro to College Improv group. I caught him checking out my knives…"

"I was wondering if I could see them, too. They look interesting," Chuck interrupted.

"Sure." I handed him the one from my belt. "Anyway, he liked the look of my knives. I liked the look of him. We got some coffee. I fixed his back. Found out we both like to fight, so we've been hanging out, occasionally sparring, since. Now we're in fencing together." Chuck spent a moment getting a feel for my blade. I spent a moment subtly moving so I could get to the gun in my pocket easily. Then he handed the knife to Chris, who also played with it for a moment before handing it back to me. I then handed the knife from my left ankle over.

"You're pretty cautious aren't you?" Chuck asked.

"Why do you say that?"

"You kept the one knife on your person instead of letting me see both of them at once."

"Look, you seem like nice guys, and I don't want to offend you, but I'm not interested in becoming a headline anytime soon. So, as long as I'm outnumbered, I'll keep at least one blade within easy reach."

"Fair enough," Chris said.

"Why knives?" Chuck wanted to know.

"I can't carry a gun on campus."

"Do you expect to need one?" Chris leaned forward like he was really interested in the answer.

"No. But that's kind of the point. Those kids at Virginia Tech didn't expect to need to be armed, either. I've been around long enough to know expecting these kinds of things isn't about them being likely to happen. They aren't. It's about not wishing you had something when you really need it."

"That makes sense. So, did you say something about 'your unit?' What's that?" Chris queried.

"Well, you might have noticed I'm a tad old for a freshman?" They nodded. "I joined the Israeli Defense Force after high school. I was a medic stationed in the Negev. That's as far south as you can go in Israel without having to swim."

"Why not the army here?" Chuck wanted to know.

"I've got automatic dual citizenship because of my birth. I figured I should do something to earn it. I bought and paid for my American citizenship. The tax bill from my brothers buying my share of the farm brought tears to my eyes, but I felt like I had done something of value here. I hadn't done anything of value there. There's also the concept of the *Aliyah*: the return to our homeland. Put them together and I'm a twenty-one-year-old freshman who can dress battle wounds, strip a machine gun blindfolded, and hold my own fighting with a gun or knife."

"Oh," Chris said. Then he and Chuck went silent, like they were thinking about it. I was starting to get uncomfortable. They weren't talking at all, just looking at each other, and I didn't know why. Finally Chris stopped looking at Chuck, and turned to me.

"So, did you say something about your brother getting kicked by a cow? How did that happen?" I told him about our farm and my family, which got them talking about their homes and families. Chuck had a sister. It was just the two of them now. His dad had died young, and his mom split a few years later. As soon as he turned eighteen, he petitioned for custody of his sister, was granted it, and they had been living in town since. Chris had three brothers and a sister. All of them younger than him, most of them still at home with his parents. His oldest brother, Rob, joined the Marines out of high school, and we talked about the U.S. military versus the Israeli for a little while.

"Where do you work?" I asked Chuck, changing the subject when it looked like Chuck was getting bored with the military talk.

"I've just got the job at Rutherford's Tool Shop now."

"A hardware store?" I asked.

"No. A lathe operator. I make tools."

"Oh." I thought for a moment, trying to remember what a lathe operator did. "That's pretty skilled work right?"

"Yes. There are six tool and die shops around town, so the vo-tech at Reevesville High does a good job of training us to do the work. It seemed like the fastest way to get a real job."

"Do you like it?"

"No. But it pays better than the grocery store. For that matter, it pays better than most jobs a guy can get fresh out of high school here. And there's a night shift, so I can go to school during the day, work from three to midnight five nights a week, and still get just about enough sleep to stay sane."

"Sleep is good. I'm quite the fan myself. Speaking of which… I don't want to be rude and boot you two out of my home, but I've still got five problems to do, and I'd like to get some sleep tonight."

"No problem. Thanks for working on my shoulder." Chris slipped back into his shirt while Chuck headed toward the door. "We usually eat lunch at the Student Union 'round about noon. If you and Pat want to join us, you're welcome."

"Thanks." They said their goodnights. I got settled on my window seat, turned on my playlist, and returned to the chemistry problems. The rest of the evening I worked on them and stopped myself from mentally undressing Chris. When I went to bed, I ran into a problem I didn't anticipate. My pillow smelled like him. The dark, spicy scent with undertones of citrus kept images of him and the feel of his skin at the forefront of my mind. After an hour, I took the pillowcase off, stuffed it in my washer, put a clean one on, and thought very intently of Ari until I fell asleep.

"I want to have a smoke." Chuck stopped in front of Sarah's house, lighting his cigarette.

"Ready to eat some crow yet?" Chris asked while Chuck inhaled.

"Looks to me like it's just hands-on skill." Chris took it from him for a drag. He didn't really like smoking, but every now and again he was in the mood for a little nicotine. Tonight was one of those times. Chuck didn't mind sharing the occasional cig. Though he didn't like anyone else to see it. It just looked 'too damn gay' as he put it.

Chris handed the cig back and said, "Bull. You know it's more than hands-on skill. So does Dave. And she's already found Ahni."

"His name is Pat here. Don't forget. And if she has it—and I'm not saying she does—it's pretty latent."

"Yeah, well, she's not one of us. Something has to wake them up."

Chuck dropped the butt and ground it out. They continued up the hill to the Writers' House. After three steps, Chuck spoke again: "You just want it to be her."

"If it's not her, why would I want it to be her?"

Chuck looked like he couldn't believe Chris would try that on him. "You know why," he said pointedly. "Same reasons my defenses jump out at her when she gets too close to me. She feels so much like Althiira it's uncanny. You want me to believe *you* didn't feel it? You want me to believe you were really just too warm to put your shirt back on? Or your attraction spell just happened to be on high while she was working on you?"

"It's not her." Chris didn't sound very convincing.

"Are you sure?"

"Of course." Chuck gave him a look that said cut the shit. "It can't be her. But… it was nice to pretend."

"Maybe you could…" He knew where Chuck was going with this. For the first time in two years, Chuck had a much better argument than usual. Still, Chris cut him off.

"No. It's not really her. I shouldn't even be pretending."

"Yeah, well, you've got to figure out a way to work with her. If she is our healer, you're going to be spending a lot of time with her. With as much as she feels like Althiira, sooner or later she'll start to want you. Judging by how she was touching you, the correct answer is sooner."

"She has a boyfriend."

"Ahni?"

"Pat, remember? No. One from home."

"Good. This could get very complicated if it was him." Chuck turned to face him. "You either have to decide this one is yours and go for her or let her go. Trying to do both is a bad idea. If you get all stupid and jealous, she'll feel it, and it will screw things up."

"She's not mine."

"Then act like it."

"Yes, Dad."

"I'm serious. Autumn and Brooke are enough drama. You don't need to make this worse by adding another one to the list."

"I'll keep that in mind."

"Good." They were standing in front of the Writers' House.

Chris took a step up to the porch. "See you tomorrow?"

"Doubt it. No classes and I've got work. I'll be up Thursday."

"Good. See you then." Chuck began the walk down the hill to his own place in Reevesville. Chris entered his home.

Mike, Dave, and Autumn were waiting for him in the living room. "Jury's still out. I say yes. Chuck says no."

"It's her. I know I've said it before, and I know you aren't convinced," Dave said in Autumn's direction, "but I'm sure."

"How's your shoulder?" she asked Chris.

"Better. She took care of everything Chuck did to it and then got the leftovers from the last time Mildred attacked."

"Really?" Mike's eyebrows lifted in surprise.

"Yes."

"Could she tell you didn't just sleep on it wrong?"

"If she could, Autumn, she didn't let on. She fixed it, though. But, here's what Chuck would add: no magic in her touch. It was all straight massage. Here's the other interesting piece: she got his leg, too. Found a spot in his knee, poked it, and did something. Next thing he knows his leg doesn't hurt anymore."

"Chuck let her work on him?" Mike sounded astonished.

"I trapped him into it."

"Ahhh…" Autumn had a knowing look on her face. Unless it was going to lead to sex Chuck didn't like having people touch him.

"Here's the really interesting bit. She's not a transfer student. She's a freshman. After high school, she joined the Israeli army and spent two years as a medic. She wears two knives and, though she wasn't openly advertizing it, a gun as well."

"I'm sold. No way that's just a big coincidence," Mike said. "And it explains how she moves in fencing class. She moves like someone who's done some fighting, not traditional fencing."

"Not the same thing?" Autumn wanted to know.

"No. If it was the same thing, I would have been in China last month," Mike answered.

"That would have done wonders for keeping your profile low," Autumn shot back at him.

"What profile? I really doubt Mildred watches the Olympics on TV. It knows where I am no matter what I do."

Dave cut into Mike and Autumn's bickering, "We've found her. Let's go get her."

"You think we've found her. This'll be a huge mess if she isn't the one," Autumn said.

"Are you channeling Chuck on purpose?" Dave snapped. "She's it. Either we bring her in or find a new one. I don't know about you, but I'm not seeing any better candidates."

Autumn sighed. "No, I haven't seen anyone else. We could keep just using me."

"We'll be dead by January," Mike replied quietly, but no one missed it.

"I'm not that bad. We've been fine so far."

"Really? Want me to fuck up Chris' shoulder again and see if you can fix it? Even with magic?" Dave's voice was sharp.

"I'd prefer you didn't do that. It hasn't felt this good for years, and I'm enjoying it. Even if she's got no magic, even if it is all hands-on skills, she blows anything we've currently got out of the water. Not to put you down, Autumn—you're as good at this as you can be, and you've patched us back up before—but she's better. With no magic she's better. If there's anything there to tap…

"At the absolute minimum, she's done two years as a combat medic. Think about that. She's used to patching people back up under fire. She's cautious. Always a good sign in a healer. Chuck asked her up to my room to finish my shoulder. She countered by inviting me to her place…where she has the advantage. She had two knives and a gun on her when we got there. Chuck asked to see the knives. She handed them over one at a time, making sure he gave the one back before giving him the new one. She's observant. She noticed me watching her and Pat…"

"That's because she never took her eyes off of you during the whole meeting," Dave said with a smile. "I doubt she noticed me watching her."

"Dave, no one notices you doing anything. Short of dancing through the room naked, you're invisible," Chris snarked.

"Yeah, yeah, yeah. Point stands. Of course she noticed you watching her. The more interesting bit is she saw you rubbing your hand and wrist and knew that meant your shoulder was messed up. Even better, she had the balls to walk up to an almost total stranger, a male one at that, and offered to put her hands on your body to make you feel better. That's a healer, lady and gentlemen."

"Chuck asked her about that. She says it's her *mitzvah*. So, she's already got the idea it's a religious duty to heal others."

"She's Jewish?" Mike asked.

"Not too many Catholics join this Israeli army out of high school," Autumn retorted.

"Okay. Yeah. I should have gotten that. But that could be a problem. Is she going to think we're witches? You know, in an Old Testament, bad sort of way?"

"Fuck." Chris looked like he had his brand new toy taken away. "That would be our luck. We finally find a healer, and she won't work with us because she thinks we're evil."

"Well, let's deal with that when it comes up. If she won't work with us for whatever reason, between Chuck and me, she'll never remember our asking." Dave checked the clock. "I've got an early class tomorrow. Bedtime for me."

"And me," Mike said, standing up and stretching. "Got to go show the freshlings, our healer included, what to do with the pointy end of a foil."

Chris followed the other two upstairs. He settled on his bed with the intention of doing some reading for his Brit Lit III class. He kept his mind on the reading for all of three minutes; then the feel of her hands on his shoulders began to slide back into his mind.

Not mine. But her hands felt the same. The touch he had been aching for was two doors down. *It's not her you twit. It can't be her…*

And if it is? He remembered the last time he saw Althiira, the last things she had said to him.

Then you are well and truly fucked!

10.

During fencing I told Pat about the invite to lunch. He told me about how he thought things had been progressing nicely with Emily when she told him about her boyfriend. The rant about how all the girls here already have boyfriends was inventively profane and punctuated with the sloppiest swordsmanship I had ever seen him perform. I actually won that round.

We leaned against the wall while another two students fenced. "How did things go with Chris last night?"

"Pretty well. He tells me he was NOT checking you out."

"Hell… at this point, I've been shot down so many times any attention would be welcome."

I nodded at him. "I'll keep that in mind. There's got to be someone here besides you who doesn't have an S.O."

"You'd think. So, did he try to get 'frisky?'"

I decided not to mention the fact he kept his shirt off all night. I still wasn't sure if that was a sign of friskiness or the fact air conditioning didn't appear to be anything my landlord had ever heard of. "Nope. He was remarkably unfrisky. And he brought Chuck along. I ended up working on him, too. Before you ask, he was also a wet noodle in the friskiness department. I mean, nothing. Not even a little spirited flirtation."

"Bummer."

"Maybe not. A little flirting would have been nice, but I can see why it's hard to figure out what the correct way to behave is when you've got a strange woman rubbing your shoulders. Or in Chuck's case, leg."

"Leg?"

"Yeah, he's got a bum right ankle, knee, and hip."

"Did he say how he got it?"

"Ladder broke under him while he was stocking shelves."

"Ouch. So they want us to come to lunch?"

"Well, I have the feeling Chuck wouldn't mind if I fell off the face of the planet, but Chris invited us."

"Then we shall do lunch with the Writers."

I didn't have too hard of a time finding their table. Autumn was already sitting there daintily eating an apple.

"Sarah, oh… I'm glad you could make it. Chris told me you and Pat might be coming. Here, have this seat next to me." She patted a chair. I put my bag on it. "Is Pat coming?"

"He told me he would and…" I scanned the room. "Yep, he's heading this way. I'll grab a drink and be back in a minute."

By the time I was back with a Pepsi and an apple the table was full. Chris was next to me on the one side, Autumn on the other. Pat sat across from me, with Mike next to him, and the dark-haired boy—I felt like I should know him, but I was drawing a blank—across from Autumn.

The four of them chatted amiably for a while. Bits and pieces about their classes.

"Is that your lunch? With the way you move in fencing class, I wouldn't have pegged you for a dieter." Mike looked pointedly at my apple.

"No, back home I've got my real lunch. I finally got some goodies from my brothers, so I've got some roast beef that'll be going on rye with some mustard and a bit of salad to go with it."

"Yum. What else did you get?" Pat asked.

"Roast beef, pastrami, a few steaks, a few roasts, hamburger, some lamb, chickens, and— thank you, Ben!—lox."

"Why are your brothers sending you meat?" Autumn looked curious.

"Two reasons: First off, I keep kosher, and they don't seem to sell much kosher meat here. Secondly, my family raises kosher beef and lamb, so that's why they're sending it to me."

"I thought eating kosher meant no pig or lobster," Chris said.

"That's true, but even allowable foods have to be raised and killed correctly. If the chicken has been fed the wrong stuff or killed cruelly, it won't be kosher anymore."

"Well, there's something for being Catholic. All bacon all the time." Chris smiled while biting into a slice of pepperoni pizza.

"Except Fridays during Lent," Autumn added.

"Does your family do that?" Chris looked curious.

"Yeah, my mom's old fashioned. No meat on Lenten Fridays."

"My parents do, too," Mike told us.

"Mine don't. But they're barely Catholic. Christmas, Easter, weddings, and funerals. The rest of the time they never darken the door of the church," the dark-haired boy said.

"Dave, isn't your mom a Presbyterian?" Mike questioned. *Dave.* I tried to burn that into my mind. It was silly to sit here thinking of him as the dark-haired boy.

"Yeah, she 'converted' when they got married to make my grandparents happy."

"Yeah, my family is like that, too. Although they are genuinely happy to celebrate St. Patrick's Day as well," Pat said while eating a french fry.

Chris took another bite of his pizza while I sipped my drink. "So, let me make sure I get this: no bacon, no lobster, no cheeseburgers?"

"Nope. Good for you, knowing the no-meat-and-milk thing. Most people miss that one."

"I try to be multi-cultural." He smiled brightly at me. "But how can you give up so many things that taste so good?"

"You want the real answer or the snarky one?"

"Ohhh… snarky, please!" Autumn cooed.

"Well, we've determined you're Catholic, right?" Chris nodded. "Well, let's see, no bacon… or no masturbation. I'll say no to pork over sex any day!"

They laughed: Pat and Dave with a full-out belly laugh, Mike with a startled snort of a laugh, a somewhat more polite chuckle from Chris, and a slightly scandalized giggle from Autumn.

Chris finally answered with a slightly embarrassed smile on his face, "Well, some of us are better Catholics than others."

"Meaning if you were Jewish you'd eat a cheeseburger once or twice a week and feel bad about it until the next time," Pat said, smirking at him. "Hey, I'm not saying I'm better. I'm a once-a-day man myself. But Catholic males under the age of twenty-five who actually obey the no masturbation thing are few and far between and probably lying as well."

Dave continued to smile. It was a pleasant smile, familiar almost. It put me in mind of bull sessions at home with my brothers.

"You all live together?" Pat asked.

"Yep, we're the Writers of the Writers' House," Autumn answered.

"But only Chris is an English major," Dave added. "Autumn's Political Science, I started out art, but I'm a poly sci/history hybrid now, and Mike's got a computer science degree in the works."

"Give me a few years and I'll be an English major with a history minor. Learn how to write and study things to write about. It seems like a good plan," Pat said.

"I'm pre-med and Middle Eastern Languages, which is me trying to get credit for one language I already speak and another I have to learn anyway."

"Which two?" Chris asked.

"I already speak Hebrew, and I need to learn Arabic if I want to be a trauma surgeon in Israel."

"Sounds like a good plan." Chris sipped his drink.

"I thought so. As classes go, it's the one I like best. Morrell and I get together and spend an hour talking about whatever, in as much Arabic as we can, and then spend the next hour on vocab and grammar. When I got here, I didn't think I'd like my language classes best of all. This is lots more fun than learning Hebrew was."

That got us talking about what other languages we spoke. Dave was the only other one who really spoke another language. He was studying the politics and history of Mexico and hoped to study there the next year, so he had conversational Mexican Spanish down pretty well. The others had all taken something in high school and were in the process of forgetting it as quickly as possible while they filled their minds with new information. That got us talking about high school and where we were from. I learned that Dave was from a place called Oilville, which was about half an hour away, Mike from Philly, and Autumn from Plano, Texas. We all chatted about our homes and how we ended up at school here. The general answer seemed to be this was the school that gave everyone the best deal. By the time that conversation was done, so was the food, so we broke off to do our afternoon routines.

Dave and Chris walked back to their house from lunch. "You try to be multi-cultural?" Dave didn't even try to keep the disbelief out of his voice.

Chris shrugged. "I spent some time Googling this morning."

"Sounds more like it."

"Seriously though, do you actually feel magic off of her or are we dreaming it?"

"It's there, Chris. It's subtle right now, but it's there."

"Good."

11.

The e-mail showed up Thursday afternoon. Party at Writers' on Saturday. I sent one back saying I'd be there after dark.

Saturday rolled around, and I waited for Pat. He said he'd stop over at my place and then we'd go to Writers'. I traded my usual cargo pants and t-shirt for jeans and a button down with the sleeves rolled up. When he opened the door, I saw Pat had a similar outfit. He had light blue jeans and a black button down. I had dark blue jeans and a red button down.

He looked me up and down. "Oh good, we match."

"Let me change." I turned around and headed back into my apartment. After staring at my closet looking for something that wasn't a t-shirt or a button down, I called out, "How cool is it out there?"

"Mid-seventies and it'll probably get cooler." A massive thunderstorm the night before killed the heat of summer pretty effectively.

I dug around and found a light gray sweater that would work. It was a little more revealing than my usual clothing—the neck was wide, one shoulder usually slipped out—but it was warm enough to be comfortable. I slipped it on and tucked my bra straps out of sight.

"Better?"

Pat smiled. "Much. Is there a reason you dress like a butch lesbian?"

"Wow," I said, blinking. "That was blunt."

"Sorry. I know you've got girl clothing, and I know you look good in it, but you almost never wear it. Half the time you look more butch than I do."

"Pat, I never look more butch than you do. However, I try to be modest. I don't always pull it off, especially if a joke is just too good. But, when it comes to clothing, it's easy. And in guy clothing modest looks better. If I wear girly modest clothing, I look frumpy. I don't want that."

"Butch lesbian is preferable to frumpy. I can see that."

"When my hair grows out, it'll look tomboyish."

"You're going to let your hair grow?"

"No reason not to. Not like I've got any fire fights coming up."

"God willing."

"So, if we're talking about unusual clothing choices, what's with the duster in the summertime?" He didn't have his coat on right now, but he rarely went anywhere without it.

Pat looked a little surprised that I asked. "Pockets. The duster has good pockets. I can keep my rock with me if I'm wearing the duster."

"Why do you carry a rock around?" I had noticed he seemed to have it somewhere on his person at all times, but I didn't see a place it could be hiding in tonight's outfit.

"Lucky rock."

"Oh. I thought this was where you'd tell me you're secretly a geomancer." I meant it as a joke. His eyes went way wide. I could feel the shock oozing off of him. Obviously not a joke. That brought me up short.

"Do you believe in magic?" he asked me seriously.

I thought about my answer carefully. I don't want to believe in magic. Magic is messy, unpredictable, and painful. Magic complicates things and causes problems. I prefer not to believe in magic. I like the nice, safe, tidy world of science. But I had a few skeletons in my own closet that didn't make sense in a world without magic. "Most of the time, no. But every now and again, you run into something that just doesn't seem to have any other answer."

He seemed to think that was a good answer. "Most of the time people claiming magic powers are little pansy-ass posers desperately trying to make themselves more important by being mysterious." That was a fairly accurate description of most of the magic crowd at my high school.

"So, are you a geomancer?" I asked.

"Yes, but there's nothing secret about it. Having the rocks on my dresser is about as subtle as a neon sign."

"That's why they're cold?"

"I feel it as warm, but yeah, that's why."

"Why do you keep the black one on you?"

"Pretty much the same reason you wear your knives. It tells anything that can see it to stay away, and I can use it for offensive or defensive work."

"Okay." I certainly understood that. "Do you find yourself needing it often?"

"Nope, but like your knives: better safe than sorry. So, are you okay with this?"

Other than the fact I didn't really know if I bought it… His rock had been cold, and there wasn't any good explanation for that. "Why wouldn't I be?" I wanted to know.

"You've got a religion and you actually seem to believe in it."

"Ahhh…" *Well, yes there was that.* "Do you conjure the dead?"

"No."

"We're good. So, party?" I wanted to put this conversation behind me. Maybe later, when I'd had some more time to think about it, we could go back to it.

"Party."

We could hear the music from my bottom step. The noise inside Writers' was deafening. A few kids were dancing in a small clot in the center of the living room. Others hovered around the sides talking, drinking, and eating. Along the far wall Dave and a few boys were playing something on the Playstation. I waved at him, and he waved back.

Pat pulled me into the center of the room, and we began to dance. His hands rested lightly on my hips as we moved to the music.

"How does this work with modesty?"

"Damned if I know. I like to dance, and I'm not about to stop anytime soon. I'm Jewish, not a Jehovah's Witness. We dance."

"And this?" He pulled me close to him, sliding one of his legs between mine.

"Depends. Is this about enjoying dancing with a friend or trying to get me to sleep with you?"

"Both." He smiled widely when he said it but not quite widely enough to make it a joke. Apparently this was the night when all our cards got laid on the table.

"That's honest. So here's the honest answer: If it's about sex, then yes, it violates modesty. If it's about you and I having a good time with our clothes on, then it's fine. So sayeth the Rabbi Sarah."

"If I want to keep dancing with you, I have to give up on getting you into bed?"

"Yep."

"But that takes all the fun out of it." He pouted briefly. Then he did manage to smile wide enough to make it into a joke. The music changed, and we slid into another beat. Autumn bopped over after the next song, looking especially pretty in a flouncy green dress. She asked how we were doing, then bopped away to greet a few others. After an hour of dancing, I broke away to go find the bathroom.

It was much larger than I would have guessed: almost twice the size of mine. I glanced at the bathtub with real longing. Maybe they'd let me take a dip one of these days. Luckily, I noticed the lack of toilet paper before I needed it. I looked around for a minute and decided under the sink was my best bet for finding more. I grabbed a roll and saw what was behind it. Black hair dye and colored contacts. Dark brown. I had to think about it for a full minute before I remembered Dave had black hair and dark brown eyes.

I shook my head. I'd seen men who dyed their hair to look Goth. But Dave wasn't a Goth. He was just a guy who wanted different colored hair and eyes. To each his own, I guess. I eyed the bathtub again as I left. I really needed to ask to borrow it one day.

Pat was dancing away with Emily when I got downstairs again. I edged around the mass of gyrating students and headed for the kitchen. It looked like Mike was playing bartender. He stood next to a counter covered in beverages.

He broke off from talking to a tall guy with dark hair and blue eyes to ask me, "What can I get you?"

"Pepsi?"

"Sure, I've got that." He handed me a cool, wet can of Pepsi. "How's it going out there?"

"Loud, hot. Hook-ups forming all over the dance floor."

"A normal Writers' House party."

"I guess. So, where's Chris? Autumn's dancing. Dave is blowing something up on the Playstation. You're here."

"Either on the back porch or in his room. He's not much of a party person."

"Ahhh…"

Mike looked at me intently for a moment, tilted his head toward the kitchen door, and said, "Back porch."

"Thanks." I headed out to the much quieter and cooler back porch. Chris lounged on a folding chair, beer in one hand, the other behind his head.

"Hi."

He looked over at me. His eyes lingered on my shoulder and collarbone, then pulled away to look out at the trees behind the house. "Hi."

"Mind if I join you for a drink?" I held up my Pepsi to him. He didn't look back at me when I asked.

"Go ahead. Enjoying the party?" I leaned against the porch rail.

"Yes. Kind of loud and hot in there."

"Which is why I am out here."

He sipped his drink. I opened the soda. We sat quietly drinking for a few minutes. His eyes stayed glued to the trees behind me.

"How's your shoulder?"

"Really good, thanks."

"Glad to have been of service."

We sat in an uncomfortable silence. I wondered where the guy who happily chatted half-naked in my house went. He watched those trees like they held all the answers to all the questions in the universe. I chugged my drink, shook the empty bottle, and said, "Good night."

"Good night." I walked back into the party feeling disappointed.

Later, while Pat and I were dancing, I knew I was being watched. Chris stared very intently at me while he and Chuck walked through the room. Our eyes met, his darted away, and he hurried up the steps to his room.

By midnight there was just six or so of us still there. The music faded to a dull background hum, and the room cooled off. Harold wandered over to the bookshelf with the games on it and picked up an Ouija board. "So, who wants to play?"

"Really, you don't want to mess with that," I said before I could stop myself. Autumn's head shot up, and she looked very intently at me.

"Come on, it's a kid's game." Harold held the box and shook it a little.

I faced two options: I could back down and look like a twit, or I could convince him it was a bad idea and look like a twit. If I was going to look like a twit either way… "So's sticking your tongue against a freezing piece of metal. You still get hurt. Kid's games aren't consequence free."

"Sounds like there's a good story behind that statement. Better than this would have been anyway." He tossed the Ouija board aside. "Wanna tell us?"

"I don't know if it's a good story. True stories usually aren't." This conversation had taken me from being just one of the group to the center of attention. Pat and Autumn were watching especially closely. I gave Pat a quick smile to let him know this was what I meant earlier by some things didn't have another explanation. Pat smiled back at me; he understood.

"As in… happened to you personally?" Harold's eyes were bright with curiosity.

"Kind of. I saw what happened but wasn't one of the main characters." Which wasn't precisely true. I didn't want to get any closer to the real story than that, not for this group, at least. Maybe I'd tell Pat the real story one day.

"Hold up. Let me make some popcorn and coffee. This should be good." Pat vanished into the kitchen.

Chris called down the stairs. "What's up?"

"Ghost stories. Sarah's gonna start us off." Harold yelled back to him. Chris and Chuck came clumping down the steps a few seconds later.

"It's not really a ghost story. It's a…" I sighed. "This sounds so melodramatic." I rolled my eyes. "It's a demon story."

"Even better." Harold grinned in anticipation of a good story.

Pat came back in with the popcorn. He handed me a mug of lukewarm cocoa. I think he forgot to put it in the microwave. Autumn's usual aura of gay perkiness faded into an intelligent seriousness. Once more her gaze made me uncomfortable. I took a swig of the drink and sighed again. "You're all going to see why I'm not a writer. I don't think this story is worth the buildup."

"Come on, tell us. How often do you know someone who was actually there? Usually ghost stories are told by someone who knows someone who read something that happened to someone else's cousin." Harold leaned toward me as he spoke.

"Here goes. Maybe you can turn it into a bestseller, Harold."

"If it's any good, I will," he said with a smile.

"This would be in the fall of my senior year. A few girls and I were having a sleepover. Just like tonight one of them said, 'Hey, let's play with the Ouija board. It'll be fun.'" I mimicked the voice and enthusiasm of a young girl.

"So, we whip the thing out and sit in a circle. Melanie was the one who had her hands on the pointer. She started asking stupid questions: 'Will we get to go to the prom? Will Shelia get the guy she wants? Can Beth pass history?' You know, dumb little girl type questions. And we get dumb little answers.

"Then Beth says, 'Let me have the pointer.' So Melanie moves over and gives the pointer to Beth. I should probably describe Beth: She's all Goth. Black hair, black make-up, pentacle ring, and a pretty cool tribal tattoo around her neck. She's the kid who used to freak Ben, my brother, out when she'd come to visit. Anyway, she says, 'Who are you?' And the room got cold.

"'I am Azzazzel.'

"'Why are you here?'

"'Because you called me.'

"'Can you move the pointer on your own?'

"She took her hands off the pointer and it shot to YES.

"Now, at this point I was shitting myself. The damn thing moved to YES on its own. The rest of the girls had gone silent. Not a giggle in sight.

"'What's my future?' Beth asked.

"'Fire.' It spelled out. 'And Death.'

"'Show yourself,' Beth commanded it. I swear… something started to form in that room. It was black and nasty: a shadow that smelled like a sewer filled with dead things. Before it could become more than a shadow, Melanie kicked the board over and shouted, 'I command you to leave this home.'

"It vanished. No one said anything for the rest of the night. None of us slept. I think Melanie spent the entire rest of that night praying. I'll admit I wasn't far behind. I never wanted something physical to touch so I could feel connected to the Lord more than I did that night. I started wearing my star the next day.

"Beth was in a car accident three weeks later. We've got a pretty nasty road outside of town. It's steep and curvy; more than one person's been killed on it. They said her brakes failed on the curve—or maybe she never hit them. Anyway, she skidded right off the road, rolled the car three times, and ended up on fire. She burned, and then she died.

"Supposedly Azzazzel is a flame demon. He burns things. He burns people.

"I stay away from Ouija boards these days." Everyone was quiet for a few moments.

"I don't blame you," Harold finally said. "I've used one a few times just for fun. I can tell you one thing; the pointer never moves on its own when I'm sitting next to it."

"My guess is it usually doesn't. After she died, there were all sorts of rumors: Like she was into devil worship. That magic books and candles and all sorts of creepy stuff were in her room. I was in her room a few times, never saw anything weird. But she might not have kept it out in the open."

"I've got a real one. It's not as dramatic as Sarah's, but it scared the hell out of me when it happened." We all turned to look at the dark-haired boy Mike had been talking with earlier. Finally, I remembered his name was Eric.

"This was last year. I had choir practice in the chapel. We don't usually practice there. Most of the time we stay in the Fine Arts Building. This was the dress rehearsal for the Winter Concert.

"So, we're singing away. I kept feeling like I couldn't breathe. Just a terrible suffocating feeling. It was stupid. I don't have allergies. I'm not asthmatic. But I couldn't get enough air.

"I excused myself from the group to try and catch my breath. I went to the bathroom to splash some water on my face. I was walking past the little room they store the extra chairs in. Out of the corner of my eye I saw something. There wasn't supposed to be anyone there, so I turn to look.

"Usually this is where the thing vanishes, right? This thing didn't vanish. It was bigger than I am and furry. The eyes were red, and the body was black but translucent. I saw the chairs behind it, and I could see it, too.

"I panicked. I turned to sprint away, tripped over my feet, slammed face first down on the floor, blood dripping from my nose. The thing moved closer to me, touched the blood on the floor, and vanished. I have never been back in that building again. I used my broken nose as an excuse to skip the concert. I dropped Choir after that semester."

"I'd call that pretty dramatic," I told Eric. "I don't like the chapel, either."

"It didn't hit me that hard, but I also didn't want to stay there a second longer than I had to," Dave told us.

"How about it, Chuck? Is there any local lore on the chapel? Was it once an Indian burial ground?" Harold asked.

"No, there's nothing about it I've heard. The local story is all about the junior high."

"Ohhhh... I've seen that. It's just nasty," Emily said before I got a chance to. Apparently I wasn't the only one noticing stuff like this by a long shot.

"Yeah, it is," Chuck answered. "You can thank God you were never a student there. Here are the bits that are factually true. Our junior high has the highest suicide rate in the state, maybe the country. At least one kid per class kills himself. The depression rate for students is way too high, as well.

"Here's what's rumor. The school was built by cultists who fuel their magic by human misery. They designed it in an occult pattern to make people feel pain. I don't know if it's magic or just a terrible designer, but retarded lab rats could have done a better job of laying out a building.

"Here's the next level of rumor. Back in the early eighties when he was a teacher, the principal decided to make a deal with the Devil to get his current job. He went from being the newest history teacher to principal in one year when the then current principal died mysteriously and no one else applied for his job. In order to keep his end of the deal he had to feed the demon one student a year.

"And—this is the perennial favorite—'insert name of freaky student here,' is a Satanist/witch/wizard, and it's his or her fault the school sucks so bad. Now I happen to know for a fact that from '02 to'04 the freaky student theory was crap because my sister had the label. For other years, I can't say for sure. But the school sucked just as bad with a non-magical freaky kid."

"Wonderful." Harold nodded.

"Yeah," Chuck answered.

Ghost stories continued for the next hour. When my eyes were getting fuzzy and I was having a hard time following who was saying what, I said, "I'm going to head home. Need to get some sleep before it's really Sunday."

Pat stood up when I did. "Late enough for me to go home, too."

He walked me to my place. At my door he said, "So, demons in the basement. Would that be what you were talking about earlier when you said 'things with no other explanation?'"

"One of them. The most dramatic one."

He nodded and looked at me for a long moment. I wondered if he was going to try to kiss me goodnight. I really hoped he wouldn't, that would just make things awkward. He winked and turned around to head back to his dorm room.

Finally, Harold left. The Writers spent a minute in the quiet alone. Then Mike spoke: "We're going to have to get them both at once. Pat makes sure she's always with him. I'm starting to think he's hoping if he keeps her around enough he can use her as a shield from us. He's not eager to rejoin the fight."

"Can you blame him? I wasn't exactly jumping for joy to find you all here either," Dave said.

"No, I don't blame him. But he's here. We're here. I don't think Mildred is going to back off just because none of us want to deal with it anymore," Chuck said.

"Look, are we sure she's the one? I still don't feel it," Autumn added her usual caution.

"Did you hear the story? Did you feel the fact she didn't tell it right? She kicked that board over. She's the one. I know it. Chris knows it. Chuck won't admit it, but look at his leg. It's four days later, and he's still feeling better. Hands-on talent wouldn't have lasted that long. She's it!" Dave looked from Chuck to Autumn.

"Then I'll bring them in tomorrow," Autumn said definitively.

"Why you?" Chuck sounded a bit annoyed.

"Because I read people better than anyone but you… and she doesn't like you. If she's got no interest, I'll know before I get into too many details."

"I hate to say it, but she's got some interest. While she was rubbing Chris, I checked out her book collection. Two out of three of them were fantasy fiction. She'll bite."

"Good. Tomorrow I'll bring them in."

Chris lay on his bed, knowing sleep was nowhere near coming to him. He'd done well. Played it cool. Kept his distance from her all night. He followed Chuck's advice and did nothing to encourage her. And he was miserable. This was worse than loneliness. He was used to loneliness. This was forcing himself to chose loneliness instead of enjoy her company.

She was dancing with Pat when he walked through, having fun, laughing with him. He had wanted to join her, pull her close, and trace his fingers over her naked shoulder…

Don't go there. She's not yours. He punched his pillow in frustration and rolled onto his side, begging sleep to come to him.

12.

At lunch Autumn asked Pat and Sarah if they would meet her for coffee that afternoon. After last night he knew this was coming soon. Before Sarah even had the chance to think about her answer, he accepted for both of them.

They were sitting in a booth at the coffeehouse when Autumn got around to it. She looked very seriously at Sarah and said, "You know things. Things most people don't. Things most people shouldn't." Pat did a good job of not rolling his eyes. Of course Autumn would go for dramatic. Why wasn't Chris or Dave doing this?

"Yes, but I usually don't talk about it," Sarah said. Pat thought that was a good answer. He could feel Sarah was very confused. He probably should have given her some warning about what was going to happen, but he couldn't think of a way to get into it in the time they had between lunch and meeting Autumn.

"And that's wise." Autumn turned to Pat. "You've been through it before."

"Yes." He rolled his eyes at her. Sure, vague sounded impressive, but this wasn't a situation that needed extra drama. The cut-and-dry version was dramatic enough.

"Are you willing to do it again?"

"Do I have a choice?" Pat asked seriously.

"No. It's here, and we need your help to stop it." That was news. Pat had felt a lot of magic on the campus but nothing from before. There was no reason for Autumn to lie about that, though.

Sarah reached the end of her patience. She asked sharply and a touch too loud, "What are you talking about? I may know things, but this isn't one of them."

Autumn hissed, "Quiet. Keep your voice down. We don't want to attract attention."

"Fine," Sarah said tensely and quietly. "Now, tell me what you're talking about."

Autumn's voice dropped. For a moment her glamour slipped, and Illyn peaked through. Pat wondered if she did it on purpose. *Probably.* Almost nothing was an accident where Autumn was concerned. "There are places where the separation between worlds is very thin, and this is one of them. There are times where Good and Evil collide, and this is one of them. In the next few months this campus will become a battleground. You are being recruited to fight for the good guys." Pat didn't groan out loud. But that was, without a doubt, the least useful and most dramatic version of the situation Autumn could have come up with.

He could feel Sarah getting ready to run. Time to talk. "That thing you saw at your sleepover. It was real. I've dealt with things like it myself. One of my friends was killed by something like it, another driven halfway to mad before we got rid of it. I ended up in a hospital for a while myself because of it. But we beat it. We sent it back from where it came from. There's something like that here. I walked into Golem with you, saw the others, and knew this day was coming."

"The others?" Autumn asked.

"Yes. You know me, I know you, and I know them."

"We were wondering if you recognized us."

"Of course."

"Yeah, well I don't recognize any of you, and you've lost me again," Sarah said, her volume increasing again.

Autumn sighed. "Let's go somewhere else. It's very public here, and you keep raising your voice when you get excited."

"How about we go back to my place?" Sarah asked. "I'm the only one of us with no roommates. Then you can start at the beginning instead of the middle, and let me play catch-up."

"Sounds good." Autumn daintily sipped her drink while sliding out of the booth.

Pat and Sarah followed her toward Sarah's. "When she's gone, I want to have a long talk with you," she said to him quietly.

"I know."

Sarah got them settled in her home. Pat watched Autumn check out the space carefully, feeling for what magic was around her and coming up with a big blank.

Sarah sat on the window seat across from them and said, "Now start at the beginning and use very small words. Pretend I'm world class stupid because I'm so lost I'm not sure what side is up."

Autumn sighed. "This campus is currently a focus in the ongoing war between Good and Evil. A group of us have shown up here, destiny having thrown us together again, and again we'll fight it to a standstill." Pat really wanted to smack Autumn. She sounded like the setup in a bad fantasy novel.

"Explain 'again,'" Sarah said. "The last time I was fighting any sort of pitched Good versus Evil battle I was taking aim at a van filled with explosives driving full-speed at our roadblock."

"Not that kind of evil. Elemental Evil. Evil like Azzazzel. As for 'again,' we know each other. Pat, me, Chris, Chuck, Mike, and Dave: we've done this before."

"Like, when you were ten? Are you going to tell me you were the real-life version of *It*?" Pat smiled; Sarah was taking this well, all things considered.

"No, not in this lifetime. Before we were here, we were in another place. The last fight there landed us here. Now, the enemy we fought before is back, and it wants Round Two."

"Uh huh." Sarah looked like she didn't buy it at all, but she didn't toss them out. Pat figured that was about as good as he could hope for at this point. "What do you see my part in this being?"

"You're a healer. We need one." That was a lot blunter than he thought Autumn would go.

"I'm a medic. I patch people up when they get wounded and take them to a doctor. Are you expecting bullets?"

"No." Autumn thought seriously for a moment. "Cuts, burns, possibly broken bones, but mostly psychic damage translated into the body."

Sarah thought about it and moved to another question. "You all know each other. Do you know me?"

"I don't think so. As far as I know, you're on your first life." Pat didn't let his surprise show. He couldn't tell if Autumn was lying or really didn't feel it. Besides Chris, Pat wasn't sure if any of the others felt Althiira through Sarah. "When you walked over to our table, we noticed your star. Dave saw you had the right kind of energy around you for a healer. We need a healer."

"Yeah, but usually I do it by sticking needles in people and sewing up holes. You want a whole different kind of healing."

"You can do it. You've been doing it. I bet your patients got better a lot faster and easier than most of the others did."

"They might have. I usually didn't see them again after I patched them back up."

"They did." Pat felt Autumn try to use her magic to nudge Sarah in the direction Autumn wanted her to go. He blocked it. If Sarah joined them, it would be of her own free will. Autumn sent a flash of annoyance in his direction.

Pat looked at Sarah. "Last time, I spent sixteen weeks in a mental ward trying to get better. Things like this break your mind if you aren't ready for them. If we had a healer with us, I wouldn't have a piece of paper saying I'm sane, neither would Marc, and Eli would be alive. You're… calming. When you give a back rub, everything feels better. The thing you fixed when you worked on me: that was left over from my last fight with these things. Once you start learning and working on it, you'll be great."

"Yeah? Who is going to teach me?"

"You'll learn on the job," Autumn said.

"I haven't taken the job, yet." There was real alarm in Sarah's voice.

"You will. Let me start at the beginning." Autumn could have sounded smug, but she didn't.

"Please," Sarah said.

"And I'll kick in the parts Autumn wasn't there for."

"Before, we were all part of the same Royal Court."

"Think Rivendell," Pat interrupted.

"You mean elves?" Sarah asked.

"Not really. We hadn't been elves for twenty-six thousand years. That's a long time, even for us. But if you think of *Lord of the Rings* and where Tolkien's elves lived, you'll have something that, if not perfect, at least has the same feel to it," Pat said.

"Chris was the High Priest, like a king," Autumn continued, "He discovered a great evil. He recruited each of us, and we fought it. It took almost a year. Eventually, we had it beaten back, almost killed.

"Then we were betrayed. Our healer turned on us and left. If she had stayed, we could have kept up the fight. But once she left, we knew we couldn't continue. We fled and ended up here twenty-one years ago. Since then we've been dealing with its Minions when they come after us. They come and go, usually every few years. Now, we're all together again. This year we're going to finish it off for good."

Autumn let her magic show when she spoke. Pat had to admit she was impressive when she did that. She glowed brilliantly. Even if she didn't look like a fairy anymore she certainly felt like a fantastic magical creature. It was almost enough to make him forget the version of the story Autumn was telling didn't really match what had happened. Then Pat saw Sarah react to Autumn's magic. She swayed slightly in her seat and began to shiver. Sarah stood up and went to her bedroom.

"Tone it down. You're freaking her out," Pat ordered. Autumn raised her shields again.

When Sarah came back, she was wrapped in a blanket. She took a deep breath and showed them she was paying attention. "Autumn, you're twenty-two."

"This body is twenty-two. My parents will tell you about the time I fell into the pool and drowned, stopped breathing, no heart beat. After five minutes, their little girl started to cough and cry. They thought she was dead. They were right. The little girl was dead. I took her body. She didn't need it anymore. Anything from their world has no tangible physical presence over here. Once I had her body, I was a child. It's almost like I have two lives. I was an adult, a member of the High Court, Protocol Master to the Ambassador from Fairy…"

"Wait. You're a fairy?"

"Yes."

Sarah turned to Pat. "You aren't?"

"No, we were something else all together."

Sarah nodded, eyes wide, her disbelief patently visible. Autumn decided to just keep plowing through her story.

"Then I was here doing little girl stuff, learning to ride a bike, being impatient with my parents for not letting me go to sleepovers, that sort of thing. I was eight when my parents started to swat my hand for telling tales. Before that, I was just a marvelously inventive child." Pat gave Autumn a very hard look. It was entirely possible a child toddled into a pool and that was that. He also knew, even without bodies, they could move small things—like, say, pushing a convenient toddler into a pool—and if Autumn had liked the family, it wasn't something he'd put past her.

Autumn smiled at him innocently. *Fucking fairies!* He loathed their whole species. Sarah was watching him, waiting for the next bit of the tale. "I'm nineteen. It took me a long time to find a body because I wanted one that had died a natural death." Pat looked pointedly at Autumn; she continued looking innocent. "I found a woman six months pregnant. The child was dead, but she didn't know it yet. The cord was wrapped around its neck tight. My parents say I'm their miracle baby: cord around the neck three times and still alive. Like Autumn I have memories of a normal childhood. But, once upon a time, I was also Chris' personal bodyguard.

"I was thirteen when I helped fight that thing. Autumn's right. Every few years we see an uptick in activity. Something happens then that allows more of them to come for us. They don't have bodies here, but they can take over other people's bodies and manifest like a ghost or demon. The thing we fought—we called it 'Bruce,' just to have a name for it. Bruce could move small things, like a nail or a razor blade. If you weren't wary, it could possess you before you knew it was near. But we beat it. Killed it good and dead." That wasn't even close to the entire story, but Pat wasn't sure he wanted either of them to know the full story.

Autumn stood up. "I bet if I go into your room, I'll find lots of sci-fi/fantasy books. I bet you've spent years wanting magic to be real and dealing with odd coincidences. The time Azzazzel showed up wasn't the first time you dealt with something along those lines… and it wasn't the last. If I were to look into your mind, I bet I'd see you were the one who kicked over the board and demanded it leave because you were the only one in the group who knew what needed to be done."

Sarah went white. Pat had felt she hadn't told the whole story; it looked like Autumn had as well. Autumn kept going, telling Sarah about Sarah, slowly closing the deal. "You like graveyards. You like churches and synagogues and mosques. Anywhere holy speaks to you. You know you're a healer. That's why you're headed toward med school. It's why you became a medic. It's why you offer back rubs to people. You see pain, and you need to fix it. If you join us, I can give you the option to become a better healer than you ever dreamed of being. You know you have a destiny. You know you were meant to confront Evil and fight it. You traveled halfway across the world to do it. If you join us, you can help us defeat Evil in your backyard."

Sarah stared at them for a long time. Pat wasn't entirely sure what she was thinking, apart from the fact this whole thing was crazy, but he knew it was the sort of crazy she felt drawn to.

Eventually Sarah said, "I'm in."

"Good. Let's go for a walk," Autumn answered.

13.

We grabbed our jackets and left the house. I felt wrapped in a muzzy film. Like my senses were far away from me.

Autumn led us up Alden Street toward the Green Grove Cemetery. She and Pat kept quiet. I found my eyes darting between the two of them. Autumn kept shifting in my gaze. I could see the cute, perky, plump wannabe cheerleader. Underneath it or perhaps through it, I caught images of a woman who had known pain and sorrow and hard choices.

Pat looked sad as well. Like something he had been running away from had finally caught him, and he now knew he'd never be free.

We stopped at the wrought-iron gate to the cemetery. I was scanning the acres of flat markers in front of me, and wondering what was past the line of trees when Autumn asked, "What do you feel here?"

"Not much of anything," I answered truthfully. "Comfortable. It's not like the junior high or the chapel for that matter. I don't like them at all. And it's not cold like Pat's rock or the Golem. Is that what you mean by 'What do I feel?'"

"Yes. Wait, the Golem? What?" Autumn looked puzzled. She pushed open the gate and we began walking down a paved road towards the trees.

"You know, the statue in front of my house…"

"I know what statue you mean. That feels like Pat's rock to you?"

"Sort of, they're both way too cold."

"Huh. None of us have noticed that. You get a sense of it, Pat?"

"I hadn't even noticed the statue on that poster had a real life version."

"I'll show it to you tomorrow or the next day," I told Pat.

"Sounds good," he answered.

The paved road led us over a small ravine, the source of the trees. On the other side of the ravine was the old graveyard. A riot of old, worn granite markets were dotted liberally with angels, weeping women, obelisks, and mausoleums. Directly in front of us was a life size sculpture in white marble of Christ on the Cross with three kneeling, weeping angels at his feet.

"What's back there?" Pat pointed at the graves behind the sculpture.

"Let's go see," Autumn said.

Pat walked straight to the kneeling angels. His hand hovered near the face of one of them. "What the hell happened here?"

"Something that needed to happen."

"Like fuck. This area is destroyed. This is sloppy work."

Autumn walked up to Pat and stood toe to toe with him. He was at least a foot taller, but they appeared to be looking straight into each other's eyes. Icy anger radiated off Pat. Autumn's posture was defensive. They looked like they were having a silent argument I wasn't part of.

It was fierce, but somehow I knew it wasn't going to come to blows, so I stayed away from their fight and walked around the statue. Once behind it, I felt what Pat was talking about. This place was wrong. The "wrong" emanated from a decrepit mausoleum. Maybe the granite was just naturally a sooty black, or maybe those long tendrils of blackened crud was the result of a fire. The windows were shattered, once sparkling gems of stained glass were dulled by the black crud. The door was gone. What was left of the hinges were ripped and mangled. On the step I saw something that scared me deeply: claw marks. What kind of thing could leave claw marks in solid stone?

My eyes turned to the interior of the mausoleum. Through the void where the door had been, something lurked, looking back at me. Palpable fear flashed electrically through my skin. I jumped back, not taking my eyes from whatever was in there. Physical space didn't help to calm my racing heart. I curled into a defensive ball, knife in hand. Crunching footsteps alerted my attention to someone coming near.

"What's in there?"

"Nothing good."

"Chris?" I had expected Pat. I wanted to turn and look at him, but I didn't want to take my eyes off whatever was in there. Keeping an eye on the thing won out. I didn't turn to him. I did stand up.

"Autumn called me. She and Pat were getting a little heated back there. Chuck's sorting them out. I figured I should get you before you got too freaked out." He rested his hand on my shoulder; I finally turned to look at him. "Yes, it's really there. No, it can't get out."

He gently turned me back toward the others. "I didn't hear her call."

"She didn't use her phone."

I looked blankly at him until I realized what he meant. "You're saying she called you with her mind?"

"Yes."

I nodded. The desire to run away washed over me. Chris smiled, and I began to feel calmer. The panic receded, but a gnawing cold grew in the pit of my stomach. Time to act more comfortable than I was.

"Yeah, well, if she had opened her mouth, I could have tackled him and that would have diffused the issue."

"But that would have been so much less dramatic." He sighed. His hand slid off my shoulder, down my arm, just brushing my fingers. It was a sweetly tender gesture, and it did help to push away some of the immense weird of this moment. "As you might have guessed, Autumn likes drama."

"What happened here?"

"Can I tell you and Pat about it back at the Writers' House? I don't like being out here after dark. That'll be soon." He eyed the mausoleum pensively. "How did Pat upset her so badly?"

"He said it was sloppy work."

Chris looked around. "He's right. But it's my sloppy work, and Autumn feels the need to defend me no matter what." I wondered about Autumn and Chris. They didn't appear to be dating, but that kind of loyalty was rare even among very good friends.

Chuck spoke softly to Autumn and Pat. Their anger had dissipated. The cold in my stomach grew. I felt like I swallowed Pat's rock. A low headache began at the base of my skull. *You feel that every time Chuck is near.* He looked up and met my gaze. The headache receded.

The walk back was quick and tense. We entered Writers' in silence. Chris' eyes closed, and the walls of the house turned to ice. Memories of sitting inside a snow fort as a little girl came back in a rush. I shivered. In a minute my teeth were chattering.

Chris looked concerned. "Are you cold?"

"Yes. You did something that dropped the temperature in here fifty degrees."

"She feels magic as cold," Pat told the group while grabbing a blanket for me off of the sofa. "Go get her something warm to drink."

"Sure." Autumn headed to the kitchen. "Coffee, tea, cocoa?"

"I'm jittery enough without caffeine. Anything decaf. Would any of you care to tell me why every time I turn around I run into something that gives me goose bumps and makes me shiver?" Pat put his arm around me. I welcomed the warmth and knowing someone here realized I was seriously weirded out.

"It's magic," Chris said. "We all feel it at different sensitivity levels. For some reason, you feel it as cold. Most of us feel it as heat."

Chuck spoke in a quiet voice, "I don't feel it, but I can see it."

"What does it look like?" Curiosity began pushing fear away.

"Your star glows. I can see it under your shirt. You glow, but at a different…color. That isn't really the right word, but it's close enough. I always know when Pat's got his rock on him; I can see it through his clothing."

"Interesting." Pat did something. Once again I felt immersed in cold. "How about now?"

"Yeah, but it's more subtle."

"Good to know."

"I felt that. What did you do?"

"Put a shield around it. I…imagine a sphere of mirror. I put it around my rock, with the mirrored side facing the stone. The energy bounces back making the stone less visible."

Autumn returned with a cup of steaming tea. "Decaf Earl Grey, one sugar."

"Lovely. How do you feel it?" Steam from the cup bathed my face in warmth for a second before I gulped the drink down.

She thought for a while. "Chris said heat, right?" Chris nodded. "Well, that's as good a description as any. It's not like putting your hand near the stove. I tend to feel it in the pit of my stomach or the small of my back. It's like a knot of warm. I can use my hands and eyes to home in on what's causing the sensation."

"You see it, too?"

"Yes, but not very well. Here." She took my hand in hers. Then she closed her eyes, and I had sense of something starting. A small ball of cold energy appeared above my hand. "You can feel it, right?"

"Yes. It's like Pat's rock, but it feels different, too."

"It's my energy. Everyone's magic should feel different as you get to know them."

"That's helpful."

"It will be. Now look at it." I looked at the place where the invisible cold sphere hovered. Nothing. "Keep looking."

I focused until I thought my eyes would fall out, but saw nothing. Frustrated, I blinked, looked away, and realized I could see it with my peripheral vision. I let my focus slide back to the ball; now it was like looking at shimmering steam swirling in a ball. "I see it."

"Look around."

I pulled my eyes away from the ball that had appeared out of nowhere and looked at the Writers' House with new eyes. All of the outside walls, all of the people, a quarter of the books on the shelf, several of the curios, and the door to Autumn's room all shimmered in different shades of mist.

"Fuck." I closed my eyes. It didn't help. The auras were still there. I took a deep breath and opened them again. "Am I ever going to see normally again?"

Chris smiled gently. "Probably not. It'll become background. Eventually, you'll only notice it when it's out of place. As of now, you'll be able to see where others like us are."

"Others from where you were before?"

"No." Chuck's voice was definitive. "We're it."

"Mike," Autumn added.

"The others you see are also magic users, just different flavors," Chuck said.

"Don't like flavors." Chris shook his head. "It's all the same stuff, just different techniques. Different schools might be a better way of putting it."

"No, 'flavors' is a really good word," Pat disagreed. "Most of the time I do feel like I can taste it. Mine tastes like earth. Mike's is like iron on the tongue. You taste like Communion wafers." Chris looked appalled. Pat chuckled.

"What do I taste like?"

Pat grinned at me. "I've been trying to find out since I saw you at the Improv." He squeezed me a little tighter. The shivering finally began to back off. I was still deeply cold, but at least my jaw wasn't shaking any longer. "Lightly spicy, cinnamon on the tongue while breathing ozone." I raised my eyebrows.

"I'm a writer."

"Yes, you are."

Pat gave me another squeeze; then his playfulness vanished. "Tell me what happened in the graveyard. That was ridiculously sloppy."

"The very short version is you two took until this year to get here," Chris said. "The longer version is this: We've been hunting for the portal Mildred—"

"Mildred?" *Who's Mildred?*

"That's what we call it. The big bad. The thing that's trying to kill us. Not it's real name, obviously. None of us want to use its real name. Names attract attention, and we've already got more than enough of that as it is. Anyway, we've been searching for the doorway Mildred uses to get from there to here. We know it's around here somewhere, but we haven't found it. The portal is likely pretty small, less than ten feet around, so we've got to really search everywhere."

"Which is it?" I asked. Chris looked confused. "Doorway or portal?"

"Oh… We've got no set term for it, door, doorway, portal… Chuck calls it the vortex every now and again. Why do you do that?" He turned to Chuck.

"That's what it looked like when Autumn opened it."

"Okay. I suppose you could call it a Fairy Circle, too."

"No." Autumn shook her head. "My circle closed after we went through. They had to open a new one."

"Okay. Anyway… last March we got to the graveyard. We had planned three different nights to go check it out. The first night was pretty easy; we got the whole front area, with the flat stones, covered.

"On the second night we thought we could get the north half of the old graveyard done."

"Well, we had been there for what… seven minutes?" Chris looked at Autumn. She nodded back at him. "We all got scared. You know the creepy stories, the temperature drops, your breath freezes in the air, and your skin breaks out in goose bumps?" I nodded. "That happened to all of us."

"Who is all of us?" I wanted to know.

"Autumn, Dave, Mike, and I." I almost said, 'Who's Dave?' But then I realized he was sitting in the corner of the room next to Autumn. Not only was he sitting with us, he had also come to the graveyard as well. I felt especially stupid for not noticing him sooner.

"No Chuck?" Pat interjected.

He shook his head. "I had broken my ankle the week before. I was home watching TV with my foot propped up on a pillow."

"Wait, when did you get hurt?" I asked.

"Last March."

"I thought the wound was older."

"I know. You also thought it was a work accident. It happened at Hurford's, but it wasn't a work accident. We can tell that story some other time, though."

Chris took over the story again. "We're all there, getting creeped out."

Dave added, "You have to remember: we don't scare easy, not by this kind of thing. Been there, done that, got the t-shirt. There's enough crap floating about this town that spooky really isn't. Autumn saw it first."

Autumn continued, "It sounds kind of dumb, like those paranormal shows where the hapless housewife talks about seeing the 'Dark Man.' Well, it was the Dark Man. It was night. We usually go search at night because it attracts less attention. So, it's dark out. But this was darker. Instead of looking at the absence of light, we were seeing the rejection of light—something that scared the light away. It stood in front of us, and I began to feel really ill. Chris was getting more and more scared. Mike had his sword out ready to attack. And Dave… What were you doing, Dave?"

"I don't think it noticed I was there. I could tell it was bad news. It wasn't human, it had never been human, and it actively hated anything human. In other words, we had walked into the territory of something big, bad, with absolutely nothing to do with what we were looking for. To make matters worse, it knew us now, and it wanted to have some fun."

Chris took over storytelling. "So, here's the choice: run and let it see where we live or fight it there without really knowing what to do. We took the gamble that our shields would hold, and headed back to Writers'.

"The shields held, but we could feel it outside. We spent the night online trying to find out what to do with it. Consecrate the ground. Kill the magic in the area. An Exorcist would have been handy." He paused and took a long look at me. I gave him an equally long look back. I'd be willing to work as a healer. I had no desire to move into exorcisms. That one close call had been more than enough.

"Ultimately, had our geomancer been handy," he looked at Pat, "we probably could have found a way to use the fact it chose a huge plot of ground filled with rocks as its home to our advantage. Or if you were around," he looked back at me, "because it sounds like you've got at least some sort of clue as to what to do with this kind of thing, we might not have needed to destroy the area.

"But no, you two were off living your lives. We had to deal with it soon because after the first night the shields were weakening and we had fifteen dead crows littered around our house."

Autumn took over. "The next day we went to St. Aggies, grabbed as much holy water as we could, and then went back to the graveyard. It didn't take a lot of brains to figure out the vandalized mausoleum was its home. We drenched it in holy water. Chris dusted off his old skills to ask God to make it leave and keep the ground holy. Then Chris and Dave built a big shield around the mausoleum to make sure anything inside it couldn't get out. Dave made sure no one would just wander into the area. And Chris killed all the magic in a fifty foot radius."

"Which is why you've got a dead zone in one of the few places that should never have a dead zone," Pat stated.

"Yes," Chris answered.

"What do you mean by 'dead zone?'" I asked. "I've jogged the graveyard several times; most of it doesn't have that cold feeling. Should it?"

"Stones have memories. Especially carved stones. Those stones are dead, just lumps of minerals. The work that went into making them markers for memories has been erased. The history that's slid by them is gone. Some stones have lots of memories attached to them, some don't, but they all should have some even if it's just the feel of the earth around them. These have nothing." Pat understood my blank look and took a different path. "Let's put it this way. You could blindfold me and drop me in the center of the cemetery, and I won't trip because I can feel the stones. Do the same thing in Chris' dead zone, and I'll be on my ass in a minute because those stones have no feel to them. They're just dead."

"And that's sloppy?"

"Yes." Pat sounded unforgiving, almost disappointed.

"It was overkill," Dave said.

"I didn't notice you coming up with anything better," Autumn fired back at Dave.

"No, I didn't have anything better. Pat probably would have." Dave sounded calm as he spoke. I got the feeling very little made him angry.

"Can you fix it?" I asked Pat.

He shook his head. "Dead is dead. Nothing will recreate those memories. Those stones will slowly soak new memories and feelings into them, but long before they become noticeable, we'll all be gone."

"If the Dark Man is trapped, why don't you want to be there at night?" I turned toward Chris.

"I don't want to be there if the trap breaks. I really don't want to find out what else is there. Things like that don't just pop up for no reason. Someone called it here. Given that it's not able to get out, they've probably called something else. People who mess with that kind of magic usually don't go home with a skip and a smile when you take their toys away."

"Did you finish checking out the cemetery?"

"No, not yet," Chris shook his head. "The rest of the cemetery became the absolute last place we'll look for the door. If we have to go there again, having Pat and his skills is a very good thing. That you turned out to be the healer, and you've got some background with this, is even better. Another mark that this was meant to be."

"Wonderful. When I told that story, did you somehow get the idea I thought dealing with things like Azzazzel was fun?"

"No. But you've got the skills, and we've got the need. I think you were meant to do it."

"Autumn, why did you bring us there?" Pat turned to her.

Autumn looked uncomfortable. "Because I still wasn't sure Sarah had any magic to her. I knew I could take her there to test her."

"Did I pass?"

"Yes."

"Lovely. So what is Mildred? Why are you fighting it? What do you think I'll need to do?"

14.

"What is Mildred?" Chris repeated Sarah's question. He spent a minute searching for an answer that wasn't an out and out lie but wouldn't send her running for the door. "There's no word for it in English," which might have been technically true although 'archangel' would have been awfully close. "It's big. It's bad. It wants us dead. 'Why are we fighting it?'" *Because I killed our God, and Mildred's pissed.* Even if that answer didn't send her running to the door, he absolutely knew it would get him killed by Pat. So he found another not terribly enlightening but absolutely true answer. "Because Mildred didn't give up after we left. What are you going to do? Put us back together when we come limping, wounded to your home."

"That's all, huh?" she asked.

"Easy peasy, right?" Dave smiled sarcastically.

"Sounds like it," Sarah answered. "It's been hunting you since you got here?"

"Yes," Chris said, pleased to turn the conversation away from how they ended up in this mess. "The first time it came for me was subtle. Hints of something ominous coming in my direction, always just out of sight. When I was seven, one of Mildred's Minions caught up with me. We were in art class. One of the other kids took the teacher's scissors and stabbed me in the leg with them.

"Usually if something like that happens, there's something wrong with the kid with the scissors. But there wasn't. We were friends. Jim was a very gentle boy. He didn't remember doing it. I watched him stab me. His eyes went blank, and Jim was gone. For a split second, I saw something looking out from Jim's eyes. I knew it was one of the Minions.

"Then it was over, Jim was back, I had a pair of scissors sticking out of my leg, and everyone was crying. Jim didn't know what had happened. I didn't want him to get in trouble. I told everyone I had fallen. He tried to catch me; the scissors just got in the way. That story made everyone happy.

"When I was in the hospital getting stitched up, I realized I wasn't safe here. Mildred had found me, and I needed to find a way to stay safe. But the magic didn't work right here. The power—the almost effortless spells I could remember—was gone. At first I thought it was just the limits of my seven-year-old body. That it just couldn't produce the concentration necessary to do what needed to be done.

"I got older and realized most humans, no matter what age, couldn't do magic. But a few humans could. I knew I had to learn how to do it all over again. By the time I was nine I was reading everything I could find on the subject. I was a model student. Spending hours in the library because I couldn't take the books home to where my Catholic parents lived.

"By the time my fifteenth birthday rolled around I was getting a handle on it. I could concentrate longer and harder than I could as a small child. The spells were coming back to me, getting easier each time I did them. Then it returned. Every time I closed my eyes Mildred came at me. I kept seeing things watching me. It haunted my dreams. My parents were worried I was on drugs because I was so jumpy.

"I was at my breaking point, so tense the slightest sound made me jump. I knew I wasn't a match for it yet. My mom decided something was really wrong with me and was taking me to the doctor. I suppose they were going to test for drugs or something. It didn't happen. We were in the car. She was telling me I was going to be all right. The doctors were going to help me. She stopped mid-sentence. The same presence I had felt in Jim came over her.

"She swerved across two lanes of traffic and flipped the van. The magic I had been studying paid off. Neither of us died. I was able to create a sort of pillow which kept us from being too badly hurt. I had a broken arm and leg; my mom spent a week in the hospital with head injuries and a broken shoulder. The van was totaled. The official story: she fell asleep at the wheel.

"In the hospital I could feel it recede again. Nothing else happened during the rest of high school.

"I got here, found the rest of them in less than two days, and a day after that, while we were sitting on the lawn a Minion showed up and decided to see what we could do. We're all a lot better at it now then we were as teens."

"Didn't everyone notice a magical fight in the middle of the campus?" Sarah asked.

"Nope," Dave answered. "I took care of that."

"Now they're here all the time. We haven't seen a possession in a while. I don't know if they got bored of it or prefer the out and out fight. Either way, it ends here. We find the door, kill them all, and close it tight," Chris finished.

"You were fifteen in 2002, right?" Pat checked.

"Yes."

"That was the year we fought Mildred, too. One minute I'm hanging out with Eli and Marc in Marc's rec room; the next a box cutter blade is flying through the air cutting the hell out of my arms. Three baby wizards in a room with a blade flying around. Eli got to it stop. Marc was so excited he just about peed in his pants. I knew what was moving that blade around and told them the real story. They were so entranced by the whole thing. It wasn't real for them until Eli got killed. Marc and I got real serious. We called in every power, every favor, every ounce of magic we could lay a hold of, and destroyed it.

"I spent that spring in a mental ward. Marc was there almost a year. Chris is right. The magic doesn't work the same way here, but there are paths to it. In Hidiri I was a fighter."

"Don't use the names," Autumn said to him. "It attracts the Watchers."

"The Watchers?" Sarah's eyebrows furrowed.

"Nasty little boogers that sit outside the shields and watch us. If we spend too long talking about the world before, or Mildred, or strategy, they show up," Dave answered.

"Lovely." Pat sighed. "We didn't have them last time, at least not that I remember. Anyway, when I got out I knew I had to find that path again. My parents were very happy to sign me up for Tai Chi lessons. It seemed so...soothing. It felt good. I got my magic back: easier than using rocks. Don't get me wrong, I like rocks," he smiled at me, "some of them are very good friends. But fighting with foot and fist was what I was made to do. Maybe you would have had an easier time in Church, Chris?"

"I'm thinking 'no' on that one." Chris smiled with grim amusement.

"I suppose there isn't a parallel path for you," Pat said.

"Why not?" Sarah questioned.

"My particular path doesn't have an analog here. Pat uses his body to channel his magic to fight. I use my mind. He could take Tai Chi or something like it, and have someone else show him how to get in tune with the local energies. I didn't have that option."

"So, you really are fucking amazing?" Sarah asked Pat.

"Yes, I am."

"But I can still beat you with a blade," Mike said as he came into the living room from the kitchen. "So, they got you to join?"

"Yeah."

"Run, little girl, run." Mike walked toward Sarah, taking off his shirt. Her eyes went wide, shocked at his actions. Then they went wider. His left arm, shoulder, and chest were covered in smooth, shiny scars. Mike had told Chris about it their freshman year; a quarter cup of flaming gasoline could do major damage.

"I got burned. Stick with us and you'll get hurt, too." He pulled his t-shirt back on.

"Won't that screw you guys?" Sarah queried.

"Yes," Chris answered. He looked pointedly at Mike.

"But you'll be better off for it if you walk out that door right now," Mike said.

Sarah looked at Pat, sitting next to her, his arm still around her shoulders. "You're with them?"

"Yes. We're in a new world, with new bodies, and one way or another it ends here."

"Then I'm in, too." Sarah leaned her head on Pat's shoulder. He kissed her quickly on the forehead, never taking his eyes off Chris. Chris felt the desire to jump up and physically pull Pat off of her so strongly his thighs twitched, ready to stand and move. *She's not yours.* He wasn't entirely sure if his mind or Chuck's was speaking. Either way, he relaxed and let it go.

"If I'm as good at this as you guys think I am, maybe this time won't lead to so many scars.

"So, what was the story with your first healer? Why did she betray you?" The mood in the room shifted; it morphed into an intensely uncomfortable embarrassment. For a while no one said anything. Chris could feel them all looking at him, waiting to see how he'd answer it. She caught the tension and said, "Okay, I can feel I just stepped in it. I'm sorry, but I still don't know why."

The others were still staring at Chris. He took a deep breath and started talking. He tried not to let the sadness shine through his voice too clearly but remembering that last week hurt like walking on knives. "She was my wife. We almost had them beaten. There were five more days until the moon would be in the right place to do the last spell when she left. I needed her for that spell. I had to cast it, but I needed her healing and protection to do it." He realized once again he had wandered into an area where he needed to lie, not for her sake but for Pat and Mike's. They didn't know he had succeeded; it had worked exactly the way Althiira told him it would. His success, his mastery of magic that would have driven most men to suicide, destroyed their world. "I tried by myself, but it didn't work. I couldn't destroy their power source by myself. Once that failed, we had to flee, so Autumn brought us here."

"And Mildred came after you?" Sarah asked.

"Sort of. We don't think Mildred is actually here, on this plane, yet. It uses the portal we're looking for to send its Minions here," Chris said.

"So, that's the plan. Find the doorway. Kill everything that comes out. Close it tight," Dave told them. "After Golem, we get together with the map, and plan where we're going that week. Then a group of us goes hunting for the door. Once we find it, we need a somewhat more detailed version of the plan."

"Yes, you do." Sarah didn't look particularly impressed with the plan. "What about you, Dave? Anything attack you?"

"I never let it get that far. You might have noticed I'm kind of hard to see?"

"Yes, I have noticed that," she replied dryly.

"There was an eight-week period between the first time I felt the Minions come for me, and the last time they saw me. During that time things never got past the creepy Watcher phase."

"Autumn? Did they come for you, too?"

"Yes. Six times in total. I have a feeling Mildred is especially pissed at me because I'm the one who let them get away. I'm not without my own healing skills, so I'm not covered in scars. Speaking of the Watchers, it's time for a new topic; I can feel a few of them outside."

Chuck nodded. "Three."

"That would be the especially cold prickly sensation in the small of my back?" Sarah wanted to know.

"Yes." Chuck looked like he was seeing her differently.

No one said anything while the Watchers slowly drifted away. After a minute, Sarah asked, "Does that mean they're gone?" Dave nodded at her. "Good, it's getting late. I want to get home, have some dinner, and finish a ton of homework."

"Dinner's a good idea," Autumn said. "How about we all get some?"

"I ate before I got here," Mike replied.

They headed to the cafeteria. Chris watched her break off from the group as she got to her steps. Pat followed her up, said something quietly to her, and returned. He grinned at Chris, a big, smug smile on his face, and joined the rest of the group as they went to dinner.

15.

Chris was the last one to get his food. He slid into his seat with two slices of pizza and a Pepsi.

"Tell me what's happened since you got together again," Pat said after he sat down.

Autumn shook her head. "Not here. No shields."

"They show up even faster if we talk outside the house," Dave told him.

"Fine. Who's free tomorrow afternoon to get me up to date?"

"I am," Dave answered.

"On a related but unlikely-to-attract-notice topic, how good is she?" Chuck asked.

"Phenomenal. Best damn healer I've ever seen."

"How many have you seen?" Chris queried.

"Many. Our kind isn't exactly rare in New York City if you know where to look. I've had five work on my back; none of them could shift the damage. She got it in one with no training. How'd she do with your shoulder," he looked at Chris, "and your leg?" he shifted his gaze to Chuck.

"As you said, got it in one."

"It's better. Not fixed, I wasn't expecting fixed; that would have been a miracle. It's noticeably better."

"What actually happened to your leg?" Pat asked Chuck.

"I was pushed off a ladder. The reason I was up there in the first place was to finish destroying a shrine that was feeding a nasty critter at Hurford's. It jumped me. I killed it. Then drug myself back up that ladder to finish the job. The second trip up is what really hurt my ankle."

"Why didn't you have backup?" Pat looked amazed that Chuck would go off on a job without Chris. Chris had been pretty shocked he had wanted to do it on his own as well.

"It wasn't supposed to be that big of a job. I was well-paid for it, though."

"Worth your leg?"

"It'll heal eventually. And yes, they did pay well enough to cover the pain. It's possible I'll be back there this summer to do it again. Looks like they haven't figured out who is summoning those things. As long as they don't, I've got an income stream."

"Wonderful," Pat said.

"One more of those jobs and I'll be able to take the time off to get my leg fixed, buy a car, and have a comfortable pile in the bank account," Chuck answered.

"If they're paying that well, I'll back you up next time."

"I've already signed up for the job," Chris said.

"Of course." Chris could feel Pat understand the likelihood of Chuck doing any fighting was just about zero if Chris was there.

"Are you going back to her place after dinner?" Autumn asked.

"Yes. I'll fill her in on more of the background. You know, little things like who you all are and stuff.'"

"Good," Chris said. "No names."

"I know enough not to use our true names. Even if it didn't attract unwanted attention, I'd leave that up to you to reveal. Does anyone else know?"

"I don't think so," Dave answered. "We've done a pretty good job of keeping it quiet."

"Plus, with us all here, there's much less need for anyone on the outside," Autumn added.

Pat nodded. "She's got a boyfriend; she'll probably want to tell him. I don't get the sense secrets are really high on Sarah's list. Can you deal with that?"

"If it gets us a real healer? Yes." Chuck picked up his drink. "He's far away, right?"

"Other side of the world. Israel," Pat answered between bites of pizza.

"Sure, that's no problem at all. Having a guy ten thousand miles away who thinks we're nuts isn't a big deal," Autumn said.

"Especially one we'll never see," Chris added.

"Sorry, Chris. I've already got a visit by him in the works. Middle of October, Ari Kogan will be flying into Pittsburgh International. She doesn't know about it, so don't let it slip," Pat replied.

Autumn looked at him softly with a hint of surprise in her eyes. "That's so sweet."

"Thanks. She hasn't seen him since January. It seemed like a good thing to arrange if it could be done. Amazingly enough, my powers of persuasion were able to get him to take a week off."

Dave gave him a half-smile. "Kind of like my amazing ability to drive as fast as I want without getting a ticket."

"Kind of." Pat looked down at his empty plate. "Well, this was lovely. I'm done with class after four. See you then?"

"Yes."

"Good. I'm off to Sarah's. Have a nice rest of dinner."

Once Pat was out of the building Chuck set a shield around their table. Chris set a similar one inside it.

"So, what's the official story?" Dave asked. "It would be a good thing to be more or less on the same page when she starts asking questions."

"Yes, it would. I noticed you did an especially nice job of not actually answering them Chris," Autumn added.

"I wouldn't have had to if you and Chuck hadn't lied to Mike and Pat right after."

"You happily lied to them all the way through before. I don't see how after changed matters," Chuck said.

"I didn't lie. I didn't tell them what we were doing. There is a difference."

"Not really, it's called a lie of omission," Autumn quipped.

"No, a lie of omission is when you tell some of the truth and leave bits out to produce an erroneous impression. I didn't tell them anything in regards to what we did. You two flat out lied to them."

"Actually it was me," Dave said quietly. "I'm the one who told them we had to run. Chuck was already on the other side with you. I don't remember Autumn saying much of anything. Did you?"

"No. I was keeping the portal open."

"Anyway, now that we've got the blame done, we're still in need of the official story. Mike and Pat were told you failed; the spell didn't work because she wasn't there. I would prefer they don't find the real version out. Pat will leave us and probably do much worse. Mike... It's harder to tell with him. He had no strong love of our home, but he might not take its destruction well," Chuck said mildly.

"Then we stay with the version they have. Home is still well and whole. The Presence is in place. Mildred was the target. We're looking for the doorway to kill it," Chris said sadly.

"Are we trying to get home?" Dave asked.

"No... damn it. Yes, the answer has to be yes. They don't know it's gone. They don't know Mildred wasn't the big boss. Once Mildred's gone, there's no reason not to go back. The door will have to be shut before the fight is over, and we've got to make them believe it can't be reopened," Chris looked weary as he said it.

"They don't know she's dead," Chuck said pointedly to Chris.

"I know. I know. Especially with Pat that'll be a sensitive area. I can handle it."

"Good. They're back," Chuck nodded to the far corner of the cafeteria. Two small, round, eyeless, white-fleshed heads, mouths open and filled with sharp teeth, faced them, patiently waiting for them to finish the conversation.

"They're getting faster, aren't they?" Dave regarded the Watchers calmly.

"I think so," Chuck agreed. He finished his dinner and stood up. "Time for me to head home."

Chris stood up, too, leaving his own dinner half-eaten. "I'll join you."

"See you back at home?" Autumn asked.

"Maybe. I'll text you if I stay at Chuck's."

Neither of them said anything until they left the cafeteria. "She waits up for you when you go out?"

"Yes. In case I might want to *talk* when I get home," Chris said with immense bitterness.

"Have you ever wanted to *talk* when you got home?"

"God, no! But about one out of ten nights she's in the living room in her lacy pink nightgown waiting for me; the other nine she's in her room with the light on waiting. If I send her a text saying I'll be out all night, she goes to sleep, and I don't have to run the gauntlet when I get home."

They walked another hundred yards down Main Street toward Reevesville before Chuck spoke again. "Looks like you're doing well on the whole, she's-not-your-wife-so-stop-acting-like-it front."

"I think I did very well."

"Only in the sense that you didn't actually jump up and punch Pat when he kissed her forehead."

"He winked at me when he did it."

"He did not! Besides, how many nights did he have to sit there and watch you cuddle Althiira?"

"I know."

"If you can't get over this, you two are going to have a hard time."

"I'm trying. I avoided her through the whole party. When she came out to see me, I kept my distance."

"I know. It's killing you, isn't it?"

"I have a whole new appreciation for the soldiers who would come to me with confessions of wanting someone else's wife."

"Fifty years too late."

"Almost twenty-two years too late. I heard confessions until the last day we were there."

"I didn't know that."

"You never paid much attention to my priestly duties."

"That's true. Also, nice attempt to derail the topic of conversation."

"Thank you. I don't want to talk about her. I already know your advice, wait until Pat's gone, go see her, charm her out of her pants, and finally pop my cherry. Right?"

"'Pop your cherry?' I doubt I would have said it like that. 'Fuck her into next week' would be more in character."

"I'll remember that. Did I mischaracterize your advice in any way?"

"Other than your appalling word choice, no."

"She's not my wife. I'll keep my distance and hold myself in check. Not let Pat bait me. In time I'll get used to her being around. In time I'll get to know her well enough that I'll be able to see the differences more clearly. It will get easier."

"You don't need to do this."

Chris stopped walking and turned to face Chuck, his voice low and hard. "Live with a woman for one hundred and twelve years, love her deeply, have five children with her, watch her put her life in front of yours multiple times, fight your battles, advise you, share your body and your bed. Then, when she asks you do to something important, ignore her because of your own pride and get her, your children, and your entire planet killed. Once you've done that, you can tell me what I need to do." He turned and took two steps.

Chuck grabbed his arm and turned Chris to face him. "It wasn't your fault! Do you remember who you were the day before you cast that spell? Do you remember him? You knew absolutely you were doing the right thing; the thing you were born to do. Remember that? Nothing changed. You fulfilled your destiny. Fulfilled the prophecies.

"If anything she's the one who fucked up by not coming with us. If she had done that she'd be here, with you, ready to finish the fight, and then live happily ever after. If she had come, there would have been enough time to get your kids, open the portal, and get all six of you over here."

Chris didn't answer him. He shook Chuck's hands off his arms and continued walking down the street.

"You're never going to believe that, are you?"

Chris shook his head. "No. I'm not."

16.

That was interesting. Pat headed toward Sarah's while thinking about what was said that afternoon. Autumn had outright lied, but that wasn't out of character. Chris' inability to come up with a name for what they fought was interesting as well, but Pat wasn't entirely unsympathetic to that evasion. He wasn't sure he wanted to tell Sarah they were trying to destroy an angel gone bad.

He knocked on her door. She let him in and settled on one side of the sofa as he sat on the other.

"Now that the rest of them are gone, tell me what is going on."

"You've got most of it now."

Sarah snorted derisively. "Here's what I've got: Great Evil and you guys somehow get mixed up in Hidiri."

"Please, don't use the real names. Names have power; they attract attention. Right now I'd rather lay low."

"Fine, give me a name."

"Osoland." They had been the Ossolyn of Hidiri, the Stone Elves. Though calling them that was an insult. *Smurfs*, he thought with a dry amusement. Osoland was close enough for him to remember easily, without being the real name of their home.

"Bear land?" Apparently Sarah had some Spanish to go with her Hebrew and Arabic.

"Sure, why not? Osoland."

"Anyway, Mildred somehow gets tangled with you guys. You almost but don't quite manage to defeat it. Your healer, who turns out to have been Chris' wife, walks away from you and joins the other side. Next thing you know you're here body hunting. Every couple years after that things get hairy, and then—which is now—you're all back together for yet another battle with Mildred."

"That's really pretty much it."

She rolled her eyes. "How about this: how did you end up fighting Mildred?"

All out or leave the sugar coating in place? All out. Better to have Sarah run now than think she had been lied to. "Mildred was Satan."

"What?" She looked stunned.

"Look, I could feel some of what Chris was thinking when he answered your question. He was afraid calling Mildred an angel would send you running. It was an angel, and it had gone bad."

Pat could feel this was intensely interesting to her. "How does an angel go bad? I mean, what was it doing?"

"Blocking us from our god, making us slaves, eating a thousand of us every twenty years."

"That sounds bad."

"Yeah. Chris was determined to get rid of Mildred. As to the actual plan, I don't know. It could read minds, and I wasn't good enough at blocking it to be allowed to know the details."

"How did you get involved in this?"

"I was Chris' bodyguard. Those of us who are especially talented warriors are tested, and those who pass are allowed to be considered for the position of High Guard. I was chosen."

"By Chris?"

"No, by our god."

"You mean you felt like you had a vocation?"

"No, I mean God, the Presence—that's about as close as I can get in English—told me my job was to keep Chris safe, no matter what." He could see Sarah was staggered by that idea. "It wasn't like it is here. The Presence talked to us, in a voice as clear as mine. It told us what to do. Told us how to best please It. I was told to protect Chris. So, I protect Chris. In my world when you sit down to pray, you get actual answers."

"Huh…" Sarah looked like she didn't know what to do with that. "So, you don't know what actually happened with them and Mildred?"

"No. There was a cave, and Dave made sure it was invisible to…well…everyone. They'd meet in the cave to plan and discuss. My job was to stand outside and make sure nothing got in."

"What did Mildred look like?"

Pat had only seen Mildred in the flesh once though it had haunted his dreams for close to six months. "It was beautiful…and terrible. Like…the most perfect person you've ever seen and the most perfect rage. What's it called? The Platonic Ideal? This was the Platonic Idea of Beauty and Fury. It spoke to me, tried to win me over, told me to stop protecting Chris, told me he was on the wrong path; I could save the world if I left him." Pat paused, his eyes grew softer, and his focus slid far away. Memories of that last year danced through his mind. "I don't hate her…"

"Huh?" Sarah looked confused, beyond the level of confusion he had been dealing with all day.

He realized he'd changed trains of thought without taking her with him. "Chris' wife. Autumn does. Mike swore to kill her if he ever saw her again. But I don't hate her. That voice, those words, it took every ounce of strength I had to stick with my mission."

He paused. It felt immensely odd talking about Althiira to Althiira. At the same time, he wanted to see if this story triggered any memories for her. "I imagine it was worse for her. She was our healer, but she also had the gift of farseeing. Really good farseeing, with enough detail to be useful for more than a minute or two ahead of time, is rare. Mildred just spoke to me. It tortured her with visions. She was a wraith by the time she left us. I don't think she had slept for a month. She would fall into trances where we couldn't rouse her. Whatever she saw—she wouldn't tell me what it was, just that it was horror beyond imagining—was bad enough to destroy her and make her leave the men she loved."

Sarah looked bleak. "Should I bail on you guys?"

Pat let out a shocked laugh. "I would. Mike's advice is good. This isn't your fight. Even if you don't get hurt, you'll get hurt."

"Can you win without a healer?"

"No," he answered immediately. "Autumn's not bad, but she's not you. You've got more natural talent in your untrained hands than she ever will. She could have made my back feel better long enough so I could make it through one more fight. She couldn't fix it."

"Thanks. So, you need me?"

Pat looked weary. "Yes. If we're all here, it's because this is the decisive battle. The last stand. Without you Mildred will pick us off one by one until everything really heats up in May. Then it'll take out Chris. If you bail, it will win. But if you bail, you'll probably still be here, in one piece, and sane, come June."

"If I bail, will I lose you?"

"Yes. I heard the voice of God tell me to protect Chris. I'm in a new world, in a new body, and I find him again. I'm bound to him."

"But you wish you weren't?"

Pat laughed grimly. "Of course. I'm tired of this. I want to be the playful funny guy who's here to get a nice piece of sheepskin. I want to be on stage or writing stories. I don't want to be charging up every stone I come across and hurling them at demonic entities trying to destroy my mind or kill me." The realization of exactly what Pat was going back to left him exhausted. Sarah put her arm around him. Pat rested his head on her shoulder, enjoying the comfort of her touch.

"What is it with Autumn and Chris?" Sarah asked him after a few minutes.

Pat turned cold. "She's his bitch." Her eyes widened. "His dog. His slave." Sarah looked more concerned with each word. "She did it herself. At least I think she did. She was an emissary from the Court of Fairy, a spy really. She took one look at Chris and fell in love. Supposedly there's some sort of compulsion magic that binds Fey to each other. She's stuck on Chris. He's not stuck on her. She's tiny, flighty, and usually not worth much in a fight until something goes after Chris. Then she turns into a ball of fury. You don't want to be near her then. She hurts everything nearby: friend, foe, and inanimate objects. She's a berserker. Then things calm down, and she turns into this prissy little princess all worried about if the fork you're using is correct or what that exact species of flower means when you give it as a gift."

"You don't really like her, do you?"

That was something of an understatement. Pat decided to leave out his history with Autumn. Sarah didn't need to know about it. "No. I've got no use for anyone who can't control her fight. If I could use her like a grenade, just toss her at the bad guys, she'd be great. But she doesn't work that way. If Autumn got in the fight, Ameena, Chris' wife, spent as much time patching us up from the damage she did as the damage Mildred did."

"You use her real name?"

"No." And damned if he knew why not. It was her name. Using it in front of her shouldn't be an issue. For whatever reason he couldn't quite do it. "But it sounds nice, and we might as well have names. Names make things easier."

"You liked her?"

"I liked her very much." Pat sighed. That was a complicated story as well; it could wait for another night. "It doesn't matter that I liked her, or she liked me, or she loved Chris, or he loved her. By the end Mildred had convinced her she was on the wrong side, so she left us."

"And did what?"

"Did what?"

"Autumn said she betrayed you. What did she do?"

"I think Autumn was being dramatic. She never liked Ameena. For obvious reasons the wife of the guy you want is going to be a problem. I think she just left us. It was down to the final conflict, a fight in the caves, a spell Chris had to do. Ameena was supposed to protect him. But she left. So he went in by himself, and the spell didn't work. I spent ten-twelve minutes outside of the cave, fighting the Minions with Mike. There was a huge blast of magic, and they all stopped. Just silent and still. Then they screamed. There were hundreds of them, and as one voice they threw back their heads and screamed.

"The world… it felt like it was knocked to the side. Everything staggered, shuddered, and fell. Then they were gone. All of them. Dave came rushing out, told us it failed because she left; we needed to run. Chris and Chuck were already gone. Autumn had opened a portal and told us we'd regroup on the other side.

"I jumped through and found myself here, alone, with no body. I found a body, spent a few days in it, just long enough to see it wasn't going to be a permanent solution, and went looking for someone recently dead. Then I found Pat. Now I'm here." Sarah nodded.

"So, where did this all happen? Are we talking different dimensions or parallel universes?"

"No idea. Osoland was a planet, in a solar system with a few other planets; we had magic to travel between planets. Fairy was another place, not on any of our planets; there was magic to go there. Here is yet another place. Alternate realities, different dimensions, parallel universes: your guess is as good as mine. We were there. Now we're here."

He watched her think about that for a while and put it aside to ask something he probably could answer. "Tell me about Chuck."

"If Chris is the white sheep of the family, Chuck is the black one. Chris is the oldest legitimate child, the one to carry on the family traditions and inherit everything. Chuck, who is older by a few months, is the son of a serving woman. They grew up together, best friends and brothers. By the time I knew them, Chris was the high priest, and Chuck was his most trusted advisor. The power behind the throne. Watch them carefully. I doubt the pattern has changed since coming here. You'll see Chris is the front man, but he doesn't really do anything until he's had a chance to talk it over with Chuck."

"What do you mean by high priest?"

"Osoland is a theocracy. It's run by a high priest. Think of him as the king. Each clan has a leader as well. Each clan leader handles whatever is going on inside the clan. The high priest handles the inter-clan/inter-planetary/inter-realm issues."

"So, wait, how old were you all when this happened?" Sarah asked.

"The years don't translate directly. I was a full adult, not quite middle aged. Call it mid-thirties. Chris, Chuck, and Ameena were all early middle age, say early forties. Dave was about my age, maybe a little older. Mike was very young for the job, about your age. Autumn? Who the hell knows? Fairies never show their real faces. She looked young, but they all do."

"Were you married? Kids?"

Pat smiled ruefully. "No. My job and a wife didn't go together. Besides, men of my class married later in life. I probably would have retired in twenty or so years, then settled down."

Sarah nodded and asked, "And Mike and Dave?"

"Dave is Ameena's brother. I probably knew him as well as anyone, which wasn't very well. He's hard to know. You see it here. If you don't actively pay attention to him he just fades into the background, never to be seen again.

"Mike was my second half. When I was off duty, he was on. Between the two of us Chris was never more than a loud whisper away from someone trained to kill for him and willing to die if necessary."

"Wow."

"Yeah."

"Did you kill for him?"

"You mean besides the Minions?"

"Real people. Osos? Is that what I should call you?"

"Osos is fine. Yes. I fought in his war for forty years. Thirty-four of them as one of his generals. Six as his bodyguard and in charge of certain operations that needed a delicate, up-close touch. Then another ten as just his bodyguard."

"The war?"

"When Chris took over, it sparked a civil war. His clan and mine went way back. When the war started, I was the general in charge of my clan's men at arms. I wasn't a great general. I am a great fighter. When my brother got old enough, I passed control of our men over to him and took the test to become a bodyguard. For the next sixteen years I was his personal bodyguard. Mike showed up fourteen years later. How about you? Did you ever kill anyone during your years in the army?"

"Yes." Pat waited a moment for her to say more, but she didn't. "Did you like it?" Sarah asked after a few minutes.

"Odd question. I'm supposed to say no, right? That my job was a necessary tragedy. But that's not how I felt about it. I love the fight. The most honorable thing on Earth is to put your physical body between the horror of war and your beloved home."

"Heinlein, right?" Pat loved the fact Sarah got him so easily.

"Paraphrasing, but yeah, it's him. I had the skills, the focus, and the talent to put my body between my king and his enemies. I was able to live in perfect accord with the Will of the Presence. I loved my job, and I was good at it."

"I'm really supposed to believe all of this?"

Pat laughed happily, very pleased to see how well Sarah was dealing with this total shitload of unbelievable crap. "Not yet. Stick with us and you will. But, no, I certainly don't expect you to believe this right off the bat. Right now I'm just thrilled you didn't show Autumn and me the door."

"I like you too much for that. If she had come at me alone, I don't think I would have said yes."

"Which is why she waited to get both of us."

Sarah spent a minute looking at him carefully. "Can you do something to prove it?"

"Which part?"

"How about we start with I'm not just hallucinating the auras."

Pat thought about it for a long time. Back home he could have started a fire with his mind. Here…

"I'm not sure. What would you consider proof? A lot of my magic is based on fighting. You already know I'm a great fighter. I can feel when an attack is coming up to three days before it happens, but that's not a right-away thing…" Pat thought for a few seconds. Well, there was one thing he could do fairly easily, and he'd enjoy it. "I can read minds in certain circumstances."

"That's testable." He could feel her inner scientist perk up happily.

"It is. But you might want to know what circumstances first." Sarah raised an eyebrow at him. "Sex. Or something close to it. It's a useful skill." He grinned. "If you think of a song and let me kiss you, I'll be able to tell you what song you were thinking of."

"Uh huh. And if you can't come up with the song?" Sarah looked amused and skeptical at the same time.

He grinned. "I'll get it. Want to try?"

"You better know what the song is when this is done."

"I will." Pat scooted closer to her and brushed his lips against hers. For a few seconds he just enjoyed the kiss, letting himself savor her skin on his. Then he stopped taking advantage and let his mind slide into hers. Pat found her thought. He knew he should pull back but let the kiss go a bit longer. He didn't know when he'd have this chance again and didn't want to let it go to waste. Before he got too turned on he broke the kiss. Pat wanted her happy with this, not feeling like he was copping a feel. "Interesting choice."

"I thought so." Sarah smiled. "What was it?"

"'One' by U2."

"Damn!"

"Yeah, I didn't know you liked U2, let alone old U2."

"My brother, Sam is a fan. I talked to him a few days ago; it's been running through my head since. So, how does that work? Why with sex?"

"I don't know. The closer I am to a person the more easily I can read them. I don't have the thoughts of strangers just wandering about in my mind. But if I'm snuggled close and happy, I can get into your mind."

Sarah thought about it. "I suppose that is a useful skill."

"It's come in handy on more than one occasion." Pat saw her check the clock. "I should probably head off. Give you some time to get your homework done and get used to all of this."

"Well, get my homework done at least."

Pat stood up. "I'll see you in fencing tomorrow."

"Bright and early."

He walked up the street thinking about kissing her. It was sweet. Would have been sweeter if Sarah knew who she was, but there was something to be said for starting off fresh. Pat passed Writers' and felt Chris in his room.

Why was Chris up in his room working? He should be camped out at Sarah's place. Pat felt Chris almost jump when he kissed Sarah on the forehead. Obviously he felt Althiira in Sarah, so why was he just sitting there?

It was almost enough to make Pat doubt it was her. Almost.

17.

It took about an hour to finish my homework. I still wasn't nearly ready to sleep. Too many ideas whirled around my mind. I turned on my computer and booted up Gmail. There was an email from Ari, talking about his last few days, local politics, and his frustrations with the Knesset.

I wrote him back. I was a page into it when I realized I was telling him about everything but what happened this weekend. I wrapped up the letter and told myself I left it out because I just hadn't had the time to really think about it yet. The fact that he would think I had gone completely insane for even thinking of believing this story had nothing to do with it.

I wanted to call Ben. He's always been a very calming, grounding presence, and right now I could use some of that. But it was late, and they get up early at the farm. I could talk to him tomorrow or the next day.

I got to Professor Morrell's office a few minutes before he did. He had given me permission to go in if he wasn't there. I opened the door and sat in my usual chair across the desk from his seat. For the first minute I was busy getting out my notes and recordings. That done, I settled back in my chair and looked at his collection of things. I'd studied them before, especially the small bronzes. This time I could see why they had attracted my attention so intensely. Pale shimmery auras hovered around the bronzes. Oddly the room didn't feel particularly cold to me. I didn't know what to make of that. Yet another flavor of magic?

It'll give you a good idea of where others like us are. Chris' voice echoed in my mind. Did that mean Morrell was a magic user?

"*Sabah al-khair, ya Sarah.*" Morrell wished me a good morning.

I jumped, then realized what he said. "Morning?" I asked in Arabic.

"Sorry, good afternoon."

"Just making sure." I slid back into English for the next bit. "It's been a crazy few days, and it's entirely possible I was here a few hours early."

"No," he answered in Arabic, "You are right. I said the wrong time." He got settled at his desk. "Good crazy or bad crazy?"

"Both. Much work. Missing husband."

"You are married?" He didn't sound shocked. Like me he was just checking to see if I had the wrong word.

"No, missing…" I fluttered my fingers trying to think of the word. "Missing man." I tried to discreetly see if he was the source of the magic, but I couldn't do it and concentrate on finding the next word I'd need. I decided to shelve my inspection of Professor Morrell in favor of getting a good mark for today's class.

"Boyfriend?" he asked in English.

"Yes." I tried not to sigh like a little twit but couldn't quite pull it off. Ari's latest email had been especially sweet.

"Sorry to hear it. What about good crazy?"

"Party. Make friends."

"It appears you are doing well keeping up with your vocabulary amid the crazies."

"I run in morning. Listen to recording when run. Eat alone. Listen with food."

"Why do you eat alone?"

That was another question I couldn't even start to answer in Arabic. "I keep kosher, at least where food is concerned. So, I cook my own food. Sometimes I pack something and eat with my friends. Most of the time I eat lunch and dinner at my place, then meet them for coffee while they have dinner."

"What about your other classes?"

"I listen recording, do math." Back into English. "That was terrible. I listen to the recordings when I'm doing math or chemistry. I'm not really paying attention but having it in the background helps."

"I can see that." He slid back into English as well. "I don't suppose we can turn you into a linguist?"

I smiled at him and thought long and hard about my answer. I wanted to get it right. "I am a healer. It is my life."

We continued to chat for the next hour. He told me about his weekend grading papers. I told him about jogging and how to make sourdough biscuits. When we wrapped up I felt calm and quite happy.

I liked the second meeting of Golem more than the first. The conversation got lively. Watching the Writers deconstruct and reconstruct a work was actually kind of cool. The mammoth *"Ode To Coffee"* turned out to be farce when read out loud. That improved it immensely. After an hour of work, the poem I had dubbed, *"Please Shoot Me In the Head,"* had gotten, well, mediocre, but since it was horrendous at the start of the hour that counted as improvement. We finished up with "Falling Cows," which was about as close to perfect as a short story could get. Very few comments for that: a few word changes, a quick grammar fix, and we were done.

An hour after that Brooke tore herself away from the group to go home. I had a feeling Chuck had something to do with her finally leaving. Then the real meeting began.

Chris came down from his room with a huge map of Reevesville. He spread it on the floor and knelt next to it. I sat next to Pat on the other side of it while Chris explained what it meant.

"Any square with a red border is one we've searched. Spots in blue highlighter are areas that have some sort of magic to them. Areas in blue pencil are the spots we want to check out next. So, say you notice something unusual, you can check the map. If it's not already on the map, and not in a red bordered square, circle it with the blue pencil. Green spots are places where we've run into Minions."

For a long time I studied the map. Pat asked the same question I was thinking, "Is there a pattern to the search?"

"Sort of. We get the spots that attract attention first. If there's nothing circled, we do the next square on the map," Chuck answered.

"Except the graveyard. We're not touching that again if we don't have to," Chris said.

"Dumb question: don't you remember where the portal was? You came through it, right?" I asked without looking up from the map.

Pat fielded that one. "Yes, trees, rocks, dirt. It's been twenty-one years. There's no way to tell if it's still the same. Could be condos by now."

"No condos here, but a new building, a new farm, totally overgrown, exactly the same: there's just no way to tell," Chuck said. "There was a big fire in the woods back in 2000. It could be a charred wreck covered in baby trees by now."

"Can't you cross off anywhere that wasn't trees, rocks, and dirt twenty-one years ago? Why were you in the graveyard at all? The sign on the gate says it's been around way longer than that."

"The thing is, just because we all came through in the same spot doesn't mean the Minions are coming through that same spot. They could be. Or because they aren't using the same portal Autumn opened, they may be coming from anywhere." Dave pointed to the different red bordered squares as he told me that. "We were in the graveyard because it was the next square on the map we hadn't yet explored."

"It's also a good idea to know what's here. You never know what will come in handy when," Chris said.

"What about?" Pat waved his hand at a huge block of what looked like trees on the far south side of the map.

"Those trees are our next target, next several targets. That's the next eight weeks' worth of looking unless something pops out somewhere else first," Chuck told us.

"We had been doing one square a week. This year we can get Autumn and Pat into the field, so we can search two squares. How about Pat, Mike, and I take Q3 on Thursday? Then Autumn, Dave, and Chuck can do Q4 on Friday," Chris said.

I watched the others nod.

"You know, I could go with you when you go doorway hunting. I'm not a bad fighter."

"No," Chuck said, his voice flat, before anyone else had the chance to even think about responding.

"I'm probably a better fighter than you are." Chuck looked like he wanted to laugh out loud but kept his manners in place. Suddenly, I knew he was a really good fighter, better than anyone else in the group guessed, and he wanted to make sure it stayed that way.

"It doesn't matter. If you get hurt, what happens?" he asked me.

"I patch myself up, and we keep going."

This time the entire group looked at me like I was the slow child in the back of the classroom.

Pat said gently to me, "Doesn't work that way, Sarah. If you get hurt, we're screwed. Things are good right now. It's going to get worse. If it's like last time, the power of what's coming up against us will continue to grow and with it the damage we'll take. Eventually, we'll end up in situations where just the healing work will grind you down. If you're hurt in addition to that…it won't work."

"I still hate the idea of sitting here waiting for you to drag back to my place so I can fix you up. If I go with you, I can get you aid much faster."

"Yeah, and if there was a hospital in the back we could go to, you could be a full combat medic for us. But you're the hospital at the back here. Surgeons don't go into battle if they can help it; neither will you," Chris said, his voice clipped and professional. He was annoying me intensely, with this I've-got-the-right-to-order-you-around feel I was getting off of him. There was something under his professionalism he was trying to cover, but I couldn't quite get what it was. Honestly, that they were right was annoying as well. Surgeons don't work in the field for the same reason you don't send pilots into the trenches: they're hard to replace.

Chuck looked at the windows. I felt a slight tingle of cold in the base of my stomach. "And that ends our conversation on the topic for the night." The cold continued to grow.

"Watchers?"

"Yes. We can usually talk for about fifteen minutes before they show up. But they seem to be getting faster these days," Chuck answered while he helped Chris fold up the map.

"I've got a lot of reading still to do. Good night, all," Chris said once the map was folded up.

We all wished him a good night as he headed up the stairs. I wanted to head back to my place to work on my homework as well, but I could still feel the Watchers out there, so I decided to stay put.

Pat called over to Mike, "What are you doing tomorrow night?"

"Nothing. Why?"

"There's no local MMA chapter, and I haven't had a real work out in a while. Care to give me a hand?"

Mike smiled. "You just want a chance to beat me after the fencing match."

"That, too. But I can feel myself getting rusty. I know you've got a real sword up in your room. If you've got two, bring them; I can put you through your paces, too."

"Can I come?" I was eager to watch them fight and join in if they'd let me.

"You want to fight?" Mike's voice mingled amazement with curiosity.

"I might. I'm not going to make either of you sweat, but I'd like to get some exercise. Fighting is way more fun than jogging."

"Fine by me," Mike said. "I'd prefer not to go up against you with a sword, though."

"Lord, no! Knives. If I ever fight either of you with a blade, it'll be a knife. I'm not good enough with a sword to want to try with a real one. Pat said I'd learn on the job, but I'm just fine with putting off working on cuts."

"Where were you thinking?" Mike asked Pat.

"The gym we fence in is free. I may not be as good at it as Dave, but I can make sure no one walks in on us."

"No need to worry. Dave's already got my sword charmed so when I'm carrying it no one will look my way. If we fight, no one will see."

"Good. I want the practice but not badly enough to get kicked out for breaking the no violence rules."

"Thursday night then?" Mike confirmed.

"Sure, say 'round about eight?"

"That works."

Chris was sitting on the sofa at Writers' working on the reading for his Brit Lit III class when Mike came down with both rapiers. "What's up?"

"Sparring with Pat and maybe Sarah. Some sword, some hand to hand. He's noticed there's no one else here to give him a good workout."

Mike went back upstairs to get the duffle bag he carried his swords in. Chris thought about it. He knew he should stay home and keep reading. That was the point of keeping his distance. But Pat would be there, fighting with her, touching her, pinning her to the ground, and pressing his body against hers.

When Mike came back down Chris asked him, "Can I come, too?"

"Sure. I'm due at eight."

Chris ran to his room and grabbed the first pair of jogging pants and t-shirt he could find. Getting into them took him barely thirty seconds, sneakers a minute more. When he came down the steps Mike was putting his second best sword into the bag.

Mike looked him up and down. "You're going to fight?" He did a pretty good job of keeping most of the disbelief out of his voice.

"Probably not."

"You want to watch?" This time he didn't even try. He'd known Chris for two years before, a little over two years this time around, and never before had Chris shown any interest in watching him spar.

"Yes."

Mike half-laughed, half-snorted and muttered under his breath, "You'd still be sitting there if it was just Pat and me."

Chris looked away, pretending not to hear him. He knew it was true. If it was just Mike and Pat, he'd still be plowing through Robert Graves. He should be sitting on the sofa reading. He should be doing anything besides allowing the absurd surge of jealousy make him walk out the door across the street and…

Really loud music hit him before they opened the doors to the gym. He paused for a moment to place it: one of the *Mortal Kombat* movie soundtracks.

"You know, it's hard to do a good job of staying invisible if you've got music so loud the entire campus can hear it," Mike yelled. He walked toward them, his long gray duffle bag slung over his shoulder. Chris was three steps behind. "Chris wanted to come, too."

"Cool," Sarah said. "What's your weapon of choice?"

"Nothing we're using today," he said with a smile.

"Are you just watching or are you going to join in?" Pat asked him.

"Probably watching. Maybe sparring with Sarah. I've got a feeling you're a lot closer to my skill level than they are." She grinned back at him. He tried to stop looking at her. The light gray yoga pants she wore were much tighter than anything he had ever seen her in. The light blue t-shirt looked like it was made for a girl her size. Her outfit wasn't particularly revealing, but it did give him a much better idea of her shape than her usual cargo pants and men's large t-shirt.

He felt Pat notice the way he was watching Sarah. He reined it in. Pat gave him a minute nod and began talking to Mike.

"What did you bring?" Pat asked.

Mike opened his bag. He lifted two rapiers out of it. One was clearly his personal favorite. He held it lovingly. With it in his hand Mike was whole and complete. Sarah watched Mike with fascination, like she had never really seen him before. The other he handed hilt first to Pat. Pat took a few steps back from them and spent a moment getting a feel for it. A grin spread across his face slowly.

"It's lovely."

"Thank you."

"Shall we?"

A look of deeply content joy spread over Mike's features. "Yes." They squared off. Chris and Sarah retreated to a safe distance away.

Chris looked at her. "Do you want to spar?"

She answered without taking her eyes off of Pat and Mike, "Yes, but not right now. I'd like to watch them fight."

"Okay."

They fought fast and hard. The blades were difficult to see beyond the occasional glint when the light hit them right. Chris kept looking at Sarah out of the corner of his eye. She was entranced by the fight. Her eyes never strayed from the flashing blades. Ten, maybe twelve minutes later, Pat's sword hit the floor. He picked it back up and bowed to Mike. Mike bowed back, then carefully put both swords back in the bag. They walked over to Chris and Sarah, sweaty and out of breath.

"It's really been too damn long since I've done that," Pat said.

"Yeah. It's nice to use my sword against someone who isn't trying to kill me. I need a break before we try hand to hand."

Pat was still breathing hard. "Me too. So, you two want to show us what you've got?"

Chris wanted to glare at Pat. Yes, the whole reason he had changed was for a chance to spar with Sarah. However, he hoped not to have the other two watching them do it. Pat grinned at him, enjoying his frustration.

"This should be interesting," Mike added with a smirk.

Sarah was already heading to the circle in the middle of the gym. She looked over her shoulder. "You coming?"

He headed out to join her. She had removed her shoes and socks and was standing easily, her posture loose and relaxed, waiting for him.

Pat said quietly but not quietly enough, "I've got five dollars on Sarah."

Chris' eyes narrowed.

"You don't have to do this if you don't want to," she said.

"Just because I'm not as good as they are, they think I'm helpless out here."

"Are you?" she asked with amusement. He knew she wanted to see what he could do with his body. He wanted to show her. Chris took his shirt off and tossed it aside. Mike whistled at him. Pat laughed. Sarah smiled widely. He toed off his sneakers, pulled off his socks, and put his necklaces in his pocket so they wouldn't bounce around.

He called across the room to Pat. "I'll take your bet... and your five dollars."

"Sure you will." Pat laughed. "I've already fought with her."

"Hey!" Mike said. "Are you trying to screw me on a bet?"

"Oh, come on. You've fenced with her, too." They continued to bicker quietly while Chris moved into fight position. Then he waited. She was going to make the first move whether she wanted to or not.

"Well…" she said to him, gesturing for him to get going.

"Okay." He still didn't move. He rested lightly on the balls of his feet, waiting for her to move first. She was getting impatient, wanting him to attack so she could stay on the defensive. He wanted to force her into the attack, away from her comfort zone.

Two full minutes went by. Nothing happened. Mike and Pat were laughing so hard he figured they'd be wetting their pants soon.

"I can stand here all night," she said to him.

"You think I can't?"

"Depends on how much you want to win that bet. Sooner or later you've got to move if you want your money."

"Hey, Pat, does it count as a win if I just wait her out?" Chris called out.

"NO!" Both Pat and Mike shouted back.

He kept waiting. Finally, her patience snapped. Her muscles tensed. Her body shifted. She was going to jump at him. He was halfway through blocking her when he realized she had jumped backward. It took a second to get his balance back. Before he could fully shift his weight, she was kicking. Her left foot caught him in the shoulder, knocking him to the side, but he was able to get his hand up fast enough to catch her foot.

He held her foot above her head, amazed at how flexible she was. He was going to tip her over, but she anticipated it. She fell back on her own. He didn't let go fast enough and went down with her, twisting at the last second to avoid landing on her.

He was face down on the ground. She pinned him with her shin pressed across his shoulders. She bent down and whispered into his ear, "Next time, you might want to act first."

"I'll keep that in mind." He focused carefully on the feel of her across his shoulders. She wasn't leaning all of her weight into him. He knew he could flip her off of him. He arched his back and pulled his arms under him fast. Moving quickly tumbled her off. He scrambled over and tackled her. It wasn't graceful, but it got the job done.

He pinned her arms to the floor, leaning his weight into her wrists. Her face was inches from his, a pretty pink from the exercise. He was immensely aware of her body and even more aware of his. He made sure he kept kneeling on the floor next to her. He was certain the fight would be over if he pinned her with his legs. He was also certain touching more of her would have very embarrassing results.

She got her legs up and pushed both feet against his hip hard, sending him back onto his haunches. She hopped up fast. He was a beat behind her, but she wasn't able to take advantage of it.

They both stood, watching each other again. Mike and Pat had stopped laughing. At least he wasn't making a total fool of himself.

He didn't want to continue this fight much longer. Pinning her had made it very clear to him this was much too much of a sexual turn-on for him. He was very aware, in a way he hadn't been since he was thirteen, of the fact boxers and jogging pants did absolutely nothing to hide an erection.

He aimed a punch at her shoulder. He knew it was a dumb move. But, on the off chance it might connect he didn't want to aim for her face. She dodged it and used his momentum to trip him over her leg. He caught her left foot from the ground, taking her down as well. He didn't spring back up this time. He stayed crouched on the floor, watching to see what she'd do next.

She had landed on her side. He might have been able to pin her again if he had jumped at her in that position, but he was thinking five dollars was a paltry price to pay to avoid showing the other three how much he enjoyed having her on the floor under him.

She was tired, panting. He could see her think her way through her next move. She executed the roll backward and up to her feet perfectly. She looked surprised that he didn't go after her while she was turning. If he had been fighting to win, he would have. She watched him carefully, trying to see what he was going to do next. Since he didn't have a plan, there was nothing for her to see.

She began to circle him, forcing him up to keep facing her. Her punches came fast and hard. He blocked each one, using both arms to keep her fists from connecting with his body. She kept him focused on her fists, so he wouldn't notice the leg that swung out to trip him.

This time, when he hit the floor, she landed on top of him. Her hands pressed into his forearms, and her knees dug into his thighs.

"You give?" Her arms were shaking with tiredness. He was sure he could flip her if he wanted to, pin her arms to the floor, lower himself against her... *Stop it!*

"Yes."

She rested on him for a moment, then shifted her weight off of her arms. For another moment she knelt on his thighs, her chest rising and falling with her fast breath. He was doing everything he could to think of anything besides the feel of her bottom against his knees and the sight of her breasts lifting with each breath. Then she stood and offered him her hand.

He took it. She gave him a boost up.

"That was fun," he said.

"Yeah. If you ever want to again, I'm interested. It's not as much fun to spar with Pat, he's so much better..."

He looked wryly at her. "Yeah, I know the feeling. Speaking of Pat..."

Pat and Mike walked over. Pat had a huge smile on his face and wrapped her in a big hug. He kept his eyes on Chris the whole time. As soon as she looked away, he glared at Pat. Pat grinned back at him and winked.

Stop it! Chris thought at Pat.

Oh, so you can still do that. Good to know. Pat thought back.

"That was the easiest ten dollars I ever made." Pat stood there with his arm around Sarah smiling widely at Chris and Mike.

"You're welcome," she said to him.

"You bet on me?" Chris asked Mike, realizing he was supposed to be doing something besides mentally glaring at Pat.

"You're almost a foot taller and weigh at least fifty pounds more."

Chris looked her over carefully, enjoying the chance to really study her without being a cad. "You're what? Five two and one hundred pounds?"

"Five two and one ten."

"I'm eleven inches taller and weigh fifty-two pounds more."

"Okay, Mr. Precise. It didn't seem like much of a reach that if you could get her pinned you could keep her down." Chris realized both Mike and Pat really knew how to watch a fight. They must have known exactly what he was doing.

"Yeah, well, if he had pinned my legs, too, that would have been the end of the fight. I couldn't have gotten him off," Sarah said it seriously, but Pat started giggling. She shoved him.

"As if there's a man alive you couldn't get off," he said with an enormous grin. Chris started to blush.

Mike snorted. "Me for one."

Pat looked confused.

"I'm gay," Mike said simply. Chris took a moment to enjoy Pat's confusion. It had come as a shock to him back when he found out in their freshman year.

Pat still looked puzzled. "But you had five girlfriends at any given time. Were you gay before?"

"No. When I got here I decided it would be cool to try," Mike said with biting sarcasm. "Of course I was gay before; it wasn't exactly a good idea to let anyone know, now was it?"

"Nooo…" Pat looked horrified.

Sarah looked curious. Chris explained, "Being gay was considered an abomination. If you were male it would get you castrated at the least, killed at the worst. What did your clan do, Mike?"

"Castration." All three of the guys winced.

"Wasn't there anything you could do about that? I mean, weren't you the guy in charge?" she asked.

"No. That was a clan-by-clan thing. The only area I had any effect on was my own clan. While I was in charge no one was killed or mutilated. But no one got caught at it while I was head of my clan, either."

They were all quite serious thinking about that. Sarah smiled slightly and said, "You know, Mike, if you close your eyes, I bet I could get you off." That broke the tension.

Mike threw his head back and laughed. "Yeah, so could Pat, but it's nothing I'm interested in trying."

"I'm really good at it," Pat said while winking at Mike. "I'm getting a lot of practice these days." He curled his hand into a very loose fist, sliding it up and down in a jerking-off gesture.

Mike laughed, reached over, closed Pat's fist so the space between his fingers and his palm was a lot smaller and said, "That's more like it."

"I do like it tight. Got anything that might accommodate me that way?" Pat asked Mike with a leer.

Chris held his head in his hands, pretending he wasn't hearing this conversation.

"Maybe. I'll keep you in mind for the next time I'm blind drunk and horny," Mike said. "Ready to fight?"

"Yeah. I'm rested."

Chris and Sarah retreated to the bleachers to sit down while Mike and Pat began their fight. Pat took off his shirt, as well. Chris didn't know if he was showing off for Sarah or making sure Mike had one less thing to grab easily. Both probably. He realized he should go put his own shirt back on but didn't feel like getting it yet.

He watched her watch them. She looked like she was seeing something of intense beauty.

"They're gorgeous," she said with a sigh.

"You like men who can fight?" Did he sound jealous? Maybe. He thought he had kept it under control. She didn't appear to notice.

She answered him without taking her eyes away from the fight, "Yes, but that's not what I mean. They're just so… fantastic. Who gets to see something like this in real life? I've watched lots of fighting… This is just so—it's Jet Li fighting Jason Statham. But real!"

Chris watched another minute of the fight but didn't see her comparison. "Which one is Jet Li?"

"Pat." They watched quietly for several more minutes while Pat and Mike kicked, punched, blocked, and dodged.

"So, what is your weapon of choice?" Sarah asked again, still not taking her eyes off of them.

"Magic," he said quietly. "I cause three blood vessels in your brain to explode, and you never get up again."

He had her undivided attention now. Her eyebrows had shot up so high they were trying to become part of her hairline. She shook her head slightly as if to clear it. "If you can do that, why did you need bodyguards?"

"I need to see you, focus on you, and it takes a minute. And, just like everyone else, I need to sleep."

She heard a thud and looked back at the boys. Mike was on the ground. Pat had him pinned. "Damn. I missed the end of the fight."

Pat and Mike walked slowly back to the others. When they got within easy speaking distance, Pat said, "So, Sarah, how about you and I in a few minutes?"

"Sounds good." She looked back at Chris. "This should be pretty fast."

"Well, he was never known for his staying power," Chris said, his tone a hair too sharp to be a real joke. Mike blinked in shock. Sarah raised an eyebrow at Chris. Pat laughed.

"When you know what you're doing, it doesn't take three hours," Pat said when his laughter died. He held his hand out to Sarah with a courtly flourish more suited to a formal dance than a gym. "Shall we show him how sweet fast can be?"

Sarah smiled enigmatically at Chris. He wasn't sure what that smile meant. Maybe she wasn't sure, either. She took Pat's hand and walked back to the ring.

Pat began the fight, letting her defend. It was fast, maybe a minute, maybe a minute and a half, but to Chris it felt longer. Pat didn't stick to his normal kickboxing heavy technique. There was more grappling than he usually used in his fighting. The final pin, where he held Sarah's arms behind her back pressing her body against his, was almost physically painful to watch. Chris made a note to never, ever come back to this. The immense chance of doing something stupid, the broken glass feeling of watching Sarah with Pat, and the gnawing guilt of watching someone other than Althiira that way, made this the perfect storm of emotional turmoil.

Pat let her go, and they both walked back to Chris and Mike. Chris stood up, ready to grab his shirt and go. Pat stopped him. "Wanna fight me?"

"Yes." It came out before he could stop it. So much for getting out before he did something stupid. He scrambled quickly for a way to save some face. "If Mike will let me borrow his sword."

"You want to fight with swords?" Mike said it, but Pat looked just as amazed.

"I was a fencer before either of you joined us."

"Really?" Pat looked shocked.

"Yes, really. I used to fence with Dave and his older brothers. When the war started, I had several occasions where I ended up using a sword. Just because I'm a battle mage doesn't mean I've never touched a blade."

"You're a battle mage?" Sarah asked.

"Not by choice. It was learn or die, and I didn't want to die. As I said, magic is my weapon."

Mike walked to his bag. "This I've got to see. You really used to fence?" he called over his shoulder.

"Yes, I really used to fence. Do I need to get Dave here to prove it?"

Mike handed him the blade. "No. You can prove it with this. Be nice to him. He's my sweetie."

"Will do."

I watched them move to the center circle again. "Put your shirts on!" Mike yelled to them.

"Why?" I asked him. "Not enjoying the view?"

"The view's lovely," he said with a smirk. "If you like tall, skinny redheads. If I wanted that, I could look in a mirror. I'd prefer they catch the blades on clothing than on skin unless you really are thinking today's the day to learn how to knit skin together."

"I'd prefer not to."

"Even with shirts, today may be the day anyway. Those two can get silly on the 'who's the better man' crap. I'll be shocked if there's no blood."

"This isn't new?"

"No. Personal bodyguards are not servants. We are not required to be deferential. Your life rests in our hands. If you value yourself, you will treat us like men, like equals. We see everything there is to see about you. We have no illusions as to the greatness of the Great Man. It's a unique relationship, and it allows us the freedom to treat him like a man."

"Makes sense."

"Anyway, those two have been doing this for as long as I've known them. We're still the same people, so the same patterns are repeating."

Pat was already warmed up. He was holding his sword lightly, allowing Chris a few minutes to get the feel of Mike's pet blade.

"How do you think he'll do?" Chris held the blade carefully, twisting it in his hand and swinging it gently.

"I think Pat will wipe the floor with him and if he's lucky, not cut him too badly."

"Great."

Mike watched me carefully. "They're showing off for you. You know that, right?"

"Yes."

"Are you sleeping with Pat?"

"No. I've got a boyfriend."

"Can I give you some advice?" I nodded. "If that ever changes, keep it discreet. They're acting this stupid when neither of them can have you. It'll get crazy if they think they've got a chance."

"I'll keep that in mind. I didn't get the feeling Chris was interested. Actually, that's not quite true. I had the feeling he was interested. Then he ran away, blew me off—I barely saw him for a week—and now he's here showing off."

"He is interested. He's not handling it well. I guess he's still married. I wouldn't be keeping the vows I made to someone who almost got me killed and made me run from my home, but he is. That colors everything else in his life. We've been encouraging him to start dating again, so far with no luck."

"Wonderful."

"Yeah, it's lovely. On the upside, he hasn't been hiding in his room in a depressed funk yet this year. That's a turn for the better. He's usually up there or at Chuck's one or two weeks a month. Sometimes more."

"And he's the leader?" I didn't keep the surprise out of my voice.

"Chuck might technically be the leader. But the words come out of Chris's mouth."

"Is he any good at it?"

Mike looked me up and down while thinking of his answer. "Yes. Maybe not on his own, but he's been lucky in his family. More importantly, he knows how to listen to good advice. Chuck is a better politician. Dave is a better tactician. Chris is immensely likeable, probably smarter than the other two, better with the whole overarching vision thing. Put all three together and you've got a good leader."

"So, they aren't going to send me to my death charging the Enzo for the seventeenth time?" Mike looked confused. "It's a World War I reference. They fought the battle of the Enzo, a river in Italy, something like seventeen times without actually taking it."

"Oh. No. I don't think so. They won the war and most of the battles against Mildred..."

We sat quietly for a few minutes while Chris continued to warm up. "He does kind of look like he knows what he's doing," Mike said quietly.

"Kind of."

"Finally, they're starting."

"Good." I watched the fight with interest. For the first minute or so it looked like Pat was humoring Chris, letting him get used to fighting. Then something shifted and they were fighting all out.

Chris was losing but losing well, deflecting seven out of ten hits, landing the occasional hit on Pat. I could see splashes of bright red on both of their shirts, but they didn't seem to think it was bad enough to be worth stopping the fight for. Then Pat sent Chris' sword flying. Chris dropped to the floor and swept Pat's feet out from under him.

Mike winced. "I really thought he was smart enough not to try that."

Pat sprang back up again before Chris could get his sword back, tripped Chris neatly, then flicked his sword, leaving a short red line on Chris' bicep.

"I can cut you again," Pat said with a hard smile.

"I'm done."

"Good." Pat held a hand out to Chris, helping him up. Pat turned to me and called out, "Medic!"

I went to them. "So, this is your idea of fun?"

"Not exactly. I prefer it when I don't get cut," Pat answered. He took his shirt off, showing me the two long cuts where Chris had managed to land hits. He was looking at them critically. "They aren't too bad, band aids and Neosporin will do them fine unless you want to try."

"Maybe. How about you, Chris?"

He was looking himself over. "Three on the chest, one on the arm, and another one in the thigh. I didn't feel that one hit."

"Feel it now?" Pat asked.

"Yes. I feel it now." He glared at Pat.

"Good. Let's go back to Sarah's. She can get us fixed up. Then I want to talk with both of you about tomorrow night."

"That's better done at our house. The shields are better," Mike said.

"Then off to Sarah's we go. We'll wrap up the night at your place," Pat put on his shirt.

"I've got homework that needs to get done. I'll see you back at our place."

"Okay. Goodnight, Mike."

"'Night, Sarah."

On the way back to my place I decided I might as well try to fix a cut, if one of them had a small, shallow one. Once we got there, I started working on Pat, mopping off the blood with a wet paper towel. He was right. They weren't bad cuts. Very straight and not too deep. One was close to five inches long, the other about eight, nothing I wanted to try for my first run. I dabbed Neosporin on his cuts and closed them with butterfly band aids.

When I finished, he held his t-shirt. "So, I don't suppose you know how to heal cotton?"

"I've got a sewing kit in my closet if you'd like to give it a shot."

"Nah. Between the cuts and bloodstains I'm thinking this t-shirt is dead. Can I borrow one of yours for the rest of the night?"

"Sure, grab one for Chris as well. His shirt is cut up worse than yours."

Pat headed into my room. "They're in the closet," I called out to him. I had a few things in my top drawer I didn't want him seeing. I gestured for Chris to sit down and grabbed a new paper towel. I gently wiped the blood off of him and began to bandage him up.

The next time you want me to touch you, just tell me you've got a headache. I'll give you a back rub. You don't need to fight Pat. When I looked up from dabbing Neosporin on his cuts, I realized he knew what I had been thinking.

I finished his chest. "So, are you going to take your pants off, or do you intend to see to that yourself?" I pointed to the hole in his jogging pants with blood oozing out of it about eight inches above his left knee.

He looked mildly embarrassed taking his pants off. I had the feeling it had more to do with Pat being there than not wanting me to see his legs. Or his boxers. I smiled to myself. Red knit boxers wasn't what I was expecting to see under his pants.

The cut on his leg was the kind I wanted to try on. It was short, less than an inch long, straight, and not too deep.

"Is this where you got stabbed?" I lightly touched two small, white scars on his thigh a little above the cut I intended to heal.

"Yes."

"I'd like to take a shot at actually healing this one."

"I'm fine with guinea pig duty."

I sat there looking at his leg. Inspiration was not forthcoming. "So, ummm… how do you suggest I go about doing something like this?"

"Mind over matter, will the skin back together," Pat answered as he came out with two t-shirts. He took a blue one for himself and placed a green one next to Chris.

"Okay." I let out a slow breath and placed my fingers on either side of the cut. For a while I sat there thinking at the skin, *CLOSE!* It didn't work. Pat knelt next to me and rested a hand on my shoulder.

"Remember what you did when you worked on my back? You felt what was wrong, and then you fixed it. Feel for what's wrong first. Stop looking with your eyes."

"Okay." I thought about what he had just told me. "Why is it you can't do this?"

"Don't know. Bodies don't do what I tell them to. Just like Mike's not very handy with rocks, and Chris—hell, what is it you don't do well?"

"I don't heal, and I almost never read minds."

"Really?" I said out loud before I could stop myself. If he couldn't read minds, was I just imagining this?

I felt like he told me I wasn't imagining it, but when he spoke he said, "Really. Chuck can read minds. He's amazing. I keep telling him to start playing poker professionally. He'd like it a lot better, and it would be a lot easier than his current job."

"I will remember not to play poker with Chuck."

"Good plan."

Back to the cut. Before it healed up on its own. I let my eyes slide shut and tried to focus on feeling what was wrong. *It's a cut, you twit! Stop that. Feel it. Don't think it.* I let my hand go soft. My fingers hovered feather light on the cut. I relaxed. Suddenly I could feel the way the energy wasn't moving properly there. *Okay, now all you've got to do is fix it.* I could feel the way the energy wanted to move. I let it gather in my fingers, then gently stroked them over the cut, showing it the way back to where it wanted to go. After a minute, it felt done. I opened my eyes. Smooth cream-colored skin met my gaze.

"Fuck! It worked. I mean it really worked. How the fuck did it work?"

Pat grinned widely at me. Then he got up, grabbed me a blanket and one of the Snickers I kept as part of my emergency chocolate stash. His timing was good. By the time he was back, I was shivering and exhausted. Once the high from healing Chris' leg faded, I was running on empty.

"Time for you to rest, Sarah. No matter what we do, the first time is always the hardest. Chris, get dressed." Chris pulled up his pants and put on the green shirt. I absently thought if they fit Chris and Pat, just maybe it was time to start getting them a tad smaller. "We'll get out of here and let you get some sleep."

"Sleep sounds good."

"See you at lunch tomorrow?" Pat asked me.

"I think so."

Chris pulled the shirt over his head. "Thank you. Tonight was fun."

"Glad you enjoyed it."

"Come on, let's get back to Mike and plan tomorrow."

"Of course."

I didn't understand the words, but I knew the content. I was demanding a blue man bring someone to me. He argued. I yelled at him, ordering the blue man to bring him—I knew it was a him—to me. Finally the light-eyed man I had seen before said something. They brought the man to me.

My husband. He was my husband. I knew that as a burst of jittery nausea swept over me when I saw him. He was hurt: horribly maimed, barely alive on a stretcher before me. The first man didn't want to bring my husband to me because he was beyond healing. But I knew he wasn't. I could do it.

His arm was barely attached to his shoulder. Worse than that, his bright blue blood was oozing slowly out of the wound. That had to be fixed first. I barely noticed the rest of the damage. If he bled to death before I got that arm fixed, the rest of the damage wouldn't matter.

I held his left arm to his shoulder with one hand. The other hand found both ends of the brachial artery and put them back together again. There wasn't enough blood inside of him. Making more right away meant it would leak right out again. Take care of the big holes first, then more blood. I got his arm back on him. Not tidy, just a layer of skin to keep his blood inside of him.

His left chest and hip were crushed. Like he was hit repeatedly with a mace. Look for the holes, the big ones. Find them, close them. Keep the blood inside.

Holes done. He needed more blood. I willed his marrow to work harder. Make the blood flow again. His heart sped up again. There was blood everywhere, sapphires pooling on the floor around me, oozing and pulsing out of him from the holes I hadn't found yet.

More focus. Find the holes. Put them back together. Eventually all the blood inside him stayed there. Now it was time to find the little holes. Now it was time to reconnect everything. Time to grow bones back together. Time to slow down and work carefully.

Exhausting hours passed. Muscles, veins, nerves, and bones slowly healed under my hands. Eventually he was well enough to start screaming from the pain. He had been far enough gone those noises were a good sign.

More hours passed, the light changed again, blue men came and went, but the light-eyed one stayed with me the whole time. Another man joined us eventually. He was tall and dark blue with dark coppery hair. He placed his hands on my shoulders, boosting me with his magic. My exhaustion fled, and I worked harder, faster, stringing muscles back together, making sure the nerves lined up properly and would still conduct messages.

I awoke before the job was done. For a minute I didn't know where I was. I expected to have dried blue blood caked on my arms up to my shoulders and the smell of destroyed flesh in my nostrils. I got up and washed my arms. The feel of the blood had been so real I couldn't shake it any other way. I was eager for my jog, anything to put some distance between me and that dream.

After dinner I went to Writers'. The guys were going out portal hunting. I'd be too nervous home by myself, waiting to hear if they had gotten home, so Writers' seemed like the natural answer.

Chris looked up at me from the map he, Pat, and Mike were standing around and said, "It doesn't matter if you can kick my ass in a fight, you don't get to come with us." The way he said it was about two-thirds joke.

"That's not why I'm here. I didn't want to sit at my place waiting to see when or if you'd come back."

"We'll be back, don't worry about it," Pat told me gently. "If the door is there, we'll locate it and run home. No fighting tonight."

"You sure?"

He smiled at me, his eyes warm and confident. "As sure as I can be."

"Good. Still, do you mind if I stay here?"

Autumn came out of her room. "No. I was on pins and needles the first time they went out without me. Stay here as much and as often as you like."

"Thanks."

I watched the three of them finished their planning. Mike went upstairs and came back with his rapier in a scabbard on his hip.

"Don't you run into trouble like that?"

"No. No one outside this house can see it." I jumped when Dave answered. He was sitting on the couch behind me working on his homework.

"Damn, Dave, you really are invisible. How do you do that?"

"It took a long time to get this good. I do everything from bend the light around me, to make sure you don't look in my direction, to modify your memory of me being here."

"Wow."

Mike stood next to the front door. "Let's go." He held the door while Chris and Pat exited.

Autumn sat down on the sofa next to Dave and turned toward me. "Now we wait." I did my homework. On the tricky calc problems, I could muster a good two or three minutes between thoughts of where they were or what they were doing. I'd do a problem, think of them, check the clock, and repeat. An hour passed that way. I was getting more nervous with each problem.

"You're worrying about them very loudly," Autumn said to me with a sigh.

"Sorry. I can't seem to shut it off."

"They'll be fine. They should just about be getting there by now. It's a four-mile walk."

"They're just getting there?"

"Yes."

"How do you stand this?"

"You get used to it. I've been doing it since the second week of my sophomore year."

Dave looked up from his reading. "Mike and Pat both know if something bad is coming. They can feel it ahead of time. If there was going to be trouble, they'd already know about it. They would have brought Autumn along for first aid."

"Since I'm working on the outline for my senior thesis, there is no trouble brewing. Try to relax. I can get you a glass of wine or beer if you want one."

"No. I'm better sober."

"Okay. Relax. Do your work. They'll be home in about two and a half hours."

What Dave said about Pat and Mike knowing when trouble was brewing did help. I got back into my homework, finishing Friday's problem set and starting on Monday's. Half way through I was in pretty good math groove. I was wrapping up Wednesday's problem set when we heard footsteps on the porch. The door opened, and all three walked in looking comfortable: not precisely happy but satisfied.

"Total bust," Chris told us.

Pat flopped onto the sofa and put his arm around my shoulders. "I've been in more danger on the subway."

"Besides the vicious mosquitoes near the pond, we were completely safe," Mike said while scratching an itch.

"That's true. Those little bastards were nasty," Chris complained while he marked the spot on the map with a red border. He looked up at me. "I don't suppose you do mosquito bites?"

"All the time. I'm famous at home for making them vanish. No, never tried before." I shook my head. "But if you're signing up for guinea pig duty, I'll give it a shot."

He sat on my other side and held out his left arm. A few grossly swollen bites clustered around the crease of his elbow.

"I always react badly to them. Maybe it's an allergy. Maybe it's just a hyperactive histamine response."

"And that would be different from an allergy how?" Pat asked.

Chris gave him a quick glare. I set to work, letting myself sense the bites. They felt hot and furious, like an anthill after it's been kicked. I worked on making the energy slow down, trying to make it match the pace of the skin around the bites. I got the energy feeling the same, but the bite didn't feel finished. There was still something foreign in the skin. I tried to see if I could make the magic push it out, the same way the body will slowly push out a splinter if you give it enough time.

That was harder. It took more effort, more concentration, but eventually it felt done. I didn't open my eyes after finishing. I traced my fingers over his soft skin, letting them tell me the itchy, swollen lumps were gone.

I felt tired but not nearly as wiped out as I did after Pat's back or the cut. I stretched for a good long minute, enjoying the feel of my muscles pulling, then slumped against the back of the sofa. "You know, I think tomorrow I'll probably be able to finish up your cuts."

"What cuts?" Autumn sounded alarmed. It occurred to me I shouldn't have mentioned the cuts.

"Chris and I did some fencing," Pat answered her.

"Why would you do something like that?" she asked Chris.

"Because it's fun. I should go get your shirt. I'll be back in a minute." He paused halfway up the steps. "Actually, would you come up with me? I would like you to look at one of the cuts."

"Sure." I stood up slowly, expecting to feel a little unsteady, but I didn't. I followed him up the steps and waited for him to open the door to his room. His room was very tidy. I'm a pretty tidy person myself, but his room had a precision my own living space lacked. My shirt was sitting, carefully folded, on the end of his crisply made bed. Two of his walls were covered in posters, mostly black and white photography. His bookshelf and desk were filled with books, many of which I had also read—either borrowed from my brothers or on my own shelf at home.

"I thought I was the only person our age to read *War and Remembrance*."

"I stole it from my dad five years ago," he said, picking up the shirt off of his light blue blanket.

The yellow cover of a book appeared when he lifted the shirt. "Why are you reading *Physics for Dummies?*"

"Research," he said cryptically. I decided not to press the issue.

"Ahhh… So what do you want me to look at?"

"Nothing really." I felt a quick flash of disappointment. I wanted to touch his chest again. "I don't tell Autumn about my injuries unless it can't be avoided. She doesn't need to know. She really doesn't need to know if I get them by being stupid with Pat."

"I'll keep that in mind." Suddenly, I wanted to push him a little; see what would happen if I confronted him about yesterday's sparring. I dug into my pocket, found my wallet, and handed him a five-dollar bill. "Next time you fight me, fight to win."

He looked up from the bill into my eyes. "Do you want a rematch? Just us?" His voice was quiet but very intense. The image of him pressing me into the floor, his hands on my wrists, legs straddling mine, was so real I could all but feel it.

I licked my lips. "Yes."

He watched me carefully. I could feel he was torn. He wanted it just as badly as I did, if not more. At the same time, he knew it was wrong.

He broke eye contact. "I can't fight you. Don't get me wrong, I want to. I enjoyed it. And the idea of going full out with you is immensely appealing, but that's the problem. I like the idea way too much." He held the shirt toward me.

"I can respect that, but honestly, I'm disappointed. I like the idea of you pinning me." I smiled at him, took the shirt from his hands, and left.

I knew it was mean. By the time I had walked the three feet from his door to the top step I felt bad about it. I turned, knocking on his door. He opened it and leaned against the door jam. I took a step back so I wouldn't have to look up quite so much.

"I'm sorry; that wasn't kind. If it's easier for you, I'll keep my distance."

"Thank you." He sighed. "It's easier but impractical. I'll cope." We spent a minute just looking at each other, not really knowing what to say.

"I should go home." He nodded at me and stepped back into his room.

I was home on my computer, reading a letter from Ari before I started to feel really guilty about how I'd been throwing myself at Chris.

18.

Ben and I were talking about the High Holy Days. He wanted to know if I was going to head home. That wasn't going to happen; there was too much going on at school. But I did need a plan because they were next week. I found what I was looking for online: a Conservative synagogue in Pittsburgh.

Apples dipped in honey, warm Shana Tovas, and the eerie, almost bleating sound of the Shofar made me feel at home among the strangers of Temple Beth Shalom. The immense beauty of the place filled me with joy. I returned home feeling refreshed. Like I had spent weeks in the desert and finally came upon not just an oasis of sweet water, but a spa with talented massage therapists as well.

I walked up my steps, opened the door, and found Pat on my sofa. He looked up from his book. "How was it?"

"It was good, really, really good. I miss having other Jews around. I mean, it's not like there's a bunch back home. I'm related to all of them. Still, it's comfortable to not have to constantly think about the rules. I could easily live in Squirrel Hill. Not only is it beautiful, it's minutes from a good medical school, things close on Friday night, there's real food, and other people will cook it for you. I could get used to a place like that."

"Good. I'd like it if you decided to settle somewhere on this side of the world."

"I'm here for the next eight years at least." I smiled at him. "I brought you something." His eyes sparked. "What?"

I put my saddle bag on the kitchen table and grabbed a fork. "It's probably a little smushed, but it'll still taste good."

He stood next to me while I opened the Styrofoam box and unwrapped the silver foil. "You brought me cheesecake?"

"It's not New York's finest, but I thought it was pretty good." I handed him a fork.

He took a big bite and smiled at me. "It's close enough."

"I was thinking, sometime later this month, would you like to go with me to Pittsburgh? Make a night of it? Go dancing, have fun, eat cheesecake. Maybe call it a reward for doing well on midterms or something?"

"Two friends having a night on the town?" I could see his hope for more but appreciated his willingness to take what I could to give.

"Two friends having a night on the town."

"I'd like that." He might have been disappointed it wasn't a date, but he did seem happy at the idea of getting out of Reevesville and having some fun in a real city.

"Good. What happened while I was gone?"

"A whole lot of nothing. I stayed here. I didn't think you'd mind."

"Do I still have any Pepsi left?" I opened the fridge. "Nope."

"Look in the pantry." There were four six-packs that hadn't been there when I left. "I just hadn't gotten around to putting the new ones in your fridge."

"Okay." I put one of the six-packs in the fridge and smiled at him. "As long as there's as much if not more Pepsi here when I get back, you can stay over anytime I'm away."

"Wonderful. Wanna bite?"

"Nah, I had close to half a cheese cake while I was in Pittsburgh."

Chris sat in front of the map and made a list of likely candidates for recorporealization.

He and Chuck got back from a less than encouraging conversation with Professor Gren in the physics department a few hours earlier. It had taken him two weeks to get a good enough handle on the physics to come up with the questions he wanted to ask. Another three weeks went by before he could get a physics professor to talk to him about the nature of energy and matter. If he had understood Gren correctly, one could turn matter into energy: break apart an atom and you get lots of energy. But it didn't work the other way around. "Lots of energy doesn't magically become matter," Professor Gren said with a laugh.

This left Chris with a few problems. First of all, he wasn't willing to give up on the idea that making the Minions, and ultimately Mildred, corporeal was the key to killing them. But getting them bodies… that was the problem.

Secondly, he didn't think he and Gren were talking about the same thing when they talked about energy. To top it off, he didn't even have a good way of trying to explain what he meant by energy. That wasn't quite true. He had a fantastic vocabulary for explaining what he meant. The fact it wasn't in English and was entirely bound in religious terms meant it was thoroughly useless to him now.

The most frustrating part was that he knew what he meant, but he couldn't put it into words in a way that would make sense to Professor Gren. Energy: that which makes things alive or move. "Like electricity?" Gren had asked him. Well, yeah, like it. Like heat, like fire, like wind, like light, like humans moving around, and like plants growing. Like all of those things but not any of them. That which all of those things had in common. *J'ruthan*: It was a great word. It meant exactly what he was thinking, and none of the five people he knew who even spoke that language knew what that word meant. If he had taken an hour or so to talk with Pat about it, he might get it. If Chris had wanted a word in English to describe what Pat had been, he would have chosen Paladin over Bodyguard. Pat's fight and magic had always been tied to a holy righteousness. He had the fundamentals upon which Chris could have built to get him to the point where *J'ruthan* would make sense. Unfortunately, since Pat wasn't a physicist, it wouldn't get him any closer to finding the link between that which made everything alive and move and that which made it solid and real.

Which left him sitting in front of the map, looking for a candidate for recorporealization, hoping inspiration would strike when he got there.

The map covered an area six square miles. In that area there were seventy-eight ghosts of varying levels of power and nastiness lurking about. He thought a very quiet, very dumb ghost would be the best kind to start with: a walking memory.

As he looked over the map, he found he had at least five options. One made its home in Grace Methodist Church, out by the edge of town. *An ideal location.* They'd been there before when they searched the woods behind the church. It wasn't locked at night. *Perfect.*

According to the map there was a strong ley line running through the woods, so he'd have a good external source of energy. Churches always had energy of their own about them, which he had an affinity for, so he'd have a decent close source as well. Several thousand calories of ice cream and he'd be set to work.

Chuck would be free Monday night, so Monday night they'd go for it.

Yom Kippur, the Day of Atonement, if not the most festive day of the Jewish year, it is the holiday that most deeply resonates with me. Like the hundreds of people around me at Beth Shalom, I sat and prayed, focusing on the old, familiar words of Hebrew and Aramaic.

I spent the day thinking of my sins and asking the Lord to forgive them. Compared to some of my previous years I had done pretty well. While sitting amid the other Jews beseeching Hashem for His forgiveness I began to wonder about my new friends. I could be legalistic. We weren't summoning the dead, and I wasn't sure if anything we were doing counted as witchcraft. Even if that were true, I had the feeling we were at least violating the spirit of the Law—if not the exact definition.

Yet, here I sat, amid my fellows in a huge room with hundreds of people, and at least four of them glowed. I could feel the Torah scroll even though I couldn't see it. When the cantor began his work, the power of his chant rose goose bumps on my skin.

Is this what You want for me? Did You give me this gift to use it on these people? Or is this the path of pride and then the fall?

No answers. Never any answers. Pat's god talked to them. For a moment I liked the idea of an easy Lord who pointed you in the right direction: all you had to do was ask. That moment passed. If Hashem answers, then kiss free will goodbye. More than anything else, I like free will.

I let the prayers seep into me. Time moved like it always does for me in synagogue, minutes of exceptional clarity and slowness followed by hours galloping by.

My stomach started growling long before the day was over. I told it to shut up. It didn't listen. I refocused on the prayers. This is the day the Lord decides if we live or die. The day when our fates are written in the book. Even if I don't believe it's literally true, I like the idea that once a year we are judged and, thus judged, granted more life or not.

Eventually it was dark again. The twenty-five hours were done, and I was ravenous. I changed into my biking gear and went looking for food. The deli where I had gotten the cheesecake was closed. All of the kosher shops were closed. Vegetarian, gentile food wasn't my first choice, but a huge salad and breadsticks followed with chocolate cake took care of my rumbling tummy and got my blood sugar high enough that I was safe to ride again.

I got home late. I expected to see Pat on my sofa, but my apartment was empty. I went to bed, hoping I'd be able to sleep through my morning jog. Of course, that didn't happen. Bright and early I was wide awake as my phone rang.

"Shalom, Sarah."

"Ari!"

We spent an hour talking before it was bedtime for him. It was so good to hear his voice. He let me know he was going to be away from an Internet connection for a few days next week—some sort of job thing he couldn't tell me about. I'm used to that and didn't ask any questions. I told him about visiting Pittsburgh for the High Holy days. He's not terribly religious, but he likes the fact I am. For whatever reason he enjoys listening to me talk about it. Mostly it was just wonderful to spend a good chunk of time solidly grounded in "normal." When we got done, I mixed up my biscuits and set them to rise, then went out into the nippy early morning air for my jog. October was rapidly turning into winter.

Six seconds later I was passing Writers' and saw Chris on the sofa through the front windows. I headed up the steps.

"You're up early today," I said quietly as I poked my head in. Autumn's room is right next to the front door, so I didn't knock.

"Technically, I'm up late."

"Can I come in?"

"Sure." He sat on the sofa with the TV on mute, eating a bowl of cereal.

"Up late good or up late scary?" I settled next to him.

"Both. We decided to head into town to see *Hellboy II*. On the way back something went after us." There it was, less than fifteen minutes after getting off the phone with Ari: a big heaping pile of not normal. "But Pat got rid of it before it could do any damage. So that's good, but that moment when you know something is wrong, that's scary."

"And you're still up...?"

"Because we spent seven hours discussing what happened. Pat left an hour ago. I'm surprised you didn't trip on him at your place."

"He wasn't there when I got up."

"So he does occasionally sleep at his place?" He kept that question light, so I answered it the same way.

"He sleeps at his place about four nights a week. We joke about him never going home, but he's only at my place about half the time."

He seemed to think about that for a minute and then switched the topic. "Anyway, I wasn't quite ready to sleep, so I got a shower and sat down for some bad TV and breakfast."

I looked over his black and green plaid flannel pajama bottoms, comfy gray t-shirt, and bare feet. "Then some sleep?"

"I certainly hope so. I've been up for," he looked at the clock, "twenty-three hours now."

"Should I scoot off and let you rest?"

"Not yet. Still have to finish breakfast and I'd like some company."

I nodded. "So, tell me more about what happened."

"We were heading home. Everything got weird a few blocks from the junior high. Temperature dropped, the colors went wrong, and I started to feel dizzy. The others felt it in different ways..."

"Who are the others?"

"Mike, Pat, and Dave. For some reason Autumn had no desire to see *Hellboy II*."

"Amazing."

"Yeah. Anyway, Dave spotted it first. This was something new. It was hiding. Like it wanted to set up an ambush. Whenever we've dealt with them before they come right at us."

"New kind of Minion?"

"No, just new tactics. It was almost anticlimactic. We knew it was there. It hadn't noticed us yet. Pat looked around for a moment. Two houses back had a gravel driveway. He loped off and came back with five nicely shaped bits of granite, charged them up, tossed them like grenades, and the Minion vanished."

"Was that an attack or a test?"

"That's what took seven hours to discuss."

"And the answer is?"

"Insufficient data. Probably a test but no way to know for sure."

"If you can blow up something's brain just by thinking about it, why are the Minions a problem? Can't you just..." I twirled my fingers and flicked them at an imaginary critter in front of us. "And have it fall over dead?"

Chris laughed. "First of all, I almost never...," he mimicked my gesture. "Autumn does stuff like that. I don't. For obvious reasons I've never seen myself do it, but I imagine I just look like I'm concentrating hard.

"Secondly, Minions, at least here, aren't the kind of thing I can just kill with a snap. My great talent—if you want to call it that—is to see how something is put together, see what makes it alive, and then stop that. Take us for example: I look at us and understand how heart, brain, and lungs work together to keep a person moving. Then I figure out which of those three options will kill easiest and do enough damage to drop the person. Most magical things without bodies were made by someone. I have yet to run into anything made by a mind like mine that I couldn't take apart. However, the Minions were not made by a mind like mine. I've had lots practice with them, so I do know how to kill them, but it takes more time and effort than I'd like."

"What about the Dark Man? What's the problem with him?"

"Same problem as with the Minions. If anything made the Dark Man, it was God, and that's very much not a mind like mine. Sure, give me a day or three of fighting nothing but demons and I'll find a way to kill them. Pick a target, and I'll eventually find a way to destroy it. But that doesn't mean it'll be fast, clean, or easy."

I sat there and nodded. Battle mage was becoming a more concrete term. "So, you really used to kill things on a regular basis?"

"It wasn't my first choice, but yes, I did it, and I was good at it."

"Why?"

"Why did I do it, or why wasn't it my first choice?"

"Why did you do it?"

"Two assassins showed up on my back porch and tried to kill me and my children. It was kill or die, and I wasn't going to let anyone hurt them. I never really did any magic before then. Didn't have a clue I could do it. But no one was going to harm them, not while I was breathing. I don't know, maybe if they had just gone after me, that's where the story would have ended. But those two idiots picked a time when my kids were with me. It was the last thing either of them ever did.

"It was a very…" He spent a moment looking for the right word and didn't find it. "It was a moment of perfect clarity. Everything slowed down. Everything was sharp and intensely real. I was whole and perfect and doing precisely what I had been created to do. Then it was over. I got my kids inside, then collapsed shaking and threw up because that's when the fear hit.

"There's…" he paused, once again thinking of a word, "an exquisite contentment that goes with doing precisely what you were created for. Pat can tell you about it, too. You can see it when Mike picks up a sword. I know it sounds terrible. When I'm killing things I'm perfectly at peace and right with the universe because it's what I was meant to do. The magic is beautiful and sharp and clear and just so perfect; it's hard to describe. Like working with molten diamonds. It's just… right."

I didn't know what to do with all of that. So many things there, so I started with the easiest one. "You had kids?" Wrong choice. I could feel the glow he had from talking about the magic fade to regretful pain.

"Yes." He sighed and tried a smile. "Five of them. The youngest two hadn't yet been born when that happened. It was autumn. We were playing… call it hop scotch. Filling the time between dinner and bedtime. My guards hated that flat. But I was being stubborn and stupid. We were in the Palace, supposedly surrounded by my supporters. We built it the way we wanted it, had lived there for sixty years, and our children had been born there. I didn't want to move to a more secure location. We moved the next day. Our children went into hiding the day after that. The day after that I declared the people who hired the assassins in formal rebellion, and the war was on."

"That's when being a battle mage really started?"

"Yes. Sort of. Took a little while for me to be able to do it on command. The first year I did fight with a sword. It was only by the grace of our God I survived. Pat and his troops showed up in the third year. That's when things started to shift in our direction. Having him around helped. I could watch how he did it and improve my own techniques. There was a war on, so I got lots of practice with my new skills. Since it's what I was made for, I had an innate grasp of better, easier, more effective ways of doing what I needed to do. Basically, I'd watch him do it, try it a few times myself, and then change it to make it work better.

"By the fifth year I was really good at it. By the tenth the price on my head was so high it would have bankrupted the other side to pay it, but it would have been worth it because it would have won them the war. By the last year of the war, no one was even willing to fight me. I won by virtue of being the biggest gun in anyone's arsenal." He paused, looked at me, got a sense for what I was feeling, and said, "You're having a hard time believing this, aren't you?"

I looked at the tall, skinny kid with a bowl of Cheerios in his lap, staring at me through small, round glasses and tried to find a tactful way of saying what I was feeling. "Well, you aren't precisely Chuck Norris, now are you? I'm sorry. I can feel you mean it. It's so very real to you, but it is kind of hard to believe. While you say it to me, it makes perfect sense. Then I realize I'm sitting on your sofa while you eat Cheerios in your jammies. It's just… unreal."

He half-smiled. "Well, first of all, me versus Mr. Norris or any other superhero—with the possible exception of someone like Wolverine who can heal really quick—and I win. Secondly, it's probably a good thing you don't just sit there and believe all of this with nothing but our stories for proof. Thirdly, one of these days, you'll see the proof. I don't mind waiting a good long time for that to happen. You're willing to heal us and haven't called campus psychiatric services to see about having us committed. That's about as good as we can hope for right now."

"I also talked to Ari right before coming here. He's very real world, very normal."

"Ahh…" I felt Chris start to shut down, begin paying attention to the TV again.

"I should probably head off. Let you get some sleep."

"Thanks."

A quick glance at the clock on the way out showed me there wasn't time for much of a jog before the biscuits would be ready for the oven. I headed home and thought about the man Chris used to be.

Monday night. Chris and Chuck walked through the woods toward the back doors of Grace Methodist Church.

"How is this supposed to work?" Chuck asked.

"You'll chase it to me. I'll trap it, then make it solid."

"Okay. What do you see me doing while you work?"

"What you usually do when I'm working: watch my flank and keep me alive."

"I can do that."

Grace was just visible through the trees when Chuck asked, "So, what exactly are you hoping to have if you make this thing solid? Not a human, right?"

"No. Not a human. Hopefully, something like a zombie. Without the brain hunger, super strength, or tenacity."

"Cell, fighting zombies does not in any way sound easier to me."

"Maybe not to you. For the three of us who actually are fighters, it will be easier. Cut the head off, and it'll die. We might have someone who's good at that. Damage the body badly enough, and it'll stop moving. Think Pat would be up to that? If I do this well enough that it has real anatomy again, I can do what I do best and take it out with a few pulses of magic. Do you remember how Pat and Mike used to fight? Fist and sword and the Minions actually died. Now what happens? Mike pokes at it. Eventually it gets annoyed and goes away. My guess is Pat'll be almost useless against one now because he hasn't gotten used to fighting something his fist goes right through. If I really work at it, I can cut it off from Mildred and starve it, but that takes minutes instead of seconds. That's just too long. There has to be a better way to do this."

"And now it's time to find it."

"Exactly."

They got inside. Chris looked around while Chuck went hunting for the ghost. He found it easily. It was a sad little thing, probably the pastor back in the 1800s, but now it just roamed around in a set pattern, doing the same routine over and over without any thought to it. Chuck let his mind settle on it and noticed a problem. He went back downstairs and found Chris setting up his shields.

"There's not enough of a mind left for me to control it. You'll have to catch it on the fly."

"Great."

"On the upside it just goes from one side of the hallway to the other, vanishes, and does it again."

"Easy enough." They headed upstairs again. It wasn't Chris' first choice of places to work. Between the huge window on the one end and the cluttery décor, it was the kind of space where a lot of things could get broken and people could see him do it. The last thing they needed was one of the neighbors calling the cops.

He blew a frustrated breath from between his lips. "Lights off." He turned off his flashlight. Chuck did likewise. After his eyes adjusted to the dark, he spent another minute watching the ghost's routine.

A simple shield should do it. He set a wall of energy in the middle of the hallway and watched the ghost walk into it. It stood there, stupid and mute, unable to finish its walk or figure out a way to go besides forward.

What came next was less than exciting. Chris studied the ghost, learning what and how it was. Once upon a time, it had been a man very deeply attached to his church and what he had done here. Now, probably two hundred years since he died, there were just a few wisps of memory left. In some ways this ghost was more a part of the building, something the stones remembered and knew should be there, than any sort of real entity. Having learned that, Chris was not coming up with any particularly good insights into how to make it tangible.

After an hour, he killed the shield and let it go. Chuck looked at him curiously.

"I've got nothing."

"I'll do more research. I've heard things about ghosts that do solid on occasion. Supposedly the reason you get cold spots is because the ghost takes the local energy to manifest in some way. Maybe there'll be something of interest along those lines online."

"That would be useful."

On Wednesday Pat lounged on Sarah's sofa, reading his way through *Moll Flanders*. It wasn't his favorite novel ever. It also wasn't *The Awakening*, which he was avoiding by reading *Moll*. Sarah was in her usual place on the window seat, reading through her biology textbook.

He looked up from *Moll* and said to her, "I don't have any papers due this Monday. Would this weekend work for the Pittsburgh outing?"

"Yes. My last midterm is Friday. Head down Saturday morning, spend the afternoon poking about, get some food, go dancing, then home again."

"Doesn't that mess up your day of rest?"

"A little, but it's supposed to be a day without work, and it will be."

"I'll tell them at lunch." Pat was looking forward to seeing Chris' face when he said it. He knew he should stop enjoying this so much. At the same time, it felt too good to completely let go of.

"Okay." Sarah thought about it for a minute and picked up on his glee. "You mean, you're going to tell Chris?"

"Yes."

Sarah gave him a disapproving look. "Be kind to him. Mike says he's a bit sweet on me and having a hard time with it." A 'bit sweet' on her might be one way of putting it; she was the love of his life would have been more accurate. Pat still hadn't figured out why Chris was keeping his distance. His best guess, that somehow Chris didn't know Sarah was Althiira, was deeply unsatisfying. It was also the only thing that made any sense.

Well, not the only thing. Pat supposed it was possible this time around God had been kind enough to drop her in his lap, and Chris could sit on the sidelines. Pat didn't mind that idea at all. He just didn't think it was terribly likely.

Sarah looked expectantly at him.

"I'm not doing anything to him he didn't do to me first."

That caught her attention. "Do I want to know?"

"Watching the two of us will probably make more sense if you do." Pat had pondered telling her about this for a while now. The more clear it became Sarah didn't remember their life before, the more he didn't want her to think he was chasing a ghost that looked like her. He also wanted her to know more about who they had been. "He loved Ameena. I loved her, too. She loved both of us. But he was her one true love, and I was her dear friend. At first she loved me because I fought for her husband. When she got to know me better, she loved me for me. In the beginning, before she knew how I felt about her, I sat through a lot of affectionate husband-wife behavior. Once she knew, she made sure they toned it down when I was around, but the looks or the quick brush of her fingers against his was almost as bad."

"I'm sorry."

Pat shrugged. Trying to explain that part of what he had loved about her was the fact she loved her husband was something he didn't want to attempt. "It was all part of the job. I could have left if I didn't want to deal with it."

"But you didn't."

"No." What to say next? Lay it out and see how Sarah responded. "It was better to have her friendship than nothing at all. Who knew? Maybe something would happen, and we'd be more than friends." Sarah's eyes flickered. Pat could see she understood how it applied to them as well. "But every now and again the desire to prove I'm better than him was overwhelming. I'm a better fighter. Three weeks ago might have been the first time I cut him. He never suggested we use blades before. But it wasn't the first time I've fought him, and it wasn't the first time I've made him bleed. He can be a little dense at times; occasionally he needs a boot to the head to keep him moving in the right direction."

"Great." She didn't sound thrilled, but Pat knew she didn't disagree with him.

"Don't get me wrong: I genuinely like him, too. I wouldn't have done it if I didn't like him. Out of deference to you, I will not rub his face in the fact that come Saturday I'll be dancing with you while he's sitting around with Dave and Autumn playing Guitar Hero."

"Thank you."

"Well, at least not too much." Sarah glared at him quickly. "He'd think something was wrong with me if I left it totally alone."

"Fine."

Pat went back to reading. Sarah worked on her biology. She looked up at him again, after a few minutes. "What was he like then? Was he a good leader?"

Pat smiled at that. "I wouldn't have taken the test if he wasn't a good leader. He was a very good general, maybe not great, but he never had to go up against anyone who was great. He is a great battle mage, and he shouldn't have been. We train for decades, lifetimes, to get those skills. As he said, it was learn or die, and he didn't want to die.

"By all rights he should have spent his life as an advisor to the high priest. He should have been a fairly anonymous member of the royal family. Life threw some serious challenges in his way, and he beat them down and made them beg for mercy. He is worth protecting. If you…" He stopped himself from saying 'remembered' and went with, "knew him then you'd understand it. He had this glow of righteousness about him. You'd see him and know he was the tool of God, doing exactly what he was supposed to. If you were with him, you were also doing exactly what God wanted. That's an addictive sensation, knowing what you are doing is absolutely morally correct. He's lost it now, but when he had it…" Pat realized he was starting to sound like a sycophantic fanboy. "Anyway, it feels good to put him in his place every now and again. If anyone has ever earned the right to do so, it's me."

Sarah let off an half-snort, half-chuckle. "You are such a guy."

"I'll take that as a compliment."

"I think I meant it as one."

The sound of a motorcycle kicking to life woke Chris from a very light slumber much earlier than he would have liked. It had taken him a long time to fall asleep. Images of Pat and Sarah dancing close and sexy wouldn't leave him alone.

Pat had been surprisingly gentle in his ribbing. He had the feeling Sarah must have asked him to take it easy. There was no way he had tired of having the upper hand. The novelty of it would eventually wear off, but it hadn't yet.

He stared at the ceiling, wanting to wrap his arms around her as she took them away on her black and chrome bike. There the fantasy ended. He couldn't go any further, even in his own head, without guilt swamping his senses.

She wasn't his, and he had no right to think about her.

He sent his mind back to Althiira. If there was a way to get his mind off Sarah and hopefully fall back to sleep, that would do it. He scooted out of his pajama bottoms and let his mind wander through his favorite images of his wife.

Althiira on her back, hips flush with the edge of their bed, legs wide, one foot dangling, toes just touching the floor, the other on his shoulder. That was a good one to start with. He could sit on the floor and lick her to his heart's content without his neck cramping. He stiffened quickly as his mind added the details: her scent, the way she tasted, and the absolutely fantastic joy of sitting there feeling her body shake and quiver against his tongue while she called his name.

He knew what came next, and his hand curled around his cock to make it feel more real. He'd get up on his knees and slide into her while she was still coming. He'd move slowly, dragging her orgasm out while warming up for his own. He'd watch himself ease into her. Marveling at how good it felt and how wonderful it looked. Her soft, wet body clinging to his while he slid out, glistening as he pushed in. *Fuck that was good.* His hand sped up as different views of her played through his mind. He felt his balls start to tighten as he settled on the image of her on her knees in front of him, lips wrapped around him, as she took him deeply into her mouth.

He forced his hand to let go. He wanted to come hard enough to fall asleep quickly and deeply. His usual three minute morning whack off wasn't going to do that. He rolled over and grabbed the bottle of lube he kept tucked between his mattress and the wall for special occasions.

He squirted some in his hand and grabbed himself again. He was about to slide it all the way down when a new fantasy came to mind. He was lying on his side, spoon position. They did that a lot when she was pregnant. Those were good memories. She was round and full, soft and curvy, and so sensitive. He'd snuggle up behind her, pressed tight against her full bottom, and very lightly stroke her nipples. She'd squirm, rubbing softly against him, but not letting him in while he'd tease her with his fingers and his words. Her skin would flush a brilliant sky blue. When he could barely take waiting anymore, she'd hook her top leg over his, and he could find that sweet angle where he could just slide in. Not too deep. Too deep hurt when she was pregnant. Not too fast. It was too easy to go too deep when he was moving fast. He slowly fisted the top few inches, mimicking the feel of shallowly sliding into her as well as he could with his hand. He'd drop his hand from her full breasts to her clit and circle it lightly as well. She would squirm and moan and arch against him. He would keep saying sexy things to her while slowly, deftly tipping her into an orgasm. He knew she liked the slow ones best because they were more intense. Her entire body would ripple with gentle spasms of release. He squeezed his hand in addition to sliding it up and down.

He breathed faster but kept his hand moving slowly. *Drag it out.* He rolled onto his back and slid into a different fantasy. She had him tied down and was blowing him. She was so very good at that. She'd suck him until he was hard and aching, on the verge of climax, and then pull back. Sometimes she'd lick him; sometimes she'd get the toy.

She walked to their dresser and grabbed the narrow black satin box it lived in. She put it on the bed next to him, then sauntered to the bath to get the oil, making sure her hips swayed enticingly. He'd just gotten to the point where he couldn't feel his pulse in his cock by the time she got back.

She pulled the dildo out of the box and coated it in the oil. Then she dribbled more of the oil down him. It was cool and slick, and he was so sensitive, aware of each drop as it trickled down his cock over his balls and down further. She'd use her fingers to make sure everything was slippery. Then she'd start with the toy. Sometimes she'd go slow, inching it in. Other times she'd go for one fast thrust.

He was biting his lip and pressing hard against the base of his cock, forcing his hands to stay still and his body to just relax and enjoy the memory. She went for fast and buried it inside him. It would burn and ache, but she knew the pain would take him even higher. Less than a second later she'd straddled him, facing his feet and grabbed the base of the toy.

Oh fuck... He wanted to grab her hips, control the speed, slam her down on top of him while the toy hit that spot that made his knees feel like water and electricity shoot up his spine. She eased it out of him while slowly rising on her knees, then back down and in, fast and hard. She didn't have to do that too many times before he was shaking with the need to climax. Before his toes, fingers, and probably hair were curled in anticipation of a shattering orgasm.

She abandoned the slow-fast duality and went with just fast. *Fuck, it was just so good.* He was using both hands, thrusting up, hips off the bed—almost there. Althiira added a squeeze to the down thrust; his hands clenched tight, and that was it. He was awash in pleasure, his body humming and pulsing with it.

He woke hours later, crusty and disgusted at himself. Blotting out images of Sarah with fantasies of Althiira was a low thing to do. He might as well visit a strip club and then head home to his wife. It wasn't right.

There had to be a way to stop this. A way to kill his desire. People got over ex-girlfriends all the time. There had to be a way to get over a woman who would never be his. He stood up, wrapped himself in his robe, and got a shower, determined this would be the day he moved on. They'd be friendly, and that would be it.

He was in the laundromat, waiting for his clothing and sheets to dry when the sound of a motorcycle blasting by made his heart beat faster, hopeful they had come home early. He buried his head in his hands and wanted to cry. *One day, fuck, not even one day. Six fucking hours.* He couldn't keep his resolve in place for six hours.

He retreated back to his room. Putting his clothing away and making his bed gave him something to do with his hands, but it did nothing to ease the wasted futility his mind felt wrapped in. That done, he lay on his bed and spent more time staring at the ceiling. Eventually the color drained out of his room. Autumn let him know they were going to dinner.

He wasn't hungry, but he hadn't eaten yet. He got up and joined them for dinner. The others notice he was in one of his funks. Autumn did her usual job of trying to jolly him out of it. Dave and Mike did their usual job of trying to ignore it. He ate half a burger and spent most of the meal staring into his tea, willing it to show him a way to get out of feeling like this. Somehow the tea didn't have the answer.

They went home. Brooke was sitting on the porch. "My roommate is having a party tonight, and I need to do some homework. Can I camp out here?"

"Sure," Mike told her.

"Do you mind Call of Duty in the background?" Dave asked her.

"No, not at all. It's fifteen drunks I mind."

Chris went straight upstairs. He spent another hour staring at the ceiling. Rain began to patter on the roof. It perked him up a little; he liked rain. The idea of going for a walk was almost appealing. Head down to Chuck's, wait for him to get home. He didn't bother with a coat. He didn't want to be shielded from the rain.

The rain helped. He felt a little less distraught at not being able to shut off his desire like a switch. He was a quarter of the way to Chuck's house when he noticed he'd picked up one of the local nasties.

It was a small critter that fed off misery. No wonder it was happy to follow him. Suddenly, he felt better. He turned on it and had it trapped, pinned to the ground by his magic, before it even knew he had noticed it.

He circled it, a very hard grin on his face. It screamed, realizing what was about to happen. The high pitched vibration of horror bypassed his ears in favor of burrowing straight into his brain. Not a bad attack, given the size and power of the critter. The scream was annoying and might cause a lesser opponent to run, but it wasn't going to even slow him down. He wished it was able to put up more of a fight.

Chris took another minute to see if someone called it here or if it just made its home here. *Probably local.* It didn't have the telltale feel of another person's magic that went with conjured critters. Chris hoped he could have found someone called it and gotten into a real fight. Unfortunately, real fights here that didn't involve Minions were few and far between.

Then he destroyed it. A few carefully placed pulses of magic sent its energy spiraling into the ethers.

He continued walking toward Chuck's, thinking about how he had destroyed it. He'd taken it apart, broken its energy, and scattered it. He'd always been good at that sort of thing. So, how to do it in reverse?

19.

I finished my conversation with Morrell and found Pat waiting outside his office. "Everything fine?" I wondered what was up.

"Everything is fine. Let's go to Writers'."

"Okay. You're acting weird."

"Yes, but it's worth it."

We walked across the campus without saying anything. I kept trying to feel what was going on. I got flashes of excitement and happiness but no context. When we were on the porch Pat reached for the door. "Remember when I said I owed you big time for fixing my back?"

"Yep."

"Well, I think this just about pays it." Pat opened the door to Writers' with a flourish.

Inside was the man of my dreams. All six foot two of beautiful Ari stood there smiling at me. Before I realized I was moving, I was in his arms, kissing him, and whispering quiet love words.

After a few moments, I pulled back from him and wrapped Pat in a huge hug. "How did you do this?"

He smiled. "You went to the bathroom while writing him an email once. I copied his address and set to planning. Five weeks later, I've got you your Ari."

I kissed him. "Thank you." Then I was back in Ari's arms. "How long can you stay?"

"Not long enough. Four days."

"Four more days than I thought we'd get."

"That is true," Ari said, pulling me close to him. I smiled, joy beaming out of me. I had longed to touch that rich brown skin and hear his beautifully exotic English for months. I don't remember what excuse I used to get us out of the Writers' House and over to my place. But soon we were in my own home, in my bed, clothing shoved out of the way because taking it off took too long, and making very happy sounds as he slid into me. Quite a while later we were enjoying a long overdue afterglow. Eventually, after the sun was gone, I started to make dinner for us.

"Your friend Pat cares about you very much."

"Yes, he does. I've been very lucky in him."

"Tell me about the rest of them. I'm afraid I'm having a hard time keeping them apart. They all look very similar, except for Autumn, of course."

I wanted to. I started to tell him about the magical saga that was the life of my friends, but, as with the email, I couldn't do it. I didn't want to defend my affections. So, I filled him in on their public lives. I told him about Golem and the Writers' House, most of the things I had already put in my emails to him. We talked about sparring with Pat and Mike. He seemed interested in joining our fight club. When we finished eating, I sat in his lap, cuddled close, and asked, "So, do you want to do my usual Monday night: hang out at Writers' or shall we go back to bed?"

He smiled. "I could use some more time before going back to bed. How about I get to know your friends?"

"Sounds good." I stood up, he took my hand, and over to the Writers' House we went.

Chris had never felt so ridiculously inadequate in all his life. It was one thing to see a picture of Ari on Sarah's mantle; it was a whole other thing to have Ari sitting in his living room, with Sarah on his lap, visibly radiating joy, while he told them about finding the tunnels under the border between Gaza and Egypt bombers were using to bring munitions in.

Maybe if he had been an accountant or something boring. Or maybe if he hadn't been so damn tall. Chris was used to having at least an inch or so on everyone around him, but Ari was another inch or two taller yet. Or maybe if it wasn't so horrifically obvious they had already had sex and were going to be doing it again as soon as they got out of here.

"I'm going to get another beer. Anyone else want something while I'm up?" Chris asked the group, looking for a decent excuse to get out of the room. She didn't even glance in his direction. He might have been invisible. She just sat there, petting Ari, listening to his story while his fingers caressed her neck. The fact that Autumn and Mike were also hanging on his every word, and in Mike's case very obviously undressing him with his eyes, didn't help either.

"How many have you had?" Dave asked from his corner of the room.

Chris took one last swallow from the bottle he was holding. "That would be number four. I have a feeling number five is on the bottom shelf of the fridge waiting for me." He stood up and walked into the kitchen before anyone had a chance to tell him what they wanted.

Pat followed him. He leaned against the fridge and cast a sound dampening spell. "It's hitting you pretty hard, isn't it?"

Chris ignored the question. "You've been a good friend to her, Pat."

"Yeah. I'm Mr. Fantastic. This is biting me harder in the ass than I thought it would."

"I know. You want another?"

"Yes." Chris handed him another beer. "How are you doing?"

"I'm fine," Chris said through gritted teeth while he opened his beer, then handed Pat the church key.

"Come on. I know how much she feels like her to me. I can't imagine this isn't driving you crazy as well."

"It's like watching my wife sitting in another man's lap happily snuggling, knowing she's going to go home and fuck him, and I can't do anything about it but hide or drink or both. In a few minutes I'll start working on homework and keep at it for the rest of his visit."

"I figured." Pat uncapped his beer and took a long drink.

Chris stared into the amber glass of the bottle for a long time before asking, "You feel it, too?"

"Of course. So does Dave. Hasn't he said anything to you about it? Or are we all walking on eggshells trying not to bring up the past?"

"Chuck's the only one willing to say anything beyond she feels like a healer."

"It's real. She feels like Althiira."

"And you want her?" He felt the old jealousy of watching Pat with her mingle with the new jealousy of Ari as he asked.

"Of course."

"That's my wife you're talking about!" He slammed the bottle down; beer sloshed out of the bottle.

Pat was annoyingly calm. "No, Chris. That's Sarah I'm talking about. Your wife is back home waiting for us to fix this and come back. Sarah is our friend and Ari's girlfriend."

"Fuck…" He said it so quietly he was practically thinking it. He took a moment to recompose himself. "And you'll respect that?"

"I did last time. Fifty years in love with her and I never once slipped and did something inappropriate. I think I can handle Sarah's long distance boyfriend."

"Yes. You were very good at that. I always wondered why you stayed with us when she left. It was clear your loyalty wasn't primarily to me."

Pat didn't say anything for a moment. Chris knew if he was less drunk or had Chuck's skills, he would have been able to feel the real answer to his question. "It wasn't to her, either. The Presence told me to protect you, so I stayed. If we fix this, I'm not going back."

"Why not?"

"I like it here. I like being free. I like letting fighting be a hobby instead of a vocation. I like not having to deal with being in love with my boss' wife. I like the fact I ended up in the one place where another version of her exists. This time…I still won't cross the line, but I will do everything in my power to make her want to."

"And if I don't want you to?"

Pat put his drink down and focused his gaze on Chris. He brought just enough of his magic to the front to let Chris know he wasn't kidding about what he would say next. "You can fight me for her if you can admit you want her when you're sober."

"I'll win." Chris looked cold sober for a second there.

Pat laughed, dry derision in his tone. "No you won't. You won't even put up a fight because that would mean His Glorious Holiness, Champion of the Presence, Defender of the Faith, High Priest Cellin Ath Dath Wa would have to break his vows and commit adultery."

Chris almost visibly wilted at and said, "Fuck you, Ahni," weekly.

Pat snorted. "No thanks. You aren't my type. But she is, and if I manage to pull this off, eventually I'll be hers."

"No you won't. Neither of us is going to win against him."

"Just give me time. I'm here. He's not. When he leaves and she's crying, I'll be there to hold her and make her feel better. He'll be the jerk who left, and I'll be the man who stayed. I am going to be the single greatest best friend a girl has ever had. She is going to forget him and fall in love with me. It might take time, but it will happen!"

Autumn poked her head into the kitchen. "Hey you two, come on out. Ari's telling us about hunting Nazis." She grabbed a soda for herself and beers for Dave and Mike. After she left, Chris looked tiredly at Pat.

"Of course he helped to hunt down Nazis. When he's not Jason Fucking Bourne, he probably single handedly flew orphan Jews out of Ethiopia and personally saved the Western Wall from a terrorist attack. Nothing either of us should ever tell her about will top that."

"Just give me time." Pat grinned: all bravado, no joy. He left the kitchen to rejoin the group. Chris picked up his beer, put it down, cleaned up the mess, then joined the others.

The one good thing Chris could think of was at least this story didn't involve Ari swooping in to the rescue guns blazing. This was all about taking photographs and running them through facial recognition software, trying to build a case that some ninety-eight-year-old in Belize used to be a minor player in the SS. When Ari finished the story, with them catching the guy, Chris made his excuses and went, in a fairly straight line, up to his room.

Laying across his bed, he realized he was more than drunk enough to have almost no control over the images in his head, but he was not nearly drunk enough to forget why they tortured him. He had done very well over the last twenty-one years when it came to not letting other women into his head. The first twelve years were utter simplicity. His child body wasn't interested, and that kept his brain in line most of the time. When puberty hit again, other women would enter his dreams, but his waking mind was focused on memories of Althiira. Once his body was under control again it was easy, well, easier, to keep his mind on the one woman he could think about that way.

Now alcohol dulled his waking mind's ability to hold his boundaries in place. Images of Sarah, naked, wet, head thrown back, legs wide, gasping softly as Ari slid his tongue against her soft pink flesh, danced in his mind.

It made him want to vomit. Then through the jealous haze he realized he actually had to vomit. Five beers in two hours were three more than a good idea. He got to the bathroom in time, and hoped the group downstairs hadn't heard what happened.

Pat decided to leave not long after Chris went upstairs. *Well, that conversation had been interesting.*

Chris really didn't believe it was Althiira or wouldn't let himself believe it. Of all the dumb fucking good luck in Pat's life, this was the absolute top of the list. He was almost tempted to turn around, smack Chris upside the head, and yell at him for being stupid. Almost. Pat was a good guy, but there were limits.

All he had to do was poke Chris about infidelity, and he would back off.

Pat felt really good for about two blocks. He'd been watching Sarah and Ari carefully all night and had come to the conclusion that she was quite fond of him, but Ari was not the love of her life. Once he was out of the way, things would get even easier. Maybe by Christmas, if he could keep Chris far enough away…

On block three the fact she was Chris' wife, once upon a time at least, and Chris trying to drink himself into a coma to hide from her with someone else, began to nibble at his elation.

By the fourth block, as Pat walked past the ravine, he pulled out his cell phone and fired off a text to Chuck.

He's had a really bad night and may want a shoulder, other than mine, to cry on.

What happened? Flashed on his cell a minute later.

Ari.

Chris woke up in the dark. His head hurt, and his mouth tasted bad. Chuck sat on the edge of his bed.

"This isn't helping anything."

"Who told you?"

"Pat." Chris looked at the clock: 2:03. Chuck must have walked here from work. "The only upside, from what Pat can tell, is she was so wrapped up in Ari she didn't even notice you being a twit."

"Did she notice him being a twit?" Chris closed his eyes again. The room spun less when his eyes were closed.

"Of course not. He brought Ari here for her. That's the last clear memory of Pat she'll have on this. Unless one of us points out to her that the only reason he wasn't winning Jealous- Would-Be-Suitor-of-the-Year was because you were in the room, that's all she'll remember about how he feels about Ari.

"You should just go for her."

"I can't."

"You should."

"I can't," Chris said, his voice sharp and pained.

"Look at it from a practical standpoint. Is this getting any easier? It's the middle of October. She's been part of your life for six weeks; are you building up a tolerance? Can you look at her and not see your wife?"

"No."

"It's getting harder, isn't it? The better you get to know her the more you like her. The more you want to be with her."

"Yes."

"Then do something about it."

"I can't."

"You think you deserve this, don't you? It's your perfect idea of penance. Her, or someone so close it might as well be her, with another man, all the time, and in your face. It's better than taking a whip and beating yourself."

"Yes."

Chuck rubbed his eyebrows. He was at a loss. His own forays into the world of self-loathing had been short and far between, leaving him with little sympathy and no practical experience for dealing with something like this. For a long time he watched Chris lie in bed and stare at the ceiling. He could see the images Chris desperately didn't want in his head and was honestly surprised at how exotic they were. He tended to think of Chris as a twice-a-week, missionary-position type. Obviously that was off.

Chuck felt like an ass. He was enjoying those images too much. "No one deserves this, Cell. Especially, not you."

Chris didn't answer.

I contemplated drifting off to sleep or rolling over and seeing if Ari was up for another round when he said, "I've gotten my newest assignment."

That banished any hint of sleepiness. "What you thought?"

"Yes."

We didn't need to talk specifics. Ari is black, speaks perfect Somali Arabic, and he had been doing in-depth espionage training for a year. I could put two and two together, and if my answer wasn't four, it was close.

"How long?"

"At least a year. Maybe more."

A year. Deep cover meant no contact, no calls, no emails, and no proof of life. Yes, it meant the chance to save lives. But it also meant danger, lots of danger.

"When do you leave?"

"As soon as I get back." We were both quiet. "Sarah…" He swallowed and wouldn't look at me.

I pulled his face toward mine. "Just say it, Ari. It'll be better after it's out."

"When I leave here… I can't promise you a future any longer. When I go, you're free to find another man."

I took a deep breath. Shards of glass pierced my skin thousands of times. I closed my eyes and took another deep breath, willing my voice not to break. "What if I don't want to find another one?"

He gave me the saddest smile I had ever seen. "In a year, if you don't have a new man, write to my mother. If I'm back by then, she'll let me know, and I'll come for you."

"In a year. And if you aren't back?"

"If you write, she'll let you know what is going on."

"How can you say 'if?' One year, Ari. On October 15, 2009 expect to see a letter."

He kissed me on my forehead. "We'll see. Do you want me to leave?"

"Only if you can't stand being with me now you've told me I'm free to find a new boyfriend."

He pulled me into his arms. "I'll always want you."

"And I you. So, why let me go?"

"You deserve someone who can promise you his life. For the next year, at least, my life isn't my own."

"Sometimes I wish you weren't so damn noble."

He kissed me deeply for a moment and then pulled back, managing to produce something that was almost a smile. "I'd rather be a bastard right about now, too."

Later that night, long after Ari was asleep, I lay against his back and began to pray. *Please God, keep my man safe, keep him whole, and let his mission be successful.* I began to trace words upon his back. The Hebrew felt old and comfortable. It tasted like safety and home. The letters flowed from my fingers, down and across his body. Although my eyes were closed, I could feel them glow. They had to glow. They'd glow as long as I could hold the prayer, hold my love over Ari. *Keep him safe.* It ran like a mantra through my mind and body. The words changed. They became a poem written long ago, in the voice of another woman, "My lover is mine and I am his… By night on my bed, I sought him who my soul loves: I sought him, but I didn't find him… Make haste my love…"

He woke up when I reached the soles of his feet. I rolled him over and continued, the letters flowing up his body, wrapping him in my love. Somehow he knew not to say anything, not to break my concentration. When I finished, lifting my fingers off the crown of his head, he touched my face with great tenderness and kissed me gently.

"What was that?"

"A prayer for your safety."

Another kiss. "Thank you." One more kiss. "Have you slept at all?"

"No, but I think I will now. I'm very tired."

"Good, you need to sleep. When you wake up, I'll make you breakfast." He wrapped around me and fell back to sleep. Within a minute I was asleep as well.

Three days later, we stood next to my motorcycle in front of the Continental entrance at Pittsburgh International Airport. He took his bag from my bike and placed it on the ground.

I curled into his arms for a last embrace. The kiss was long, soft, and sad. He cupped my face while he rested his forehead against mine.

"Goodbye."

"One year, Ari. I will wait for you."

He held me closer, kissed me again, then turned, grabbed his bag, and walked into the airport without looking back. I gulped air, trying to keep tears from breaking free. With fast, sharp movements I pulled on my helmet and kicked the cycle into gear.

Speed helped to numb the hurt. The focus required to ride well kept the pain out of my mind. It's ninety-three miles from my home to Pittsburgh International. I made the trip in an hour and four minutes.

Pat was waiting for me when I got home. He opened the door for me as I headed up my steps and greeted me with open arms. I sunk into his embrace, and he held me while I cried on him. He rocked me and told me it would be all right. In a year I'd see Ari again.

"You don't know that…"

"Shhhh…" Pat cut me off, touching my face. His words were gentle, and I felt calm ripple through me. "Nothing's going to happen to him. I saw your protection spell. As long as a bomb doesn't go off directly under him, he'll be fine. The next time I do anything even kind of dangerous, I want you to do that for me."

"I don't think I can."

"Why not?"

I won't die if something happens to you. That wasn't a polite answer. "I'm not sure how I did it in the first place."

"Yeah, right. You need to really love someone to make that work. I'm just not that valuable to you." Pat paused and kissed me on the forehead; he smiled. "Yet."

"Yet." I managed a smile at him. "Keep working your way under my skin and I'll do it for you as well."

Pat pulled me close and stroked my hair again. "Sounds good."

20.

Pat and I were sprawled in my living room working on homework. I was on the window seat slogging through yet another problem set for Calculus. Pat was on the couch reading. We'd work some, chat some, work some more. It was an easy way to spend an evening. I had finished yet another problem when we heard steps on my stairs. Pat looked up. "Chris. I think he's looking to hide out from Autumn."

"You can tell by the footsteps?"

"I can tell it's Chris by the footsteps. I can tell he's hiding because I was over earlier this afternoon and watched her paw him while trying to look sexy. She was working on a new outfit and kept coming out to ask us how it looked."

"Not good?"

"No, it looked fine, but it was less than half done and strategic bits of her kept sliding out of it. Then she'd quickly cover up, say, 'ooops!' and scurry back into her room. Come on in," Pat called out before Chris could knock.

He came in, holding his laptop and a small pile of books. "Can I work here?" I shifted over and cleared a spot for him.

"There's a plug on that side. Plug in, grab a drink, and get your homework on."

"Wonderful." He plugged his computer in, placed the books on the seat next to me, and went to the kitchen. "Do you have tea stuff?"

"Sure." I got up, wondering why he had chosen to come here. I was pleased to see him, but he'd never come over to hang out and work before. I pointed out where the mugs, tea, and sugar lived, then showed him how to work my microwave. "I don't have any lemon right now, but if you like it, and if you're planning on coming by regularly, I'll make sure I have some for you."

"I'm not a big lemon-in-tea fan. I do like Earl Grey."

"I can keep that on hand for you."

"Thanks." I left him to his tea making and returned to my homework.

"Is she still sewing?" Pat asked.

"Worse, she's designing. She's in my room every few minutes to ask what I think about this sketch or that one."

"Ugh."

"I told her I was off to the library."

"And the warmth and comfort of Sarah's waylaid you?" Pat cocked an eyebrow. There was some context I was missing, but I didn't want to seek clarification.

"It's cold and rainy enough out there that cutting a thousand yards off the walk sounded like a good idea."

The microwave dinged. He poured hot water over his teabag. We got back to homework. An hour passed with almost no sounds beyond the turning of pages, the clicking of Chris' fingers on his keyboard, and the soft scratching sound of my pencil as I juggled numbers.

Pat put his book down and got himself another pop. "Any word from Ari?"

"He got home safely."

"Now he's off the grid?"

"Yes."

More homework. More clicking, scratching, and turning pages. I moved from calculus to chemistry. More numbers danced in front of me. Chris stood up, stretched, and got himself another tea. He returned to his computer but didn't start to write again.

"How about Friday night for Good Dialogue Movie Night?"

Pat looked up. "I'm free. *Serenity*. That's the movie we need to do."

"Good one. You in, Sarah?"

"Not on Friday night."

"Busy?" Chris asked.

"Sabbath."

"Oh."

Pat looked at me with interest. "I thought you could study on the Sabbath. That it doesn't count as work."

"You want to call watching a movie with you guys studying?"

"Sure. You're learning more about the fine art of writing good dialogue."

"I'll think about it."

We returned to our work for another ten minutes before Pat looked up again. "I've been wondering about this for a while now. You keep kosher, stay home on Friday nights, and you went to Pittsburgh for the High Holy days, but, unless I'm sorely mistaken, Ari wasn't sleeping on the couch while he was here. What gives?" Chris had stopped writing and was listening with interest.

I smiled. "What did Chris say? 'Some of us are better Catholics than others?'" Chris nodded at me. I got his quote right. "Well, some of us are better Jews than others, too."

"Yeah, but if you were Catholic you'd have a load of guilt on about it. I'm not seeing it."

"I'm not guilty."

"See, that's what I'm not getting. I'm fairly sure you guys aren't supposed to be having sex with people you aren't married to."

"You'd be right-ish about that. Do you want the real reason or the sophisticated —And by sophisticated I mean total load of crap but it sounds good—theological justification I came up with?"

"Both, if the theological justification is good, I may borrow it myself," Pat said with a smile.

"It won't work for you; Paul calls out fornicators. But read my Bible, and you'll notice gobs of sex between unmarried people. What's not allowed is adultery, and from what I can see that means having sex with another man's wife. Having sex with another woman's husband isn't a big deal. Sex with prostitutes happens all the time. Sex with servants, just dandy. Sex with concubines, no problem. Most of the sex restrictions I can see are about protecting the value of a man's property, in this case his women. Women like me aren't anyone's property. My parents are dead. My brothers bought out my share of the farm. I'm a free agent, able to do whatever and whomever I wish as long as I don't infringe on the value of another person's property. How's that for a sophisticated?"

"Sounds good. What's the real reason?" Pat asked.

"I like sex." Both of them laughed. "And I'm not about to feel guilty about it. As a biologist, I know liking sex is the reason for my existence. Spread those genes around. The biological imperative. As a Jew, I know I shouldn't be screwing around. I'm conservative enough I'm not interested in the hook-up culture. But I figure if David, Solomon, and Abraham could do it, than I can, too."

"Any female fornicators on the list?" Pat winked salaciously.

I thought about it for a minute. "Rahab. Tamar. Lot's daughters. Bathsheba Judith. Well, maybe not Judith. She used her wiles to get close enough to cut Holofernes' head off. The story is vague as to how many wiles she used to get him in a compromising position. Enough so he didn't put up much of a fight." Pat smiled. I grinned back at him. We went back to working. I felt like Chris was watching me, but every time I looked up he was focused on his computer screen.

"When would you do 'Good Dialogue Night?'" I asked.

Chris looked up at me. "Eight? That's usually a good start time."

I thought about it some more. Sunset was six-thirtyish these days. It was less than two hundred feet from my house to theirs. Yeah, there'd be some electricity going, but I was never strict about that.

"I'll be there. I keep hearing good things about this movie. And I'll be a better Golem member if I know more about good dialogue."

"Shiny," Pat said. I looked puzzled at him. "You shall learn, Grasshopper."

"Okay."

I was the last one to leave Writers' after *Serenity*. It was a blast. Pat promised me he'd be over with the entire *Firefly* collection and we'd watch them together. Dave made sure we did it at their place, so he could see, too.

By Sunday night I was thinking about getting myself a brown coat and changing my name to Zoe. Yeah, I may look more like River, but I want to be Zoe when I grow up. I really hope they make a sequel. Lots of sequels. I had the feeling *Buffy* and *Angel* were in my future as well. The assorted Writers were appalled I hadn't seen them.

When I got home after the *Firefly*-a-thon, I sat on the window seat and began the homework I really shouldn't have ignored all weekend. I'd be hurting to get it all done by tomorrow morning. I worked on chemistry problems until my eyes felt like they'd fall out of my head.

I closed my eyes, twisted my head and neck, and enjoyed a long stretch. Then I caught sight of something out of the corner of my eye. It was in the spot on my window where my body's shadow blocked the room's reflection. Something white, round, and face-shaped looked into my window. My second story window. I ran to the light switch, turned it off so I could see out, and grabbed the knife I wore on my boot.

With the light out I could see it clearly. The irrational desire to turn the light back on and make it go away was so strong my arm almost moved. Words from role playing games came to mind: wraith and ghoul, but neither was quite right. It was white and kind of human-shaped, standing at my window facing me. No eyes or ears I could see, just a mouth, an open, toothy mouth.

I kept my eyes on it while fishing my phone out of my pocket. I'm not sure which one of the Writers picked up the phone. It didn't matter: any one of them would do.

"There's something outside my apartment. Get here fast."

"What kind of something?"

"The kind of something with no face, just a mouth. It's looking in my window, but it doesn't have any eyes."

"Less than five minutes. Stay cool. If it could have gotten in, it would have."

Three minutes later, as I heard footsteps outside on the porch, the thing vanished. Even with it gone I couldn't pull my eyes away from the window or force my heart to slow down.

A minute after that, I heard Autumn's voice from the street. "Hello, Allan."

"Hello. I think we'll have snow tonight."

"Really?" she asked politely. *Stop fucking chit chatting!*

"You can't be too sure. Still, it doesn't hurt to put the salt out early. It's always a good idea to have some salt on the ground. You never know when it'll get slippery."

"Yeah. We're off to see Sarah." *Finally! Get your asses up here!*

"Have a nice visit."

Footsteps came up my stairs. I whisked opened the door, pushing them into my house as fast as possible, and then slammed the door shut. I hadn't turned on the light and had no intention of doing so anytime soon.

"I'm fucking shaking. There was a thing… in my window… and it vanished when Allan came out. I don't mean it moved away quickly. I mean it fucking vanished. There one second. Gone the next."

"That's good. It probably means it was just checking you out," Dave said as he looked out my window.

"I don't want eyeless, earless, open-mouthed heads checking me out!"

"They've been doing it for a while now. You've just described a Watcher. I'm sorry. We didn't realize you never actually saw one before. They're usually around." Autumn pointed across the street to the three of them lurking on top of the Fine Arts building.

"Fuck. What was it doing here?"

"How about we turn the lights back on?" Mike asked.

"No. If it comes back, I want to see it."

"It won't come back," Chris told me.

"How do you know that?" I hoped he was right and felt certain he wasn't. That thing had been less than five inches from my face, only a pane of glass between us. The only reason it didn't come in was because it didn't want to.

Chris moved so he was standing between me and the window. Forcing me to look at him instead of whatever might be out there. "Allan said he was putting salt down. In addition for being good for snow, it also can't be crossed by most of the assorted nasties out there," Chris said patiently. "Nothing is coming back until it rains."

"Snow?" Dave asked.

"Yes, Allan said snow," Autumn answered.

"There's no snow coming. Hell, it won't break forty tonight. Winter comes early here, but it's three weeks early for snow," Dave responded.

Autumn looked curious. "Interesting. That might explain why we couldn't find you here in the beginning. What do you think, Dave?"

Dave focused on the man in the home below mine. "I don't feel anything. Not even another living person down there. Yeah, he's one of us, just with the kind of hiding skills that make me want to ask for lessons."

"Did you just actually say that?" Autumn was amazed.

"Yes. Feel it for yourself. There's nothing down there, which should have set off all the bells and whistles, but he's got it cloaked so well you don't notice it."

At any other time I probably would have found this discussion of Allan's potential talents fascinating, but right now it was just annoying.

"They just watch?" Fear and annoyance made my voice sharp.

"They just watch," Chris said gently. "We thought when you could see us you could see the rest of it as well. Here…" He took my hand, tugging me back to the window seat, and began pointing. His other hand rested warmly on my back. "There are three Watchers across the street. They always have our house under surveillance. When they brush up against the shields we feel them. My guess is they finally decided to check you out as well. See the roof of the gym?" I nodded. "Look more carefully."

I couldn't see what precisely it was, but something, vague and gray and wrong, sat on the roof of the gym. "Is that a Minion?"

"No. That's just one of the local critters. For all we can tell it just hangs out there. It doesn't seem to do anything. There are three ghosts in Fullings. Some sort of thing hangs out in Lemmon. If it's real or just too many feelings trapped in one place, is open for debate. If you look at the map, you'll see the whole area is glowing with activity."

"Great. They really only watch?"

"They really only watch. Do you want to come over to our place? You can stay under our shields until you get used to it."

I shook my head. "No. Nothing is forcing me out of my house." The little voice in the back of my head was shouting *ARE YOU INSANE? GET UNDER THE SHIELDS!*

The sound of footsteps on my stairs made me jump a good three inches.

"What's up? The lights are off, and you're all here?" Pat asked when he opened the door.

"I actually saw one of the Watchers."

He didn't say anything as he pulled me into a firm hug. I dropped my head to his shoulder, and he stroked my hair. "They're not very pretty are they?" Pat whispered to me.

"No they're not. It's fucking real, isn't it?"

He pulled back and held my gaze. For a second I felt like I was looking at the white-eyed blue man from my dreams. "Yes, it is."

The next week was not fun. Every sound, every person who walked by my apartment, every image caught by my peripheral vision made me jump. I was cold all the time: aching, bone deep, standing in the shower with the heat on high and shivering cold. I started to hear disembodied voices call my name as I walked around campus. I was very aware of everything that wasn't supposed to be at Sylvianna.

Most of them were just vague shadows of wrong. Walk past the cafeteria, look up at one of the dorms, and there's something indistinct looking down from one window on the floor no one lives on. That sort of thing. Jones, where all my science classes were, whether because of its shiny newness or pervasive scientific bias, seemed immune. I started spending a lot of time up there. Nothing was going to jump out at me. Except the other students.

I could feel them all as well now. It made resting impossible. Someone would walk by my place at two in the morning, and I'd run to my window to see who or what it was.

I was ahead on my homework. That moment or two when a hard problem would take my mind away from the world was my only respite, so I continually chased it.

On Wednesday I couldn't spar properly. The thing over the gym kept attracting my attention. I couldn't concentrate on anything else.

On Thursday when Pat, Chris, and Autumn went out hunting, Mike came over to stay with me. We were quiet. I wasn't talking much those days, and he was working on homework. After an hour, he stood up and asked me, "Can I smoke in here?"

"No. Back porch."

"Okay. It's not tobacco. Is that a problem?"

"No. I didn't know you smoked."

He quickly rolled himself a joint. "On occasion. Want some?" Mike offered. "I can roll another one."

"The entire world moved three feet to the left on Sunday. I'm cold all the time and hearing voices that don't belong to anything human. I don't need anything else mucking with my perceptions."

"Are you sure about that? You look like you'll snap if you don't relax soon. This is good for that. It takes the edge off everything nicely."

"I think I've earned the right to be on edge."

"You're right. But we don't want you breaking, either." That helped to put this in perspective. Back in the IDF I'd seen this happen occasionally. Someone would get too stressed, and his buddies would try to get him drunk enough to relax. It didn't work all that well. Interesting that he'd be the one to try. I would have expected Pat or Chris.

"This isn't going to break me. I helped to pick body pieces off of a street while looking for survivors from a bombing. I thought I had found someone. There was a hand in the rubble, and I was too excited to notice it was cold. This is freaking me out and it's painful, but it's not nearly as bad as the moment I found that hand wasn't attached to a person."

"Not yet." He stood up and waved for me to follow him.

"That sounds ominous."

He kept talking while walking to my back porch. I grabbed my jacket and followed him. "There were hundreds of them by the end. We fought them with fist and sword and magic... Magic I can't even believe I saw. Chris' worst spell is called 'Flesh Melt.'" He lit up, inhaled deeply, held it, and then exhaled. His eyes asked me again if I wanted any. I shook my head no. He continued his thought, "I don't know what, if anything, it'll do on this side of the line. Probably nothing because we aren't fighting anything with bodies. But, before we came here, it got pretty nasty."

Flesh Melt made me uncomfortable. I didn't want to think about it. "What was yours?"

"I'm barely magical by their standards. Most of what I did was with a sword. I'm good with a sword, and most of my magic makes me better, faster, able to cut through magical protections. I get hit less often than I would otherwise. When I'm really on fire, I know what my opponent is going to do a half-second before he does."

"Useful."

"Yes. I think it's something a lot of us bodyguards have. If we know something's coming, we can do a better job of deflecting it. I always know when an attack's coming. I can feel it, usually a few days in advance, sometimes, rarely, as little as a minute. Pat's got it, too."

I felt my interest peaking. Maybe the second hand smoke was helping to get me interested in something besides the things out there. Maybe I was finding some of myself inside the scared girl. "So, wait…how does a sword work if you're fighting something without a body?"

"It's not the physical blade that does it. The sword is a focus. Here I'm fighting with my magic and my mind's ability to focus that into a weapon. I don't actually need the sword. It's just a whole lot easier to do it if I've got it."

"Oh." He finished, and we went back in. He did look pretty relaxed. We went back to our homework. I felt the fear creeping back up. Three different times I jerked up to look out the window to see who or what was outside my house.

"You're really sure you don't want any? If anyone could use less reality right now I think it's you."

"I'm fine. Was this your idea?"

"Was what?"

"Getting me high."

"Probably, but I was talking to Chuck at the time. He's really good at making you think what he wants to you think."

"What else is he good at?"

"What else does he need to be good at? If he wants you to do something, you do it. If he wants you to forget something, you forget it."

I thought about that while Mike went back to his programming. His fingers didn't seem to be slowing down. I wondered if the code he was coming up with was any good. After a few minutes, he looked back up at me. "Chuck can fight, too. I mean, with spells. I've got no clue if he can use his body to fight. I've never seen him do it. He and Chris fight together. They're better at it together. Chuck's pretty damn scary on his own. He's not Chris. I don't think Chuck ever killed an entire clan's worth of men at arms in one sitting, but he's still scary enough on his own."

I thought about that, too. I know alcohol tended to cause people to exaggerate, but I wasn't sure if pot had that effect. I was hoping it did. "How many men are we talking about?"

"Small clan. Eight hundred. Something like that. Chris went in and melted them. Sundown, men in camp. Sunup, goop with bones sticking out of it. Then Pat burned them to ash."

One of the Watchers came close. I could feel the cold deepen. My teeth started chattering again. I turned to look at the faceless head inches from my window.

Mike giggled at it. "Time to stop that topic." He saw me shivering, staring at it. "Did you ever see a scary movie as a kid, one that gave you bad dreams?"

"Yes. *The Neverending Story* freaked me out."

"How did you get over it?"

"I knew vampire wolves weren't real."

"They are, but that's not the point. You found a way to put the fear away. You've got to find it again, or this will break you. Chris likes you. Pat likes you. If it looks like you are in real danger of snapping, they will wipe your memory of us clean before that happens. They'd prefer you didn't remember us than end up a broken person."

"You know this?"

"They were talking about it at lunch."

For the first time in a week I was so angry I didn't feel any fear. They'd take my memories over my dead body! "That isn't going to happen."

"Good."

21.

Mike's warning stayed in my mind. I kept the fear toned down where the others could see it. I physically forced myself to stop jerking at every sound. I stopped looking at the things I saw out of the corner of my eyes. I acted more relaxed and did a better job of paying attention to the conversations around me.

I was still cold all the time, still couldn't sleep, and Pat didn't seemed nearly as fooled as I would have liked him to be.

On Saturday night he stopped working on his homework and sat next to me on the window seat. He motioned for me to sit on the floor in front of him and spent ten minutes rubbing my shoulders. Finally he said to me, "You need to sleep."

"I can't sleep."

"I'll stay and watch. You sleep. When you wake up, we'll use every bit of magic you can muster to protect your home. I know you can do it. You did the best protection spell I'd ever seen for Ari; you just need to find a way to do it for your home. But first, you sleep."

"I don't think I can."

"Well, the likelihood of sleep gets a lot higher if you get in your jammies and go to bed. If you want, I'll even stay in your bed. I remember how scary it was the first time I felt these things. Being alone at night made it worse. So, I'll stay with you. But you need to sleep."

"Okay." I put on some soft clean sweat pants and a plain t-shirt and got into bed. Pat sprawled on the left side of the bed, book in hand.

"I figured you'd like the light on."

"Yes. It's stupid. I feel like a little kid using the light to keep the monsters under the bed at bay."

"It's only stupid if the light doesn't work. Since in this case it helps, you may as well have it on. Go to sleep." He gave me a chaste peck on the forehead and opened his book.

I just lay there for what felt like a long time. Too tense to sleep. Then I was dreaming. Most of the night was filled with common dreams, helping with the cattle at home or being naked in class with a report I had to give and no idea what the subject was.

Then it wasn't normal. I was in a different place than anywhere I had ever been. I stood on a balcony thousands of feet in the air, overlooking a deep valley with a slow river at the bottom of it. I was the blue woman again. There were two little boys in my arms, two older ones, almost men, held me. We were crying. Above and through the tears was the sound of roaring. I looked up. The sky was on fire. Oppressive heat roasted everything. Ornamental trees burst into flame. The stones cracked from the heat. Screaming blotted out the roar. Millions of voices screamed as the fire got closer. Then it was gone, and I was awake.

I should have been scared. But I didn't feel fear nearly as much as sorrow and curiosity. Pat was curled into a ball next to me, snoring lightly. The clock said 4:23. I switched off the light and went back to sleep.

No dreams the rest of the night. For the first time in a week I woke up feeling better.

I went for a jog at six like usual. Also a first for the week. My muscles had missed their daily workout. Long before I was up the hill, my legs were burning, but I pressed on. While I jogged I tried to think about how I would protect my house. I wrote on Ari, a prayer to cover every inch of him. I could do that with my rooms. Paint brushes should work just as well as fingers.

By the time I was home I had a plan. I popped the biscuits into the oven and got a shower. Pat slept through all of it. I ate mine while making a shopping list. Latex paint, brushes, and a few paint trays. I figured I could just about get it all in my saddle bags.

I left Pat a note and wrapped up his biscuits so they'd stay warm.

There are things I don't like about Walmart. The ability to buy latex paint, brushes, paint trays, and a pound of salt at eight in the morning on a Sunday wasn't on that list. In fact, I was just about in love with Walmart by the time I left. The lady behind the paint counter even helped me pick a nice combination of light blue for my walls, cream for the ceiling, and dark brown for my trim.

When I got home, Pat was still asleep. I envied his ability to sleep through pretty much everything. Then I grabbed my MP3 player, mixed up some peppy tunes, and got to work.

My plan was simple. If the nasties couldn't cross a salt border, I was going to salt my whole house. I mixed the salt into the latex paint, putting as much in as it could hold without looking grainy. It took about thirty minutes to do the east wall. That was the easy part.

Then came the hard part. I began in the top right corner, working my way to the left. I let the Hebrew roll out of my head onto the wall. "Yea though I walk through the valley of the shadow of death, I will hear no evil, for Thou art with me." I let the words gather energy and felt them start to glow under my hands.

Pat came in while I was working my way around my door. "My God, woman! What are you doing?"

"Protecting my home."

"I can see that. With paint?"

"Salted paint. Prayers written with salted paint."

He sat down and noticed the biscuits. "For me?"

"Yep. 'Round about four hours ago they were warm."

"Still taste good," he said between bites. When he finished eating, he looked at what I was doing. "So, the mojo is in the writing. The base coat is just about making sure the physical barrier is in place?"

"Yes."

"Give me a brush." I handed him a brush. He looked at it, put it down, and vanished into my room. A minute later I heard him talking on the phone.

"Get over to Sarah's and bring brushes... Paint brushes... Because the least we can do for her is help her keep her home safe... Good... Bring lunch and some drop cloths, too..."

He re-emerged a moment later. "I called in the cavalry. Now, I haven't done this before, but how hard can it be?"

I gave him half a grin. "It's not that hard. How about you start on the ceiling over there?" I pointed to a corner.

"How am I going to reach?"

I pushed a chair at him. "Let me show you how to mix it up." I mixed more of the salt-paint blend and then handed it to him. "Dip the roller into the part with all the paint, rub it on the grate so the extra comes off, and then rub it against the ceiling. Stay away from the walls. Someone who's done this before will cut in."

After a few minutes Pat asked, "If I turn on some music will it mess up your concentration?"

"I don't think so. I'm pretty much wrapped in myself right now."

He booted up my computer, set up a playlist to his liking, and blasted Blue Öyster Cult while he rolled paint and moved his chair every few minutes.

I continued to move across the wall, words flowing from my hands. Each word was written carefully with maximum intention. Once again the mantra ran through my head. This time it wasn't "Keep him safe," it was "Keep this space safe."

An hour later Chuck, Chris, and Autumn showed up with more brushes, plastic plates, and pizza. Veggie pizza. I smiled when I saw that. Then I stopped. I needed the break and the food. Physically, this was the hardest thing I had ever done. My shoulders ached, my legs were on fire, and my hands could barely hold a brush anymore. I had two of the three outside walls in my front room done. The four of them whipped through the rest of the painting.

Autumn paused in her work. She saw what Pat was doing and immediately started to cut in the edges. "You know, I have a feeling next weekend we'll be painting our place. It's looking a little shabby, don't you think, Chris?"

"It could use some new paint, come to think of it."

"I have a feeling my place could use a new paint job, too." Chuck said from inside my bedroom. He was working on the far wall and doing a more precise job than I would have pegged him for. He stuck his head back into the main room. "This is actually a really nice bit of magic work here. When you pour the salt around your home the line gets broken, it gets washed away or kills the grass, and it's hard to do it without being obvious about it. The neighbors talk when you wander about the house spilling salt like the Morton's girl."

Pat hopped down from his chair. "Ceiling done. Pizza time." He sat next to me and dug into a slice. "So, what are you writing? I can see the letters. I know they aren't English, but besides making me feel safe and cozy, I don't know what they are."

"You know them. 'Yea though I walk through the valley of the shadow of death, I shall fear no evil, for Thou art with me.'"

"Good choice."

"I thought so. Plus, I think it sounds really nice in Hebrew."

"You're going to paint that over and over on each wall?" Autumn asked from her corner. She had almost finished cutting in the ceiling. I was going to put her in charge of trim next. She had a very precise hand for this.

"Yes. Assuming I can get back out of this chair again."

"The salt will act as a good stop gap, and when you've got more energy you can do more of the apartment. Don't try to do it all at once. If you burn through too much energy, you'll be hurting," Autumn said while working around where my cabinets and the ceiling met in the kitchen.

"Like when you exercise too hard?"

Chris stopped painting my mantle to answer. "Not really. Dave ended up in a coma." My eyebrows shot up. "He did too much too fast the first time he realized he needed a way to hide. You know how he becomes invisible?" I nodded. Anyone who was paying attention knew Dave could become invisible. Chris continued, "Well, the first time he actually made himself invisible he burned through so much energy it stopped his breathing. He fell unconscious, but no one could see him. The spell held for something like two minutes before it broke, and his mom found him not breathing on the floor. He spent two days in a coma and a week in the hospital. Don't burn yourself out."

"Yeah, it'd be a bitch if the healer ends up in the hospital," Chuck added.

"Yes, that's the real reason I wouldn't want to end up in the hospital. I wouldn't want to leave you without a healer."

"Just take it easy. If you burn yourself too low, and something comes after you when you're not here, you'll get hurt. Then we'll have to leave you to Autumn's tender mercies," Pat said.

"Hey. I'm a pretty good healer." Autumn hit Pat with a quick glare.

'No, you're not. You're a decent first aid person. Sarah's a healer," Pat replied seriously. Autumn looked affronted but too polite to say anything about it in front of me.

By dinnertime my whole apartment reeked of paint. The base coats were done as well as two walls of prayer. I offered to make dinner for everyone. We spent a pleasant evening talking about normal things and eating spaghetti and meatballs. At one point I even found myself smiling at Chuck, when it turned out we were the only two who loathed *Catcher in the Rye*. Yes, I get how subversive it was at the time, but whiny protagonists who do nothing in a book with no plot make me want to throw the book away in disgust. Chuck agreed. The others thought we were bonkers. The discussion made for a lively half-hour.

Then, because they were on Tuesday, the elections came up, and that ate another hour and a half. Judging by the group around me Obama was going to win. That didn't fill me with joy, but a McCain win wouldn't do it, either. Autumn and Dave were looking at me like I was some sort of exotic species. I had a feeling they may have never met a real live libertarian in the flesh before. They were intrigued because I didn't know if I was going to vote. When you loathe both choices, it's hard to work up much interest in going to the polls. Then Chuck and I got into an argument about whether or not it was moral to not exercise your right to vote even if you loathed both choices. He took the 'civic duty' position. I argued counter: if everyone is swine, you don't have to cast a vote. When they left after dinner, I had the feeling I might have made a more convincing argument, but I still hadn't won because on Tuesday I was going to get up and vote.

It took me a week to finish my home. I'd do a few feet of wall in the morning, a few more in the evening, and slowly warmly glowing letters inched across my walls. When I celebrated my next Sabbath, I gave an extra prayer of thanks for the power to keep my home safe.

22.

The three weeks that followed were very quiet and peaceful. Schoolwork, sparring with Mike and Pat, reading more poems for Golem, and going home for Thanksgiving filled those weeks.

The Monday after Thanksgiving break I walked down my steps to join the others for dinner. The day's snow had tapered off in time for sunset. Halfway down the steps the dull headache that now said "magic" to me started. I rubbed the back of my neck and shivered with a cold deeper than the snow. Nothing seemed out of place in the area around my house. A few more steps toward the ground level and my eyes landed on the Golem.

This time it met my gaze. I stopped dead. The statue didn't have eyes. It didn't have a face. It was only the vaguest outline of a human. But it had turned its head and was looking at me. It was sad. The emotion was so strong it made me nauseous. It overwhelmed the whispered words gently lapped at the edges of my consciousness. The light leached from the air, but somehow I could still see the Golem perfectly. Words danced around my conscious mind, almost, but not quite, letting themselves be heard.

Then it was a statue again. Chris stood on the sidewalk in front of me. "I thought you were going to meet us for dinner."

I jumped. "I am."

"We finished ten minutes ago. I'm on my way to the library."

His words and the fact it was night sapped the strength from my legs. I collapsed into his arms, shaking, teeth chattering.

He stroked my hair, holding me close to let his warmth sink into me. "It's okay. Everything is fine. What happened?"

"How long has it been dark?" I realized there was no answer that would make me happy. "Never mind," I said through rattling teeth.

"Let's go back to your place." He kept an arm around me while we walked up my stairs. I still shivered, but at least my teeth were no longer chattering.

Back in my own home the shaking stopped. One good thing about my shields is they do a decent job of keeping me warm. Chris led me to the kitchen table, put a blanket over my shoulders, and began to make some tea. "Tell me what happened."

"The Golem looked at me, and it was sad. So very sad. Millions of people screaming sad." He looked in the direction of the statue, but the light in the room reflected off the window giving him a perfect mirror image of himself.

"I know you guys don't feel it. It's not on your radar, but it's been on mine since my first day here. Today it looked at me. It tried to tell me something, but I couldn't hear it over the sorrow."

"It was crying?"

"No, it was so sad, sad beyond tears, so powerfully sad it made me sick. I couldn't focus on what it was saying, couldn't understand it. But it was saying something to me."

"We can go and check it out if you like."

"Not right now. I'll try going back on my own when it's light." I sipped the tea he handed me. "This is insane. I've got nasty critters watching my house, statues trying to talk to me, and disembodied voices calling my name. It's just wrong." My head fell to the table.

Once again he stroked my hair. Then he took my right hand in his and gave it a friendly squeeze. "I wish I could tell you it gets better. It doesn't really, but you'll cope. None of us thought you'd get so much better with this so quickly after you saw the first Watcher."

The threat of being magically overpowered and having my memories stolen was very motivating. Chris caught my thought and looked deeply embarrassed. He let go of my hand. For a moment we just watched each other.

"Do you want me to stay?" I thought that was an odd question. I was expecting him to leave.

"You were on your way to the library, right?"

"Yes. I've got a paper due tomorrow, and my chances of getting it done in time increase dramatically if I actually start it."

I yawned. I felt tired more often these days, probably because I still wasn't sleeping as well as I would have liked. "I've got some things I need to read, too. I'll be a mess in my lab tomorrow if I don't have some idea what I'm doing."

"Good, get into those books. Normal helps. It doesn't make the weird or evil go away, but it helps you remember what else is here and what will come after this is done. There will be life after May, and you've got to be in a position to take advantage of it."

"May. Why May? You all seem to know it'll be done by then."

"Every time they've come in the past things heat up until May, then there's the final big attack, then they go away again."

"My birthday is in May. I'll be twenty-two on the eighth."

"So is mine: the fifteenth."

"You're a lifetime older and a week younger than I am."

"Precisely." He squeezed my hand again and stood up. "I only need to go to the library to pick up some books. I can come back here after. Do you want some company?"

"I'd like it if you came back here." I had absolutely no interest in sitting here by myself trying to work on my bio while pushing that horrendous feeling of sorrow away.

"Then I will. I'll be back in twenty or so minutes."

Going back probably wasn't the brightest idea Chris ever had. Her looking shaken and vulnerable probably wasn't quite as much of a turn on as fighting her, but it was close.

He could see it in his mind. He'd walk back up there; she would look at him with those wide eyes, fear barely held in check and a slight tremble in her hands. He'd wrap her in his arms again. She'd nestle against his chest, her head tucked under his chin. She'd relax against him, stop holding her emotions so tightly in check. Trembling would turn to small, sniffly tears. He would pet her hair, whisper comforting nonsense to her, pull back a little, lift her face to his, and kiss her.

At the foot of her steps, he took a deep breath to calm himself and thanked all that was good and holy he had a paper to work on because it would keep his hands busy and his lap covered.

He walked up the stairs, knocked at her door, heard her yell out for him to come in, and did so. Sarah lay on her stomach on the floor near the window seat, a pillow propped under her chest, textbook in front of her, music playing softly on her computer.

"I left you the window seat, so you can plug in."

"Thanks."

Her eyes were still wide, and she still had that irresistible edge of fear about her, but she looked determined to master it. Laying on the floor meant she was in a position where he couldn't easily offer comfort to her. The hope that this would be easier than he thought glimmered at him. "If the music bothers you, I can put my ear buds in."

"I'm fine. What is it?"

"Brendan James." She watched him plug in, set his books down, and sit across her window seat, his back against the right side. "What are you working on?"

"Critiquing a critique."

"Sounds like fun."

"Oh, yes, spectacular fun. It's not enough for us to dissect the original work; now we're attacking what other people had to say about it."

"Have I mentioned how happy I am not to be an English major? I see you and Pat reading—it looks like fun—then I remember what you have to do later, and yuck! I'm much happier with the clean elegant lines of science."

He laughed about that. After mucking about with *Physics for Dummies,* neither clean nor elegant were words he'd use to describe the subject. She went back to her reading, and he started on the paper. He spent about ten minutes outlining his argument before looking back up at her. Her head was propped on one hand with her fingers through her hair. It was getting longer, about chin length now. His eyes moved down her back, lingering on the curve of her ass. *Stop it!* He pulled his eyes back to his paper and spent another ten minutes working very steadily, making sure his eyes didn't leave the computer screen.

Where was Pat? This would be a lot easier if he wasn't alone with her. He was tempted to see if he could get Pat to come over. But the part of him looking over the edge of his computer screen at her lying on the floor really didn't want to share this.

He pulled his eyes back to his work again. Three paragraphs of critique flowed down his computer screen when he realized she hadn't turned a page in a long time. Chris looked up again. Sarah was asleep, her head pillowed on her arm facing away from him. *You should wake her up. She's told you she needs to get that reading done. She also needs to get more sleep. Those black circles under her eyes aren't a fashion statement. Besides, if you being here lets her relax enough to sleep after feeling whatever the Golem showed her, you should let her enjoy it.*

Come on, this isn't about her enjoying anything. This is about you enjoying it. Well, that was true. He could watch her openly, without having to worry about her catching him at it though he did try to keep his eyes at her shoulders or higher. This was hard enough without letting his eyes travel down to map out the luscious, inviting curve of her ass. He jerked his eyes back to the computer screen.

In the end it was almost a matter of self-defense. He stood up, found the blanket he had gotten her before, and carefully draped it over her. Then he went back to his paper. His eyes would wander to her face and neck from time to time, but they were safe… ish. At the very least they didn't inspire a hard, urgent desire to get on the floor with her, slide his knees between hers, press himself against her back, and remind himself in full, glorious detail why he loved that position so much.

It was close to three when he finished his paper. He debated leaving. On the one hand, he'd sleep better in his own bed. On the other hand, he'd be alone there, and his hands and thoughts would get even further out of line.

She stirred a little when he got up. When he returned from the bathroom, she was on her side facing the sofa. *Of course.* He went back into her room and grabbed another blanket, turned off the light, and then settled onto her sofa. If it had just been a bit longer, he would have been quiet comfortable.

I woke up sore and perplexed to be on the floor. As I became more aware, the sense of being out of place increased. I had a blanket over me, which I knew I didn't when I started to read, and I could hear breathing, but it wasn't Pat's telltale snore.

I sat up. My neck ached, letting me know it did not appreciate me sleeping on the floor. The breathing was coming from Chris, who was, much to my surprise, sacked out on my sofa. My bio book was still next to my head, so I must have fallen asleep working on my reading. Chris must have decided I was cold and put the blanket on me.

I looked out the window: no new snow. I could kind of see staying over if he didn't want to go out in bad weather. I looked back at Chris' things. All piled up neatly. He must have finished his paper. Odd he was still here, though. Pat lived a good quarter mile up a very steep hill and a whole lot of steps. Not much fun in the cold when you're sleepy. Chris lives two doors up, and judging by how he fit on my sofa, he was going to wake up with a neck very similar to mine.

Why stay over here when his bed was more comfortable and very close? I didn't have a good answer for that.

I headed into my room and got dressed to jog. Back into the kitchen. I mixed up biscuits for both of us, very quietly. Then wrote a note for Chris, saying I was going for a jog, and he was welcome to join me for breakfast.

For a moment I just stood there and watched him sleep. He looked soft and relaxed and almost like a kid. A kid who had kids of his own. A kid who had been a king. A kid who was right and perfect with the universe when he was killing things.

I sighed and went out for my jog. As I headed down the steps, my mind focused on something more immediate than Chris' past. I went over to the Golem and rested my hand on it, trying to make it talk to me. Nothing.

"Come on, you talked to me yesterday. Talk to me now." It did. Images washed over me like a tidal wave. Once again the sky was on fire, and I could hear screams.

I tried to focus beyond the image, tried to hear the words, but it was so hard. I didn't want those images in my head, but I couldn't make myself look away. People screamed, smoke filled my nose, and the world around me was burst into flame. My lungs burned, the oxygen inside them turning to flame. Then a wave of shattering force burst through me.

It went dark. Blessedly dark. The fire was out. The screams were gone. Nothing but black and glorious cold. I'd never been so happy to feel cold in my life. Now I could hear the words.

"Ahom maun illit unc. Ergun ol wellm." Meaningless sounds wrapped in a dread feeling that it would be a very bad idea to try to find out what they meant.

I went back up the stairs feeling shocked out of myself. Like I was watching myself from far away. I put the biscuits in the oven without thinking about it, just moving on automatic. I did the same with my shower, getting dressed, and eating. My body knew what it was supposed to do in the morning, so it did it. My mind was still reeling from the sorrow and the pervasive awfulness of the fire and screams.

Chris slept through all of it. I was pretty glad for that because I didn't want to talk, and I knew I couldn't pull off acting normal in front of anyone who was paying attention. When I got to the lab, I threw my whole mind into it and let the science blast fire and screams out of my mind.

By the time I got home Chris had left. I found a note on my kitchen table.

Sarah,

Thanks for the biscuits. They were delicious. I hope you didn't mind me sleeping on your sofa, but I didn't feel like walking through the cold at 3:00 when I finished my paper.

-C

Chuck watched Chris try the spell for the sixth time. It really wasn't working at all.

"You thinking about how useless this is isn't helping me," Chris said without looking away from the ghost.

"What would be helpful?"

"A good idea for how to do it would be helpful and, short of that, quiet. Or, if you're feeling especially helpful, go find me a low-level Minion or a Watcher and trap it."

"We've tried that, remember?" Unfortunately, he did. It had been a complete disaster. In his rational mind Chris knew the Watcher hadn't been laughing at him as he tried to trap it, but it had certainly felt like it. "That's why you want to make them solid, so we can get one."

"I know. It'd be nice to have a chance to practice this on one of them before trying to whip it out on Mildred."

"Nice to have you good enough at it so you can do it in the background without it noticing while still throwing regular spells."

"Yeah, that'd be nice." He closed his eyes and focused on the ghost again. It didn't even appear to notice they were there. It was just a memory walking around. Something with its own intelligence would be even harder to deal with. Eventually he'd want to try on one of them as well. He'd need the practice if he was going to be able to do it in battle. Ten minutes passed, and the ghost was still remarkably incorporeal. "This isn't going to happen tonight." He dropped the spell, and the ghost vanished.

"You let it go?"

"Sure. If we want it again, we can find it. It'll be at Grace Methodist just waiting for us to grab it and take it home."

"It's very predictable, isn't it? So now what?"

"Let's go fight something. Pat and Mike are right. They need to keep in practice; so do we. Want to go pick a fight at the junior high?"

"What happened with Sarah? Every time you come down here and want to throw yourself in the line of something dangerous, something happened with her."

"Something scared her last night. I spent a while holding her and petting her hair."

"Are you trying to get hurt so she'll have a reason to touch you, or are you hoping to get hurt to punish yourself?"

"Both."

"Idiot. What scared her?"

"The Golem talked to her."

"Really?"

"No, I'm making it up. Yes, really."

"What did it say?"

"She couldn't tell. It was very sad."

"That doesn't sound good. That's how it started last time."

Chuck's words hit Chris upside the head like a brick. It hadn't occurred to him last night, but that was just how it had started last time. Althiira had been on the staircase beyond the Great Hall when the vision struck. He'd been walking up to meet her, and she fell into his arms sobbing. "Yes, I know. Just like last time I was right there when she came out of the vision, and she pretty much fell into my arms. Another reason I want to go fight something." Though that hadn't been true a minute ago, it certainly was now.

"Not tonight. I don't have the energy for it. Didn't she tell you to just ask her to touch you?"

"Probably. I felt her think something along those lines."

"Then go to her house with a headache. I can give you a real one if you want."

"I spent last night watching her sleep. I'm frustrated enough without having her touch me."

"If you want to throw yourself into combat and kill things after spending time with her, that's not a good thing."

"Better than sitting in my room feeling guilty."

Chuck nodded. "That's true. No luck at all on getting past that?"

"No. I look at her and see Althiira. I touch her skin, and it feels like home. But I'm not home, she's not my wife, and I'm the asshole who can't keep himself in line."

"No, you're the asshole who can't figure out he's drawn the line so high no one could possibly stay on it."

"Thanks. That's helpful."

Chuck's eyes gleamed. "I could help you with this. I could make the guilt go away. I could banish your memories of her. I could make you happy if you'd let me."

"You could make me a mindless puppet. No. I've earned my pain. I deserve my guilt."

"If you say so." Chris stood up and put on his coat. "Heading home?"

"Yes. I've got work I need to get done."

Chuck didn't look like he believed Chris. "Sure. Don't get into a fight with anything you can't beat. I do not want to come to your rescue."

"Yes, Dad."

"It's not like I just met you two weeks ago. I know that look. You're going to find something to fight. Just make sure you can take it."

"Not much purpose in that."

"Go home and ask Pat to fight you. He'll beat you to a pulp without actually damaging you. Then she can practice on bruises."

"I at least want the option of winning."

"Then go fight her."

Chris sighed. He was fairly sure he had mentioned something about being frustrated all of a minute ago. Fighting Sarah would not help relieve those tensions at all. "No. I'll be fine. Don't worry about me."

"It's hard not to when you get up to things like this. Yes, it's better than you hiding in your room thinking about killing yourself, but with the way you're acting now it's possible you'll let something else do it for you."

"Not today." Chris walked to the door.

When his hand was on the knob Chuck said to him, "Be careful."

"I always am."

"That might just be the biggest lie I've ever heard you tell." Chris gave him a hard smile and left.

If not the biggest lie, it was certainly in the top ten. Chris headed straight for the junior high. He hadn't been in a one-on-one magical fight against anything that could put him through his paces in a long time, and today he wanted the fight. He wanted the high that came with danger and the satisfaction of destroying something with his will.

He walked around it slowly. Getting a feel for what was there. At least three separate critters: fat, happy, lazy monsters sucking off the misery of the eight hundred students that spent ten months a year in that building. On his second pass around the building, he felt one of them notice him. *Good.*

He walked into the parking lot and focused on the one that noticed him. It was still in the building. Time to make it attack. He gathered the energy into a ball in his palm. It would annoy the critter, make it hurt a little, but not nearly enough to actually damage it. A quick thought sent the magic flying.

Oh, yes, he had its attention now. It was coming for him. The smile on his face was as hard as the stone his eyes resembled. *Come and get me!*

He drew the energy to him, let it spark between his fingers, arcing around him like an electric storm. It came for him. He felt the familiar fear and cold that went with danger and the more heady power of the magic around and through him. A bolt of energy, invisible lighting, coursed through the monster. It growled at him, hurt and angry, then leapt. It probably wanted to hit him, touch him, somehow hurt him, but he had his shield up and ready. It bounced off and landed a few feet away.

He felt it gather its magic, ready to try an attack along those lines. The magic felt like old, rusted dead things and made his head feel wrapped in fuzz. He knew that trick and blocked it. Then he focused on the heart of the creature, on the magic that made it. He felt it, tasted it, let himself steep in how it was made, and started to pull it apart.

He ripped the threads of its existence away from each other and left them to fly into the air. When he was done it was gone, not dead as much as eradicated.

The magic tingled through him. He wanted to go after the other two, but he would have to find a way to go after them. They cowered deep inside the school, hoping he couldn't get to them.

He turned and headed back toward home. Less than fifty feet later he felt something watching him. A new sort of something. Something hard and dangerous and manmade. *Perfect.*

This one rushed him, probably attracted by the fight at the junior high. Once again he had his shield ready, but this didn't bounce off. This one latched on, sucking the energy out of him. He felt sick and weak. Falling to his knees, he knew his only option was a simple attack. He focused his magic into a blade and stabbed the thing between the eyes. It screamed and let go, running away. It wasn't dead, but it didn't have any desire to tangle with him again.

He realized he was in trouble when he didn't start to feel better when it ran. Chris tried to stand up but couldn't. The last thing he thought before passing out was he was never going to hear the end of this.

23.

I knew Chuck was coming before I could hear his feet on my steps. I opened the door, fear and magic a cold lump in my back. He was still a few yards from the steps. Chuck half-carried, half-dragged Chris. I bolted down the steps and put my arm around Chris' other side to help Chuck get him up the steps. He gently put Chris on my couch while I hovered next to him.

"What happened?"

"The fucking idiot got into a fight he couldn't easily win." He could tell that answer wasn't helpful to me, so he expanded on it. "I felt him call me, but I don't know what specifically happened. He was a third of the way home and unconscious on the ground when I found him."

I stood over Chris looking at him. His breathing was fast and shallow. His skin was a chalky gray. I propped him up for a moment, sat on the couch, and laid him back down so his head was in my lap.

"Now we get to see if you're as good as Pat says." I didn't like Chuck's tone. It was dismissive, challenging, and angry.

"Yeah, now I get to see. Time for you to leave, Chuck."

"What?"

"Time for you to leave. I don't need you watching over my shoulder. I don't need to be distracted by your scorn. I need all the concentration I can pull together, and you breathing down my neck won't help. Go away. Go hang out at Writers'. Chris or I will let you know when he's better."

"You're telling me to leave?" He was stunned.

"I'm telling you to leave. I don't need you here for this."

"Our last healer betrayed us, so forgive me for being wary." His voice was defensive and a touch sarcastic.

"I'm not her. Go be wary somewhere else. Now."

The gaze he shot me was hot and mad, but he left. Chris' head rested in my lap. I sighed. Now what? I had known what to do before, but I knew what was wrong with him before. Chris was cold, pale, and unconscious. *Feel it. Don't see it.* I laid my fingers on his temples, closed my eyes, and tried to get a feel for what was going on.

He felt like a piece of fabric washed too many times in acid, faint and weak, ready to tear at the slightest tug. I began to gently push some new energy into him. Something to make him more vibrant, stronger. I had been at it for less than five seconds before I was dizzy, nauseous, freezing, and wanted to run away.

My head fell back on the couch while I took gulping breaths. I didn't want to run to the bathroom, dumping him on the floor, no matter how much I thought I was going to puke.

"You're here." Chris' voice was tired and very quiet.

I took another deep breath. "So are you. Can you sit up?"

He did, slowly. As soon as he was off my lap, I raced to the bathroom and threw up. I rinsed my mouth and returned to my front room. He was lying on my couch again. This time I sat on the floor next to him. "Can you tell me what happened?"

He turned his head toward me but didn't open his eyes. His voice was still weak; he looked like he had just come out of a very high fever. "You tripped one of my defensive spells when you tried to help me."

"Oh." That explained the desire to puke and run. "I meant, what put you into the state you're in."

"Psychic Vampire. I thought I got it in time. Once I finished it, I couldn't get back up again."

"Is it dead?"

"Maybe. It wasn't when it ran away, but I've got some pretty strong defenses that work on automatic and have lasting effects. The fact it was able to hang on that long says it was very nasty and strong."

"Lovely. Now what?"

"If you can help me, I'd certainly like it. Otherwise I'm looking at a week or so on your couch eating chicken soup to build myself back up."

"You're good company, but I don't think I want you around quite that much." I touched the side of his face. He smiled at me.

"How do I do this without tripping your defenses?"

"There's a hard way and an easy way."

"Let's go for the easy way tonight. I'm still feeling pretty shaky from the first run."

"Take my necklaces and rings off."

"I can do that." The rings slid off his slender fingers with minimal coaxing. It took me a moment to get the necklaces off. Trying to get the latches toward me, and undone, took more dexterity than my shaky hands could muster easily.

For a moment, as I removed the silver capped bit of moonstone, he looked different. His colors changed, his hair was flatter, less silky, a less intense dark red, his skin went from chalky to sallow, and his features became less perfectly symmetric. His eyes were closed, but I had the feeling they would also be less dramatic. I put the necklace on the floor next to me. When I looked back up at him, he was his usual self again.

The seven pointed star came off. I was enchanted with his vulnerability and the immense intimacy of this moment. Had he ever been this naked in front of anyone else? Of course he must have. But recently?

Lastly I removed the hemp string of bone beads. It was difficult to untie, and I wanted to cut the string to speed things up, but that would destroy it.

I joined him on the sofa again, laying his head in my lap. This time, I touched his temples tentatively but only felt a little cold. He sighed as I began to refill him with energy. I remembered from the spell on my house that I'd be exhausted long before I finished with him if I just used my own power for this. So the prayer began. No real words this time. Just will and intention. The Lord knew what I was trying to do, and He was kind enough to aid me in that endeavor. The color slowly crept back into Chris' features. He warmed up. Eventually he felt done, and I was perfectly content, warm and right. I knew with absolute certainty: this is what I was meant to do, and how I was meant to do it.

He lay in my lap. Awake? Asleep? His eyes were closed. He was breathing softly and evenly. He looked peaceful. Beyond that it didn't matter. My head fell back, and we rested on the couch. I stroked his hair, enjoying the smooth wavy feel of it. Eventually my hand drifted to his throat; his pulse thrummed strong and regular under my fingers. I felt an overwhelming desire to continue stroking his skin, trace his collar bone, or caress his ear. Touching him was my right; his body was mine.

That possessive feeling jerked me out of my comfort zone. I had no right to his body and no desire to overstep my place. I looked down at him. His eyes met mine.

"Feeling better?" I said with a bold smile. The best way to deal with an uncomfortable situation is to bluff your way out of it. So I did.

"Yes. You really are good at this."

"Of course I am," I said with a wink. "Just don't forget to tell Chuck. He sees your old healer when he looks at me. I sent him away before working on you."

Chris sat up slowly, looking like he expected to be dizzy but wasn't. "She would have done that, too. They didn't get along. He loathed the fact I had another person I trusted implicitly. She thought he was a bad influence on me. Not a fun thing when your wife and brother don't get along."

"I'm sorry."

"I was, too, but it's a moot point. He's here. She's not. Where are my things?"

I bent down to the floor and gathered them, holding the necklaces by their chains. "So, what's the hard way?"

"You figure out what each one does. Learn how not to trip it."

"Do you mind letting me figure out how to do that before you actually need me to put you back together in the middle of a fight?" I asked as he layered on his protections.

"No. Not tonight, though. It's pretty late."

I looked at the clock; three hours had passed. "Yeah, Chuck's probably about to chew nails. He's waiting for you at Writers'."

He gave me a weary smile. "He and Autumn will be worrying. My two mother hens."

"Go home. Let them see you're all right."

Chris supposed one of the good things about magic was that he and Chuck could have an absolute flaming argument without letting anyone else hear it. Chuck was well into hour two of yelling at him for being so horrendously stupid when he started to laugh.

That brought Chuck up short. *What?*

You really think yelling at me about how I could have gotten killed is really the best way to encourage me not to do it again?

Chuck thought for a minute, then spent another minute feeling Chris' emotions. *Fuck.* This was a new version of Chris' self-destructive tendencies, a more active, less morose version.

Yeah, now probably isn't the best time to yell at me about how I almost got killed. That was part of the point.

I'd miss you. She'd miss you.

Chris switched to speaking out loud. He didn't like having conversations in his head if he could avoid it. "That's a better tactic."

"It's more than a tactic. I would miss you."

"But would *I* miss me? You know what the highlight of my week has been?"

"I know. I can feel you enjoying it still. Say it anyway, I know you want to."

"Two of them really. I absolutely destroyed one of the things at the junior high. I absolutely unmade the fucker, tore its magic to shreds and scattered the ashes. The other was lying in the lap of a woman who doesn't love me, who I can't have, and feeling her stroke my neck and twine her fingers in my hair. Destruction and lust: those are my shining moments. I am better off dead at this point. But I'm not going to let it get that far. If I do, it means I don't get to spend more time with her, torturing myself with not only what I can't have but can't even allow myself to think about."

Chuck sat down next to Chris and wrapped his arm around him. When he spoke this time it was in their old tongue, words he wouldn't be willing to say in English, "Let me help you, Cell. I hate seeing you like this."

"I deserve this, Anthur," Chris answered in the same language.

Chuck sighed. "Then let me help you sleep. I know you're tired."

"I'd like to sleep." Chuck held his brother and let the magic flow. He eased Chris down onto the bed and tucked him in. For a long time Chuck sat next to Chris. Three times he almost put his hand to Chris' temple to take the guilt away. Three times he pulled his hand back. Chris was right: he wouldn't be Chris unless he somehow managed to get past it himself. Chuck stroked Chris' hair, concentrating on him having good dreams, dreams from their childhood before anything shaded with guilt or pain had touched them.

24.

When I got home from class Chris was sitting on my couch, looking significantly perkier than he had been the night before.

"You're looking good today."

"I slept well last night. Good dreams."

"I'm glad to hear it."

"Want to learn how my defenses work?"

"Yes."

He patted the sofa next to where he was sitting, and I joined him. "Tell me about them," I said.

He shook his head. "You tell me about them."

"How do you suggest I do that?"

"However you think it'll work. I'll keep them reined in enough so you don't end up puking on the floor."

"Well…" I sat there and looked at him. "Come over here." He scooted to my side of the couch, his leg an inch from mine. I swallowed and gently pulled his necklaces out from under his shirt. The hemp cord with the bone beads seemed like a good place to start. For a moment I let my fingers hover over it, purposely not touching it. It felt like Dave. Then I touched the beads. If I didn't pay attention, I'd think it was Dave's neck I was touching.

"It feels like Dave."

"Good, he made it for me. What does it do?"

"Knowing Dave it makes you hard to see, but I don't feel that. I'm just reasoning it out based on what Dave does."

"You're right about what it does in general. Now, try to feel exactly what it does. It has a specific purpose."

"Can you sit on the floor in front of the sofa? This position isn't working for me." He complied with me, looking amused. I moved so he was seated in front of me on the floor between my legs. Now I could touch the necklaces easily.

"You pay more attention to your position than anyone else I know."

"You're a foot taller than I am. This is hard enough without having to reach up to your neck. Down here it's easy to get to." Touching the necklace was still a little awkward. I wormed my fingers under the cord, placing the fingers from my other hand over the beads. "I'm not choking you, am I?"

"It's not that tight."

"Good." *What does it do?* I spent a few minutes willing my fingers to come up with the answer. The answer didn't come.

He turned to look at me and smiled. "Relax, Sarah, let it come to you. Stop trying to force it and just feel. It'll tell you if you let it."

"Great. Relaxing isn't exactly my thing."

"It's time to make it your thing. Just let it come to you. It will."

I took a deep breath and let out a long sigh. Quieting my mind was harder than focusing it. I'd start to get a feel for the magic, my attention would snap to it, and that would force it away again. It would almost whisper to me, then dance away when I asked it to speak up. Six times it happened. Six times my brain hopped on it like a trout after a bug, and each and every time it eluded me. Seventh time was a charm. I could feel the glimpse of it start to build; I kept my brain soft and relaxed. It was one of the hardest things I had ever done, like keeping something you desperately want to see in your peripheral vision. It paid off. The magic moved to center stage. I knew exactly what it did, and how it did it. The necklace kept the other defensive spells hidden. Most of the beads attracted attention to themselves, but some of them were linked to the other defensive talismans. It made them dim and quiet.

"It's a cloaking spell. It attracts attention to itself and keeps your other protections hidden."

"Good. What does that mean healing-wise?"

"I can ignore it. It's not going to bite me."

"Exactly. What next?"

"Your star. That's what it's working hardest to hide." I slid my fingers out from under Dave's necklace to the leather cord with his star. It rested about heart level on Chris. I lifted it off of his chest, trying not to be too touchy as I picked it up.

"I really don't like touching this." I felt queasy and panicky; it made me want to drop it and run away.

"No one does."

Keeping my mind soft was easier this time even though the sensations of nausea, suffocation, and fear were distracting. A very familiar headache began low in my head.

"This is mostly yours, with some Chuck, too."

"Exactly right. What does it do?"

"This one bit me last time." I let it drop back to his chest. "When you're in trouble it calls Chuck and makes whoever is causing the trouble want to get away as fast as possible."

He gave me that familiar half-smile. "It does more than that."

"Yeah, I get that feeling." Another sigh. I really didn't want to touch it again. I also couldn't think of a way to get around it without finishing figuring out what it did. Gritting my teeth, I inched the cord into my hand until the star rested in my palm. Something in my mind said look, so I did. I could see the energy moving along the line of his star. My mouth started to move before I really knew what I was saying. "It pulls you into it… through the points. You get mixed up and lost in the corners. Next thing you know it's vamped you." I blinked, feeling startled. It almost felt like someone had talked through me.

Chris also looked somewhat surprised at how I had said that. "Yes. The trick to getting around it is to not get pulled into it. It won't hurt me if I end up vamping you. It will hurt you."

"Here, let me try something." I rested my fingers against his temples again, and gave him a few gentle pulses of energy. This time I could feel the points and avoid them. As long as my energy didn't touch them, I could work with him without getting vamped.

"That was nice."

"You might as well get a little lift in the middle of the day."

"I'm guessing you figured out how to avoid it."

"I think I did. This begs the question: the thing that got you yesterday, did you vamp it or did it avoid this spell?"

"No, it tripped it. That's how Chuck got called. It was nasty. I pulled some of its energy into me, and that's what made me ill."

"Ah…lovely. Onto the moonstone?"

"Sure. Most people don't know what it is."

"How many people get to see your necklaces?"

"Good point. Autumn thought it was some sort of opal. Brooke didn't have a clue. Chuck thinks it's kind of dumb to begin with, but he thought it was milk quartz when I first showed it to him."

"I've got a ring with a little face carved into a moonstone gem. The face of the man in the moon."

"Cute."

"I thought so. My aunt gave it to me when I turned eighteen."

I lifted the silver capped moonstone gem into my palm. At first I felt happy, enjoying Chris' company. He's fun to have around. Then I became very, very aware of his physical presence. His scent, the warmth of his skin, his shoulders pressed against my legs. The longer I held it the more distracted by him I became. I couldn't focus on the gem, let alone something nebulous like magic. The curl of his hair and the curve of his ear pulled my mind away from his defenses. He became more beautiful by the second. I wanted to drop the gem and touch him, stoke his face, twine my fingers in his hair, lick the line of his collar bone, slide my hands under his shirt, and stroke his chest. I wanted him naked, in my arms, in my body. Then his eyes met mine.

He was blushing. He gently took the gem out of my hand; his fingers brushed mine. For that second when his hand was on mine, I felt like there was nothing I wouldn't do to touch him. He was my man, and it was high time I had him.

Then he was holding the gem in his own hand. My mind started to clear. I was sure I was blushing, too.

"No one's ever held it that long," he told me. His voice was huskier than usual. I had the distinct impression he knew exactly what I had been thinking and liked it as well.

"Urgh," I said or something similarly elegant.

He was still blushing prettily and looking me in the eye very carefully. I knew he was keeping up eye contact because he didn't trust himself to look anywhere else and didn't want me looking elsewhere. "It makes people like me. It keeps me safe by making sure no one wants to attack me." I suppose that was one way to put it. Although, if I had held it any longer, I was fairly sure I would have tackled him, pinned him to the floor, and—I was leaning toward him. Now seemed like a really good time to get a drink.

I stood up, which posed its own interesting challenge because he was still sitting between my legs. Delicious images of naked Chris danced in my head while I gulped the first glass of water. Cool water helped. Space between us helped. I downed a second glass of water and went to the bathroom to buy myself more time. I'd heard of guys using really unappealing images to turn themselves off. It was worth a shot. Images of the Watchers worked just fine for that purpose. Five minutes later I returned to Chris and sat cross-legged in front of him. I did not need him sitting between my legs right now. Fortunately the rest of his defenses were rings, so that position worked nicely.

There were two rings on his right hand, a high school class ring and a thin Celtic knot in gold. I let my hand hover over his, careful not to touch. By now letting my mind go soft and just receive the information was almost, well, not simple, but routine. The class ring was the easier of the two to read. It didn't feel like it did much. Just an energy sink. Like having a back up battery.

"Extra energy?"

"Never know when you'll need an emergency boost."

"Did you use it last night?"

"No. It attacked too quickly. I was unconscious before I had the chance to use it."

"Wonderful. Let's see what this one does." My focus shifted to the Celtic knot. It was all his magic and covered him all over. Finally it hit me. It was his personal shield.

"I feel silly for not recognizing this one faster. It's your shield."

"Yes it is. It's not very active unless something gets tossed at it; then you'll really see it."

I shifted my attention to his left hand. I briefly touched the plain silver band he wore on his wedding ring finger, but I didn't feel anything that made me think it was magic of any sort. It was warm to the touch. "If it's magical it's too subtle for me to pick up."

"It's only magic in the same way any symbol is magic. It's a wedding ring. Women see it, and they stay away. It's a constant reminder to Autumn and Brooke to keep their distance."

"Oh." After the experience with the moonstone, not mentioning my name was a kindness. Though, while I held the stone, his wife could have been sitting next to us and I wouldn't have cared.

"It's easy for Autumn to think I should be free. Brooke doesn't know the real story. She's under the impression I had a girl I loved dearly and deeply who died on me."

"Which is more or less true."

His look was tinged with dark bitterness. "More or less."

I decided to change the subject. "So, wedding rings: did you do them before?"

"No. We, men, wore clan markings: a tattoo extending from the tip of the left middle finger to the shoulder. The body of the tattoo was the same for each member of the clan, but the individual details were different to each man. When we married, the woman would take his mark. Kind of like taking his last name."

"What did yours look like?"

"It looked like a Celtic knot done in ivy vines. The vines were black, the outline of the leaves green, the hearts of the leaves red. Here..." He unbuttoned his shirt and slid it off. Then he rolled up the left sleeve of his t-shirt to show me his tattoo. My eyes lingered too long on his arm, stroking the curves of his bicep and deltoid. "This isn't exactly right, but it's close. I didn't want to redo the whole thing, but I wanted something like it. A reminder of who I used to be."

"I think I have an image." A very clear picture of loops and swirls of black that crossed and intersected itself, each line terminating in a kind of leaf shape with a red heart with a green outline, formed in my mind.

"It looped around your wrist," I said, knowing it was right and having no clue how I knew.

He looked sharply at me. "Yes, it did." He didn't ask me how I knew, but I felt his curiosity.

"I don't know. I think you were seeing it in your mind, loudly. The image of the tattoo looping around a wrist popped into my mind. Kind of like how I know you want to know how I know about it." I couldn't fully read his look, a blend of hopeful skepticism, maybe? "So, does it work?"

"Yes, it does remind me of home."

"No, I meant the wedding ring. Does it keep the ladies at bay?"

"Somewhat. On the upside, I see women check my hand, see the ring, and change course. That usually happens when I'm out with Chuck. On the downside, Autumn and Brooke think it's the most romantic thing in the history of the universe."

"Ah. Kind of dumb, really." He looked slightly hurt. I felt bad about being that blunt. Unfortunately he didn't just drop it there.

"You don't think it's romantic?" He looked expectantly at me. I was feeling worse by the second that it really didn't strike me as romantic.

"No, well, the version of the story Brooke's got is romantic. The version of the story Autumn has says 'I'm a doormat' in huge glowing neon letters."

He looked insulted. "Go on."

"She betrayed you, left you, and just about got all of you killed. If that doesn't sever your marriage vows, what will?"

He sighed. "That's Autumn's version all right. It wasn't like that. If it had worked the way I thought it was going to, I would have seen her again in five days. But it didn't work.

"She thought what we were doing would end very badly, so she tried to stop us. When I wouldn't stop, she left us. She was the kind of woman who would walk away from... from what and whom she loved if she thought they were doing the wrong thing. She thought what she was doing was for the greater good."

"I hate that term. People tell you it's for the greater good when what they mean is they don't care how many bodies end up buried because of what they did."

"It really wasn't like that. She was trying to save lives."'

"Was she right?" He looked very... I was having an especially hard time putting my finger on his emotions.

"I think it was a self-fulfilling prophecy. She had farseeing. Which is good but not perfect. She could see the problems arising, and she didn't want to be part of what caused them, so she left. Her leaving set up the situation where we ended up having to flee, instead of stopping it from happening."

"She could see you banished and didn't want that to happen, so she tried to get you to stop. When you wouldn't, she left thus resulting in your banishment?"

"In a nutshell." He looked horrendously uncomfortable with that answer.

"And you still love her?"

He looked intensely at me. I could feel it. He loved her. He had always loved her and would always love her. His love was threaded through with exquisite pain and shaded with guilt. Before I could stop myself, I was stroking his hand, trying to comfort him. Then his eyes met mine, looking for something, but I didn't know what. The moment passed, and he recomposed himself.

Finally, he smiled again. "Still think I'm a doormat?"

"No. That is kind of romantic."

"Hmmm... Maybe I was better off with you thinking I was a doormat?"

"Why? Because now I know you're the most tragically romantic soul in the entire universe, I'll start mooning over you? Fat chance." I let go of his hand, realizing my hold on it was illustrating exactly how little truth there was to my words.

"Just making sure."

"Is there any chance of you two ever seeing each other again?"

"No."

"Oh. I was kind of hoping for a happier ending. Like she'd come here and join you or you'd get back to her."

"Not in this lifetime."

"Wait. You aren't dead?"

He smiled. "My low body temperature and remarkably pale skin aside, no I'm not dead."

"That's not what I meant. You back there. That you isn't dead?"

"No, I'm not dead. Our bodies are long gone, but I'm not dead."

"I'm not seeing how that works."

"No break. My life is one continuous line. Granted, when I started over again as a baby was strange, but I was always an adult playing a child. Past life people I've read about were genuine children who just had memories or dreams of times when they were something and someone else. Not even that sometimes, many of the past-lifers had no idea until something triggered the memory. Until that point, they're just like everyone else. We were never just like everyone else."

"So, what happens if something kills the body you're in now?"

"I imagine we'd die. I'm not terribly interested in finding out. But I hope that's how it works."

"Then why didn't you die when your old bodies vanished?"

"I don't know this for a fact, but my guess is since we lost our bodies somewhere between home and here, they ceased being important to our existence."

"So, you're stuck in your body now?"

"I think so."

"Hmmm... So why come here? Wouldn't a place where your body came along have been a better choice?"

"Autumn picked here. Our old world and this one don't really work the same way. If we had gone somewhere our bodies would have come with us, that would have also been true about what was chasing us. Autumn figured this would give us a better chance of laying low and healing up before we had to deal with them."

"That's smart. How did Autumn know about here?"

"The fey hung on the longest here, but they left about five hundred years ago."

"Why?"

"In Christian lands the Catholics won the battle. Slowly, one by one, people like us got picked off. Autumn can tell you one requirement of any treaty with the Catholics was the removal of every member of the species from this plane of existence. She should know. She's one of the signatories on said treaty.

"The fey folk had been here longest, in the largest number, but finally they decided it wasn't worth it anymore. Humans weren't that interesting to them. Rather than have their hostages killed, they left."

I thought about all the fairy stories, fantastic creatures, and legends of old. "Once upon a time, they were all real?"

"Once upon a time dragons roamed the land, fairies danced among the flowers, brownies kept house, and goblins hid in caves. But once upon a time is no more." He sat quietly for a moment. "That's not necessarily true. There are probably some holdouts. Some subspecies that were never prevalent enough to attract notice. For the most part, it's just you humans here now."

"'You humans…' You're one of us now."

He smiled wryly but didn't say anything. I got the feeling he was thinking that he was as much a human as a person wearing a bear coat was a bear, but he didn't want to insult me by actually saying it.

"Is turn about fair play?"

"Huh?"

"Can I see your star?"

"Sure." He scooted up onto the couch and leaned down to pat the floor where he had been sitting. I sat between his legs, pulled my star out from under my shirt, and handed it to him. Resting my back against his left knee, I half-turned so I could watch him work. I did a very good job of keeping my hands to myself and felt pretty happy about it because I really wanted to start petting his thigh. He wasn't looking at me. His posture was relaxed: his eyes were closed, my star on his palm, his middle finger resting lightly against it.

"So, what does it tell you?" His arm lay on my shoulder. I fought the desire to rest my head against it.

He didn't open his eyes when he answered. "It's old. That's usually hard to tell with jewelry because the metal is old, but I have the sense of many hands holding this. It's been in your family at least four generations."

"Close, my grandfather, father, brother, and now me. Not quite four but close. What else do you feel about it?"

"I don't think it's magic so much as just a holder of hopes and prayers. I know your brother held it and prayed. I feel that very strongly." It looked like he was trying to listen hard to catch a faint whisper. "Did your brother go to school here?"

"Yeah, class of '89."

"He was here when you were born?"

"Yeah."

"I feel him very strongly on your star. He looks like you, right?"

"I guess."

"I've got an image of a dark-haired guy about our age holding this and praying while another man, one I should know, is pacing around and smoking…" His voice trailed off. "Fuck! You have to call your brother."

"Why?"

"The brown-haired one, he's the first person I saw when I got here. He was leaning over me, talking, and… and he's so familiar… I know him. He's still here somewhere, and I can't lay my mind on him."

"You want me to ask Ben who the brown-haired chain smoker was when he was holding the star and praying?"

"Yes."

"Just in case there's more than one, can you give me something more specific than that?"

"Yes." He leaned toward me, pulled off his glasses, and set them on the floor. He placed his fingers on my temples and looked directly into my eyes. I knew exactly what the brown-haired man looked like because I could see him in my own head.

I pulled back blinking and shivering. "Got it?"

"Yeah. I do. I didn't know you could do that."

"I usually can't."

"Oh." I pulled my cell out of my pocket and saw what time it was. "Look, he's never in this time of day. Can you wait until tonight to find out?"

"Yes. I've got to go find Chuck. Show him the image. He might remember him and have a better clue as to who he is now."

"Okay. I'll come over after I talk to Ben."

"Good. See you tonight." Chris was halfway out my door as he said that.

25.

Chris found Chuck half an hour later. He started talking, and Chuck listened very intently. He showed Chuck the image of the men, and Chuck had the same reaction. The brown-haired one was shockingly familiar, but he couldn't place him.

"Why were you holding her star anyway?" Chuck asked as the conversation wound down.

Chris told him. As he talked, Chuck looked more and more annoyed. He stopped Chris and said, "Are you trying to get me to take those memories away? Seriously, the more you act like this the more tempted I am to just knock you unconscious and let you wake up believing the lie. If I did it and told Dave and Autumn, they'd back me in a heartbeat."

"There's a good tactical reason for it. She won't get hurt trying to help me now."

"It would be if we ever let her come along for a battle. Since we don't, it isn't. She does not need to know how your defenses work. No one needs to know. *I don't need to know.* I know you're in an 'I don't give a shit about my own safety' mindset this week, but if you go down, that seriously damages the chances of the rest of us coming out of this alive. Unlike you, I want to see my next birthday."

"She won't hurt me."

Chuck smacked him upside the back of the head and sent him a look of such withering disdain it could have turned a steak into jerky. "Tell me what Mildred does."

Chris nodded at him. "I know."

"Then stop acting like an idiot."

Chris was quiet for a minute, then started talking about the real reason he let her do it. "Last night, after she took all of my necklaces and rings off, I felt her enjoy the intimacy of it. She liked having me naked in her home. When she asked me to learn how to get around the defenses before she needed to know, I said yes. I wanted the chance to enjoy it, too."

"That could possibly be the lamest substitute for sex I've ever heard of."

Chris didn't bother to bury his annoyance at Chuck's very limited, mechanical view of sex. "You would think that, wouldn't you?"

"Yes. I'm sure you found it just as satisfying as a good afternoon in bed."

"No, but it's the closest I'm going to get in the foreseeable future, so I might as well enjoy it."

"It doesn't have to be." Chuck paused. Something about those words triggered an emotionally dense memory for Chris. Then he felt it and saw the image that went with it. "You let her hold the moonstone? You really want another version of Brooke on your hands? A version you actually like? This is your grand plan for more pain, isn't it? She'll be throwing herself at you. You'll keep saying no, tormenting yourself with her willing and eager two doors down and just outside of your reach."

That held enough truth to make Chris uncomfortable and defensive. "She was learning what my talismans do. What was I going to say, 'You survived the star, but this one you can't touch?'"

"That would have worked. She would have asked why. You would have told her what it does. Then you could have pointed out the absolute debacle that's been your life with Brooke since the day she touched the damn thing."

"Brooke was bad before she touched it. She wouldn't have reached for it if she had any sense when it comes to boundaries."

"I still can't believe you even made that thing, let alone let her touch it." Chuck shook his head.

"I was thirteen and getting beaten up at school every week for being the weird redhead. I prefer not getting into fights in the first place. It's good at that. It's not like it puts something that isn't there in your head, it just makes what's already there stronger. She liked me before, now she just…"

"Wants you as badly as you want her."

"Probably not."

"Probably not. But she's got absolutely no reason not to act on it."

"Ari."

"On the other side of the world and out of contact for almost another year. Can you break it?"

"I don't know. I haven't tried on Brooke. I'd probably need to touch her to do it, and I don't trust her long enough to do it."

"Find a way to break it. Unless you intend to sleep with her, leaving that magic in her system is cruel."

Chris blew air from between his lips, frustrated Chuck was the one telling him the right way to behave and more frustrated that he was right. "I'll find a way."

"Good. Now come on. We're going to her house, and we're sticking around to listen to her talk to her brother."

Halfway through dinner, I heard two sets of footsteps on my stairs. Chris and Chuck. I opened the door before they could knock.

"So?" Chris asked.

"Haven't called yet. Dinner should be done a bit after seven. I'll call then. How do you suggest I do this? 'Hey, Ben, so… ummm… I've got this friend, and he was holding the star you gave me, and when he did, he got the image of you and a guy with brown hair and a beard chain smoking and pacing around. Anyway, he feels like he should know who the guy is, and I was wondering if you could tell me for him?'"

"That's better than anything I'd come up with," Chris said while looking at the clock to see how much longer they had to wait. It was 6:15.

"Look, how about you two go get dinner? Come back after, I'll set the phone on speaker, and you can talk to him, too." They nodded and headed off. At 6:55 they were back again.

I dialed quickly, then placed my phone on the kitchen table.

Anna, my brother Sam's wife, answered. "Hello." The sound of a large family finishing up dinner made her sound indistinct.

"Hey, Anna. Is Ben around?"

"Sure. I'll get him."

A minute later Ben asked, "Sarah?"

"Hi. Do you have time to talk?"

"Sure. What's going on?" I could hear him moving away from the rest of them. The sounds of the kids got quieter in the background.

I took a deep breath. "I've got a weird question for you. My friend Chris," I waved at Chris. He looked alarmed, then said, "Hi."

"Hello, Chris."

"Anyway, he was holding the star you gave me and saw the image of you and another man. He had brown hair, a beard, and was chain smoking. Chris feels like he should know who the smoker is. He asked me to ask you."

Ben said nothing. We sat there and waited for a few more seconds. Finally I said, "I know it's a weird question. You still there."

"Yes. I'm turning on the computer. I don't want any of the others to overhear this. I can see you on chat. We can do it like that."

"Okay." Ben hung up. I went to my computer and took it to the sofa. Chris sat on my right and Chuck on my left.

You there? Flashed onto my chat box.

Yeah. So, who's the smoker?

I don't know.

Then why the cloak and dagger?

Because he erased himself from my mind with my blessing. That part I remember. There were six of us. Three of us vanished. One of them was very dear to me. By the end of it, I asked them to make the memories go away.

What happened?

Two people were hurt. Not two of us. Two other people. We were the best chance of stopping anyone else from getting hurt. We had to stop it because they were hurt bad enough I couldn't fix it.

Why would you fix it?

Because that's what I do. Mostly. That I remember. That's how I met the one with the brown hair. Helping him with his asthma though the smoking made sure my fix never lasted long. He was friends with the one... Ben stopped typing. I waited.

The one?

The one who was dear to me. That's how I met her, through him.

Oh. How were you going to stop it?

I don't know.

"Where?" asked Chris.

Where? I typed.

I don't know. Woods. There were trees and moonlight. Steep walls of rock and dirt rising around us with trees growing out of them. The light was wrong. It was too dark.

On campus?

I don't know.

"When?" Chuck asked.

When? I typed.

The year you were born. Springtime.

"Eighty-seven," I said to the guys.

"We were gone by spring," Chuck said. "Ask when it began."

When did it start?

Fall. The leaves were orange. September? October?

"That's when we got here," Chris said. He gestured for me to hand him the computer, and I did.

You were holding the star, praying intensely for protection. Your friend was trying to set the record for most cigarettes smoked in the least time. What was happening?

Sarah? Ben replied.

Chris

Why were you holding her star?

Because she had just finished with my talismans, and I wanted to see hers.

You let her see yours?

Chris' fingers hovered over the keyboard, like he was thinking of what to answer. She's our healer. It seemed like a good idea for her to know how they worked.

I could feel Ben wasn't buying that. Chuck also looked very doubtful as well.

Who's the third one with you two?

How do you know there are three of us?

I am letting you know formally that just because I don't remember that year does not mean I've given it up or I'm not very good at it.

Chris smiled. I wasn't sure if he knew he was doing it. Message received. The third one is my brother. What was I watching you two do?

We were waiting for something. And, no. I don't know what. But it was important, and the fact it was only the two of us was odd. There were usually others with us.

What else do you remember about the brown-haired guy?

I liked him. We were friends. Something really bad happened to his... Ben stopped typing. I could feel he was thinking about it, trying to remember. Sister? Girlfriend? Friend? It was a girl, and she was close to him. I don't think I knew her well, though.

Ben stopped writing again. I could feel him thinking about the brown-haired one. Right before they took my memories, we built something. Something made of clay, and the dirt mixed in the clay was from the place where it happened. I remember kneading clay with dirt and slapping it on a wooden skeleton. We used a lot of magic to hide something. And the thing made of clay was its anchor. Then we went back to my house, he and the blonde one did something, and my memories of that year have been fuzzy at best since.

Where did you live? Chris typed.

"Why are you asking?" I asked Chris.

"Because maybe the brown-haired one was a roommate or something."

"Oh. That makes sense."

1236 Alden Street.

The three of us stared at each other. That was the Writers' House. "Was it the Writers' House then?" I asked them.

"No idea. But we can find out," Chris answered. What room? Chris typed.

Upstairs, next to the bathroom, why?

I live there now. In the room across the hall from the one that used to be yours. Was it The Writers' House then?

I don't think so. I'm not a writer. I doubt I was then.

What else can you tell us about that year?

Nothing useful.

How do you know it won't be useful?

Because the classes I took, time spent with my lover before she vanished, and talking about Regan isn't going to tell you what you need to know.

How about anything else on the brown-haired guy? What kind of magic did he do?

I don't know. Whatever it was, he was there with me, instead of off with the others. I think that must have been the night they vanished, but... I know the image you saw. I dream about it sometimes. He grinds out his cigarette, I stand up and go to the door, and it ends in black. We built the clay thing after that. Then I was home, and even with almost no memories of that year, heartbroken. What's your brother's name?

Chuck.

Chuck, back off. I don't want those memories back, and unless it's literally my sister's life on the line, you don't get to have them, either. Got it?

Chuck looked stunned. I hadn't even noticed he was trying to work any magic, but apparently he was trying to get into Ben's head. Chuck nodded.

He's got it. This isn't a life or death matter. Not yet. The school keeps copies of the yearbooks in the library, and that's our next step.

Then go to the library. I want to talk to her alone.

We will go.

Chris handed me the computer. He and Chuck put their coats on and headed off.

I'm alone.

I remember telling you to be careful.

I'm being careful. They're being careful. They don't ever let me get near anything dangerous because they don't want to risk their healer.

At least one of them is a pro then.

All of them are.

Why didn't you say anything earlier?

Why didn't you? Like, when you saw this school on my short list?

Because the best I could do for you was a vague warning. And that I did.

Until he was holding the star telling me you had held it and prayed, I didn't think there was any reason to tell you.

So, really, why was he letting you touch his talismans?

So I could figure out what they do and not get attacked by them when I'm putting him back together.

He let you study all of his defenses?

Yes.

Wow.

???

All of them?

Yeah.

No wonder his brother is pissed. That wasn't a helpful answer at all. I decided to deal with something else I was wondering about.

How can you even feel that from home?

They were sitting next to you, and I made your talisman. I've got a pretty good feel for what you're doing, who is near you, and what they're up to.

Oh. That was a bucket of ice water down my back. Having my older brother following me around was not my favorite idea. How good of an idea?

I don't snoop.

Keep it that way, or this goes in a drawer, and I get another one.

I keep myself to myself.

Good. So, once again, why is him letting me see his talismans a big deal?

It wouldn't be if you were very close friends, or lovers, or something. It's just not the sort of thing you let someone you're just fond of do. Like looking through his underwear drawer or reading his diary.

Oh.

So...

I knew what he was asking. We're just friends.

Sure... It was kind of amazing how intensely I could feel Ben not believing me. We spent the next hour talking about magic in general, what he could do, what I was doing, and bits and pieces from his last two years of school here. I told him about the great magic saga that was their lives, but it didn't trigger any new memories for him. Finally we broke off, and I went back to my homework.

After an hour, I got a text from Chris. Copies of Sylvianna's Yearbook 1987, 1988, and 1990 do not have a picture of the brown haired man in it. They didn't make a yearbook in 1989.

Great.

We're looking through team photos, old student newspapers, etc...

Want me to check Facebook?

Sure.

I got online and looked. Twenty minutes of searching showed me there were only seventy-eight people listed as Sylvianna Class of '89. It took me half an hour to look through, select everyone who might have been the brown-haired boy twenty years ago, and send the list to Chris. I texted him to let him know I didn't feel like anyone I found was the guy. Chris sent me a last text around midnight. They were giving up. The brown-haired boy didn't turn up in any of their searches.

26.

I asked Autumn if I could use their tub sometime when no one was home. She told me they all had class on Thursday morning, and if I felt like it I could come over. All I needed to do was let her know which day, and she'd leave the back door open for me. I told her I'd be over as soon as possible.

It felt strange to be in another person's home with no one there. I knew Pat was used to doing it, but this was the first time I had been in a home without my host around. The desire to snoop around Chris' room pulled me up the stairs. I'd been thinking about him almost nonstop since what I was now thinking of as the moonstone incident, but my better angels got a hold of me and took me straight to the bathroom.

Two hours before anyone was due home. Two glorious hours where I could lounge in the tub, suck up hot water, and just relax. Two hours to lay in the same bath he used, be naked in the same room, and... *Stop it! Hello? Remember Ari?* That helped pull my mind back to where it belonged, for a little while at least.

I turned on the water and drizzled some of my shower gel into it. Bubbles foamed richly in the water. Cocoa seemed like a good idea. I got to the door of the bathroom, then decided to wrap up in my towel. Just in case. *Although... if Chris were to come home early.... Really, stop that. What the fuck is wrong with you?*

Downstairs in the kitchen I found a mug and a packet of cocoa. I was walking with the full cup from the sink to the microwave when Chris bounded up the stairs and burst into the room. I jumped, dropped the mug, and let out a high-pitched, girly shriek. Sure I had been thinking about it, but I didn't expect it to happen. The only redeeming thing about this huge embarrassment was Chris looked equally horrified when he saw me.

"What are you doing here?" He was out of breath and visibly pulling himself out of fight mode.

"Getting a bath. Autumn said I could use your tub. What are you doing here?"

"Having a heart attack."

I wrapped the towel tighter, thanking the Lord I was wearing it, and grabbed a paper towel to wipe up the water. "That's not a helpful answer to me. You look ready to fight."

"Wards." He was still breathing fast. "I've got wards on the house. Anyone enters when no one is supposed to be here, they go off, and I come ready to fight."

"Is Chuck coming, too?"

"Probably not, but Pat and Mike will be here in a minute."

"Great. Does Autumn know about these wards?"

"I thought she did. I've certainly mentioned them, and she should be able to feel them. But this might also be her idea of a practical joke." He went quiet, calmed his breathing, and closed his eyes. I could see and feel him working some sort of magic, but I didn't know what. When he finished his spell, I looked at him quizzically. "I just let them know it was a false alarm."

"Oh. Is it a good idea for you to come running to a battle against an unknown foe all by yourself?"

"Probably not. But, if it's in my home, I'm going to go after it."

"I'll remember that. So, do you mind if I go get a bath?"

"No. What were you heating water for?"

"Cocoa."

"How about you head up and turn off the water before it starts spilling out of the tub, and I'll make you a cup?"

"I forgot about that," I said while scooting back toward the bathroom as fast as I could go. The bubbles were already above the rim of the tub when I got up there, the water less than an inch below. I turned off the water and fumbled for the plug to let more of it out. I heard Chris come up the steps.

"Here." He handed it in to me, unwilling to cross the threshold while I was in there. I stood up, made sure the towel was snug, and then took it from him.

"Thanks." I sipped it. "Are you familiar with the concept of serendipity?"

"Yes."

"Good, then you'll see how this applies. I almost didn't wrap up in the towel."

"Well, that would have been interesting."

I chuckled briefly, smiled too brightly, and pushed my breasts together at him in a thoroughly immodest way, which I stopped the second I realized I was doing it. "To say the least."

He turned and walked the four steps to his room. I closed the door and settled into the water.

Chris actually being in the house helped with getting my mind out of the gutter. I wasn't sure how well he could feel my thoughts, but I didn't want him feeling what had been going on in my head lately. Better to think of chaste things, like wards. I'd have to remember to ask him how that worked. I could see some real value in knowing if anyone got too close to my home or bike.

Once upon a time, I'd sink into a tub of hot water, laze about, maybe read, maybe dream about beautiful men. Now I'm thinking magical home defense though beautiful men might be on the menu, too. *Stop it!*

Chris watched her close the door to the bathroom. He retreated into his own room and closed the door. He stood with his back to it. *Fuck!* He still had too much adrenalin pumping through his system from the panicked run home. It heightened everything else.

She had been bending over to pull the plug out of the tub when he got far enough up the steps to see into the bathroom. Her towel hadn't been long enough to cover her. Soft, tawny legs and a luscious, round bottom were burned into his mind.

He felt somewhat proud of himself for staying cool and not jumping her when she mentioned skipping the towel. Cool left the building the second he closed his door. Her skin and how it would feel dominated his thoughts. She was less than twenty feet away: wet, naked, skin dappled with soft, foamy bubbles. All he had to do was knock. She'd let him in. His mind raced to the view of her legs. That position, if she just straightened up a little... The idea of running his tongue from her ankle to the back of her neck and the feel of her pressed against the length of his body, made him bite his lip. He'd kneel behind her, slide into her, his hands on her breasts, her head against his shoulder while she'd gasp and call his name.

He leaned against the door. His hands moved to his fly without conscious thought. He could lie back in the tub, and she'd straddle him, kiss him softly while sliding against him. He spit on his palm and curled his hand around his cock, moving his hand fast and keeping his fingers tight. Out of the tub, up against the outside of the shower, where he could see her in front of him or look to the side and see both of them in the mirror on the back of the bathroom door. He could lean against the sink, clutching onto it to keep his hands from grabbing her head and pulling her against him while she sucked him deep and stroked his balls. That image did it. His head thudded against the door in defeat seconds after his body finished spurting. In all the years since leaving Hidiri he'd never let another woman into his head. Not like that.

He cleaned up slowly, his mind far away from the cold linoleum floor and the tissues in his hand. He couldn't even talk to anyone about it. Chuck would laugh at him, tell him that he should have gone into the bathroom and taken her for real. Pat would have laughed over feeling guilty about a fantasy. None of the others would have any sympathy for the idea that fantasizing about another woman was a kind of adultery.

He dropped the tissues into the trash can and remembered his wedding day. *My one and only as long as I shall live.* He stood there, her hands in his, and said those words, promising her, her family, his family, his king, and his God he would honor her for all the days of his life.

His favorite image of Althiira formed in his mind. It was the morning before the Choice. Before everything fell apart. They had been lying in bed together, enjoying the few minutes between first waking and getting up for the day. She had been resting on her stomach, her head pillowed on her arms, face toward him as they talked about what needed to be done that day.

He held that image in his mind as he went to get the box he kept in the back of his closet. He built the dark, burnished oak cube years ago as a place to hold things he didn't want anyone else to know about. These days it held only one thing: an antique straight razor.

On very bad days he'd play with it. Stroke it against his skin and imagine pain and blood. Once, last year, when he was especially lonely and distraught, he'd spent an hour cutting himself. Today he wanted the pain, wanted the punishment. There had to be something he could do to atone, even if this was only a miniscule drop in the ocean of things he had to atone for. He took off his pants and left sock. Chris grabbed his towel and laid it on the floor under his calf. He held the razor in his hand, pressing the flat of the blade against his skin.

This is insane. He closed the blade and put it back in the box.

Chris leaned against his bed, his shoulders against the side, his head on the mattress, and his hands in fists on his thighs. He wasn't Arthur Dimmesdale; he couldn't own up to his desires, and he couldn't burn them out of his flesh, either.

The image of Althiira re-entered his mind. "I can't do this." Like always she didn't answer him.

Sarah's footsteps sounded on the floor outside his room. *Please don't knock.* Either she felt his wish or knew how to read his shut door. She called, "Goodbye." The sound of the front door closing behind her followed it.

Chris was ready to bite Autumn's head off when she got home from class. He stood, glowering, waiting for her at the door.

She felt his anger and asked, "What?"

"What? I came running home ready to kill something and found Sarah making cocoa and getting ready to have a bath."

"How is that my fault?"

"She told me you said it was fine for her to come over."

"I did. I also texted you this morning to tell you she'd be over. Not my fault you didn't check the message when you saw it was from me." She turned and went into her room, not interested in letting him vent further on her.

Chris searched with Pat that night. They were deep in the woods, far away from anyone else, and finding absolutely nothing of any interested amid the snow-covered trees.

"Fight me," Chris asked, an edge of desperation in his voice.

"You're kidding."

"No. I need to fight something. You're here, and I know you aren't adverse to it."

"I'm not pissed at you enough to beat you into a pulp today."

"I saw Sarah naked."

"Yeah, see, that really doesn't do it."

"I saw her naked, bent her over the side of the bathtub, and fucked her 'till she was crying with joy."

Pat laughed. "Not going to do it. She already told me about your close call today. No crying with joy in her version of the story, and she wasn't precisely naked, either. I am not going to beat you because you've got a hard on for her and you don't know how to deal with it." Before Chris knew he was going to strike, Pat was blocking his punch. Chris landed the second one, and then Pat had Chris' arm twisted around his back, keeping him still by holding his shoulder just on the verge of dislocation. Pat hit him hard, three times, in the ribs.

"You are one sick fuck. Can I let you go, or do I need to start breaking ribs?"

"Let me go." Pat released Chris, and Chris rubbed his shoulder.

"If you want to fight me, you know where I am on Wednesday nights. Then and there. I'll even let you have the first two punches."

"She'll be there."

"Of course. She's always there: in your life, in your sight… beautiful, friendly, fun, and always there. You can run and hide or learn to deal with it. But you don't learn to deal with it by hiding, so come and spend some time with us, and you can at least fight out your frustration then and there."

"How did you handle wanting a woman you couldn't have?"

Pat paused, looking annoyed. "I knew Althiira didn't love me. And I did it knowing it would go on for the rest of my life. You had one hundred and twelve good years. Years most men would kill for. And you want to throw that away for at best a few months with a girl who feels like her? You're so damn horny you can't hold out for another six months? Trust me, if you can't hold out I will go back and make sure your wife knows. She deserves better than you're acting now. She's not back there lusting after someone else."

"I hate this."

"Too bad for you. Learn to deal. Or don't. But keep it in your pants for the next six months. And you don't get to go over to her place to have her fix those bruises. You think I don't know that's why you're picking fights?"

"I want something to punish me."

"It won't be me. Not here; not like this. Come on, let's keep searching. The sooner we find the door, the sooner you can be with the one you really want."

27.

Three nights later Chris stood in the sculpture garden and watched Sarah through her front window. For once, Pat wasn't there. She sat on the window seat reading. After a quarter hour, she stood, stretched, and walked out of his view. A second later the light turned off. He could feel her in her bedroom. His image of her taking her clothing off and sliding into her pajamas led him to wonder about what kind of pajamas she wore. *Flannel pants and tank top.*

He wanted to go up and watch her sleep. If he did wake her when he entered, she'd probably think it was just Pat coming over to crash.

He was in her living room, walking silently to her bedroom door. Chris rested his hand against the knob slowly, making sure to turn it soundlessly. Heart beating too fast, he eased himself to her bedside and watched her sleep. Her chest rose and fell slowly. The cleft of her breasts under the scoop neck of the tank top mesmerized him. Her eyes opened, and she invited him to her bed with her hands.

"You know what actually happens? You creep in there, open her door, and she shoots you in the head. Pat doesn't sneak around in her home." Chuck stepped out from behind one of the statues. "Come on, let's go see if we can find the Vamp that bit you and kill it."

"Sounds good." Chris turned quickly away from Sarah's house.

"Pat tells me you stopped eating." Chris shrugged. He ate, just not much. He hadn't felt hungry in days. "Autumn says you haven't been sleeping at home. I know you haven't been at my place. Are you spending your nights watching her?"

"No." The last two nights he'd gone out looking to fight something. The last two nights he hadn't found anything that had taken him more than a minute to kill. He'd actually been thinking about heading up to the graveyard to see what kind of fight the Dark Man really could put up when it started to get light this morning.

They walked in silence for another ten minutes.

Chris stopped in front of the junior high. "I was here, destroyed one of those things. See how they're hiding now?"

"Yeah. I might have to flush one out for you."

"That'll work. Anyway, I killed it with a huge flashy display of magic, attracted the Vamp, and by the time I had gotten fifty feet it had attacked me."

"How about this? You hide. I'll kill one of them. If those mindless bastards in the school know it's you, the Vamp probably does, too."

"Good point. It probably doesn't want to fight me again." Which might explain why he hadn't seen it over the last two nights. He pulled from Dave's bag of tricks. His invisibility spell wasn't perfect. He was still visible to the human eye, but nothing about him screamed magic anymore. The things in the junior high relaxed and start checking out Chuck.

"Gluttons. How's that for a name for those things? They're so interested in you as a meal they've forgotten I was here two seconds ago."

"You're easy to forget. When you said flashy, were you thinking something like this?" Chuck let off a blast of magic to call one of the Gluttons to him. It was loud, bright, and definitely flashy. Everything in western Pennsylvania knew he was there.

Chris was ready with a snarky comment along the lines of lighting up half the state was probably overkill, but he kept quiet. Chuck was already attacking the Glutton and didn't need distractions. Chris leaned against a tree and watched with professional interest. Chuck was getting better. He'd never be the fighter Chris was, but he was competent. It took a good three minutes for him to kill the Glutton, and by the end of the fight it was just dead. Chris didn't think Chuck actually could unmake something. But destruction was his pet tool; control was Chuck's. Chris knew he'd never be able to make someone do what he wanted the way Chuck could. When it came down to it, mind control was probably handier than ripping the fabric of something to shreds, burning the threads, and scattering the ashes to the wind.

It occurred to him that the Vamp would probably be more interested in Chuck than it was in him. Chuck was much tastier to things that feed on emotion and the powers of the mind. It also occurred to him school in Reevesville was likely to be less painful now. He was halfway through thinking about how to get the third one out of the building to finish it off when he felt the Vamp come.

He watched it carefully, looking for a better way to deal with it. It had an actual physical body. That made him grin. He felt for its anatomy as it circled Chuck, drunk on the power radiating from him. It didn't appear to have a brain or heart; that was annoying. Finesse and finely tuned power wasn't going to do this job. It continued to circle Chuck, waiting until it had finished its appetizer before heading for the main course. Chris tried to feel why it had a body. It didn't seem to need one. Watching it feed answered the question; it became more solid as it ate. That was how it stored its energy.

He couldn't just sit there and watch it feed. It had to be killed before it really attacked Chuck. Chris hoped he'd learn more as he worked. He set a spell for just inside its chest. A small energy sucking vortex. He watched with satisfaction as it became translucent. The Vamp still hadn't noticed him, but it knew something had happened. It rushed Chuck, ravenous, but Chuck stopped it. It had more than enough of a mind for Chuck to be able to control it.

Chris walked toward it. He could feel the magic keeping it together. He knew why it was created and how. Then, with a delicate touch, he pulled it apart. After a minute, a fetid cloud of magical ick hovered where the Vamp used to be. One last pulse of magic cleared the miasma of vaporized Vamp.

"You know, there's someone really powerful and nasty in this town."

"I had come to that conclusion," Chuck replied.

"Maybe that will be next year's job. Go find whoever makes these things."

"How about next year you write your senior thesis, graduate, and get a job?"

"Sure, but what will I do with the rest of my time?"

"Read, watch movies? I don't know, whatever the hell it is normal people do."

"Like I'd ever be 'normal people.'"

"That's up to you. I need to go home and get some sleep. Killing things agrees with you. Let's do this tomorrow as well. Finish off the school."

"Sounds good."

On Wednesday Chris joined us to fight again. I was very surprised to see him there. He had been avoiding me since Thursday, so showing up at the one place he absolutely knew I'd be was something of a shock. I didn't offer to fight him, and he wasn't really interacting with me. If I spoke directly to him, he'd reply. Otherwise he tried to ignore me.

Tried being the operative word. He wasn't quite successful. Especially while I fought. It was distracting to know how closely he was watching me. Between him watching me, and me wanting to watch him, I lost all the gains I made over the last two months. Pat had me on the floor in a matter of minutes. I was far enough along with my fencing that Mike had started training me on swords two weeks ago, but today I slipped, let one of his thrusts get by my guard, and ended up with a nasty cut on my right shoulder. I stopped the fight. Unlike Pat and Chris I had no desire to see if I could fight through the blood.

I excused myself to the ladies room, keeping pressure on my shoulder to slow the bleeding. Once there, I took my shirt off and looked at the wound critically in the mirror. He stabbed clean through the fleshy part of my deltoid. If I was a character in an old western movie, getting shot there would be a pretty good hint that I was one of the good guys.

Healing myself was easier and harder than working on the others. I knew exactly what I needed to do. That was the easier part. It hurt immensely and trying to focus on healing while my own blood slid down my arm and dripped off my fingers was the harder part.

I was just getting the muscle fibers knitted back together when Pat knocked and poked his head in. "How are you doing?"

"I'll be fine. It's just slow going. Hard to work through the pain, and this is the first time I had to knit muscle together as well."

"Okay. I'll let them know you aren't bleeding to death in here."

I snorted and half smiled. "Not from this. It's messy but not life threatening."

"Good."

He leaned against the door while I finished up the skin. A few minutes of clean-up left the bathroom and my arm blood free. I looked at my sticky, bloodstained t-shirt.

"Can you get me my coat? I don't want to put this back on." Even though I didn't mind Pat keeping me company while I wasn't wearing a shirt, I didn't want to just streak across the gym in my bra for Chris and Mike to see. If Chris was going to see me in a bra, I wanted it to be one of the nice ones.

"Let me get you my hoodie. You'll be more comfortable while we're here. It's not like I'm using it right now." Pat hadn't gone for topless fighting since the first time Chris joined us, but he also didn't see any need to keep his hoodie on over his t-shirt.

"Thanks." I waited for a few minutes for him to return. He handed me his black and gray hoodie. I rolled the cuffs up so my hands actually stuck out of the sleeves and returned to the gym.

"Are you okay?" Mike looked guilty.

"I'm fine." I rolled my arm through its entire range of motion. "My own fault, I should know better than to let myself get distracted while fighting."

"You're really fine?"

I unzipped it far enough to slide my shoulder out. "Look. All better. You can't even tell I was hit unless you look at my shirt."

"Good. You scared the shit out of me when I realized you weren't going to get your sword up in time."

"I'm sorry. I'll do better next time." I zipped back up.

Chris hopped up and said to Pat, "Let's fight."

Pat grinned at him. "By all means."

I headed to my coat. "Do you all mind if I head off early tonight? I've got a pile of homework waiting for me."

"No problem," Pat said as he walked across the gym. Mike was looking concerned at me.

"I'm really fine," I said to him, "I've got a lot of homework left to do."

"Okay."

I did have a lot of homework, but more than that I really wanted to get a shower. The dried sweat from my two fights wasn't too much of a big deal, but the memory of the blood on my arm wasn't going away as quickly as I would have liked. Really washing would help.

On my way out I stopped to watch Pat and Chris fight for a moment. Chris wasn't showing a lot of finesse, but he was certainly enthusiastic. He wasn't going to win, and he didn't care. It was just about hitting as hard and as often as he could. If that's where he was, Pat was the best person to do that with. Pat wouldn't hurt him too bad, though I noticed a few bruises already on Chris' torso, and wouldn't let himself get hurt, either.

Once home and in my shower, I finally lost the sensation of my own blood sliding down my arm. That bothered me more than the pain. I really don't like the idea of my life sliding out of me and dripping onto the floor. When I got out of the shower, I realized I wasn't alone in the apartment. I wrapped up in my towel, wishing I hadn't left my robe in my room or the door open. Leaving the bathroom, I saw the door had been closed. That told me it wasn't Pat in the other room. He wouldn't have thought to close the door to my bedroom because he'd be sitting on the sofa with his back to my room.

I toweled off my hair and got dressed. When I opened the door, Chris was sitting at my table, waiting for me. His lip was split, chin bruised, and he had the start of a black eye. "'The first rule of Fight Club is do not talk about Fight Club.' You look like shit."

"Thanks."

"How's Pat?"

"Good enough he's still fighting Mike."

"Ahhh…" I walked from my doorway to the kitchen table and sat down in the chair next to his.

His eyes were glued to my shoulder. "You're really okay?"

I gently cupped his chin, avoiding the bruise extending down from his split lip, and angled his face so he was looking at my eyes. "Asks the guy bleeding at my table. Yes, *I'm* really okay. Now tell me about you. What's going on?" I realized that was too intimate of a gesture and quickly stood up, using making an ice pack as an excuse to put more space between us.

"Lots of bruises."

"I can see them. Tell me about this glorious frenzy of self-destructive bullshit you've been on this last week. You're picking fights, you're barely eating when you show up for meals, and, until a minute ago, you weren't talking to me."

"You wouldn't understand."

"Try me. Lots of people think I'm marvelously understanding." I wrapped the ice in a paper towel, put it on the table in front of him, and leaned against the kitchen counter. "I'm not healing any of this until you start talking about why you're doing it."

"I can't tell you."

"Bull. You want to tell me. I can feel that." He sat silently, holding the ice against his eye, watching me with the open one. I almost expected him to stand up and kiss me. I almost expected him to turn and run away. What I wanted him to do was start talking. "Just say it. Whatever's in there is like an infected tooth. Lance the fucker and let it out. You'll feel better for it."

He closed his eyes and turned away from me. "Everyone says it's no big deal. Fantasies happen. If you enjoy them, who's hurt? No one."

"You appear hurt."

"Not hurt enough." He looked back at me again.

"I won't help you with that. Go see Pat if you want someone to beat on you again."

"Do you fantasize about other men? Would you hate Ari if he did?" he asked quietly, holding my gaze.

I wanted to joke about how I'd be disturbed if Ari was fantasizing about men, but he was so serious I let the joke drop. I felt like the honest answer would be better for his guilt. At the same time, I didn't know if it would make things worse on the desire side of the equation.

I decided to go with honesty anyway. "Until recently, no. I wouldn't hate Ari for it. I'd prefer I was the one in his mind when he touches himself, but if I'm not…. Yeah, it hurts. I don't want him fucking other women in his head. But I'm not holding myself to that standard, so I don't see how in good conscious I can claim it for him."

"Did you start the day you held the moonstone?"

I smiled at him wryly. "How much of that did you feel?"

"Enough."

"Me in a towel the next day didn't help did it?"

"No. May I hold your hand?"

I looked curiously at him but held out my hand. He cradled it in his left hand and stroked his thumb down my palm. Only the fact that I was sure I'd hurt him kept me off of him.

While his thumb slid down my palm I wanted to hop into his lap, wrap my hand around his neck, and pull his face to mine. I was barely aware of the magic in his touch.

Then he let go of my hand and said, "That should help."

"Help what?" The urgent need to jump him faded away. "Oh, that," I said stupidly as I felt the change.

"It took me a while to figure out how to do that. As Chuck said, unless I intend to sleep with you, leaving that magic in place wasn't kind."

"Off to Brooke's next?"

"No. I didn't invite her to touch the stone. She grabbed it, and she can deal with the consequences herself." His words hung between us as he moved the ice from his eye to his lip.

I wasn't sure what to say to him, but both of us sitting there mute wasn't helpful. Finally, I came up with something. "I can't imagine she expects you to spend a lifetime with no contact and not, at least occasionally, think of another woman. Did she like sex?"

He looked shocked at the question but answered it anyway, "Yes, very much."

"Then there's absolutely no chance she hasn't thought of another man."

"That is remarkably uncomforting."

"Why? She's a real woman, a real person, with all the ups and downs and good and bad that goes with a real person. And real women who like sex don't go two decades without some sort of release. It just doesn't happen. I don't know, maybe she is back there still thinking of only you. Maybe she knows just as well as you do you aren't coming back, but unlike you she doesn't know you're alive. She might be remarried by now or taken a new lover. Just because you know you made it through doesn't mean she does."

He didn't have an answer to that. Whatever he was thinking, my last words didn't seem to hurt him nearly as much as I thought they would. "Nothing I just said hit you? Why?"

"Her breaking her vows doesn't absolve me of mine."

"Then you've got two options: Have an absolute bacchanal in your head, imagine it as fully as possible and revel in it until it's out of your system. Or use the same skills you used to discipline your mind to relearn magic and stop thinking about it. You learned how to kill a person with your mind. How hard can keeping your sex drive in check be in comparison to that?"

I saw a hint of a smile hit his lips. "You really aren't a guy, you know that?"

"I had indeed noticed that."

"How are you dealing with it?"

"I have a firmly entrenched 'no guilt' policy. If I think I'll feel guilty about it, I don't do it. If I do it anyway, I forgive myself, move on, and don't do it again."

"So, if you slept with someone else, you'd be okay with it?"

That was a jump. I pondered my answer. As much as I had been thinking about Chris, I was *just* thinking about it. I didn't intend to do anything about those thoughts. "Yes, but that's a line I'm not crossing anytime in the near future. I can wait for a man I love. If I were to actually fall in love with someone else... well, that changes the rules."

"In your case it does. Bacchanal or self-discipline?"

"I was thinking that was what you were actually asking the first time." He sat and stared at me, moving the ice from his lip to the knuckles of his right fist. "If I answer, am I setting you up for a harder time?"

"Not if the answer actually worked."

"Define worked."

"Got me out of your head."

"Nope." I shook my head. "I came up with a... workable, guilt-free compromise."

He looked intrigued and happier than I had seen him in a week, and gestured with his left hand for me to keep talking. "Judging from how strongly you reacted when I asked if you were gay, I'm thinking it would bother you deeply to know."

His eyes went wide. Then he winced because it hurt the bruised one. "I'm not that vanilla. I just really didn't want you thinking I was gay."

"I do not think you are gay though I reserve the right to tease you about it from time to time."

"I'll keep that in mind. So, what is this compromise you think will bother me?" His interest was perking up nicely. I had no idea if this was a long-term good thing or not, but I was willing to play with it if it would buy him a little happiness.

"Honestly, is hearing what I'm thinking about while dancing with Mr. Lefty really going to make this any easier for you? I don't want to put images in your head that you'll spend the next week trying to erase with pain."

"Mr. Lefty?"

"See, I'm already giving you images you don't really need."

"If you tell me this, I promise I will be perky next week."

"Promise?"

"I will win a fucking Academy Award for perkiness if need be." He tried a smile. It didn't work all that well, a fresh drop of blood oozed out of his split lip. He blotted it with the paper towel holding the ice.

I sighed, then wiggled the fingers of my left hand at him. "I'm usually, but not always, a righty, hence, 'Dancing with Mr. Lefty.' It's a somewhat more elegant bit of slang than jerking off, especially since, as a woman, I don't *jerk*. As for the compromise, Ari told me he'd try anything once, so it's the three of us. Now that I've been so horribly frank with you, how about you answer one for me?"

I had the distinct impression watching him right now was similar to when he watched me hold the moonstone. His eyes were far away, and I could see a trace of pink light his cheeks. After a minute, he blinked very slowly are refocused his eyes on me. "What do you want to know?"

"Why me? Autumn's cuter. Emily's absolutely gorgeous. There are lots of women who have crossed your path over the years, what's different about me?"

"Being near you makes me happy. It's hard to even want sex if there's not enough joy in your life. You bring me joy, and that wakes up my interest in sex."

"That's the kindest thing anyone has ever said to me."

"Thank you."

"So, what are you going to do?"

He leaned back in his chair and exhaled deeply. "The only option I can live with: self-control."

I nodded. It was the answer I expected him to come up with. "Can I fix you up, or are you better off if I don't touch you?"

"Fix me up, please. After all, compared to the image of you between Ari and me, your fingers on my skin are... well, that's pretty hot, too."

I touched the bruised and split skin of his right hand, planning to get working. I looked up from his hand to his eyes. "Too? The idea doesn't bother you?"

"As I said, I'm not that vanilla. As a general preference, I don't like to share, but..." He paused, looked me in the eyes for a long minute, then continued without finishing that thought. "Just because this body is a virgin doesn't mean the mind is."

I held his hand in mine but totally forgot healing it. "Have you ever done something like that?" If the answer was yes, that would certainly explain more about how he and Pat got along.

"No. Just her. One hundred and twelve years, during that time I never had enough interest in another woman to even seriously think of it. It's not like I had never heard of it happening. Most men of my class had a concubine or two, in addition to a wife, and if the ladies really liked each other, things like that could happen. You?"

"Only in my mind. We talked about it once, which is where the 'open for anything at least once' conversation happened, but we never found a person both of us liked enough to invite into our bed. It's probably one of those things that sound like fun but get complicated later. As much as I like Heinlein's happy multi-spouse families, my sense is they don't actually work out that way."

"Not in my experience. Being one of the few men in my class with only one woman in his house also meant I was one of the few men in my class with a truly happy marriage. You're welcome to speculate as to that being a cause or effect."

I realized I was standing there holding his hand, not doing anything with it, and got to work. A few minutes got the skin back together and back to its original color. I moved to his left hand next. It was in better shape, no splits, just bruises.

His face came next. I wanted to stand between his legs, tilt his head up to me, and rest my fingers on his lip while watching his eyes. That would be too intimate. I circled behind him, so he wouldn't be looking me in the eye, and began with the black eye.

"Where are your glasses?"

"I took them off to fight Pat. They're in my pocket."

"How's your vision?"

"It went red for a minute when he hit me, but it's as good as it ever gets now."

"Good."

I really tried to do a professional job on his lip. He sat very still while I traced my finger over it, willing the skin to close. I only stroked it two or three times more than was strictly necessary. It was so soft and warm and pleasant to touch. I finally pulled my hand away and studied his face a moment. It looked the way it was supposed to. Nothing left to do there.

"What else? I saw the bruises on your torso when you were fighting."

"He didn't break any of my ribs, but I'm sure I look like a punching bag. He got a few kicks in to my hip and legs, too."

"Bruises everywhere?"

"I'm certain the bottoms of my feet are bruise free."

I handed him my computer. "You might as well set up a playlist. I have a feeling we'll be here a while."

I stood up, got my quilt, folded it in half, and laid it on the floor. "You're just too tall. I'm not going to stand over you trying to reach everything." Back to my room for some pillows and one of my other blankets. One of the pillow went on the quilt where his head would go and another about where I thought his knees would go, then I laid the blanket on top of it.

"Take off whatever you need to for me to get to the bruises. Then lay down face up, and put this pillow under your knees. The blanket goes on top of you."

"What about your homework?"

I looked at the clock. It was already ten and the chances of getting done before eleven were minimal. "I don't have a class with actual turn in homework tomorrow. I was hoping to get a jump on Friday. I'll have less goofing-off time tomorrow, but I can deal. Holler when you're ready." I went back into my room to let him strip down without me watching.

After a few minutes, I heard him say, "Ready."

"Oh, Lord!" escaped my lips in a low sigh. He was a mess. The blanket was pulled up to his chest, leaving only his arms and shoulders visible. Both arms were mottled with bruises from blocking Pat's hits. "I really hope this made you feel better."

He turned to me. "Maybe it's being here with you, maybe it's finally feeling like I paid for my sins, but yes, I'm feeling better."

"Does the rest of you look like your arms?" I asked, settling next to his left side.

"A lot of it does."

"I may burn out long before we get done."

"Whatever you do for me is fine. The rest I can deal with by eating Advil and taking cold showers."

If I tried to do this one bruise at a time I'd be at it all night. "Have you ever had a massage?"

"Back rubs, never a full-body one."

"Tonight's your lucky night. If I try to do this the way I did your face, it's just not going to happen. I'm going to use my massage skills a whole new way."

"Sounds good."

I went to my pantry. Normally, I don't use oil for a massage, but tonight I needed soft glide. If those bruises were going to fade under my hands, my hands needed to flow from one to the next. The almond oil I use for sweet challah would do for a massage also.

Sitting next to his left arm again, I poured a little oil in my right hand. I rubbed it between my hands to warm it up, molded my hands around his wrist, ran them up his arm, cupped around his shoulder, and then back down again. My hands were moving practically without any conscious thought. I held the prayer and felt the energy gather in my hands. My mind went back to where I had sent it when I worked on him after the Vamp attack.

Eventually the flesh of his arm felt finished and looked bruise free. I pulled the blanket down to his hips and surveyed the damage to his torso. 'Punching bag' was a pretty good description. Pat had been careful: Chris' stomach was only lightly bruised; his ribs were spattered with fist-sized splashes of ugly, dull purple. My fingers rested against his abdomen and gently stroked up to his shoulder. I added more oil and kept the pressure light; the last thing his skin needed was heavy hands.

Time passed. I had no idea how long. My only focus was the feel of the energy in my hands, the feel of his skin under them, and the feel of the one slowly suffusing the other until it was full and healthy.

Chest and stomach done, I folded the blanket back over him and gently slid my fingers under it to touch his hip. He was naked under the blanket. I carefully draped the blanket around his leg, keeping the bits I was sure he didn't want flashed around covered, but giving myself access to his left leg. It wasn't too bad, not compared to his chest. Three distinctly foot shaped bruises marred his thigh, one more marked his calf. If he got hit in the hip, it wasn't this one.

I silently thanked Pat for not damaging his inner thigh. It was more than surreal enough to be stroking the front and outside of his leg without having to run my hands up his inseam. I finished his leg and covered it with the blanket.

His right leg required more careful folding of the blanket. When he said hip, I had been thinking the outside of the top of his leg. Apparently he meant Pat's heel had pounded into his hip bone and very low abdomen. The area I would have referred to as pelvis. One more inch down and toward his midline and I would have skipped that one. As it was, I had a much better idea of what his pubic hair looked and felt like than I really needed. *More fodder for Mr. Lefty. Stop it. Focus. Be professional.*

I finished messing with the blanket and went back to his ankle. My best guess was Pat had stomped it because both the ankle and the top of his foot were bruised. The rest of his right leg was in good shape.

"He got your left more than your right."

"I defend left, attack right." I hadn't realized I had said anything out loud until he answered me. I hadn't realized he was still awake until he spoke as well. I started at his foot and stroked my way up his leg, trying to get the focus back. After the first few passes, I was back in the zone again. Only aware of the work of healing.

Eventually I had him roll over and started on his back. This was easier to keep the focus on. It was familiar territory and much less damaged than his chest. I finished up and covered him in the blanket again.

I lay my hand on his tush, over the blanket, and asked, "Anything here?"

"No."

"Okay." I got to work on the back of his left leg. Only one bruise left to do. I just lay my hand on it and let the energy flow through me.

I finished up, covered him again, and leaned against the back of my sofa, feeling immensely proud at having done it and limp with tiredness.

If he wasn't asleep, he was very close. I didn't feel any need to poke him or make him get up. For several minutes I watched him rest, then slowly got up, grabbed the blanket from my couch, and went to bed.

I should have fallen into a deep sleep in a matter of seconds, but thinking about fantasies kept me awake. I didn't feel nearly as bad about the idea of Ari thinking about other women as I should. More importantly, I should be feeling worse about thinking of another man. Those weren't errant little daydreams; it was full out fucking another man in my mind. Deeds are more important than thoughts—I know that, and I believe that— but at the same time I'm allowing myself to lust after someone else.

Do better. That resolved, I fell asleep.

Chris knew he should get up. But for the first time in—he didn't know how long—he actually felt good. He was warm and comfortable, nothing hurt, and his skin still glowed from her magic. Getting up, dressed, and back to his own bed seemed like way more work than he wanted to do. He let himself slide into a happy, relaxed sleep.

He woke up the next morning when he felt her footsteps. She was in the kitchen making biscuits and, from the looks of it, getting ready to go for a jog right after. He realized casually chit chatting naked under the blanket with his morning erection was just something he couldn't pull off. He rolled onto his stomach, pretending to be asleep until she left.

He waited a few more minutes to make sure she wasn't going to come back and got up. There was something surreal about being naked in her living room. He pulled on his clothing and headed to the bathroom. There wasn't a note on the table this time, but he did notice enough biscuits for both of them rising on her counter. After last time, she probably expected him to sleep until she had gone to class.

He folded up the blankets and put them and the pillows back on her bed. He went to her sofa and to doze until she got back. Biscuits and her company for breakfast seemed like a pretty good idea to him.

Maybe after breakfast he'd take another stab at trying to find the man with the brown hair. Spend an hour or so sitting in the Student Union watching people walk around. He knew the brown-haired man was around here somewhere, it was just a matter of laying eyes on him.

28.

"Do you really want to go out this week?" Autumn asked as Chris and Chuck looked over the map.

"We still haven't found the portal, and we won't have a chance to search again for a month. You don't have to come if you want more study time," Chuck answered.

"I don't want to come because it's freezing out there, snowing, and both Pat and Mike are busy. Going out when both of them cannot come is never a good plan."

"Neither of them report anything brewing," Chris said, looking up from the map.

"Neither of them are coming tonight, and we'll be far enough away they can't get to us fast if need be," Autumn pointed out again.

"Do you feel something coming, or are you being cautious?" Chuck wanted to know. Autumn did occasionally whip out a flash of prescience. They had all learned listening to Autumn's warnings was worthwhile, even if you didn't want to.

"I'm being cautious. I'd like to make it all the way through one semester without getting hurt. Just one out of eight would be enough."

Chris looked at her, hope lighting his eyes. He wouldn't mind at all if she didn't go. "Then stay home. We can handle anything that pops up tonight."

Autumn put on her coat and headed to the door. "Why couldn't we be in Texas? It'd be seventy-five degrees right now."

"Yeah, but it would have been 110 in August. I'm happier in the cold," Chuck said as they headed out.

They didn't get to the target area. They barely got out of the house. Across from the ravine was a tree-filled lot. As they walked by, a deep roaring sound hit them.

"Goddamn it! One semester!" Autumn cursed as she turned toward the sound. One of the lower-level Minions stood in front of them. It looked like a huge blue lion with silver dragon wings. It roared again and pawed at the ground. Chris turned and began trying to make it real in this world.

"Cover Chris. He's been working on a new trick," Chuck said while he tossed his first volley at the Minion.

"I always do," Autumn said to him. Her magic wrapped around the Minion, pinning it to the ground beneath its paws.

Chuck's next volley hit it hard. It screamed and leapt, breaking Autumn's hold on it and tearing through Chuck. He cursed quietly, pushed the pain aside, and turned to face it again, putting himself between it and Chris.

Autumn pinned it to the ground again. Chuck worked on making sure it wouldn't move. The Minions were hard. Not to say they were particularly intelligent—the smarter something was the harder it was to control—but because they were rage incarnate, they would not take orders from him without an immense battle of wills.

Change it or kill it, Cell. I can't hold it much longer.

Chuck's voice in his mind stopped him from trying to change it. It wasn't going to happen today. *Kill it,* he thought back to Chuck. He had found only one good way to kill the Minions: cut them off from Mildred. It took him a few seconds to cast the spell, and a few minutes for it to finish the job. The Minion withered in front of them, starving without the continuous flow of power Mildred provided.

"Home then?" Autumn asked.

"Yes," Chuck answered. "Are you hurt?"

"No. You?"

"I'll find out when we get back. I pushed everything into the background to hold it. It'll take a few minutes before I can feel my body properly again."

"Then let's go straight to Sarah's house. Every time you've pulled that trick you were hurt once you could feel yourself again," Chris watched him critically. He could already see Chuck was hurt worse than he knew.

They were ten feet from her house when Chuck started to limp. Chris got his arm around Chuck to help him walk as his steps faltered. Autumn darted in front of them and opened the door without bothering to knock. Chris carried Chuck the last few steps.

"What's up?" Sarah called from her room while heading in their direction.

"It's us. Chuck's hurt," Chris said.

She was at Chuck's side in less than a second. "I thought it was Pat when I heard the door open. What happened to you?"

"One of the Minions jumped through me."

She knelt in front of Chuck, her hands on his. He tried to focus enough to get into her head and see through her eyes, but didn't have the power on hand to do it.

"Stop blocking me. Your shields are in the way." He lowered them just enough to let her peak through. Her eyes slid out of focus. Whatever she was seeing it wasn't his physical person. He slumped against the back of her sofa and let her work.

"It tore you to bits. Does it hurt?"

"Not yet. Get me back together fast enough and it might not."

"I can try." He felt her magic wrap around and pull the scattered pieces of his magic back together. They weren't fused back together, just closer, like a stitched cut before it healed. She leaned back onto her heels.

"Chuck, either turn down your defenses or heal yourself. I am not going to keep doing this while you attack me."

"Sorry. I'm not doing it on purpose."

"Tell that to my blinding headache."

Chris put his hand on her shoulder and added an extra layer of shielding. "I don't think he can turn that off. Not now, at least."

She took Chuck's hands in hers again and began to fuse his magical self back together. Not fast enough, he was really hurting now. The Minion had teeth and claws and used all of them on him while it went through. His body throbbed in sympathy for his soul.

He gritted his teeth and breathed slowly, then pulled his mind away from the pain. That required no magic, just will. He went back to his last stats lecture and focused on the lines of the formulas. He made the math dance, working his way through each example the professor had given them. Chuck finished one class and let his mind go back to his body. It still hurt but not as badly as before.

He watched her work on him. Her technique was entirely wild magic. With training she would be a formidable wizard. On just pure intuition, she was better at this than anyone had any right to be. Pulling the disparate pieces of another person's magic back together and knitting them into a whole should take years of practice.

He looked at Chris' shield over her, his hand on her shoulder. It looked right on her. She could wear his magic too easily. His pain dropped to the dull toothache level. He thought about the look of Chris' shield over her more. Maybe she had years of practice.

"Stop it Chuck. I can work through pain. I will work through pain. But if you want to get done anytime soon you've got to rein this in."

"Sorry. Better?"

"Yes. What happened there? I was going along fine and then ice picks in the eyes."

"I had been keeping my mind away from my body. I came back to check how things were. It hurt."

"I'm working as fast as I can."

"Thanks." She bought it. Autumn hadn't. She'd hold onto his lie until she could find a way to use it to her advantage. *Fuck!* It was too easy to forget exactly how good Autumn was at reading people.

He pulled back into his head again, went back to his stats class, and focused on it again. He was halfway through the lecture when Chris poked him. He came back.

"All done?" He still ached all over.

Sarah lay on the floor, her eyes closed, her skin tinged gray; her picture could go next to the word 'weary' in the dictionary. He wondered how much of that was exhaustion from working on him and how much was the result of his defenses attacking on automatic. She didn't open her eyes or look at him when she answered. "As done as I'm going to get you. What happened? That was… different."

"How so?" Chuck asked.

"What was I fixing? It wasn't your body. I know that. It didn't feel like working on Chris after the Vamp attack. Your energy level was low, but that was because of whatever happened to you. It didn't cause the problem."

"You were working on me. You know we're basically wearing these bodies like coats. The Minion clawed and bit me while moving through this body."

"Great. You're put back together, but not the way you were before. I could feel an order to you… but I couldn't duplicate it."

Autumn smiled at her from her place on the window seat. "That's because he's a wizard. They're highly organized."

Sarah almost turned her head to look in Autumn's direction. "Aren't you all wizards?"

"No. Chuck is. Pat is. Dave is. You, Mike, and Chris most definitely are not."

"Still not getting the difference."

"Training. They've had formal magical training and end up with a different relationship to the magic. All of us can use it, but they've got a precisely structured way of working with it. We just wing it," Chris answered. He sat cross-legged on the floor between her and Chuck. While he spoke Chuck noticed Chris still hadn't taken his hand off her shoulder or let his shield down. "They get more reliable results. The ability to do the same thing exactly the same way over and over is easier for them."

"More powerful?"

"Usually. Not always. New magic is harder for them. They'll eventually be able to do new things, but it takes more time, study, and effort."

She opened her eyes to look at Chris. "What are we?"

"Mages. Masters of the wild magic. Instinct, feeling, intuition: those are our tools. We can pull some immensely powerful magical tricks out of the ethers. The only thing limiting us is our will and imagination. Anything can be done with magic, and we're the ones who manage to do what was previously unthinkable the first time. They're the ones who figure out how to do it again and how to rein in the side effects."

"Why aren't you a wizard?" Sarah looked up at Chris.

"I wasn't very good at the kind of magic my clan valued, so I ended up in the Priesthood where we didn't study much magic. Chuck excelled at the kind of magic my clan valued. Our father made sure he got all the training he could take. In a different clan I would have been trained as a battle wizard and ended up a general. Chuck probably would have been sent into spying."

"What are you?" Sarah asked Autumn as she sat up slowly and leaned against the couch next to Chris. Chris took his hand off of Sarah's shoulder, seemingly just realizing it was still there. Chuck noticed Chris didn't lower the shield, and he kept his hand less than a quarter of an inch away from hers on the floor. He very gently poked into Chris' mind to see if he knew he was doing it. Nope.

"None of the above. I'm a fairy. Magic is like breathing to us. We don't train in it. What would be the point? It would be like learning how to blink. That's why I have a hard time here. I have to figure out new ways to make what should be automatic work for me. Back when we still had formal contact with this world, it was easy. Our realms are detached from each other now, and that makes everything more difficult."

"So, here you're a mage?"

"Not really. I don't have any formal training, like Chuck had, and I am using the same basic skill set as you and Chris. But I'm a magical creature. You're creatures that use magic. It's not the same thing."

"How so?" Sarah asked.

"My magic is mine. I supplement it with the background magic. Which is why things are harder here. The background here is weak and tricky to work with. But the core of my magic is intrinsic to me. You all can store the local magic internally, but if you end up in a magic free place, you're powerless."

"I can honestly say I'm too damn tired to think about that right now."

"You do look beat. Shall we head off and let you get some sleep?" Autumn asked.

"I'd like that."

Chuck stood up. He felt Chris wanted a moment alone with Sarah and gently nudged Autumn toward the door.

Chris knelt on the floor next to her. "You want help getting to bed?"

"No, but I'll take it." He put his arm around her and lifted her to her feet. "I hate feeling this weak and dependent."

"You just ran a marathon with no training. You're going to feel weak after. Muscles you never knew you had are getting Olympic-quality workouts. There's no shame in being exhausted." He slid his other arm under her knees and carried her to her bed.

He laid her on the bed and knelt on the floor, his elbows resting on her mattress. "Thank you for fixing Chuck. This time last year an injury like that would have kept him off his feet for a month, maybe two."

"Glad to be of service." He squeezed her hand, stood up, and left.

29.

Compared to putting Chuck back together my finals were easy. By the time I was done I felt like every cell in my brain had been squeezed dry, but I didn't need to be carried to bed after.

Pat gave me all seven seasons of *Buffy* and five seasons of *Angel* for Christmas. Only the fifth season of *Angel* was new. The rest were his personal copies. He told me they were a gift with a string attached. He wanted to be able to see them whenever he wanted. I was more than cool with that. Then he said, "Come on, Dave made me promise to bring you and them over after I gave them to you. He's looking for a Whedon fix."

"Then we shall have to make sure he gets one. What should we start with?"

"I like *Angel* better. Knowing Dave, he does too, but it won't make much sense if you haven't seen *Buffy*. Grab *Buffy* seasons one and two." We went over, and Pat put the DVD in while Dave made popcorn.

"All done, Dave?" I leaned against the counter in the kitchen, watching the popcorn spin in the microwave.

"As of eleven thirty this morning." He took the bag out and poured it into three bowls. He handed one to me and took the other two out. "Day after tomorrow my parents show up, then home for three weeks."

"Sounds good," I said, sitting on the sofa. Pat took one of the bowls from Dave and sat next to me. Dave grabbed the cushy armchair and dragged it to a good spot in front of the TV.

"What are you doing for break?" Dave asked me.

"Pat's coming to the farm with me for a few days. Then I'm heading to his place for a few more. Then back here."

"That's why I gave her all of *Buffy* and *Angel*. She's got to have something to keep her company while we're all off at home." Pat hit the play button.

Three episodes later Mike came in, kicked the snow off his boots, and shouted, "I'm done! I have programmed faster, harder, and longer than any man before me. I am the King of SQL, the Master of Python! Bow down and worship my greatness!"

"Good for you. Sit down and watch some TV with us," Dave said.

"In a minute." Mike held up a box of Duncan Hines brownie mix. Dave laughed. "Can I borrow some eggs and oil from you?" he asked me.

"Sure. What's funny about you making brownies?"

"Something of a Writers' House winter break tradition. It gets so cold I don't want to go outside to smoke, so the year ends with pot brownies. Chris made them last year. Since he's still working, I figured I could make my own."

I laughed. "Chris bakes?"

"Yeah, he's really good at it. Have him make you brownies, with or without pot one day," Dave said. "He makes them from scratch."

"Okay. Help yourself to oil and eggs. While you're at my place, can you get my blanket? It's kind of chilly in here."

"The joys of deep winter at Writers'." Dave smiled. "The heater can't keep up when it gets below zero outside."

"Another reason to do some baking. It'll help keep it warmer down here." Mike put the brownie mix down and headed back out into the snow. Several minutes later he returned with a few eggs, my blanket, and a bottle of vegetable oil. He handed me the blanket, put the eggs and oil in the kitchen, and then joined us for more *Buffy*.

After two more episodes Mike said, "I'm thinking we should order pizza and subs and have a proper celebration."

"Sounds good," Pat said. "We could use a proper celebration."

Autumn came in. "Celebration sounds good to me." Then she walked over to the fireplace, tossed two of her books into it, and got a lighter out.

"Are you going to set fire to them?" Pat looked pleased.

"Yes. I hated each and every single page of this dreck. I just got back from the bookstore. I can't sell them back. I checked on Amazon; they're going for less than a tenth of what I bought them for. Setting fire to them seems like more fun than selling them for a combined eight dollars."

"Don't forget to open the flue," Mike told her. Pat paused *Buffy*. It's much harder to get a textbook to catch fire than it should be. Unlike newspaper, they don't just burst into flames when you hold a lighter to them.

"I can light them for you," Pat said as he watched Autumn's third attempt fizzle out.

"If I wanted to do it with magic, they'd already be burning," Autumn replied. Finally she got enough vodka poured over the books, and for a few moments we sat around a roaring textbook fire. Mike got on the phone and called for three pizzas, asking the lot of us for sub orders.

We got back to watching *Buffy*. Suddenly I was in love. I looked at Spike. I looked at Pat. I looked back at Spike… and back at Pat.

"This is where you got the black coat idea, isn't it?"

He looked sheepish. "Mine isn't leather." I laughed.

Chris came down when the pizzas showed up. He ate two slices quickly, looked longingly at the television, and headed back up, grumbling about symbolism and how much he wanted to do some anatomically impossible things to his Brit Lit III professor.

An hour later, Mike decided it was time to do some baking. Chris bounced down as the sound of the mixer died. He helped himself to another slice of pizza and a beer and sat next to me. "I have emailed the fucker off. Never, ever, again am I taking a class taught by that bastard. Do I smell chocolate?"

"Mike's making brownies."

"Ahhh…."

Mike came back out. "They should be ready in half an hour. I stole some of your chocolate chips," he told Chris.

"Which ones?"

"A handful of the Ghirardelli white and another handful of the dark ones."

"You have multiple kinds of chocolate chips?" I asked.

"You may have noticed we have no sex lives. As a result, there's lots of chocolate in this house," Autumn answered.

"Speak for yourself," Dave said.

"When did you get a sex life?" Autumn giggled.

"About the time I turned eleven."

"Oh. That. Yeah, well, on that level I guess we all have sex lives. None of us have partners. Is that a better way of putting it?"

"Much."

"As a result, we go through a lot of chocolate, fiction, movies which I'm sure get more interesting when I go to bed," she looked pointedly at Dave and Mike. I thought that was odd because I didn't think there was any sort of porn both of them would watch. "And other chemicals that make you feel good." She sipped her glass of wine.

"I see. What do you two watch that Autumn would consider interesting?"

"Anime. Nothing too racy. Our tastes don't run in the same direction on that scale," Dave answered.

"Yeah, right." Autumn rolled her eyes. "You both like big-eyed, impossibly large chested heroes and heroines with not nearly enough clothing."

"Well, we are guys," Mike said. "And if the girls don't do anything for me, I don't find them disgusting. I imagine Dave feels the same way."

"Pretty much. I tend to sort of look around the guys."

"Okay. I know Dave is on beer number four. How much of the batter did you eat before putting them in the oven?" I asked Mike.

"Not nearly enough."

"Shhhh. This is the best line this season," Pat said. He was right. The image of happy meals walking around made me laugh.

At the end of that episode, Mike got up to take the brownies out. He came out a few minutes later and began offering them around. I turned him down. Chris followed my refusal with one of his own. Mike looked like he couldn't believe Chris was turning him down.

"My brother's picking me up tomorrow morning. I don't want to face him puffy eyed and stoned," Chris explained.

Pat reached for a brownie. I got up and grabbed myself a Pepsi. I stuck my head back into the room. "Dave, mind if I help myself to some of your rum?"

"No."

"Thanks."

"Would you get me another beer?" Chris called out.

"Sure." I grabbed a Sam Adams, popped the cap off, made myself a Rum and Pepsi, and went back to my place on the sofa between Pat and Chris.

I got myself situated under the blanket. "Mind if I share?" Chris asked me.

"Not at all." He slid closer to me. His shoulder pressed against mine as he arranged the blanket around him as well. A few minutes later, Pat also ended up under the blanket. He put his arm around me and, by default, some of Chris as well.

Mike laughed quietly at us. He looked at Autumn, looked at us, and then said, "Look, it's Angel, Buffy, and Spike." Autumn thought that was the funniest thing ever. When she noticed I hadn't gotten the joke, she spent a minute explaining. I looked over at Mike, the image of innocence, watching the TV and minding his own business. Then he caught my eye, flashed a grin at me, and went back to watching the show.

I spent the next hour enjoying the show and the feel of Pat on one side and Chris on the other. I was probably drinking my rum and Pepsi too quickly because daydreams of both of them kept tugging at the corners of my mind. Trying to force those thoughts away kept me a bit distracted from the show. I had the unsettling idea Chris could read my mind. I knew Pat was close enough to. And I was certain neither of them needed to know I was thinking about being pressed between the two of them, Pat's lips on my shoulders, Chris sucking my ear lobe. Let alone the racier images.

Pat stood up to grab another brownie. I asked him to get me more soda. While Pat was in the kitchen, Chris put his arm around my shoulders. I leaned into him.

Pat came back and looked at us. "Harlot!"

"He's nice and warm. And you got up!" I may have pouted at him. He handed me my drink, sat down, got under the blanket, and then picked up my feet so they were resting in his lap. I twisted so my back was against Chris. He also shifted. I ended up with my back against his chest and my feet in Pat's lap. Pat began to rub his fingers into the soles of my feet.

I sighed happily, let my head fall against Chris, closed my eyes, and sipped my drink. "Whoa, Pat, is there any Pepsi in this?"

"Some."

"Yeah, when I made mine up it was a shot of rum to a full can of Pepsi. This is what, half and half?"

"Thereabouts."

I took one more sip and leaned down to put it on the floor. "If I drink all of that I'll get silly."

"Can I have it then?" Chris asked.

"Sure." I reached back down and handed him my drink. "I may ask you for a sip or two."

"No problem." He wasn't tearing through the drink, either. He'd take a sip, watch a few minutes of *Buffy*, then take another. At the rate he was going, it would take him two hours to finish it. Pat continued to alternate between munching on his brownie and rubbing my feet. After fifteen minutes, I touched Chris' hand and took the glass back, took another sip, and then gave it back to him. I closed my eyes, rested my head against his chest, and sighed happily again.

I heard Mike snort in our direction. "You three should just go upstairs and get it on."

"Nope. Too comfy right here. You go upstairs if you don't want to watch. Or come join us. I bet Pat's other side is cold." Then I realized I actually said that out loud. "And we have reached Sarah's cutoff point for the night."

"You sure? I'll happily make you another if it'll get you upstairs," Pat said.

"You'd share me with Chris if it meant getting me into bed?"

"Better than nothing."

"You know I'm right here, right? And, also, I'm not nearly drunk enough to let your skinny, red-haired ass into my bed."

"How do you know it has red hair?" Pat asked him.

"And we have reached Chris and Pat's cutoff points, too," I said.

"Nah. I'm still good. No need to cut me off until I do invite both of you upstairs," Chris said while smiling at me.

"Yes, but by the time you've had that much both of us might just well say yes." I caressed his face.

"It'd be fun. I could show you my tricks," Pat gently stroked my ankle. Very welcome shivers slid up my leg.

"You think you've got anything I haven't seen yet?" I grinned at him.

"Ohhh…" He smiled widely. "Well, I could show the virgin over there some tricks."

"The virgin over here was married for over a century. I've got tricks you've never dreamed of."

"I doubt that. I've got some pretty wild dreams."

Autumn stood up. "Well, we have certainly reached Autumn's cutoff point because if I have to watch much more of this I will start to puke."

"Sorry, Autumn." I started to straighten up into a less loungey pose, but Chris kept me tight against him. "Looks like I'm not going anywhere."

She shook her head. "Good night. If I don't see you before I leave tomorrow, Merry Christmas and Happy New Year."

"Happy New Year, Autumn," I said to her. She went up the stairs and a few minutes later vanished into her room.

I settled in close to Chris, feet snug against Pat, and let my mind drift.

"Is she asleep?" Pat asked quietly after Mike and Dave went to bed.

"I think so," Chris answered.

"I guess we aren't going anywhere anytime soon."

"Feel free to head home. I'll keep her warm."

"How drunk are you?"

"Drunk enough to enjoy this. Not so drunk I'll end up throwing up. It's pretty nice."

"And you think I'm going to leave?"

"I can hope."

"Ain't gonna happen."

"Why am I not shocked?" Chris stroked her hair, letting his fingers trace down her cheek.

Pat caressed her knee. "Did you feel her thinking about both of us?"

"Yes. You will have to get me a lot drunker before that happens."

"How much?"

"I honestly don't think there's enough alcohol on Earth to get me to share."

"I was afraid that was the answer. Still, nice images. The girl has an intense imagination to her."

"Yes, she does." Which was putting it mildly. As she was falling asleep, some of the images were vivid enough Chris could practically feel them.

"What was your favorite?"

"We are not having this conversation."

"Come on. The one where she was kneeling in front of me with you behind her, or the one where she was on your lap, and I was behind her?"

"I am not talking to you about this."

Pat snorted. "So, are we the kind of gentlemen to carry her upstairs, tuck her in your bed, then come back down here and camp out of the sofas or do we stay here snuggled with her?"

"I don't care what kind of gentleman you are. I'm staying here, with her. I haven't been this content in twenty-two years, and I am not about to cut it a second shorter than necessary."

"If I was on your side of the sofa, I'd feel the same way. Good night, Chris."

"'Night, Pat."

He didn't fall asleep for a long time. He didn't think Pat did either though they both stayed quiet and relaxed. He shifted further so his back was against the arm of the sofa, and she in turn scooted around so her face was against his chest. He continued to very slowly stroke her hair and cheek. Eventually he drifted off to sleep.

He felt someone watching him. Chris looked up and found his little brother staring at him. "Well, this is cozy."

"Tom? What time is it?" They had all shifted during the night. Sarah's head and back were in his lap, her legs across Pat, who had slumped over and was leaning against his side.

"Nine o'clock. You know, when I said I'd be here to get you."

Sarah jerked awake in his lap. "Chris? Pat?"

"Good morning," Pat said to them with a huge smile while straightening up. "You fell asleep during *Buffy*. Chris and I, being proper gentlemen, were too kind to move and wake you."

"You let me sleep on you all night?"

"Well, it was that or dump you on the floor. You looked so happy where you were neither of us had the heart to move," Pat answered.

"Oh." She pulled herself out of Chris' lap and took her feet off of Pat's. Sarah ran her fingers through her hair and looked up at Tom. "Hi."

"Hi."

Chris remembered his manners. "These are my friends, Sarah and Pat. This is my brother Tom. Give me a few minutes, and I'll have my things ready to go."

"Okay." Tom surveyed the room filled with beer bottles. He reached for the lone remaining brownie.

"You don't want that," Pat told him.

"Why not?"

"They suck. Really bad. Mike made them, and he can't cook to save his life. We were using it as proof there actually is something in this world worse than cafeteria food."

"Oh. That bad?"

"Worse," Sarah said.

Chris came back down the stairs with his backpack bulging. "See you all next year."

"See you," Pat said.

"'Till next year," Sarah said.

"What? No hugs?" Tom smirked.

"Come on." Chris poked his brother out of the house.

When they were both in the car, heading toward I-79, Tom asked, "Was she the one we saw when you were moving in?"

"Yes. I told you I'd find her again. She lives two doors down in the gray house."

"Judging by your farewell, I'd say she's not your girlfriend."

"No, she's not."

"But you'd like her to be?"

"I often wake up with women in my lap. It's no big deal. Yes, I'd like her to be my girlfriend."

"Why isn't she?"

"She's got a boyfriend."

"Mom and Dad are going to be so relieved."

"You'd think I was a cross dresser with a rainbow tattooed on my forehead and a great big Gay Pride flag on my side of the room."

"You're a twenty-one year old English major who was way too attentive in church and has never had a girlfriend. And you do have a tattoo of, what, ivy leaves? You wear necklaces and rings. What were they supposed to think?"

"I'm not gay."

"They will be very pleased to hear it."

"There's nothing to tell."

"There was a girl in your lap when I came to get you. Before you woke up, you were petting her hair. That's big news."

"Do you really have to tell them?"

"Depends. Can you make it worth my while not to?"

"What do you want?"

"Our room empty all night on New Year's."

"I can do that."

"Then Mom and Dad don't have to know about Sarah." They drove a few more miles. "Tell me about this boyfriend of hers."

"Say you wanted a girl, what would be your worst nightmare to compete against?"

"Don't know. I've never thought about it."

"He's a handsome, taller than I am, twenty-eight-year-old Mossad agent who's currently undercover in a terrorist cell in Somalia and used to hunt down ex-Nazis."

"Really?" Tom sounded like he didn't believe Chris.

"Really. She met him when she was in the army in Israel. He was trying to stop a bombing. It didn't get stopped. She swooped in and patched him back up."

Tom thought about it for a minute. Then he looked at Chris and said, "You're fucked."

"My thoughts exactly."

30.

Pat slung his backpack over his shoulders and hopped on the bike behind me. Three hundred and eighty-three miles later we were half-frozen but at my brothers' farm. He looked a bit shell-shocked through the introductions. I think that came from being very, very cold and suddenly enveloped in a mad whirlwind of Metzes ranging in age from three, Yael, to forty-one, Ben. Once he thawed out, got some food in him, and started to come back to life, I could see my oldest nephews watch him like he was the coolest thing ever.

Pat probably is the coolest thing that's ever walked into our home. He kept the group interested by telling stories of us at school, heavy on the fencing and hand to hand, light on the magic. Jon and Eli were looking at him like when they got him back to their room they'd be quizzing him intensely on the pieces of college life he wasn't talking about.

After dinner Pat, Ben, and I settled back to chat without the others. Mostly we covered the ground we had gone over with Chris and Chuck. Pat had a few new questions that also got no useful answers. I told Ben we'd had no luck in finding the guy with the brown hair. Though I was able to get confirmation he had been in Ben's class, the year without a yearbook, another dead end.

Then Ben and Pat spent an hour talking general magic. Ben found Pat and how he did what he did absolutely fascinating. They got to the point where they were actually doing small spells, shields and glamours, and talking technique. I just sat and watched. With each word I could see Ben's magic more fully. It was quiet and calming, putting me in mind of Morrell. There was nothing defensive or shivery about him. What really struck me was how comfortable Ben was with Pat. The sharpness I felt when he was chatting with Chris over the computer was gone.

I got the chance to ask him about it the next morning.

"So, what happened to Mr. This-Is-Your-Formal-Notice-I-Can-Magically-Kick-Your-Ass?"

Ben laughed. "Tell me this, has Pat let you check out his talismans and learn how his defenses work?"

"I've touched the rock."

"Not the same thing at all. Have you let him hold your star and feel what all it can do?"

"No. He's never asked."

"That's why he's not getting a view of Big Bad Magical Big Brother. Honestly, most of that was directed at Chuck. I'm not thrilled with that one."

"Me either. But he's part of the package. So, you like Pat?"

"I like him very much. He's welcome here."

"Good."

"Keep one thing in mind. He doesn't want to be your friend. He'll settle for it if it's all he can get, but he wants more."

"I know."

"You aren't leading him on, are you?"

"I'm trying not to. He knows I've got a boyfriend."

"Ahhh... so how is Ari, who you haven't mentioned in a month?"

"How would I know?"

"Maybe this is a more direct way to put it: do you still have a boyfriend?"

I sighed. "I'm trying to. I live in a very intense world filled with lovely men who are very dear to me. Doing the right thing by holding onto a ghost is hard."

Ben spent a few minutes looking me over and then asked, "What makes you think it's the right thing?"

I didn't have a good answer for that.

When the weather was clear again, we headed toward Christmas at Pat's. The family I come from is well off, granted most of our capital is wrapped up in land and cattle, but we've got money. Pat's family is *rich*. I knew they had to be well off because they live in Manhattan and his dad's in finance. Still, having a valet park the bike, a doorman usher us into his building, and realizing I was in an apartment with at least 3,000 square feet overlooking Central Park, was a shock. Our entire farm isn't worth as much as Pat's parents' apartment.

Having grown up with a very large family I didn't think the Calumn Christmas extravaganza would be anything I wasn't used to. I was wrong. Not to indicate my family is in any way quiet or reserved, but the Calumns are a loud, cheery, occasionally tipsy sort of crowd.

By the end of Christmas I was pleasantly buzzed, tired, and a little upside down feeling. Like a small redheaded hurricane had whipped through the apartment. I was leaning against the fireplace, watching Pat's twin cousins play with something—I don't remember what, but for the moment they were quiet—when Pat came over next to me to hand me eggnog. Grandpa Calumn started to laugh loudly, with much joy. He had the sort of laugh that, especially if you're a bit tipsy, makes everyone around him laugh.

"Give her a good one, boy!" It took a minute for me to register what he said; then I knew what he was talking about. I looked up to confirm. Yep, the dratted Christmas weed, mistletoe, hung above me.

Pat gave me a look that was half-devil, but he didn't move until I nodded at him. It was a very nice kiss or, as the hooting around me indicated, a good one. Maybe he's got lots of natural skill. Maybe the whole mind reading thing really is a handy sex skill. Either way, he knew what to do with my lips. I pulled back after a minute or two. Probably much longer than was necessary, but it had been an awfully long time since anyone had kissed me, and it really did feel good.

Pat looked stunned I had let it go on that long. I felt bad about it. Kissing a guy like that might as well be the definition of 'leading him on.' I'd have to apologize when there weren't a dozen Calumns around.

When I woke the next morning, I could feel the rest of the house sleeping around me. I got my jog in and headed back upstairs. Katie, Pat's twelve-year-old sister, was in the kitchen eating breakfast when I came in; I joined her.

"You and Pat are friends, right?" she asked when I sat down with a bowl of cereal.

"We are friends."

"Is that going to change?" I thought back; she had watched that kiss with very big eyes.

"I very much doubt it, but it's not impossible."

"Why?"

"I have a boyfriend."

"Oh. Why aren't you at his place?"

I smiled. "Because he's a million miles away pretending to be someone else." Katie looked confused. "He's infiltrating a terrorist organization in Somalia. At least I think that's what he's doing. I don't know for sure and probably won't ever know for sure."

"Oh. When did you see him last?"

"A little over two months ago."

"Do you get letters or anything?"

"No. Two months with no contact down, at least another ten to go."

"That's a really long time."

"Yes, it is."

"Would he have been bothered by last night?"

"I don't know. I hope not." I tried not to think about how, of all the things I had done since Ari left, last night was probably not on the top of the list of things that would have bothered him. I figured having my hand less than an inch away from Chris' penis while I worked on his hip and waking up on the sofa with him and Pat would probably be higher on the list, with the incredible magic saga being at the absolute top of the list.

"You look like you aren't very sure about that."

"I'm not very sure about that. Perhaps mulling it over in the shower would be a good idea." I finished my cereal and headed to my room.

I opted for a bath. Not only did the guest room I was staying in have its own bathroom, it had a soaking tub big enough for me and a few friends. As it filled, I thought about Ari and felt guilty. Two months had passed, and I hadn't been thinking about him much beyond the first three weeks. Three or four days could go by now without him crossing my mind.

So much for true love. No. That was too cold. It's just easier not to think of him. A defense mechanism. A way to not have to hurt too much because it did really hurt those first few weeks. *Sure. It's all about avoiding pain. It's got nothing to do with the redheads that fill your life now.* I was startled at exactly how much sarcasm I could pack into the little voice in my head.

Okay, it's got everything to do with the redheads. Heads? Fine, redhead! Much better. Still, I had been doing better. I'd kept Chris out of my head from the day I healed him until the *Buffy* extravaganza. Really, the bigger issue—the one I should have been more concerned about—was the fact I never told Ari about all of this. Why not? I could put a cut back together when I saw him last. Yeah, he wouldn't have taken it well, but once I did that, it's not like he'd be able to deny it. I should have told him. Compared to that, I could have slept with Pat last night and it wouldn't have been that big of a deal.

Do better! If you want a future with that man you've got to tell him. If? Fuck. Do better!

When I got out and headed back to their kitchen, I found Pat in his jammies eating breakfast.

"What'd you have for breakfast this morning?" he asked me.

"Cereal, milk, fruit."

"Good. How about I introduce you to some real cheesecake for lunch?"

"I could stand an introduction."

"Wonderful. I was thinking we could bop around town today."

"Sounds good. How's the weather report?"

He felt for a minute. "Tomorrow will be good and again on the thirtieth. How long do you want to stay?"

"I'll probably head off tomorrow. Your mom is doing a wonderful job making me feel welcome, but I don't want to impose on her."

"It's not an imposition," Ellen said as she came into the kitchen to pour herself some cereal.

"Thank you, but I'm still starting to feel a little homesick." If she thought I meant for the farm, I wasn't going to correct that. Some alone time was sounding pretty good 'round about now.

"I understand that. It's good to see your family when you've got the chance."

"Yes, it is."

Pat and I floated around New York doing touristy stuff. A little ice skating. Some roaming about looking at the Christmas decorations and the preparation for New Year's. Then he took me to the Stage Deli.

"This is, at least in my opinion, the best Pastrami and cheesecake in New York."

"I'll have to have the cheesecake then." I had it for lunch, and it was *good!* He packed away a sandwich so tall just looking at it made my jaw ache and finished up with a slice of his own.

I finished off my slice about the time he finished off his. "We really have to do this again," I said to him.

"This summer. Celebrate finishing off the year."

"I'd like that."

"Me too."

We headed into the street. "I'm sorry I let the kiss go on so long last night."

"It wasn't that bad was it?" He kept his smile in place, but I could feel his uncertainty.

"What? No. Quite nice actually, that's why it went on so long. I was using you because it did feel good, and I haven't kissed anyone in a long time."

Now his grin was genuine. "I'm amenable to being used for such purposes."

I laughed. "Yeah, but I don't want to be that kind of person."

"You're bothered about it. I'd say you aren't that sort of person."

"Still, it's not kind to kiss someone like that and not mean it."

He turned to look at me, resting his hand on my forearm. "It's really okay, Sarah. I would have told them to stuff it if I hadn't wanted to. Whether you meant it or not, it felt pretty damn good."

"Yeah, it did. You've got skills."

"Thank you. No guy on earth minds hearing that. So, wanna see what else I can do?" He smiled brightly at me.

"Nope." I smiled and shook my head. "He'll forgive me a kiss. I really doubt if I finish up the story with, 'and then we got a hotel room and fucked like bunnies all afternoon,' he would forgive me that."

Pat grinned at me again, but this time the smile wasn't quite as bright. "I know I wouldn't. Since fucking like bunnies is out, what do you want to do with the afternoon?"

"No idea. We've skated, we've eaten, and we've wandered about. I'd say let's catch a show, but we aren't dressed for it."

"The dress code isn't too strict for matinees. Let's go see if we can find tickets to anything."

"Cool."

When I got home, I found a package with Chris' handwriting on it waiting for me. I had it opened before I was halfway up the steps. Inside was a paperback copy of *The Things They Carried*.

I got inside and opened the book. He had a note tucked inside.

> Sarah,
> Not sure what the etiquette is on this. Autumn would know, but she isn't here. I saw this and thought you would like it. I wanted to give it to you.
> Merry Christmas,
> Chris.

I unpacked, started my dinner cooking, and began to read. Dinner was burned before I pulled back from the book enough to get it on a plate. I cut the black bits off and ate absently while I read.

Hours later, I finished the book. I couldn't sleep. I sent off a thank you email to Chris and puttered about my apartment, not sure what to do with myself. The stories weren't letting me go.

My cell beeped to let me know I had a text while I was thinking of putting a *Buffy* DVD in my computer. It was from Chris.

I'm glad you liked it.

I really did. What are you doing still up?

I wasn't. John messed with my computer and left the volume high. When it beeped to tell me a new email was there, I woke up.

Sorry about that.

Not your fault. So, you're home then?

Yep, got in a few hours ago.

Got New Year's Plans?

Not yet.

Want to go out with Chuck and me?

Sure. Where?

No idea yet. Might just be Writers' or your place.

Sounds good. Let me know when you've got a plan.

Okay. I should go back to sleep. I'm taking Helen to the orthodontist tomorrow morning.

Goodnight Chris.

Goodnight.

31.

"And the reason we are walking up to her place to then walk back down into town is…?" Chuck asked as they left his house, turning north, toward Sarah's, instead of heading east toward the bar.

"You don't have to come if you don't want to," Chris responded.

"That does not answer my question. I'll understand if you want to walk her home tonight. What I'm not getting is why we're walking six miles out of our way to pick up a girl neither of us is dating, and who is perfectly capable of walking, or better yet *riding*, down to meet us at the bar."

"Because I'm a very nice guy."

"You must be. This certainly isn't anything I'd do on my own."

"As I said a minute ago, you don't have to come. We can meet you there."

"I'm tempted. My ankle aches and heading all the way up and all the way back isn't making me sing for joy."

"Then don't do it. I'm not a baby. I can get to her place on my own. Go get us a booth, a round of drinks, and we'll be there in…" Chris' voice dropped off as he looked across the street. "You see it?"

"I do now." It was one of the Minions. The winged serpent. *Sypheleem.* Taller than either of the men, with a ten foot wingspan, it was silvery gray with glints of orange from the reflected lamplight. They stopped and watched it warily. It didn't appear to have noticed them yet.

"What's it doing?" Chris asked.

"Waiting for us?" Chuck's eyebrows furrowed. "This is wrong."

"I know. Let's loop around it. See if we can get a better view. Maybe it's bait?"

"They've never tried anything like that before."

"Always a first time."

They circled widely around it, cutting across a few yards to keep it in view without crossing the path of its unmoving eyes. They finished the circle and stopped back at Chuck's house to talk under the shields.

"What the fuck is it doing? There's nothing else there, and it's just sitting," Chuck said, looking agitated. He was used to all sorts of attacks, but stupid blatant ones that didn't actually attack were unnerving.

"Calm down. Maybe that's the point, to get us jittery."

"Well, it's working. I'm jittery. I don't like it when the bad guys start acting like something lobotomized them."

"I'm not enjoying this, either. Keep an eye on my back. I'm going to go get it."

"Why?"

"Because that's why it's there. Get her number up, and call her before you come running in if you need to."

"Great. This is exactly what I wanted to do for New Year's."

"Yeah, it wasn't on my list, either. At least she can get to us fast."

"Wonderful. Have fun."

"Watch my flank."

"I always do."

Chris found a comfortable point to attack. A minivan blocked him from the view of most people on the street and made sure nothing could sneak up behind him. He took a few seconds to pull the energy to him, mold it into a ball of force, and toss it at the serpent. When it connected, the Minion turned to him sluggishly; he felt a warm glow fill his heart. Chris smiled widely and thought to Chuck, *It's got anatomy!*

Wonderful. Go kill it before whatever else is out there jumps you.

Chris focused on the way the creature in front of him was built. It slithered jerkily toward him. He realized it was cold blooded and slowly freezing. That made his smile wider. He pulled energy out of it, heat vamping it instead of psy vamping it, letting its blood freeze in its veins. Its hammered pewter eyes slowly tracked him. He knew it was trying its best attack, a mental one. Those eyes could confuse you to the point of no longer knowing up from down, but with its blood crystallizing into ice, the *Sypheleem* couldn't do it.

He reversed the heat he had taken out of it and focused it on a tiny point in what he knew was the serpent's brain. For half a second he could feel it rejoicing at the heat. Then the blood began to boil, destroying the brain tissue around it. It fell over, dead.

That was anticlimactic. He walked over to touch it. It was real, solid and cold under his hands. *So, what do you suggest I do with a dead winged serpent?*

I think that's a question for Dave.

Because he's oh so handy right now?

If that was an ambush, it was a really bad one.

I don't think it had enough of a brain left to really plan. Too cold for those things here.

That'd be nice if it's true. Go to her place. I'll keep a few minutes behind you.

Okay. And the serpent?

There's a trash can at the end of the next driveway. It might fit in there.

It's taller than I am and frozen. It will not fit in the trashcan.

Then drag it behind the pile of snow at the end of the driveway and hope the people who live here don't call Weekly World News when they find it.

Chris bent down to drag the Minion out of the way when he got another surprise. *It's gone.*

Well, that was convenient.

Yeah. Too convenient. I don't think we're going out drinking tonight.

No. We aren't. See you at her place.

Chris got up the hill to her house in a little under an hour. She opened the door. For a moment he was struck by how pretty she looked. She had on a skirt and the soft gray sweater that left her one shoulder bare. He looked more carefully and realized she had on some makeup.

"Let me get my coat." She turned to the hook where her coat hung. As she turned, he caught a faint scent of something floral and spicy. It made him want to nuzzle against her shoulder and inhale deeply.

He stepped into her place, pulling his mind away from her scent to what had just happened. "Change of plans, we're staying here tonight."

"Okay. What happened?" She shut the door.

"Chuck's a few minutes behind me. I'll tell you about it when he gets in."

"Okay." He stayed tense and ready to jump until he heard Chuck's steps on her stairs. Chuck came in and nodded to him; there was no sign of anything following him.

"What happened?" she asked after getting them drinks. They told her. She looked perplexed. "So... that's just weird."

Chuck nodded. "Yeah, it's weird."

"Have they ever done something like that before? Just sat there and waited for you?"

"That one time coming home from the movies."

"Why did it have a body?" Sarah chewed on her lip while waiting for them to answer.

"No idea. It certainly backfired on it. It's just not a good plan for them to have bodies at all. I can kill things with bodies like..." Chris snapped his fingers. They sat quietly for a few minutes trying to think of why this had happened.

"So, has there only been one real attack this year?" Sarah asked.

"Yes," Chris answered, "and we've only seen low-level things since we arrived here."

"Assistant Vice President in Charge of Accounting is about as high up as we've gotten. The members of the Board haven't bothered to visit," Chuck said.

"And if we're lucky, they won't," Chris replied.

"But we aren't that lucky," Chuck answered.

Chris looked far away and fiddled with his drink while he talked. "We might be. What if they've got bodies here and now because they have to pull off the local energy to keep going? We know we got their power source. Sooner or later they've got to find something new or starve."

"Are you thinking through this, or is this what you're feeling?" Chuck watched Chris critically.

"Does it matter?" Sarah didn't get Chuck's question.

"He's a mage. If he's thinking, that's fine. If he's feeling it, he's likely to have a better idea of how the magic is working."

"Okay. So, if it was you, we'd prefer you were thinking?"

"If it was me, you'd prefer I was doing research on it. I'm not plugged into the magic the same way he is."

"To answer your question," he said to Chuck, "about half and half. Either Mildred's keeping the big guns hidden… or it's eating them. I like that idea. It feels right. Mildred would have to decimate or worse its foot soldiers to keep going, but one of the higher-ups would keep the rest of them going for a long time. Might be why we haven't seen any of the higher-ups. Might tell us why now. If it's out of them, this might be about finishing the fight before it starves…" Chris let that idea linger, rolling it through his mind.

"Is there any way to know for sure?" Sarah questioned.

"Well, if one of the higher-ups pops out, it proves all of them haven't been eaten. Beyond that, no. Not like we can test for it," Chris replied

"So… if you really think that's true, shouldn't you…" she gestured to indicate not just Chris and Chuck but the members who weren't here as well, "scatter? Make Mildred burn through its reserves faster hunting for you, then just wait it out?"

"If there was any way to know it's true, yes. If it isn't, then we just lost our best protection," Chris answered.

"You're not sure enough of that idea to bet on it with your life?"

"No."

Chuck warmed up to the idea. "You know, that might also explain why we're seeing less of them this year. Mildred might be keeping them close to conserve energy. Maybe it's planning to bring them all out in one last attack. It knows we've got a healer now. Instead of nibbling at us with little attacks you can take care of, Mildred'll mass its power, attack us with full force, and overwhelm us."

"These things aren't known for tactical brilliance, are they?" Both of the guys looked at her like they had missed something. "They know I'm here. They know I'm the healer. They know you don't have a backup. I should have a great big price on my head and a huge target painted on my back. I should be fighting off attacks every day."

"You really should." Chris looked a little puzzled. "I can't imagine they believe in the Geneva conventions…"

"It could be they just haven't really figured out what you are yet. They've never seen what it is you really do," Chuck said though he didn't sound sure.

"They know enough to keep my place under watch."

"True, but we don't know what they see. We couldn't feel you here until we knew you were here. Your place has some really impressive shields on it courtesy of Allan, and the job you did on it was some tight magic as well," Chris replied.

"I thought you were all able to identify me as a healer by feel alone."

"Dave and Chris were. Pat probably was too, but we weren't talking to him then. Autumn and I couldn't feel it. Mike didn't feel it but was willing to believe it based on the rest of your story."

"So, that means, what? There's a fifty-fifty chance they know what I am?"

"The fact you aren't being attacked every day lends credence to the theory they don't actually know." Chris looked out my window toward where the Watchers usually lurked.

"How do you go about making it attack more so it burns through its energy faster?"

"The same way we go about moving to any of the next steps: we've got to find where they're coming from." Chris turned back to her.

"Who has the locator spell?"

"Been watching *Buffy* lately?" Chris smiled.

"Not a whole lot to do here by myself with the bookstore closed and the roads bad enough I don't want to take my bike out. On a more serious level, could some sort of locator spell be done? Isn't this the kind of thing a mage is handy for?"

Chris answered, "This would be precisely the kind of thing a mage is handy for. There's a reason we've got a huge map, and it was to do exactly what you're suggesting. Magic and logic are not incompatible. When you get an answer you know to be impossible, the Minions are coming from nowhere, you know you're dealing with magic stronger than yours."

"Freshman year, first semester, Chris spent a lot of time working on the locator spell. He's still annoyed it didn't work," Chuck said.

"Mike made up the map for me. I did the spell. Nothing. Okay, they aren't in Reevesville. So, a bigger map. Not in Pennsylvania. Bigger map, not in the Northeast. Bigger map, not in the Western Hemisphere. We were pretty sure the spell wasn't doing its job, but just for kicks, I tried a globe. They aren't coming from anywhere on Earth."

"So, magic stronger than yours is hiding them?"

"Yes."

"That doesn't bode well for you guys winning. Does it?"

Chris replied, "Not necessarily. None of us can find Dave if he doesn't want to be found. If we could find him, any of us could take him. The only thing it doesn't bode well for is us finding the doorway."

"Which is step one on the to do list."

"Yeah," Chuck said.

"If it's that well-hidden, why do you think walking around looking for it will do the trick?"

Chris and Chuck looked at each other. "The alternative is sitting on our hands waiting for Mildred to do whatever it wants to do. Look, we probably can't find the portal by walking around looking for it, but that's our best shot of taking charge and making Mildred fight on our terms," Chris told me.

Sarah thought about that for a moment and moved onto another question, "So, if logic and magic aren't incompatible, how about magic and science? The reason I bring this up, shouldn't bodies take more energy than no bodies?

"Fuck!" Chris let his head drop to the table.

"What Chris is so eloquently saying is, yes, bodies should take more energy. He's feeling very frustrated by this new incomprehensible development."

Chris stood up and made himself another cup of tea. "I've been trying to make these things develop bodies all year long, and now suddenly they're doing it for me? They know me. They know how I fight. It's a death sentence for them."

"Did they know you were trying that?" Sarah asked.

"I tried it on the one who attacked us before the break."

"What do they gain by doing it for you?"

The three of them thought about it. When Chris spoke sounded weary: "I told you it was a good plan. The only reason to do it for me is to keep me from learning how to do it myself.

Mildred keeps most of its pieces close, occasionally harassing us with solid attacks, maybe weakening us, but mostly testing its forces and what they can do here with bodies. Then, at the time of its choosing, it attacks en masse without bodies, denying me the ability to make Mildred and the Minions real."

"Well, that's better than thinking it suddenly went stupid," Chuck said.

"Yeah. Great. Mildred's not stupid. We already knew that."

"So figure out how to make the solid ones incorporeal again, then reverse engineer it. Be smarter than it is," Sarah said to him. "Or go at it from both sides, find something that doesn't have a body and work from that side. When the solid Minions show up, make them fade."

Chuck shot her down. "Nothing here feels like the Minions, so there's nothing to practice on from that side."

"From the other side it means not fighting when I run into one: solely working on taking them apart. Or I have to work on something alive. I don't want to do that. Nasty critters with real bodies are very few and far between here, not common enough to make working on one of them likely. I'd have to catch or buy something, a mouse say, and figure out how to turn it into just energy."

"Oh." Sarah looked sick at the idea of what that involved.

"What will probably happen is I'll stop fighting. When I'm on patrol, I'll be looking for a solid one, hoping for a shot to break it."

"Which means when he goes on patrol the rest of us are more likely to get hurt. If something with a body shows up, he can kill it quickly or study it, but he can't do both, not at first anyway. We're left in a situation where the guy who's best at killing these things isn't fighting and needs extra protection. And the things we're protecting him from just got harder for the rest of us to fight."

"None of the rest of you can try to do this?"

"Mike doesn't have the power. You don't go anywhere near a battle if we can help it. The rest of them are wizards." Chris' voice was tired and stressed.

"What about Autumn?"

Both of the guys shuddered. Chris picked his words carefully. "If Autumn could figure out how to do it, she's got the power for it. Remember, fine-tuned control is not her thing. If she figured it out, one of us would be just as likely to end up a ghost as the Minion she was aiming for. Because control isn't her thing, it's also quite likely she wouldn't be able to then turn the trick around if she did figure out how to do it."

Chuck took over. "Autumn's more like a nuclear bomb than nitroglycerine. She's usually pretty stable, just sits there doing nothing. But if you hit the right buttons she goes boom."

"Boom is really not what we want happening with her," Chris finished.

"If nothing here really feels like a Minion, what were you practicing with before?"

"Ghosts. I was still at the proof of concept stage, seeing if it could be done."

"We know it can be done now. Mildred's done it for you. Skip to stage two," Sarah said.

"Can't. I still don't know how to do it on any level."

"You know it can be done now. Keep trying!"

"Go Team!" Chuck chirped at her. Sarah glared at Chuck. "What?" he asked innocently.

"You know exactly what! You mean it as a slap at me for being cute and enthusiastic. It's especially annoying since you aren't exactly overflowing with problem solving plans."

"You want problem solving? Here it is: Mildred doesn't want us dead. We'd be dead if that was the case. Mildred wouldn't have pulled its punches back when we were kids and couldn't protect ourselves if it wanted us dead. Mildred wants us in pain. All of this is designed to annoy us, hurt us, and grind us down until it finally comes through and destroys us. Our best hope is killing Mildred before it kills us, and that rests almost entirely on him," Chuck gestured at Chris, "pulling some sort of wild trick out of his ass. Like turning Mildred solid and blowing up its brain. When it comes down to it, all the practice on Earth isn't really going to help. Mildred isn't like anything else. It is not a Minion. It is not a mouse. At best he'll have a general idea it can be done and sort of know how to do it. Our job is to keep him alive long enough to pull it off."

Chris sighed. Granted he hadn't solved the problem yet, but he was sure Chuck was underestimating his ability to kill Mildred. "At best I'll know it can be done, and how to do it. I'll have the ability to tailor the spell to Mildred while fighting and keeping it distracted."

"You hope."

"You don't have anything better do you?" Chris asked pointedly.

"No. We've been over that."

"So, is now the time to head over to the physics department and have a chat with one of the professors about the nature of energy and matter?" Sarah questioned.

"Been there, done that, and courtesy of Chuck, Gren doesn't remember it. It was an exceptionally frustrating conversation. There's a connection, obviously. The magic is making energy into matter."

"What happens when I heal something? I mean, that's energy becoming matter, right?"

"Is it?" Chris looked interested.

She gave Chuck a hard grin. "Guess what Chuck? You just volunteered to be a guinea pig."

"What are you going to do with me?" Chuck eyes were wide with alarm.

"I'm going to cut a small bit of your skin off and then fix it. Chris is going to watch and try to learn what I'm doing."

"Making cells replicate faster is not the same thing as making something out of nothing," Chuck said defensively.

"I'm not starting with nothing. I'm starting with your energy and turning it into new cells."

"Is that how you do it?" Chris asked.

"Maybe. I think so. If Chuck's right and I'm just speeding things up, the technique will be useless. But if I'm just speeding things up, I should leave scars when I heal you, and I don't. If I'm turning his energy into new Chuck, then it will be quite useful for you to feel how I do it." She turned to Chuck. "I'm thinking your arm. It won't bleed too much."

"You're really going to do this to me?"

Sarah had a hard gleam in her eyes. "Go Team!" She got out her paring knife. "Stay still. It'll hurt but not for too long. Ready to watch what I do?" Chris nodded.

She did it quickly. Two small cuts lifted a quarter-inch-long strip of skin off of Chuck's arm. "Good job of not moving."

"Get on with it." He didn't look at the damage she had done to him.

Chris felt her heal before. The last time she did it for him, when he had hours to see how she had been doing it, he had been paying way more attention to the feel of her hands on his skin and hoping she didn't notice how hard he was than the magic she had been doing. This was the first time he tried to see exactly what she was doing and how it worked. About fifty percent of it was making Chuck heal himself faster. The other half was sort of like what he was looking for, but it wasn't quite right. The cut was done before he could figure out exactly what he was seeing.

"She just speeds things up." Chuck said when she finished. Chris was already rolling up his sleeve.

"No. It's not just that." Chris grabbed the knife and started cutting himself.

"Whoa. That's a big cut." Her eyes were wide as blood slid down his arm to drip on her table. He casually flicked the strip of skin aside. "What are you doing?"

"Making sure I have enough time to see what you're doing. Have at it." He held out his arm with a three-inch-long strip of skin cut off of it. She went back to healing. He focused on what she was doing. From the edges in the skin was reforming faster than normal. In the middle, though, that was something different. It felt like she was making him real, taking whatever there was beyond his body, and giving it form. He could feel her doing it but not how.

"Get into her mind and tell me how she's doing it."

Chuck did, and everything came to a screeching halt. "Ow!" Sarah clutched her head and ran to the bathroom. They heard retching and vomiting.

"Maybe a lighter touch next time," Chris said to Chuck sharply.

"That was a light touch."

"She's not usually that sensitive to you."

"I've never gotten that far into her mind before."

"Could you see how she was doing it?"

"No. I had just found what you were looking at when she bolted," Chuck said as the toilet flushed.

She came out looking gray and shaky. "Let me finish." She glared at Chuck. "Stay in your own fucking mind. You," she said to Chris, "don't ever tell him to go into my mind again. Now, give me your hand. I'm going to use your magic to do it."

"You can do that?" Chris looked eager and surprised.

"I can right now. If I stop to think about it, it won't work. So be quiet and pay attention." She took his hand in hers and began again.

Chris felt a dull shock of recognition when she took his hand in hers. Rewind twenty-two years, back to, practicing the magic that would keep him alive for the last spell. It wasn't precisely the same, couldn't be. It wasn't the same sort of spell. But the feel of it! She held his hand and pulled his magic through hers, using his power and her technique to heal him. He could feel her make his skin grow and close. She was giving his energy physical form. He felt like he almost had it, and once again the healing was done before he really could get a handle on it.

"Can you do that again?" Chris' breath came fast with the excitement of being on the verge of knowing how to solve the problem and the immense intimacy of what she was doing with him.

"Maybe," she said. He rolled up the other sleeve. "Stop it. That's enough of your skin cut off tonight."

"I'm not doing it again," Chuck said.

"Fine." She handed Chris the knife while pushing up her own sleeve. "Do it for me."

His eyes met hers. Chris knew she had felt the magic just as intensely as he did and she was fully aware of what she was asking him to do: cut her skin, spill her blood, and let her use his power to put it back together. His mouth went dry at the thought of it. He held the knife, spending a moment looking at the smooth skin of her arm. He put it down. "I'm not sure I can."

"Yeah, well, self-mutilation is against my religion, so you or Chuck can do it. I'm not cutting myself on purpose. I really shouldn't be cutting you, either."

"You really shouldn't be doing any of this. Magic is against your religion," Chuck said.

"Consulting the dead is against my religion. Healing isn't. There's a famous Jewish healer who got called out for a lot of things, but the only thing in regards to his healing was about timing issues, not about the healing itself. Now, one of you, cut."

Chris looked at Chuck. There was absolutely no way he'd let Chuck do it. He picked up the knife again, took a deep breath, and pressed the knife to her skin. Two cuts. Her blood welled up, and he shivered at the feel of it against his fingers. Before he could focus too closely on her blood on his skin, she was holding his hand in hers again and pulling his magic into her, using it as her tool to heal her skin.

He focused on the center, ignoring the edges of the cut. In the center she was dealing with her own energy, using his magic to feel what her energy wanted to be, how it wanted to be, and making it become that. Her energy knew what belonged there. It knew how her body should look and act. It knew what skin was and what it should be. She used his magic to allow it to turn that desire into fact.

Then she was done. The connection broke, and he felt achingly alone. His fingers rested on a soft, smooth, hairless patch of perfect, new skin. He caressed it.

"Got it?" Sarah asked him. He knew what her look meant. He felt her skin and blood under his fingers. If he didn't get out of her house right now, he'd start kissing her and wouldn't stop until he had found that connection again.

"Yeah." He turned to Chuck. "Give me a cigarette and your lighter. I'll be back in a few minutes."

"They're in my coat."

Chris walked over to Chuck's coat and put it on. He closed the door behind him, not caring they were both looking at him oddly.

He headed down her steps to the sidewalk, letting the cold clear his head a little. He didn't want a smoke nearly as much as the excuse to get out for a minute. He felt around in Chuck's pockets for the cigs anyway. It'd look even stranger if he went back in and didn't smell like smoke.

He lit it and was pleased to see how steady his hands were. He noticed there was still blood on them—hers probably, but it could be his, or both of theirs. The buzz of the nicotine helped to distance him from what they had just done. Her will using his magic to touch her soul. He inhaled deeply, watching the coal glow orange. He could have stripped her naked, sunk into her body and her mind without touching her with that level of intimacy, without her touching him with that sort of intimacy. She used his magic while her blood coated his fingers! He shivered at it and fought the desire to go back up there, kick Chuck out, and see if he could find that connection again.

Chuck came down a minute later. *You okay?*

He inhaled savagely, savoring the buzz with the burn of the cold air. *Sure.*

You know how to do it now?

Yeah. At least I know how to start.

Good. You want me to excuse myself and leave you two alone.

NO! He knew exactly what would happen if he spent any time alone with her. He'd set her on her table, hike up her skirt, pull her panties to the side, and fuck her, desperate to recapture that feeling of her soul under his fingers, her magic wrapped around his, and her life in his hands.

Okay. Got anything to drink at Writers'?

Yeah. Go get it?

Sure. Keys in your pocket? Chuck patted the pocket of Chris' jacket.

No. Chris reached into his pants and handed Chuck the keys. He took another cig from Chuck's pack and lit it off the first one. He couldn't remember the last time he smoked two in a row, but he needed a few more minutes in the cold by himself.

Chuck came back up with a few bottles of alcohol and no Chris. The few minutes alone had been a good thing. Right now a drink sounded like a good plan, too. I didn't know what had come over me while rinsing my mouth out after Chuck's exceptionally unwelcome foray into my mind, I suddenly just knew how to do what I had done.

What had I done? That was the real question. Vulcan Magic Meld? Twenty-one years, plenty of sex, secrets shared late at night, mourning with my brothers, and nothing had ever come close to that level of intimacy.

I kept seeing the image of my blood on his hands while I used his energy. I couldn't shake the feel of his magic sliding through me, bending to my will. I took a deep breath trying to chase it from my mind.

"Pour me a drink," I told Chuck.

"What do you want?" He turned to my cupboard and grabbed three glasses.

"I don't care."

"Are you okay?" He sounded genuinely concerned. That shocked me out of the post-magic daze.

"I'm probably better than he is, but that's not necessarily saying much."

"No it's not. What did you two do?"

"You couldn't tell?"

"I could feel it was very intense. And it has both of you rattled. Beyond that, no. I didn't want to mess up his concentration by going into his mind, and yours is currently off limits. Now you've both got walls up around whatever happened, and I don't feel like breaking in."

"Thanks. I'm not even sure I could describe it if I wanted to." He handed me a glass of something brown. I took a sip. Whiskey. One more sip. My mind felt like it was getting clearer. "Okay. Here's what I think I did. Don't ask how; I don't know. I used his magic to heal us. My technique, his magic. The blood on top of that... his blood on my hands, mine on his, and... just...." I took another swallow. "It was very intense, very intimate; I wasn't expecting that when I suggested it."

"How did you know you could do it?"

"I just knew. One minute I was tossing my cookies. The next I knew how to show him what it was I do."

We heard Chris' footsteps on my stairs. Chuck poured two more glasses. Chris' was brown as well. I think Chuck had vodka because his was clear. I washed my hands and arms quickly, then looked at my table.

"Chuck, can you get that?" I gestured at the mess on the table as Chris opened the door.

"Yeah."

"Thanks." I really didn't want to touch our blood or skin. Doing so would suck me back into the depths of the magic again, and I was having a hard enough time pulling myself out of it. Much more of that and I'd find myself chasing it, looking for the chance to do it again. To be that open and connected to another human being would be addictive.

Chris hung up Chuck's coat. Chuck handed him the drink. Chris knocked it back. "Happy New Year." He went to the sink to wash his hands. As the blood rinsed clear of his hands, I felt the magic recede further.

I looked at the clock. 12:03. "Happy 2009."

"Happy New Year," Chuck said as he tossed out the paper towel he had used on my table. "Now what?"

"What we were going to do originally. Drink. Listen to music. Eat." Chris walked over to my computer and set up a playlist.

I didn't have a lot of food in the house, but I did have ice cream and cookies. Maybe not the greatest thing to go with drinking, but it was that or start cooking from scratch.

"I've got cookies and ice cream."

"Anything salty?" Chuck wanted to know.

"Not really. I could make popcorn."

"That'll do."

I made popcorn. We spent a tense hour listening to music, half-heartedly eating and drinking. I did a good job of not jumping Chris, dragging him into my room, and trying to recapture that feeling of being with him any way I could. I knew he was doing precisely the same thing. At one Chuck decided it was time to head home. They left. I took an extremely long shower trying to wash off the feel of his blood, magic, and skin under my hands.

When that didn't do anything to relieve the issue, I tried it from the other side, wallowing in it, imagining it as fully as I could, trying to feed the ache that way. It didn't help much, either. Eventually I drank enough I could sleep; all the while imagining the pillow I was wrapped around was him.

"What happened?" Chuck asked as they walked back to his place.

"I'm honestly not sure I can describe it for you. I doubt you've had the kind of sex that most closely resembles it, and I know you've never done anything magical that even came close." He thought about it for a few blocks. "Okay, you can read my thoughts and feelings. Now imagine me doing it back to you at the same time while using your magic to do something. Add to that the way she heals. She does speed things up. She also links into your... soul, for lack of a better word, uses how that feels to know what you healthy should be like, and then works the magic to make that desire a fact. Then, on top of that, because that's just not intense enough, let's toss in some blood."

"What do you mean 'using your magic?' Like an energy boost?"

"No, like directly manipulating my energy to do what needed to be done while I was still using it. If you give someone a boost, you don't feel the energy after they've got it. This was different; the magic was still fully mine, just under her control."

"No wonder you were rattled." Chuck got himself a cigarette. He offered one to Chris. Chris nodded and slipped the cig between his lips.

Chuck inhaled. "No wonder she was rattled. She wasn't thrilled when you went sprinting out of her house the second she let go of you."

"It was get out or fuck her on the table chasing that connection, trying to get it going again."

"Which you didn't want to do."

Chris closed his eyes and said softly, "Which I want to do so badly I'm literally aching for it." They smoked quietly for a few minutes. Chuck knew pressing Chris on the whole turn-around-and-head-back-to-her-place thing wasn't going to go anywhere, so he decided to start talking shop again.

"Tell me more about how the healing works."

"Okay. There's a purely mechanical level. The speeding things up bit you felt on the first pass. It makes sense she's got to have more than just that, or else she wouldn't have been able to do anything for you last month. Your soul, energy, whatever you want to call the 'you' that isn't body, has an idea of what your body should be like, a Platonic Ideal of your form. Your body does not have any idea like that. It's just a collection of cells working together. If you damage something, the cells do their thing, but they don't have a master plan for what you should be. That's the trick, getting that image and making it real. She lets the cells know what they need to do to match up with that plan. She gives the energy form. I don't want to test it, but I bet she could regrow a finger or something because the soul knows there's supposed to be a finger there."

"Now your part of the trick is figuring out how to make it happen for something with no cells."

"Yeah. We're getting a ghost and going to work as soon as I can get back here again, next week probably. It's going to take a shitload of energy. We'll need something with enough of a brain to know what it should be like. Those walking memories I was practicing with before won't do it. They have no soul left."

"Define 'shitload.'"

"I'm thinking six to eight thousand calories of my own energy, probably similar amounts of yours, and pulling from all of my favorite usual sources as well."

"I foresee a grocery run in our future."

"I'd say you're right."

"You're still going to try to make the solid ones incorporeal?"

"Probably a good idea. I'll have a much better idea of how they became solid if I can take one apart." Chuck finished his cigarette and ground it out. Chris finished his a few seconds later. Chuck could feel him thinking about another one.

"It's a bad substitute for sex."

"Fine. Can I drink more when we get to your place?"

"If you like. A long hot shower and a lot of sleep might be a good idea as well."

"Alone time or dreams wouldn't be a good thing right about now."

"Then keep talking shop with me."

Chris thought about the rest of the night's conversation. "They really should be attacking her."

"I know."

"Do you buy the idea they just don't feel her?"

"No."

"Then why aren't they?"

"I don't know. The more I think about it the more I don't like it. Think they're hoping for a repeat?"

"Maybe. A straight-out attack would be easier."

"Yeah it would. Especially since she isn't wearing any defenses. You should have a chat with her about that."

"I'll do it when I can be alone with her without doing something inappropriate."

"If you both want it—which you clearly do—it's not inappropriate."

"Tell that to Ari."

Chuck laughed. "You're scraping the absolute bottom of the excuse barrel if you're pulling him out. He's not Pat. You owe him nothing and…"

"Yeah. Fine. Mildred doesn't want us dead. It wants pain. Is that your professional opinion as a reader of intentions and minds, or were you just BS-ing for her?"

"It's my professional opinion."

"Then that's why they aren't attacking her. Can you think of anything that would hurt Pat and me worse than having her around for a good long time and then taking her out?"

"Maybe. It would certainly put both of you out of commission for about two days; then you'd blow the town off the map in an explosion that would make Autumn look like a master of control. Maybe Mildred does want you as mad as it is, but it also knows what you and Pat can do when you're mad. If Mildred's got any sense, it doesn't want a repeat of that. Unless this is suicide by mage, Mildred doesn't want you that mad."

"It might. I still like the idea it's eating the higher-ups to keep going. It has to get energy from somewhere, and I'm not feeling any better options. Suicide while extracting maximum pain might be preferable to winning and then starving."

"Then round about… what, mid-April? Or when you, or Pat, or in what I suppose Mildred would consider the best of all possible worlds, both of you, finally sleep with her, the target shows up on her back and everything jumps at her?"

"I think so."

"Think or feel."

"Can't tell for sure. I'm way too close to it right now. I'll let it sit in the back of my mind for a while. Go at it again when I'm less emotional."

"Okay. Let's get home. More to drink is sounding pretty good to me right about now."

32.

Chris looked at the empty plate in front of him and felt ready to burst. That looked true for Chuck as well. But, if he somehow managed to pull this off, they'd both be eating again ravenously in a few hours. One of the few things the books never talk about is how the use of magic takes energy—not just in the mystical pulling from the ethers sense though there would be plenty of that as well—but the actual flesh and blood physical energy of the mage as well. There was a reason why fat magic users were few and far between.

He found the target by going over the map carefully. The ghost in question spent its time hanging out at the Reevesville Historical Society, keeping visitors on edge and occasionally tormenting the curator and docents. The ghost was scary. It made sounds that shouldn't happen. It moved things around the one-time mansion that now housed the historical society. It dropped the temperature uncomfortably. Occasionally, it caused full hallucinations to scare off the more stubborn employees. Basically, it hadn't gotten the message it was dead and wanted the interlopers out of its house.

Because of that, Chris thought it might be the perfect candidate for recorporealization. All he had to do now was break into the historical society and turn the ghost into something with a body. Then kill it.

Breaking in wasn't nearly as difficult as he was afraid it would be. When Chuck had told him, "Trust me," he felt nervous. He should have known nervous was a waste of time. It became very obvious Chuck spent closing time across the street watching the curator wrap up the day. Her key was neatly dropped on the front porch. After picking it up to open the door, Chuck quickly punched the code into the security system.

"Same game plan as before?" Chuck asked after he relocked the door.

"Yes. Chase it to me when I'm ready and give me a boost when I need it."

"Okay."

Chris scouted. He wanted a room with two good exits without a lot of clutter. Sure, if the place was a mess when they left, it'd get chalked up to the ghost. If it could be avoided, that would be even better. In the end he had two options: a parlor with good access points filled with fragile-looking antique furniture or a basement with only one exit filled with sturdy locked filing cabinets. The basement won out. There wasn't much in there that could be used to distract him. He decided that was a better choice than an easy exit.

Next came the set up. He knew he'd have to be able to pull an immense amount of energy to make this thing real, which meant setting up the flows ahead of time. Energy in the mystical sense was vitally important for a job like this. When it came to that, Chris preferred working with fire or wind. A big fire or a thunder storm would be nice, but that wasn't going to be an option for today. He concentrated for a few minutes, finding the closest ley line. *Not bad.* But not his favorite either, it ran along and through French Creek, picking up a lot of water energy in the process. He could work with it though he preferred a less water-tinged energy source. If this had worked exactly the way he wanted to, he'd be pulling off the line that went through the smelting plant. That line picked up the feel of molten iron nicely. He worked very well with it. That line was also seven miles away, which made using it almost impossible.

The basement walls were stone. Also a good thing. He wasn't Pat, but, like all of his kind, he got along well with stones. Chris turned the stones into an energy sink, pulling as much energy as he could off of the ley line and embedding it into the stones around him so he could use it like a battery.

He realized Chuck put up shields, which was something he really should have done for himself. He sent a quick thanks to Chuck and went back to building up his reserves.

When the stones had all they could hold, he began to build the trap. Some people would have gone for flashy symbols drawn on the floor with some candles, crystals, and maybe a knife for show. He didn't work that way; the fewer marks he left the better. Chris didn't need a physical focus to keep his mind in place. Not for this sort of work.

He went with a circle: a glowing ring of energy to hold whatever was inside it. It was simple and did the job. Once the ghost was in it, he'd set it to spinning fast enough to become a sphere. Then the ghost would be stuck.

Send it down.

Okay. This particular ghost had enough of a brain Chuck could locate it, make it go into the basement, and step into the circle with no problems. If it had been brighter, there might have been a fight. As it was, it meekly obeyed.

Chuck knew not to distract Chris, so he just sat on the steps watching. He kept his mind in Chris' to monitor him. If Chris managed to pull it off, he'd be able to see how Chris did it. Then he could start working on how to do it better, easier, and most importantly, on the fly in the middle of a battle while doing something else at the same time.

Chris set the trap spinning and began to study the ghost. Chuck felt him slide into the almost trancelike state he needed to really understand what was in front of him. The ghost started to yell at them. It wasn't happy about being trapped. Chuck shut it up.

Let it talk. I need to feel what it is well enough to get into it.

Chuck lifted his will from the ghost. It went back to cursing at them. He could feel it trying to make them hallucinate. That the ghost wasn't able to succeed made it angrier. The filing cabinets started to rattle. Chuck was fairly sure it couldn't muster the energy to move them, but a redux of the opening scene from *Ghostbusters* with the flying catalogue cards didn't seem like much of a stretch.

Chris kept studying it, making sure he fully understood what was standing in front of him rattling the filing cabinets. It was about one-third memory still walking around and two-thirds stubborn soul that didn't feel like leaving its home. He had the feeling one hundred years ago it was all soul.

He wasn't sure how or if the fact it wasn't just a soul walking around would affect what he wanted to do. That was the point: experiment and see what happened.

Now came the hard part. *You can shut it up.* He'd work better without having it cursing at him in the background.

Chuck got it quieted down again. Chris fed the energy to it, felt what it wanted to be, and gave it the tools to become that. He made his magic feel as much like Sarah's as he could while pouring energy into the ghost. It seemed to be responding positively. It became visible, brighter, harder for Chuck to control. But from what he could tell solid wasn't on the list of adjectives.

He wondered if it had been so long since it had a body it didn't know precisely what it wanted along those lines. Then he noticed it cast a faint shadow. It wasn't solid yet, but it was starting to slow down light. That was a good sign.

It was almost opaque when he felt Chuck flood him with more energy. He hadn't been paying attention to how he was doing. When he felt Chuck's energy, he realized he had been pretty low.

At some later point, he wasn't sure how much later, he stopped trying to make it real and started studying it to see how real it had become. It was... goo; a five-and-a-half-foot-tall, pissed-off man made of goo. The details were good. It was holding together nicely. But a pile of ectoplasm wasn't precisely what he had been aiming for.

He spent a minute on an internal inventory. *Keep going or stop?*

Stop. Chuck's voice in his head. *You've still got to kill it. I'm thinking you can keep this up for another three minutes before you pass out, leaving me with an annoyed ghost to clean up.*

Which left the final question: how to kill a pile of goo? Five minutes of thinking and feeling what was standing in front of him left him with the start of a plan. Okay. No anatomy yet, so he couldn't do that. Pulling all the energy back out of it was his best bet. The easiest way was to blow it up.

You might want to get out of here.

What are you going to do?

Make it go boom.

Chuck got out of there. He felt the house shudder and a flash of energy sweep over him a minute later. Three minutes later Chris dragged up the stairs from the basement.

"Ice cream?" Chuck asked him.

"Good idea."

They had borrowed Chuck's sister's car. Chris slumped into the passenger seat. Chuck's advice had been good. Another minute or two working on making the ghost solid would have left him unconscious on the floor when he killed it, instead of weary to the bone.

Chuck stopped at the grocery store and went in. Chris didn't bother to move. He came back a few minutes later with two bags filled with as many calories as could be packed into the least possible space.

"My place or Sarah's?" Chuck put the car into drive.

It had been a week since he had seen Sarah last. They had texted a little, so she knew why he was in town today. She was annoyed they wouldn't let her come with them for this experiment, but maybe she'd forgive him when they showed up with ice cream.

"Sarah's. When does Becky need the car back?"

"Not tonight. She's in Erie with her friends."

"Good, I don't feel like walking much."

He pulled out his cell phone. He texted Sarah. Feel like some company?

Sure.

We've got ice cream.

Well, there's a stroke of luck. I had pizza for dinner. How'd it go?

Tell you about it when we get there. Five minutes or so.

Okay.

I put my cell phone down and got out bowls and spoons. Then I turned off *Angel* and waited. I could feel exhaustion radiating off of both of them before they got into my home. They shuffled into my place after a long, slow climb up the stairs. Chris had graying skin, deep circles under his eyes, and was barely moving. He looked like he had been awake for three weeks, doing hard work the entire time. Chuck looked weary.

"Coffee?"

"Nope. Nothing that'll make it hard to sleep," Chuck answered.

"I've got tea and milk. What's your preference?"

"Tea," Chris collapsed into one of my kitchen chairs.

I made a pot of hot water and got out mugs. Chuck unpacked the ice cream. He saw my bowls. "We don't usually bother with bowls."

"This is something you do regularly?"

"Ice cream is his 'large quantity of calories in the least possible space' of choice," Chuck said while opening a pint of New York Fudge Chunk for Chris. "If you want your own, I've got mint chocolate chip, java chip, vanilla, chocolate, or Cherry Garcia. Or you can just dig into whatever we've got open."

"I'll graze if you don't mind my germs."

"Somehow I'm not worried about catching something from you."

"I haven't been sick in… five years, maybe more." I took a spoonful of Chris' New York Fudge Chunk. It might as well have been solid chocolate. As density of calories went, I couldn't think of anything to top it.

Chris began perking up with the infusion of extra calories, but I laid my hand on his and gave him a boost anyway. "Tell me about your experiment that was so dangerous I couldn't be allowed anywhere near it," I said as I took a bite of the java chip Chuck claimed for himself.

"You haven't talked with her about this yet?" Chuck half asked half said to Chris.

Chris shook his head, ate another bite of his ice cream, and then opened the mint chocolate chip. "I've been home all week. It didn't seem like an over-the-phone/text/email conversation."

Chuck turned back toward me. "Look, it's this simple: if I had my way you'd never be out from under the shields. I don't care if we're doing the magical equivalent of babysitting sleeping toddlers. I don't want you around."

"Thanks. Your confidence in my abilities is overwhelming."

"You don't get it. You are the only member of this group we cannot afford to lose. You have to make it to the last fight. None of the rest of us do. It'd be nice if we all do, but if not, we can still fight and maybe win. If you don't make it to the last fight, we die. So no, I'm not taking you along for anything that might involve you getting damaged in some freak accident or lucky attack. In fact, let me make it even clearer: I will never voluntarily take you along for anything that involves any likelihood of magical attack. You are not a medic anymore; that's Autumn's job now. You are not a fighter anymore; that's Pat and Mike's job. You are the healer. You stay home and put us back together when we need it." Chuck took another bite of his ice cream while I tried to think of a way to respond. Nothing sprang to mind, so I copied Chris and took a bite of mint chocolate chip with a bite of the New York Fudge Chunk. They tasted pretty good together.

"That's what you didn't want to talk to me about over the phone?" I finally asked Chris.

"No, but it's related." I waited a minute; he still didn't say anything. He kept plowing through the ice cream at a mind-boggling rate.

"So…" I gestured with the spoon for him to keep talking.

"You have no shields," Chris said between bites.

"I kind of remember you and Chuck helping to paint them in place."

"You have no personal shields. I wince every time you leave your house or Writers' because you're naked out there," Chuck said.

"Oh. I never really thought about it."

"Start thinking. Just because they haven't noticed you yet doesn't mean that's likely to stay true." Chuck took another bite of ice cream.

"So… how?"

"How?" Chuck looked confused. He wasn't getting why I would ask. Obviously, I knew how to do a shield.

"Yeah, how? I did a version for Ari, and I did my walls, but I don't think I can do myself. Among other things, I can't reach all of me."

"That would be the conversation I didn't want to have with you over the phone. That's not a question for him. He'd give you a very technical and not terribly useful answer." Chris' voice sounded more alive. I was astonished to see he had already finished a pint of ice cream. "The shields you did for the house, they work by wrapping your space in a prayer right?"

"Yes."

"Then that's how you do it again. The physical act of the writing is the way you focused your mind to make the prayer real. You don't actually have to touch or write. It just makes it easier. You could focus it on your star if you wanted to, or your skin, or just keep it in your mind. You could do it by wrapping the words around the parts you can reach and letting the energy stretch between the words."

"You could have him do your back." Chuck grinned.

"Or, if you really do need the physical words, I could do your back." He glared at Chuck. "However you chose to do it, sooner is better than later. What Chuck said was true: we can't replace you."

"Let's table shields for a while. I'll work on them when you guys head off. Can't I teach one of you to heal? Can't I teach all of you to heal?"

"You can teach. We can learn. In the end, we'll be able to deal with little cuts and bruises and almost burn ourselves out to do it. We've all got specialties, things we can do easier than others. Yours is healing, mine is reading minds, and his is destroying stuff. When you go outside of your area, you can learn how to do other things, but it takes really hard work. Econ 101: Do what you do best. Let someone else do what they do best. Don't muck around with your second or third best options unless there's no one else who can do them. We've got your second and third best options covered."

"Fine. Tell me about ghost hunting. I'm guessing it wasn't a total success or failure, either of those things and you'd have told me by now."

"You'd be right. I made goo."

"Goo?"

"Yeah, goo." And with that Chris started to tell me about the creation of ectoplasm.

I woke up the next morning and headed to the gym to jog. The treadmill was much more pleasant than pavement in this weather. While jogging I resolved to have shields by the end of the day. Maybe they wouldn't be great, but they'd be functional. When either Chris or Pat came back, I could work on going from functional to great. I got home, showered, ate, and rested. The last two times I had done shielding work it had left me pretty tired, so I wanted to go at it with a good energy reserve.

I lay on the sofa watching more *Angel* when a small brainstorm hit. I grabbed my cell and texted Chris. How's your Google-fu?

A few minutes later I got one back from him. Why?

Look up 'photosynthesis.'

Like plants?

Like how plants turn sunlight into sugar. Energy into a solid. I actually felt his interest perk up when he read those words.

A minute later I got another text. I'm borrowing your bio book when I get back.

That's cool.

What are you doing tonight?

Probably talking you through Bio 101. I could feel him smile.

Good. Let me spend a few hours reading, and then I'll have questions for you.

Okay. I'm going to work on my shield. I'll have some for you, too.

Good.

By afternoon I felt ready to try.

I didn't need a battery for this. I didn't need to hook it into my star. This was a prayer, a direct connection to my Lord. All I needed to do was hold the love of my Lord close to me, let it wrap around me into a protective shield. Should be easy as breathing. It wasn't. But it was easier than the first two times I had done it. I let the letters glow, this time entirely in my mind, and wrapped myself in the Psalms.

I wasn't sure if I was different afterword. I didn't know if I had built myself some shields or spent an afternoon intensely praying.

You home? I sent the text to Chuck.

Yeah.

I'm heading out. Tell me if you can find me. I went outside and stood in front of the Golem. I brushed the snow off of it, wondering if it would talk to me today, and waited for him to text me back.

No.

Good. I think I've got shields.

I think you do, too. Let me know if you feel this.

I waited for a minute. A very slight tingle at the back of my neck made me look around. I couldn't tell if it was from Chuck or the Watchers checking me out with renewed interest. After another minute, I sent him a text. I felt something. Could have been you. Could have been the Watchers. They're all staring at me right now.

Wasn't me. I still can't find you.

What was I supposed to feel?

I was hoping to find you and send a very gentle attack in your direction.

I guess you not finding me is a good thing.

Yes.

I'm going back inside. It's awfully cold out here.

Where were you?

Standing next to the Golem.

Yeah, they're good shields. I should have been able to pinpoint you.

Okay. Thanks for letting me test them. Not sure I like all the Watchers staring at me, though.

They do that whenever any of us change anything. They'll stop after reporting back.

How do they report back? Can we follow them?

No. They're tuned into Mildred, no need to go anywhere to do it.

Ahhh...

Time for me to go to work. Let him know you've got some shields.

Okay.

That was the last magic of the break. Chris and I spent a few evenings talking about how plants make food; in the end, he thought the healing trick was a more direct route to what he wanted to do. I spent a lot of time watching TV, chatting online, and reading. The snow piled up deeply enough I didn't go out until I absolutely needed something. And finally, when I was on the verge of full-on stir crazy, my buddies came back to school.

33.

I typed the last word of the last page of the abomination that was my paper on Pre-Roman Britain. How I let Pat talk me into taking a class on English history still boggled my mind, especially since we had a short paper due each Friday. Had I the brains of a sponge, I would have taken one of Morrell's history courses and gotten my social science credit out of the way much easier.

Bedtime. I was half-undressed when the sound coming from my steps forced me to pull my t-shirt back on again. Nothing good accompanied the sound of someone falling down my steps. I opened the door and saw Chris struggling to get Pat into my home.

"Let me help you." I ran down the snowy stairs as fast as I dared in bare feet and got his other arm around my shoulder. I gasped. Pat was icy cold, even through his coat.

"We're taking him straight to my shower." Chris nodded at me. He was out of breath and shaky. I kicked the door shut behind me, and Chris cast another shield on top of mine.

"What happened?"

"Something bad. Don't know what," Chris answered.

We got Pat into my bathroom. Chris set him on the toilet seat and turned on the water. "Why are we putting him in the shower?"

"Because he's frozen. We're going to warm him up as gently as possible." Chris cranked the water to hot while I unlaced Pat's boots. "Gently. Put it on cold. What'll feel warm to us will burn him."

I had Pat's boots off and started on his coat. "Pat, can you talk?"

"Yes," he said slowly through a jaw clenched to keep his teeth from chattering.

"We're going to warm you up. Chris and I are going to get you in the shower."

"Can't stand."

"I didn't think you could. We'll keep you up."

Chris looked alarmed at the thought of getting into a very cold shower. "Stop being a wimp. Get out of anything you don't want to get wet, then get in there."

He quickly shucked off everything but his boxers and stepped into my shower. His muscles tensed and goose bumps appeared on his skin. I got Pat undressed, standing up, and gave him to Chris. Pat shrieked when the water hit his skin. I undressed to my t-shirt and panties and got in with them. I took most of Pat's weight off of Chris. Chris was shaking from the strain.

"I've got you, Pat." I held him close and let the water and my rapidly dropping body heat warm him gently. "I'm good for about eight minutes before I'll need help holding him. You can get out if you want," I said to Chris.

"No point. I'm starting to get used to it."

Pat's color started to get better and the shivering less violent. His forehead pressed against mine, and his jaw relaxed as he warmed up. "Turn the temp up a few degrees," I told Chris.

Chris squirmed to reach the dial. My shower is okay for one, tight quarters for two, and all I can say for three is it's a very good thing we're thin and friendly. There would have been less room in a sardine can but not much.

"Want to tell me what sucked every degree of heat out of Pat?"

"Something we haven't seen before. We were walking back from searching, over the bridge across the little ravine, past the chapel."

Pat croaked, "Warmer."

Chris turned up the dial again. Pretty soon we'd be at swimming pool temperature: outdoor, unheated, after a rain storm in April, swimming pool temperature.

"We were behind the chapel. You know how the light comes out from behind the stained glass and looks really pretty?"

"Yes. It's one of the pictures in all the promotional literature."

"Something blocked the light, then moved out of the chapel through the window. Pat got between me and it. He got three rocks off at it. Each one made it stagger back but didn't seem to do much beyond that. I was working on shielding spells and trying to get an attack in on it. My first few spells had no effect on it."

"Different," Pat said. "N-n-not ours."

"I'm getting there. Warmer?"

"Yes."

Chris turned up the temp further. That made me happy because I was shivering, too.

"Pat hit it twice more before he began moving back. Any of the local critters should have been running away or dead. This was different. It felt more like the Dark Man than anything else. It also wasn't paying any attention to me. Then it reached out to Pat and poked him in the chest.

"I cut its hand off. It faded away, quickly, and we came here as fast as possible."

"You cut its hand off?"

"In a pinch I can make a blade. Mike's is much better. Mine doesn't last very long, but it'll get the job done."

"It had a hand?"

"No. It was like an out-of-focus shadow, all fuzzy and black. It touched him with something kind of arm shaped." He turned the temp up again. "You take a break. I've got him for the next few minutes." Pat was still far enough gone not to complain when I shifted him back to Chris.

Over the next half-hour we slowly turned the temperature up to steaming. I knew Pat was going to be okay when he started to hold up his own weight and began snarking about being pressed against an almost-naked Chris when I was just as close and much cuddlier.

At the end of the hour, the three of us sat around my kitchen table, the two boys wrapped in blankets as their underwear tumbled around in my dryer, me in my fuzzy, gray robe. All three of us were drinking hot tea.

"I think this is new. Either Mildred's gotten some local talent on her side or we tripped into something else," Pat said as he stared at his drink.

"I think you're right," Chris replied. "But that's the question. Were we just in the wrong place at the wrong time, or was it looking for us?"

"I don't know. I couldn't feel it until it was right in front of me," Pat answered. I had the feeling that wasn't all of the story, but I also got the sense he didn't want me pressing the issue.

"Same here."

"I haven't liked that chapel since day one. It makes my skin crawl. You said there was light before it came out?"

"Yes." Chris nodded.

"After?"

"Maybe," Chris looked like he was trying to see the details of his memory he hadn't noticed while it was happening.

"Wrong place, wrong time. Nothing's supposed to be happening there tonight. You've felt every attack at least a minute before it occurred, usually days. You don't get caught flat footed," I rested my hand on Pat's arm.

"No, we don't."

"Once we get done with the drinks, let's get you on the couch and see what else happened."

"More than hypothermia?" Pat sounded like he was too tired to be properly alarmed, but, if he had more energy, he would have been.

"Honestly, I don't think so."

"Great." Pat sighed. "You know, in other circumstances this would have been one hell of a night. I got to spend the evening pressed between you and Chris with warm water streaming down all three of us. That could be the start of a 'Dear Penthouse' letter."

"Yeah, but you'd have to turn Chris into a girl." Chris looked indignant. "They don't sell with two guys and a girl. Not if one of the guys is in the middle. It scares the readers."

"You'd know this how?" Chris asked.

"I spent two years in the army. I know something about the kind of guys who read *Penthouse*. Two girls are great. Two guys are icky."

"Icky? Wonderful word choice." Pat stood up, wrapping the blanket tighter around himself. He walked slowly over to the couch and flopped down. "Could you toss another blanket on me?"

"Sure." I grabbed my quilt off my bed.

"You know being cold really sucks."

"Yeah, I'm kind of familiar with it." I smiled dryly at him and spent a few minutes with my hands on his shoulders. Nothing jumped out at me.

"It just froze you."

"That's good."

"Lord, what's become of us that frozen friends are our idea of good?"

Chris half-smiled. "We're veterans."

"How about you guys stay away from the chapel and the cemetery until we get done with Mildred?"

"Sounds like a plan," Pat said.

"I can handle waiting until next semester for a whole new round of evil," Chris answered.

Chris left Sarah's place. He had wanted to stay. He was safer at her apartment; there was no place in her home to be alone with his thoughts. But there was no good reason for him to stay. She didn't need any help with Pat, and it's not like he could have offered much if she did. So, when Pat fell asleep on her sofa, he left.

When he got home, Autumn and Mike were downstairs working on their own homework. He joined them, told them what had happened, dragging the story out, trying to find a way to keep himself downstairs longer.

After half an hour, Mike got up and left them. Chris debated staying with Autumn, but if it was just the two of them his mind would wander, and she was good at reading what people were thinking. He didn't want her to get even the slightest hint of what was in his head. She seemed to like Sarah, but any idea of what he was desperately trying to not think about would shoot any affection she had for Sarah to hell and gone.

So he wished her a good night as well and headed up to his own room.

His own remarkably distraction free room.

He tried to work the images away. It didn't help. The first assignment he grabbed was Andrew Marvell, "To His Coy Mistress." "Two hundred to adore each breast..."

Each breast. Her gray t-shirt had been sopping wet. It wasn't translucent. It didn't need to be. Cold water made sure every contour was visible. She had been wearing white panties. They were translucent by the time they had gotten out. That delicious dark triangle just begging to be nuzzled and kissed.

NO! Not again! He found an econ text. It wasn't even homework. Just something, anything to keep the images at bay.

Less than a page in his mind was wandering again. Images flashed through his mind: the v-neck on her t-shirt, water droplets sliding down her neck to vanish into the gray, her nipples hard and pointed on soft, round, little breasts. Images dissolved into fantasies: his hands sliding her shirt up her chest, her breasts free and pressed against him, hooking a finger into her panties and sliding them to the side while he knelt in front of her and slipped his tongue against her...

He groaned in frustration and dropped the book. He looked in the direction of his razor. *No! You are a grown man. Control yourself. Now read.*

He picked his book back up and focused on it. An hour went by with the images in the background. He began to think about going to bed. He was tired and sleepy, his muscles weak from holding Pat up. Lying in bed he began to relax, his muscles letting the day go.

He was almost asleep when the images started again, half-dream, half-fantasy. The wet, gray t-shirt plastered to her skin. Translucent, white panties clung to her body. Her fine breasts in his hands while he licked a pink nipple. Her back pressed against the wall of the shower while she wrapped her legs around his waist, and he held her ass in his hands and lowered her onto him. Kissing her throat while she threw her head back in joy. Drops of water sliding down her skin.

He was so hard he ached. He welcomed the pain. If he was going to do this, it better hurt.

He let his hand slide under the blankets and his mind run wild. She was on her knees in front of him, his hands fisted in her hair while the water streamed down both of them. Lips soft, mouth wet and warm, her hands stroking, pressing him while her mouth sucked. She stood up, turned her back to him. Once again he slid into her, this time his hands cupped her breasts, his lips slid against hers, and beautiful, soft moans danced in his ears as her body pulsed around him. He spun her around to face him. He wanted to look into her eyes as his body tightened and his hips moved faster. Her eyes watched his as everything else slid away.

He was asleep before his hand released.

His shoulders ached. His hands tingled. His mouth tasted dirty and dry. The space around him was white. No details: no walls, or doors, or ceiling. Just him, hanging by his arms, toes barely brushing the ground, in a blinding expanse of white.

Then Althiira was there. She was armed with a whip. She uncoiled it slowly, letting him watch the braided leather fall to the ground.

The first lash caught him around the chest. He hissed at the pain, electric thorns wrapping and writhing around his body. She moved behind him and ran the whip slowly down his back. He shivered at the sensation. She pulled back. The second lash fell upon his back. The third one wrapped around his leg.

It hurt. God, it hurt! He tasted blood on the fourth lash. He knew he had bitten through his tongue.

She didn't speak. She didn't need to. He knew why she was here.

She beat him until his skin hung in wet red ribbons. As she rolled up the lash, he said one thing, "More."

34.

I wasn't horribly shocked to see Chris keep his distance the week after getting Pat warmed up. I didn't mind, to be honest. Between the magic over the break and the image of him in wet and not completely closed boxer shorts, a little breathing space was useful for helping me do a better job of keeping my promise to Ari.

From what I could tell Chris was mostly hiding out in his room. I wasn't sure if that was better or worse than running around picking fights. It did mean I didn't spend any time running my hands over his skin.

It also meant I ended up working with Pat when it came to making my shield better. When I asked him for help, he looked me over and said, "You're wearing a giant, flashing, neon I'M MAGIC! sign. Let's see if there's a way to make it less noticeable."

"When I asked Chuck, he couldn't find me."

"Yeah, he can't find you under the glow of this thing. Trust me, he could feel the shield. He just didn't know it was you."

"Okay. How do I tone it down?"

"Well… you just sorta…" Then he did something.

"I didn't follow that."

"I realized I could turn down your glow a lot more easily than I could teach you to do it for yourself. If Chris ever gets out of his snit, have a chat with him about it. He'd do a better job of showing you how."

"What about Mike?"

"He's not wearing his own shields anymore. Dave does his. He can whip one out if he needs it, but these days all of his magic is used for fighting."

"Great. They tell me you're a wizard, and I'm not."

"Yep. If you want to start at the beginning, Magic and You 101, I can teach you how to do it the way I do. In the process it'll fuck with how you do it now. Not a good plan."

"I'm having enough fun learning this without having to lose everything I've already gained."

"Yeah, I don't think you want to go back. It is kind of insane, just about everyone here is a mage; your brother is a mage. Actually, he'd be a really good person to talk to about this. If I had to guess, I'd say there's fewer than one hundred of us on this planet, and you're smack dab in the middle of the highest concentration of us on Earth."

"Where are the others from?"

"I trained one of them. As to the others, it's just speculation. I can't believe no one else has ever stumbled onto it. I can tell you outside of this group and my one friend, I've never seen another wizard."

"The rest of us?"

"Mages, neo-pagans, witches, wiccans: there are more words than varieties of magic user. You're all doing it by feel. We're doing it by formal training. Cooking versus baking. Intuition versus education."

"Why would you want that? It seems limiting."

"It is limiting. It's also protecting. Magic is like any extremely powerful tool. It's dangerous. You don't want to use a table saw just by eyeballing it and saying, 'I think it works like this.' That's a recipe for having 'Stumpy' for a nickname. We do what others have done before, and we take what mages like you come up with and make it safer. Enough magic and you go bonkers. You can do anything with magic, and we're the ones trained to not do it. You guys are the ones who push the edges, come up with new stuff. We're the ones who figure out how to protect our minds from the side effects. You guys can have long and glorious magical careers if you've got the control to use it sparingly. We can do it every day for the rest of our lives without deciding to see what kind of monsters we can create or if it really is possible to end the world." He thought about it for a minute while I watched him in fascination. This would have been useful to know before I signed on.

"Okay, here's a good example. Buffy is fiction. Willow might as well be real. She's a great example of a mage who tastes the power and goes bonkers on it. Better example: you may have noticed Chris is a tad more delicately balanced on the edge of sane than the rest of us?"

"I've noticed he's a bit variable as to his mood."

"That's a nice way of putting it. He used to have moods between happy and depressed. My guess is they burned out on the last spell he cast on the other side. Maybe since then. But once upon a time he had them, and he doesn't anymore."

"You think that's a side effect of the magic?" I didn't have to add, 'as opposed to the family he left behind.' Pat knew I was thinking it.

"I know it hasn't helped. I know he's put buffers in place between him and a lot of the power he carries. I assume it's because Chuck sat him down and explained why going completely off the deep end wasn't a good plan. Chris actually has enough power on hand where 'end the world' is a possibility for him. Most mages, most people, don't."

"What do you mean, 'buffers?'"

"He keeps most of his magic external to himself. Chuck's got two pendants; they're his contingency plan. If he's ever unconscious, they take over. I've got my stones, but I use them mostly as backup power and distance attacks. If Dave carries anything, I've never seen it. Mike has his sword. Autumn's a whole different sort of magic so we'll ignore her. Chris has three pendants and two rings. He doesn't need all that stuff; he's got it to minimize the amount of constant magic he uses."

"Should I have my shield linked into something external to me?"

"No. Protection and healing seems to be what you're really good at, so it'll give you less problems. You'll notice Chris doesn't bother with things when it comes to destroying nasties. That's what he's good at. It takes less effort and less of a toll on him to do it. He's a fighter. For all practical purposes he's wearing full plate armor he forged himself. Back home he wouldn't have bothered. She and Dave did his protection spells."

"Dave did one of his here, too."

"And he's got Chuck linked into another of them. Like full plate armor, his protections aren't terribly subtle. Now take Dave: none of us have any idea what he's got on him. I'm not even sure if any of us even know what Dave looks like over here. He could be six three and two hundred pounds or four eleven and one ten—no way to tell. We know what he wants us to know about him and that's it. But Dave is a wizard. He knows how to keep the magic from worming its way into his brain and making him think things he shouldn't. Dave's got his mental protections in place. If he was trained the way I was, they started just about as soon as he could walk."

"What about Ameena? Mage? Wizard?"

"She should have been a wizard, would have been a fantastic one, but farseeing is a wild magic skill. Tame her magic too much, and that would have been the end of her farseeing. She ended up being an immensely well-trained mage. That in and of itself was amazing. She had wizards for tutors, and she must have driven them bonkers. All they were there to do was to show her what could be done and the easiest possible way to do it.

"By the time the war ended she very rarely used any magic because she knew how close to the edge she was. When she started slipping away from us, that's what we thought was happening. She had finally looked ahead one time too many without enough buffers in place. It might have been true, at first. Maybe Mildred just took advantage of what was already happening; maybe it was all Mildred. It was very likely, if the stuff with Mildred had never happened, within fifty years she would have had to stop using magic completely."

"What happens? You go permanently mad? You end up like an addict and have to stay on the wagon? You end up like Willow and become a wizard so you stop going bonkers?"

"Back home you went on the wagon or died. The problem with a mad mage is they don't know they've gone bonkers. Raising a legion of undead nasties is perfectly normal for them. By the time it gets that far the only option is to take the mage out. If they could hold onto enough sane, then on the wagon they went. She would have gone on the wagon. She knew the edge was close and had been dialing back her magic use for a decade.

"Here, who knows? The world hasn't ended, and really nasty monsters are few and far between. My guess is most of the mad ones get eaten by the things they call. On this plane it's a self correcting problem. Mad with enough power and enough control to handle something like the Dark Man is a very rare combination. Mad with enough power to call it— sure, I can see that. Then it shows up and sucks you dry because you don't have the control to fight it or the will to dominate it."

"Is that what you think happened to the person who called the Dark Man?"

"Probably. It's possible for a sane person to call something like that. If you ever need a really high caliber gun, the Dark Man is a good one. If you can give it what it wants, it'll take care of your problem for you. It'll make a whole lot of new ones, but whatever it is you're looking for, it can do."

"How do you know that?"

Pat looked like he wasn't sure he wanted to answer but did it anyway. "Because the thing that froze me was a reminder of some pissed off skeletons in my closet. Remember, I'm a battle wizard. Control and power are my calling cards. Six years ago, I was a thirteen-year-old wizard with a big problem, two friends I was trying to protect, and not enough local power to keep them safe. I made a deal, and it kept its part of the bargain. Neither Mildred nor any of the Minions have been seen within a hundred miles of my home in six years, nor will they ever be. I kept my end of the bargain, but it keeps trying to rewrite it. Every now and again, when it thinks it can get the upper hand, it jumps out at me."

"Fuck." I felt cold, remembering the way Azzazzel smelled. Understanding exactly how scared they had been when Mildred came around and they didn't have the magic to fight it hit me viscerally. "You made a deal with the Devil to get rid of Mildred?"

"No. I made a deal with a demon. That's the most power anyone can readily get at on this plane. For some reason angels are not easily summoned or controlled. At least not by me. Maybe you could do it, but that was six years before you and I would cross paths. I would have preferred to work with something along those lines, but it didn't happen. When I called out, only unsavory characters answered."

"What was your end of the bargain?"

"Blood. I profaned an area. My first born." My eyes went wide. "I'm kidding about the first born. The area I profaned was my side of the bargain. It hurt. It took a lot of energy. But, besides my own arms, I didn't hurt anything. I did as much as I was willing to do for the protection of me and mine; that didn't extend to harming anyone I didn't know."

"How good of a bargain could it have been? Your friend died. You and the third one ended up in the hospital for a long time."

"Two of three of us are alive. When Eli was killed, I knew I was in over my head. At that point, I hadn't gotten the magic figured out on this side. Now, I wouldn't have to make that sort of deal. But then I was still relearning it, starting from almost scratch getting used to the new energies. That's another area where you and Chris have the advantage; you can work more easily in a new place."

"Which is great, other than the whole insane by thirty thing."

"Well, for him, maybe. Remember he had over fifty years as a battle mage on his first run, plus I don't know how many years of whatever magic he did before that, and twelve or thirteen years on this side. If you keep to what you're good at, you'll probably have a good long run. If he stops or uses it sparingly once this is done, he'll have a good long run, too."

"And if he doesn't?"

"Chuck will take care of him. He won't let Chris go supernova."

"Lovely."

"Yeah, this was one happy and bright conversation..."

"Well, let me perk it up further." I spent the next hour telling Pat about Chris trying to make the Minions solid, about showing him how I healed things, about the feel of that magic, and Chris using what we did to turn a ghost into goo. Pat looked disturbed at the whole thing.

"Well, if he's going to learn how to do something like that, that's how to do it. But let's drop that estimation down from thirty to twenty-five."

"Should I not be doing things like that with him?"

"I don't know. I can't believe Chuck just sat there and let you two do it. It's magically right up your alley, so it probably didn't hurt you much. Are you feeling okay?"

"Well, I keep having this odd desire to go to the graveyard and see if I can make the Dark Man leave." Apparently I didn't manage enough of a smile to let him know I was joking. He looked really troubled. "Like the first born comment, I'm just kidding. Other than the desire to do it again, I'm fine. Mostly I was annoyed when they wouldn't take me along for ghost recorporealization."

"At least he's not totally gone. You really shouldn't be doing stuff like that."

"Yeah. Chuck read me the riot act. I stay put. You guys go off and do interesting stuff."

"You stay put. We go off and do stupid, dangerous stuff. You fix us up and do interesting stuff when we get back."

"My question stands. Should I be trying any sort of magic with Chris, or should I be leaving him alone?"

"See, this is also a conversation you need to have with him. I don't know how this feels to him. In theory he's probably better off with a partner to help him do this stuff. In theory he and you are better off with him working with Chuck because Chuck does know how to create the necessary buffers. But I don't know how much together they do versus how much Chris does version A and Chuck then refines it into version B.

"If he's working on his own with Chuck hanging out in the background taking notes, then yes, he's better off with your help. As long as you two stay on your end of the magical spectrum, you're probably fine. If you slide over into helping him destroy things, he gets the better end of the deal and you the worse. At least, that's the way it works in the books. I started training as a wizard before I could talk, so I don't remember what it was like to be a mage. I've never done the kind of magic you're talking about. There's a wall between me and the magic making it impossible for me to do it.

"You're talking about... emotional sex magic... for lack of a better term. We don't do that sort of stuff." Pat gestured to indicate he was trying to put his thoughts together. "Regular sex magic and blood magic is about the essence of life being used to fuel magic. That's part of what you did, and I can do that. It's well studied, well defined. But you aren't talking about sex in the mechanical sense, rather the emotional sense, and that's something I can't tap into. You felt the desire to chase the magic, the desire to go after it again. That's where the danger lies. The healing was in your element. Grabbing his magic and using it isn't."

"Are we setting Chris up to go supernova in his effort to find a way to kill this thing?"

"I hope not. Killing things is what he's good at. He's at least as good of a fighter as Mike and I are. In fact, if you want me to be painfully honest, he's better because he's not limited by his physical range. My guess is he can get this sorted without going bonkers. It's a fight, and that's what he does best. If he gets a good long rest after this is over, he'll probably be fine."

"Wonderful."

"I think I'm scaring you to no purpose. There are probably a million, if not more, mages roaming about this country, and most of them are just fine their whole lives long."

"Most of them won't ever stretch to use magic that isn't in their sphere."

"True."

"Tell me how many of Chris' caliber end up just fine their whole lives long. I don't need to know how many Mikes, who never go past their comfort zone, end up dandy."

"I don't know."

"What percentage from before went bonkers?"

"Mages were very rare before. If it looked like you had enough talent to cause problems, you were trained. Chris had the dumb, silly luck to be born into a trading clan that didn't take any notice of what he could do until it was much too late. I don't know if he ever used any magic before he was an adult. Ameena was kept a mage on purpose; people like her were even more rare."

"That didn't answer my question."

"Almost all of them."

"Fuck."

Pat took my hand and looked at me for a long time. "Look, we're talking about the far, far future here. I promise you, as long as I'm around, you won't get the chance to go bonkers. I'll install buffers if you want them, or if you want the power, I'll keep an eye on you."

"I want the power."

"I figured you would."

I almost didn't say it, but fear of pain got my mouth moving. "If you ever need to… take care of me… make sure it doesn't hurt much."

He half-smiled at me. "I won't let you go out in pain."

"Thanks."

Pat headed into Reevesville that night. He didn't know where Chuck lived, but he figured finding it wouldn't be hard. It wasn't like he was trying to find Dave's place.

He set the spell and let the magic pull him to Chuck. After an hour's walk, he was in front of a shabby gray house with a green Subaru parked in the driveway. He knocked on the door, and a woman about his age with black hair and dark brown eyes opened it.

"Is Chuck here?"

"Yeah. Come in." She stepped out of his way and yelled up the stairs, "Hey, Chuck!"

Chuck came down, surprised to see Pat. "Hi. Becky, this is Pat. Pat, this is my sister, Becky."

Pat made all the proper sounds and flirted lightly with Becky until she was smiling at him. Chuck stopped that and led Pat up to his room.

"I suppose 'How did you find me?' is a silly question."

"Yes."

"Then let's get straight to why."

Chuck settled back on his bed and lit up a cigarette. Pat made himself comfortable on the chair next to a desk covered in books. "Mind if I have one?"

"I didn't know you smoked."

"I fight better without it, so I don't do it often."

"Okay." Chuck tossed Pat the cigarettes and his lighter. "So, why are you here?"

"I had an interesting conversation with Sarah on some magic I can't believe you just sat there and said, 'Oh, this looks cool, let's see what happens' about."

Chuck sighed. "They're both adults. And, in case you haven't noticed, neither of them are particularly easily led when they don't want to be. He had a good two inches of skin peeled off before I realized what he was doing. At that point, she had to heal him, and if she was going to heal him anyway, there was no reason not to see what I could learn from it."

"What did you learn?"

"I'm not a mage."

"The eighty years you spent training to be a wizard didn't tip you off to that?"

"Funny," Chuck said sarcastically. "I'm used to his magic. I've spent years getting a feel for it. I don't have those skills with hers. It was like watching a film in a different language with no subtitles. I could see what was happening, but I missed most of the action. I got a much better idea of what he learned from her when I watched him go after the ghost."

"Is it a good plan?"

"Good enough Mildred co-opted it. Good enough that on the first try he turned a ghost into... well, a much more substantial ghost."

"Have you talked to him since Wednesday?"

"Yes."

"How's he doing? Can he handle this?"

"Let's put it this way: he's handling the magic much better than he's handling her. I prefer him out trying new and dangerous magic because I can help control the side effects of that. The three of you practically naked in the shower together is a whole different kind of crap, and I'm less useful with that. He's hurting over Sarah, guilty about wanting her, and he desperately wants to do right by the last one. I really wish he'd go pick more fights. It's good for him to kill things on a regular basis, helps him get rid of the tension he can't let go of any other way."

"That would be why I can't believe you let them do that. You had to know how that would feel for him."

"'Let' really isn't the word with those two."

"Still. When she said 'I'm going to use your magic,' shouldn't that have been the time to say, 'Whoa! Bad plan!'?"

"I'd just broken into her mind and sent her running to the bathroom puking. She didn't want to hear anything from me, and neither did he."

"Why did you break into her mind?"

"She left that part out?"

"Apparently."

"He wasn't sure what she was doing, so he asked me to get in there and find out. By the time I was close enough to see, she was sprinting away."

"How is it every time you get near her you set her off?"

"Because she feels too much like my sister-in-law for comfort. We weren't exactly BFFs before. Being near her sets my defenses off, which set hers off."

"God, what a lovely dysfunctional family we are!"

Chuck snorted. "Anyway, is that what you wanted to know?"

"Mostly. I want to know if he can handle this. I want to know if you think the magic will tip him over the edge."

"Why are you asking?"

"Because he's only got two speeds now, and once upon a time he had five. When we left he didn't spend his time ricocheting from depressed to happy to depressed. Did the last spell push him that far?"

"No. At least I don't think it was the spell. I think it's being here, being alive, that did it. Magically, he's pretty stable. Well, as stable as they ever are doing this kind of work. If anything tips him over the edge, it'll be her and not the magic."

"Okay. Next question: are they better working this together, or should I be running interference on her end?"

Chuck blew smoke toward the ceiling. "I don't know. From a purely magical perspective, I think he's more stable working with her. He's coming up with some unique insights. From the 'potentially saving all of our asses because he'll be able to come up with the trick that finally kills Mildred' perspective, I'm very interested in seeing them continue working together. From a personal perspective..." Chuck paused and looked like he was thinking about what to say next. "If he can't get over this whole undying fidelity to Althiira thing, working with Sarah will be torture for him. While he's doing it he's happy and forgets

Althiira for a while. When the magic clears, it all comes back, and he's banging his head against the wall or bumming too many cigarettes off of me in an effort to drug the desire out of his system. I keep trying to get him to focus on how much he enjoys working with Sarah."

"So, you're encouraging him to go after her?" *Even though I want her?*

Chuck understood both questions. "Yes. But I've been encouraging him to go after pretty much anyone who isn't Autumn since we found each other again. He actually likes this one, and that's a good start. He'd be happier with some attachments to this side."

"That's a cold way of looking at it."

"I was never known for my warm and fuzzy personality."

"True."

"I'm sorry if it fucks your chances with her."

"That's not my main concern. I don't need farseeing to envision a future where he gets close to Sarah and pulls back and gets close and pulls back, over and over, hurting her worse and worse because it hurts him, and he seems to like it."

"You always did see him too well.

"Why do you think Mildred hasn't attacked Sarah?"

Now it was Pat's turn to think. "I don't have a good answer for that."

"I don't think it's trying to kill us, not now at least. Mildred is here to cause us pain. Tell me what hurts you two worse than something happening to her? I know for a fact you can pull some astounding magic out of the ethers. Can you work together well enough to do it now? If one of you actually gets Sarah, will you be able to?"

Pat didn't like thinking about that. Yet another complication to something that should be simple. Finally he answered, "I don't know."

"Keep it in mind. Especially when you're thinking about kissing her in front of him."

"Okay." Pat stood up. "That covered what I wanted to talk about."

"See you at Golem tomorrow?"

"Yeah. I'll see myself out." Pat left shaking his head. He had never gotten the dynamic between Althiira and Anthur, watching it play out here again was interesting. Pat wondered as he headed back up to campus if Chuck knew it was the same woman and wasn't saying anything to him about it for some reason, or worse, wasn't saying anything to Chris. There was always more going on in Chuck's head than was comfortable to deal with, knowing it was her and not saying anything about it was his sort of mind fuck.

If Chuck knew Sarah was Althiira, that would explain him trying to push Chris in that direction. *How could Chris not know?* It'd been close to four months, and Pat still didn't have a good answer for that. Chris obviously didn't know. This tortured, romantic crap would dissolve in a minute if he knew.

So, why didn't Chris know? *Because he doesn't want to.* Pat didn't find that answer terribly satisfying. Which led Pat to the next question. The question he had very carefully avoided since seeing how entranced Sarah was as she told him about the sex magic. Could he step back and let Chris have her again? *No.* Pat might be a good guy, but he wasn't about to just let Chris have her. If it meant rubbing broken glass in Chris' wounds for a while longer, he'd do it and a small, mean part of him would enjoy it. If Chris ever figured it out…

That hurt too much to think about for too long. He'd set fire to the bridge when he finally came to it. As long as Chris didn't know, Pat had no incentive to tell him.

Next question: what had happened to Althiira? Whatever brought her here left her without her memory. Maybe to protect her? As Sarah, she was safe from Mike and Autumn. As Althiira, she was safe from Mike. Pat knew Mike would never reach his sword in time if it came to a fight with Althiira. Althiira versus Autumn was a whole other story.

Maybe it was the lack of memory keeping her off Mildred's radar? That didn't feel quite right to him, but he had the sense he was onto something with that. Pat knew not to force it. If he just let it simmer in the back of his mind, it would eventually click.

He walked past Sarah's apartment and decided not to go up. Pat looked up at Chris' window as he went past. This really would have been much easier if he didn't actually like Chris. He was tempted to go up and spend a bit of time with him, get a feel for how close to the edge he was.

Chris' light was off, and his shields were good enough Pat couldn't tell if he was asleep or not. He let it pass. Either tomorrow Chris would be up and about again or he wouldn't. If he wasn't, Pat could go and visit then.

35.

Golem had finished, and most of the group had left. Emily and Brooke were the only outsiders left; neither of them looked like they had any intention of heading home soon. I guess that made sense. They could see I wasn't going anywhere, neither was Pat, nor Chuck, so why should they leave?

Emily finished talking to Autumn about one of the submissions and said to all of us, "I was hoping to go to the Winter Formal, and I was wondering if you'd..." she gestured to indicate the whole group of us, "...like to come, too? You know, since none of us have a date, just go as a bunch of friends?"

Autumn hopped on the invitation with both feet. "Oh, yes. That'd be great. We'd love to go!" The boys ranged from enthusiastic (Pat) to horrified (Dave). Mike and Chris looked—amused was probably the best word to describe it. I didn't get much of a sense of how they felt about dancing, more about how they felt about Autumn answering so quickly. Brooke licked her lips. I think everyone in the room could see her planning on how to turn this into a night of romance with Chris.

"I'm working," Chuck said.

"And don't dance," Dave added.

"I've got to bow out, too. I don't have a dress or shoes. I'm not really interested in spending a bundle of cash to get them," I replied.

"You dance, right?" Autumn asked me.

"Yes. I like it a lot."

"Stand up."

"Okay." I felt very exposed as Autumn looked me up and down.

"If I can make you look like a princess for less than fifty dollars, are you in?"

I could swing that. "Yeah. Are we going to Salvation Army?"

"No... I can sew. We'll get patterns and fabric online. I'll make it long enough you can wear your sneakers."

Pat grinned. "'Bippity boppity boo,' ladies. We're going to a ball. Which one of you will I have on my arm? Emily, you game, my lovely?"

"Of course I am." She giggled. "I wouldn't have it any other way."

"And you on the other arm, Sarah?"

"You would want to show up with two girls." I gave him a gentle eye roll while chuckling softly.

"If I had two more arms, I'd offer to Autumn and Brooke, too," he said with a saucy grin.

"Even if you had those extra arms I'd have to turn you down," Brooke said jokingly, "Four women to one man, it just looks silly."

"And we couldn't have that." Autumn's voice had a joking veneer laced through with scorn for Brooke.

"What's the point of us going then? You could just take Pat. He'll be happy as a clam surrounded by his harem, and the rest of us can have some real fun. Play Guitar Hero and drink until the room goes blurry," Dave said with enough sarcasm to show he wasn't really kidding.

"Sounds like Dave doesn't want to go," Brooke observed. She didn't sound crushed.

"No, Dave does not want to go. Dave hates suits, hates dancing, and hates the idea of jumping through those kinds of hoops if there's no chance of sex at the end of it." Dave kept his voice deadpan, but the rest of us broke out laughing.

"Well, Dave, I like your company, but I'm just not willing to have sex with you to get you to go," Emily answered with the same deadpan Dave had used as soon as she stopped laughing. That sent the rest of us back into a tizzy of laughter.

Then Chuck did whatever it is he does that makes people decide it's a good idea to go home. Emily and Brooke headed off talking about dresses. The rest of us waited for Chris to bring down the map.

He got it laid out, and they set to planning. The number of unsearched squares had dropped to ten. Our conversation about not being able to find the doorway by just looking rung in my mind. I felt a deep temptation to try to come up with a locator spell of my own. Just because Chris hadn't been up to it didn't mean I wasn't. Didn't mean both of us working together weren't up to it.

He glanced at me while I thought it. He'd been in a pretty good mood today, eating and joking. I wasn't sure if spilling him back into a depressed funk right away was a good plan. I wasn't sure if working with him would spill him back into depressed funk. On top of that, I wasn't sure if I could work with him without ending up in his bed. Well, that was easily avoidable. Invite Pat along. Three magic users might be better than one. Thinking of Pat made me feel wary about trying any sort of magic that involved going outside what I already knew how to do. So maybe not. But, for a few minutes there, I really wanted to try it.

Wednesday afternoon, Autumn had time to begin dress making. Emily was already there when I got there. They were bonding with each other like Professor Higgins and Colonel Pickering in *My Fair Lady*. I was half-expecting elocution lessons.

"What kind of dresses do you like?" Autumn asked as she, Emily, and I were sitting in front of her computer looking at formal dresses.

"Elegant. Nothing poofy. Nothing lacy. No sparkles."

"Ahhh… you like boring dresses," Emily said with a laugh.

I offered her my hand as if to shake and kept my tone light to let her know I was mostly joking. "Hi, I'm Sarah. Maybe we've met before? You've seen the rest of my clothing, Emily. It's not like I'm hiding a burning passion for bling under these cargo pants."

Jill looked me up and down. "I guess not."

"Okay, let's try this, I know we're going long so you don't need new shoes, what would you like to have exposed?" Autumn asked.

I thought for a moment. "I like my shoulders and neck. Something that shows them off would be nice."

I saw Autumn type in some terms I didn't know; then a few images popped up. One caught my eye. "Can you make that?"

"I think so. It's not very complicated. Basic A-line skirt, fitted bodice, off the shoulder, long fitted sleeves. I can make that. Let's find a fabric. We're going to need a lot of it, so we're not going for anything high end. It's only got to last one night, so I'm thinking polyester or a blend of some sort. Velvety texture with some stretch to it…" Autumn was already seeing the dress in her head. I sat back and let her go.

They both looked at me critically. I could see they were thinking colors. "Red," Autumn said.

"Or plum," Emily added.

"Ohhh…I know what we want!" With that, Autumn was off looking through fabric websites. Ten minutes and more clicks than I could follow later, she said, "This!" It was a deep winey red. "We'll get four yards and go from there." She continued to click. Next thing I knew she had my credit card out.

"Should be here tomorrow. Let's get you measured." She got to work with her tape. Emily wrote down measurements. I felt like a specimen in a jar, both of them watching and recording everything about me. Autumn got to my bust.

"Do you have a strapless bra?"

"No."

"Are you going to get one?"

"Not much need. I can go without for a night pretty easily. B cups don't flop around too much."

"Okay, then take the one you're wearing now off so I can see where they fall and get the right measurement. I'll add a little extra padding to the dress so your nipples don't poke out."

"Thank you." I did that little shimmying trick where you thread the bra through your shirt.

"You could just take it and your shirt off." Autumn seemed very amused at my contortions.

"In your living room? I know it's just us here now, but come on! Any of the guys could walk in any second."

"Yes, but only two of them would care: One is in class for the next hour. The other one is at Chuck's place."

"You just want to see them yourself," I said to Autumn with a joking smirk.

"Oh yeah." She grinned up at me. "I've been trying to get you naked since day one. This whole dress thing is just my lascivious plan. You know what they say: once you've been with a woman, you've got no use for men."

"I don't know about that. Sarah's got a fine-looking man." Emily laughed.

"Thanks, Emily. He is pretty fine, isn't he?"

"Yeah."

"We'll have to make sure he gets pictures of you all dressed up and ready to party," Autumn said.

"He'd like that. We used to go dancing on Sunday nights, but never anything fancy like this." Emily and I spent a while talking about night life in Tel Aviv. She found the idea Friday night isn't a big party night interesting. Autumn wrapped up measuring, and we spent the afternoon hanging out talking about girly stuff. It was kind of nice. A reminder of what normal looked and felt like.

At lunch on Thursday Autumn told me the fabric had come in. They weren't kidding about the whole next day shipping thing. Once I finished my chat with Morrell, I headed back to Writers'. She had all the pieces cut out and wanted to start sewing.

When I got into her room, Autumn was in a deep funk.

"What's up? Paper going badly? More delays on your resources?" That was the first thing that came to mind. Autumn had been working on her senior thesis on comparative diplomacy methods for months and had gotten as far as she could without one book. Unfortunately that one book was still on back order at the library.

"Oh, no. Not that. They tell me it'll get here on Tuesday. He isn't going to go."

"Just because he wants to hide in his room, doesn't mean we can't have fun." I tried not to admit to myself how disappointed I was.

She smiled sadly. "That's not why I'm down. I'll be there, and you'll see me set fire to the dance floor. Dancing and parties are something of a specialty of mine. But he used to dance and laugh. There were some really happy times. I'd hoped because Emily asked and she doesn't know the background maybe he would go. I'd like to see him dance again."

"Dance with you?"

"I wouldn't mind. But me, you, her, by himself. Anyone but Brooke. If he does dance with any of us, he'll have to dance with her. From what I can tell—though he isn't saying it— that's why he's not going."

"What is he saying?"

"Big paper due on Monday." Autumn stood up. "Well, let's get working on that dress. It's not going to sew itself."

"I really am grateful for you doing this for me."

"One of these days you'll literally save my life, and this will look like nothing."

"Well, for the time being, it's a big deal to me."

"Thank you. It's a shame Ari can't be here to dance with you in it."

I felt a quick flash of shame. It had been three days since I had thought of him without prompting from someone else. "Yeah, it is. I'll make sure to get pictures for him. Come next fall…" I could see him for another two days and go back to having him on the other side of the world totally divorced from my day-to-day life. *Stop that! Him on the other side of the world was your choice. Him not knowing about what you've been up to here was your choice. What does that say about him being your choice?* I decided not to answer that.

"Yeah, next fall…"

Autumn got to work. Every few minutes she'd have me stand up and pull a piece of the dress on to see if it was properly snug. When she got to the bodice, I asked her, "Is it possible to make it a little less low cut?" Autumn was draping the fabric for the collar, and the dress was in danger of showing off way more bosom than I was comfortable with.

"Yes, but it will look better like this."

"How about here?" I pointed to a spot on my chest about two inches above where she was aiming for.

"I can do that, but why do you want it so high? They're nice breasts; you should show them off more often."

"That's not so high." There was still a hint of visible cleavage. "I don't show them off for the same reason I don't eat pepperoni pizza."

Autumn looked confused. "I thought the dress code was skirts and long sleeves?"

"I'm not modest by the standards of the Orthodox, but for my time and place, I am. There's a reason you've never seen me in shorts, tank tops, or tight clothing. Unless I intend to sleep with you, you won't see me flashing my bits around."

Autumn thought about that. "I can do it higher."

"Thanks."

"Kind of a shame to keep it all covered, though."

"Trust me, under the right circumstances, it all spends very little time covered. I've even got some interesting outfits for going out dancing with Ari. But unless he's the one on my arm, my skin stays undercover."

Autumn giggled. "Well, that's good."

I smirked kindly at her. "Glad to hear you approve. There's a big difference between modest and prudish. The one I try to be, and I know I don't always pull it off, but I do try. The other is anathema to me. How about your dress? Will there be boobs on display?"

Now she laughed full out. "Nah. Mine aren't that nice. It's a short halter dress. I have nice shoulders and legs. They'll be on display. Unlike the tradition you come from, the one I come from makes sure it's all out to be admired by anyone nearby."

"Sounds cold." She looked at me oddly for a second, then realized I meant temperature-wise.

"I have ways to work around that."

"True."

When dinnertime hit, she was almost finished. Autumn was handy with a sewing machine and fast. At dinner I asked her why go into diplomacy when she had an actual saleable skill. Opening up a tailoring shop might not be the road to riches, but it certainly seemed like more fun than kissing up to various and sundry high muckety mucks.

She didn't see it the same way as I did. We spent most of dinner talking about it. Apparently she'd been in the diplomacy business for roughly four thousand years, and she did like it.

After dinner we went back to Writers', and she finished up. I stared at myself in the mirror and just couldn't believe what I was wearing. I did look like a princess, in a medieval European way. Just yesterday this marvelous concoction of wine velvet had been a pile of fabric and thread.

"You really are amazing."

"Thank you. It's good to have useful skills."

"That you do. This is the best fitting dress I've ever worn."

"Thanks."

I took it off carefully, got dressed, and hung the dress on the door. I was thinking about heading home and starting on some homework when it occurred to me Autumn might be able to shed some light on working with Chris.

"You aren't a mage?" I asked.

"Right."

"And you aren't a wizard, either."

"Yes."

"So, I don't know if you know the answer to this but maybe you would. One mage has a certain power level. Add another mage to the mix. Do you get more power, or are you limited by the upper level of whichever mage is the stronger of the two?"

"You get more power. That's how it works with all magic. The question is: do you get enough control to deal with it? Most magic users have a direct relationship between their power and their control. Up the power level, and you need to have enough control to deal with it. Smart mages or wizards know that and work with others sparingly."

"Good to know."

"Why are you asking?"

"I understand the locator spell didn't work the first time. Since now he's got another mage to work with, I'm curious to see what would happen."

She thought about it. "Might be worth a try. If it works and saves us tromping about all of Reevesville, it's certainly worth it. Here's the downside: you don't have the control. You have the power, and eventually you'll learn the control, but you don't have it yet. That means he'd be driving..." She let that thought trail off.

"Does he have the control?"

She thought about it for a long time. "I don't know. I saw what you did with Chuck, so I know you can call on some serious power. I've seen him work, so I know he's also got some serious skills. I don't know if you plus him is just too much. Still, he's up there. Go up and see. If it works, you've saved us a lot of time."

I headed up the stairs to his room. When he opened the door, he didn't look surprised to see me. "Am I interrupting anything?"

"Not really. I'm looking through the back copies of the *Reevesville Gazette* to see if there are any pictures of the brown-haired boy."

"Anything?"

"Nothing. I know it's a really long shot, but it's that or work on my paper, and I'd prefer not working on it right now."

"If you're looking for a way to procrastinate, I've got a proposition for you. Let's redo the locator spell."

He stepped out of the doorway and let me into his room. "Do you have any idea how to do a locator spell?"

"Not a one. I don't know what we're looking for, either. But, if the problem is whatever's hiding it is stronger than you are, I see the question as being: is it stronger than you and I are?"

He smiled. "How do you suggest working this?"

"The same way I showed you how to heal: reversed. Do the spell again, and use my magic as well."

He seemed to think about it for a minute. I could feel he was interested in trying to do any sort of magic with me, so I guessed he was pondering the mechanics of doing it.

"Sounds worth a shot. Let me get the map." Chris opened the top drawer of his desk and took out a folder. He slid the map out and unfolded it on the floor of his room. "There's not enough room to unfold it all the way in here. But that's not too important. If it works, we'll find a little glowing spot where the doorway is."

"So, how does it work?"

"Two ways: First off, it homes in on anything that feels like us. Secondly, it looks for weak spots in the world here. Put those two things together and that should be the doorway to home."

"How do you do it?"

"Do you want to watch me do it, or do you want me to try to explain it?"

"How easily can you do it by yourself?"

"Easily enough. I'll have plenty of energy for a second go at it."

"Then do it for me. I'll watch/feel."

He sat cross-legged at the edge of the map. I settled next to him. "Do you need your hands for this?"

"No."

"Then give me your hand. When I say 'feel it,' I mean it in the literal sense."

"Why my hand?"

"I don't know. Because it's there. It's skin-on-skin contact. I suppose I could just let my hand hover near you, but I don't know if I'd still feel what you were doing well enough. Why? Do you have something you'd prefer I touched?"

He laughed, and I found myself grinning. "Yes. But my hand is probably as good as anything." He took the rings off his right hand and switched them to the left. Then, with a gentle flourish, he offered his hand to me.

I shifted a little and took it in both of mine. It was soft and cool and nice to hold it without him bleeding on me. "Why take the rings off?"

"Did you want extra distractions?"

"Not really."

"That's why. Ready?"

"Not quite yet." I spent a moment identifying the magic whirling around him, then sorted out the background magic of his room. I could feel there were things in here he had made, and while holding his hand I had a more intense sense of them. "Okay. I've got the lay of the land. Whenever you're ready."

"Here goes."

He hooked himself into one of local ley lines and began to pull power out of it. I felt him gather it close to him. Somehow he used it to amplify his own senses so he could feel what he was looking for. The map worked into it, but I didn't know how. By the time he was done I was pretty sure there were some big holes in my understanding of what he was doing, but I had the basics of it.

"How does it get from your head to the map?" I asked when he was done. I didn't let go of his hand. I probably should have, but I liked holding it.

"It was originally a hunter spell. You focus on what you're looking for. The magic allows you to find it and draws you to it. Instead of walking all over Reevesville, I let my magical self walk over the map, then plant a little glowing spot where the thing is."

"Neat."

"Thanks. As you can see from the total lack of glowing spots, Mildred's cloaking is still better than I am."

"Let's see if it's better than we are."

"Sounds good. How did you do it before? Last time I felt you take charge of my magic and use it, but I don't think you were using it in tandem with yours. It felt like you were using it instead of yours."

"Hmmm…" I thought more carefully about what we had been doing that night. "You might be right. I was working completely on instinct, so I can't tell you how I did it. I'm not one hundred percent sure I can do it again, especially on anything that isn't healing. Do you think you can do it? Use my magic with yours?"

"I can use you like a battery. I've done that sort of magic before. That's what I was doing with the ley line. It's not a power multiplier, at least not in the breaking-someone-else's-magic sense. In the keep-going-when-you-should-pass-out sense, it is."

"Well, last time I was rinsing out my mouth and inspiration just sort of hit. I knew I needed to take you in hand and do it through you because without that you couldn't get close enough to the magic to figure it out. I suppose we could call Chuck and ask him to break into your head, stab you in the eyeballs with ice picks, make you throw up, and then see if that causes you some inspiration on how to work this."

He laughed. "Let's not. Not only can he enter my mind without that side effect, but dinner wasn't particularly bad tonight. I'd like to keep custody of it."

"Well, if you aren't willing to sacrifice for your art..." I gave him a half-smile while I said it.

"Yeah, selfish of me." He turned so he could face me. I watched him slip his two magical rings and his star off. Then he took his ring-free hand and slid it between mine.

"Unshielded? No defenses?"

"I'm in my shielded room, in my house that's been shielded by me, shielded by Autumn, hidden by Dave, and warded by Chuck. There's not much need for protections on my skin here. I'd ask you to take yours off, too, but it doesn't work that way does it?"

"Probably not. Can you see the letters?"

"Just the glow."

"Okay." I thought about it for a minute, felt the letters on my skin, felt the prayer that made them glow, and tried to let it drop. I shook my head. "Looks like it's not going to turn off. I'm stuck with it now."

"Not a bad thing to be stuck with. Besides, Pat might come barreling up the steps looking for a fight if you turned it off. I can feel he's providing you a dimming layer on top of the shield. If the shield went away, he'd probably get freaked out."

"I wouldn't want that."

He closed his eyes and took a minute to get the same sort of feel for me that I had for him before the first spell.

"Okay, your hands in mine." We shuffled our hold so his hands were on the outside. "Your eyes on mine." He took his glasses off. I guessed he was aiming for nothing between us. I made eye contact. For the first few seconds I enjoyed the chance to really look at them up close. Then he was in my head, in my magic, and I was out of control, out of myself, a will without a voice. I started to panic. He felt it and sent a wave of calm in my direction.

I didn't know if I was feeling the magic myself or feeling him feel the magic. Either way, I was much more in tune with its flows and ebbs than normal. I suddenly knew what he was feeling for, a sort of fraying in the magic around us, a worn and weak spot. Like a threadbare heel of a sock.

This was beyond any sensitivity to magic I had ever had. I could feel everything. I could feel my house, the Golem, each individual layer of magic on Writers', and every little "glowy" thing in the house. I knew where all of us were, including Allan, who I hadn't thought of since the night I saw the Watcher at my window. I knew were Morrell was. That answered my question as to if he was magic or just collected old things with a certain feel to them.

I could feel Chris sorting through all of the magic around him, trying to find whatever it was that said home to him. His eyes were still on me, but he wasn't seeing through them anymore. I didn't think he was really even in the room with me anymore.

Then he was back. His eyes refocused, and he started seeing with them again. He held my magic for a few breaths longer than the spell required, then slowly pulled away from me.

I started to shiver violently as his magic slipped away. By the time I was back in my own head my jaw was shaking and my skin had broken out in goose bumps. I hadn't felt that sort of magically induced cold in a while and had forgotten how remarkably unpleasant it was. He had goose bumps as well. I tried to laugh, but my teeth were chattering too hard to do it well. He squeezed my hands to let me know he caught what I had been thinking.

He stood up, pulled his quilt off the bed, sat on the bed with his back against the wall, and gestured for me join him. He wrapped his quilt around both of us and his arms around my shoulders. "There's got to be a way to shut that off."

I nodded at him and forced my jaw to stop shaking so I could speak intelligibly. "I haven't felt it in a while. It's not much fun."

We sat there and warmed up for a minute. "Did it work?" I didn't see anything glowing on the map, but I also couldn't see the whole map.

"Sort of. I had a lot more sensitivity to what was around us. I found things I hadn't noticed before, but I couldn't find the portal."

"Is it in the Federal Witness Protection Program?"

"Just really well hidden."

"Want to try a bigger map?"

"Not really. I'm sure it's here somewhere. I'm going to put this in the success column. It's good to know I can team up with you and improve my reach."

"Yeah, that is good to know. Next time something rips Chuck to shreds I'll probably ask you for a boost as well."

Chris nodded. I thought about it for a bit. "Actually, should I be asking you to do stuff like that? I mean, play my game, not work magically together. Pat was telling me there's a downside to the great power that goes with being a mage, and you might be closer to trouble than I am."

He gave me a grin of such immense bitterness it took my breath away. "All Peter Parker had to deal with was great responsibility. I've got dead by twenty-two. If I somehow manage to survive, there's the fun of insane by forty. But, I'm not so close to the edge I need to stop working even if it is outside of my range of expertise. Especially if it's the difference between one of us crippled or not; that's worth the trade off."

I nodded at him. His eyes were pointed at the wall across from us, but I didn't think he saw it. When he started talking again, entirely new chills raced through me. I don't think I had ever heard a human voice so devoid of any hope.

"It might actually be fun. By the time you're that far gone, you don't know any better anymore. There's just the power and the joy of the magic. Chuck will kill me fast. He's learned at least one of my tricks: the one that causes an aneurism. It takes less than a minute. He's learned enough of Dave's tricks so I won't know he's coming. It'll be unexpected. I'll be designing sharks with laser beams on their heads one minute and dead the next. There are worse ways to go."

I wanted to find a way to pull the bitterness out of him, but I didn't think there was one. "You spend a lot of time thinking about this?" I stroked his cheek.

He turned his eyes toward me. "More than I should. Not as much as my reputation might indicate."

"Great."

He looked like he didn't know what to do with my obvious distress at the topic, so he smiled at me and held me a little tighter. "It was a good try. Mildred never had any skills when it came to hiding things before, but it has certainly mastered them by now. It had eighteen years to get the door hidden, plus whatever it's added since we've gotten here."

"So, tomorrow night off you go into the snow to see if anything jumps out at you and says, 'Look, here I am!'"

"Yes."

We sat there quietly for another minute. "I should probably head off and get some more homework done." I didn't really want to go, but I didn't have any good reason to just sit in his room and snuggle under his quilt, and I did have to write a quick sum up of the Norman Invasion.

"I'll see you at lunch then?" he asked as I got up.

"Yeah, I'll brown bag it and join you guys." That was my usual Friday pattern because I wouldn't see them again until Saturday night.

"Good." I had my hand on the door when he added, "If I can get a ghost under our shields, would you want to give me a hand with it?"

"Very much so."

"Good. It probably won't happen, but if I can pull it off, I'd like to try it with you."

"Then I won't get my hopes too high, but if you can do it, I'd like to help."

"I'll see what I can do. There are a few things floating in Lemmon Hall. Chuck and I are going to check them out and see if any of them are appropriate candidates. If one of them is, we'll chase it to your place and have at it there."

"Sounds good. When are you scouting?"

"Monday or Tuesday night. His days off."

"I'll await your text." I opened the door and headed back to my own place.

36.

Pat came over after dinner on Saturday with a large bag and a smile on his face. I had already gotten my shower and was wrapped in my robe, thinking about what I could possibly do with my hair. After six months without a cut, it was almost shoulder length. He hopped in the shower while I kept brushing it, thinking maybe I could curl it. I finally realized not only did I not own a curling iron, I also didn't have any pins, pony tail holders, or gel. By default I'd be wearing my hair exactly the same way I usually wear it, but it was really well-brushed today. I stopped tucking it behind my ears so it would look a little different.

The shower stopped a while ago. I wasn't sure what Pat was up to in there, but I was hoping to get a hold of the mirror at some point so I could put on some makeup. If he was doing his hair, he could share a mirror with me. I knocked on the door.

"Yeah?"

I poked my head in and then rapidly pulled back. He was standing in front of my mirror in just a pair of black boxer briefs, doing something with his hair.

"You can come in."

I did. For a brief second I thought about what I had told Autumn about modesty. Well, at least I was covered from neck to shins.

"After all, it's not like you haven't seen this before," Pat said. Since it wasn't wet, white briefs, this was actually less revealing than the last time I saw him in his underwear.

"That's true. Don't you usually wear white or blue?"

"Lucky underpants."

"Lucky like your rock is lucky?" I didn't want to look closely enough to see if they had any magic of their own.

"No. Lucky in the sense of I like to wear them if I think the possibility of sex is good." He grinned. "What did you want?"

"You to budge over and share the mirror with me."

"Okay." He scooted over, and I began to put on my makeup. It took about five minutes. By the time I was done, he seemed to approve. I finished before he did and headed out to get dressed.

"Damn, woman, you clean up well!" He leaned against the door to my bathroom, watching me carefully. I stood up and did a little spin to show off the look.

"I should say the same for you." Apparently Pat had style. Hiding under his usual scruffy exterior was a guy who could pull off a slim cut black suit, charcoal shirt, and cobalt tie. His hair looked carefully tousled instead of its usual just-got-out-of-a-tornado appearance.

"Damn, indeed," I said while licking my lips. He smelled wonderfully yummy and his eyes looked especially large and intense. "Did you do something to your eyes?"

"Shhhh…it's a little mascara. Makes them look more dramatic."

"You're kidding me, right?"

"Would you like me to be?"

"I'm not sure."

"How about this? It's magic. I'm still all butch, just borrowed one of Autumn's tricks."

"You know, mascara might be more butch than that."

"Either way, I'm dressed up and ready to dance. Shall we head over to Writers'?"

"Sounds good to me." I kept looking at his eyes as we headed down the steps. "Is it really mascara?"

He laughed. "You aren't supposed to see it like that. It's one of Autumn's tricks. It's supposed to make you want to look into my eyes."

"It's working. I'm looking."

"Yes, but you aren't thinking, 'Gosh, you're fascinating, let's go have sex.'"

"Well, no, I'm thinking, 'Are you wearing makeup?' This might be why it's one of Autumn's tricks. On girls the idea is to put on makeup but look like you aren't wearing any."

He stopped in front of my house. I felt him change the energy around him. Then he looked back at me. His eyes were still interesting but less lashy. "Better?"

"Yeah."

"Then we shall continue on." One minute later we were inside Writers. Emily and Autumn were fluttering around Autumn's room doing some sort of last-minute hair thing.

"Mike's still in the bathroom, and Brooke isn't here yet," Autumn called over her shoulder while pinning something sparkly into Emily's hair.

"Chris upstairs?"

"Yeah. Going to try to get him to come?" Emily asked.

I held up my camera. "I'm going to try to get him to take a picture of all of us before we go. I know I'd like one." I headed upstairs and knocked on his door.

"Yeah?"

"It's me, can I come in?"

"Sure."

I opened the door and went in. He sat at his desk, mound of books on one side, his laptop on the other.

"Looks like you're working hard."

"Quite hard." He clicked from the window with the paper to another one with a computer game. "Did she send you up for a last-ditch effort to get me to go?"

"How am I supposed to do that? Stun you with my loveliness?" I did a little twirl and winked at him. "I get why you don't want to come. I've heard you can dance, and I'd like to see it, but I'm up here to ask about your other talents. Specifically, would you be willing to come downstairs and take some photos of us?"

"If I come down, Brooke will try to get me to go."

"She's not here yet, and it won't break my heart to get a group shot without her. Besides if you don't come down, she'll just come up to you. She might even decide to stay here and keep you company while the rest of us go dance."

"That's a horrible thought to plant in my mind."

"It's in character for her, isn't it?"

"Unfortunately, yes. I may end up going with you just to avoid being alone with her." I noticed a suit through the open door of his closet. From the looks of it, he was ready to jump into it in a minute if he needed to. "Anyway, if I'm going to get shots before you leave, I might as well head down now."

"Sounds good."

"Can I get one of just you?"

"Yeah."

He pointed his cell at me. "That wall." He gestured to the wall that didn't have anything on it. "It'll be a good background." I wandered over to it. He looked at the screen and turned on another light. "Smile big."

I did. He flashed a shot. "Let me get one more. Got a sexy look?" I gave him a saucy smile, then slid into a sultry look. I had a hard time reading his look in return. Pleased, with some other layers I wasn't getting. He shot another picture. Chris taking pictures of me for his own collection made me warmly happy.

We went downstairs. Mike had descended while I was talking to Chris. He looked smashing in light gray. I was starting to think Emily and I were the only ones trying to compete on just our looks alone. Then I caught the faint outline of Autumn's energy around her. It was subtle: her hair was just a hint darker and shinier than usual, her lips a bit more plump, her voice was slightly less nasal, her tone a little more mellow. Apparently Pat's spell was working, too. Emily couldn't tear her eyes away from him.

Okay, I was the only one trying to compete on my looks alone. Lucky for me a successful night meant getting some time on the dance floor and nothing more.

Chris got us all into a group in a hurry, hoping to get the shots before Brooke showed up. He took three pictures fast and almost sprinted back up the stairs.

"Well, so much for tempting him to come by seeing us all dressed up and ready for fun," Autumn said to me. "I'm surprised you even got him to come down."

"That really wasn't the plan. I just wanted pictures of us."

"You could have asked Dave." She gestured to Dave who sat on the couch talking with Mike while doing something on his laptop.

"Autumn…" I pitched my voice low so Emily wouldn't notice. Granted, with the way she was watching Pat, it was entirely possible she might miss a marching band coming through the living room. "I never remember Dave exists unless he's actually in front of me. Even then half of the time I just don't see him. For whatever reason his invisibility thing works way too well on me."

Autumn seemed to think about that. Then the phone rang and Mike picked it up; he listened with a serious look on his face. "I'll let them know. I hope you feel better soon… Yeah, bad idea to eat shrimp salad the night of a dance." Autumn looked hopefully at Mike.

"She's sick." Mike put the phone down and gave Autumn a very long, very accusatory look.

She made sure Emily was out of earshot, and said quietly, "Wasn't me."

"Sure." If sarcasm had a face, Mike was wearing it now.

"Chuck wanted him to go, too." Autumn wasn't terribly convincing. Her pleasure at Brooke's misfortune was too obvious.

"Uh huh."

"That doesn't mean I won't enjoy heading up to tell him the unfortunate news." She scampered out of the room, her steps bouncy with joy.

Mike rolled his eyes. "God save me from the fangirls," he said under his breath.

I raised one eyebrow at him. In the same quiet tone he said, "Chuck's not above poisoning someone if he thinks it'll please Chris. But if it had been Chuck, Autumn would be puking up her guts, too."

"Ahh…she really doesn't seem like much of a problem."

"She's worse than Brooke but better at hiding it. And, we've had a long time of dealing with her."

"Okay."

He thought about it. "You've only seen it in this world, and you don't live here so you don't see much of what happens when she thinks they're alone. She keeps forgetting Dave is still around. She's clingy, intrusive, a little too touchy, and a little too familiar. She's much more likely to hang out in her short bathrobe if she thinks it's just them, or an extra button mysteriously comes undone, that kind of thing. Did you notice the extra lock on the bathroom door?"

"Yeah."

"The first one won't keep her out. She had an unfortunate habit of accidently walking in until Chris and Dave set up the second one."

"Oh."

"On the other hand, he does like to dance. And he does like you and Emily. So the question is: will he face Autumn's restrained public facade for the chance to dance with you two lovelies?"

"What about you? Will we be dancing?"

"Possibly. There's a guy going as well. I'm hoping to grab him at some point. Dancing with you girls might send the wrong message. Or not. It'll depend a lot on the kind of music."

"Which guy?'

"Matt Fresk." The image of a muscular blonde from the swim team popped into my mind.

"He is cute. I didn't know he was gay."

"He's not out, but he was at the last few Lambda meetings. I'm hopeful."

"Good luck then. It'd be nice if one of us didn't have to be celibate."

"Even better if it's me." He grinned and looked deliciously handsome. Makeup was overrated. I really needed to figure out how to do a glamour.

I laughed. "I'll be rooting for you."

"Let's wait a few more minutes. He's coming," Autumn said as she descended the stairs. "He decides to brave one dragon for a chance to get on the dance floor."

Three minutes later Chris joined us in the living room. Mike and Pat had chosen slim cut suits. Chris' was a more conservative dark blue with the traditional white shirt and lighter blue tie. Something that looked more like banker wear and less like fashion model clothes. Maybe it was a difference between growing up in the middle of nowhere versus a big city?

We took a few minutes to pull on coats and headed into the night. While we were inside it had started snowing. Pat offered an arm to Emily, and she happily wrapped around him. The other four of us walked in a clump across the campus and down to Fullings. The ancient girl's dorm also housed a large all-purpose room, transformed for the night into a dance floor.

Miles of Christmas lights had been wrapped, stapled, and tucked against everything that could support them. The whole room had a soft golden glow to it. We deposited our coats at a snowflake and glitter bedecked table set for eight. It looked like most of the others had come in large, co-ed, friendly but not romantic groups like ours. Maybe three couples were out on the dance floor already. Everyone else lingered around the edges talking and getting drinks.

The music was fast and easy to move to. Nothing too complicated. Anyone with a pulse could manage to dance to this. Pat grinned at Emily and I, grabbed both of our hands, and swept us out onto the floor. In a minute Mike joined us as well.

I was impressed. Mike could really dance. I don't know why this surprised me. I've fought with him so I know he can move, but somehow fencing, fighting, and dancing hadn't connected in my mind. Emily and I were giggling, having a good time keeping up with both boys. Eventually the music slowed down, and I got a dance with Pat while Emily danced with Mike. I had looked around but didn't see Matt Fresk anywhere. Obviously Mike didn't see him, either.

When the music sped back up, we went back to a foursome. Chris and Autumn joined us, shifting our square to a circle. After a few more songs, I saw Mike's eyes focus on the far side of the room. He had spotted Matt. I looked over and saw the same thing he did: Matt had come alone.

"Good luck!" Pat and I both said as he went off in search of true love or at least some company for the night. The five of us continued to dance, but more and more of the songs were becoming Pat and Emily, with Chris, Autumn and I on the side. Then three other Golemites joined us. Harold, Josh, and Amber were happy to have some extra company to dance with. We spent more time with them. With each passing song Pat and Emily danced closer to each other and further from the rest of the crowd.

I hoped tomorrow morning Emily wouldn't remember her boyfriend and have a fit.

A song I didn't much care for started. Time to sit down, cool off, and suck up some punch sounded pretty good to me. I returned to the table with a drink and found Chris already sitting there.

"Taking a break?" he asked me.

"Yeah. I wanted a drink, and this song doesn't do anything for me, so here I am. You?"

"Pat's got Emily. Autumn seems to have made a new friend." He tilted his head toward Autumn and Josh.

"They look like they're hitting it off."

"Yep." Chris sat quietly for a few minutes, then, out the blue, asked me, "Did you pick that dress, or did Autumn choose it for you?"

"Odd question."

"I suppose it would seem like that." He waited for me to answer.

"I picked the dress, Autumn and Emily picked the color." He nodded at me and looked relieved. "Why ask?"

"It looks like home."

"Is that good or bad?"

"Good question. If it was something Autumn had done, I'd think it was something of a bad joke. Since you picked it yourself... it's just... I don't know. Lots of memories." He looked a little melancholy, and I didn't know what to do with that.

"This was all me. I asked her for something to show off my neck and shoulders, she showed me a bunch of styles, and this is one I've always liked.

"So, this was the fashion where you're from?" I asked lightly, trying to perk up his mood.

"Almost, take off the left sleeve so your clan mark could show, and it would be dead on. With two sleeves, it's just similar."

"How about you guys? Suits back there?"

"No. Leggings, tunics, and cloaks. The occasional formal toga looking thing. Left arm bare to show the clan mark."

"Wow. There's an image. Cod pieces?"

He perked up. "Is that something you'd like to see?"

"I wouldn't mind." I flashed my sexy look at him.

"Unfortunately for you, the tunics came to below mid-thigh. As societies go, it was quite modest."

"How about music and dance? You look pretty comfortable out there."

"It's totally different. The desire to move when you hear certain kinds of music is the same no matter where you are, but here there are no rules. There, dance was very formal, very stylized, ballroom-type stuff, so was most of the music." He looked far away from me. Back in the home he no longer had.

"I'm doing a fantastic job of keeping you cheery. You look so lonely you could start to cry soon."

He smiled slightly. "I'm not that bad today."

"You sad and lonely wasn't the plan. Dancing and laughing and fun was the plan."

"We could dance."

"We certainly could. New song will be up in a minute. I'm game if you are."

"I'd like that."

We headed out toward the dance floor. The current song wound down, and the first few notes of the new one slid into place. I could tell it was slow and wondered if Chris would want to dance to a slow one. He slid his hand around the small of my back, took my right hand in his, and held it against his chest. We began a slow box step. The music continued. More and more dancers fled the floor for the safety of the tables. I didn't know the song, but it wasn't what I'd call dance music. Chris looked annoyed.

"What?" Had he been hoping for something faster and now felt trapped into a slow dance with me?

"Listen to the lyrics."

"This one goes out to the one I left behind..."

"They're playing our song." I smiled gently at him, hoping a reminder he wasn't totally alone in his loneliness would help a little. Even if I hadn't exactly been pining for Ari lately.

"I'm sorry. I'm being an ass. This is just as much your song as well."

"It's just not hitting me too hard today." *Or yesterday, or the last week, or really, the last month.* "I've got my down days, too." *Just not since December.*

"It's hard to tell that. You always look pretty perky."

"I cried for an hour when I got back from dropping him off at the airport. But this will sound so dumb…"

"Go on, I promise not to laugh."

"Ever read *New Moon*?"

"Will you think less of me if I say yes?"

"No, but it may add your gayness quotient."

He smiled dryly. "In that case, no, I've never read it."

"Okay. So the heroine is named Bella, and she's a twit. She's got no life of her own and is just a big ball of Edward-crazy mush. Anyway, he leaves, and she spends like three months moping."

"You don't want to be Bella?"

"I didn't stay in Israel because I wanted more from life than being Ari's girlfriend. Now I've got it."

"But you love him."

"Yes," I answered on automatic. "But I love me, too. I was barely eighteen when we met. I'm not even twenty-two yet. I want some time to be *me* before I become *us*. It was too easy to just be part of him. When I thought about it, it scared me. So I came home for some away time."

Chris looked thoughtful. His voice dropped. He dipped his head so his mouth was near my ear. Words for only me to hear. "I was never just me. We were married when I was 102. Say, eighteen and a month by local standards, just barely an adult. She was younger, seventeen-ish. My entire adult life was spent with her. Our first child was born before I was the age I am now. I was head of my clan by twenty-three. High Priest by thirty-ish. Where I started and those things ended, I couldn't tell you." We danced quietly for a few more beats.

"Autumn's watching us closely," he whispered to me. His lips almost brushed my ear, and his breath raised the hairs on the back of my neck.

"Josh isn't as fascinating as we are?"

"Not now, apparently."

The music changed—sped up. I knew this song and was surprised when Chris didn't let go of me.

"You want to dance to this?" "Butterfly" by Crazy Town was raunchier than anything I pictured him dancing to.

He dipped me low, swung me back up again, pulling my hips flush against him, and once more he whispered in my ear. "She's been watching me like she wants to pounce all night. All of her glamours are on high and aimed at me, and I'm sure she made Brooke sick. Do you mind helping me get a little revenge?" This time his lips did touch me. I enjoyed the sensation of warm skin and soft breath too much.

I grinned at him. "How mean do you want to get?"

"Dance close to me on this one. Then we'll leave together."

"My, you are pissed at her, aren't you?" I cocked an eyebrow at him. Then I slid down his body, scooted back up, and ground my hips against his.

He gave me a wicked grin. One I thoroughly enjoyed. Chris could really dance. I would have been thrilled to have him as a partner anytime he wanted to go clubbing. By the time the song ended I had the glow that goes with a good, sexy, fast dance, and he had an erection. I took it for the compliment it was. He kept his hand on my back while we walked to our table, then held my coat for me while I put it on.

"Well, goodnight, all," he said. Autumn looked like she was about to swallow her tongue. The rest of them wished us a pleasant night, and off we went. I wrapped an arm around him, and he slid his over my shoulders as we walked out into the night. My breath steamed. I felt and welcomed totally natural shivers. He pulled me closer as I began to shake.

"Danger?" His voice was serious and tense.

"No." I smiled kindly at him. "It's just cold."

"Oh. I'd do a warming spell for you but that would backfire wouldn't it?"

"Just possibly." He hadn't moved his arm off my shoulders, so I kept mine wrapped around his waist. I knew I should drop my arm, but I liked having him near. I wanted another body close to mine. "Is Autumn properly punished?"

"Probably. She wasn't actually green, but it was close."

"Green?"

"Jealous."

"Got it. So, now what? Any plans for the rest of the evening?"

"I do have a paper due on Monday."

"And it's not getting any closer to done."

"That's true, but I really enjoyed dancing. If you're game, I'd like to do some more."

"I'm game. What are you thinking? The streets aren't too bad. We can get to Erie in a little under an hour."

He looked up and judged the sky. "It'll be snowing again in less than three minutes. You've got a whole apartment, a Rhapsody music subscription, and no roommates."

"We could scoot my couch out of the way."

"I was thinking that."

"Are you any good with sound-dampening spells?"

"I'm competent but not fantastic. Why?"

"I doubt Allan wants to hear us clomping around above his head."

"Makes sense."

"So, both Autumn and Mike know you like to dance. But Autumn tells me she hasn't had any luck getting you on the dance floor. So, is that memories of before, or is there a more recent story there?"

"A more recent story. The year before last we were all at a party where I had a beer or two more than I really needed. Everyone who was there got to see I do like to dance, and I can do it pretty well, too. Autumn's been trying for a repeat ever since."

"Ahhh… were you dancing with her?"

He sighed. "It really was a dumb move on my part. She was in front of me. Brooke at my back. There's a reason why I rarely have more than two beers now."

"Staying sober always seems like a good plan to me. I also don't enjoy feeling drunk." The snow began to fall again adding a pleasant softness to everything.

"It's not normally something I enjoy, either. Like cigarettes. Every now and again I just want a buzz. Sometimes it's nice to let go of being in control and just let it all fall where it may."

The words came out before I could stop them. "You like being tied up, don't you?"

He smiled at me, his eyes warm and flirtatious. "It's been a very long time, but yes, I do recall enjoying that."

I smiled back at him. "I've always got to be in control. That's a part of why I don't like being drunk."

"Always?" He seemed intrigued.

"Well, I do let loose in certain intimate settings, but they're few and far between these days."

"Ah."

"And yes, in that case, I do like being able to let go and let it fall where it may."

"Good to know." He was smiling, and I was enjoying this risqué talk immensely.

"Really? And what are you going to do with that information?"

"You'll just have to wait until the time is right to find out."

"That sounds promising." We were at my place. I let go of him to walk up the steps. At the top stair, I turned to look at him for a moment before unlocking the door. A little voice in the back of my mind said this wasn't the smartest thing I had ever done. The possibility for going too far was much too real here. Looking at him, snowflakes in his hair, those huge gray eyes level with mine, I squashed that voice flat. It would be fun, and it had been too long since I had had this kind of fun.

"Computer's on the table. I'm going to change out of this into something I can really move in. How about you set up a playlist?" I hung my coat on the back of the door and kicked off my shoes. He followed my lead, then settled in front of my computer while I went to change.

I opened my closet door and stared at my clubbing outfit. It isn't modest, in fact it's practically anti-modest. It is easy to move in, and it's cool when you're dancing hard. Out of my dress and standing in my panties I still hadn't decided if I should go for club wear or my usual cargo pants and button down.

Go all out. Let it fall where it may.

I grabbed the clubbing outfit. It's a tiny white tank top, cropped a good three inches above my hips. I didn't bother with a bra. It wasn't supposed to be worn with one anyway. The pants are low-rise, dark blue, skinny jeans. Low enough I took the panties off, too.

I went to the bathroom and stared at myself in the mirror.

What are you doing? Trying to seduce him?

Yes.

Stop it. You're friends.

Yeah, but he started this game, and he's the one who wanted to keep dancing.

He's not the one who picked an outfit you're all but naked wearing. That's all on you. If you wear it, you're telling him, 'Let's have sex.' Is that what you want to say to him?

Yes.

Well, too fucking bad! He's not yours, doesn't want to be yours, and you aren't doing him any favors by flaunting yourself at him.

I went back to my room and pulled a flannel button down over the tank top. I didn't button it. Still sexy. Not quite so blatant.

Back in my living room he was putting the finishing touches on his playlist. He had taken off the jacket, loosened the tie, and unbuttoned the top two buttons. All he had to do was roll up his sleeves a bit, and he'd be a pale version of my perfect idea of sexy.

"Do you want a drink?"

"Yeah. What do you have?"

"A bunch of stuff. Help yourself, and grab me a pop while you're at it."

Music I couldn't identify flowed through my apartment. I slid my coffee table against the window seat. When I started on the couch, he came over to help me. We had it out of the way in a few seconds. He handed me a soda, and took a sip of a beer.

"Isn't that how you got tongues wagging last time?"

"I trust your discretion." He smiled at me and drank.

"Good to know." I smiled back at him. The music was getting a hold of me and a warm, happy relaxation flowed through my limbs. I'd be dancing in a minute. For everything my brain had to say to me when I was looking in the mirror, being out here with him was comfortable and friendly. As I started to move, things got a little sexy, but a pleasant, safe, friendly sexy.

Most of the music was fast. Two people dancing in the same room kind of music. We were bopping along to a swingy sort of song with an upbeat sound and not very upbeat lyrics when I realized I didn't know what one of the terms meant.

"What's an Arab Strap?" He looked uncomfortable. "How bad can it be?"

"It's a cock ring, with leather straps attached to it."

"How does that work?"

"You ask me?"

"You're the one who tells me he's not that vanilla and knows what it is."

His smile was a blend of chagrin and amusement. "I looked it up on Wikipedia. No picture. So, I can't tell you how it works."

"And if there had been one?"

"I could have probably figured it out," he said dryly. I laughed. Slow violin music filled my apartment as the previous song faded.

"Is this a waltz?"

"Yes."

"If there's any line dancing in here, I might have to pinch myself."

"Sorry, none of that. A few more 'real dances' but it's mostly fast stuff."

"Where did you learn to dance?" I asked as he swept me around the waltz's box step.

"My mom thought it was something everyone should know. All five of us have or had lessons. You?"

"Most of it I just picked up here and there. Things like this came from high school gym."

He whirled me around as another fast song came on. "Finally, one I know!" Shakira's "Hips Don't Lie." Also pleasantly raunchy.

"How is it you like to dance but don't know any dance music?"

"I know gobs of dance music. Israeli dance music."

"Oh." His hands settled on my hips as we moved to the music. He pulled me close and our bodies rubbed together deliciously.

By the second verse I took the button down off. I wanted to send him a clear message of intent. He got it. My hips weren't lying. Apparently he liked the outfit, too. His fingers traced distracting figures on the bare flesh of my low back. I had one hand on his neck and the other moving toward his face when the song stopped. The song that followed was slow. He took the hand that had been sliding toward his face and twined his fingers with mine, once again holding that hand against his chest.

I slid close to him, nestled against his chest with my face inches from his neck, his chin pressed against the top of my head. His skin was a soft pink from the exertion and he smelled so good I wanted to lick him. His hand was flat against the small of my back now, anchoring me snuggly against him.

My free hand still rested against the back of his neck. If I just lifted my face, we'd be in perfect kissing position. I pressed tighter to him, a thrill shooting through me at the feel of him hard against my abdomen. The idea of his tongue on mine started a warm glow I very much wanted to see spread.

I trust your discretion. That thought stopped me cold. Discretion didn't just mean not talking about what happened here. It meant making good decisions. Like not throwing myself at a man I knew wanted to stay away and was having a hard time of it. I moved my hand away from his neck and stepped back. He didn't let go but did stop dancing. His eyes questioned me. "I'm enjoying this too much."

"That's a bad thing?"

I smiled sadly at him. "No, but where enjoying this too much will lead probably is."

Disappointment radiated off of him as he let me go. "Should I leave?"

"Only if you don't want to end up in bed with me." He actually thought about it. For a moment I was sure he was going to take my hand and start dancing again, letting the consequences fall where they may. I held my breath, hoping, almost praying, he would. But he didn't. He slid his shoes and jacket back on.

"I had a really good time tonight," he said, standing in front of my door.

"I did, too. If you ever want to go out dancing again..."

"Yeah." I wanted to grab him and pull him against me again. I wanted the warm, hard press of his body against mine and the soft, wet slide of his mouth on mine. Instead, I opened the door, smiled at him, and watched him head into the night, feeling world class stupid for stopping instead of kissing him. Watching from my window seat, I was perversely satisfied to see him head down the street toward Chuck's house, instead of toward the home he shared with Autumn.

I put my furniture back, turned off the music, and went to bed. For a long time I tried to remember Ari's touch, the way his skin felt and smelled, but, like everything else, that was fading. The slide of Chris' fingers through mine as he took my hand and pressed it against his chest kept intruding.

Sleep stayed away for a long time. Images, both real and fantasy, of Ari and Chris kept tumbling through my mind. When I finally did sleep, I found myself wrapped in erotic dreams of the light-blue-skinned man I knew was my husband. After, we lay spooned together. I looked at his arm against mine and saw the matching clan tattoos.

I jolted awake. The clock said nine. Time for a shower and a chance to get that dream out of my head. I had gone beyond fangirl mad crush into dreaming I had been her. The last thing he needed was another silly girl who couldn't get it through her head he was just a friend. There was a line, and I had come too close to crossing it last night and fucking trampled it in my dreams.

I got out of the shower determined to put the romance behind me. Then I fell right back into it. Pat was sprawled on my couch, snoring softly. He was still in his suit, and, unless he had developed a strange rash, there was lipstick, Emily's color, on his neck and cheek.

He looked up at me and smiled. Smiled huge. "Guess who finally got lucky?"

"Mike?"

"Probably. But more importantly, ME!" He sprang up and swung me into a big hug. "This has been the longest, saddest, driest spell of my life, and it's OVER!"

"Are you sure?"

"She broke up with him last week. We've got a date tonight."

"Yay!" I was happy for him and doing my best to sound enthusiastic.

"You slept late. Any fun last night?"

"Yes, there was fun last night. Just not the kind you had. After we left, Chris and I came back here, boogied for a few hours, then I went to bed"—he had a salacious sparkle in his eye—"alone."

"What was up with you and him dirty dancing?"

"He wanted to piss off Autumn."

"It might have worked too well. She went home with Josh." I blinked in shock. "She used to do it all the time. He and Ameena would be especially close, get all romantic over something. Then she'd head off, find the first guy who would fall for the glamour, and fuck him into next week."

"Wow. I wouldn't have thought—"

"She's a fairy. It's what they do."

"Okay. Don't know much about fairies."

"As long as it didn't muck with her ideas of proper protocol, she'd be happily boinking anything that moved. It's just part of what they are."

"Good to know. It doesn't seem like she does that here."

"Nope, but it does seem like patterns repeat themselves. As soon as you two left, she was all over Josh. I imagine when Chris got home there was a loud concert under his room."

"Lovely. Why were you watching her? Weren't you all wrapped up in Emily?"

"I was, but she wanted to take a break. I watched you and Chris leave. Then Autumn and Josh sucked face for a few minutes and left right after."

"And after that?" He gave me an immensely smug and satisfied look. I turned to my biscuit starter. "I was going to make biscuits. Do you want me to make some for you, too?"

"I could use some breakfast."

"Need to replenish your energies?"

His grin was infectious. "Oh yes! Then it's home for shower, a mound of homework, sleep, and another date! Thank you God! It's OVER!" He swung me around in another hug.

"You and celibacy really don't get along well, do you?"

"I've been fucking since I was fourteen and much, much longer than that before. The last six months have been torture."

"Yeah, I haven't been enjoying them much either, but I doubt I'll be dancing a jig when I finally get some again."

"Only because you'll be pulling Ari back into bed for yet another round."

I grinned while mixing the biscuit dough. "You might have something there." I had a terrible feeling part of why Pat and I could be so comfortable and happy together was because I was with someone else. If that ever weren't true, things would change in ways I didn't want them to. Even in his distracted state right now, if I got too serious he'd wonder what was up. I found a light question to ask him. "What was the score last night?"

"I don't want to brag, but it had been a long time for both of us. Seven to four, her advantage."

"Liar." I smirked at him.

"Swear to God!" He gave me his most innocent look.

"That mind-reading trick of yours really does come in handy, doesn't it?"

He winked at me. "Sure you don't want to try it yourself?"

"In your dreams, baby." I grinned at him.

"Every night, love, every night." I giggled. "So, really, nothing happened with you and Chris? You were looking pretty hot before you left."

"Just dancing." Which might not have been strictly true, but was as much as I wanted to say to Pat about it.

37.

"Only if you don't want to end up in bed with me." Chris' hopes for things just happening came crashing to a halt. He should have known she was too honest with herself, too honest with him, to let them slide into sex as an accident. If it was going to happen, he'd have to take responsibility for it. He stepped back, barely aware of what he was saying as he left. She shut the door. He stood on the stoop, desperately wanting to knock on the door and go back in. He knew she'd let him. All he had to do was own his desire and lay it at her feet.

He couldn't do that.

He didn't want to go home. His empty room was a very bad idea right now. Chuck's then. He checked his cell. Chuck was still an hour from getting home, but he had a key. The walk down left him frozen and breathless. It couldn't be much above ten degrees, and he didn't bother with a warming spell or even closing his coat. Let the cold punish him. Let it purify him. Drive the lust away. It worked. By the time he had gotten to Chuck's the lust was gone. Misery and guilt replaced it. Old, comfortable feelings he knew how to deal with.

His hand could barely hold the key. Several minutes of trying to get it in the lock caused Becky to open the door for him.

She looked annoyed at having been rousted out of bed in the middle of the night. "Are you drunk?"

"I wish."

"Come in."

"Thanks."

"You look like you should be drunk."

"I should be drunk. If I had been drunk, I wouldn't be here now."

Becky sighed. She knew she wasn't going back to bed anytime soon. He collapsed on their couch, still in his coat. "Want to tell me about it?"

"Not really."

"Tell me anyway. You walked four miles in the cold with an open coat. Obviously something is bothering you."

"She gave me the choice: stay and end up in bed with her or leave."

"You made the right choice. No matter how horny you are, you don't want to end up in bed with Brooke. You'd never get rid of her if that happens."

"Not Brooke. Sarah."

"Why didn't you stay?" Her unspoken, 'You idiot!' rang through his head.

"It's complicated."

"No. It's not. You need to take off that ring and start moving on. Sarah sounds like a fine way to start. She's not psycho."

"I can't."

"Fine. Be miserable, but stop showing up here in the middle of the night to spread it around."

Chris didn't respond to Becky's last comment. He stared at the fake oak paneling on the wall seeing images of Sarah dancing in front of him. "She has a boyfriend," he said quietly.

"It sounds like she's not too worried about it if she's inviting you to stay."

Chuck walked in. Becky looked up at him. "Lover boy here shot down another one and is wishing he didn't." She stood up. "I'm heading back to bed. Work in the morning." She headed out of the living room, up to her own room.

"What happened?" Chuck asked in a low voice.

"Autumn poisoned Brooke…"

"I did that. Autumn didn't get sick?"

"No."

"Her shields are getting better. With Brooke out of the picture you decided to go dancing?"

"I should have stayed home."

Chuck rolled his eyes. "But you didn't."

"No, I didn't. She picked a dress. It looked a lot like home, and Sarah feels so much like her. I was lonely. Autumn was pissing me off, all of her glamours on high. I asked her to dance. It turned out to be a slow song."

"Accidently, I'm sure."

"It was that time. We talked and danced. The next song came on; it was fast and sexy. I grabbed the first excuse I could think of to keep holding on to her. Playing a trick on Autumn. I got her to leave with me. Next thing I knew my mouth was on automatic and suggesting we go back to her place and dance some more.

"We danced for a few hours. Most of it just fast and friendly. But I made the playlist. As the list wound down, there were more slow songs, more sexual songs. If it just happened... I could live with that.

"Of course, it couldn't just happen. We were so close. She was in this tight little tank top and jeans..."

"Wait." Chuck looked up from taking off his boots. "Let me imagine that for a moment. Sarah, queen of the loose fit cargo pants, boots, and flannel button down, was wearing skimpy clothing?"

"Tight, skimpy clothing. She was in my arms, pressed against me. Her hand around my neck. I had one hand on the naked small of her back and was holding her other hand. It could have been home. The way she fit against me... the way her body moved. If I had closed my eyes... I felt her think it. She was going to kiss me. Then she stopped. She pulled back, told me she was enjoying this too much and if I didn't want to end up in bed with her, I needed to leave."

"And you, King of the Idiots, left. You need to turn your ass around and head right back over there. Hell, I'll drive you."

"Don't tempt me."

"Why the fuck not? Getting laid would do you a world of good."

"I don't want to get laid," Chris said, pain radiating off of him.

Chuck shook his head. "It doesn't always have to be about lifelong commitment and everlasting love. Sometimes it can just be friendly and fun. If any of the girls could handle friendly and fun, it's Sarah."

"I don't want friendly and fun. I want what I had."

"And she feels like what you had. I know. At first I thought that was why you thought she was our healer. Look, you aren't going to get it back. There's no going back for us. You know this. You might as well go forward with someone who feels like home." The words felt old and tired to Chuck, but he didn't have anything else to offer Chris. Then an insight hit.

"Wait. Are you afraid you'll fall in love with this one?"

"I..." Chris stopped to think. Chuck felt the emotions running through Chris. He considered it a good sign his question pushed Chris' guilt into the background. "I'm afraid I'll end up pretending she's Althiira. I'm afraid I'll hurt both of us by wanting her to be someone she isn't."

"You don't think..." Chuck didn't need to finish that idea. Chris was as much in his head as Chuck was in his.

"Oh God. Half the time I hope it's true. But if it is, and if she ever remembers..."

"She can finally punish you."

"Or forgive me."

"That's not what you want." Chuck could see the image in Chris' mind. Chris laying at Althiira's feet, beaten, bloody, and broken in a hundred places while she slowly healed him and broke him again. Chuck shook his head. "She'd never do it for you. She'd never hate you enough for it. She never liked pain enough for it. No healer does. They can't do their jobs if they like pain."

"She'd hate me enough now. She told me what would happen. Told me the price was too high. I made her doubt her visions because I couldn't take the fact they were right and the only honorable thing left for me to do was die."

"No, Chris. You defended yourself and your people. You did the honorable thing. It just didn't work out."

"I destroyed our world because I couldn't bear to believe her!"

Chuck hated talking about this. They had been through it before too many times, and it never got any easier because Chris never really believed it. "You destroyed our world because it's what you were born to do. The Presence set you up to be its tool for the end. There was nothing you could have done to avoid it. When you fought for the position of high priest, when we raised your banner in the name of the Presence, all of this was set in motion. You knew the prophecy as well as, if not better than, anyone else. When our clan took over, the end was near.

"Hell, Chris, when you decided to be a priest instead of a king. When you decided what was right was more important than power. Because you were you, it was going to happen. No one else could have done it. It was always going to be you. The warnings, the prophecy, her visions—they were never designed to stop you. Otherwise, they would have worked.

"Seriously, what kind of god has a spell sitting around to unmake it if it doesn't intend to have it used?"

"If this was my destiny, why does it hurt so much?"

"Because no one ever promised you a good time."

"I should be dead." Chuck knew this litany by heart as well.

"Yeah, well, more and more I'm wishing I hadn't taken you with us." Chris looked up. This was the closest Chuck had ever come to apologizing for bringing him here. "But right now we've got one piece of our destiny left, one loose thread to tie up, and that's Mildred. Stick around long enough to defeat it with me, and then do what you want. Go fuck Sarah into the next century. Close your eyes and pretend she's Althiira. Make her forget Ari ever existed, raise a bunch of kids, and try to be happy. Or take that razor I'm not supposed to know about and find a quiet place to end it. Trying to live in a world that's gone isn't working for you. It's not working for me. And if she's half the woman I'm afraid she is, it's not working for her, either."

"Why so concerned with her all of a sudden?"

"I'm not concerned for her. I'm concerned for you. This one might just make you happy. Which isn't illegal. But it will never happen if she comes to her senses and realizes you are a moron. Twenty years is long enough to mourn. Time to move on."

"And if I can't?"

Chuck took a deep breath and finally made the promise he had been avoiding for the last two years. "Then fight this last battle with me, and I'll help you end it. There's no point to living like this."

"You think we're going to survive?" Chris might have been asking about the weather. His interest in the topic was minimal.

"We did last time. Try not to piss this healer off so much that she leaves and, yes, I think we'll survive. Maybe not all of us—I've got a bad feeling about Dave. Do not tell him that. I don't want him even more worried going into this. But you and me, and for some strange reason Autumn because she's the fey equivalent of a cockroach, we're going to make it through, if you can keep Sarah with us. Now, it's almost morning, and I've got to get some sleep. Do you want to crash here, or should I drive you home or, better yet, to Sarah's?"

"Here."

Chuck started up the steps. He could feel Sarah inside her home and knew she was alone. A minute of casting made sure no one else would be coming over. This would get awkward if Pat or Chris showed up.

He didn't want to have this conversation. On top of that, he didn't like being alone with Sarah. He kept expecting her to attack when he turned his back. She may not have been able to hate Chris enough to destroy him, but he had no illusions about how much his former sister-in-law had cared for him.

Sarah looked puzzled when she saw he was alone. "Are you hurt?"

"No." He gritted his teeth and fought the desire to turn and leave. Two steps forward and he stood in her blue apartment.

"Do you want a drink?" She always asked that. He knew it was polite, but it annoyed him.

"No. I wanted to talk to you about Chris." He had her full attention now. She gestured to one of the chairs at her kitchen table and sat across from him.

"I'm listening."

He had been debating how to start this all the way up to her place. Nothing struck him as a good way to say it. If there were no good ways, then he'd go with a bad one.

"You need to just sleep with him and get it over with."

Her jaw didn't drop. It should have. Her eyes went wide. Whatever she had expected him to say that wasn't it. He continued quickly, "You know you want to. You know he wants to. But if you keep leaving it up to him, he'll keep saying no and spending the next week torturing himself about it. If you took the decision out of his hands, everyone would be happier."

She blinked slowly at him. Acting like she had never seen anything his shape and wasn't quite sure what to do with it. The silence stretched beyond the comfortable point. He wondered if something was wrong with her. Even if he had insulted the hell out of her, she should have said something by now. Another minute of quiet passed. He was ready to go into her mind and see what she was thinking when she finally spoke.

"If I rape Chris, we'll all be happier?"

"What? No! Seduce him. Let it happen without making him take responsibility for it. Don't give him the option to back out."

He was a little surprised to see how much loathing she could pack into one look. "You can leave now, Chuck. I'd prefer it if you didn't come back."

"No." He turned the full force of his frustration with this situation on her, and she twitched away from it. "Listen to me about this. He's so close to being able to move on, but he can't because he's so tied to ideas of fidelity and nobility and all that crap. If you kicked his feet out from under him, he'd see the world won't end. He can still love the first one and love another person, and it doesn't have to be all about pain and torment, and just maybe he could put some of the demons behind him finally."

She let her own frustration and anger out at him. "Do you think I want to be Autumn or Brooke? If he needs someone to kick the feet out from under him, go see one of them. I'm not interested in anyone who can't own up to wanting me."

"Damn it! You're both being stubborn twits."

"Do you think I enjoy this? Yes, I want him. I know he wants me. I also know he's a cracked eggshell, and any push from the wrong direction will break him. I don't want to deal with the clean up. Do you remember that week of self-destructive shit he went through last year? That was over a fantasy! Remember the one two weeks ago where he was in a snit for a week? I'm fairly certain that was the result of him seeing me in a wet t-shirt and panties. What sort of fantasy land do you live in where the two of us sleep together and he bounces out of my room a new, happy man? So much of who he is is tied to her. If I help break that tie, will there still be any Chris left?"

"If you don't, I'm not sure there will be a Chris left when this fight is done. Once Mildred is gone and we're all safe, he's got nothing to tie him to this life."

"What do you mean?" She thought she knew but wanted to make sure.

"I mean he never wanted to be here in the first place. I brought him here. He wanted to stay there with her and the children and take what was coming, but Autumn and I brought him here. I hoped he'd remember what he liked about being alive; that he'd be able to start over. It hasn't worked. He's at my place fantasizing of ways to kill himself or picking fights trying to get something to do it for him at least once a month. That's where he goes and what he does when he vanishes.

"Staying with us to finish this last fight, to give the rest of us a good chance at getting through alive, that's all that's keeping him here now. Once that's gone—this morning I finally promised to help him kill himself if he can't get past this. He is my brother, my best friend, and I do not want to lose him. I do not enjoy his misery. I want him to have a new attachment."

"You do not get to lay that at my feet."

"Yes, I do. You're the healer."

"Yes, I'm the healer. So listen good. A quick fuck isn't going to fix him. If I thought it might—Well, I don't think that. He doesn't want it. He doesn't need it. And if something with us does actually happen, and it turns out I can't give him what he needs that might make him so much worse he stops just thinking about it and actually does it. I can't promise to love him the way he needs or wants to be loved. I can't say I want someone that broken bound to me. Right now, I can't even say I want him for more than some friendly sex. I have a man, remember?"

Chuck probed her mind, not caring that she felt him do it. He saw her wince and rub her temples, but she didn't run away, so he didn't pull back. He dug into the places she tried not to go herself too often. "No, you don't. Right now what you have is a shield. Ari's a way of keeping feelings you don't want to deal with away. He's a way to keep yourself in line and Autumn and Pat happy with you. As for the real Ari, you don't know if he's alive or dead or still loves you. You can't claim him in good conscience anymore because you don't love him, not the way you did in October. You'd slide back into loving him if he came back, but it's fading away as each day passes. If you keep spending time with Chris, you will fall in love with him."

"It hasn't happened yet, and I'm not fucking him until he wants it enough to agree to it."

"He does want you."

"Not enough. Until he can say yes to me, with his eyes open and of his own free will, nothing's ever going to happen between us."

"But you want him."

"Do you want me to be ridiculously honest with you? Yes, I want him. I like touching him. It feels too good. Feels like what I was born to do. It makes me feel whole, and happy, and useful. But you know what? It doesn't matter. Not one bit. It doesn't matter if he feels the same way. That this is what he was born for because right now he's not willing to do anything about it, and I've got too damn much self-respect to chase a man who doesn't want me, especially a married one."

"He's not married anymore."

"He thinks he is. Are we done?"

Chuck glared at Sarah in frustration. He felt Althiira in her very strongly. *What she was born to do.* It was her. He decided it was time to get a lot more cautious as to how he dealt with her. If there was any chance of bringing Althiira back through Sarah, he didn't want to risk it.

"Yes." He stood up and left.

38.

"Are you done?" Pat asked as Chris poked the food he wasn't eating with his fork.

"Yeah."

"Good, let's go. We'll get Sarah and head back."

"I can head back on my own."

Pat looked around. No one paid any attention to them. He spoke quietly anyway, "No you won't. Something's coming, soon. Tonight or tomorrow. That means you don't go anywhere by yourself. As long as I'm on duty, neither does Sarah."

"Fine," Chris said tensely. They headed toward the doors of the cafeteria.

"What the hell happened after the dance? You've been in a snit ever since and avoiding her. She's not saying anything, but I can feel an edge on her, too."

"Nothing happened." They were outside in the cold. Pat grabbed Chris' arm, forcing Chris to look into his eyes.

"Bullshit. Something happened. Did you fuck her?"

Chris could feel Pat trying to read him, trying to feel the truth of what happened. "No. I turned her down." He let Pat see him leave Sarah's home.

"Good."

"What gives you the right to ask?"

"Because I love your wife. You know, the one for whom you're supposedly forsaking all others. Because I love Sarah. Who is one of those others." *God, I'm a real asshole for laying it on so thick.*

"The only other," Chris said very quietly. Then louder, "Says the guy who actually was in bed with someone else on Saturday night."

Pat turned and started walking again. "Emily is warm, friendly, and a lovely person. She's not looking for anything beyond a person to get over her ex with, and I'm not looking for anything more than someone to keep me toned down enough so I don't do something stupid with Sarah. In that regards we're a perfect match."

"Just perfect."

"Do I detect disapproval?"

"Only if you're paying attention."

"And what gives you the right to disapprove?"

"Nothing. But you claim to love Sarah, and you're off fucking another woman."

"Look," Pat turned to face Chris, letting Chris feel his own immense frustration at the situation. "If I didn't find someone else, I was going to do something horrendously stupid with Sarah. It's very clear she doesn't want me for a lover." Pat gritted his teeth. "Yet. I was finding myself getting closer and closer to grabbing her and... and you know I've got enough magic to make sure she'd agree to it. The next morning I'd have lost her friendship and any chance I have with her. I couldn't read my homework when I was sitting next to her because she smelled so good. My eyes kept drifting to the open collar of her shirt, so I could ogle that little mole at the base of her neck. Want to know about the little freckle on her wrist or the tiny scar on her index finger? If I could draw, I could do a perfect rendition of her hands because they're pretty much the only skin she keeps visible. I'd sit there and stare at them while she did her homework. I was too close to the edge.

"So, yeah, I found another woman. And yeah, it's cold. But I found one who isn't looking for something serious. Emily is happy with good sex and pleasant companionship. I can be a better friend to Sarah if I'm sleeping with someone else. I get you're in the same boat and on a much, much longer voyage. And I don't know how you've done it because six months with no sex was driving me crazy. You've held out twenty-one years. You can make it the three more months to May."

Chris let Pat feel his own struggle and the tinge of pain and guilt he was never fully able to remove from his interactions with Sarah. "I don't want to cheat on Althiira." Chris looked so distraught Pat almost broke and told him. Almost. Then he thought about exactly how much he'd lose when Chris found out.

"Good," Pat said. They walked quietly to Jones. "Let's go get her. By the way, her lab partners think it's ridiculously cute I pick her up and walk her home after lab. If you notice them snickering, that's why."

"Run!" My legs began to pump before I even fully knew what Pat had yelled. Like his word went straight to my legs without entering my ears.

The crack of especially sharp thunder, followed by a muffled yelp from Chris, stopped me dead in my tracks. I turned to go to him but couldn't move. In front of me was Mildred. It was magnificent. Taller than I would have thought possible, more terrible than anything I could have imagined on my own. It looked like sapphires made of brittle, angry, elf-shaped flesh. Red hair—redder than any color I had ever seen or imagined seeing, red in the perfect mathematical sense—floated behind it. Red leathery wings, reminiscent of dragons, extended beyond its body. In Mildred's right arm was a whip.

Once again the sharp cracking sound snapped across the campus. This time the whip caught Chris around the leg and yanked him off of his feet. This time the yelp was not muffled. He made a sound verging on a short scream. Then Pat was yelling some sort of battle cry. Glowing rocks sliced through the air, striking Mildred with horrific crunching sounds.

Mildred turned its attention to Pat and jerked the whip off of Chris. He whimpered when the whip released. I knew the plan was to strike Pat with the whip. Mildred's arm moved fast; then Pat was hissing. He had let the whip strike his arm and wrap around it. He wrapped it around his arm one more time, caught it in his fist, and pulled. Mildred fell. It landed on its hands and knees in front of him. He leapt, driving his knees into its shoulders. Mildred landed flat on the ground. Instantly Pat was up with his arms around its head. Another terrible crunching sound and Mildred was gone.

Pat rested on the ground for a moment, then picked something up. He walked over, handing it to me.

"Hold it carefully. It's sharp." His voice was a little shaky, and he was out of breath from the fight. He handed me a foot-long piece of thorny vine. The thorns were wicked, at least an inch long, and much too sharp for a normal plant.

"Let's get Chris," he said.

I felt my skin burn in shame. I had forgotten Chris. I was doing a brilliant job as a Combat Healer. He was on the ground, not making any noise, and not moving. I ran to him and began assessing the damage. He wasn't bleeding. Anything more detailed than that would have to wait to get back to my place.

He opened his eyes to look at us. "So, it's gone?"

"For the time being," Pat answered.

"Can you walk?" I asked him.

"Probably not." I looked at Pat. He cradled his right arm in the crook of his left. As his adrenaline level faded, his face tightened in pain.

"Come on." I handed the vine back to Pat and got an arm under Chris' shoulders. He winced when my arm brushed his ribs, but he stood when I began to lift him. "Can you get the others to meet us?"

"Mike and Chuck are already on the way."

"Good. Pat shouldn't be carrying anything, and I can't get you all the way back to my place by myself."

We had gotten about fifty yards when Mike joined us. He was armed and tense, ready to fight, but he shifted out of fight mode when it was clear no more attacks were forthcoming. He draped Chris' other arm around his shoulders and took a good deal of his weight off of me. We continued toward my place, not talking. It occurred to me Dave had to be the most powerful of all of us. We were dragging a wounded friend across campus—one of us cradling a damaged arm, another one openly carrying a Spanish-style rapier—and no one even looked in our direction.

Chuck met us just outside of the library. He took my place helping to carry Chris. I fell back beside Pat.

"How are you?"

He answered through gritted teeth. "I'm hurting. My arm will be a fright show."

"The sleeve isn't damaged."

"No, the whip, the Minion, they aren't real in this world."

"The Minion? That wasn't Mildred?"

"Yeah, Mildred's… beyond that. It doesn't need weapons. It doesn't really fight. Once Mildred's there, you just… endure." We got to my apartment. Chuck and Mike put Chris on my couch. I started undressing him. Pat was awkwardly taking his own shirt off one handed.

"Oh fuck!" Pat moaned.

I stopped unbuttoning Chris' cuff and looked over at Pat's arm. 'Oh fuck!' was an understatement. At least 100 white welts wrapped around his arm to his fingers. Each one had a small puncture wound in the center oozing some sort of black sludge.

"Get Chris out of his clothing," I told Chuck while moving to Pat. I very tentatively touched one of the welts. The skin was frozen solid. Some of the black goo got on my finger. It was so cold it burned. I saw the skin around the goo freeze white as well.

I grabbed Pat and got both of us to the sink. The water was cold but not cold enough. My finger burned while the skin thawed. Pat looked like he wanted to pass out as the black ooze washed off of him and his arm slowly regained some color. I left him there, biting on his lip and whimpering softly as the water slowly thawed his flesh, and went to Chris.

Chuck had taken everything but Chris' boxers and socks off. Pat's arm was bad. The welts twisted from bicep to fingers. Chris was worse. The first lash had wrapped around his chest, just below his pectoral muscles to the bottom of his ribs. The second lash had gotten him from just above the knee to just below the groin. Any skin the ooze touched was frozen white.

"Get him in my shower. Keep the water as cold as possible. I want all of this black shit rinsed away. Don't touch the wounds. Don't touch the ooze." I showed him my rapidly blistering finger. "When the marks aren't white anymore, you can take him out. Can you do that?"

"Yes." Chuck got Chris up and with Mike's help got him into my shower. I heard the water start and a long, profane tirade in Chris' voice as the water warmed his skin and rinsed off the black stuff.

I went back to Pat. His arm was now free of the ooze but still covered in red, puffy welts with small, white punctures. I took his arm out of the water and gently poked one of the welts. The white ring around the puncture cracked under my finger; more of the black goo oozed out. Pat's eyes were closed, and he was sweating.

"Let's get your arm back under the water." He did so, hissing when the water hit the frozen skin. I checked on Chris. Mike was holding him up in my shower. The black goo was gone from Chris' skin. Like Pat, he was now covered with hundreds of red welts with frozen white punctures. Chris let out an anguished groan. I couldn't tell if he was sweating, but he was shivering and flushed.

I called Autumn, asking her to bring whatever hard alcohol she had. She didn't ask any questions. Almost before I had hung up the phone, she was at my door with a bottle of bourbon.

"Thanks." I said to her, pouring two large portions. Holding the glasses, I prayed they would ease pain. Pat got one. He shot it back fast. I motioned for him to follow me into the bathroom. This would be easier if I had both of them in the same room.

Chuck held Chris now. "Can you get out?"

Chuck got them out. I held the glass. Chris drank gratefully. "That's not enough to make me pass out."

"I don't think that would be a good idea. With any luck it'll help, though."

"What's next?" Pat put his glass on the sink.

"The core of those welts aren't thawing. I think there's some of the black goo in there. I need to draw it out, get it off your skin, and get those holes to close up."

"You think it'll hurt?" Pat asked me. The booze was taking effect; he looked like he was having a hard time making his eyes focus.

"I can't see how it won't."

"Then do it fast." He held out his arm.

"Hold on for a second." I looked at his arm and Chris' chest more closely. The frozen cores had grown while they were out of the water. "Back in the water, both of you. Autumn," I said as I headed into the kitchen, "if you see me do something, do you think you can copy it?"

"Maybe. Dave's really good at that, though."

I wanted to say, "Dave's here?" But he was sitting at my kitchen table, looking at the thorny vine, and checking something online.

He looked up. "I was looking to see if I could find out what kind of thorn this is. Nothing yet. Let's see you do it, and then Autumn and I can take a stab at it."

"Thanks. There are hundreds of these little bastards, and I doubt I can get them all."

We went back into the bathroom. Mike held Chris in the shower. Pat had his arm under the faucet in my sink. The frozen white cores of each welt still looked terrible.

"How are you feeling?" Pat looked less tense than he had a minute ago.

"Drink is starting to kick in. It's fucking skippy."

"Do you mind if I try on you first?"

"Sure, I'll be your guinea pig. No reason for the beloved leader to get hurt on the first run."

"Okay..." I placed my fingers gingerly on one of the welts. "Here's what I'm trying to do. I want to thaw the tissue, push it together, squeeze out the black goo, and then have it stay together." Then I did it. Will over matter. My mind, my love, and my magic forcing the tissue to warm, soften, and squeeze shut. Black goo oozed out of the first welt and washed away under the spray from the sink.

When I was done, the welt was smooth and pink. "Can you do it?" Autumn was already shucking off clothing to get into the shower with Chris. Dave turned to work on Chris' leg. "Be careful the black stuff doesn't touch your skin. It'll freeze it."

I worked solely on Pat. After two hours, I had finished with his arm. He was flexing his fingers and wincing, but at least he could move them—an improvement from before. He was also hot, sweaty, delirious, and his eyes had completely stopped focusing about an hour earlier. I dried him off, put him in my bed, and told Mike to keep an eye on him.

Autumn and Dave were still working on Chris when I joined them. A third of the welts still needed to be fixed. He was flushed, feverish even with cold water pouring over him, his eyes were no longer tracking, and he was speaking a language I couldn't understand. Chuck kept answering him in the same language, with a gentleness I didn't think he had in him. We worked as fast as possible, coaxing more and more of the black goo out of his flesh. Adding me to the mix sped things up. After another half hour, he was finished.

Chuck wrapped him in a towel, patted him dry, and laid him in my bed next to Pat. Mike helped the rest of us to my couch. None of us could stand on our own anymore. Autumn was gray, her limbs limp, and her eyes slid shut before she was even fully seated. Dave didn't look much better. I didn't imagine I'd be winning a beauty contest anytime soon. All three of us had blistered fingers from the repeated freezing and thawing.

Chuck took over after Chris was settled. He made cocoa for all three of us and, while the water warmed, bandaged our fingers. Chuck isn't a healer, but he was able to do some basic first aid. His energy was surprisingly gentle as he soothed our burns with aloe and magic. If it weren't for the splitting headache that started the second he began to minister to me, it would have been a very comforting moment.

The cocoa was delicious and laced with a hit of energy. I was fairly sure I could lift the cup myself after the first few sips, but I let Chuck keep feeding me. He put my cup down after a few more swallows and made sure Autumn and Dave got some.

"Do they need anything besides sleep and food?" Chuck asked.

"I don't think so."

"Then I'll get them home. Come on, Autumn." He lifted her bride-over-the-threshold style, "let's get you home. You can sleep in your own bed for a good long time and come back and hover over Chris soon."

Autumn made a sound, which I assumed wasn't assent. She wanted to stay near Chris but didn't have the energy to fight Chuck. I don't know how he got the door open while holding her, but somehow he did. Fifteen minutes later he was back.

"I can't lift you, Dave."

Dave didn't open his eyes or turn his head in Chuck's direction. "I'm not going anywhere under my own power."

"I still think you would sleep better in your own bed."

"Then get Mike. Between the two of you you'll manage. I doubt they'll drop dead without anyone watching for ten minutes."

Chuck gave me a questioning look. I nodded. "They won't die on my watch. I can get up if I absolutely have to."

"Lucky you. The building could be on fire, and I could probably just about flop off the couch."

"Dave, have I ever told you how much I love the fact you've always got a sense of humor?" I asked.

He gave a small, tired, half-laugh half-sigh. Mike joined us. After some awkward maneuvering, they got Dave up without sitting on me in the process.

"I'll be back soon," Chuck told me as they left.

"I'll be here." My eyes slid shut. I wanted to sleep, but that wasn't going to happen. No matter how tired I felt I wasn't going to fall asleep with two wounded men in my bed. Not until there was someone else in my house to keep an eye on them.

I've never had a fever so high I've been delirious. If I had to guess, it was pretty similar to those minutes waiting for Chuck to come back. My mind kept hopping around, seeing things I was fairly sure weren't in the room. My mom, for example. I was pretty sure she wasn't actually there, but I kept thinking she was sitting on the couch next to me, stroking my hair. It was a nice fantasy. I absolutely knew the pictures on my wall weren't moving. In fact, part of the reason I was sure they weren't actually moving was the fact I could still see them even though my eyes were closed.

Chuck came back and rested a hand on my forehead. "How much of the goo did you get on your fingers?"

"More than I should have? Why?"

"You're hot. Not as bad as Chris and Pat but you've still got a fever."

"Oh. I thought I was just really tired. Can you get me more of the cocoa?"

"Yes." When I finished drinking the second cup, the tiredness cleared just enough to realize I ached all over and was running a fever.

"I need to sleep. Can you keep their fevers under 103?"

"I think so."

"Good. Wake me if you can't or something changes. Worst comes to worst, we're all going to the hospital."

"I don't think it'll come to that."

"Good."

"Sarah?"

"Yes?"

"I couldn't have fixed this. Neither could Autumn."

"You're welcome." I spent the rest of the night drifting between exhausted wakefulness and fever dreams. During one lucid moment I found myself thinking if I was this bad off just from the stuff I had on my hands, I should really get Chris and Pat to a hospital. But I couldn't muster the energy to call to Chuck, and all too quickly I was enjoying my mom's hands on my hair again.

Then I was aware of the light of day, the smell of rye bread toast and Earl Grey tea, and feeling like I had pulled a full week of all-nighters. As I became more awake, I realized the fever had faded and my mind was clear.

Pain bit at my fingers as I pushed myself up from the sofa. Chuck heard me gasp and looked up from his breakfast.

"Let me help you." He got me sitting up and unwrapped my fingers. They were an angry, swollen, blistered red. The sores where I had gotten the worst of the damage were leaking a clear fluid.

"Fuck." I was tired, mind-bendingly tired, and hungry—eating a cow didn't seem like a problem this morning, but, unless I wanted Chuck hand feeding me breakfast, the first thing I had to do was fix my fingers.

"Can you give me a boost?" Chuck looked worn out. Black circles under his eyes and a aura of weariness didn't instill much confidence as to his ability to give me a little extra energy.

"A bit. Keeping those two from burning up has been taking it out of me."

"I understand. But until I get my hands fixed, nothing else is going to happen."

He put his hand on my shoulder and a bolt of cold arced through me. In a second I was shivering and headachy. I also had the energy I needed to get my fingers under control. They still ached. They were still red. But the swelling, blisters, and weeping sores were gone. Best of all, I could use them well enough to eat.

Food helped. Toast, tea, fruit, spaghetti left over from last night's dinner, and the last of the chocolate chip cookies left me achingly full but almost human again. An exhausted human but better than before. Chuck didn't say anything, just watched me eat with amusement.

"Do you want to catch some sleep? It's a good couch for sleeping. I can take over on sick watch."

He nodded at me. Before I had even gotten out of my chair, I could hear snoring coming from my couch.

Both boys were in exactly the same place they had been laid. If either had moved in the last ten hours, I couldn't prove it.

I checked Pat's arm first. On the upside the welts were no longer frozen. On the downside they had swollen to the size of quarters and were leaking yellow pus. Checking Chris proved he was in much the same state, but he had three times as many welts as Pat. They were both feverish. True to his word, Chuck had kept them at under 103. Which left me with something to ponder: get us to the hospital and get massive antibiotic doses into them, or stay here and let their bodies fight it off?

Which led to the next question: would antibiotics even help? Was this just a run-of-the-mill infection due to a very nasty magical attack, or was this part of what that attack was supposed to do?

If I had been in better shape myself, I would have hopped to and figured out what was going on. Instead, I slumped in the chair, making sure neither of them looked like he was getting worse. Eventually I realized it wasn't the snow-filtered light in my room making their skin look gray. They were both dehydrated. I hadn't told Chuck to keep them drinking.

I very slowly got them drinks. The human head weighs much more than it looks like it should. I did manage to hold up Pat's head and get about a cup of juice into him. He made some small unintelligible sounds while drinking but didn't open his eyes or give me any indication he knew I was there.

Getting Chris to drink was harder. He wasn't swallowing well so most of the juice dribbled down his neck. I put the cup down and looked him over more carefully. He wasn't breathing well, either. I got him mopped off and started spooning the juice into his mouth. Time to figure out if they had to go to the hospital.

Feverish, red, swollen, and leaking pus. Classic infection signs. The pus didn't smell bad or like much of anything. When I touched one of the welts to try and see what was going on, I got some of it on my finger. I pulled back hissing, burned again, acid this time.

The hospital wasn't going to be much use for this. Even if it was an infection, acidic pus wasn't on the list of symptoms they knew how to deal with. We'd need to get them rinsed off again. This stuff wasn't doing their skin any good.

A moment of inspiration hit. I had baking soda. *Acid plus base equals neutral.* I shuffled into the kitchen. Making up a paste of baking soda didn't take too much effort.

I dabbed the paste onto Chris' welts. He moaned, a reaction to having something cool and wet placed on burned skin instead of pain. The paste hissed and bubbled. Eventually it calmed down and, I hoped, neutralized the acid on his skin. I had to spend half an hour resting after that. Holding Chris on his side so I could get to his back and the back of his leg took a lot of my minimal energy stores. Once rested, working on Pat took a few more minutes.

I knew two things for certain. This was not an infection. The magic from the attack tingled my senses. The other thing I knew was trying to fix this one welt at a time would leave the rest of us as weak as newborn kittens.

"You'll learn on the job." I didn't need to learn, I needed to know how to fix this. Inspiration wasn't bonking me over the head.

I placed a hand over Pat's arm. What was the point of this attack? Why this weapon? Would it kill? Could it kill? The answer I could feel wasn't useful. *Revenge.* The Minion wanted revenge. Great. That didn't tell me how to fix it. It didn't tell me what kind of damage it was trying to inflict.

I looked up again and saw an hour had passed. I got more juice for the guys and dribbled it into them. Pat started to look a little better. The gray was gone, and he didn't look like he was in quite as much pain.

After another hour, I heard knocking on my door. Autumn stood on my porch, tired and determined. Chuck stirred, cracked one eye, saw Autumn, and went right back to sleep.

"How is he?"

I mentally rolled my eyes. Pat was in there, too, and the only reason he was hurt was protecting Chris. "*They* aren't good. Come on in."

She walked into my room and went straight to Chris' side. She was about to touch him. "Don't touch the wounds. They've changed since last night. Instead of black goo that burns cold, we've got yellow acid pus."

"That's why you've got him covered in this white stuff?"

"Yes."

"I didn't know you did salves and potions."

"I don't. It's baking soda. I don't have the strength to get them back in my shower to rinse the crap off, so I neutralized it."

She stroked Chris' forehead. I wondered what he'd think of that if he was conscious. I doubted he'd go for it. Maybe it was comforting, though.

"Why don't you have Chuck do it?"

"He was on duty all night and needs some sleep. You look like you need to go back to bed, too."

"And you don't?"

"No idea. I haven't seen myself yet."

She wanted to give me a snarky response but decided against it. Instead she turned crisp and businesslike. "Now what? Can I do anything?"

"Can you tell me what the point of this wound is?"

"I don't know what you mean."

"If it was a gunshot to the back of the head, I'd know the point was to kill the person. If it was a burn to the foot, I'd know it was about pain. I don't know if this is just about pain and will eventually clear up on its own, or if it's supposed to be slow death. Do I need to risk putting all of us in comas to take care of this?"

"I can try." She sat quietly next to Chris looking intently at the wounds. I went into the kitchen and made myself lunch. More food helped. I put a sandwich and chips on the coffee table next to Chuck and one on the floor next to Autumn. Food would help them, too.

I got more juice into Pat. Autumn wouldn't let me feed Chris. She did it for him. She did come up with a more clever way to do it than I had. She used a straw to drip the juice into him. Less mess and more liquid in Chris. It was a clever trick. Once finished, she sat down and ate the sandwich.

"Good chicken salad."

"Thanks. What do you think?"

"It's about pain. The thing that did this could kill if it wanted to. It didn't want to. It's playing with us, waiting for Mildred to finish us."

"You know what did it?"

"Yes, I have an image. Tall, red hair, wings, blue skin, whip. It's upper-middle management."

"Great. What do I do about it?"

"That's your specialty. I can get more alcohol and baking soda if you think that would help."

"Can't see how it would hurt."

She stood up. "I'll be back in a bit. Want dinner?"

"Dinner would be good. Chicken broth for the boys, eventually I'll want to get some food in them, too." She was almost at the door when I remembered to ask, "How's Dave?" I understood why I had a hard time remembering, but I still felt like a heel for not asking sooner.

"Still sleeping when I left. He can do almost anything but not easily. I think it took a lot out of him when he worked on Chris last night."

Chuck sat up when she left. "Did I hear you say something about getting them rinsed off again?" He tore through the sandwich.

"Yeah. They're oozing acidic pus. I don't have enough strength back to lift either of them yet. Can you?"

"Not by myself. I'll call Mike, and we'll get on it."

"Thanks."

Mike looked pretty good. Then again, he had gotten a good deal of sleep and hadn't had to do any healing last night. His arm shook a little when he and Chuck lifted Pat out of my bed. I watched it with mild interest, noting that was what muscles do after you ask them to work too hard for too long. I moved one of the kitchen chairs into my bathroom, and they set Pat on it. Mike held him in place while I put his arm under the water. His eyes jerked open when the water hit his arm.

"Still alive, huh?" His voice was rough, pain filled, and barely audible.

"As long as I've got something to say about it." I smiled at him and kissed him on the forehead.

"Last thing I remember clearly was sucking down the hooch. Got any more?"

"When we get done with this, I'll fix some more for you. Can you move your fingers?"

He slowly flexed them and ran his hand through its full range of motion. "It hurts. It's hard to do."

"Good. I don't think I got it all out last night."

Once the paste and yellow pus was fully rinsed off, I could see what we were dealing with. The punctures had opened again. I stopped looking with my eyes and tried to feel the wound. After a few minutes, I knew what was wrong. Each puncture still had a very tiny bit of thorn in it. Yesterday's work didn't force it out.

Time to try a new tact. This time I lay my hand on his arm over the wounds. I winced as the pus burned me. My hands would be a tragedy tomorrow, and tomorrow I could take the time to deal with it. I willed the magic to pull the tip of the thorn out. I could feel the little bastards; now I knew to look for them they were obvious. They felt hard and sharp and evil. Pain steeped in poison and filled with rage.

I felt world class stupid for not finding them the first time. Once I could lay my mind on them, removing them was easy, much easier than trying to squeeze out the black ooze. In a few minutes I had at least thirty of them out.

Chuck watched me carefully. "That's the root cause?"

"I hope so."

"Do you want me to get Chris in the shower? You look like you'll be done with Pat soon."

"I will be done with Pat soon. Can you make up my pain-killing whiskey from last night?"

"Sorry, didn't see you do it."

"Then wait until I've got Pat back in bed before moving Chris. You know what you can do? Strip off the side of the bed Pat was on and get some new sheets on it. When we get Chris up, we can finish changing the sheets and put them both in a clean bed."

"I can do that. Where are your clean sheets?"

"In the closet. Look to the left. Third shelf from the bottom."

He left. I heard him rummaging about in my stuff while I worked.

"Clean sheets?" Pat was starting to look better as I got more and more thorns out of him.

"Only the best for you. You're looking better."

"I'm feeling better. Every one of those little fuckers you get rid of I can feel. Each one makes me hurt less."

"Good, maybe you won't need the magic-laced hooch."

"Maybe not, but I want it. It felt fantastic, and, right about now, I could use some fantastic."

"Then I'll get you some in a bit. Do you think you'll be able to eat?"

"You're kidding, right? Put food in me, and I'll puke. I'm not that much better."

"Then I'll get some juice and magic hooch for you. Can't let you dry out."

"I wouldn't want that. How long was I out?"

"About sixteen hours. With any luck you'll go back to sleep as soon as I get this done."

"I can handle sleep."

Chuck poked his head into my bathroom. "I don't think you're going to want to keep those sheets. They're beyond ruined. So's the mattress pad. Looks like the timing on this was good; longer and the pus would have started to eat into the mattress."

"Great. Under the sink I've got an extra shower curtain liner; put that under the sheet. I don't want to have to get a new mattress, too."

Chuck bustled around while I finished up Pat. Mike continued to hold him in the chair, keeping him from toppling over onto the bathroom floor. I got two more glasses, poured a slug of bourbon into each of them, and doctored them with magic. It was amazing how much easier it was to do this time. Pat drank his, and within a minute a blissful look spread across his face.

"That's fucking excellent. Screw medicine. Set up a distillery and sell that. You'll be millionaire before you can blink."

Chuck finished Pat's side of the bed, and we got him settled. Then Mike and Chuck got Chris in the shower and the water on him. Chris yelled when the water hit him. He started babbling again in the language I didn't know. Chuck kept whispering back at him in the same language. Whatever it was Chuck was saying didn't calm Chris down, his voice kept rising as he asked the same thing over and over. Once the paste and pus was washed off, the guys held Chris up while I dried him off. The skin on his chest and leg looked like it had been boiled. Pink blisters interspersed with open welts. He'd have some interesting new scars to go with the old ones.

Like the drink, pulling the thorns out was also getting easier each time I did it. They had surrendered and were just waiting for me to collect them. It took less than twenty minutes to get them all out of him. When I was done, his fever was down and his eyes were open again.

"I've got some more of the painkiller for you. Can you drink it?"

"Yeah."

"It's good to hear you speak English again."

He looked blearily at me and then back to Chuck. Chuck nodded at him. "Sorry. I don't remember it."

"No problem. How are you feeling?"

"Like a poisoned pin cushion."

"That's not a bad description," I said while feeding him the drink. His eyes slid shut and the tension left his face. "It's time for you to get some more sleep."

"Sounds good," he said without opening his eyes. Chuck and Mike put him back in my bed. Chris was dead to the world before they even had the blanket all the way over him.

"Now what?" Chuck asked me.

I spent a moment very carefully cleaning my hands, making sure I had all the pus off and there wasn't a tiny tip of a thorn wedged into a wrinkle somewhere. Then I made up a shot of the painkiller for myself. I drank it fast, not caring if I ended up drunk. Since I wasn't healing anymore, my hands would be screaming soon. "I think you guys can go home if you want. Unless there's yet another level of crud here, it's just a matter of waiting for them to heal up. They'll sleep. I'll nap and feed them juice. When Autumn comes back, chicken soup. Eventually they'll feel well enough to walk home, and I'll get my bed back."

"How about I stay, and you get more solid sleep?" Chuck offered.

"You sure? You've got work tonight, right?"

"Nope. It's Tuesday. We should have Golem. Go, get some more sleep."

"Oh. How about you Mike?"

"I've got a pile of homework. Some of which I need to be in the computer lab for. I'll head off. If you need anything, text me, and I'll be back in a minute or two. While I'm at it I'll let the Golemites know tonight's meeting has been cancelled due to flu at the Writers' House."

"Sounds good."

I returned to the couch, pulled the blue blanket up around my shoulders, and was also dead to the world in a matter of minutes. Autumn's and Chuck's voices filtered through my sleep, but I couldn't rouse enough energy to come fully awake for it.

When I woke, it was dark. Checking the clock on my stove showed it was a little past eight. I could smell chicken soup. The stove was on low, keeping it warm. I flexed my fingers. They ached but were in better shape than they had been when I went to sleep.

I checked on the boys. Chuck was sitting next to Chris, his hand resting on Chris' arm, concern radiating off of him. I crept over to him and put a hand on his shoulder. He got what I was thinking, and we both walked to my kitchen.

"I'm turning on the light."

He nodded at me, and we shielded our eyes against the light.

"I'll get him fixed up. Maybe some scars but he'll be functional again. I promise."

"I know you will." He sat down at my table. I started to mess around with dinner.

"You like biscuits?"

"Yeah."

"How about biscuits and chicken soup for us? Should be ready in an hour."

"Sounds good." He sat quietly while I got the biscuits ready. Once they were rising, I didn't have anything to do, and quiet chit chat with Chuck was something we had never attempted before. He looked like he wanted to go back and sit with Chris.

A thought hit me. "What were you saying to each other before?"

"Nothing really. He didn't know where he was, or what was wrong with him, or who you were. I kept telling him what was happening, and he'd know for a minute or two. Then he'd be lost again. He thought he should have been home."

We sat quietly for a minute before another question came to mind. "Why are they still hunting you?"

"Because it's not over until we're dead or they're dead. I'm hoping it will be them."

"I don't know what 'it' is. Or why you fought them."

I had the feeling he was testing me as he spoke. "It was Mildred's boss. An immensely powerful magical creature. Every twenty years It would select one thousand people to 'ascend' to It. Chris learned the 'ascension' was crap. It was eating our people. Sucking the life out of them and leaving withered husks. So we fought It. He killed It. In the stories you kill the Big Bad and all the Little Bads run away. It didn't work that way for us, so we ran. Mildred and all of its underlings are still out for revenge."

"If Chris' wife had stayed, you could have ended it there?"

"I like to think so. It's not certain, but if you've got a good healer, you can fight a lot longer than you can without one."

"So it would appear."

"Yeah."

We sat at the table for a while longer.

"I don't enjoy his misery, either," I said, thinking of our last conversation.

"I know."

I felt sluggish and fuzzy for a moment. Like my mind was wrapped in cotton. Then the food was on the table, but I couldn't remember getting it. *If you're forgetting things like that, you're too damn tired!*

"How much soup do you think they can take?" Chuck asked me as he ate. He was eating with his left hand. The right one was under the table.

"We'll try to get a cup or so into each of them. What's up with your right hand?"

"I burned it on the baking sheet." I really was too tired if I was forgetting stuff like that.

"Do you want me to heal it?"

"Sarah, you just asked me what happened two minutes after it did. You're stretched too thin to heal me."

"Great."

We finished dinner quickly. Chuck poured broth into cups for Pat and Chris. I put the cups on my bedside table and touched Pat's shoulder. Chuck hung back and watched me work.

"Hey, Pat." He woke up and looked tiredly at me. "Think you can drink some soup?"

"In a minute." He very slowly rolled to his side and started to push himself up.

"Bathroom?"

"Yeah." Chuck joined us and gave Pat a hand, helping him get up and do whatever needed to be done on the other side of that door. Chuck mostly carried Pat back to the bed. But Pat did sit up and was able to hold the cup and drink himself.

"Are you hurting?"

"No. Just more tired than I've ever been or ever imagined being."

"Good. I mean about not hurting. When you finish the soup, I'll check your arm again."

"Okay. I wouldn't mind my pjs if you feel like putting me in them."

"No problem." I grabbed the set he kept here for the nights he slept over. "One decrepit t-shirt and a pair of Joe Boxer smiley face pajama bottoms."

I could feel Chuck was very interested in the idea Pat had pajamas at my place. I waited for Pat to finish his soup and got to work on his arm. The punctures had closed and now looked like blisters. The magic moved through me, making his wounds smaller, less swollen, helping his body get rid of the poison coursing through it.

Putting clothing on a grown man is not as hard as putting it on a baby. Even a very tired grown man can sit up on his own long enough to get a shirt over his head. In this regard getting Pat into his t-shirt was a lot easier than doing it for my nieces or nephews when they were babies.

On the other side, getting jeans off a grown man is harder on a different level. I don't know if guys usually wear briefs under their jammies—Ari didn't—but that isn't a definitive sample size. At least for this night, Pat was wearing his.

Pat lay down again. He looked pretty content to be doing so. "Better?"

"Much."

"Good. We'll get Chris taken care of, and you can go back to sleep." Pat snored back at me. "Or you can fall asleep now, and I'll work on Chris anyway." Chris didn't wake up when I touched him. I got a straw and began to use Autumn's technique. It was slow, but it got the job done. All of the soup ended up in Chris.

"Has he peed today?" I asked Chuck.

"No."

"Then drag him over to the bathroom and don't bring him back until some of those liquids end up on the outside. I don't want him peeing in my bed."

Chuck gave me a sardonic salute and got Chris up. I don't think he fully woke up, but his eyes opened for a few seconds. He said something—once again not in English—to Chuck. Chuck said something back to him, then shut the door. Several minutes later I had Chuck hold Chris up so I could work on the wounds on his back. By the time I had finished with his leg, I was ready to sleep again, too.

I grabbed some yoga pants and a long sleeve t-shirt. "You want the sofa or do you want to use the cushion from my window seat to make a bed in here?"

"I'll stay in here."

"Okay." He headed into my living room to grab the cushions. I went into the bathroom to get ready for bed. While brushing my teeth I looked at myself in the mirror for the first time that day. My earlier estimation of not winning any beauty contests had been wildly optimistic. My skin was gray with exhaustion, and black circles rested under the bags under my bloodshot eyes. My hair was sticking up at about thirty odd angles, and I had smears of yellow goo, black goo, and blood on my clothing. I peeled off the clothing and thought about getting a shower before a yawn practically popped my jaw out of joint.

I'd get one tomorrow. Before class. The class I hadn't gotten my homework done for. *Fuck!* I moaned quietly in frustration. I was way too tired to even think about differential equations, let alone do them.

I headed toward the sofa. Chuck leaned against the wall, waiting for me to get out of the bathroom. I was almost to the door when he asked, "Why does Pat have pajamas here?"

A wave of exhausted snark overtook me. "I'd think that's obvious. Because he sleeps here."

"What does he do before he sleeps here?"

"And the reason it's any of your business?"

"Because if that's the reason you aren't willing to do anything with Chris, he deserves to know."

"Pat has pajamas here because he crashes on my sofa two or three nights a week. The blue toothbrush is his, too. He just started seeing Emily."

"Okay. Good night."

"'Night." I crashed into a heap on the sofa and didn't move again until seven, just in time to grab a quick shower and get that problem set done.

39.

When I got back from class, Pat was sitting at the table very slowly eating cereal. I didn't see Chuck or Chris and assumed they were both still sleeping in my room.

"You're up."

"I'm up. I feel like I've been awake for a month, but I'm moving under my own power again."

"Wonderful. How's the arm feeling?"

He slowly picked up the spoon and fed himself, his hand shaking only a little. "It's sore, weak, and feels about three sizes too big. Other than that, it's just dandy."

"Let me give it another shot on the healing-things-up front." I took his arm in my hands and once again worked on getting the swelling down and the poisons out of his system. I'd be able to do this blindfolded soon.

"Want me to head over to your place and get you some clothing?"

"Depends, do you mind me laying about in my jammies today?"

"Not at all."

"Then I'm going to finish this, get a shower, and spend the rest of the day napping on your sofa."

"Sounds like a plan."

He continued to eat. I got out my crock pot and tossed in stuff for pot roast. Then I poked my head into my room. Chuck was snoring, and Chris looked like he hadn't moved all night. I sat on the Pat's side of the bed and pulled down the blanket to check his chest. He didn't open his eyes, but he said something to me in the other language. If Pat hadn't been in the shower, I would have asked him to translate.

I put my hand on his shoulder and said, "It's me, Chris. I'm just checking your wounds and doing a little healing. Then I'm going to get you a drink."

He said something else, settling more deeply into sleep. I rolled him onto his side with the bad leg on top, and got to work. By the time I was done, the skin between the welts no longer looked scalded. I called that a victory and gently pushed him back onto his back.

I brought him a large glass of orange juice. He woke up just enough to help me help him drink it and was asleep again.

I checked the clock. Time to head off to meet with Morrell.

He watched me collapse into the chair on the far side of his desk. In his slow and precisely accented Arabic he said, "You look terrible. Was it a good weekend? Partying hard?"

I thought for a long time and answered with my faster, less precise Arabic, "No. Bad weekend. Sick friends at my house."

He hadn't expected that answer. It took him a good minute to compose his response. "Why were they at your house? Why not the hospital?"

I doubted I'd ever get a better opening for what I'd wanted to ask him since the middle of September. I gestured to his collection of figurines. "How did you get them? Did you make them? Did someone do them for you?"

He looked at me for a long time. When he spoke this time it was in English. "I don't suppose you're asking me if they're forgeries."

"No," I answered in Arabic.

"I didn't think so," he replied, once more speaking in Arabic. "And this has something to do with your friends being at your house?"

"Why hospital not the right place."

"Ahhh... your house is?"

"Yes."

He nodded. "That is good to know." Once more he switched into English. "Occasionally it's useful to know people with such skills."

I switched back to English as well. "Yeah. It seems like those occasions are happening more and more these days."

"Can I help?" His concern was real.

I smiled tiredly at him. "Probably not. If the need arises, I'll let you know."

He nodded at me. "If you ever need a place to crash or a safe place to hide out, you know where my home is, and you can always call."

"Thank you. That's very comforting. Don't take this the wrong way, but I hope to not have to take you up on that."

"I understand. But really, anytime—three in the morning, whenever—feel free to show up on my doorstep."

"Thank you."

Once more he switched into Arabic. "Now, let us conjugate verbs."

"Let us. I could use some normal."

I got home an hour later and found Pat sleeping on my sofa. I felt an overwhelming desire to get a nap as well. I dropped my books on the table, lifted the lid off the crock pot, gave everything a stir, and then tried to decide where to sleep.

Sofa was out. Investigating my room showed me Chris and Chuck were still in their respective places. That left the floor or Pat's side of the bed. The floor looked remarkably hard and floor-like. Fuck it—he's too sick to even notice, and I'm too tired to care. I'd sleep in my own bed.

I woke up at some later point when I heard Chuck moving around. I rubbed my eyes and sat up. *Food. Food would be a very good thing.* Apparently Chuck thought the same thing because he was in my kitchen making lunch. I sat down at the table, and he put a roast beef sandwich in front of me. I picked off the cheese and ate. Pat stirred on the sofa.

"Could I get some food, too?"

"Sure. You want a sandwich or more soup?" I asked.

"Solid food sounds good."

I got up and made him a sandwich while still eating mine. Then I grabbed some cookies for me, and put the bag of them in front of Chuck. He looked pleased to see them and helped himself. I took Pat's plate and sat next to him on the sofa.

"Good nap?"

"Yes. I'm starting to feel alive again."

"Good."

"How's Chris?"

"Somewhere between deeply asleep and unconscious. That reminds me… I need to feed him, too." I left Pat with his food and poured another glass of juice for Chris.

Chuck took it from me. "I can do this."

"Great." I sat down next to Pat again, put my arm around him, and gave him a long hug. "Don't scare me like that again, okay?"

He gave me a half-smile and took another bite of sandwich. "As long as you stay nearby, there's nothing to fear." I smiled back at him.

The rest of the day passed quietly, Pat and Chris sleeping, Chuck and I doing homework and napping as well. Chuck called off work so he could stay by Chris. Autumn stopped by after dinner. When she realized there was nothing for her to do and none of us wanted her just sitting in my room watching Chris, she went home again. Once she left, Pat headed back to bed. By nine I was having a hard time keeping my eyes open.

I woke up feeling better the next morning and started breakfast. While the biscuits rose, I checked on the two redheads in my bed.

Pat opened one eye when I touched his arm. "Let me get up; then you can mess with me."

"Okay."

He headed to my bathroom. I noticed Chris was awake, too. "Good morning."

"Hi."

"How are you feeling?"

"Tired."

"That sounds about right. You want to try some real food for breakfast?"

"Not really."

"I'll get you some more juice." I headed into the kitchen, poured him a glass of juice, and put the biscuits into the oven.

He sat up and drank the juice without help. "Could I get some clothing?"

"Yeah. I think Autumn brought some of your stuff over."

I found the bag of things she had brought over. There was clean clothing in there. "Do you want blue flannel pants or red ones?"

He half-smiled. "Why not red? It's a good 'I'm alive' color."

"Yes, it is." I took the pants, a pair of boxers, some socks, and a sweatshirt out of the bag. "Can you get dressed on your own, or do you want help?"

"I don't want help, but I'll take it."

"I'm up," Chuck said from his place on the floor. "Once Pat's out we'll get you set."

"Good."

I handed Chuck the clothing and sat next to Chris. "Let me take care of these for a minute." I let my fingers hover over his skin, doing the same thing I had been doing the last two days. Another day of this and I'd be able to do it blindfolded in my sleep.

Pat came out in my bathrobe. "I put the clothing in the washer. When it's clean, I'll get dressed."

"Might as well toss your boxers in there, too," I said to Chris as he and Chuck moved slowly toward my bathroom.

"You look cute," Chuck said to Pat.

"Thanks. I think the color goes well with my eyes."

Pat and I went into the kitchen. The biscuits were just about done. I started to make eggs to go with them.

"The color does go well with your eyes."

"It's not too hard to match gray with gray."

"You've got a point."

Chuck headed off after breakfast, and Pat felt good enough to go to his room once his clothing was dry. I got Chris set up with more to drink, told him to text me if he needed anything, and headed off for my lab.

Chris was on my couch when I got home, still sleeping. At least he had moved of his own accord, and gotten himself some tea and what I assumed from the crumbs had been toast. That was a very good sign. With any luck in a day or two I'd have my space back. I settled on the window seat and started my homework. At least I tried to do that. Chris and I hadn't spent any time alone with him functional since the night of the dance, and some of the things Chuck had said to me began to work their way back to the front of my mind.

I looked up, planning to watch him sleep. But he was already watching me.

The desire to walk over to the sofa and hold him startled me with its intensity. It also made me very aware that I really should talk to him about whatever was happening with us. Might as well get it out and done with. "Chuck thinks I should just fuck you and be done with it."

He made an odd strangled sound and coughed embarrassedly. He calmed down and started breathing normally after a minute. "I did *not* put him up to that."

"I didn't think you did. It's not your style. Some of what he said does seem to go with your style, so I figured I'd save both of us some confusion and heartache and go right out and say it. Yes, I'd like to sleep with you. No, I'm not going to do anything about it without your express consent and preferably hearty agreement. I don't want anything to just kind of, sort of, accidentally happen between us."

He didn't look like he knew what to say. I got up off the window seat and started to make dinner.

"Are you up for some solid food or more soup?"

"How can you do that?"

"We've got to eat. I want meatloaf and that takes time, so I need to start now."

"Cut the shit. How do you switch gears like that?"

"I said what I needed to say. You've got the information you need. Obviously it makes you uncomfortable, so onto something else. I may not be perfect when it comes to keeping my heart off my sleeve, but I'll do my damnedest to try. I'm the healer. If you aren't safe and comfortable here, I'm not doing my job."

He digested that thought and said, "If you're making meatloaf, I'd like to try some. It's probably a good idea to make soup, too because I don't think I can take too much."

"Good. That I can do. Did you see Autumn brought over your books and laptop?"

"Yes, but I don't have the energy to do much with them."

"I can understand that. I got no schoolwork done last weekend, either."

"You know what I'd really like?"

"What."

"Television. It'd be nice to have some easy, mindless entertainment."

"Hmmm… well, I've got the Metz family Netflix subscription password. I can hook you up with some streaming video."

"I'd like that very much." I grabbed his computer and set him up, then started dinner. Meatloaf takes about an hour and twenty minutes all told. I wasn't really paying attention to him while I cooked; occasionally I'd hear some low laughing, and that made me happy. If whatever he picked perked him up, all the better. When the meatloaf was in the oven, I walked behind him and watched over his shoulder for a minute. Two guys were doing something with a pig and a closed car.

"What on earth is that?"

"*MythBusters*. They take urban legends, myths, stuff like that, and debunk them. The myth here is the car gets found with a dead body in it, and it gets all cleaned up but can never be sold because the smell is so bad. They've got a car and a pig. They're letting the pig decay in the car, then cleaning it up to see if they can get the smell out. And they blow stuff up. Lots of stuff."

"Okay." I slowly nodded my head. "This is your idea of quality TV?"

"It's light, funny, and requires no introspection or character development. And, I'm a guy. I like things that go boom."

"I like things that go boom, too."

"Good. I'll do the episode where they blow up the cement truck next."

"Why would they blow up a cement truck?"

"You'll just have to come over and watch it with me."

I dragged the coffee table over so he could sit forward on the couch with his legs in front of him, instead of across it as he was now. He propped up his legs, then took a moment to lean back, close his eyes, and rest. I sat next to him so I could half-watch the show while working on my biology.

"It's discouraging to be this tired by moving from one position to another."

"I know, but you're awake and got all the way to the couch by yourself today. Neither of which happened yesterday."

"I had to crawl from the kitchen to your couch."

"Still, better than yesterday. You made tea."

"I did make tea and toast. That's why I ended up crawling from the kitchen to the couch, standing for three minutes burned too much energy."

"Today or tomorrow, when you start really eating again, you'll notice another big step forward. Pat was able to walk home a day after getting some real food into him."

"You're thinking, what, two days for me?"

"Day and a half, thereabouts. We're just waiting for the poisons to work their way out and for your body to stop spending all of its energy healing up those holes.

"I've got a few more pages to read. How about I get them done, and then we watch things go boom with dinner?"

"I can handle that."

I worked on homework for about twenty minutes before he said something. I didn't catch it the first time and asked him to repeat it.

"You know what else I'd like?"

"What?"

"A shower. I'm so sticky and gross I can barely stand myself."

"Do you want me to call Dave or Mike to give you a hand?"

"Nah... I spent enough time being held up by someone else. I'd like to be able to get in there and steam myself and wash until my hair is so clean it squeaks, without any help."

I suppose I could think of things more appealing then wet, naked Chris. Wet, naked Chris with the energy to do something, for example. Either way it was pretty high on my list. As it was, I knew that wasn't what he was looking for.

He watched me think of ways to get him a shower and said, "I'm fine. I can stand me for at least another night. When you go to class tomorrow, I'll take a stab at it."

"How about you try after I'm back? Taking a shower alone when you can barely stand for three minutes is a dumb move."

He didn't have a good argument against that. "I'll wait. Maybe after dinner. Once I get some more calories into me, I might feel like it."

"Maybe. It would make sitting next to you to watch some TV more pleasant." Half a second after saying it, I realized it was a bad joke. He ran his fingers through his hair and grimaced. He didn't have to say anything. He was personally fastidious; four days without a shower was demoralizing for him.

"You aren't bad, not really. How about we come up with a compromise? We'll put some clean clothing on you tonight after I take care of the wounds. That should make you feel better. I'll ask Mike to come over after fencing tomorrow so you can get your shower earlier instead of later."

"How long until dinner?"

"Fifteen minutes?" I sniffed, got up, and checked the meatloaf. "Call it eighteen. It needs to brown up a little more."

He stood up very slowly and shuffled toward my bathroom. I rolled my eyes. "Here." I put an arm around him and helped him get to the bathroom. "If you slip and fall on your ass in there, I will not only kick it into next week, I'll also take pictures and post them on Facebook."

"I'll keep standing. Just get me to the shower." He looked around for a moment; then asked, "Do you have a razor?"

"Yes, and I don't care how itchy your stubble is, I am not giving it to you. You may find it hard to believe, but I'm pretty tired, too, and I do not want to add knitting your throat back together to my list of healing tasks." He nodded at me, and I left him standing next to my shower. After a minute, I heard the water turn on. Then it occurred to me he was in there with no clean clothing. I gathered up his clothing, knocked on the door, called in, "Clean clothes," and then quickly tossed them in without actually entering the bathroom.

Ten minutes passed. I didn't hear him crash to the ground. Then fifteen. At eighteen I took the meatloaf out and made up plates for us. At twenty I started to get worried. At twenty-five I was seriously debating heading in to see if he had passed out or something. I was standing up to head in when I heard the water turn off. I sat back down and began to relax. After a few more minutes, he called out, "I could use some help."

He was half-dressed, sitting on the floor of the bathroom, leaning against the shower stall. "I don't think I'm going anywhere else tonight."

"Okay. Was it worth it?"

"Oh yes! This feels much better."

"Good. Let me get you up, and you can have dinner in bed."

I'm a soldier. I know how to move a man. This is a good thing because at a foot taller and fifty pounds heavier I don't think I could have gotten him off the floor and into my bed without the training I got in the IDF. As I picked him up, I noticed there was something off about him. I couldn't place it. He didn't seem any more hurt than he had been before, and it didn't set my danger sense tingling, so I pushed it away. I got him seated on the side of my bed. He dropped back to rest against the mattress.

"Might as well do your wounds now."

He nodded tiredly at me. The burst of energy that got him through the shower was gone.

I slid the pants leg up around his thigh, trying to move it gently over the welts. Now it looked like his leg had a long nasty spiral of deep blisters. I worked on reducing the swelling and making sure no infection set in. That took a minute. I scooted onto the mattress, pushed him into a sitting position and balanced him against my knee while I worked on his back. Then I gently lowered him to get his sides and chest. Like yesterday and the day before, I was once again amazed at how much easier this got each time I did it. It looked like I'd get them healed up with no scars. That felt good.

I helped him get his shirt on and the pillows arranged so he could sit up to eat in bed. While he set up the next *MythBusters*, I got our dinner. Sitting next to him in bed, eating dinner, watching two guys trying to remove cement from a cement mixer with dynamite was deliciously fun. We were halfway through the episode when I finally realized what the nagging sense of wrong in the back of my mind was. He smelled like my soap and shampoo. It wasn't bad, but it wasn't that distinctly Chris scent, either. Once I figured it out, I was able to focus on the show completely. Without much conscious thought we watched two more episodes, sitting close together to see them on his tiny screen.

At eight Pat let himself in, saw us in bed watching the computer, and hopped in next to me to watch, too.

"And it didn't even take a rum and coke," Pat said.

"Huh?" I asked.

"The three of us in bed. All it took was *MythBusters*." He grinned at Chris and me.

Chris snorted. "Not my bed. Still not enough alcohol on Earth to get you in my bed."

I threw my head back and laughed. "Hmmm... you two in my bed together. I wasn't in the middle in the shower, either... and weren't you lying on Chris when we all woke up together? I'm your—what's the term?—beard?"

Pat reached around me to stroke Chris's cheek. "You got it, baby. By the way, you smell good in her shampoo."

Chris made a little kissing gesture at Pat that absolutely floored me. I could tell I had wandered into some sort of strange male one-up-manship, but I wondered when which one of them could act the gayest became something two straight guys tried to compete over.

"Okay, that's just weird," I said. "It took me a good ten minutes to figure out he smelled like my soap instead of his, and you get it right off the bat."

"I probably pay more attention to scents than you do."

"I guess so."

"Shall we watch another?" Chris asked.

"Yes!" I said.

Chris shifted the computer from his lap to mine, and the three of us watched another two episodes. While the last one was loading, I checked Pat's arm. It looked much better. Another day or two and he'd be back up to full strength.

By the end of the last episode Chris' eyes were drooping. Pat and I left him to sleep and headed into my living room. We talked for a few more minutes before Pat also started to flag, and I sent him home. I turned off the lights and waited in the dark living room for a few minutes so my eyes could adjust to the low light.

After grabbing my clothing, I watched Chris, a quick stab of envy piercing me. He was stretched out flat on his back looking quite comfy in my bed. His eyes flickered under his lids. Walking closer, I wondered what he was dreaming about. I tried to get a feel for it, but whatever it was that allowed me to have a better than normal sense of his waking thoughts didn't seem to work when he slept.

I stroked the lines of his throat, shoulder, and arm with my gaze. He was too thin, his bones and muscles much too visible under his skin. I remembered the feel of his chest and abdomen under my hands, the sharp curve of his hip bone, and the edge of soft curly hair, as I healed his bruises.

Stop it. I let the images go and went to the shower. *Ogling him while he sleeps is not providing a safe and comfortable environment.*

I didn't bother to turn the light on. No need. Getting in the shower triggered the image of him standing in my shower in wet boxers that weren't quite shut as I handed Pat to him. He had been distant the week after that as well. Had he gone home and thought about me, touching himself as images of my body played in his mind?

Was he masturbating again? Did he feel well enough for that yet? Is that why his shower took so long? Did he slick up his hands with my soap? One hand, both hands?

Stop it. If you keep thinking that way, you won't be able to work on him properly. Keep thinking those thoughts and eventually you'll let them slip at the wrong time and he'll feel it.

I let the images go. There'd be time enough for them when he wasn't sleeping in my bed waiting for me to heal him up. I did realize the almost-naked image I had of him was from when I was working on Pat. I didn't have a clear recent image of him in his boxers, his only clothing for almost three days. I took that as a good sign: when the chips were down I could be professional. It was just after that I had a hard time holding it.

Do better!

40.

"Is your house still a hospital?" Morrell asked me at the start of our next class.

I slumped into my chair, happy to be in a class where I could relax. My Arabic wasn't great, but it was still easier to sit around chatting with Morrell than working on Diff Eq or the functions of the cell. "Yes. One gone. One still there. Go home tomorrow, next day."

"Good. Are you looking forward to having your home back?"

"Yes." I smiled broadly. "Sleep in my own bed. Very good."

"You are not sleeping in your own bed?"

"No. I have the... Chair... No...." I switched into English, "Couch."

"I hope your friend appreciates this."

"I think he does."

Morrell looked a little surprised. "He? What does your boyfriend think about this?"

"He does not think about this. He does not know. We have not spoken in four months."

"Oh. I am sorry." He must have thought we broke up and I hadn't mentioned it.

"It is not like that. He is...," once again into English, "There's no way I'd have the words for this in Arabic yet. He's undercover, so I have no way to contact him. I imagine if he knew, he'd be fine with it. Most of my friends are male, and most stay over at my place now and again. But I don't actually know and won't for quite a while."

"How old is your boyfriend?"

"Twenty-nine."

"That makes more sense. I was thinking of someone your age."

"He was when he started."

"When will you see him again?"

"Fall? Maybe. There is no way to know."

Morrell gave me an odd look before he spoke. Like he wasn't entirely certain the next bit was a good idea or not. "You must really love him."

Great. I sighed. Was he trying to get me to talk to him about it or just looking for a chance to use some extra vocab words? I felt raw. Like the boundary between proper behavior and TMI had been scoured away with a sand blaster. I might as well ask him right out and go from there.

"Are you asking as friend? Or is this part of the class?"

He slid back into English. The energy in the room shift subtly, making me feel slightly more calm. "I'm asking as a friend. I can feel there's a huge pile of stuff on your plate right now. If you're doing as well in keeping up with your other classes, then it looks like you're doing a good job of handling it. But I get the feeling you want to talk about it. So I'm here."

"Are you an empath?"

"Among other things."

"Then just read the feelings. I can talk all week, and I won't get the words right." I spent a moment allowing myself to just feel the confusion, the desire, the anger, the pain and the joy of it.

"No wonder you look awful these days. If I can offer some advice, don't love someone just because you feel like you should. That never works out well."

"He told me it was okay if I found another man. But..." Once again I just felt it.

Morrell looked like he understood, but he spoke anyway: "But? It'll be better if you actually say it."

"I don't want to be the woman who sends the 'Dear John' letter to her guy when he's off invading Normandy while she's safe at home. I can't even send him a proper 'Dear John' letter. The buddy I'd normally talk to about this kind of thing has a crush on me. He'd be hurt if he found out that, in addition to not being the woman with a love far away, I'm not slowly falling in love with him. And, just to make matters more interesting, the new man I found couldn't be a bigger cluster-fuck of emotional damage if I tried to find one for a week. Dropping the one is a character flaw and loving the other is going to end badly."

Morrell thought for a moment. "It's not exactly like you're home safe and sound. If he's invading Normandy, you're on an aircraft carrier headed for Midway. More importantly, it doesn't seem like you've got much of a choice at this point. Feels to me like you already love the one, and the other is becoming less of a person and more of a shadow with each passing day. You've already dropped him. I think you already know it, too."

"You're the second person to tell me that. The one in my house—"

"That friend?" Morrell looked amused in spite of himself.

"Of course, that friend. I live smack dab in the middle of the Land of the Law of Murphy. Of course, he's the one in my home twenty-four hours a day, sleeping in my bed, eating my food, being pleasant and tired company. Of course, he's the one with the wounds on his thigh and chest that require daily wound checks, so I have to spend at least a few minutes a day with my hands on his practically naked body. Of course, I'm a healer, so there's nothing more up my alley than a wounded man. Of course, he's the one who suggested we go dancing and then backs off when things get too hot."

"It sounds like he was meant for you."

I looked at Morrell carefully. I wasn't sure if he was kidding with me or not. I decided he was being serious, but he was obviously getting more from my feelings than my words because I really wasn't doing a good job of explaining how I felt about Chris. "Maybe he is. But he doesn't think he's meant for me. He's still in love with his wife and doing a pretty damn good job of staying in love with someone who isn't there because he may be a wreck, but he also has character, which apparently I don't. He's already got a small troop of fangirls following him around mooning over him. They drive him crazy because they can't understand he doesn't want them, once again because he actually loves his wife. I have no desire to join them. Although, judging by how this is going, it looks like I'll be the president of his fucking fan club any day now."

"And the world is scheduled to end right about May 3, and none of this helps with that."

I looked alarmed. "May 3?"

Morrell smiled. "I'm just making it up. I know you've got something bigger than this on the horizon. I can feel it, and you wouldn't have ended up with two wounded guys in your house otherwise."

"Yes. The drama here isn't helping with the bigger issue, and it's not making me a better healer, scientist, or linguist."

"You're doing fine on the language front. I still think you should drop this whole med school thing and start working full-time with me on becoming a linguist. You don't have to be a doctor to be a healer."

"I can't think of a better way to run into hurt people and use these skills than being a doctor."

"You have something there. However, it looks like you're getting plenty of practice right now."

"I'm hoping in the not too distant future that will be done."

"Your lips to God's ears. What are you going to do with your soap opera?"

I rolled my eyes at the absurdity of my situation. "It really is a soap opera, isn't it?"

"Are any of you pregnant? Unable to name the baby's father?"

I laughed. "No, pregnant would require sex. Not a lot of that with this group. Which is probably the only reason this isn't really a soap opera..." I looked at his bookshelf for a few minutes, then answered his question. "Nothing I can do with the one. He's literally out of the picture. I suppose I can work on trying not to feel like a fraud because I couldn't keep him in my heart for four months. As for the other... I'm trying to be a good friend to him. He could use one. As for me, I'm spending all of my non-healing time working on homework because one thing they have all told me is, 'Keep attachments to the real world,' otherwise—"

Morrell cut in, "They're right. I spent too long outside of the real world when I was younger. It's not a good thing. Do you have any friends who are totally outside of this?"

"Not here."

"Well, as soon as you get the one in your apartment out of it, go call one and spend some time in the real world. It'll help." Once again the energy in the room shifted, and I found myself feeling very calm and mellow. The problems weren't better, just further away.

"Thanks. I needed that. Speaking of the real world, how about we work on some more Arabic?"

We talked later than usual. I didn't really want to break off the conversation, but it was time to go to town and get my Sabbath supplies. As I left, he said to me, "Shalom, Sarah," and, having done so, I did feel a wave of peace wash over me.

"Thanks," I said to Morrell and headed into the cold in search of flowers and candles.

"That smells good." Chris looked sleepy as he leaned against the doorway to my bedroom two hours later.

"Good nap?"

"Yes. This is the first time I've woken up feeling halfway decent. What are you making?"

"Right now, Kosher Onion soup, which is just like French Onion soup but I use olive oil instead of butter. Challah will go in the oven soon. Once it comes out, I'll toss the beef and some veggies in there to roast."

"You keep feeding me like this, and I'll never leave."

"I enjoy it, and cooking's even more fun when you've got an audience. It'll be nice to have a proper Sabbath."

"It's Friday?"

"Yeah."

He traced a finger over the lilies I had in a vase on my table. "I lost a day somewhere. I thought it was still Thursday."

"That's easy enough to do when you sleep three days straight."

"You're okay with me here for your Sabbath?"

"Sure. It's nice to have company. Visiting with friends and having people over for the meal is part of the observance. Does it bother you being here for my holy day?"

"No. As long as you don't mind me asking questions."

"Not at all."

He walked over to sit at the table. "Can I help you?"

"Carrots, turnips, and potatoes need to be chopped up to go with the beef. Are you handy with a kitchen knife?"

"My mom made sure we could all cook. When I'm home, Wednesday is my night to make dinner."

"Good." I handed him a knife and a small pile of vegetables. "Call it an hour and a half in the oven."

He started chopping a carrot and held up an inch-long piece. "Should be nice and tender by the time it comes out."

"Looks good."

I brushed the egg wash on the challah and put it in the oven. Then stirred up the onions, making sure they were browning evenly. "What's your signature meal?"

"Do you mean what do I make most often or what do I like best?"

"Either, both."

"Each month we'd get twenty dollars to make four dinners that had to feed seven people, at least two of whom were teenagers. Fried rice is what I did most often. It's easy. It's cheap.

Everyone eats it, and it's halfway decent for you. As for what I like best, barbequed spare ribs. Somehow I have a feeling I won't be making them for you anytime soon."

"You might be right. How are you coping in the land of the pork-free kitchen?"

"I've been enjoying your food. Granted, I've got a craving for bacon; probably because I can't have any here."

I smiled wryly at him. "It's always bacon. Ally, Ben's wife, converted, and she came up with a kosher substitute. I'll make it for you one day though it's horrendously bad for you. Very, very tasty, though."

He raised an eyebrow. "Tell me more."

"Take the skin off the chicken. Rub it with equal parts salt and brown sugar, add a little finely ground pepper. Cut it into strips. Then put it in a low oven until it's crispy."

He looked intrigued. I was quite pleased to see him look interested in food. "You're right, that sounds really tasty and horribly bad for you. Now what?" He gestured to the pile of cut veggies in front of him. I stood up, filled a bowl with water, and put them in to stay cool and fresh.

"Now, we wait. In forty minutes the challah comes out. Then season up the beef and into the oven it and the veg goes."

"Pat usually comes over for your Sabbath, right?"

"Yes. I think he's out with Emily tonight, though. I have to ask him how he's explained what happened to his arm. Don't want to contradict that story."

"If they both have roommates, she might not have seen it yet."

"We can hope. A long spiral of blisters isn't something you can come up with an easy lie for."

"No, it's not. Whatever he comes up with, I'm sure he can make her believe. He doesn't have to survive on wits alone on this one."

"That's true." We were both quiet. "I think I understand why Mike and Chuck just go for one-night stands and weekend flings. Trying to keep something like this from someone you actually cared about…I wouldn't want to even try." Then I realized what I said. I blushed for a long moment.

"What?"

"I never told Ari."

"You didn't?"

"No. This isn't the sort of thing he'd respect."

Chris looked shocked; I caught a layer of pleasure as well. "He doesn't know any of this?"

"None of it."

"Why wouldn't he respect this?"

"I'm Mulder. He's Scully."

"Scully came around in the end. If Mulder had grown her skin back together, I think she would have decided he was onto something a lot sooner."

"He might have, too. But when the time came, I didn't want him to look at me like I was gullible or stupid for believing you. Even if I can cut myself and regrow the skin, it doesn't mean you are what you think you are." I stood up and stirred the onions again; it seemed like a good way to change the subject. "I think this batch is going to turn out especially well."

"Good. I like French onion soup."

"I should probably warn you. There's no cheese with this tonight."

He pouted at me a little bit, and I smiled back at him. "I'll survive. What's next on your list of things for this evening?"

"Getting as much homework done as I can between now and four thirty, a shower, and dressed. Then I'm ready for candle lighting."

"Should I get dressed up? Mass at home means a button down, tie, and slacks."

"Do you have anything here to 'get dressed up' in?"

"I've got what I was wearing when we were attacked. It's not dressy, but it's not pajamas."

"Yes, getting a shower, if you haven't already, and dressed up would be in the right spirit."

"Then let me get a shower and dressed." He got up. Eventually I heard the water running in my bathroom. He popped back out wrapped in a towel a minute later.

"Can I have your razor now?"

"Sure." I headed into my bathroom, grabbed it from under the sink, put a fresh blade on it, and handed it to him. "No shaving cream. I just use my shower gel."

"I can cope. Getting rid of this will feel good."

"It doesn't look bad." Which was me being cool about it. Five days of stubble looked dangerous and rugged but not nearly a beard. It looked really, really good, and I wanted to see what it felt like.

"It itches and feels wrong," he said, scratching his chin.

"Never did a beard then?"

"Nope. Didn't have facial hair of any sort the first time around. Never had any desire for it this time."

"Why not just make it stop growing?"

"I tried. I didn't like the side effects. Normally I keep it slowed down enough so I only have to shave twice a week." He smiled dryly at me. "The last few days I've been a bit too tired to run any magic that wasn't vitally important."

"Just a bit." I felt myself gazing too long at his naked stomach. "I should get started on my homework," I said and left him in the bathroom. I spent several minutes very carefully not thinking about how he had looked. Between the dark blue towel low on his hips, the stubble, the tattoo, the necklaces, and his comfort with me in that state of undress, I was having a very hard time seeing anything else. Finally, I gave up and let myself imagine him, taking the time to really enjoy the view. *Good Lord, he was delicious like that!*

He popped out of my room again fifteen minutes later. This time wet, clean shaven, and wrapped in a towel. "Do you have an iron?"

"Yes. In my closet. Top shelf. There's an ironing board in there, too."

"Good." He vanished into my room again. I heard the squeak my ironing board makes when it's set up. I wanted to go in and watch him iron. *That's not a good plan.* I had more than enough fantasy fodder as it was. I didn't need to add the image of his arms while he ironed to my collection.

"Challah done?" Chris asked when he came back out of my room dressed in his jeans and a green button down. He ironed the jeans as well as his shirt. I was very impressed.

"Yeah. I think so. You want to get that while I get the beef ready?"

"Sure. Where are your hot pads?"

"In the drawer next to the stove." He nodded and got the challah out. I applied salt, pepper, garlic, ginger, and coriander to the beef, then slid it into the oven.

"A bit more homework and then shower time."

"Yes. I think there's about enough time for me to get my paper on *The Wasteland* started." He settled on the window seat with his computer and got to work outlining.

I fought my way through another problem set, then headed for my bathroom. The lighting of the candles might be the official start of the Sabbath, but for me the day of rest begins with my shower. Hot water washes the rest of the week away and puts me in the mindset for a day of rest. I got out and dressed, enjoying having my room all to myself again.

I checked the clock as I left my room. Three more minutes. I found the matches and lit the candles around my living room. Two might be customary for a woman with no kids, but I like more light than that. His eyes followed me as I moved from candle to candle.

"You look very pretty."

"Thank you." I feel very feminine in my Sabbath clothes. The rest of the week I go for tomboy modest; for Sabbath I get dressed up. Today's was one of my favorite outfits: a straight gray skirt that landed just below the knee and a soft, wide-necked, black sweater. "Not that your jammies aren't snazzy, but you look nice in outside clothing as well."

"They feel pretty good, too." I headed over to the table and waved at him to join me. He did.

"It begins with the lighting of the candles." I lit them. "Then the gestures." I waved my hands through the smoke the match left and covered my eyes. "Then the blessing. *Barukh ata Adonai Eloheinu Melekh ha-olam, asher kid'shanu b'mitzvotav v'tzivanu l'hadlik ner shel Shabbat. Amein.*" I removed my hands and smiled at him.

"What does that mean?"

"Blessed are You, Lord, King of the Universe, who sanctifies us with His commandments and commands us to light the candles of Shabbat. Amen." I doused the match and tossed it in the trash. "If we were at the farm this would be followed by the blessing of the children."

"What comes next?"

"Kiddush: the blessing of the wine. The washing of the hands. Then the blessing of the bread. Then eat, drink, enjoy each other's company." I poured a glass of wine for each of us, took mine, and started to pray, "*Vay'hiy erev vay'hiy voqeir yom ha-shishiy...*" The Hebrew tasted rich and lovely in my mouth. I let the words slide through me as I tuned myself into their meanings. "*...Barukh atah Adonai, m'qadesh ha-shabat. Amein.*" I put the glass of wine down. "Want me to translate?"

"No. I could feel what you said. God who made the seventh day. God who made the wine. God who rested. Blessed are you, God, who made this day of rest. Who chose us from all people. This our most holy day. Something about... slavery... the exodus... blessed are you, God, who made this day."

"That's a good paraphrase."

"You're feeling the words so intently while you say them it's giving me goose bumps." He pushed his sleeve up to show me his forearm, which was speckled with goose bumps.

I smiled. "Supposedly, if every Jew manages to celebrate the Sabbath properly two Sabbaths running, the Messiah will return, and we'll be ushered into paradise on Earth. I might as well do my part."

He smiled back at me. "It sounds nicer than the elect being sucked into heaven, seven years of war, plague, famine, and all the rest of it."

"Much less dramatic."

"There is that. Hand washing?"

"Yep. Over to the sink. Take the cup. Pour the water on the top of your right hand and on the bottom of your right hand. Then on the left." I went through the motions as I talked. "Then comes, *Barukh atah Adonai, Elohaynu, melekh ha-olam, asher kid'shanu b'mitzvotav, v'tzivanu al n'tilat yadayim.*" I dried my hands and handed him the cup.

He wet his right and then left hand. "Say it slowly. I'll repeat."

I did. He followed a beat or two behind, not doing nearly as badly as most people do when confronted with an entirely new language with entirely new sounds.

"Very good."

"I didn't know I could even make half of those sounds half an hour ago. What was that, 'Thank you, God, who made the washing of the hands?'"

"Pretty much." I handed him the towel, and he dried off his hands.

"Now I bless the bread, we each take a slice, and dinner is on."

"Good."

He stood next to me at the head of the table as I held the loaves and blessed each one. "*Barukh atah Adonai Elohaynu melekh ha-olam ha-motzi lechem min ha-aretz. Amein.*" I put one of the loaves down and tore two pieces off of the other one, handing the first one to him and keeping the second one for myself.

"Blessed is God who gave us the bread?"

"Yes. Do you just hear it in English?"

"No. I just know what you mean. You don't hear it in English in your own mind when you say it. Do you?"

"No. I learned it in Hebrew as a baby. It didn't even have English words until I was four or five. Can you read my mind, like Chuck?"

"No. Well, sort of. When you're feeling something intently, I can feel it. I can catch phrases or images of what's going on in your head when you're thinking loudly. But that's not how Chuck works. He's absolutely phenomenal at reading people and better at making them do what he wants. You, Chuck, Pat, a few others, I'm close enough to feel. I can't do it with anyone else."

"I sometimes think I know what you're thinking, but I'm never quite sure. Since the first Golem meeting…"

"Reading for writers." He grinned warmly at me.

"Ahhh… so that was real."

"Yes. You know, that's a conversation we haven't had yet."

"By all means. I'll carve. You start." He sat down and began to talk about what writers need to know most from their reader. I made us plates and put them in front of each of us.

He took a bite of the beef and stopped talking. For a moment he just tasted and chewed. I loved the look of intense pleasure on his face. "Oh. That's really good."

"Grass-fed, organic, kosher beef lovingly raised by my family. Now you know why I'm willing to eat vegetarian instead of settle for less."

"Yes, I do." He took another bite. "That's insanely good."

"Thanks. Remind me to feed you lamb sometime."

"I'll happily do that," he said while raising another piece to his lips.

We passed an hour comfortably talking and eating. After dinner, we headed for the sofa. I sat on the left side, feet curled under me, facing him, and leaning against the back of the sofa. He reclined across the sofa, his feet on the cushion next to me. We had brought our glasses and the bottle of wine with us and talked about how the rest of the Sabbath is celebrated; he seemed especially interested in the idea, at least for married couples, sex was part of it. Then we moved to him talking about Easter at his parent's house. If sex was part of the traditional Easter celebration, it wasn't something anyone had bothered to mention to him.

We were wrapping Easter up when he said to me, "You know I'm not really Catholic, right?"

"I know you don't go to Mass every Sunday, and I know most priests would be horrified if you were to explain what your necklaces do. I just figured you were a… Cafeteria Catholic? Is that the term?"

"That's one of them. I'm not even one of them. I'm not a Christian of any stripe. My family is Catholic. I'm not. I just see no reason to rub their faces in it."

"You don't believe in the Lord?"

"Quite the opposite really: I know for a fact God exists."

"Oh." I took another sip of my wine, feeling a little foolish for forgetting. "Tell me about being a priest."

"What do you want to know?"

"Anything. I'd like to know more about who you used to be."

He settled back against the sofa more comfortably, one hand behind his head, the other holding his wine glass. "I was something of a hot-shot seminary student, finished in almost record time. Mostly I spent my time kissing up to my higher ups, arguing theology, and coming up with newer and even less intuitive ways of expressing the Will of the Presence.

"Theology is sort of like literary criticism. You get brownie points for coming up with oddball interpretations that are hard to understand. Sprinkle in some counseling, which I was remarkably ill-suited for—not that I didn't want to be good at it, I was just too young and too innocent. It's hard to be sympathetic and useful to someone dealing with an issue when not only the issue but the desires that caused it are alien to you. I was on track for my own parish. It would have been some little, out-of-the-way town with probably nine people in it. Then my mother swooped in and told me to pack my bags. I was getting married and moving to the Palace of the High Priest.

"That radically changed the direction of my life. Had I ended up in that parish I would have probably stayed a theologian, spent most of my time stuffed in books. When my father died, I would have taken over our clan. Chuck would have done the actual ruling. I would have spent my time writing about the ins and outs of how best to interpret the Will of the Presence, chatting with the bishops about the role of evil in the world, and should we choose free will or submit ourselves to the Presence.

"Instead, I ended up in the Palace of the High Priest. For the first few months they didn't have a position for me. Nice honeymoon. I got to know my wife and the lay of the land, but there wasn't much use for a barely adult, brand new, lowest-possible-level priest. I went from being the pet of my instructors and a few old bishops, to the son-in-law of the high priest. Think of it as going from being a star of the local seminary to living in the Vatican eating dinner with the Pope every night.

"Anyway, instead of let me poke about the Palace and turn into a full-time scholar, my father-in-law made a position for me. One of the perks of being the high priest. Each clan sent at least a tenth of their men at arms to the Palace at any given time. I became the Soldiers' Confessor. He knew it would be useful for his son to have a brother-in-law who was intimately acquainted with all of the soldiers who went through their home. When I became high priest, those relationships proved immensely useful."

Chris stopped, took another drink, and thought. "That's more politics than theology. Say you knew, absolutely, that if you prayed you'd get an answer. The *right* answer. No doubt, no excuses, no refuge. No option to say, 'I thought it was for the best' or 'I meant well.' How often would you pray?"

It occurred me I rarely prayed for guidance. "Probably about as often as I do now."

"Then you'd be unique. In a world where God answers, very few people ask. That's where my job came in. Say you don't want to be told with absolute certainty you're just fooling yourself by trying to start a life as an actor. Say you want someone to guide you but leave the decision in your hands. You'd come to see me, and I'd tell you about the Will of the Presence. Then you could make your own decisions. If you asked It, It would answer, and you'd never have the option of going against It. Once you knew Its will, yours vanished.

"That was my life. Confessions and counseling during the day. Getting to know the soldiers. Building relationships with them. For fifty years I did that. Over that time things changed. More politics. I was never supposed to be in line for succession. Her older brothers died, and Dave did not want it. He wanted to name her as his successor, but he couldn't. So it landed on me."

"Why not her?"

"One of the less savory aspects of our home. To say women were property would be a gross generalization; it would also be more or less true. There was no law saying he couldn't have done it, but the clans would have rebelled. He was trying to avoid a civil war. The great irony was setting me up as his heir sparked one, nonetheless. However, I did win the war in my own name. I'm not sure I could have done it in hers. Pat's clan showed up very early on in the fight, and they made a lot of difference. I don't think they would have showed up to fight for her as high priestess. Honestly, I'm not entirely sure my clan would have shown up to fight for her as high priestess, and I was in charge of it."

"Oh."

"Yes. Once I was named his successor, being a priest changed once again. Now it was all about politics. I had ten years to learn to place a veneer of holiness over political practicality before he died. Chuck moved to the Palace then. He was always better at the politics than I was. That was also part of my father-in-law's plan. I think he figured between her, Chuck, Dave, and me we'd do a pretty good job ruling our world. It started off pretty rough, though. There were political priests and religious priests in our world, and I was the first high priest in a thousand years trained as the latter instead of the former. The best analogy I can think of, I went from being a priest in the Vatican of Pope John Paul II to being a Medici Pope.

"There was a reason why other high priests weren't religiously trained. The holiness got in the way. My father-in-law was a better ruler than I was because he'd know what to do and steep it in the proper language. I actually believed the tenets of the Church and let that form my actions. Then I'd have Chuck try to find a way to make it work.

"One of my less-stellar moves: food aid for the poor. Sounds great, right? Feed the hungry, that's one of our basic duties. I almost bankrupted the treasury and put a huge number of farmers out of work, thus increasing the number of poor in need of food aid while simultaneously lowering the food supply and raising food prices."

I nodded at him. "That's why charity should be a personal thing, not a state thing."

"I know that now. I didn't then. Another of my great ideas: no one could charge interest. Chuck was able to talk me out of it. That would have been a disaster, especially since that great idea hit me less than a year after the Food Aid Catastrophe. What he was finally able to do was let me see a government and a person are not the same thing. What's desirable in a person is not necessarily so in a government.

"Mostly, though, I liked theology. I liked being the hot-shot student who could tie knots in the arguments of my professors. I would have made a great theologian. Instead I became a decent confessor, and eventually I was a good ruler."

He liked theology… well, let's talk theology. "Once upon a time Hillel was asked to explain the whole of the Law standing on one foot. He said, 'Do not do what is hateful to yourself to another. The rest is commentary. Go and learn it.' So, on one foot what was your theology?"

"Hmmm…" He looked at his wine glass. "I may have had too much wine for doing this on one foot. How about comfortably reclining on the couch?"

"Sure." I smiled at him.

"We are the Will of the Presence made flesh and bone. Our highest calling is to be the tools of Its desires."

"Sounds like Islam."

"Not a bad comparison. Submission to the Will was a very big theme."

"But you didn't have to submit?"

"You could do whatever you wanted, but if you ever prayed about something, if you asked for directions, that was the end of your will on the matter. In some ways it was a good thing. Say you know your desires for your neighbor's wife are totally inappropriate. Ask the Presence for guidance, and that would be that. If you still felt the desire, it was meant to be. If it wasn't, it would never bother you again.

"That's why being gay was an abomination. It didn't have anything to do with the sex. The Presence could have just as easily picked wearing orange or eating apples. If you asked, it would go away. No struggle. No pain. Just ask, and it would be lifted from you. It wasn't like it is here, if you asked your desire for sin really would vanish. That someone would willfully choose to exile himself from the Presence… That's why death or mutilation was the result. I didn't know it at the time, for obvious reasons, but Mike explained it to me once we were here. He loved himself the way he was, and he loved his mind. He didn't want to allow anyone else's will into his head."

"Brave or stupid?"

"Definitely brave. Possibly stupid. He didn't get caught. He was always extremely careful, and he was a good enough fighter he was chosen by the Presence to watch over me and my family."

"So, even with an all-powerful deity who would show you the way, there was evil, and inappropriate desires, and all the rest of the sins of man?"

He smiled wryly at me. "Of course. Men like their sins. I certainly liked most of mine. You like yours."

I laughed. "I certainly do. I like them so much I consider free will the highest and most precious gift the Lord gave us."

"You believe in free will?"

"Absolute free will."

"Even though God hardened Pharaoh's heart?"

"Even though. I believe the Lord spent a long time giving us the rules and showing us how to behave. Then He slowly moved away. Now we're on our own, and it's up to us to actually use what He showed us in our everyday lives. Pharaoh and Job were special cases. Illustrations for our benefit. That kind of thing doesn't happen anymore."

"Why not?"

"No idea. Because that's the way He wants it? Because my theology doesn't work if He's still out there meddling in people's lives? Take your pick."

"That's honest."

"No reason not to be. Can you see any good coming out of pretending to yourself you believe something about the Lord you don't actually believe?"

"No. But I've spent a good deal of time with people who don't want to face certain ideas. God is all good. Really? Define good. Because I don't see any way anyone is going to define it that fits. There's a major discomfort to saying, He's an all-powerful bastard, who picks and chooses, and sometimes you win, and sometimes you don't." He was looking at me very intently. I could feel the last bit especially was very personally relevant for him.

"Yeah. I'm not going that far. I'll agree with you on doesn't meet any definition of good but capricious and cruel? Nah... not going there."

"Really? Tell me about Job."

"How did I know you were going there?"

"Because it's the only example in your Bible where God screws someone over for the fun of it."

"You've got Herman Wouk's *War and Remembrance* on your bookshelf. Do you remember his explanation of Job?"

"That even in the face of God one must hold onto the truth. Job knew he was a blameless man, and he would not lower himself or insult his God by admitting to sins he had not committed."

"Exactly."

"Take that a step further, what if God really isn't good?" he asked while sitting up.

"I would have thought that was obvious."

"What if you could do something about it?" His eyes were bright with excitement.

"Like what, stand there like Job going, 'It's not fair...?' He's the Lord; I'm not."

"No, I mean really do something."

"Once again, like what? Life isn't fair. The world isn't nice. That's the cost of free will."

"Why should you worship that which is unjust?"

"I don't know He is unjust. I know the world is. I know bad things happen to people. I don't know the scales don't eventually balance. How about you? Can you tell me it never evens out? That evil will get away with it in the end?"

He leaned back into the cushions and took another sip from his glass. "No. I can't tell you that. Like you, here I've only seen what I've seen. Back home, if you wanted absolute justice all you had to do was ask for it. When given the option, almost no one asked. You had to immensely hate someone or be insanely sure of your own goodness to ask for that.

"Seriously though, what if God isn't good? Are you morally bound to do something about it?"

"Once again, like what?"

"Deicide," he said it quietly, his eyes and magic searching for my response.

"Umm… is that even a word?"

Apparently that wasn't what he had hoped for. His intensity faded as he answered me: "I think so."

I stood up and put my wine glass on the coffee table. "Back in a sec." The book I was looking for was on my bottom shelf, next to the rest of the DragonLance books. *Test of the Twins*. I pulled it off the shelf and carried it back to the couch. Tossing it in his lap, I sat down, sure he had read it because he had a copy in his room.

"It didn't work all that well for Raistlin. He killed his entire world and everyone he had ever cared about."

Chris looked oddly serious. "No, it didn't work all that well for him, did it?"

"Here's a better question. What defines good and evil? At least in the tradition I come from, the Lord makes the rules. He says what's what. Given that, how am I supposed to know He is evil?" Chris thought about my words. "The way I see the world, He makes the rules for good and evil. If you ditch that, all you've got is personal preference. Say the Lord and I disagree on something, like, I don't know, pork. Not that eating pork is evil. Anyway, I can argue with Him about it; we've got a long and glorious tradition of that. I can ignore him; we have an even longer and more storied history of that. I don't get to say He's wrong about it because He makes the rules."

"If God told you to kill a bunch of people or something just wrong…"

"If He starts talking to me, I'm going to assume I've been with you all so long I've finally gone off the reservation and it's time for the loony bin."

That brought him up short. He thought for a moment. When he spoke again, he was quieter, more thoughtful. "The Presence did talk to us. If you asked, It told you. And sometimes, even if you didn't ask, It told you."

"And what? It started telling people to do evil?"

"No, nothing like that."

"Then why ask?"

"Theological question. A good way to exercise the mind. Are you morally bound to attack evil wherever you find it even if it's in God's hands? Isn't that what Wouk is saying about Job? After all, Job can say, 'Yes, God, I must have sinned because you don't punish the innocent.' Or he can hold the truth and say, 'I've done nothing wrong. You're treating me badly. Stop it!'"

"Then I guess it's your duty to stand up and always hold the truth because Job is rewarded for holding onto the Truth in the face of the Lord. He gets everything back and then some because he does not admit to faults he did not have."

"Now, if it had been in Job's power, should he have done something to God for picking on him? For using him for His amusement?"

"No. Job does not know the mind of the Lord. He can hold onto the Truth, but he cannot attack. He does not know he has been chosen as an example."

"So, no matter what, God is always right?"

"Well, in my world that's part of the definition of 'god.'"

"Is that the first time I've ever heard you use that word?"

"Possibly. I said it with a lowercase g, though."

"I got that from context. You usually say the Lord."

"Yes, I do. Another observant Jew thing, we don't speak the name of the Lord. I also use *Hashem* at home and in Israel. No one knows what it means here, so I say the Lord instead."

"What does it mean?"

"The Name."

"And what is the name of God?"

I rolled my eyes at him. *"Yod Het Vov Het."*

"I Am. That's what we were taught in Catechism."

"More or less true. There's debate as to what precise case or tense of being verb should be used. But there's a debate about everything. Imagine four thousand years of highly skilled lawyers all pouring over the same base text and all of each other's opinions, then continuing a constant argument with each other over what it all means. That'll give you a pretty good idea of what Jewish theology is like. We have no pope, no infallibility, and a long and glorious tradition going back to Adam of telling the Lord…"

"You can use *Hashem* around me."

I smiled at him. "I'll keep that in mind. Anyway, we've been arguing with *Hashem* since Adam said, 'Well, it does look mighty tasty, let's see what happens.' Abraham's another good example. He stood up to the Lord and argued about the people of Sodom. *Hashem* took it and let himself be whittled down. I think He expects us to argue when it looks like things are wrong. I guess you didn't have any of that before?"

"You could argue, but what was the point? You'd say your piece, and then The Presence would say Its, and you'd be filled with peace and acceptance. All would be right with the world, and you'd do whatever it was."

"That's not much of an argument."

"No, it's not. Where does Abraham fit in your arguing with God theory?"

"Didn't we just cover that?"

"Wasn't he Isaac's dad?"

"Ah… I don't know. I'd still be arguing with Him. Maybe after Sodom he decided *Hashem* knew what he was talking about?"

"Maybe."

I felt his mood darken; there was something deeper to this than just talking about one of the Patriarchs. "What?" I felt silly as soon as I asked. Chris' children were as good as dead to him.

"Just thinking about being told to kill your child. Maybe he was too horrified to argue? Or so sure the promise of descendents as the stars meant something would stop the blade? Maybe he knew he couldn't finish it? He could raise the knife but never lower it."

"Or maybe, as the story said, he trusted the Lord to tell him to do what was right?"

"Maybe." He sighed. "We always did."

"It's more than just a story to you, isn't it?"

"It's more than a story to anyone with kids." I could tell that wasn't all of it. At the same time, I could tell he didn't want to spend more time on that.

"Well, part of the Sabbath is avoiding unpleasant topics of conversation. So, set a new topic."

"I like free will."

"We've got my view on the topic but not yours."

"I'd like to hear more about what you think."

"Not willing to hazard an opinion?"

"Not yet. Let me collect my thoughts. Tell me more about absolute free will."

"It's pretty easy. Everything you ever do is entirely up to you. Hashem's greatest gift to us is the ability to choose. You know we're made in His image?" He nodded and drank. "Okay, well, I don't take that to mean He's an upright biped with minimal body hair. I take that to mean He made us to choose. Now that's not a terribly unique position, but I think this one is…" I took another sip of my drink. "Evil is the Lord's greatest gift to us. Not only is He directly responsible for evil, but without it we cannot have free will. Satan is the highest of the angels precisely because he is the one who brings us evil. He was designed to allow us the joy of choice. Choice makes us men instead of sheep."

"That's unique. That's also hard."

"That Hashem created evil?"

"No. I believe that, too. If you define God as the creator of all things, evil's one of His, too. That you are responsible for everything you do. That's hard."

"I take it you don't believe in absolute free will?"

His eyes drifted away from mine. He spent a moment looking at my wall, then returned his gaze to me. "I'm afraid there is absolute free will, especially here. I'd like to have the luxury of being able to blame bad decisions on fate or God or something else. Chuck tells me it was fate. But late at night, when I'm being honest with myself, I know it's just me."

"I can see that. I've certainly made decisions I'd have preferred to be able to blame on something else. When it comes down to it, I make better decisions if I've got to live with the fact it's all me."

"Do you think we're held accountable for our sins?"

"Yes. I think the scales balance eventually."

"In that case, I better pray there is no free will."

I looked questioningly at him. He shook his head. "Not for tonight. A long life gets you some interesting sins. I thought Jews didn't believe in Hell."

"We generally don't. I know there are some who believe there's a place of judgment for a year after death, but it's not universal."

"Then how do the scales balance?"

"When the Messiah comes, the righteous rise from the dead. They get to live, bodies whole, fully alive again in a world of no pain or hate, wrapped in the perfect joy that is the love of Hashem. Everyone else stays dead."

"I like that idea. It's very comforting." I wasn't sure I agreed, but I gestured for him to keep talking so I could hear him out. "Knowing there's a finite end, that was true where I came from as well. I found the lack of that very frightening about being Catholic. My family here believes that it never ends. Everything you've ever done will follow you forever. Tiny unconfessed sins can result in eons of punishment."

"Okay, compared to that, I can see how everything being over is comforting. In my case, there are people I want to see again. My mom for one. I'd like to have the chance to know her at some point. And I miss my dad."

"Then I hope you find them again."

For a while we didn't say anything. Then I found something I wanted to know more about. "What happened when you got here and reached out for the Presence? I mean, your god isn't mine, right?"

He didn't say anything for a long time. I felt like I had wandered into something important, but I couldn't tell what exactly it was. "More unhappiness?"

"No." He shook his head and drank. "Well, yes, but I'd like to tell it. Just trying to think of a way to describe it. Quickly...no, my God is not yours." Another drink. I took a sip from my glass as well and noticed it was empty.

"Anymore left?"

"Just what's in my glass." He offered me his glass, and I drank from it. "I thought you didn't like feeling drunk."

"I have enough alcohol tolerance to drink a glass and a half of wine in three hours without getting drunk. I'm just nicely relaxed."

"You look it. Very soft, peaceful."

"Thanks. You're looking pretty laid back yourself."

He had a very warm, fond expression on his face. "Once upon a time I looked this way most of the time. Well, most evenings after work at least. Dinner, wine, play with the kids, then laying about and relaxing."

"I would have liked to have seen that."

"Maybe, come next year, you'll get a chance to see more of it."

"That would be nice."

He sat up so he was facing me on the cushion closest to mine. His one arm rested on the back of the couch, the other one held the wineglass between us so I could get to it easily. I took another sip and gave it back to him.

"Let me take a shot at answering your question now. Part of what happened before was we were cut off from the Presence. It stopped talking to us, but we could always feel It. When I got here, I didn't know what had happened. I was in a strange place with people I didn't know speaking a language I didn't understand. For the first time I could remember I was alone. It was horrifying. I'm roughly 235 years old, give or take, and a decent-sized chunk of my life was not all sweetness and light. Those first two days, alone in a way I had never been, were the most terrifying of my life.

"Chuck found me and told me what had happened. Then it was time to find new bodies. Babies made the most sense. We knew nothing of this place, and no one expects a baby to know anything. Christopher Luke Mettinger should have been a SIDS baby. I swooped in and grabbed his body."

"Your middle name is Luke?"

"I've got two of them now. I picked Augustine for a confirmation name."

"Why?" Christopher Luke Augustine Mettinger was a lot of name.

"Because in a new place, with a new body, and a new name, I'm still the priest who enjoyed theology for its own sake." He drank again but left one more swallow in the glass and handed it to me. I finished the glass. "I've enjoyed this very much. Could I come back next week?"

"I'm glad you've enjoyed this. Come back for Sabbath as often as you want. I light the candles eighteen minutes before sunset. If you're here by five, you'll have plenty of time."

He stood up and stretched. "I should probably go home tomorrow."

"I think you're just about better. Stick around for breakfast tomorrow. I usually get up, do my reading, and then have breakfast. It'd be nice to have someone to talk to about Exodus and the plagues while making food and eating."

"I'm good with plagues. That's my best hope for no free will." He smiled lightly at me, his face at odds with his words. "You want the bathroom first?"

"Nah, go ahead."

A few minutes later he came out, once again in his pajamas. "I've never seen you in your pajamas. I know you get up earlier than I do and go to bed later, but it's been three nights and not even a glimpse. Are you hiding them from me? Are there cute, pink bunnies or something else you're keeping secret?"

I laughed for a long time and then walked over to my dresser. "Majorly cute, pink, fluffy bunnies. With bows. And sparkles." Another laugh. "You've seen me in the clothing I sleep in every morning before I get my shower."

"Your running clothing?"

"Yeah. I sleep naked in my own bed. I don't actually own pajamas. Yoga pants and a long sleeve t-shirt are doing double duty these days. Speaking of which…" I grabbed a pair of gray pants with a black stripe down the leg and a blue shirt. I headed to the bathroom. He was standing next to my bed when I got out.

"Good night, Chris," I said while heading back to the couch.

He took a step in my direction. I had a feeling he was going to hug me, but he stopped. "Do you want your bed back?"

"I can do one more night on the couch. Besides, I fit nicely on the couch; you're kind of tall for it."

"Thanks. Good night, Sarah."

Chris lay back in the bed. He was very aware this was her bed. Tomorrow night she'd be laying here. Resting her head against this pillow. Lying under this quilt and between these sheets. He wished she was here, next to him, just to talk. Well, and more than talk, that was always there, but mostly tonight he wanted the intimacy of another mind next to his. Another voice in the dark. He wondered what she would say if he asked her to come lay next to him and talk until they were both asleep.

She had looked very soft tonight. The edges were gone, rubbed away. No knife, no gun, no defensiveness. Very open. He wondered if she was like that all the time before her father died, before magic and the army.

The image of her curled on her side of the couch, head resting against the back, wine glass cradled in her fingers filled his mind. He thought through their conversation about God. It had been a long time since he had used those skills, that mindset. It was nice to have someone to talk to about it again.

At the same time, their conversation hurt. She'd never understand what they did. That wasn't right. She'd never condone it. That was a better way to think about it. Unlike Chuck, in front of her, he was responsible for all of his actions. He found that idea appealing and terrifying.

Her head resting against the sofa, her neck long and fragile, and her eyes bright with questions: he studied those images. She asked better questions than he had dealt with in a long time. More interesting. It was a real conversation. How long had it been since he had had a real conversation with a woman?

He found himself looking forward to coming back next week and the week after. He happily anticipated the opportunity to spend more time with her like this. He'd have to share her with Pat and Emily, but that would be good, too. Fun. A day for fun, joy, and remembrance that God wanted you to have good things. He liked that her God wanted His people to have good things.

He lay on his back with his hands behind his head, looking for the word to describe how this night had felt. *Cherished.* She had bent her will to pleasing him, physically and mentally. He pondered what he could do in response; how he could thank her for this night, for this week.

He wanted to go into the other room and watch her sleep. He got as far as the door before turning around and going back to her bed. That would be a step too far. She'd drawn the line for him and asked him not to cross it unless he wanted to deal with the consequences. Which he wasn't. *Not yet.*

Better to just enjoy this night for what it had been.

He lay down again, feeling more peaceful about himself and her then he had in a long time.

41.

Saturday night Chris was back eating dinner in the cafeteria with the rest of them. The tough, indifferently cooked food left him wanting to head back to Sarah's place to see if she'd be willing to feed him again. He caught Pat's eye and knew Pat was thinking the same sort of thing.

He and Pat broke off from the rest of them when they got to her place. This was Pat's last wound check. Chris' would probably be after the next Golem meeting. At the base of her steps, he stopped and motioned for Pat to stop with him.

"I want to get something for her."

"So, get something. Why tell me?"

"I want you to give it to her with me."

"You're being weirder than usual, Chris."

"Sheets. I want to get her a set of really nice sheets. Since we destroyed her previous ones."

Pat grinned. "You don't want to give her a set of sheets by yourself."

"Exactly. From me it says more than I want to say."

"No, it says exactly what you want to say but shouldn't."

Chris looked mildly annoyed. "Fine. From both of us it says 'Thank you for putting us back together, and we're sorry we wrecked your bedding.'"

Pat nodded. "Okay."

"I'd say let's give it to her next Sabbath, but Emily will be with us, and I don't think you want to explain why we're giving our female friend sheets."

"That's a conversation I can happily avoid."

"I'll send you a link to whatever I find. It'll probably be from Amazon." They headed up the stairs.

While he hunted for sheets online another thought occurred to him. He fired a text off to Pat.

Do you cover your head when you're at her house for Sabbath?

Yes.

What do you wear?

Only hat I've got, Yankees cap. Why? Looking for a yarmulke?

I'm looking for something. Maybe not that far but a hat of some sort.

She's right here. Let me ask her.

A second later another text flashed at him. Yarmulke not necessary. I like fedoras.

Sarah

Good to know. Chris cruised around Amazon.com looking at hats, wishing there was some other dress requirement for the Sabbath. He was firmly convinced he looked dumb in hats. They did have a nice selection of basic fedoras. He thought brown looked pretty good until it occurred to him that was Indiana Jones' hat. *Black. Black goes with everything.*

He added it to his cart and went back to sheet hunting. Chris couldn't shake feeling silly about the hat, but it would look better than a ball cap. Except Pat knew he had bought the hat, and he'd probably have something that showed some effort by Friday. Knowing Pat, he'd look stylishly retro in a Rat Pack sort of way while he'd look like a twit in a hat.

He found a set of sheets he liked and sent another text to Pat.

Done.

Good. When are they coming?

Wednesday.

She tells me you can cook.

Yes.

You're cooking. I'll get her out of her place after four. We'll be back by six.

I can work with that.

He could work with that. He knew the basics: no pork, no shellfish, and no milk and meat at the same meal. He didn't know if milk and poultry were fine or if butter counted as diary. Twenty minutes online and he felt more secure. His fried rice would work for dinner. Add vegetarian eggrolls and crispy beef and that would be a fine dinner.

Wednesday morning. While she was in class, Chris stood in front of her freezer looking at a very large collection of small packages wrapped in white paper with little notes on them. He really hoped she didn't go in there between coming back from class and dinner. Chris knew there was absolutely no chance he was going to get them back in the order they were in now. Sorting through them showed him a nice selection of chicken, beef, and a bit of lamb. Eventually he found something roughly the right shape labeled 'sirloin.'

He grabbed it and inventoried her pantry. It'd be nice if he didn't have to spend forty dollars on spices he'd use less than a tablespoon of. She had most of what he needed in there. He wrote a grocery list: lemongrass, lemons, celery, sprouts, mushrooms…

He grabbed his phone and texted Pat, Does she eat mushrooms? I don't see any here. He went back to the list while waiting for the reply. She was low on soy sauce; he'd get more along with ginger and garlic. He added cabbage, sake, and egg roll wrappers to the list. Some sort of sweet thing if anything looked good. If nothing great jumped out at him, he'd make brownies.

His phone beeped.

Don't know if she does. I don't.

Like allergic to them or you just don't like them?

She'll spend the night stopping me from breaking out in hives.

No mushrooms.

Good.

He looked at the keys to her motorcycle hanging on their hook by the door.

Don't be stupid. You don't know how to ride it, and inspiration is not going to strike just because you sit on it.

He grabbed his phone again. What are you doing?

Sleeping.

Feel like stealing a motorcycle and giving me a lift to Walmart?

Not really.

He took the package and left her house. After he put it in the fridge at Writers', he headed for Hurford's. Grocery Store of the Damned it might be, but it was also three miles closer than Walmart. He was a third of the way there when Pat pulled up to next him on Sarah's bike.

"I feel like an idiot with you on the back of this thing."

"Thanks."

"You need to ask her to teach you how to ride it."

"I will before tonight is over."

"Good."

Pat sped through a U-turn and got them to the Walmart in a few more minutes. Chris did his shopping. Pat got his hair cut. A quick run to the state store finished off Chris' list. They were poking around the wine selection when he said to Pat, "There's a decent state store in Erie, right?"

"Supposedly."

"How about you pick up something worth drinking with dinner there?"

"I can do that."

Wednesday afternoon, cooking time, Chris turned on his music and laid out his ingredients. The Indelicates and cooking went well together. He hunted for knives and a cutting board while "Point Me to the West" played. The knives were exactly where he expected them to be; the cutting boards hid from him. Finally, he noticed them in the few inches of space between the fridge and the wall.

He was prepping away when he heard a truck pull up. A quick glance out the front window showed him UPS dropping off his package. He went back to the stove and finished getting the vegetables ready for the eggrolls.

Chris hit a lull in the cooking. The eggroll filling needed to cool down before he could work with it. Time to get the box. He brought it up to her apartment and slit it open. Everything looked the way he expected. He put the hat on the table, stared at it for a minute, and tried to imagine it on and not looking stupid, but his talent for fantasy didn't lend itself to that image.

He started filling the eggrolls, his hands working automatically. Once done, it was time to wait. No more prep work. He made himself a cup of tea, settled onto the couch, and began to read. After about five minutes, he got curious enough to go try on the hat. Looking at himself in her mirror he decided it looked not nearly as dumb as he thought it would. Which wasn't the same thing as looking great, or good for that matter, but it wasn't awful. He decided that was a victory and took it home.

Autumn and Mike were downstairs when he came in, and both of them were quite interested in why he was carrying a black fedora.

"Put it on!" Autumn said with a very enthusiastic look in her eye.

"I've got to see this," Mike seconded.

Chris brushed his hair back and set it on his head.

Mike spent a minute coolly appraising him. "That looks better than I would have thought."

"Not bad." Autumn nodded.

"Why did you get a hat?" Mike asked.

"Because I really enjoyed Sabbath at Sarah's, and it's part of showing respect."

"You'll be spending your Friday nights there?" Autumn did a very good job of not sounding too interested.

"I hope so. I like the tradition. I like the prayers. I like having someone to talk theology with. Wrap it all up with good food, a few glasses of wine, and some music and it's a very civilized way to celebrate your faith."

"You really were a priest, weren't you?" Mike said dryly.

"I still remember your confessions." Chris smiled. He put the hat in his closet and headed back down.

"What's up for the rest of your day?" Autumn asked him.

"Back to Sarah's. Pat and I are saying 'thanks for healing us.' He's got her out of the house, and I'm cooking. Then we're giving her new sheets to replace the ones we destroyed."

"Always a good plan to keep the healer happy." Mike turned his eyes to his computer screen.

"That's the idea. She certainly didn't sign up to have to constantly feed us and replace her stuff because we destroy it."

"Good point," Mike replied as Chris headed out.

I glanced at Pat as loud music that put me in mind of Chris echoed from my house. He looked back at me like the soul of innocence.

"Should I ask?"

"Why bother? You'll know in a minute."

I got off the bike; he followed. Pat stopped me at the base of the steps. "So, I don't make him jealous…" He hugged me warmly and gave me a kiss that sent hot tingles to my toes. "Thank you for getting my arm working again."

"You're welcome.

"He's up there?"

Pat tilted his head and smiled. "Or it's a pretty bad trap. Either way, you get to go up first and find out."

I laughed and bounced up the stairs, eager to see what was behind my door. I found Chris standing at my stove, spoon in hand, cooking something that smelled awfully good.

"Hi." He looked perfectly comfortable in my kitchen.

I grinned. "Honey, I'm home. What's for dinner?" I asked while I took off my coat. Pat came in behind me and also got out of his cold weather gear.

Chris grinned back at me. "Egg rolls, fried rice, and crispy beef."

"It smells excellent," I said, walking over to see what he was making. "Can I help?"

He very gently whacked the back of the hand I was reaching toward his food with the spoon. "No. Sit down, relax. Pat, glasses are over there." He pointed to the wine glasses on the counter. "Pour something for us. I'll have this ready in a few minutes."

Pat got busy with the wine he had supposedly bought for time with Emily. One bottle went in my fridge and another in the pantry. Two stayed in his backpack. Apparently some of it really was for Emily. A third one he opened and poured for us.

There was something richly satisfying about having both of them serve me. Chris plated up the food with care and easy movements. Pat set the glasses on the table and put the open bottle in the fridge as well.

"So, to what do I owe this pampering?" Pat gestured for Chris to answer.

"For healing us, feeding us, and giving up your home for a week." Chris put a plate in front of me and squeezed my hand. "Thank you."

"You're welcome. Thanks for not taking it for granted."

"Never," Chris said to me. I felt a pleasant thrill at his word and touch. Then he released my hand, turned around, and grabbed his and Pat's plates.

They're pretty well trained. When they eat in the cafeteria, they just dig in. At my place they know to wait for me to say the blessing. I added an extra line, "Thank you, Lord, that blessed us with good friends."

They smiled, and we got down to eating. It was good. Really good. "You can cook for me whenever you feel like it. This is wonderful."

"Thank you."

"When did you learn how to cook?" Pat asked.

"'Round about the age of ten."

"It's an improvement."

"Sounds like there's a story there," I said.

Chris looked like he was on the verge of smiling but kept it reined in because he was supposed to look serious.

"It's a story all right," Pat answered with something halfway between a grin and a smirk.

"It's not that big of a story," Chris responded, keeping the mock seriousness about him.

"Yeah, well, so far it's not a story at all. How about one of you tell it?"

Pat leaned back, sipping his wine. "Okay, so the first time I met Mr. Mettinger, he had just started a civil war, was fighting for his life, and not doing nearly as well at it as he would later on. Anyway, his clan and mine went way back, so as oldest son, heir apparent, scion of the Buis, off I went with some of our men at arms to join the fray, render our fealty, and all the rest of that. He was in the field when I first met him. Unfortunately someone had left him to his own devices to procure food for that night."

Chris broke in. "You should probably know our class didn't cook. It just didn't happen. Now, until that night, because Pat showed up at exactly the wrong time, I had always had someone around to cook for me. We had servants. Even in seminary we had servants. If you wanted something, you asked for it, and a person brought it to you. That's how it worked."

"I show up three nights earlier than expected with three thousand of our men at arms. And, as the great commander, it's his job to do proper honor to me because I'm here with the best troops money can buy, a ton—literally—of money for his coffers, and I'm putting my life on the line to pull his nuts out of the fire."

"Proper honors means food for him, drink, and making sure his men are settled. Getting his men settled is easy. I've got people to take care of that. So, I'm sitting in a tent with Pat staring at me waiting for the reception he deserves. I didn't have it. We're in camp, so I don't have access to the usual pile of cooks I've got in our castle, and the people I had planned to bring in to provide him with that reception are still three days away."

"You have to realize he's the high priest. He's not supposed to be showing any sort of weakness, lack of grace, or skills here. He's the direct link to our God, my ruler, and the guy I've just signed up to put my clan's money and blood on the line to defend. And he's standing there looking like a deer in the headlights, not sure what to do with me."

"I planned on eating with the troops, but that won't cut it. Finally, I swallow my pride and explain what has happened. I offer to make him some tea because it's the only thing I've got on hand. I've completely muffed the protocol for welcoming him, so I decide to make him the tea myself. That would be a sign of immense favor and will hopefully make up for the fact I wasn't ready for him."

"It really would have if you had a clue how to make tea."

"I'd never done it for myself before. I had a fire, water, tea, and a tea pot. It didn't seem like it should be hard. Tea didn't come in nice little packages, it came loose in little tins. You put it in the teapot to steep and then poured it through a little metal strainer. But I didn't know that. I got the water boiling well enough—that was pretty easy—then I tossed a handful of tea into the pot."

"Which was about six times more than he needed."

"I let it stew for a few minutes, still on the fire. I got the cups, handed one to him, and tipped the pot. Nothing came out. He's sitting there, trying not to laugh because we aren't friends yet and he's not allowed to laugh at me."

"But he's holding the tea pot and nothing's coming out. Bear in mind, it's not like I've done much cooking, either. But at the least I'd been in the field enough to know how to make a pot of tea. He's put so much tea in there the water's plumped the leaves up, and he's got a pile of hot, damp tea leaves. Finally, I can't hold my composure anymore, and I start to laugh."

"And grabbed the tea pot, said some unflattering things about our chances of winning the war if I couldn't make fucking *tea*, emptied out the wet leaves, and showed me how to do it right. By that time I was laughing, too."

"I'm just glad you were a much better general than cook."

"I didn't end up in charge because of my pretty looks." Chris smiled at me.

"No, you didn't. And I am glad to see you've learned how to cook."

"Thank you. It's fun. I don't know about you, but I prefer the self-sufficiency we're allowed here." He turned to face me. "Believe it or not, Pat and I were actually paragons of masculine self-sufficiency back there. I laid out my own clothing and would run my own bath. He spent years fighting with his valet about doing his own hair."

"I had forgotten that," Pat said with a laugh. I looked at him in wonder, eyebrows high. He explained, "We wore our hair long. Civilians just pulled back. Military in a long braid down the back. A man of breeding and class got into the bath after his valet had filled it and applied whatever bubbles, oil, or scent to it, washed himself, got out, dried off, wrapped up in a robe, sat down at the mirror, and had his man brush out his hair and do whatever with it. That just seemed undignified to me. I was an adult. I could do my own hair. As for this world over the last one, I prefer the privacy here. Until I've got a three-foot-tall pile of laundry, I prefer doing things for myself."

"What do you mean about privacy?" I asked Pat.

"You were never alone in our world. Well, not quite never but very rarely."

"At least in our class, that was true. You grow up with nurses and whatever other siblings sharing your nursery, and then off to school—in my case seminary—where you share a room and a valet with another student..."

"Which was considered almost roughing it. Instead of seminary, I was at our home with my own valet and tutors, being trained as a battle wizard. I think I had a good sixty years where I was never alone outside of the bathroom. Then off to the camps with the soldiers where I shared a tent with my valet. From there to active fighting with his army. After that, as a member of his house where I finally got a room of my own, and having a room of my own, I made sure there was a woman in it as often as possible."

"I had finished school but hadn't moved out yet. I lived at the seminary, still sharing a room and a valet. Then I was married. For the first eight months I had my own room. Then we moved in together."

"You moved in with your wife after you married her?"

"Yes, and it was considered... cute is probably the right word... that we'd share a suite. Most married people didn't. That we had the nursery off of our rooms and actually spent time with our children was even more shocking."

"I was still a kid when they got married, but I remember hearing about it because everyone was talking about how in love they were, and how sweet, and just cooing over it. No one thought it would last because they were so young, but it did. Sixty years later, when I brought our troops to join in, they were still living together. Though the children were in hiding because of the war." Pat paused, chewing a bite of eggroll. "I know you're ahead in the British history reading; have you gotten to the Victorians yet?"

"I haven't gotten that far yet. I'm still slogging through the War of the Roses."

"Skip ahead. It'll give you a good idea of the home life of the world we grew up in."

"No problem. So, is that how you two became friends?"

Chris smiled. "It was the start of it." He went on to tell me about how Pat had become a friend of his wife, and how through her they had become friends. Pat added bits and pieces about how the war worked. How Chris, Chuck, Dave, and Ameena had each had a part of the war under their control. She had handled the diplomacy. Over time Pat became her personal guard; often he and his troops went to back her up.

"Negotiating from a position of strength is a very good thing. Having three thousand armed troops and one of the finest battle wizards in the field show up with your negotiator tended to make things go more easily," Chris said. He noticed we had finished dinner and began to clean up. Pat took over from him.

"Go get it," Pat told him. "I've got this."

"It?" I asked as Chris disappeared into my room.

Chris came out with a medium sized brown box. "I hope you don't mind the lack of wrapping paper."

"I happily accept presents in all states of wrapping."

He handed it to me. Pat came over to watch me open it. I slid my finger under the tape and popped the flaps of the box apart. Inside was a package of deep brown sheets. I pulled them out and looked over them, then looked up at both of my guys. "Sheets?"

"To replace the ones we destroyed," Pat answered.

"Oh." I blinked slowly. "Can you believe I had forgotten that?" I tore into the package and ran my fingers over the sheets. "Oohh... these are fantastic." They were very soft and dense and felt lovely.

"Supposedly they get better after a few washes," Chris added.

I smiled. "I'll test them out tonight." I got up and put the sheets in my washing machine. They did feel fabulous, and if softer was on the menu, I was going to be really impressed. When I came back, Pat was finishing up with the dishes while Chris sliced strawberries and put them on top of brownies. Pat was the closer of the two, so he got the first hug. After a moment, I went to Chris and hugged him, too.

"Thank you." I smiled at both of them.

Pat finished up the dishes and made coffee. The three of us headed to the sofa for dessert. A glance at the clock showed me it was 7:30 on a Wednesday. "Did either of you tell Mike about this?"

"I mentioned what we were doing. Why?" Chris put down his cup of coffee.

"Is he expecting us to meet him for sparring in half an hour?"

"Good question. Do you want to fight tonight?" Pat asked while he texted Mike.

I shook my head. "A glass and a half of wine and too much excellent food. I can do it if I have to, but I don't have to. What about the rest of you?"

"About the same," Chris said.

"He wasn't expecting to," Pat replied when his phone beeped a few seconds after his first text. "He wants to know if a Saturday morning rain check is in order."

"Not for me, but you two feel free to go ahead."

"I'm free." Chris nodded.

"Eleven?"

"That works."

"We're set for Saturday before lunch."

We talked about the world before this one until my washer buzzed. On the way back from moving the sheets, I leaned against my door and watched them for a moment. Pat doctored another cup of coffee, and Chris said something with friendly sarcasm. I liked seeing them this way, at ease and enjoying each other. It felt intensely familiar and very right. Chris turned to look at me. I was halfway across the room, ready to sit in his lap before I realized what I was doing and shook it off. After snagging another brownie, I curled up on the left side of the sofa.

"You both coming to Sabbath on Friday?" I asked when they got done talking about one of the English professors. They both let me know they'd be there. Pat mentioned Emily would be coming as well.

"Good."

"So, would you be willing to teach me how to ride your motorcycle?" Chris asked.

"Sure. Why do you want to know?"

"If I ever want to surprise you with dinner again, I won't have to look like a dork on the back of the bike with him."

Pat laughed at that. "Very good reason."

They were walking home when Pat remembered the conversation he had had with Chuck two weeks ago. "Do you want a hand with the whole trying-to-make-ghosts-solid thing?"

"Yes, I would."

"Good."

"I'm thinking of trying to get one of the ones in the psych department under our shields and then taking a whack at it there. If I can do that, Sarah'd like to join in, too."

"No."

"No?"

"I won't help you put her anywhere near danger. Neither will Chuck. I understand the advantage of working with her, and I know the risk is minimal, but if she gets hurt…"

Chris remembered the last time Pat had told him not to take a risk involving a woman. "Fine, just us then. You, me, and Chuck."

"Sounds good. Let me know when you want to move."

"Whenever the three of us have a free night with nothing going on in Lemmon Hall."

42.

February turned into March uneventfully. Though there were five separate nights where Chris, Pat, and Chuck were free, every single one had something happening at Lemmon. Chris spent hours fiddling with ideas for the spell, doing dry runs on it, but until they had a chance to really practice, it was all academic.

The highlight of that month was spending Sabbaths with Sarah, Pat, and Emily. Chris would go over to her place Friday afternoon, earlier and earlier each week, help her cook, listen to music, chat, get a shower and dress, and then wait for Pat and Emily to join them. They'd have dinner. Pat and Emily would wander off eventually, and he and Sarah would finish off the bottle of wine, sharing a glass and talking. He'd sleep on the sofa and join her for morning *Tanach*. She'd sit at the kitchen table, reading to him while he'd cook breakfast. It was a pattern that felt very much like home, leaving him deeply content and guilty at the same time.

On their third Sabbath they had been talking about Israel, Palestine, and the proportional use of force. She wasn't a fan of that doctrine. He had been talking about it as a moral choice when she said, "Mike once told me your pet spell was called 'Flesh Melt.'"

That brought him up short. If there had ever been a time when proportional use of force hadn't been in play... She looked at him expectantly. He wasn't really sure he wanted to tell her that story. "I try not to think about that very often."

"Oh. I don't want to dredge up bad memories." He knew she wouldn't ask again or say more about it, but the idea of the spell bothered her deeply. It should; it was a deeply disturbing spell. He decided to tell the story.

"You'll forgive me a dark topic on the Sabbath?" She nodded, and he continued, "Remember me saying a long life got you some interesting sins? This would be one of them— a very big one of them. When I became high priest a civil war broke out—you know that part of the story. My father-in-law was the previous high priest. By tradition the title should have gone to Dave or, because he vehemently rejected it, to his oldest male cousin. Allt, my father-in-law, didn't think much of Loeb, the cousin, so he named me as his heir. For ten years, I ruled in Allt's name. Everyone thought the succession was set. Then he died. His brother, Jresh, Loeb's father, split the clan and our planet over the succession. He didn't think I'd put up much of a fight. Obviously, he was wrong. My wife, Dave, and about a third of their clan followed me; the rest went with their uncle. The other clans lined up with whichever side seemed most beneficial to them.

"For the first forty years I fought a polite war. Casualties kept to a minimum. No torture. No pillaging. We hung our own soldiers publicly for theft and rape. I was always willing to grant a truce because, eventually, I'd have to rule these people.

Chris thought about pouring himself more wine, or something harder, and decided against it. If he was going to talk, it'd be better with a clear head. "Our main army, the one I was in control of, had been setting a trap against the combined army of our four biggest opponents. I had seventy thousand men directly under my control, and they had close to three hundred thousand. We had been slowly moving through the mountains. Weeks of skirmishes where we'd pull back again and again had gone by, but now we had the trap set. They were still in the mountains. We were on the plains below, and winter was coming. Dave and Pat had a secondary force, twenty-thousand men, moving behind their army, harassing them, destroying their supply chain. Chuck had a third force, three hundred thousand men, that made sure the rest of their army couldn't enter the mountains to reach them. My enemies were in the mountains, winter was coming, and they were getting hungry.

"My army was in front of them, on the plains. I had to keep sending my men against them, convince them we wanted that pass, keep them in the mountains. They had the high ground and were happy to use it to their advantage. Rule of war number one: If your opponent suddenly goes stupid, retreat as fast as you can. You've walked into a trap.

"We did it because the snow was coming. Pat kept telling me it'd be there soon, two or three days probably, no more than another week. Once it started to snow, he was going to use the mountains as a death trap. Two carefully placed avalanches would trap their men, and a third one would kill them all if they didn't concede. All I had to do was keep them in the mountains until a few days of snow made the mountain tops unstable and Pat could move.

"My wife sent word the Cluns wanted to lay down arms; she was going to their fortress to negotiate the treaty. Usually, when she went off, she took at least a few hundred Buis and Pat. He was much more her guard than mine those days. But the Buis were tied up, snaking through the mountains doing what they did best.

"Remember what I said about when your opponent suddenly goes stupid?" Sarah nodded.

"The Cluns sued for peace for no good reason. We weren't actively fighting them. We didn't even have troops near them. They were a tiny clan, eight hundred men at arms, and they were practically on the other side of the planet. She thought, and it had happened before, so it wasn't a silly conclusion, that they were looking to change sides so they could take advantage of being part of the winning side.

"She sent word that she was heading off. Because it would be good practice, Iyan, our daughter, went along, too. My daughter was a young woman, old enough to begin lerning the skills of a princess of the royal house. They didn't travel unguarded; she brought a hundred men with her. It just wasn't enough.

"Four days, one there, two to negotiate, one back. I didn't even notice they were late at first. We were still waiting for the fucking snow. Pat's telling me to keep strong; it'll come. I'm hating this because I'm feeding my men into a meat grinder. Every day we go into those mountains and fewer and fewer of us come back out. I have no idea what Chuck's up to; I hadn't heard from him in three days. He might be in a fight for his life or just strolling around out there.

"Finally, late on day four, Pat asks me how things went with the Cluns. He was nervous about the whole thing, told my wife to hold off until he and his men could be free. But by the time he and his men would be free, we'd need her to negotiate the surrender of the army we were trying to trap. So, against his advice, she went. When he asked me the fourth day, I realized I hadn't heard from her. She never went that long without letting me know what was happening.

"I try to contact her, nothing happens. Pat tries, nothing happens. I'm stuck; I don't have the men to send to go looking for her. She took most of the men at our fortress, and the rest need to stay there as security for our boys. Pat and Dave immediately send two hundred of their men to go hunting. They can do that without our enemies wondering what's going on, but they're also in the middle of the mountains. It'll take a few days before they can get to a portal and start looking in earnest. That was the fifth day.

"On day six, Chuck finally reports in. He had been fighting for his life, but the good news is that the other half of the enemy army has laid down arms. He's bringing his men to me, and he's a day out.

"I keep trying to convince myself it's nothing. She's busy. Negotiations have gone long before, and if Iyan was handling them, that could mean they were going longer. I want to spend every minute I can trying to find her, and if I couldn't find her by scrying, then get out there and start searching myself. But I can't. I'm running my men into that fucking mountain, and I have to go in there with them. If I leave, they won't keep attacking. They're getting slaughtered in there, and the only reason they're willing to do it is because I haven't let them down, yet. Too many more days of this and they may very well decide I've gone bonkers and take off anyway, so the one thing I can't do is leave.

"On day seven finally it starts to snow. Chuck and his men show up just before sunset. I still can't leave, but I can pull my men out of the grinder, give them a rest, let them heal up, and put his in. And Chuck can leave. He's not my first choice for going after my wife and Iyan, but he's what's available. I'm screaming at him to leave, and he's telling me he isn't going anywhere; I'm not fighting well and need to sleep. She's a big girl and can take care of both of them for another night, while I get some rest.

"He was probably right about not fighting well. I don't really know. I don't remember. Blood and screaming, worry and fear all blended with watching the skies for snow, waiting for Pat to strike. He was certainly wrong about my wife and daughter, but none of us knew that yet.

"He finally knocked me out. You don't feel particularly rested when he puts you to sleep, but it's better than nothing, which was the amount of sleep I had gotten in close to three days at that point.

Day eight I wake up ready to kill him, but he's not there. He'd already left to go after them. I went back into the mountains and killed the men unlucky enough to attract my attention. And thank the Presence, it's still snowing.

"Pat's telling me he needs one more day of snow. Then he'll set the trap. Dave's already moving their men out of the mountains. In a few days I'll have my army whole again.

"I get back to my tent that night and Chuck won't face me. He tells me they never made it to the meeting. The Cluns waited for three days at the portal before heading home and writing us an irate letter about being blown off.

"Chuck already knows that story is absolute shit, has contacted Dave, and put him in charge of finding them. There's no chance they went missing from one side of the portal to another, but I'm so exhausted I can't see it. I'm trying to think through what sort of magic can corrupt a portal and how to find them if they went missing in transit. Once again, he puts me to sleep. This time he leaves instructions that I'm not to be woken up. I slept through the avalanches. He took control of the ultimatum: surrender or die in the snow."

"They surrendered in a matter of hours. Pat melted a path out of the mountains for them, and Chuck set his diplomats to dealing with their men and their officers.

"We went back to the Palace. That was day nine. Still no word. Dave had returned. He found proof they made it to the meeting but not what had happened after. The Cluns had vanished, and they had lied about what had happened. It didn't take Chuck's skills to figure out at least part of what had happened.

"Day ten, nothing. Dave was off hunting the Cluns. They were the best link he had to what had happened. Chuck was doing everything in his power, which is quite a bit, to keep me from going insane, which I was pretty close to by that point. There was nothing to do. No one to kill." Not that he didn't try. On the tenth day he got into a massive fight with Pat, both of them half-mad with anger and guilt. He'd ended up with six broken ribs, a broken wrist, and a ruptured spleen. Chris didn't think she needed to know that part of the story, though. "Just hours and hours of guilt, recriminations, and waiting.

"Day eleven I needed to put on my fearless leader hat again and finish the terms of the surrender. I was sitting in a room with some nameless diplomat, occasionally nodding my head when he said something. Chuck was handling it. I just needed to be physically there. Pat broke into the meeting and motioned for me to join him.

"My wife was back. Alone..." For a long time Chris said nothing, reliving the feel of Althiira sitting in his lap, his face buried in her hair, turned white from rage and grief, her face against his shoulder as they both sobbed for their daughter. Sarah had never seen him so distraught.

"I'm sorry."

That seemed to jerk Chris back to the present. He tried to give her a reassuring smile, but it didn't quite come off right. "She was back, so we knew that the Cluns overwhelmed our men, killed them, taken Iyan..." He took a moment to collect himself and steady his voice.

"I'll never know exactly what happened to her, and handed my wife over to Loeb. He offered her a deal: she'd marry him, advise him, use her powers for his benefit, and our daughter would be kept safe. She wasn't much of an empath, but if she got close enough to a person, for a long enough time, she could read him. When she learned our daughter was dead, she killed Loeb, killed Jresh, killed her guards, and escaped. That was day five. It took her another six to get back to us.

"On day thirteen Dave found the Cluns. They had sold my women to Loeb. We snuck in. I killed them. Two days after that Dave got us into the fortress of his clan. They were scrambling to figure out what to do now Loeb was dead and she had escaped. Obviously they were in no position to sue for peace, and they had no claim on the throne, either. I killed them, too.

"The war ended less than a year later.

"Mike was... call it nineteen. I know he was already with our army at that time. It must have made an impression on him." His tone shifted, cold anger piercing the pain that had accompanied the rest of his tale. "I don't usually like pain for the sake of pain. Until that night, I'd never hurt anyone. I'd killed before, but it was always fast and clean. That night was about pain. They screamed for hours while I tortured them, and I screamed with them. They killed my daughter and raped my wife. If I could have found something more painful than melting the soft tissue off their bones, I would have used it.

"When it was done, when I was sane again, I knew I had tortured and murdered more than two thousand men."

She didn't say anything. Really there wasn't anything to say to a story like that. She gave his hand a gentle squeeze, which he returned. They sat there, quietly sharing the glass of wine; after a few more minutes, he wiped the tears from his eyes and pulled himself away from the story. Time to start thinking about a new topic. Something lighter. Something that wasn't going to make him cry. He remembered back in November she still didn't know if she was going to vote. That seemed like a safe topic.

"Who did you end up voting for? Or did you stay home?" She blinked, not expecting that shift.

"No. I voted. Thinking about what Chuck said about staying home being immoral made more sense than I liked. I voted for McCain and felt... dirty about it."

"He wasn't my first choice, either."

"It was like..." She paused, seeming to think about if she wanted to finish that sentence. "Like?"

"I realize the comparison may not mean much to you and is very immodest." She gave him a quick smile. Chris knew she was trying to pull him away from the darkness of his story.

He grinned and looked tantalized. "You absolutely have to tell me now. No way you say that and leave me wondering what you were thinking."

She smiled. "I think it'll mean more to Mike or Autumn but here goes. It was like having a guy you don't like come in your mouth. You choke and gag and end up swallowing something you don't want. At least, I think it's a good comparison. I don't know firsthand."

"You've never?" he asked, watching her mouth more intently than he wanted to. As topics to get his attention away from his life before went, this was a fine one.

"Not with someone I didn't like. It's a very different story when it's with someone you do like. I assume all sex is like that."

"So, you have had a guy—"

"Yes." She chuckled. "You know I'm not a virgin. I don't have Pat's record. I don't think Pat actually has Pat's record, but I've done most things at least once."

"Did you like it?"

She smiled and licked her lips. He knew she was doing it on purpose and enjoyed it too much to pull back from this line of conversation. "Yes. I like all of it. It's smooth and round and tactilely pleasant. It feels good in my mouth, and the slide against my lips is luscious. I wouldn't say I love the taste, but it's effecting and powerfully erotic. I love the sounds and the control. Knowing you're bringing another person that kind of pleasure is exquisite. I never got the girls who didn't want to do it or spit after. That just always seemed wrong. You don't want him getting up to brush his teeth right after. Why would you do it to him? How about you? Been there, done that?"

He grinned and leaned back against the sofa. "If it can be done with a woman without props, I've done it. If it can be done with a woman with props, I've probably done it. So, yes, been there, done that: tasted myself on her after and have always been very appreciative of her not getting up to brush her teeth right after. As the converse of your statement, it's soft and wet, and it smells and tastes so good it's hard to put it into words. Like swimming in sex." He loved the way she was watching him as he said that. "I've never gotten guys who didn't want to do it. It's everything we're designed to want, up close and in our face. What's it like when you do like the guy doing it?"

"Beyond nice?"

"As a counter to your first example."

"Ahhh…if you're paying attention, you know it's going to happen. If it's a guy who's worth doing it to, he hasn't grabbed your head and choked you. You pull back a little so it's not blocking your airway, and hold still while sucking for a few seconds. You use your hand as a buffer and let him thrust. No choking, no gagging. Once he's done, you swallow, milk him with your tongue, and swallow again. Maybe one day I'll trade war stories with Mike and Autumn and see how they handle it."

"I think that's a conversation I could safely miss."

"You only want to hear about the mechanics of a blow job when I'm talking about it?" She laughed.

"I don't really want to imagine either of the other two doing it."

She laughed again. "I think Mike and another guy would be very pretty to watch."

"You would. One naked guy is good, so two naked guys is better?"

"Something like that. But for Mike specifically, he's always very intense when he's doing something physical. I assume you don't watch him the same way I do when we fight, but he's remarkably present. There's not a single cell of his brain anywhere else. Watching him do something sexual with that kind of concentration would be immensely enjoyable."

"Very few of us are thinking about anything else when it comes to sex."

"You'd think that wouldn't you? I keep getting reports that's not actually true. Especially as guys get older and have more other things to think about."

"That's when you most need to shut everything else off and just focus on sex."

"This would be something you know from experience?"

"This would be something I know from experience. Lots of experience. If you let yourself, you can have an hour or two of vacation every day. That's much healthier than full-out, all-the-time work. You sleep better if you've got some down time. If you're sleeping, you think better, make better decisions, and the work gets easier."

"Better leadership through sex."

"Exactly."

"I wonder if that was what Bill Clinton was thinking."

He laughed. "I somehow doubt he got much past the 'I want sex' part of that train of thought."

"So, politics to blow jobs and back to politics. I really enjoy talking with you."

"And I you." He offered her the last sip of wine from their glass. She took it from his hand, drank, and put it on the coffee table. He checked the clock; it was late. "What's the reading for tomorrow?"

"More Exodus."

"Sounds good. You want the bathroom first?"

"Nah, go ahead." He stood up, grabbed his book bag, and did a quick job of getting ready for bed. When he left the bathroom she was lying on her bed, reading something in Hebrew. She put the book down, rolled onto her side, and wished him a good night as he walked out of her room. He closed the door to her room behind him and settled on her sofa.

This was always the hardest part of the night for him. The peace he had found after the first Sabbath had been fleeting. He hadn't been able to recapture it. His mind was too free at this time, too likely to wander into her room and start imagining things it shouldn't. He already had way too many images in his head he really should stay away from.

He scooted around, looking for a comfortable position. The sooner he was asleep the sooner he'd be safe again. He preferred to sleep on his back, but that didn't quite work on her sofa unless he wanted to wake up with his neck stiff or his feet asleep. So he curled onto his side, tucked his hands under his chin, and stopped himself from feeling if she was already asleep. He'd done that the week before, caught a hint of what she was doing, and it was not sleeping. That had been an especially difficult night. His hand had been on her door, ready to turn the knob, before he turned around and went back to the sofa.

He sighed. He knew he should stop doing this. As each week passed, being her friend became harder. He wanted her too much for his own comfort, but it hurt too much when he wasn't here to stay away. He knew he'd be back next week.

On their fourth Sabbath, Pat handed Emily the computer. "Pick your five favorite songs."

She held the computer. "This should be interesting. I love that one."

"Don't tell what I put on there. We'll see if we can guess who picked what based on the music."

"Sounds good." After several minutes, she handed the computer to Chris.

"Five?" he asked.

"Well, more if you have to," Pat said, "but with five each that should get us through dinner and then some."

"Okay." Chris held her computer. Five songs, most of them should just be songs he liked, but he had a chance to pick one for her. One to start off tonight's conversation. He found it quickly. As long as he got her to listen to the lyrics, it should slide by the other two. He found three others and realized he didn't have a handy number five. He thought for a minute and remembered the one he wanted.

Sarah came out of her room. He handed her the computer. "We're picking songs. Put your favorite five on the list. We'll listen and guess during dinner."

"Okay. Will you light the candles?"

"Sure." He lit all but the two on the table while she picked her songs. While putting the matches on the table next to her hand, he glanced at her list. "Spending most of your time on one letter, huh?"

"Hey, don't look."

"Don't worry; I don't know them by their names."

"Great." She gestured him aside. "Shoo." He sat down as she finished up her list.

She had made lamb, and they were tucking into it when Pat reached over and turned the music on. Sarah started to grin a few beats in, and Emily also looked pleased. Chris didn't have a clue as to what it was. Pat looked appalled.

"It's yours, right?" Sarah asked Emily.

"Yes."

"Taylor Swift? Really?" Pat sounded disgusted, but grinned to soften his tone.

"Really. I heard her talking about how dumb she thought Romeo and Juliet was. So she came up with a happier, saner version. It's cute, perky, and fun. I like fun music."

"I like this version better, too," Sarah said.

"You like country pop?" Pat stared at Sarah in disbelief.

"You've seen where I grew up. It's a miracle I don't have Keith Urban and Shania Twain posters plastered all over the place. Rock, dance music, and pop are all from the last four years." "Love Story" faded, and a few very familiar beats filled the room.

"Are you the Space Cowboy?" Sarah smiled at Pat.

"That would be me. Though I prefer Maurice."

"Care to tell us what a *pampatus* is?" Chris queried.

"Nope, trade secret." Pat and Sarah started singing along. Pat eyed Emily suggestively when the song got to the peaches line. Emily laughed. When "The Joker" ended it was replaced with music Chris knew he had heard Sarah play before but didn't know the name of.

"I know this one is yours," he said before the lyrics let the rest know it was a song about a soldier. "I'm surprised it's on your list."

"Why?"

"It's more anti-war than I'd think you are."

"Listen harder."

"I still don't know what it is," Emily added.

"Brendan James, 'Hero's Song.'"

"Still not seeing it as one of yours." Chris looked mildly perplexed.

"Been there, done that, felt it, lived it. The only difference is I get why they need to fall, and thank the Lord it didn't happen, but I was willing to die for that. The flood of hate is very real and something you just don't get here in the US. Walk in the middle of Compton in a KKK outfit; that'll give you an idea as to what it's like to wear an IDF uniform in Gaza."

"Were you there?" Emily asked.

"No. Once again, thank the Lord. I spent most of my time in Tel Aviv or the Negev. The city or the desert. Most of us have walked into a place where people didn't like us. You know that feeling. Well, in my case, one time that feeling was accompanied by a truck filled with TNT. I get shooting at me. I'm a legitimate target. I met Ari when a restaurant was blown up. The chef in the back, the kids in the booths, they weren't."

That pretty much killed the conversation for the rest of the song. Then the first beats of "Butterfly" sounded and broke the quiet.

"Did you add that after I looked?" Emily asked Pat.

"Not mine. Sarah?"

She turned to smile at Chris. He felt her satisfaction at his adding that song. "Yours?"

"Yes."

"This is one of yours?" Emily looked at Chris in shocked disbelief.

"Yes, this is one of mine. It's good for dancing. What kind of music do you expect me to have?"

"I don't know. The musical equivalent of the way you dress. Upright and conservative?"

He laughed. "Not too much of that."

"He's got a tattoo under that preppy clothing," Sarah told Emily.

"Really? What of?"

"I'm not showing it off."

"Celtic knot around here." Sarah touched his arm where the band was. Emily looked from Chris to Sarah and back again. Chris didn't need magic to see Emily wasn't buying the two of them weren't a couple.

"Cool? Do you have any?" she asked Sarah.

"Nope. I like the way they look but not having any is a religious thing. I've worn the henna ones on occasion, though."

"Where?" Chris liked the image of Sarah with tattoos.

"Both hands and the small of my back."

"What did you do that for?" Pat also looked like he enjoyed the image.

"I just felt like doing something pretty. A bunch of us went to the beach the summer after tenth grade. There was a place that did it. It seemed like fun. I've got a picture of it buried in my computer somewhere." A new song started. "Who picked Muse?"

Chris and Pat said, "I did," at the same time.

"'Starlight' is mine, too."

"I've got 'Uprising.'"

"This sounds more like you," Emily said to Chris.

"Just a different facet of my personality."

"Emo-fest: yeah, that sounds more like you," Pat snarked.

"I wasn't thinking Emo-fest, but you are an English major, and I usually see you with a poetry book. This fits better with that. More imagery, more meaning, deeper, less lust." Emily took another slice of challah.

"Lots of lust in poetry," Chris answered, trying to keep his eyes off of Sarah and doing a bad job of it.

"Not the ones I see you carrying around."

"That's because the English department has deplorably bad taste on the subject. What I read for pleasure is less... constrained."

"What are you reading for pleasure these days?" Emily wanted to know.

Chris grinned, "I'm brushing up on my Old Testament. Song of Songs." Sarah rose an eyebrow at him, and he nodded back at her.

"The Old Testament is less 'constrained?'" Emily didn't sound like she bought it.

"That part is," Sarah answered. "'Come, my beloved, let us go forth into the fields, and lodge in the villages; let us go out early to the vineyards, and see whether the vines have budded, whether the grape blossoms have opened and the pomegranates are in bloom. There I will give you my love.' It's also one of the earliest examples of female sexuality in literature."

"I'll have to give it a read at some point," Emily replied. "Starlight" faded, and another song started.

Pat listened to the first few beats. "Let's see, it's a twee Emo-fest from the nineties. Must be Chris."

"Says the guy who can identify a twee Emo-fest from the nineties on the third word of the song."

"You are such a girl," Pat fired back with a smirk.

"Is this thing even on shuffle? That's three of mine in alphabetical order in a row."

"It's on shuffle. You're just lucky," Emily said.

Sarah was listening carefully. "You've played them for me before—a lot, actually. But I don't remember this one's name."

"It's Belle and Sebastian, and yes, I do listen to them a lot. I'm especially fond of this one; it's called 'The State I Am In.'" The song wound through its lyrics and finally got to the words he was waiting for. He focused on Sarah, singing them in her head.

"Oh, love of mine, would you condescend to help me..."

She had been mid-chew listening to Pat and Emily talk about what counted as twee. As soon as she felt his voice in her mind, she stopped and turned to him. He could feel her surprise, not only at his voice in her mind but at the content of his words. Her foot pressed against his under the table. A quick affectionate touch, a promise to talk more later.

"If the next one is mine, I'm going to start thinking you've fooled with the computer," he said to Pat. The Rolling Stones started to sing. "No, it's not." He listened for a few more beats. "Loud, thumping beat, random violence, and massive waves of testosterone. Must be Pat."

"'Sympathy for the Devil.' He needs it. This is my all-time favorite driving-fast song."

"You have driving-fast songs?" Emily questioned him.

"Yes. You can't really drive in Manhattan. But I like to drive. Every now and again, I'd make up a playlist of loud, thumping, testosterone-drenched music, take the car, and head upstate. Lots of room to go crazy with speed out there."

He and Emily talked about driving for pleasure for a while. Two more of her songs and one of Pat's whizzed by.

Then he heard a quiet guitar accompany a female voice. Chris knew Sarah wanted him to listen closely to this one. She wasn't able to sing in his mind. He had the feeling she was trying but couldn't figure it out. He touched her foot to let her know he got the message.

"This one's very pretty. Yours, Sarah?" Emily asked.

"Yep."

"What is it?" Pat listened more intently than Chris would have liked. So much for song lyrics slipping by the other two.

"'Okay,' by Kaiser-Cartel."

"Short little thing." Pat poured another glass of wine and offered the bottle to the rest of them.

"Yep, is says what it needs to and wraps. This next one is mine, too."

"I wouldn't have figured you for The Killers," Emily said.

"I had a hard time picking between 'Human' and 'Mr. Brightsides,' but I think I like 'Human' better. It's more me. Either of these two can tell you about how cold my hands get."

"Seriously, this is the only person on Earth whose hands are naturally below the room temperature." Pat smiled.

"How do you know?" Emily asked, one eyebrow high.

"Between sparring and the occasional back rub, he's felt my hands."

"Until she warms up, she's got two weapons: the force of her fist and the fear those icy little things will touch you." Pat mimicked dodging a punch.

"That's right, you all fight on Wednesdays."

"Yep. Do you want to come and watch? Maybe join in?" Sarah invited her.

"There's something I'd like to see. You and Sarah, hand to hand. Oh yes…" Pat grinned widely.

Emily stuck her tongue out at him. "Probably not. I don't want to see him get beat up," she gestured to Pat, "and I know I don't want to fight."

"It's a good skill to have and more fun than jogging," Sarah said to her.

"I'll stick with yoga for my workouts."

"Okay." Sarah stood up and began clearing plates. Emily joined her, and the two of them got dinner out of the way. Sarah put Chris in charge of getting dessert out. Pat made coffee for the other three. The noise of the coffee maker drowned out half of one song. Chris went to the computer and started it from the beginning again.

After the first line Emily looked up, shocked. "Did I actually just hear that?"

Chris smiled at her. "This would be what I mean by my own tastes are less constrained. It's called 'New Art for the People' and my current favorite."

"'But for the cum in your hair…' Yeah, that's a tad less constrained. Is that all of yours?"

"I've got one more kicking around in there."

Dessert wrapped up. It was becoming more and more obvious Pat and Emily were looking for a polite exit. As soon as the food was done and the kitchen tidy, they made their excuses and left.

Once they were out the door, Chris sat down on her sofa. He knew she would sit sideways resting against the back of the left side of the sofa. He settled himself in the middle cushion, facing the left side. Sarah poured a glass of wine. She handed him the glass and sat down. He took a sip and handed the glass back to her.

Her finger circled the rim of the glass. "So, love of mine, what do you want help with?"

His eyes slid shut as he savored those words in her voice. After a moment, he opened his eyes and looked at her again. She leaned against the sofa, her hand inches from his. "Enjoying this. Not feeling ripped in two when I look at you."

"I can't do that for you. I can't make you forgive yourself."

"Can you forgive me for not being a better man to you?"

"There's nothing to forgive."

"Yes, there is. I'm not yours, can't be yours—not now at least, but I can't stop acting like I am. As Pat will remind me tomorrow, possibly with his fists, that's not kind."

She walked over to her computer, brought it to the coffee table, and turned on "Okay" again. "Listen."

She took the glass from him and kept her eyes on his while the song played again. When it wrapped she said, "I'll take what you can give me. If that means this chaste romance, then that's what it is."

"Chaste romance. I guess that's a way to put it. Though I'd prefer something less chaste."

She shook her head. "That's a bad bargain. All or nothing, Chris. I... want you too much to just fool around. If you won't sleep with me, don't kiss me." He thought about it as her computer moved through a few songs. She was right. He didn't want to fool around either, and he was fairly sure he couldn't handle the tension of just making out with her.

She took another sip from the glass and one more. He had the feeling she was working up to asking something that made her uncomfortable. Finally, Sarah asked, "Why are you here? She's the love of your life. I can feel how much she means to you. I think I know how you feel about me, and if this isn't adultery, it's certainly infidelity."

He looked at her very intensely and stopped his hand from stroking hers. "I'm here because it hurts too much to not be here. That's why I feel ripped in two. This isn't me living up to the words of my vows or, for that matter, the intent."

"And her?" He realized how much she didn't want to ask that question. Sarah's pride made it difficult to allow herself to wonder, let alone ask, about his wife.

"Her." He took the glass from Sarah and drank more of it, half looking for words, half working up the courage to say what he felt. "We lived together for more than one hundred years, had five children, and mourned one of them. She fought my war and advised me. She saved my life: held my body in her hands and put it back together when I was so far gone the greatest healers of our clan were getting my tomb ready. She loved me more than I had any right to be loved. When she left it was because she couldn't love me more than what was right. It's been twenty-two years, and she is sliding further and further into memory. I come here, I laugh with you, talk with you, study with you, and I enjoy you. I want you. It tears at me because I should be honoring her. She and our children deserve better than me."

Sarah thought for a moment and then asked, "When you find the portal, is there any way for you to go back?"

This turn in the conversation made him feel sick. He didn't want to lie to her. He didn't want to tell her the truth even more. "No. It's a one-way trip. That's why we haven't seen Mildred yet. It won't come out until the end because once it's out it can't get back."

"I thought you said anything was possible with magic."

"It might be, but I don't know how to do it, and I don't know anyone else who knows how to do it."

"How did Autumn get you here in the first place?" He realized she was trying to find a way for him to get back; it made him ache with guilt.

"She opened a door. She doesn't have the power to do it now. If she can find an existing door, she can go through, but she can't make one from scratch here. We tried when we first got here. It didn't work." They had 'tried' for Mike's benefit. Going back and taking the fight to Mildred had been one of his first suggestions. Chris honestly didn't know if Autumn couldn't do it anymore or, knowing opening the door was a ridiculously bad idea, didn't do it.

"There is absolutely no hope of you ever seeing her again?"

"No." He hoped that answer would shut down this line of conversation.

"If she had died, would you have remarried?"

"No." He felt her mood crash. "I couldn't have legally remarried. It's the easiest way to protect your heirs. No stepchildren to fight over the inheritance. No one would have blinked if I had taken a lover or a concubine. Would I have? If you had asked me this time last year, I would have said, 'No.'" He took another drink. His pinky brushed her hand when he returned the glass to her. "You said you'll take what I can give. Can you share me with a ghost?"

Sarah brushed his face gently with her fingers. It felt like a kiss on the forehead, a gesture of acceptance and understanding. "When she's a ghost, when she's the love of your youth, when she's dead and mourned and you are at peace with it, yes, I'll share you."

"Fair enough. Can I stay here tonight? I'll make us breakfast in the morning."

"You can always stay over, especially if you're offering to make me breakfast."

"Good. What's the reading for this week?"

At lunch Pat had asked him to spar. Chris wasn't surprised. The lack of Sarah and Mike was also not shocking.

"So, out of curiosity, do you think I'm deaf in addition to stupid?" Pat asked between punches.

"I do not think you are stupid or deaf." Chris blocked Pat's kick.

"Then you've gotten to the point where you no longer give a damn about making love-sick noises at her in front of me?"

Chris landed a punch to Pat's torso. "Yes."

"Six." Chris blocked that punch. "More." That one made it through his defenses and snapped his head back. "Weeks." The kick caught Chris in the knee and knocked him to the floor.

Pat knelt on the floor next to him. "Come May you can go home. What the fuck are you doing?"

Chris looked at Pat with an expression that gave him chills. "Don't kid yourself. There's no 'back home' for me. The first thing Mildred does when it comes through is kills me. And, if I'm very, very lucky, it does it quickly."

"Mildred didn't manage to do it before," Pat said, trying to backtrack away from whatever new well of emotional crud he had managed to tap on Chris.

"It's a lot more pissed off this time," Chris sat up.

"This is your plan? Go off in a blaze of glory wrapped in the love of a good woman?"

"No, nothing like that. Starting something up now would be cruel. I'm just not interested in keeping myself so tightly bound. As you said, I don't give a damn anymore."

"You'll hurt her."

"No way to avoid that now. She likes me too much for me to get killed and have it not hurt."

This was really not the conversation Pat wanted to have with Chris. Using guilt to get Chris to back off from Sarah was what he had been hoping for. "There's nothing like expecting to end up dead to make sure it happens."

"You've seen it. You've felt it. You've fought it. What are my chances?"

Pat felt a quick stab of desire to sugar coat it. Chris without any hope was scaring him. At the same time, Chris with a better-than-realistic picture of the danger in store was likely to make bad tactical decisions. Honest assessment won out. "Worse than the rest of us. But you aren't dead yet; no need to give up hope. You've survived what, four things that should have killed you?"

"Sounds about right."

"Then stop being a twit and bet on snake eyes again. By the way, thinking love songs at her is starting something up."

"You think she doesn't know?"

"I know she knows. Emily knows. Autumn knows. Harold has a pool running on when you two finally get together, which Josh thought he won after the dance. As a heads up: Chuck has next week scoped out. This is the worst-kept secret of all time. Still, if you don't want to hurt her worse than just losing a friend, back the hell off. Not sleeping with her won't do it. Friends don't do what you did last night."

"How would you know?"

"Because I have the good sense not to do it! Since that's true, it's pretty damn certain it's not something a friend does. There's no straight guy on Earth who has a closer friendship with a woman than I do with her. You two are not friends. You're lovers who haven't slept together. If you don't want her to feel like your lover when you go off to die, stop acting like hers." Pat stood up, and Chris followed.

"She sent one back to me."

Pat's voice and manner went hard. "I know. I felt it. I heard it. I am doing everything in my power not to beat the shit out of you because somehow you're winning this one, too."

Chris extended his arms to his sides. "I'll give you a free shot."

"If I hit you as hard as I want to, I'll stop your heart. That would piss her off."

"Might just possibly piss me off, too."

Pat was relieved to see Chris was not interested in dying right this minute. "You'd be too dead to care. You know, if you are going to go off and die, I might have to spend some time on the other side consoling your widow. If I plan this properly, I can do it for both of them."

Chris answered him seriously, "There's no one I'd prefer do that."

"You really don't give a damn anymore?" Pat's horrified look caught Chris' attention.

"It's remarkably freeing." He smiled grimly at Pat. "I'm not that far gone. I'm almost certain I'm not going to make it, and I'm beginning to wish I would. Six more weeks. Hell, if I can make it through, I will really fight you for her. And I'll enjoy beating you. Then we'll find someone who loves you the way you should be loved, and I'll dance at your wedding."

"Great." Pat rolled his eyes, a wedding that involved Chris dancing with Sarah wasn't precisely on his list of favorite images. "I suppose it's better than being Gurney Halleck."

"Gurney got Jessica in the end."

"Well, my Duke, try not to let the Harkonnens kill you. I don't want her over your dead body."

"You really are a good man."

"I'm Mr. Fantastic. I need a spandex costume with a big fucking F on the front of it. It doesn't seem to be doing me much good, though. Does it? Maybe if I spend the next six months being haunted and tortured she'd love me?"

"If you think it'll work, you're welcome to try. But six weeks from now, assuming you haven't put me in the ground, I'll fight you tooth and nail for her. If tortured and haunted is what she wants, I can do that better than anyone on Earth."

43.

My cell phone buzzed. 911 South Corner V4.

"This is an emergency. I've got to go." My lab partners were under the impression I was an EMT. I had done nothing to disabuse them of that notion.

I ran out of there as fast as I could go. A quick stop at my place for my bag and bike had me set to deal with whatever was coming. V4 was four miles away. I gunned the bike; I could be there in three minutes if the lights were right. The lights were right.

I felt the fear long before I could see them. Screams pierced through the engine noise of my bike. It was Chuck. My own fear made my skin feel electric. Flames glowed and flickered through the leafless trees. Another hundred feet and I could smell it: smoke and burnt flesh.

I didn't want to keep going. I wanted to turn around, run home, and hide. Chuck was screaming. Chuck sat in my house, his soul ripped to shreds, barely blinking. Chuck walked thirty miles a week on a badly healed ankle and never mentioned it. Whatever was in front of me was going to be horrible.

Keep going. You're the healer. You need to be there when things get bad. Through the trees, and…

"Fuck." The trees were on fire. The ground was scorched. *Look at him!* Chuck's face was gone. An eyeless, charred, pulpy mess screamed into the night. I had my phone out and was dialing before I even knew I was doing it.

"Hello?" Morrell's voice on the other end.

"I'm in the forest behind Tenth and Sutton. I need help."

"Ten minutes."

I forced my feet to take me forward. I'd be seeing this in my nightmares for the rest of my life. Images of blackened skull, wet sticky ooze from charred, cracked flesh, and shiny yellowish goo where his eyes should have been carved their way into my long-term memory. I sat next to Chuck. The hot dull glow of his pendants scorched into his skin pulled my eyes away from where his face used to be.

"I'm here, Chuck. More help is coming." I don't know if he heard me; the screaming didn't stop. I numbly got some of the magic hooch. I didn't have much hope it would help, but it couldn't hurt. His screams stopped while he swallowed. I poured more, and he swallowed again. His screams faded to mewling whimpers.

Examination. His face, neck, shoulder, and right arm: all burned. To make matters worse, nothing here was life threatening, not with my skill at killing off infections. He'd survive this. He'd be a blind monster, but he'd survive. Whether he'd want to was a different story.

Look more closely. I forced myself to analyze the damage. His eyes were gone, cooked empty sockets. His lips were gone, blackened cracked teeth with a swollen blistered tongue behind them. His nose, melted cartilage. His right ear, gone, left ear, a melted nub. His jacket and sweater must have been some sort of polyblend; the parts that hadn't full-out burned were melted into the edges of his wounds.

I didn't know where to even begin. *Pain. Begin with pain.* I lay my hands on his left arm and worked on killing the pain. His magic hit mine. I stifled an agonized scream. My head was going to explode. He attacked me on automatic. Where was Chris? If anyone could stop this it was him.

Quick glance around. Chris was twenty feet away on his back. Autumn hovered over him, doing something. Smoke rose from his clothing. He didn't make any noise. Mike stood next to me.

"Which one is worse?"

"Chuck."

"Can you shield me?"

"I can try."

"Do it. Now."

I felt the cold wash over me. I put my hands on Chuck and went back to easing his pain. Mike's shields helped. I felt less pain and could concentrate better.

Chuck went silent and relaxed. Either I'd killed his pain or he passed out. *What next? Pray.* That came next. *Please, Lord, lead my hands. Show me the way because I am lost. Please.* Then I knew what came next. I grabbed my boot knife and cut off his coat and shirt. Next came peeling off the melted plastic and the charred skin under it. I tried not to think of the small pile of blackened mess that used to be living man growing next to me as I kept cutting off the damaged tissue. Several minutes later I had the plastic and last remnants of charred skin off of him.

I stood up, walked a few steps away, and threw up, welcoming the sour burn of vomit because it muted the sweet smell of charred flesh. That done I went back, sat on his right side, and found the edge of the healthy tissue. I lay my hand on it and began to do something. I still don't know precisely what, but his skin began to reform around the edges. Fresh, pink, healthy skin very slowly crept back up his arm, one new cell at a time. At some point Morrell and a beautiful woman with long white hair knelt by me. I could feel them adding their magic to mine. The healthy cells continued to creep in from the edges a little faster.

Later. The fires were out. Autumn was next to us now, lending her energy as well. Chris was letting me use his magic to heal Chuck.

Eventually the sky grew light. Eventually Chuck's face was back, lips in place, ears where they should have been. His hair was gone, no telling when or if it would come back. We were done. Nothing more any of us could do now. Time to go home.

I collapsed back on the ground and lay there for a few minutes, unsure if I had the strength to ride my bike.

Chuck's voice got me off the ground. On the surface it was calm, but under his calm lay a deep well of fear. "I can't see."

I sat up and looked at him. His eyes looked like two soft boiled eggs, all white and barely set.

Mrs. Morrell answered him, "You're all right. It'll take a while for everything to heal up. Two hours ago you didn't have eyes period. Now you have to wait for them to start working. The cells have to remember what they do and get back to it."

He turned to the sound of her voice. "I don't know your voice."

"We've never met. I'm Claire Morrell. Sarah called Eric and me in when she saw how bad you were."

"I thought you were healing me," he said in my direction.

"I was."

"She's the one who figured out how to do it; the rest of us added to her energy," Claire added. "You're lucky. I've never seen a healer who could do what she did. When I first saw you, I thought she had called us in to end it easily for you." I looked at her in shock. She smiled gently and nodded. "It never even crossed her mind."

"What happened to Chris?"

"I'm here. I'm fine now. Eric?" He looked at Professor Morrell, who nodded at him. "Got my arm back in its socket and took care of my burns."

Eric stood up. "Let's get you home."

"I can't go home like this. My sister doesn't know about any of this."

"My house then. I'll lead the way." I dragged myself to my bike and got on.

"You're kidding me, right?" Mike put his hand on my bike. "You try to ride now and we'll be taking you to the hospital. Scoot back." He hopped on and kicked the bike into gear.

Somehow everyone was in my living room. Chuck sat on the couch, Chris next to him, holding his hand, making sure he wasn't alone in the dark. Autumn was trying to hide in plain sight and doing a terrible job of it. She was just about as noticeable as Dave was when he wanted people to see him. Morrell was in my kitchen making food. I rested on the floor and let the world spin around me.

"What happened?" Claire asked.

"Autumn finally remembered how to make a fireball," Mike said with a look that should have cut Autumn.

"It was ripping his arm off," she answered quietly.

An image formed in my mind. I had the feeling I was seeing Chris' memory, but the point of view was off. Something, like the Minion we had faced last time, but larger, angrier, meaner looking, a gleaming sword with a blade of solid electricity in one hand, had a hold of Chris. Autumn was right, it was trying to rip his arm off. It had his arm twisted behind him and was pulling straight up. Chuck ran toward him, right arm out, casting something. Then the world exploded. The Minion was on fire. Chris was smoldering. Chuck looked like someone had poured napalm over his head and arm. The Minion vanished. Autumn got Chuck put out, but it was too late. Mike looked around to see if anything else needed to be fought, then texted me.

Morrell handed us each a plate of eggs and toast. As we ate, he silently cleaned up. He gestured to his wife; they left us.

"I'll see you tomorrow?" he asked me from my door. I knew there was more he wanted to say to me but not in front of the others.

"Yes."

I collapsed in my usual chair. Morrell stood up and closed the door.

"You're still exhausted?"

"Yes."

"Here." He put his hand on my shoulder and gave me a boost before sitting in the chair next to mine instead of his usual one behind his desk. I sighed, closed my eyes, and enjoyed feeling just bone deep weariness for a moment.

My eyes were still closed when he asked, "The blonde one... is she your friend?"

"More like an associate. We're friendly but not close."

"She's the reason your friend got hurt?"

"Apparently. I was working in the lab, running gels with my partners when I got the 911 text."

"How did she end up with your group?"

"Why?"

He leaned toward me, looking concerned. "Just tell me, please."

"I don't know the whole story. She's an old acquaintance of the others. They go way, way back. When they got tangled in this mess, she joined them, helped them, and then got them here when it looked like they'd be killed where they were before."

"Do you know what she is?"

"Yes. Why?"

"Her kind don't belong here."

"Once this is done, she intends to go home."

"Good."

I leaned back in the chair. "How do you know what she is?"

"Claire's older than I am. A lot older than I am. She knows they're trouble. Nothing good ever comes from working with fairies. And that particular fairy..."

"Wait, she knows Autumn?" I sat back up.

"Not by that name, not in this body. Her name was Illyn the last time Claire saw her. Illyn's idea of fun didn't fit with Claire's. *La Dame Belle Sans Merci*: it's based on a story about her. She can stay until all this is done, but if she's here more than a week after, Claire will make sure she leaves."

"What is Claire?"

Morrell smiled at me. "She's human. Just a very, very old one. Illyn recognized her— that's why she was trying to hide and unnerved enough to be doing a bad job of it. I imagine seeing a three-thousand-year-old human would be unnerving, especially to a fairy."

My mind jumped quickly. If she was a human who had kept herself alive that long, what other tricks did she have? "Did I heal Chuck?"

"Yes, that was you. We just added to your power, kept you going when you should have collapsed with the job half done. Claire wasn't kidding. When we first saw Chuck, we were sure she was going to have to help him on."

"The wound wasn't mortal."

"That's why he would have needed help. No one wants to live like that. One of her less-fun jobs: coming at the liminal times to push them one way or another."

"Great." I thought for a moment. Clair looked no older than early thirties, besides the white hair. Morrell looked barely five years older than I am. "How old are you?"

"Seventy-three." He laughed dryly. "It's been a long time since anyone asked me that."

"You know, once upon a time, I would never have even thought to ask."

"Your friends are human?" He sounded like he meant it to be a statement, but it came out a question anyway.

"Their bodies are. They tell me names have power, so I don't know what they were before they were here. Your wife doesn't recognize them, does she?"

"No. She's never seen them before. Illyn is old, very old. The fey didn't leave here without a fight. Claire fought on the one side. Illyn was on the other."

"Claire fought alongside the Catholics? I didn't think they were big on magic-using women warriors."

"I doubt they knew she was on their side. Her kind tried to avoid the priests."

"What is she?"

"A witch. A good, old fashioned, proper Celtic witch. What the Wiccans want to be. I was working on a paper on Britain under the Romans back in the early sixties. She was a source for some of the best research on early Celtic Pagan religion. We met. Hit it off. Later I found out the reason she knew so much is because she was there the first time."

"Wow."

"Yes." For the next hour I sat quietly, resting mostly, asking questions when warranted, while Morrell told me about his days as a young grad student in Oxford. He really should write a novel about how he went from being a staunch Presbyterian to a Pagan, discovered his magic, and won himself a wife.

When I got home, Chuck was on my sofa staring hard in the general direction of the windows.

"Is it sunny out?"

"Nope, about ten minutes away from rain if I had to guess."

"Damn. I was hoping I was starting to see brightness over there."

"It's darker out there than it is in here. Chris left the lights on for you."

"That wasn't particularly useful."

"I'd imagine not turning the lights off in a room with someone in it is deeply ingrained polite behavior for him."

"Probably."

I sat on the sofa next to him. "Face me." He did. I looked at his eyes carefully. "I think you're starting to grow lenses. Your eyes aren't perfectly round or white anymore. Where your pupils go is starting to edge toward gray."

"Great," he said flatly, pointing his face back to the window again.

"Your enthusiasm and gratitude are overwhelming."

"Can't feel it over my anger at Autumn."

"Fine. I'm going to get a nap. I need rest if I'm going to kill this headache I've had since healing a good quarter of your skin, both eyes, both ears, your nose, your lips, and half a tongue. Then I can work on getting your eyes functional again."

In retrospect I was glad he couldn't see me stomp out of the room in a pissy huff. I'm sure he heard the door close. I didn't exactly slam it, but it wasn't quiet, either. I knew being annoyed at the scared, wounded man on my sofa wasn't the right way to deal with it. If anyone had good reason to be snippy, he did. Of course, if anyone had good reason to be snippy, I did, too.

I fell asleep much faster than I thought I would. My dream took me to a fierce argument with a dark blue man with coppery hair. We were both seconds away from screaming at each other when a second blue man entered and calmed us down.

When I woke, I really wished I knew what everyone was saying in those dreams. I know I dream in other languages, but usually I know what's being said, even if it's not English or Hebrew. It's insane to sit there, look through this woman's eyes, watch her go about her life, and never know what's being said.

The smell of food and sound of two voices talking got me out of bed. Chuck sat at my kitchen table. Chris was at the stove making… "Hamburgers?" I asked from the doorway.

"Yes. I thought something easy to eat with your hands would be a good plan."

"Okay."

"Do you mind if I put cheese on mine and Chuck's?"

"Nope. Just don't let it touch mine and clean the pan carefully."

"Easy enough. How well-done do you want yours?"

"Medium." He plated up Chuck's burger and put Chuck's hands on the food so he could find it easily on the plate. A minute later he plated his and then mine. Food took the edge off the headache and helped with the tiredness.

"Is your head still hurting?" Chuck asked.

"Yes. It feels like you drove two ice picks through my temples, and I haven't been able to remove them."

"Sorry about that."

"You didn't do it on purpose. It's just frustrating. You might have functional eyes now if I didn't have shut down half my brain to work through the pain."

Chuck looked deeply annoyed, then resigned. He reached under his shirt and showed me a pendant made of copper wire twisted around a smooth, oblong, dark green stone. I was surprised to see it around his neck again. Last time I saw it, I was using the tip of my knife to flick the glowing hot pendant and scorching chain off of him. "If it happens again, take this one off. Better yet, loop it around your wrist and mine, especially if you're working on me under fire."

"I'll keep that in mind."

He put his pendant back under his shirt. I could tell he didn't want me to spend any real time learning what it did or how.

"After dinner, I'll work on your eyes some more. Pat will probably join us. Then I absolutely need to get my Diff Eq problem set and taxes done."

"Sounds fun," Chris said.

Even though fun wasn't the word I'd use to describe it, once I got into the problems my headache faded a little. Not totally gone, not even close, but I could go a good minute or two without really noticing it. Unfortunately, my taxes did not have that effect. I put numbers in the blanks Turbo Tax told me to and shuffled through the small mound of papers that went with my finances. An hour later I finished filling out the forms and hit the send button with a little triumphant cheer.

"And I am done!"

The other three congratulated me. I checked the clock. It was nine thirty, and I was ready to sleep. Pat decided to head off when I went to bed, leaving me home with Chris and Chuck.

When I got to bed, I wanted to strip off my clothing and slide between my nice soft new sheets. Chris and Pat had chosen well. Those sheets felt extremely good against bare skin. But Chuck was staying over, which meant Chris was staying over, too. If Chuck couldn't tell I was sleeping naked should he have to head to the bathroom at some point, Chris had nothing wrong with his eyes. So, instead of happy naked skin, I was once more pulling on a pair of yoga pants and a long sleeved t-shirt.

I headed back out. "Are both of you staying over?"

"Yes," Chris answered.

"Do you want my bed then? I fit better on the sofa than either of you, and there's enough room for both of you on my bed."

"Thank you," Chuck said to me. "It would be nice to stretch out a bit more than I can on your sofa."

"I'm not sharing a bed with you. By 'a bit' he means take up the entire mattress and boot me off in the middle of the night."

"I haven't done that since we were kids."

"We haven't slept in the same bed since we were kids, and none of your girlfriends have reported you getting better over the years."

The window seat cushion was four and a half feet wide. I moved the coffee table to the side of the room. Then I snagged the cushion and a few of the pillows off of it and made up a bed on the floor. I looked over at Chris. "Do you want the softer and shorter sofa or cushions on the floor where you can sprawl out?"

"I'll take the floor. My neck feels odd after sleeping on your sofa."

"Common side effect of sticking a six-foot, one-inch man on a six foot wide sofa."

Chris got Chuck up and led him into my room. They did whatever pre-bed routine they did. I settled on the sofa, let my eyes slide shut, said my prayers, and began to put the day behind me. Eventually Chris came out and settled down on the floor in front of me.

I didn't open my eyes. "Bring some pajamas tomorrow. At the rate you sleep here, you might as well have some here, too. I don't like sleeping in jeans. I can't imagine you do, either."

"I took them off." I opened my eyes and rolled to my side to look at him. He lay on the floor, hands behind his head, covered in my blanket. Unfortunately, he still had his button down on. He rolled to his side and propped himself on his elbow. "I didn't think you'd mind."

"I don't mind." I smiled. "Kind of annoyed I had my eyes closed when you walked by, but I do not mind."

He smirked happily at me and rolled onto his back. "'Night."

"Goodnight, Chris."

The dirty gray light of pre-dawn rain pried me away from sleep. I looked at the pouring rain, the sleeping man on the floor in front of me, and decided I didn't want to go anywhere. I'd be sparring with the guys tonight anyway, no need to jog. I closed my eyes, scooted around to get comfy, and thankfully fell back to sleep.

The downside of not getting up for a jog was waking up with a jolt at eight thirty, half an hour late for my Diff Eq class. My less-than-silent string of curses woke Chris up.

"What?" he asked blearily, blinking at me.

"I just missed a class, which means I can't turn in the homework, so there's a zero for the day."

"Sorry."

My head began to ache again because what was the promise of a new day without ice picks in the skull? I headed for the shower grumbling and once in there, wet and naked, I realized I didn't have any towels in the bathroom. *Lovely.*

Poking my head out of the door, I saw, much to my relief, Chuck was no longer in my bed and the door to my room was shut. The towel was in its usual drying spot, draped over the chair at the desk I almost never use. I dried off and dressed quickly. When I came out, Chris handed me a spatula, told me to keep an eye on the eggs, and headed for the bathroom. He was back a minute later, taking the spatula back from me. Chuck was looking much improved from last night. In addition to the start of some hair, he had the beginning of all the major parts of his eyes.

"Can you see?"

"Better than yesterday. Everything is a milky blur."

"You've got cloudy lenses now and irises. They aren't the same color they were before—much darker now—but maybe by tomorrow we can send you back to your sister."

"I'd like that. My head itches this morning."

"It should. Your hair is growing back."

He touched his scalp. "I didn't realize it was gone."

"And your eyebrows, and eyelashes, and all the hair on your right arm. All of the freckles on your right arm are gone, too."

"Great."

"At least you've got plenty of time to come up with a good lie."

"Nah, I can make sure no one sees the difference." Chris put plates of eggs and toast in front of each of us. I spread jam on mine; Chris did theirs up with butter. Chuck ate quickly and got to my bathroom without any problems.

"I could get used to having you cook for me."

"Show me how to make your biscuits, and one of these days I'll do them for you."

"I'll do that. Will you stay tonight as well?"

"I'll be here as long as he is."

"At least one more night. I'll show you how I make them tomorrow."

Thursday morning, while I was introducing Chris to the fine art of sourdough biscuits, Chuck came in grinning. "It's still blurry, but I can see you." He walked over to me, wrapped me in a hug, and then, much to my surprise, dipped me back into a very long and tingly kiss. "Thank you," he said after he let me go.

I blinked in surprise. "You're welcome. Sit down; let me look at your eyes." He sat down, still grinning, while I looked him over.

"They're baby blue. I guess it'll take a while for the pigments to come in. How close can you focus?"

"About two feet."

"Baby range as well."

"Sounds wonderful. Stop scowling at me, Chris."

"Can you see that?"

"No. I can feel it. He's saying some very rude things in my head right now about not just grabbing you."

"I make allowances for moments of extreme rejoicing. You're not a bad kisser, either."

"Lots of practice." He winked at me. I was floored to see him so playful. "Come on, Chris, you can say it in front of her. No need to yell in my head."

"You're in a really goofy mood today."

"I'm happy. I didn't think I'd get my sight back, and that would have fucked everything. I need my eyes to work. I need them to support my sister. Now the biggest thing on my plate is making sure no one notices I look odd."

"I can see how that's a relief. Stop kneading, Chris! They'll get tough. You two want to talk. I want a shower. Can you be trusted to roll those out and let them rise?"

Chris nodded without breaking the glare he had aimed at Chuck. "How thick?"

"Half an inch, thereabouts."

I got my shower, pleased I'd be able to lie back in my own bed, stretch out, and enjoy the feel of those ridiculously soft sheets against my own skin tonight. It looked like it might be the start of a good day.

44.

Or not.

The headache jumped out and beat on me after I got out of the shower. Breakfast was on the tense side. Chris and Chuck were still arguing but not out loud. I would have preferred they spoke in the other language; at least I'd have a better gauge for how the conversation was going.

My chat with Morrell was pleasant. Of course, to date, my chats with him were always pleasant. I looked forward to a time when we could properly be friends. Then I went home, sat down to recheck my taxes, and make sure they had gone through.

They didn't. Somehow my computer had eaten the entire first filing, and I had to do it again. To say I wasn't thrilled would be an understatement. I made sure to save them to my thumb drive as well as the hard drive because I did not want to spend another hour putting fiddly numbers into a form. Once again I hit the send button, hoping this time it worked.

During lunch Ben called to see what my Passover plans were. I told him I'd be coming home for the *Seder*, probably with Pat. We had an uncomfortable chat about whether or not I was leading Pat on. I assured Ben Pat was well aware of the fact we weren't dating. The fact he had a girlfriend seemed to indicate he had gotten the message. Ben was less sure.

"Can I bring him home or not?"

"He's welcome. Just make sure he knows you think you're friends."

"Yes, Ben. Tell me about the rest of the crew. What's up with them?" We talked for twenty minutes about the family and farm.

Then came homework. I spent three hours working on a paper for the history class Pat got me to join. Three hours produced three pages of utter shit. Yes, I had answered the question 'What were the causes and effects of ascension of James I?' but I hadn't produced any interesting insights or particularly decent prose. If I had done it my way, it would have been a page long list of bullet points, but the history department thought it valuable to learn how to write a decent argument.

I put the computer down when something outside my window made me shiver. A quick look around showed me more Watchers than usual outside. *Wonderful.* Dave, Pat, and Mike were heading out tonight. I restocked my first aid bag and made another batch of the magic hooch.

Naptime. If I was going to end up putting hurt friends back together again, I might as well try to be rested for it. An hour later I was still awake. I couldn't keep the pain at bay and relax enough to sleep. I didn't want to risk being fuzzy, so I couldn't drink the hooch. Finally, I gave up on the nap and started my math homework.

The math wasn't behaving. Usually I could do these problems with half my brain, but today the little bastards wouldn't obey. The numbers and symbols kept bouncing about giving me crap answers. I made myself a sandwich and ate dinner while struggling with the numbers.

I was on my fourth try on the same damn problem when Chris knocked on my door.

"Come in." It looked like misery loved company today because he practically had a little black cloud hovering over his head.

"So, what's fucked all the way to hell and back in your life today?" He looked taken aback. I guess that was snippier than I usually am.

"I can leave if you want."

"No, just having a bad day myself. I can feel the cloud hovering over you. What's up?"

"Homework hell…" He slumped next to me on the window seat and plugged his computer in. "Autumn's all over me today. Supposedly trying to make up for practically killing Chuck. My shoulder aches something fierce. I can feel something's coming, but I don't know when or what it is, so I can't get ready to defend against it properly. How about you?"

"Let me work on your shoulder. I'll tell you about it while I work. Is it dumb that doing stuff like this always makes me feel better?"

He took off his sweater and unbuttoned his shirt. "Doing what you were born to do makes you feel good. No, I don't think that's stupid."

He sat on the floor in front of me, between my legs, while I lay my hands on his left shoulder. I didn't talk while I got a feel for his shoulder. The tendons were still stretched further than they wanted to be. But they were snapping back a lot faster than without magic. The muscles had healed up with a minimum of scar tissue. Morrell had done a good job there. For someone who had had his arm ripped out of its socket four days ago he was in vastly better shape than he had any right to be. I reduced the swelling of the tendons further and gave him some pain relief.

"Better?"

"Much." He turned to face me, his head resting against my knee. "Tell me what's up."

I continued to work on his shoulder while I talked. Nothing magic about this. Just good old-fashioned massage. It didn't do much for my headache, but it helped release some of the frustration from the math. "Let's see. The numbers won't co-operate. For some reason I just can't get the equations to work today. Of course, the little fuckers are due tomorrow, and of course these are for a grade, and because I've been busy healing you guys I didn't get the last two sets in, so I really need to do this one.

"Then there's the headache I've had since I worked on Chuck. I still can't rid of it. It's not making it any easier to work on the problems. And I've just written the least inspired essay in the history of Sylvianna College, so there's one more mediocre grade in a glorious line of mediocre grades I've gotten in my British History class. And every Watcher in town is camped out across the street..." I was working up to a good head of steam on my rant about how the entire world sucks when he cut in.

"Can I ask you something?" He stopped me rubbing his shoulder by placing his hand on mine. He was debating something and hadn't yet decided what the right answer was.

"Sure."

"Are you in pain now?"

"Yes. I'm having no luck killing this headache."

"Can I help?" His mood improved the moment he said it. Like, by saying it he had made a decision, and once made he began to feel free.

"Can you?"

"Let's see. How about you lie down on the floor? I'll try my hand at some of your tricks. You've done them enough to me I should have them down by now."

"Should you be doing that?"

He laughed. "Even I can give a back rub without getting into trouble."

"Oh, those tricks. Sounds good." I took his place on the floor. He didn't put his shirt back on, which gave me more of an idea of what he had finally decided before asking me if he could help. I smiled. That's good for headaches, too. It felt odd to be the one to lie down. He settled himself cross-legged at my head.

"So, where's it hurt?" he asked with his hands hovering near my head.

"My whole head, neck, shoulders. I still feel like I've got ice picks stabbed into my temples. Magical tension headache with a side of Chuck-induced crud."

"If this is a tension headache, time off and relaxing is the cure."

"Sounds right."

"Tell me about something fun. Something that isn't stressful." He slid his fingers down my eyebrows, circling my eyes, and brushing across my forehead. I closed my eyes, slowed my breathing, and relaxed the muscles of my head and neck.

"That feels really good. Do you have any idea how long it's been since someone gave me a massage?"

"Not off the top of my head."

"Too long." I tried to remember the last time, but Chris' fingers were making firm circles on my temples. That felt too good to spend time thinking about the last massage.

"How about when all this is done, you and I set up a standing appointment to work on each other. You know, next year, when all we've got to deal with is classes and homework."

"Maybe I'll even lay out the four hundred dollars to get a massage table."

"That would make this easier. I'm developing a new appreciation for why you pay so much attention to your position all the time." He lightly pressed his thumbs down the line of my jaw and stroked his hands back up my face. Then he settled his fingers at the base of my skull and pressed up into the knotted muscles there.

"That's excellent," I said with a sigh. His touch was careful, focused, and warm. I felt the pain start to drift away. A deeply content sexual glow began to replace it. He moved away from my neck and began making small circles with his fingertips on my scalp.

I opened my eyes to look up at him. He was watching me carefully, seeing how I reacted to his touch. With his eyes on mine and a smile on his lips, he very delicately, with just the tips of his fingers, stroked from the base of my throat to the top of my skull.

"Mmmm…" My eyes slid shut. Before I could stop myself, I licked my lips. He traced his finger tips over my eyebrows again, very lightly along my eyelashes, then down to outline my lips. For a moment I fought the desire to lick him. *Fuck it! He's stroking my lips. He knows how I feel about this. If it makes him uncomfortable, then he shouldn't have been touching my mouth in the first place.* I took his index finger between my lips and gave it a gentle suck. He didn't pull away. He did cup my face with his free hand.

"How about you roll over? I'll work on your shoulders." His voice made my skin feel warm and happy.

I rolled over for him, and he began to move from my head to my hips. "When you work on my shoulders, you have me take off my shirt. Pat, too."

I sat up, turned to face him, and undid the first button on my shirt. I don't think he was breathing, and my heart was beating faster than was strictly necessary. His eyes followed my hands down my shirt, tracing the line of flesh my fingers revealed. I shrugged off the blue flannel button down and crumpled it behind me.

"Bra, too?" I asked him, giving him a chance to back out.

His eyes pulled back up to mine. "I can't see how it won't get in the way."

I unhooked it and slid it off my shoulders. He watched me very intently. Lord, I wanted to burn that look into my mind and keep it for my personal viewing. If he somehow managed to back off and leave, I'd keep that image for fantasy fodder for the rest of my life. No one had ever looked at me with that much longing. I expected him to reach out and kiss me then and there. But he didn't. He just watched.

I lay back down, tucking my shirt into a pillow under my head. Absurdly, I found myself thinking I really did need to get a massage table or something because the carpet was scratchy. Then he sat on my thighs and slid his fingers up my spine. Whatever else happened he seemed determined to give me a good massage. The way he was kneading my shoulders sent thrills all through my body.

After a minute, he stood up, wandered off, and began rummaging about in my cupboard. I looked up to see what he was doing, but my couch blocked the view.

"Hungry?" I asked more sharply than I intended. This was not the ideal time to be looking for a snack. Unless he had images from *Nine and a Half Weeks* in his head.

"Getting some oil. My hands aren't sliding as well as I'd like." A minute later he straddled my hips again. I heard him open the bottle. "How much of this do I use?"

"Not much, a teaspoon, maybe less. You can always add more. But too much and I'll be a slippery mess."

"And we wouldn't want that."

"Nope. Soft and slick is good. Oil spill with suffocating wildlife, not so much."

He rubbed his hands together. Then they cupped around my shoulders, slipped down my spine, and back up again to the base of my skull. I sighed happily.

"Soft and slick is very good," he said while circling his knuckles into the muscles next to my spine.

"Very good." Another happy sigh. A bit more of this and I'd be purring at him.

He started with his hands at my waist and slid them up to the tops of my shoulders, leaning into them, letting his weight stretch my back. This was good, too good. His palms slid back to my waist again, and his fingers inched under the waist band of my pants to press into my low back.

"Lift up for a second." I wanted his hands lower.

He rose off of my legs. I scooted out from under him and took off my jeans.

"Better?"

He sunk back onto my legs. "Yes." Half-sigh, half-word, all desire. I wanted to keep that sound in my mind forever.

He cupped his hands around my hips, his thumbs pressing into my sacrum. Then once again he slid his hands up my spine, once again leaning his weight against me as he slid upward. This time, as he stretched to reach the top of my shoulders, I felt his pelvis rub against my tush. Twice more he did that. Sliding his hands from the base of my spine back to the top, gently rubbing against me at the top of the stroke, then sinking back onto his heels.

On the fourth stroke, I arched up to meet him. He let out another sound, this one somewhere between a hiss and a moan. Then he shifted, scooting back. I was starting to think I had gone too far when I felt his necklaces cold on my back, his lips on my neck, and his arms slide under mine. I turned my face toward him, and finally he kissed me. His one hand cupped my face, the other around my shoulder.

It was good. Too good. Impossibly good. Dark chocolate laced with opium good. His fingers and hands knew exactly what and how to touch, and I was playing him like Mozart with a piano.

We were in the doorway of my bedroom when I spoke again. "Do you want this?"

He looked up from the breast he was nuzzling. "Yes."

"Good." I hooked one leg around his hip and pulled his lips back to mine.

Golden light, their skin tinged green by it, his fingers gripping her hips, slowly easing into her, keeping the pace languid and relaxed, wanting to just gently, easily tip her into another one, and then, when the quivers slowed, speeding way up for a fast one. That one for both of them.

Ahhh… just like that. Slowly, gently, just a bit more, another inch, one more flick, and *yes…* soft little quivers around him. His eyes rolled back in his head as he began to move faster.

There, slide, *oh fuck… so good…* faster, deeper. Fingers gripping harder. Her heels pressed into his hips. Her fingers reaching behind her, gently twisting him. *Oh… oh… yes…* faster and again faster. *Tight, so, so tight.* Muscles straining to go faster, fingers clenching, heels and shoulders on the bed, the rest of him arching up into her as his body melted into hot, liquid pleasure.

Limp and sated. Wet and twitch. Breath and pulse. Her soft weight on his chest. Her hair against his chin. The smell of sex and her perfume. Golden light through amber windows…

Chris' eyes opened.

The light was orange-gray; the color of halogen lamps reflecting off of rainclouds.

He closed his eyes again, willing himself back into the glow of the golden light. The smell was right. The feel of her skin was right. But little details, the pillows were wrong and her hair didn't drape across his chest, kept pulling him away.

She got up to go to the bathroom. Alone in her bed, he couldn't hide in the fantasy any longer.

I left the bathroom, looking forward to a nice snuggle and some sleep, but Chris wasn't in the bed anymore. He sat on the edge of it, head drooping as he looked at the floor, radiating an aura of pained guilt. *Fuck.* This was exactly what I didn't want to deal with. He walked into the living room, without looking in my direction, and started gathering his clothes. I knew if he left here feeling terrible, it would hurt worse than anything I ever wanted to feel. I also knew my best guess of how to deal with this wasn't likely to be good enough.

I watched him for a few minutes while trying to think of what to say. He still wasn't looking at me. The hunt for his boxers was either the most fascinating thing ever or he literally couldn't stand to face me.

"We were still in the doorway when I took them off you. My best guess is they're in the kitchen somewhere." They lay on the floor behind the table. I picked them up and handed them to him. Forcing him to look at me.

"I thought you could handle this."

At least he was looking at me now, uncomfortable, rumpled, and naked, but looking at me.

"I was wrong."

"I don't know how to help you deal with this. I felt it when you made the decision. You were at peace for a minute there. Why did you change your mind?"

He pulled on his boxers. I couldn't properly read his emotions. I felt like I was supposed to see sadness and regret, but there was something else there, and I didn't know what it was.

"Because I'm lonely," he snapped at me. He was rapidly going from guilty to angry. *He's baiting you. Picking a fight because it's easier to fight.* "It's been more than twenty years since I touched a woman, and I miss it. I miss fucking. And you're here. And she's not. And you want me. And sometimes I'm just so miserable all I want to do is grab the nearest woman and fuck until it all fades into the background."

"Did it all fade?" He looked surprised I would ask him that. It disarmed some of his anger.

"Yes."

" Are you less miserable?"

"Yes... no... a whole new kind of miserable."

"Why?"

"Why?" His voice rose as his anger rushed back. "I broke my wedding vows! I promised her in front of God and both of our families I would never touch another woman as long as I was alive."

Suddenly I was angry. Stupidly angry. I wasn't even sure if the anger was mine or his, but I wanted to make sure it was me, not ghosts of promises made a century ago in a different land, that had his blood boiling. *You want a fight? I'll fight you.*

"You fleeing to a different dimension didn't violate those vows? You left her. You got up, walked away, and went where she'd never see you again. That's okay, but fucking me isn't?"

He was sitting on my couch pulling on a sock and stopped dead, sock halfway up his foot. My question worked. He had passed from angry to furious. The air around him felt hot and electric. While he spoke, I caught a hint of the kind of man who could use something called Flesh Melt on another person. "I shouldn't be here. I should be home with her and our children. I never wanted anyone else, and I never wanted to be apart from her. One hundred and twelve years, that's how long we were married for. I've loved her since the first time I saw her. And yet you can't wrap your mind around why I hate the fact I broke my vows!"

I wanted to slap him for being a liar. If there was ever a time to do it, it was now. "That's shit. Twenty minutes ago when you had your dick in my mouth you wanted me! Yesterday you wanted me! This one true love forever stuff is crap. You've wanted me from the minute I put my hands on your shoulders. And no, I can't wrap my mind around how leaving her in a different dimension was okay but fucking me isn't. I don't get why sexual fidelity is a bigger deal than actually, physically staying with her. If she's the love of your life, why did you leave her? You told me she asked you to stop. Well, if you loved her so much, why the fuck didn't you?"

"I didn't want to die!" he hissed at me. "That's what she was asking me to do. If I had stayed, I would have died." He pulled his shirt on and tried to get it buttoned without much luck. Once he had two buttons done, he gave up on the rest. He started to put a shoe on.

"If you had died, that would have been the end of your marriage. When you left, your marriage ended! Get over it. She's gone. You're gone."

"Get over it!" He was yelling at me now. "Get over it! This wasn't some fling."

I was yelling back, "Yeah, and it hasn't been two weeks since she left you, either. Twenty-two years, Chris, twenty-two fucking years! She's not coming here, you've said it yourself. You aren't going back. So it's over. Your marriage is dead. She's dead! What do you think happened to her? And to your kids when they decided to stay in the presence of your enemies? Do you think they're just fine and dandy in a place where the people who want you dead are still strong enough to send creatures to another world to hunt you down?"

He looked like he wanted to hit me. His arm twitched, and I was ready to grab it before it could connect. He turned fast and stormed out of my home.

I sunk onto my couch, wanting to cry, but I couldn't quite do it. "Fuck!" I yelled and punched the back of the sofa as hard as I could. I looked around the room. One of his socks, his belt, and sweater were still on the floor. So was my clothing.

I slowly picked things up. My hands folded his sweater without any conscious thought on my part. For a long insane moment I wanted to smell it. I shook my head and very deliberately laid it on top of his sock and belt, and put them next to his laptop and homework.

I debated getting dressed and taking his things over to the Writers' House. A mean, petty part of my personality enjoyed imagining the look on Autumn's face and the fall out he'd have to deal with because of it. I couldn't do it. There was no reason to hurt Autumn and seeing his clothing, especially his belt, left at my place would hurt her. If he had been dumb enough to go home half-dressed, he could do his own damn explaining.

A shower sounded like a good idea. Looking at the still pink finger marks where he had gripped my hips finally started me crying. I rested my head against the wall of the shower and let the tears fall. A bleak certainty that there was no good way out of this tore at me. Worse, I had the horrible feeling Chris wasn't going to be able to act like nothing had happened.

I stayed in the shower until the water went cold, then a bit longer. The cold water washed away red puffy eyes and the marks left by Chris' fingers. I wrapped a towel around my body and opened the door to my bedroom.

The door made a satisfyingly loud crash when he slammed it behind him.

He didn't know where he was going. Not home. He was still sensible enough to know going home missing half of the outfit he left in was a bad idea. Not Chuck's. He really didn't want to deal with Chuck about this. Chuck would be smugly pleased, especially since kissing her this morning was entirely about trying to goad him into doing exactly what had just done.

Fuck. The one person he could have talked to about this was the one person he couldn't face right now. If it had been anything else, he'd go over to her place, and just being near her would make him feel better.

That was the problem. He had felt too much better. For an hour, two hours, he hadn't bothered to check a clock before leaving, there was no pain. Just skin, touch, and soft, wet, sliding sensations he had missed for far too long.

Far too long and far too familiar. Blindfolded he wouldn't have been able to tell which one he was with. For a few brief minutes he was home with Althiira again, wrapped in the one person he wanted more than any other. Then he was in a small bed, in a tiny apartment, with a woman who didn't share a century of memories with him. A woman who felt so much like his wife he had a hard time telling them apart with his eyes closed.

What if it was her? If she had somehow made it here without her memories? If it was her, if she ever remembered, could he take losing her again?

If she wasn't? If it was just some sort of sick cosmic joke to end up with two versions of the same woman, could he get past Althiira and find Sarah? Could he love her the way she deserved to be loved if every time he touched her he felt a different person?

He stopped and leaned against the back wall of the library. His forehead rested on the rough brick as rain streamed down his skin. Now, more than ever, he hated the lies. He wanted to go back, beg her forgiveness, and tell her the whole story. See if it brought Althiira out. If it did? What then? *Lie at her feet and hope she kills me quickly.*

At least he now had an opening to tell more of the truth. He could admit Althiira was dead, but that meant more lies, and he was sick of lies. There was no simple fix to this. No way to hold onto reality and make it better.

He wanted to run back to her home, close his eyes, and slip back into the fantasy of the world before. Chris didn't know if he was strong enough to resist the fantasy.

He had to go back. Eyes closed and breathing deeply and slowly to calm himself, he spent a moment working up the temerity to face her. He had to make things right, or as close to right as they could get, and do it without sliding into the fantasy.

Chris walked slowly back to her house. Sarah didn't answer when he knocked, but she was in there. After a moment of focus, he realized she was in the shower and couldn't hear him. He let himself in. His clothing was in a tidy pile next to his homework. He put it on, realizing too late dry clothing over wet clothing wasn't a great idea.

He sat on the edge of her bed, waiting for her, very aware the water dripping off his clothing wasn't the only wetness on the bed right now. The room still felt like sex. The smell, the energy, the all-too-fresh memories left him uncomfortably aroused in addition to the rest of the emotional turmoil.

She was crying. He could feel it across the room. Time passed, and he worked on what he'd say to her. Trying to think of a way to minimize the lies. Then she faced him, wrapped in a towel, drops of water sliding down her skin.

"I'm sorry." She stared at him. "Of course they're dead."

She sat down next to him, not quite certain what to do. She wanted to comfort him, but her first line of comfort was touch, and she didn't know if that was appropriate anymore. Her hand tentatively rested on his shoulder. Chris rested his cheek against it, closed his eyes, and sighed, content to feel her skin on his. He wondered if she knew how soothing her touch was. Did she do it on purpose, or was it just part of being her? Sarah inched closer and wrapped her arms around him, no longer nervous. A few more quiet tears escaped; then he took a few deep breaths to calm himself.

"As long as I kept acting like she was still here, as long as I kept my vows, I could pretend she was still alive somewhere. That somehow I didn't get her and our boys killed. That's the real reason Autumn sees no reason for me to maintain my vows. She knows they're gone. Dave thinks me keeping my vows is silly for the same reason. Pat's the only one with any sympathy because he's hoping just as much as I did that she's still alive somewhere." She gave him a sympathetic squeeze. He felt ill, wanting to vomit out the lies and tell her the whole story. He couldn't do it. The fear that she'd hate him if she knew the real story bound his tongue.

They sat quietly for a long time.

Her voice was low, and she stroked his hair when she spoke: "Chris, I want you. You know that. But I don't want to be with you if you can't enjoy me. I don't want your guilt. I don't want you to try to hurt me or yourself because of it. Tonight was your one freebie. You do not get to kick me because you're mad at yourself. I won't put up with that. Do it again, and you don't get to come back here."

He nodded. "I don't know if there's a me without the guilt."

"Find him. When you do, I'll be here."

"I should leave." His voice was flat.

"Are we all right?"

"We are. I will be, eventually."

She nodded, gathered him close, and let him free. He retreated into the dark and rain, scanning his own house. Autumn's light was out. That made his night easier. He crept in quietly and was in his room before anyone could have noticed him enter.

He lay on his bed, staring at the ceiling. No words. No thoughts. Just a silent, blank mind. Given the last few hours the silence was a blessing. He might have slept. Or not. Hard to tell. Eventually sounds from the rest of the house began to move around him.

What was the quote? "If I love you enough to sleep with you, I love you enough to leave my wife for you." Something like that. Of course, Pug's wife left him and took the choice out of his hands, but the quote remained relevant.

Was he leaving Althiira or going back to her?

There had to be some way to find the answer. Was she just Sarah? Was it just luck they felt so similar? Or was she Althiira? If she was Althiira, what was she doing here? How did she get here? Was she truly a past-life case, alive and dead and back again with them? Why? Could she have done it herself? She had more magical talent than any of them, herself included, had ever guessed. But that? It was possible. With magic anything was possible. Plausible, no. Likely, no. But possible, yes.

He tried to look at it logically. Her energy felt like Althiira's. Her manners were similar. At least, he thought that's how she'd have been if she had been raised as an ordinary girl instead of a princess. The body was different. Of course it was different—so was his—but how it reacted was the same. Not just similar. It was identical. His memories made real once again. Her touch… it had taken them years to learn each other that well. Ten years? Fourteen? He didn't remember exactly. He knew it had been more than eight because their daughter had already been born, and less than seventeen because their first son hadn't.

He could hear Chuck laughing in his head. It had taken them years because they started as two shy kids with no experience and learned entirely on each other. Of course, to hear Chuck tell it, he was born knowing everything there ever was to know about sex. But the point he knew Chuck would make was Sarah had done this before, probably lots, so she already knew what to do with a penis.

The image of her legs wrapped around Ari's back formed in his mind and with it the bitter taste of jealousy. Had he been her first? Had there been others? How many? He found himself desperately wanting to believe she just knew how he liked to be licked. That some part of her remembered that little extra bit of friction and how to pull back just enough to keep him on edge. He hated the idea another man held her hand and showed her how to touch or told her what to do while his hands fisted in her hair.

Too much doubt. He couldn't count on the sex as a way to tell who she was. "Fuck!" he said it louder than he had intended.

Footsteps padded up the stairs. "Chris?" Autumn asked outside his door. He didn't respond to her voice or the soft knock that followed. After ten minutes, she headed back down to her room.

Magic. Sarah can heal. Althiira could heal. Some of the techniques are the same. Some are different. But that was true for all magic here. Protection. They were both better with protective spell than anyone else he had ever seen. Only Dave's invisibility came close. Of course, that was because they were siblings.

Dave felt her more strongly than any of the others. He didn't need convincing she was the one. He knew it on the first meeting, and his magic worked better on her than anyone else. That was a good sign. That was how it had been before.

Pat: It was the relationship they would have had if they could have. The relationship they deserved. Not the relationship Pat wanted for them. That was another good sign. She had loved Ahni deeply but never was in love with him.

Autumn: that was new. Autumn had actively disliked Althiira. Since the dance she hadn't been thrilled with Sarah, but she didn't hate her the way she had hated Althiira.

Chuck. He sighed. They hadn't even spoken five words between the three of them and the same dynamic started all over again. *Does he really think it's her? Or is it just an automatic response?* That might be worth seeing him and talking about.

Mike: He didn't have much of an idea. No real feeling one way or the other. They'd had a friendly, professional relationship before and a friendly relationship now.

Her magic: She could heal. She could protect. Could she farsee? That would be one way to know for sure. It was also a question he couldn't bear to ask her. He continued staring at the ceiling trying to think through a problem that couldn't be answered by thought alone.

45.

I didn't sleep that night. After an hour, I gave up and did more math homework. This time the numbers obeyed. I got two more problem sets done and used them as a way to not think about Chris. It worked pretty well. The muzzy feeling of not nearly enough sleep kept me fairly numb throughout the morning.

Chris wasn't at lunch. He didn't come for Sabbath though all through the afternoon I kept hoping to hear his feet on my stairs. During dinner Pat kept looking like he wanted to ask what was up, but I let him feel I didn't want to talk about it with Emily there. They headed off early. Sleep was probably the best thing I could do for myself, so I went to bed.

I found myself in a dream almost before I was asleep. It took a minute to understand I was back in the head of the blue woman. There was more distance here than usual. I was still experiencing her point of view, but wasn't her. There was a man on top of her, kissing sloppily, fumbling with her body, looking for entrance. I couldn't see. Her eyes were closed, and she lay still and tense. It was viciously painful but over fast. As he moved away from her, she curled into a ball and cried. I wondered if I was feeling a rape, when the voice I knew belonged to her husband began to whisper. I still didn't know the words, but the content was clear. He was immensely sorry for what had happened.

A very bad first time then. I sat in the back of her head while her husband curled around her and cried with her. When I woke, I was still wondering how they had gotten past that.

I missed him in the morning. I had gotten out of the habit of spending my Saturday alone and found it lonely.

When I joined the Writers for dinner on Saturday, he wasn't there. According to Autumn, he was in his room, but he didn't answer when she knocked, and he didn't eat the food she left for him.

Pat came home with me. "Tell me what's up," he said as we sat on my sofa.

I almost did. I was seconds away from telling him everything. The desire to confide almost overrode everything else. But it couldn't overcome the fact I didn't want to hurt Pat. Also, I didn't want him getting overprotective and heading over to Writers' to beat up Chris. When I told him, I wanted it to be happy news, on my part at least.

I opted for something pretty close to true. "More fun with Mr. Mettinger."

"You deserve someone better than him," he said with great sincerity.

I smiled sadly at him. "You're right, but I like him."

"What is it about tortured, wounded guys? Seriously, why do girls like them?"

"I like them because I'm a healer. As for other girls... no idea. I didn't used to like tortured, wounded guys. It wasn't particularly appealing until I got here."

"Is this a new flavor of fun?"

"No. Just more of the 'He's married/I'm not.' The frustration really sucks."

"Want me to go over there and kick the shit out of him for you?" He didn't smile. The realization that he really meant it: that he'd practically kill Chris, or anyone really, for me was deeply comforting and terrifying at the same time.

"Nah. I'll do it myself if it ever comes to that."

"Good. Nothing wrong with him a few serious ass kickings by you wouldn't fix." This time he smiled, lightening the mood considerably.

I almost laughed. "You think so?"

"Not really, but I'd enjoy seeing you do it."

I did laugh at that. "I'll make sure to invite you if we ever get to the serious ass-kicking stage."

"Good. I'll make popcorn." He put his arm around me and kissed my forehead. "You deserve a man who can love you, Sarah."

"I know. So, tell me about how things are going with Emily. I'll spend a little while in your head vicariously enjoying a functional relationship..."

After Pat left, I went back to the James I paper and tried to rewrite it into something more fun to read. It was better—not good, but better. Then more math, more reading, I pushed anything besides the work away.

Asleep again. Dreaming about sex again. I was back in the head of the blue woman. This time I felt like I was actually her, not just riding along in the back of her head. The sex was significantly better, too: still very fast, but playful and happy. Obviously they did get past it somehow.

At Sunday dinner Autumn speculated he had gone to Chuck's house because he wasn't at Writers' anymore. I hoped he'd come back to me. As I got ready to go to bed alone again, I didn't think the odds were good. He was probably right; there wasn't a man without the guilt.

Sunday night brought a new dream. The result of all that sex. I was sitting astride his lap, legs wide, pushing hard. Burning, splitting pain was replaced by a feeling of relieved emptiness. Then the cry of a very small person who was quite unhappy to be out its nice, warm womb had my entire attention. The woman who had been kneeling in front of me showed us it was a girl, cleaned her off, wrapped her up, and handed her to me. We held her, gently touching her moist scarlet hair and wrinkly azure skin. I ran my finger over the floppy, blue point of her ear. She wrapped her hand around her father's finger. He grinned at us while crying and saying something quietly joyous to her.

I woke up Monday morning and decided to run hard. I had to get these dreams out of my head. They made me feel dirty for inventing a past with him I had no right to claim. But I had started dreaming them before this had begun. Before Chris was really on my radar. Was I seeing Ameena's life? I watched her die. The fire killed her. I knew that. What was the fire? Was that Mildred's wrath? Was that what they were trying to stop and failed? Or was it just some sort of fantasy my brain was creating for the fun of it?

My feet pounded against the pavement, propelling my body forward hard and fast. It was time to ask about the dreams. On Wednesday, I would have asked Chris. But Wednesday was gone, and Thursday had made sure, 'Hey, so I'm having weird dreams, and I'm wondering, were we married once upon a time?' was one question I couldn't bear to ask him.

Which meant waiting for Pat and I to get some time alone together. After Golem, maybe. I could wait a day for that.

Chuck had found an immensely determined-looking Chris sitting in his room waiting for him when he got home from work early Monday morning.

"Tell about the 'best first time with a new person' sex you've ever had."

That question snapped the sleepiness right out of him. "Who are you, and what did you do with Chris?"

"Do I look like I'm kidding here? I need information I don't have, and it's either talk with you or Pat, and I really don't want to talk to Pat about this."

"No, you don't. What do you want to know?"

"Everything. How it felt. How well she knew you by instinct. How well you knew her. What girls here know. What's expected."

Chuck got out of his coat and sat down on his bed before answering. "None of the first times were exceptional. Plenty of great sex. Don't get me wrong. But the finger curling, toe clenching, Oh My God! sex: That's not a first time thing, at least not for me. For her is usually a different story," Chuck said with a satisfied smirk.

"Yes, you're a sex god. I know. You've been telling me about it for more than one hundred and fifty years. Now cut it and tell me."

"How well she's known me is always a crap shoot. Some of them seem like they can get in your head. Some are just fumbling in the dark. Because of my talents, I can read her way better than anyone else she's slept with. It takes conscious effort, though. It's me actually looking into her mind to see what she wants, not instinct. Don't think I've ever fucked on straight instinct before, in either body. Not sure I'd want to.

"What they know here..." Chuck smirked happily. "Way more than they did before. If she's over sixteen, she'll have a clue as to what to do with you. She might not be interested in going down on you—you know what that is, right?"

Chris rolled his eyes. "Yes. I was married for a while, you know. And I wasn't raised in a convent for nervous virgins, either."

"You were married the last time we talked about this, and you weren't overflowing with information then."

"I was one hundred and two, had been married for less than one day, and it had been less than twelve hours since I had lost my virginity when we last talked about this."

"Fine, you've racked up gobs of experience over the decades, just none of it applicable to sex in this world. Anyway, she's certainly heard of it. If she does it, she likely expects you to return the favor and have a clue as to what you're doing." Chuck didn't ask again out loud; he didn't even think the words into Chris' head. Chris still knew they were there.

Chris sighed. "I'm really not that straight laced." Asking for advice from his older, more experienced brother right after his wedding night and being shocked at his advice was backfiring now.

Chuck continued on, "Her on top isn't scandalous, and it might be her preferred position. Hell, she probably has a preferred position or two. She'll know what she likes. At the very least, she'll have done it to herself enough she'll have a clue there. She'll expect you to have a clue to. She'll want you to know how to get her out of her clothing. She'll want you to know what to do with a clit and how to tell when she's done. You lose major points if you finish up and leave her hanging. That's not considered acceptable here.

"Why? Are you finally going to fuck Sarah?"

Time to shock Chuck back. Let him know he had grown up since that conversation so long ago. "So, say we're sixty-nining, and I've gotten her off so many times she's hit the continuous orgasm stage. I'm just very slowly finger fucking her with a few very soft licks to keep the quiver going. She's got me to the point where I know I'm going to climax so hard I see stars. She's sliding her mouth up me, and I can feel everything tighten, but instead of sliding back down on me she bites me hard on the inner thigh. The pain endorphins hit like an orgasm, just racing through my body. Of course it isn't one, so I don't get soft. She switches positions so she's riding me. She's not coming anymore, and I want to feel her quivering around me while I ride this one home. So I grip her thighs and ease into her real slow, using the tip of my thumb to just slip her into another orgasm. Once that one hits, we speed way the hell up; every muscle in my body has tensed to the snapping point; only my heels and shoulders are still on the bed. I'm straining so hard to press even further, harder, faster into her. And with one gliding motion she slides all the way down me, presses under my balls, pinches a nipple, and the entire world explodes. I'm not just seeing stars but on the verge of blacking out it feels so fucking good.

"That's not usual first time sex? Not here? No matter how many times she's done it with someone else?" Chris found the look of utter, stupid shock on Chuck's face immensely satisfying.

After a minute, Chuck's brain started working again. "You've been waiting one hundred and thirty-three years to gloat at me like that."

"If I had known how lame your sex life was, I wouldn't have waited so damn long. 'Toe Curling, Oh My God! Sex,'" Chris gave a derisive snort, "That was the kind of quickie we'd get in on late nights with an early morning the next day.

"But that's also what I needed to know. This isn't common. Not everyone gets that kind of connection. That level of knowing another person comes from years, decades of practice. It's not luck, and it's not something she's picked up with someone else."

"Why are you here?" Chuck looked at him in wonder. He sure as hell wouldn't be sitting in Chris' room looking for advice after an experience like that. "Shouldn't you be with her making up for lost time?"

"Would you be shocked to hear I managed to make a total ass out of myself after, picked a fight with her, stormed out of her place, then came back, kind of made up, and wandered into the night a lost soul?"

"No." Chuck sighed. At least Chris had gotten past the first step. If he was reading Chris right, he was just about ready to go back and see her again.

"I didn't think so."

"Your mood seems pretty good now."

"I've just about got myself convinced she's Althiira. It helps."

"Based on what?"

"Did you hear what I said to you? That was just the last five/six minutes. Want to hear what came before? She feels the same, has similar magics. She reacts the same way to each of you…"

"Except Autumn."

"Except Autumn."

"Sarah has no farseeing talent, no diplomatic skills, and a very limited empathy."

"Sarah didn't spend eighty years being continually tutored by the best wizards money could hire or grow up a princess in the Court of the High Priest."

"Look, it could be her. Pat's certain it's her. I know Dave is convinced it's her. The few times I've talked to her alone I've felt Althiira very strongly. But there's a reason why I hope it's not her. If it is her, if she ever remembers, we are all fucked.

"Let me add one more level of devil's advocate: Sarah is a Touch Empath. She can't read your thoughts, but if she puts her hands on your body, she knows what needs to be touched and how. It's part of being a healer, part of her magic. The first time she saw you she touched you exactly right. She did it for Pat, and she did it for me. The fact *she* can fuck you senseless first time out may just be part of who she is."

"And that I could do it for her?"

"Are you sure you did?" Chris rolled his eyes and punched Chuck on the arm. "I'm serious here. If sex is your deciding factor, you better damn well make sure you were as hot as you thought you were."

"It's been a very long time, but I can still identify a female orgasm when it happens a quarter inch from my nose. I may not be able to read minds like you do, but in that position I can read hers. That's something else I could do before."

"Tell me what happened. Preferably with less detail this time. I really don't need the image of your naked ass bouncing around in my head. Feel free to tell me all about her, though." Chuck lit a cigarette. Chris motioned for him to give him one as well, and he did.

"Have I mentioned how off-putting I find your interest in my wife naked?"

"Only about once a decade." Chuck smiled at him. "I'm not really interested. I just like having the chance to tease you."

"Great," Chris said sarcastically. "We were both having a bad day. Talking with her helps. Being with her helps. Her hands on my skin helps. It helps her, too."

"And you just helped her into bed?"

"Cute. She told me she was still having headaches from working on you. I realized that was it. I could touch her and end up in bed or back away again and spend a pleasant evening sitting next to her doing homework. I didn't want that anymore. I wanted to touch her, not just have her touch me. I offered to work on her, try my hand at her skills. My fingers brushed her forehead, and it felt right. That's the reason I was a jerk after. It was too right. I didn't know where I was those last five minutes. I was home. When I realized I wasn't… that was unfortunate.

"I'm not a total idiot. If it is her, and as more time passes the more I think she is, this won't end well. What's worse, I don't want to believe it isn't her any longer."

"How much worse can it be than last time?"

"Do you think I can take that again?" Both of them knew the answer was no. Once had been enough.

"It could be reincarnation," Chuck said as he exhaled. "Her soul could be back, but the memories are gone."

"It would be silly to pray for that, wouldn't it?"

"Depends on who you're praying to. Look, how long have I been telling you this was how it was supposed to be? You did your part. Now you're inches from being done, and your reward has shown up right on schedule. Does it matter if it's really her or not? She feels like her. She acts like her. Close your eyes, and you can barely tell the difference. When she finishes growing out her hair, you won't be able to tell the difference with your eyes closed. Can't that just be a sign you're on the right path? You did what needed to be done, when it needed to be done. Now the one person you want more than any other falls into your lap. Call it your reward and enjoy it.

"You know what else? If you let it, you can have it all back again. Keep fucking her, and she'll turn up pregnant, binding you to her and your children again." Chuck felt Chris' flash of fear. "Forget something?"

"Shit. Yes. I hadn't even thought about it until now."

Chuck thought about it for a minute. "She's got to be on something. She doesn't menstruate. At least, not so I can tell, and I can usually tell."

"How do you know that?"

Chuck looked a little annoyed. "I can feel her emotions. She's either completely unaffected by her cycle or doesn't have one. I've never met a woman who was completely unaffected by it, so I'm thinking she doesn't have one."

"I hope you're right."

"Even if she isn't, it's something like a one-in-twenty shot. One in four you hit the week where you can get her pregnant, and one in five it implants."

"I'm used to much lower odds."

"Yet you still ended up with five kids," Chuck said with a smile.

"That's not comforting!"

"Sorry." Chuck was enjoying this more than he should. For the first time in two decades Chris looked like he might believe he didn't need to spend the rest of his life wrapped in pain. "Did you two plan to have that many kids that close together?"

"No. As I said, I'm not that straight laced. We had three kids in twenty-three years because we had sex practically every night, same with the two youngest ones being six years apart. The only time we actively tried to avoid getting pregnant was during the war."

Chuck pondered that and something he had long suspected but never asked about Chris' fourth child. He looked at Chris and felt he had enough distance to talk about it now. "Was Gerrath yours?" He felt a weary sadness in Chris and wanted to kick himself for asking.

"I had tried not to think about that around you." Although he had told Sarah the full story of what had happened when Althiira was captured, when it had happened only he and Pat knew about the rape.

"It slipped out of you when we killed the Cluns, but it was already old news to me by that point, I had gotten it from both Pat and her before then."

Chris nodded. He spoke quietly: "We had just lost Iyan. I understand it's common to try to have another one as quickly as possible. When she got back, there was a lot of sex. To comfort each other, to forget what had happened, to show her she was still mine, to show me she was still mine. When she told me she was pregnant with the first three, there was a million-watt smile and palpable, electric joy. That time she was nervous, a tinge of fear in her voice. She didn't know if I would want this child. It was too soon after her capture. There was no way to know for sure which one of us fathered him. I couldn't do that to her. I couldn't not love the child. No matter which one of us fathered him, he was still hers." Chris paused to remember, and Chuck quietly watched the images in his mind as he spoke. "I'd slide into bed, snuggle up against her at the end of the day, rest my hand against her belly, and feel him move. All five of our children were born with her sitting in my lap. My body supporting hers while she pushed. My legs under hers. My hands stroking her face. My voice in her ears to encourage her. After, with both of them in my arms, him hungrily nursing away, they were mine. Gerrath was mine. It didn't matter that he didn't look like me."

Chuck had a hard time fathoming loving a woman so much you'd love a child who wasn't yours. He hadn't claimed four he was sure were his. "You really never wanted another woman, did you?"

Chuck felt Chris check his sarcasm. "I'm still a man, and not a blind one, but beyond appreciating the scenery, no."

"It's got to be her again. You wouldn't feel this way about someone who was merely similar."

They were both quiet. Chris smoked slowly and thought carefully. After ten minutes, he looked at Chuck and asked, "Which one of the jewelry stores in town is any good?"

Chuck sighed. Pat's comments about Chris having more than two speeds once upon a time seemed especially relevant now. "Are you seriously trying to scare her off? Do not show up at her house tonight with a ring. She will run away and move back to Israel."

Chris ground out his butt. "I'm not that stupid, but if I want something custom made, it will take time. By the time it's ready, maybe she will be, too."

"It's not going to take two years. Which is about the speed normal people do stuff like this. You're moving too quickly."

"Just tell me."

"Harn's is supposed to be good."

"Is it actually good?"

"How exactly do you think I'd know? I made both pendants I wear. If I wanted someone to make me custom jewelry, I wouldn't be doing it in a little, middle-of-nowhere town. I'd go online, find someone who specializes in it, and do it that way."

"Good point. You're right. This is insane. One minute I'm so happy I can barely stand it. The next I'm terrified it will all explode and fall to shit."

"When did you see her last?"

"Right after."

"And it's been what?"

"Three days."

Chuck smacked Chris upside the back of the head. "Piece of advice number one: the likelihood of everything falling to shit increases dramatically with each day you don't go see her. Trust me on this, they don't like it when you sleep with them and then vanish."

"She told me not to come back until I could face her without guilt."

"So, she never expected to see you again? I suppose that's in your favor. Still, don't wait too much longer. Go see her. We'll deal with shit if it happens; for now enjoy being happy. And go buy some condoms before you get there. If you really want to impress her, read the directions and practice putting them on so you can do it quickly and easily. Now get out of here. I've got class in eight hours, and I'd like a decent bit of sleep between now and then."

Chris stood up. "I already know how to put on a condom. I assume, like a bicycle, it's something you don't really forget how to do."

Chuck rolled his eyes. "The same basic principle is in play."

"Good. See you tomorrow?"

"I'll be up for Golem."

46.

I almost didn't hear the knock. The rain and thunder were roaring, my music was on loud, and I was reading for tomorrow's lab. In fact, I probably didn't actually hear the knock. But I knew Chris was at my door, and I knew he was alone. A fierce flare of joy shot through me. He had come back! Even if it was just to pretend nothing had happened and go back to what we had last week, I wanted it.

He stood on my landing, soaking wet, looking at me in a manner I couldn't name. Something I hadn't seen from him before. It was intense but not sad.

"Are you in love with me?"

"Come in. This isn't a conversation I want to have in my doorway."

He stepped into my home. I went to grab a towel. When I returned, he was still standing in front of my door staring at me with those huge gray eyes. "Here, give me your coat and dry off." He handed me the coat and just held the towel, water dripping off him.

"Are you in love with me?" he asked again.

"Yes."

His hand whipped out faster than I could see and grasped me by the back of my neck. Next thing I knew, he had pulled me to him, and we were kissing like it would soon become illegal. Once again, his tongue knew all my tricks. The first time hadn't been a fluke. He had me pinned against the wall and gasping before I had the presence of mind to reach out and turn the light off so we didn't give the whole neighborhood a show.

I was wrapped around him very happily enjoying where this was going when he pulled back.

"What now?" My voice snapped with the fear that he was having second thoughts again. He smiled reassuringly. "Condom."

"Don't need one. Norplant."

I could feel relief and pleased lust from him as he said, "Good."

We didn't get to the bed until the third time that night. Much later, because that was a very long, very slow, very lazy fuck, we both lay there, flat on our backs, limp like cooked noodles when he spoke again.

"What about Ari?" The intensity was back. This time I had a feel for what part of it was.

"You're jealous?"

"Yes."

"Ari told me I was free to find a new man before he left."

"You two broke up when he left?" Chris turned his head to look at me. He sounded surprised.

"Your presence here certainly indicates that. In October I'll send him a letter. I owe him that."

"Do you still love him?"

"I think the better question is did I ever love him? I thought so. I imagine if I had stayed in Israel with him I would have been happy. But I couldn't hold it. I saw you, and he started to fade."

"Why didn't you tell us when he left?"

"Mike said if my relationship status changed I should keep it quiet. Having seen you and Pat cut each other up, I decided he had given me some good advice." We lay quietly for a minute. I rolled onto my stomach, rested my chin on his chest, and lightly kissed his chin. He stroked his hand through my hair. He returned his hand from my hair to behind his head. While doing so, I noticed something.

"That's your left hand, isn't it?" I propped myself on my elbows and pulled it from behind his head to look at it. It was naked. I felt irrationally angry seeing it naked. I knew it was a gesture for me, a sign of moving on, but his wedding ring belonged there. "What about Autumn? Or Brooke? Won't they be on you the second they see your naked finger?"

He kissed me. "I wanted you to see me not wearing it, at least once. I'll put it on when I leave here. I don't want to deal with Autumn on that level. Maybe she'll graduate, go home, and it'll just fade."

"The easy way out."

"Can you blame me for wanting at least one thing to be easy?"

"No. I don't blame you for wanting some easy." I twined my fingers between his, feeling the naked skin on his ring finger. It still felt wrong to me, and I didn't know why or what to do with that. I pushed it aside, more than enough time to deal with it later.

"Why ask if I was in love with you?" He looked at me intently for a long time. I could tell he was very aware of the question I didn't ask him.

He kissed me again and rolled to his side so he could face me easily. "Because I couldn't stand just being a warm, friendly body to you. I don't want to be your fuck buddy. I don't want to get laid. I want this kind of pleasure to mean something."

I draped one of my legs over his and snuggled close. "It does."

"Good." I could see he was struggling with something.

"What do you want to know?"

"I'm not sure I do."

"Oh." I had a pretty good feeling I knew what he was thinking. "Will it make you feel better if I say I've had no interest in getting laid, either?"

"Yes."

"That you aren't my first is driving you crazy, isn't it?"

"I'm trying not to let it."

"If I say this has been the best?"

He smiled briefly. "If it's true, it helps quite a bit."

"I wouldn't lie to you about something like that."

"What would you lie to me about?" He cupped his palm around my shoulder and slid his hand down my arm. His eyes followed his hand on my skin.

He looked me in the eye when I answered. "I don't know. Never felt the need. I probably won't ever lie to you, but I recognize it's not impossible."

He stroked his finger along my eyebrow. Still fighting the desire to know with the dread of what the answer might be. "How many others?"

"Two. I was with Matt from the age of fourteen until I was seventeen and Ari from eighteen to twenty-one. That's not as bad as you were afraid of, was it?"

"I don't know." I could see from the way he was looking at me he really didn't. "How old were you?"

"Fifteen." I could see him trying to imagine my fifteen-year-old self. "My hair was long then, my eyes were less... well, everything. The rest of me is about the same."

He kissed me again. A long slow kiss. Trying to block out the image of my other men? Branding me as his? I didn't know, didn't much care.

When he broke away from me, he asked, "Aren't you going to ask me if I'm in love with you?"

"No."

"Why not?"

Too proud to ask. "You'll tell me when you can."

He spent several moments stroking his fingers down my back. Gently playing along the line of my spine. "I'd really like a cigarette."

"Huh?" Of all the things I could have anticipated him coming up with, that was nowhere on the list.

"They go nicely with sex."

My eyebrows scrunched together. "How would you know?"

He wiggled his right hand at me and smiled. "They go well with all sorts of sex."

I smirked back at him and chuckled quietly. "Yeah, well, freezing your butt off on my porch doesn't go well with sex."

"True."

I kissed him. "Do you want to stay?"

"Yes."

"Good."

In the morning I woke up at my usual time. I slipped out of bed and went for my run. An hour later I was back; he was still sleeping. I hopped in the shower.

He knocked on the door a few minutes later. "Yeah?" I called out.

He came into the bathroom, fully dressed, hair sticking up at odd angles. "I'm going to go home. I need to get ready for class. See you at lunch?"

"Sure." He looked me up and down. I had the feeling he was a heartbeat away from getting in the shower with me.

"Get going," I said kindly. "You'll miss breakfast if you spend too long dawdling around here."

He blinked. "Right." He pulled my hand out of the shower and kissed my wrist softly. Pausing at the door, he said, "If Autumn asks, I'll tell her I came here from Chuck's house, and fell asleep."

"Fine by me. It's even true."

"All part of the fine art of the lie. Keep as much true as you can."

47.

Chris got home and headed straight for the shower. He couldn't smell himself anymore, but he was certain he had to smell like sex and Sarah, neither of which was a good thing to smell like with Autumn hovering around. He undressed quickly and spent a minute looking at himself, seeing himself the way she had seen him: new, beautiful and delicious. Several explicit memories of the night before ran through his mind. His hand on his own skin made those memories feel more real.

He heard beeping. Mike's alarm. Usually, he was out of the shower by now. He got the water on and stepped in, planning on a quick shower. The shower part was pretty quick. He washed as fast as he could. The images in his head made sure washing wasn't the only thing he got done.

Mike was wrapped in his towel, leaning against his door, and scowling at him when he got out of the bathroom. "Sorry." Mike glared at him and went to do his own morning routine.

Chris got into his own room and dressed, barely paying attention to what he was putting on. Any pair of boxers, jeans, and shirt would do. He didn't bother with his hair. Class was less than twenty minutes away. If he wanted to eat before getting there, he didn't have time to tame it.

He definitely wanted to eat. He hadn't had a real meal in... four days, he thought. He'd scrounged bits and pieces here and there. But a real, sit down, get-enough-calories-to-keep-going-without-burning-what-little-body-fat-he-had-meal had been a while ago.

He was sitting in the kitchen, plowing through a huge bowl of Cheerios and a cup of cocoa when Autumn joined him. Her small, flouncy, pink nightgown slipped off of one shoulder.

"You're back!" She gave him an enthusiastic and too long hug. "Feeling better?"

"Yes. I am. Thanks," he said between bites.

"What happened?"

"Just the usual."

"I'm glad to see you out of your room again."

"Nice to feel like being up and about again." He shoveled the Cheerios in faster. Two minutes later he finished the bowl and had a legitimate excuse to leave. "Gotta go. I got in late this morning."

"I know."

"I stopped by Sarah's and had her work on my shoulder."

"All better?"

"Just about. It still aches when the weather changes."

"It'll probably do that for a while."

"It probably will." He put on his jacket and grabbed his books.

Class was supposed to be about "A Lullaby" by Auden. He hadn't done the reading and had no intention of paying any attention. He made sure the professor knew he was there and used one of Dave's tricks to make sure he didn't get called on. Instead of poetry, he thought about rings. She wouldn't wear a tattoo. He knew not to ask. But a ring, one that matched the mark of his clan... if it could be done. There had to be someone who could turn his mark into metal and hopefully get closer than the man who had done his tattoo. It wasn't quite right, and he hadn't had the artistic skills to show him what right actually looked like.

Something to do when he got home: go online and see who made things like that. There should be a stone on her ring, something warm, that felt like her and home, and a symbol of an intensely felt commitment. Not a diamond, they were too cold and generic. Opals. His clan had become rich trading and mining them. A fire opal with sparks of red, gold, and orange would be perfect. He wished he could actually touch the stones before purchasing one.

He wished he could tell Pat what he wanted to do. Pat had the skills to pick the right stone on the first shot out. A brief fantasy of the Pat helping him pick out the stone dissolved into the reality of Pat hurt, angry, and beating the hell out of him. Chris sighed. He should tell Pat. That would be the honorable thing to do. But the code was different now, and honorable wasn't quite the same here. It occurred to him Sarah might not appreciate him telling Pat without talking to her about it first.

His mind drifted back to opals. He'd have to find one online and hope the one that looked right on a screen was the right one in person.

When he got home, he began the search. Twenty minutes online landed him on the Etsy Alchemy page. It looked perfect for his needs. He set up his request and how much he was willing to spend. He used his phone to take a picture of his tattoo so potential artists could get a general idea of what he wanted. That done he went stone shopping.

It was pretty. The pictures of the little red and gold cabochon showed a lot of fire for a stone small enough to not overpower her finger. His credit card whimpered for a moment when he put its numbers into the computer. *Shut up!* He had the cash to cover it, and that was that.

He checked the clock. Five minutes before his eleven o'clock class. Then lunch. She'd be at lunch. He smiled, gathered up his books, and headed across the street toward the English building.

Tuesday night, practically Wednesday morning, Chris was sitting against my headboard while I rested on my side next to him. "I don't suppose you'd let me smoke in here?" he asked.

"You brought cigarettes?" He nodded. "No, you can't smoke in here. I don't want my house smelling like an ashtray." He pouted at me. It was the most ridiculously cute thing I had ever seen. I didn't even know he could be cute.

"Okay. In the bathroom, with the window open, and the fan on."

He stood, stretched, and moseyed over to his pants. I enjoyed watching him move, feeling contentedly possessive of the naked man in my home. He fumbled around, grabbed the cigs and a lighter, and settled himself against the wall of my bathroom next to the window.

The cold, wet air from the open window poured in. I wrapped myself tightly in my blanket before joining him in the bathroom. I flicked on my shower and set it to steamy. He leaned against the wall, one leg drawn up, the other supporting him, and slowly inhaled, looking more relaxed and happier than I had ever seen him.

I took the cigarette from him, sucked down a drag, quickly exhaled, and replaced the cigarette between his lips. The smell isn't as bad if you've been smoking, too. Two years in Israel taught me that. "Yep, does nothing for me."

His eyes closed as he inhaled again. "Don't always like them myself, but right now..." He took another drag, held it for a few seconds, and exhaled. "Right now feels quite good."

I stepped into the shower. "This feels good to me." A moment later he slid in next to me, cupped my breast, and nuzzled against my neck.

"You're right. This does feel good."

I moved his hand off of my breast. "I've got class early tomorrow, and I'm kind of low on sleep. So after this, I'm going to bed, to sleep. You can stay if you want."

"I do want to."

"I was hoping you would."

We had settled into bed when a question hit me. "How often do you sleep at home?" He thought about it. "Three, four nights a week."

"You should probably keep it up if you don't want Autumn to start wondering."

He sighed. "I know you're right, but I'd rather stay here."

"Anytime you want to take this public…"

"Not yet."

"I should tell Pat."

"Just give me a half-hour of warning. He'll beat the hell out of me after, but he won't be pissed enough to kill me. He knows we've been… falling in love, for a while now. I told him when this mess with Mildred was done I'd fight him tooth and nail for you, and I'd enjoy beating him at it. He knows I'll win and seemed resigned."

I wasn't quite sure what to do with that. Both of them were old fashioned on the whole sexual politics front. Sitting them down and explaining I, or any other woman for that matter, wasn't something they got to fight over and win seemed like a waste of time. They'd been here twenty years, if it hadn't sunk in yet, it wasn't likely to.

"I'm afraid it'll change our friendship." A related thought that wasn't going to run head first into the brick wall of two hundred years of entrenched sexual mores.

"It probably will. But there's nothing to do about that."

"I was planning on him coming to the farm with me for Passover. Maybe then? Give him time to cool down before you're within convenient punching range."

"That'd be nice. I like my ribs in one piece."

Finally a night when Pat, Chuck, and Chris were all free and nothing was happening Lemmon Hall rolled around. All three of them were standing in the lobby, ready to see about the next step in making a ghost real.

Chuck had briefed Pat about how making these things corporeal worked. He felt like he had a pretty good idea of what was going to happen, and what sort of help he could lend. The biggest problem was the total absence of anything to practice on.

"I thought you two said there was something here?"

Chuck was busy concentrating on finding any of the things that called this building home. Chris looked annoyed. "There was something here. Three somethings. We didn't know precisely what they were, but they were here."

"They aren't now," Chuck said as he pulled his mind away from looking for them. "Nothing's here."

"When did you check the first time?"

"We were here last year. Spring. Mike had a class here last fall, and he didn't report them being gone," Chuck added.

"Come on, let's go to Fullings."

"You want to go to the girl's dorm at two in the morning?" Pat asked Chris.

"Yeah, I'm playing a hunch."

"Fine, lead on." Chris' hunches were usually worth listening to.

They tromped across the campus. Chris lead them behind the girl's dorm. "I don't think we have to go in. Take a look, Chuck."

Chuck focused in on the inhabitants of the building in front of them. "Just students."

Pat shook his head, realizing where this was going. "No one has seen anything on campus since the last attack, have they?"

"I don't think so. Besides the uptick in watchers last week, nothing new has been added to the map in five weeks," Chris blew out a frustrated breath. "The whole place is dead."

"It's a good tactic. How close did you get to figuring it out before the Minion tried to rip your arm off?" Chuck asked Chris.

"Not very. There was a glimmer of understanding, a hint about what came next, and then searing pain. I didn't even get far enough to really tell if it was solid or not."

"It was solid," Chuck added.

"I get them hiding. But everything else as well?" Pat's eyes scanned the building.

"As I said, good tactics. If the idea is to make sure Chris doesn't figure out how to make them solid, chasing all of the practice material out of the area is a good plan."

"I'm not asking about it being a good plan. I'm asking how Mildred's pulling it off. That's a ton of power, and none of us felt it happen."

"Oh. Yes." Chris looked distracted, his mind far away from the other two.

"Not like you two have been paying much attention lately."

"True." Pat shrugged. "But it doesn't explain why none of the rest of you noticed."

Chris jerked slightly. "Okay, I'm back. There's nothing on campus."

"Wonderful. I'll put out feelers for something farther afield." Chuck turned towards Writers'; Chris followed. Pat stayed put. "You coming?" Chris asked

"No. You two go chew over this. Theoretical magic with dead things isn't really my area of expertise. Plus, Emily lives here, so I'm going to visit."

Chuck grinned. "Have fun."

"I intend to." Pat turned and headed into the dorm.

Chris got the email Thursday morning. Autumn told him Sarah was coming over for a bath. Her text message showed up a minute later. He sent one back to let her know he got it. As he headed off for class, she mentioned it on his way out of the house. "I've got it, Autumn. I will not come charging home when I feel the wards go off 'round about one."

"Good."

He did not allow himself to think that at five minutes after one he'd walk happily into the house to join her. He knew thinking that near Autumn was a bad idea. Pleasure sparked through him when he saw Autumn didn't join them for lunch. He wasn't able to keep Autumn out of his head when she was right near him, and he had things he'd rather think about than the conversation going on around him. He shielded his mind and allowed himself to daydream about what he'd be doing in an hour. If Mike had to ask him the same question three times before giving up on trying to get him involved in a conversation, that wasn't precisely odd behavior for him. Sarah watched him curiously from time to time. To keep his mind closed to the others it had to be closed to her. He smiled at her though, and she went back to chatting with Pat about their history class.

He heard water running in the bathroom as he walked up the steps. Like last time his heart and breath were both faster than normal. Unlike last time he was enjoying the sensation. He opened the door quietly and stepped inside.

She sat on the edge of the tub, her feet already in the bath. She didn't hear him enter over the sound of the water. For a moment he stood there, enjoying the view. "Hi."

She jumped slightly and turned to face him. "Hi, yourself. Feeling the need for a bath?"

"After last time, Autumn made sure to email, text, and personally tell me you'd be here today."

"That was very considerate."

"Yes, it was." He began to unbutton his shirt, reveling in her watching him like he was a particularly delicious morsel she was planning on savoring. "By my count we've got close to two hours before anyone else comes here."

"That sounds right. Autumn gets out of class at three."

He sat on the side of the tub next to her and put his feet in the water. "So, what do you usually do when you get a bath?"

She turned off the water and slid into the tub. For a moment, she lay submerged in the bath. Then she came back up. "I usually start like that. Then I pray. There's no *Mikvah* here, so this is the closest I get to ritual purity without a trip to Pittsburgh. After that... read, drink cocoa, fantasize about lovely men."

"I noticed you didn't bring any cocoa or book."

"I didn't think I'd be spending much time alone." She smiled warmly and kissed his knee.

"That leaves fantasies then."

"Or realities."

"If you'd like to tell me, I'd like to hear them." Chris grinned. "Much more likely to become realities." He slid into the tub on the opposite side. He grasped one of her feet in his hand and tugged her closer to him. He lifted it to his mouth, kissed the arch, then licked to her ankle. "Such pretty little feet."

She closed her eyes and let her head rest against the side of the tub. "You really want to hear this?"

"Oh yes."

"Will you tell me some of yours?"

"I'll trade you one for one."

She took a deep breath and started. Her voice sounded charmingly embarrassed. He was deeply pleased she'd tell him this and very amused she kept her eyes closed while she talked. "Since you were staying at my house, I've been thinking about how you play with yourself. You took so long on that first shower after you were hurt. It got me wondering what you were doing in there. Were you in my shower stroking yourself? One hand? Two hands? Did you use my soap for lube? Were you thinking about me when you did it? What did you have me do in your fantasies?

"It grew out of that. I hadn't seen you fully naked yet, but I had enough bits and pieces to put together a pretty complete image. It starts with you in my shower, washing yourself, your hands moving over your skin. You're thinking about me, and you start to get hard." She opened her eyes and gently traced his stiffening erection with her toe. "Kind of like now. You reach down with your right hand and start to fondle yourself, stroking and stretching as you get fuller and harder."

He let his hand fall and curled it around himself, slowly pulling up to the tip. She licked her lips. "Damn, that's hot."

He grinned. "One of these days I'll give you the full show."

"I certainly hope so."

He let go of himself and started massaging her foot. "Anyway, I'm in your shower…"

"With your hand on yourself. But your hand isn't sliding as well as you'd like it to. You reach for my soap and squirt a little in your hand. You're thinking about me rubbing the soap all over my body. Seeing my hands on my skin while you touch yourself. Your eyes are closed, and your hips are moving now. Your skin pinks up. Your nipples get hard. You're breathing faster, jaw clenched, body moving faster. You aren't making any noise, besides the wet slippery sound of your hand. Your hand tightens, moving faster, and your…" He realized she was looking for a good word to apply to that particular bit of his anatomy.

"If you call it a manhood, I'll giggle."

"You giggle?"

"When properly motivated."

"I'll keep that in mind. Anyway, your head falls back against the shower wall, and your *cock* twitches, spurting into the spray from the shower."

"Good choice."

"Thank you. I don't use that word often, but I like the way it sounds, hard and strong. It's got a good sound for this sort of conversation." He traced his fingers from her foot to the inside of her knee and back again, lost in memories of a similar conversation long, long ago, when Althiira said something almost identical to him. "So, what did take you so long that first time?"

He blinked, remembering where he was, and answered, "Nothing that exciting. I was enjoying the hot water and feeling clean again. Then came staring at what I hoped wasn't going to be a long and interesting chain of new scars. Using your soap did start some images, but I put them aside. I still couldn't think about you then."

"When was your first happy fantasy of me?"

"The morning after our second night."

"I would have thought you'd have been all fucked out that morning."

He smiled warmly. "There are some perks to a twenty-one-year-old body. I know for a fact this level of stamina won't hold forever."

"You mean eventually I'll have to trade you in for a newer model?"

"Hush. Between my tongue and fingers I can keep going as long as you can."

"That sounds promising."

"It should."

"So, you've gotten home…" She looked directly at him, and he was pleased to see she wasn't at all shy about hearing him talk.

"I headed straight for the bathroom. Mike's alarm is going off, so I know I've got to get moving. I bend over to turn on the water and remembered the first time you got a bath here. You were leaning over the edge of the tub to pull the plug out, and your towel didn't come down far enough to cover you. When I walked up the steps, I got quite an eyeful. That day, I couldn't really enjoy it. I had my hand on cock less than two minutes after you closed the door, but that wasn't fun or enjoyable. I hated not being able to keep myself under control."

"I didn't know you saw that much."

"I was pretty certain you didn't know. I doubt you would have made that serendipity comment if you knew what I had seen while bringing your cocoa. I almost dropped the cup and grabbed you when you said it."

"That's what you were thinking about?"

"Not really. I was thinking about what I should have done instead of hiding in my room, wacking off, and feeling guilty about it for the next week. I was thinking about walking up behind you. You look over your shoulder and see me. You smile, and I grin back. You straighten up so you're kneeling in front of the tub, holding onto the edge while I slide into you from behind, one hand on your breast, the other on your clit. You're half-turned so we can kiss. I tend to fantasize in snap shots instead of storylines, so that image morphed into you and I on the floor. Your legs are wrapped around my back as we slowly rock together. The final image was me standing in your shower, you on your knees in front of me sucking me deep into your mouth, your one hand wrapped around the base of my cock, the other pressing me behind my balls."

"You really like oral sex, don't you?"

"Are there any guys who don't?"

"Not that I've met." She knelt between his legs and licked her lips. "Would you like me to?"

He sat up as well, turned her so she was facing away from him, and pulled her so she lay against his chest. He wrapped one arm around her waist and used the other to stroke her from hand to shoulder. "Not yet. I like talking with you. I'm enjoying the anticipation."

"What are you anticipating?"

"Another fantasy from you."

She laughed. "You really aren't twenty-one, are you?"

"Because I like to fuck with my brain almost as much as with my body?"

"Yeah. So, let's see…" She settled back against him more comfortably and lifted one leg to rest her foot against the soap dish. He cupped her knee, tracing his palm down her leg, just lightly brushing her pussy, then back to her knee again.

"You told me, once upon a time, you weren't that vanilla. Another time you told me you liked to be tied down."

"This sounds like it'll be good."

"I hope you like it. I've got you tied spread eagle on my bed."

"Sounds even better." He kissed her ear.

"It starts with just massage: petting, stroking, kneading. Taking the time to really look at your body. Getting to know the curves and flats. What I wanted to do but couldn't when I took care of your bruises. We're kissing, and I'm getting wetter and wetter as your tongue dances with mine. I'm sliding along you, letting just the tip in before pulling back." He moved his hand back down to cup her sex and very lightly circled her clit with his middle finger. Her eyes slid shut and she sighed. "That feels very good."

"Good. Keep talking to me. I love the way your voice sounds right now."

"I move up your body and straddle your face, lowering myself so you can lick me." A deep, rumbling moan escaped Chris. "I turn around so I can lick you, too. I'm slowly sucking you when a really dirty thought hits me. I get up. You make a little disappointed noise. I say something like, 'Trust me,' while going to my dresser to get a bottle of lube and one of my toys."

"Toys plural?" He was very pleased his voice stayed even. Just the idea of her and toys was making all the blood in his body rush to his cock.

"Toys plural. All that time in my house and you never snooped in my drawers?"

"No." He forced himself to calm down. "Probably a good thing, I'd have been unable to look you in the face or make my erection go down if I had found something like that."

"You like the idea of toys?"

"Do you not feel me against your back? I could pole vault with it if I needed to."

She laughed. "I doubt it will come to that."

"What do you pull out of your drawer?"

"It's not very long, it's thin, and it vibrates." She kissed his middle finger. "About that size. I watch you watch me take it out. I know what you expect to see—me playing with myself with it—and I do give you a show. I ask you again if you trust me, and you say yes. I settle myself between your legs and open the bottle of lube. Your eyes go wide when you realize I'm going to put the lube on you. I warm it in my hands and then slick you up. Then I add more to the vibrator and very slowly ease it into you. You don't look like you're sure this is a good idea yet. But when I go back to sucking on you and turn it on, you start making very happy noises. I turn around again, so you can lick me, and… well, that's usually where it ends. I've never made it past that part."

He forced himself to breathe slowly and let the lip he was biting slip from between his teeth. He held her firmly against him, certain if she moved he'd come. "When you do that to me for real, you better not leave me hanging."

"You like the idea of me doing that to you?"

"That's the closest I've ever come to climaxing from words alone."

"Really?"

"Really."

"So, if I were to turn around and slide onto you…"

He tightened his hold on her. "Please, stay still. I'd be done before you got all the way down."

"Interesting. That fantasy would freak most guys out."

"Most guys don't know what they're missing. We've only got four major erogenous zones, and that fantasy gets three of them at once."

"I bet I could get all four."

"I bet you could."

"You're on a hair trigger today."

The urgency faded, and he let his arms relax. "I've been thinking about this since breakfast."

"Is that why you were so distracted at lunch?"

"I wasn't distracted. I was extremely focused. I was thinking about fucking in the tub with you, but people kept trying to get me to have conversations with them."

She laughed. "Inconsiderate people. Maybe you need a little sign, 'Fantasizing About Sex. Do Not Disturb.'"

"Maybe I do." He began kissing her neck while his fingers continued circling her clit. She let him do it for a few minutes, her hips rocking against his. Then she turned around and straddled him, very lightly brushing against him before sliding onto him. His head fell back against the side of the tub. He cupped his hands around her hips, holding her tight to him. "That feels so good."

"Tell me about it."

"Can't. No words for how good that feels." She leaned in and kissed him slowly, keeping her mouth soft and lips wet against his; then she sucked his tongue and squeezed around him at the same time.

"How does that feel?"

"Better."

"If I start to move it will feel better yet."

"Yes it will." She eased upwards, keeping her motions slow and gentle. "Fuck, love, that's good." For a few strokes he just enjoyed the sensation, then he opened his eyes and started talking, "I still owe you a story."

She smiled down at him and squeezed him again. "Then by all means, tell me one."

He smiled wickedly at her. "A long time ago in a galaxy far, far away…"

"If you tell me the plot to *Star Wars*, I will hit you."

"Just fooling. It's Saturday morning, and, for once, you're sleeping in. The sun's just over the trees. Bright enough to color everything yellow. You're lying on your stomach, sleeping, quilt down around your hips. I wake up before you do…"

"This really is a fantasy, isn't it?"

"Shush. My fantasy. I can wake up whenever I want." His fingers dipped below the water line to stroke her clit. Her eyes slid shut, and she leaned back a little to give him better access. "For a while I just lay there, enjoying being in your bed, waking up next to you for once, and watching you sleep. After a few minutes, that's not enough. I have to touch you. I run my hands down your back, very lightly, like this." He slid his other hand down her arm, barely touching her, feeling goose bumps raise on her skin in response. "I start at the nape of your neck and stroke everything between it and the top of the quilt.

"But that's not enough. I want to taste you as well. I move so I'm leaning over you and begin to kiss and lick my way down your back. I get down to here," he used his free hand to stroke the line between her cheeks. Her hips added a slow rolling motion. He exhaled and closed his eyes. "God, that's good… and I can smell how turned on you are. I love that smell. Delectable wet pussy. I know you're awake now. You're moaning as my tongue rubs against you. I pull your hips up so I can lick you easier, so I can get to all of you," her hips moved faster, his fingers kept pace, "and I get my fingers going, too. Sliding in and out of you. I can feel you start to tighten. I know you're going to climax soon, and I don't want to miss feeling you clench around me. So I switch my fingers to your clit and slide into you." He began to thrust against her. Opening his eyes so he could watch her ride him. "You're on your hands and knees. I can see myself sinking into you with each stroke, and I love the way that looks." She moaned softly as he pressed more deeply into her. His fingers rubbed faster with a bit more force. "You're making sounds just like that. And you're so tight and so wet and so soft and just feel so incredibly good. You get louder. You're calling my name. And then you're twitching around me, your legs shaking, your sweet, sweet pussy's clenching around me." She was rippling around him, head back and eyes closed. "I grab your hips and pull you against me harder and faster," he pulled her tight against him and used his legs for extra leverage to thrust deeper into her. She pushed against him, meeting him on each stroke, squeezing him further. "Fuck, love! Just like that." His jaw clenched, his eyes slid shut, and his fingers gripped her hips as his body spasmed.

At some later point she lay on his chest, breathing softly against him. "The water's getting cold," she said after a few very content moments.

He turned the hot water on with his foot. "Better?"

"Yes."

"Good. I don't feel like going anywhere soon, and I don't want you going anywhere, either."

"I'm not going anywhere. Except maybe your bed if you're willing to try this somewhere conventional."

"Are you interested in conventional?"

"I was thinking about your image of us on the floor, and it occurred to me, we haven't done it that way yet. And I'd like to, but cold tile and a small, wet bath mat sound much less comfy than your bed."

He laughed. "Give me a few minutes to feel like moving again, and sure, I'll show you exactly how comfy my bed is."

"Good."

Chris stood next to the map on the table and pointed out exactly where they had come in contact with the last Minion. That left a good three quarters of V4 still to be searched.

"Here's what I'm thinking. We're going to start on the northeast corner and slide to the southwest. We'll stay in two groups: me, Pat, and Autumn on one side, Chuck, Mike, and Dave on the other. We'll move in parallel lines. If anything jumps out, the five of us who are not Autumn go into combat mode."

She squeaked indignantly. Chris, for the first time, let her feel exactly how angry he was with what happened to Chuck. She visibly wilted. "I do not care if a Minion has actually ripped my arm off my body and is beating Chuck over the head with it. All you do is First Aid. Got it?"

"Got it."

"The only time I want you doing any combat is if we are all down. Every single one of us. If Pat is the only one still standing, and he's doing a version of the Black Knight, standing on one leg with no arms and bleeding on the Minion, you do nothing. The only time you fight is if you need to buy enough time to get Sarah there."

"Got it."

"Good. Have you been practicing?"

"No."

"Then that's your other assignment. When you get to the point where you can burn individual branches off a tree, then you can fight again. Now, anyone else with any other ideas?"

The others didn't have any.

"Good luck," Sarah said as they headed off; he caught a hint of fear in her voice.

"I'm coming this time, nothing will go wrong," Pat answered with a grin and a hug as he headed out the door.

"See you in three hours." Chris sent a gentle pulse of desire and comfort to her.

Oh, stop it! You aren't going off to charge Fort Wagner, Chuck said in his head. *And really, stop that when Pat and Autumn are with us. The last thing I want you to do is piss her off so much she burns my head off again.*

Fine. It has to suck to just sit there, waiting for a call to let her know we're all right.

I imagine it does. When we get home, when the others are away, you can soothe her all you want. Right now, STOP IT!

Yes, Dad. Now get out of my head. I need to act like the fearless leader.

An hour of walking landed them at the northeast corner of V4. Another hour of searching showed them it was empty. Chuck could feel there had been Minions here, maybe it had been a gathering place for them or something, but they were gone now.

"God damn it!" Pat yelled as they finished the square. He might have been the only one to say it, but the rest were thinking it. The entire map was almost done, and they had found nothing.

"We'll find it." Autumn put her hand on Pat's shoulder. He flinched at her touch.

Pat spoke with a frustrated anger, "We should know where it is by now. We should be planning. We should be training. Dave should be spending his evenings on recon getting a feel for its strengths. We should be working on new spells to fight it. But no, we're here mucking about in the wilds of suburbia looking for the battleground while Mildred watches us and learns all of our tricks. This is a recipe for a lost battle. This is how we all end up dead. It knows more than we do, and it gets to pick the battleground."

No one had anything to say to that. Pat snapped opened his cell phone and sent Sarah a text letting her know what was up.

Alone in his room, Chris kept listening for the shower to shut off. He wanted to brush his teeth and go to sleep. What he really wanted to do was go to Sarah's, but, not only was it odd for him to spend five nights in a row away, Pat was there. Finally the water stopped, but Dave didn't come out for a long time.

After fifteen minutes, he leaned against Chris' door jam in his towel. Chris waved him in. Dave stepped in, winced, and stepped out.

He kept his voice low. "There are three rooms in this house all of us use. Because of that, they are unshielded. Two people in this house are empathic and can feel the ghosts of intensely emotional moments. In my case I can catch images of it. Thus, it is a bad idea to have sex in any of the unshielded rooms. May I also add, since one of the empaths is your wife's brother and the other one is obsessively in love with you, for you and Sarah especially, it is a remarkably bad idea to have sex in any of the unshielded rooms. I mean, yes, it would be uncomfortable to step into the shower and get the image of Mike screwing away, but that would be that. Unfortunately I now need to go visit Chuck and have him remove the images of you and my sister I now have burned into my mind."

Chris didn't know what to say. He tried to form a few words but stopped before getting through the first sound.

"I'm glad you finally realized who she was and got over yourself enough to get back with her. But please, for the sake of my delicate sensibilities, clean up after yourselves properly. I got another flash of it when I stepped in there," Dave gestured at Chris' room, "and I have absolutely no desire to walk into anything like that ever again."

"Sorry. What about?" Chris pointed at the bathroom.

"I took care of it. I'm not terribly interested in hearing Autumn step in there and start shrieking."

"Thanks."

"I'm assuming—evidence to the contrary notwithstanding—you are interested in keeping this fairly quiet?"

"Yes. At least until the fight is done."

"No problem."

48.

Then it was Friday. Chris packed up his book bag with good clothes and his hat and strolled towards Sarah's. He knew Pat and Emily would be there tonight, so he'd have to keep himself reined in during the meal, but when they were cooking and after dinner... He was very much looking forward to sitting on her sofa tonight, drinking a glass of wine with her, talking about whatever, then taking her to bed and properly celebrating the Sabbath.

He got to her place an hour after lunch. Sarah lay on the sofa, eyes closed, one of her British history textbooks open on her chest. Chris quietly put the bag down and looked around to see what she had started. Nothing yet, but a package of lamb thawing on the counter looked fated to become dinner.

No flowers, no candles, he didn't see anything for dessert. He'd had three lessons on how to ride her motorcycle but wasn't feeling confident enough to just grab the keys and head into town to get the rest of her table setting.

He decided start on the challah. He quietly pulled out the flour, sugar, oil—he couldn't look at the almond oil without grinning—eggs, and yeast. As he measured the flour, she pressed against him from behind, wrapping her arms around his waist.

"You started without me."

He turned to kiss her. "You looked pretty peaceful sleeping there. I didn't want to wake you up."

"Thanks. I appreciate my naps."

"I would, too if I got up at six every morning."

"I'm sleeping in a lot more often these days. It's difficult to get out of bed when I've got you spooned against me."

"Good. It's one of my goals to get you to spend as much time in bed with me as possible." She giggled and let go of him, moving over to see what he was doing with the cooking. "Do you want to get this made and do the grocery run while it rises, or do you trust me with it and want to head off on your own?"

"Do you want to come shopping with me, or would you rather bake?"

"I'd rather bake. I like making food. Shopping for it isn't my favorite thing."

"Then I'll be back soon." She put on her jacket and helmet and slung an empty backpack on her shoulder. "See ya."

He waved a flour-covered hand at her and went back to mixing up the ingredients. After four weeks of helping with the challah, his hands knew the drill and moved automatically. For a moment he wondered what his Catholic mom would think of him cooking for his Jewish girlfriend's Sabbath dinner. She'd be pleased he was doing a tidy job of the cooking, beyond thrilled there was finally a girlfriend, the Sabbath thing would bother her. Nothing he could do about that. For the time being his mom didn't need to know about it. If he made it to summer break, he could tell her about it then.

Sarah got back while he braided the challah. She put the bags on the table and leaned against it, watching his hands move. "My brothers are going to be so happy with you."

"I had been wondering what my mom would think of this."

"And?"

He finished the braid, tucking the strands under, then turned to face her. He took a step closer, leaned into her, and kissed her neck just below her ear. "I think she'd be pleased I'm cooking well, very pleased to see I have a girlfriend, and disconcerted by my long-terms plans if they involve someone who isn't Catholic."

She rose an eyebrow at him and asked with mock seriousness, "Do you have long-term plans?"

He grinned and kissed her lips. "I've got some short-term ones."

She smiled back at him. "What would they include?"

"Taking your hand, heading into the shower, and getting soaped up and clean for tonight. Then, after dinner, breaking into that drawer of yours, seeing exactly what kinds of goodies you've got in there, and getting very dirty."

Hand in hers, he pulled her toward the bathroom while she answered, "Far be it from me to mess up your plans though I might want to add to them."

"Really?"

"Yeah." She dropped his hand, headed back to the kitchen table, and grabbed one of the bags. "Wanna guess what's in here?"

He licked his lips. It was a Walmart bag, so he knew it couldn't be too risqué, but he was warmly pleased at her gesture.

"Can I get a hint?"

"It's red."

He smiled widely. "Do I get to see it before you get dressed tonight, or are you going to make me wonder about it all night?"

"I'm thinking you should see it first, so you can imagine it every time you look at me."

"I'm thinking the conversation on the sofa tonight might be short."

"How long do you want to sit there anticipating what comes next?"

"About ten seconds." He took her hand, pulling her against him. "Shower, now!"

"Yes, Sir!"

He leaned down to her lips, kissing hard and deep. When he pulled back he said, "I think that might be a game for another day. Especially if you've got a plaid skirt."

She laughed. "I don't. I can make or buy something along those lines, though. White button down, plaid skirt, knee socks. That what you're thinking?" He nodded. "Call you 'Sir' and ask for help with my homework. If you wait a few months my hair will be long enough to put in a proper ponytail."

He grinned, backing them into her bathroom. She smiled up at him while unbuttoning his pants. Her hand pressed against him while he pulled off his shirt. "You really like that idea, don't you?"

"I do." He reached behind himself to turn the water on. "You know what else I like?"

"Tell me." She let go of him and began to take her own clothing off.

"You and me, in your shower, wet, naked and soapy. My skin sliding against yours. Picking you up, pressing you against the back of the shower, and slowly sliding into you while you bite on my shoulder because it feels so good."

"Then get in."

He stepped back into the water and hopped back out again. "Fuck! It's still cold."

She laughed. "I didn't imagine you wouldn't reach in to see what temperature it was first. How about now?"

This time he reached back and stepped in. "Much better. After this winter, I could go the entire rest of my life without ever having to get a cold shower again."

She stepped in after him and pressed close. "Let's not think about that now. You said something about soapy."

"I did." He picked up her shower soap and poured some in his hands. He slid them over her body, watching the suds slide down her skin along the path of the water. She made happy noises as he stroked her skin.

"You like that?"

"Yes."

"How about this?" He began to work the shampoo into her hair.

She leaned against him and sighed deeply. "That's excellent. Very happy scalp sending happy little tingles everywhere else."

"Good."

She turned so the water could rinse the shampoo out of her hair. He moved his hands to her shoulders, pressing deeply into the muscles where her neck and shoulder met. "You really are good at that."

"Thanks. I like doing it."

She finished rinsing her hair and turned them around so he was in the direct line of the spray. Sarah looked up at him. "I'm not doing this over my head. Do you mind kneeling?"

"Nope." He got on his knees, his head at her breast level. "Perfect for nipple kissing." He began to nuzzle and lick her while she reached for the shampoo.

He moaned, a long, relaxed sound as she soaped up his hair. She did it longer than necessary, her fingers rubbing into the tight spots on his scalp and neck. As the last of the shampoo rinsed out, he stood up and pressed against her for a long kiss. She wrapped her leg around his, pressing harder against him. When that didn't get him moving faster, she took him in hand and began stroking. He continued kissing lazily.

"You said something about picking me up…"

"Am I moving too slowly for you?"

"Yes. Now would be good. Two minutes ago would have been better."

"Have patience." He took both of her wrists in one of his hands and pressed them above her head against the back wall of the shower. "We'll get there." The fingers of his free hand traced over her breasts. "I should do this to you more often. You look wonderful. So glorious, wet, back arched, breasts high, arms trapped above your head. And you know what'll look better?" he licked her lip as he asked.

"What?"

He slipped his free hand down from her breast to her pussy and whispered, lips against her ear "You climaxing against my hand. Then I'll pick you up and fuck you into the wall." She moaned, biting her lip, and thrust against his hand. He made sure his fingers moved the way she liked them.

He pulled far enough back to watch. Eyes closed, mouth slightly open, her head fell back against the wall of the shower. Sarah's skin flushed as she made small moaning noises. Her hips rocked faster, and he moved into a steady rhythm to keep up with her. Her face was soft and open with a very intense expression. In another setting, he might think it was pain. She moved faster against him, looking for more friction, more pressure. He debated keeping his fingers light and drawing this out or moving harder and faster to send her over the edge.

"Please, Chris." Her eyes opened slowly and focused on his. "Please, baby, fuck me."

So much for his first plan. That was a request he couldn't say no to. He let her arms drop and picked her up. Her legs wrapped around his waist and her arms around his neck. She slid down him in one quick thrust.

"Ohhhh… so good." He didn't know if he said it or she did. Either way it was true. He didn't bother with slow or gentle. She wasn't looking for that right now. Now was about fast and hard and catching up to her. He could feel her body tightening around him, but he wasn't quite there yet. Then her teeth clamped down on his shoulder, enough force to add to the endorphins, not enough to break the skin. She sucked hard on the bite and that did it. Pain arced bright and hot, taking him higher, intensifying his pleasure. He was thrusting fast and erratic, pulsing inside her while her thighs quivered around him.

His head rested against her shoulder while his heart slowed down. Chris realized he should put her down because pressing her into the back of the shower probably wasn't comfortable, but he didn't want to be free of her body yet. She wasn't saying anything, so he decided to stay there a little longer. Eventually he let her go, and they finished getting showered.

She winced at his shoulder as he got dressed.

"What?" he asked, as he buttoned his pants.

"I bit the hell out of your shoulder." Her fingers rested gently on the bruise. "Do you want me to fix it?"

He remembered how it felt when she did it. "No. I like that you marked my shoulder. I like that I know it's there and you know it's there but no one else does. I like you on me." He cupped her neck in his hand and kissed her. He kept his hand on her neck, pulled back enough so he could look in her eyes, and said, "Any mark you want to put on me, I'll proudly wear." He kissed her again, then let her go and picked up his shirt. "So, what's in the bag?"

She grinned at him. "Go put the challah in the oven, and when you come back you can see it in all its glory."

He hurried out of the bathroom without bothering to button his shirt. When he came back forty seconds later, she wasn't quite dressed. She was smoothing one stocking up her leg. The other was draped over the door knob. The rest of the outfit was as far from her usual cotton panties and bra as an outfit could be. It was a red, silky corset and garter belt all in one with a very tiny red thong.

She finished the first leg, looked up at him, and winked. She very delicately reached past him for the second stocking. Sarah balanced on one foot, put her other foot on the sink, and slowly eased the nylon up her leg.

"Do you like it?"

He bit his lip and wrapped her in his arms. "If it had been more than ten minutes since I came last, I'd be fucking you again. As it is, I'm very, very tempted to get down on my knees, pull those hot little panties to the side, and lick you until you're quivering on my tongue. By the time that happens I will be ready for another go."

She grinned and pushed him away. "Later. Our friends, who do not know we're sleeping together, will be here soon, and we've still got to do some cooking. So, for the rest of tonight, you get to enjoy knowing what's under the conservative outfit I'm about to slide into."

And he did enjoy it.

During dinner Sarah asked Pat if he wanted to come home with her for Passover. He watched Pat look at Sarah, then look at Emily.

"How long will you be gone?"

"The ninth and tenth, maybe stick around for the eleventh, depends on how I'm doing on my class work," Sarah answered.

"Could I borrow your apartment instead?" Pat leered happily at Emily. She blushed prettily.

Sarah grinned at both of them. "Yes. How about you, Chris? Feel like spending sixteen hours on a motorcycle and meeting my family?"

"I'd like that very much."

"Let's see how you feel about it after that much time on a bike," Sarah replied with a warm smile.

"Will you let me drive?"

"If it's clear, yeah."

"You didn't let me drive." Pat sounded mock insulted.

"There was half a foot of snow on the roads when we went to the farm and your place. I don't trust my life to anyone else in the snow. If it makes you feel better, you're the only person I'd let ride with me under those circumstances."

"What?" Chris questioned. He genuinely felt a little insulted.

Sarah stroked her foot down his and answered calmly, "Get a few hundred more miles under your belt, and I'll change my mind. Right now I know Pat knows what to do if we get into trouble."

"Thanks." Pat smirked at him. Chris almost smirked back at him, thinking about what he had been doing with Sarah two hours ago. However, it wouldn't make sense in the context of the conversation, so Pat would wonder why he was smirking back. Emily began to ask about Sarah's motorcycle, how she had gotten into it, what she liked about it. That conversation got them through the rest of dinner.

After Pat and Emily left, Sarah turned on the dishwasher, turned to him, and flicked open the top button on her shirt. A little red peaked out at him. "So, wine and conversation now or later?"

"Later."

Later he did walk naked across her apartment, grab the wine bottle and a glass, and return to her bed. For as much as he had enjoyed sharing a glass of wine with her and talking on the sofa, he liked doing it in her bed even more. She lay on her side, her head propped on her hand, and took the glass from him. He very carefully and gently sat back against the headboard, then took the glass from her.

"You okay?" She had the same look of concern on her face as she did an hour ago when he said, 'How about that one?' and picked a much bigger toy than the one she had selected.

"A little sore, in a very, very good way."

She laughed. "I could fix that, too."

"Nope." He smiled at her. "I want my body to remember this." She took the glass from him and had a sip. "So, your place for Passover?"

"Sorry about ambushing you with that."

"I'd like to go. Can I sleep with you there?"

"No. That'd give my brothers' heart failure. It was one thing for my dad to have a girlfriend who slept with him; their little sister is a whole other story."

"Damn."

"Eight hours there and the *Seder* goes late. Neither of us is likely to feel like much fooling around."

"Even if we aren't fooling around, I like your warm, soft body sleeping next to mine."

She grinned and kissed his thigh. "I do, too. But, that's the price of Conservative Jewish siblings: no fucking around at home with someone I'm not married to. If we were staying longer, I'd show you some of the less obvious spots around the farm. Come back with me in the summer, and I will show you."

His first impression of her home was a sea of smallish people with dark hair flowing around Sarah, wrapping her in embraces, and then flowing away. One of her brothers, Sam, introduced him to everyone. He got most of the names but didn't know which kids went with which adults. They all looked enough alike he couldn't trust that as a way to guess. Sarah's sisters-in-law grabbed her and pulled her into the kitchen. He started to go and offer to help when Jon, her oldest nephew, pulled him aside and said, "You're staying in our room. Let's get you settled."

"Thanks."

"Besides, you don't want to be in there when they get cooking. It's a girly talk-fest."

"Okay." He wanted to watch Sarah in a girly talk-fest, curious as to how she'd handle herself, but had a feeling that wasn't the kind of thing to admit to her nephew.

"Everyone'll start showing up in the next hour or so. Which means it's about time for us to get changed. You can have the bathroom first if you want it."

"Thank you." He got a very fast shower and changed into dress slacks, a button down, and tie. He put his fedora on, noticing fedoras were the headgear of choice among the Metz men. Maybe he was getting used to wearing it. Maybe the fact Jon and Eli had similar hats. Either way he didn't feel nearly as silly about wearing it as he usually did.

"Come on; let's get out there with the rest of them. My mom will be running through here making sure we're all dressed and moving soon," Eli said with a final tug at the knot on his tie.

"Which one is your mom?"

"Anna's our mom," Jon answered while pointing at Eli, "And Maddy's. The little ones belong to Uncle David and Aunt Beth." Jon led him to a room filled with more new people and made yet more introductions. After a few minutes, Sarah came out and held his hand while he explained what he was studying and where he was from and answered all the other polite questions that get asked of the new boyfriend when faced with a huge extended family. He was chatting about being an English major when Anna called out, "Dinner!"

Everyone shuffled toward the dining room. He was in the middle of one table, with Sarah on one side and Jon on the other. Ben lead the proceedings. He knew it wasn't precisely the same prayer Sarah said for Sabbath, but it was similar. A minute or two in he realized he wasn't just remembering the similar bits from Sabbath with Sarah but understood Ben's Hebrew as well. He didn't have as good of a feel for it as he did when Sarah said the prayers, but he was definitely getting the gist of it. He drank his cup of wine along with the rest of them.

For most of the first part of the meal he watched Ben and tried to keep up with everyone else. It wasn't too hard. As long as he ate the right things at the right times, he was fine. That he could do while getting a sense of Ben's magic. Ben had the ability to call on some very serious power and he sensed Ben hadn't done so in a very long time. Chris could feel the blocks in Ben's mind. They had been very well done. Someone on Chuck's level had taken care of Ben's memories.

Then he noticed something surprising. Ben had been magically bound to a woman at one point. When they had chatted on the computer, he had thought the 'Dear One' was just a girlfriend. The magic blocking Ben's memories made a whole lot more sense to him now. Whatever else had happened that year, Ben had also lost his mate.

Sarah nudged him, and they went to wash hands again. This time with the blessing he knew. Her brother, David, looked surprised to hear him say it without stumbling.

"You know this?" David asked him.

"I've got all of the Sabbath prayers but the *Kiddush* down by now. Your sister tells me I make a mean challah as well."

"She's got you baking for Sabbath?" David's eyes were wide.

"She's got him cooking as well," Sarah answered. "He's a good cook, and I'm not about to let that go to waste."

"This I have to hear more about, maybe at breakfast tomorrow?" he asked as everyone shuffled back to the table to continue dinner.

Once back at the table everyone made themselves a small matzo and horseradish, Chris knew it had another name, but it had slipped his mind, sandwich. The little kids made faces as they ate it.

Then came dinner, starting with a hardboiled egg, which he didn't understand but ate happily. Followed by roast beef, roasted potatoes, mounds of succulent looking veggies, and what he knew was challah based on taste but was rolled into a spiral instead of a braid. The others were freely drinking from their wine glasses at this point, but Sarah had said there were four cups of wine this night, so he stuck to his water glass. Most of the conversation was family stuff about who had been up to what lately, kind of like Thanksgiving at his house.

When the meal wound down, the kids went hunting for the matzo, and Dan found it. He held it ransom and got ten dollars for it. The wine bottles were passed around again, and everyone topped up their cup. Then small pieces of matzo were passed around and eaten. Ben prayed again, and, on his lead, the others joined in. They drank the third cup of wine when the prayers wound down.

Ally, Ben's wife, opened the door. As she did that, another cup of wine was poured and placed at the empty seat. Then more prayers, more songs, more wine, and finally, "*L'shanah haba'ah b'Yerushalayim!* Next year in Jerusalem!"

The small children had gone to bed. The rest of the group had moved to the family room to study. They were reciting *Song of Songs* when Ben touched his shoulder. "Come take a walk with me."

"Sure." Chris got his coat and followed the older man outside. He felt sluggish from the wine, food, and the fact he had been awake for close to twenty hours. The cold air and a good sense of what Ben wanted to talk to him about sharpened his mind. Ben led them down the driveway, across the street, through a fence, to the far side of a field with a pond in the middle of it. Ben stopped when he got to a lone oak tree. He leaned against it and looked Chris up and down very thoroughly.

"You're going to marry her."

That was more blunt than Chris had expected. He went for the blunt answer. "Yes."

"Tell me why you are the right man for her."

Chris spent a long time debating his answer. He wished he had Chuck's talents. Any clue as to what Ben was thinking would have come in handy, but the oldest Metz was a blank to him.

He picked his words carefully. He could tell from Ben's broken binding one word would resonate more strongly with him than any other. "She's my mate."

"You know this after two weeks?" Chris thought through every conversation about the two of them. Neither of them had mentioned how long they had been together. Granted, she might have told Ben over the phone, but he didn't think she had. He spent another minute trying to decide if Ben was reading it off of him or immensely in tune with his sister. He settled on Ben reading it off of him. He hadn't been particularly guarded in her brother's presence, and that was the easier way to go about doing it.

"If you know it's only been two weeks, then you also know it's been much longer than two weeks."

Ben gave him a sharp half-smile. "Tell me why you're the right man."

Chris took a deep breath and started to talk, very aware this was either the exact *right answer* or the absolute wrong one, and there was no way to know until he had said it. "Because I've been married to her for almost one hundred and thirty-four years. Since the first time my hand touched hers, I've been in love with her. And if that was a boy's infatuation when it began, it was love as strong as any man has ever felt for a woman when we parted. It took me twenty-one years to find her again, six months to convince myself it was her, and I don't want to wait another second to get our life together going again."

Ben smiled, and Chris relaxed. Right answer. "She doesn't know that."

Chris shook his head. "No, she doesn't."

"Why not?"

"She didn't survive."

"And you haven't told her…" Half-statement, half-question.

"She's probably happier not remembering. I'd be happier not remembering." He figured Ben would be sympathetic to that answer.

Ben looked thoughtful. "When she came home for winter break, she had another friend with her. He's stronger than you, a better fighter, possibly a better magic user, and loves her very much. What about him?" Chris smiled at Ben and let him feel a little flash of the magic he was capable of. Ben looked impressed. "So, he's not a better magic user."

Chris smiled dryly at Ben. "She's not in love with him. When he realizes she's mine again, he'll give up and be happy for her. He's a good man, and he loves her enough her joy is more important to him than his own. He loved me for her sake before. He'll do it again. Granted, he'll probably beat the crap out of me before he gets to that point, but it won't be the first time, and she can put both of us back together after." Ben nodded. That fit his assessment of Pat as well.

"What is your plan?"

"To bind us together as soon as she'll let me. Graduate next year, get a job, convert, and marry her formally before she starts medical school. Follow her wherever she goes. Twenty-one years was long enough. I'm not leaving her again."

Ben looked more at peace leaning against the tree than he had at the beginning of the conversation.

Chris decided to ask something he had been wondering since he first held her star. "Why did you give her your star?"

"After I married, I made a new talisman. The boy you saw when you held it had long since vanished, and his talisman was no longer appropriate for me. But she needed one, and I could fill it with comfort and ease, which we all needed that year…"

"You will convert?" Ben was staring in the direction of the farm as he switched from one train of thought to another.

"Yes."

"That'll make the family happy."

"You seem very understanding about this."

"She was born two days after I got home from an absolutely horrific year of college. It's odd; I know that year was bad. On an intellectual level I know some of the things that made it bad. But most of it is very far away now. Like it happened to someone else, and I just watched it. When I got home, even with those blocks in place, I was still shell-shocked from it. I was also so magically sensitive I could feel everything within twenty miles. I held her less than an hour after she was born. Her eyes were old. Her soul was old. She lost it shortly after that. After a week, she felt like any other baby. But from the day she was born I knew someone from whatever had been before would come back for her again. Then I'm on the computer chatting with a guy who feels like he knows someone from my past and has let her see all of his defenses. Speaking of which, did you ever find the brown-haired boy?"

"No. It's galling because I know I know him. But I can't make myself connect the twenty-year-old version to the man who's walking around out there somewhere."

"I don't want those memories back. I couldn't deal with it when it happened and getting them back would be like rewinding twenty-two years and jumping right back into it. But if it's her life on the line then I'll let your brother have them."

"If it was her life on the line, we'd already have them. I lost her once. It will not happen again."

Ben seemed pleased. "I'm assuming you're not planning on proposing tomorrow."

"Not before finals. I should hold off longer, but I doubt I'll make it. The rings will be ready soon. Once I've got them, waiting will be hard."

"You already ordered rings?"

"Yes."

"You really weren't kidding about the whole 'as soon as she'll let you' thing, were you?"

"No." Chris shook his head. "The next time you see her, she'll have a ring, and I'll have the matching one."

"You're very sure that she'll agree."

Chris thought about that for a moment as well as Chuck telling him to slow down. "She may not remember the specifics, but she knows it's right. I think she's known it since the first time she saw me though I don't know if she was willing to admit it to herself. She'll say, 'yes.'"

Ben seemed to consider that for a moment, offered Chris his hand, and said, "So, youngest of my brothers, tell me your name."

Chris took it. "Technically, I'm the oldest of your brothers."

Ben smiled. "Not this time around."

"*Cellin Ath Dath Wa.*"

"Well then, Christopher—who was Cellin—welcome to the Metz clan."

49.

The day after Chris and Sarah got back, Pat pulled Chris and Chuck aside as they walked home from lunch. "I've been kicking around an idea for a while now, doing some research, and I think I've got something."

"What sort of something?" Chris asked.

"Hopefully a how-every-creepy-crawly-thing-got-scared-out-of-town-without-any-of-us-noticing sort of something."

"That would be good to know," Chuck said.

"If I'm right, it's brilliant."

"Mildred pulling brilliant magic is not a good thing." Chris looked worried.

"Sure, but still, you've got to respect a good enemy." Chuck nodded and gestured to get Pat talking more about what he found. "Okay, so here's the thing, one of the ideas on what a ghost is has to do with electro-magnetic energy. Now, we're all tuned into the magic, but we don't really pay much attention to real world stuff. It's in the background. Anyway, I'm watching *Ghost Hunters* with Emily, and they start talking about the EMF changes that go with ghosts. That gets me thinking, and I started to check around. The first test was easy; I got a compass. It was slightly off, just a few tenths of a degree. And, a few weeks ago there was a story in the school paper about how radios aren't working properly anymore, everything has just a little static to it." Chris nodded. Chuck didn't. He didn't read the student newspaper or listen to the radio, so the whole thing had missed him. "That's another sort of thing that would be messed up by a subtle shift in the electro-magnetic signature of an area."

"Is that why the wifi's been slow lately?" Chris asked.

"I'm thinking, yes. And, not that I know anyone I could ask to check, but I'd bet an analog TV would have fuzzy reception right now, too."

"So, you're thinking Mildred somehow shifted the electro-magnetic current of this area?"

"Something like that. And just a little. More and we would have noticed. The computers and the rest of the electronics would have really stopped working. But this is just enough to make this area inhospitable to ghosts."

"But not inhospitable to them." Chris added. Chuck could feel him warming to the idea.

"Exactly. And here's the brilliant part, if Mildred can give it a big tweak at will, it'll fuck with our magic as well."

"Yeah, brilliant, great." Chris ran his fingers through his hair. "Here's hoping that's just too damn much magic for it to pull."

"It probably is. What Pat's talking about is a subtle effect, but it's got to take a massive amount of energy."

Pat nodded. "So, one of two options. We can either see if we can put the background back the way it was and get the ghosts back. If they can come back, which is a question in and of itself. Or Chuck can step it up on finding several of them out of town for us."

"I've got people asking around for me. The tricky bit is I don't want to get a lead on something that is us just retracing our steps. Another walking memory won't do it. Hopefully I'll have a lead for us soon. Then, road trip."

"Good," Pat said. "So, should we try to put the energy back?" He looked at Chris, the only one of the three of them with any chance of even thinking of a way to pull something like that off.

"I'm stretched as far as I can go on figuring out how to get them into a form we can kill easily. If you" he indicated Chuck and Pat, "think you can do it, go for it. In fact, if you think you can really do it, find a way to tweak the background so they can't be here, but our magic still works."

"I don't think that's possible. We use the same magic they do. If we burn them, we burn ourselves," Chuck replied.

"That makes sense," Chris added.

"Actually..." Pat was thinking strategy. "Sarah and Autumn don't. If we tweaked the background and left the clean up to them..."

"Do you really think crippling us and the Minions and leaving the clean up to Sarah and Autumn is a good idea?" Chuck asked him.

"No, not really." Pat shook his head and said to Chuck, "So, road trip, huh? Do you even have a car? Because the three of us on Sarah's bike just isn't happening!"

Two days later Chris found a small Priority Mail box on the porch with his name on it. He walked inside holding it lightly, wanting to run upstairs, tear into it, and see how they turned out.

Autumn sat on the sofa next to Dave watching something on the TV. "What'd you get?" she asked him.

He didn't have an answer off the top of his head. He blushed, looked flustered, raised his mental shields against Autumn as fast as he could, said, "Something private," and headed upstairs fast as both of them stared at him in wonder.

"That was interesting." He heard Autumn say to Dave.

"No weirder than he usually is," Dave said back.

"What precisely do you consider weird behavior from him?"

He shut the door and made sure his shields were reinforced. Autumn's mind snooping around up there while he opened the box was not something he wanted. He ripped open the Priority Mail box. There sat a small, gray, velvet bag amid the packing peanuts. Untying the cord and shaking the rings into his palm sent a quick thrill through him. *Stop being a girl!* But they were worth a thrill. He had given a picture of his tattoo and described his mark as best as he could to the artist. This was... just... well, not perfect, it couldn't be because it was only one color, but it was as close as it possibly could be. He felt a sharp surge of desire to rip the ring he already wore off and put the new one on. Finally he gave into it, slipping the new ring onto his finger. He didn't want to take it off or put the cold, generic silver band back on his finger.

Chris also didn't want to wear it until he had given Sarah the matching one. He slid hers to the first knuckle of his pinky and twisted it around, watching the stone catch the light. It was certainly the right stone. Small flashes of red, gold, and orange convinced him of that.

He put them back and tied the bag. A voice eerily similar to Chuck's told him to put them away. They had been together for three weeks by her calendar and had never been on a real date. It was still much too soon to give it to her. He held the bag, realizing just carrying it around for the next however long was not a good plan. Not only would it increase his temptation to give it to her, but the next time he pulled her close she might feel it in his pocket.

He looked around the room. Plenty of places to put it. Nowhere jumped out as particularly good should the next attack land him at her house with Autumn getting his clothing for him again.

Which left him with a not particularly good place. The box. It was shielded. He didn't think anyone besides Chuck could even see it. But it wasn't a place for happy things. Secret things—which these certainly were—but not happy ones. Maybe it was time to change that. He took the box down, removed the razor, put the rings inside, and returned the box to his closet.

He held the razor for a long time. He couldn't decide if he wanted to throw it out or use it for shaving. It wasn't beautiful. It was antique and extremely functional. The part of him that spent two decades in Ohio with a woman who made sure nothing useable got thrown out rebelled against getting rid of it. The more rational part realized he didn't know how to shave with one. Even if he did love a healer, he had no desire to learn on his own skin. He tossed it in the trash can.

The top button of her shirt was undone. Chris could just see the dip of her collar bone and the tiny mole at the base of her neck. It kept attracting his view, pulling his eyes away from his reading. He wanted to lean over and kiss it, nuzzle against her neck, slowly unbutton her shirt, reveling in what was under it. And, if Pat hadn't been sitting on the sofa, he would have done just that.

By 9:30 p.m. he had finished his reading. Chris sat on the widow seat next to her and opened Gmail. He began writing about what he wanted to do as soon as Pat left. It took him ten minutes to get it out of his head and into a letter. He hit send. Two minutes later her eyes met his, and she began typing.

9:45: Pat finished his work. Chris hoped Pat would go home, but he just grabbed another pop and picked up the *Diskworld* book he was reading for fun.

10:00: Chris kept looking at Pat, lying on the couch, reading. There had to be some way to get him to go home. She wasn't typing anymore, and his inbox had a new letter. His eyes ran across the screen. Half way through the letter he was looking for a position where his pants weren't quite so tight. He wrote her back, very glad his laptop also worked well for camouflage purposes.

10:12: Pat went to the bathroom. The second the door closed he leaned over and kissed her lips, neck, and ear. Her hand was in his lap, squeezing him, promising him good things for later that night. If Pat would ever leave the fucking house.

10:30: She finished her homework and began to read his latest missive. She sent him a one word reply, Soon.

10:45: Sarah stood up. "Okay. I want to go to bed. I can feel you both want to talk to me without the other one around. How long of a conversation are each of you thinking?"

Chris wanted to smile but didn't let it show on his face. It didn't need to. She could feel the smile without seeing it. He figured ten minutes would do it. Short yes, but after the last hour on the computer, ten minutes was more than long enough.

"Ten minutes," he said with a smile that didn't reach his lips.

"Longer," Pat said, a smile of his own lighting his face.

"Okay. Chris, come with me. Pat, see you in ten minutes."

He followed Sarah into her room and cast a muting spell.

"Silencing spell?" She was getting better at identifying the magic around her.

"Yes."

"I'd think you'd be all out of words after the last hour. What do you want to talk to me about for ten minutes?" Her eyes were warm and playful, and her tongue ran over her top lip.

He sat on the side of her bed, took her hand, pulled Sarah to stand between his legs, and unbuttoned her shirt. "Sex." He kissed the base of her throat.

"You want to *talk* about sex?" She didn't quite giggle when she said that.

"Yes. I want to talk about your sweet, luscious pussy and how, if I had the time, I'd lay you on the bed and lick it until you were quivering around my tongue." Her eyes sparkled, and she licked her lips again. He unbuttoned her pants and eased the zipper down, his fingers tracing along the skin of her lower abdomen.

"And since you don't have the time?" she asked while stepping out of her pants. She took his belt in hand, opened it, and slid his pants to his knees.

He hooked one finger into the crotch of her panties and stroked her, then pulled them off. "I'm going to lift you into my lap" he did, "and slide into you." His eyes slid shut and he hissed softly as she lowered herself onto him.

"I love seeing you like that," she said while licking his ear.

"I love it when you do that to me. So soft and tight and hot…" She moved again, and he inhaled sharply. His eyes held hers. He cupped his hand around the back of her neck, pulling Sarah close for a very deep kiss.

When he pulled back, he traced her lips with his finger. "I want you to suck on my finger." She wrapped her lips around it, and her tongue flicked it while he sighed at the wet suction.

"So beautiful," he whispered and kissed her neck. He took his finger from her mouth and gently slid that hand down her back between her cheeks and began to stroke her.

This time she inhaled sharply. "Oh."

"You like that?" This time the smile did make it to his lips as his finger slipped over her.

She was having a hard time keeping her eyes open. "That's fucking brilliant." She pulled the collar of Chris' shirt to the side and bit him gently on the shoulder. He moaned softly.

"And this?" He slipped his other hand down to her clit and followed the rhythm he had begun with the first hand. She whimpered softly and her hips rocked faster.

"Fuck, Chris, don't stop doing that."

"Never baby. I want to see your eyes. Want to see and feel you come. Look at me, love." She pulled her head back up and locked eyes with him. "You're so beautiful like this, your skin's pink, lips wet and open, eyes soft. You feel so good, soft and wet, hot and tight, and just so, so good. Please, love. You're so close, and I want to feel that exquisite pussy of yours pulsing around me." Her fingers clenched on his shoulders as her eyes lost their focus and her hips jerked erratically. *Deep breath… ride it out.* "Just like that, baby. Best feeling in the world being deep in you and feeling you ripple around me."

She rested against him for a moment, then stood up. He looked at her with a question. Her getting up wasn't part of his plan. Standing up, turning them around, and going full out on the bed with her legs over his shoulders was the plan.

She grinned at him. "Best feeling in the world, huh? I can make you feel better. Stand up." His smile was back. He knew where this was going and decided that was a good plan, too.

She knelt in front of him and took him into her mouth. "Fuckkk…" he breathed through clenched teeth. His eyes slid shut, and his hands fisted in her hair. He knew not to try and control her, just hang on for the ride. He forced his eyes to open so he could watch her do it as well as feel it.

One hand stroked with her mouth. She took the other one and slid it down, out of his view. Then he felt a slippery finger slide from the base of his spine to behind his balls. She began to touch him the way he had been touching her.

"Please, love…" She sped up and squeezed him a little harder. Fast breath and soft moans replaced his words. Pleasure pulsed through him. She swallowed and very lightly, very gently sucked. He rested on her tongue while he calmed down. Then Sarah stood up, kissed him, pulled up his pants, and tucked him in.

He checked the clock. Nine minutes. She smoothed out the blankets on her bed. He picked up her panties. Plain, white cotton, bikini cut, the same kind she almost always wore. A really dirty thought hit him; he grinned again. He stepped behind her, kissing her neck. Then he gently wiped her dry with them.

"Later, when I'm alone in my room, I'll be thinking of tonight. Just thinking about this will make me so hard. I'll be holding these, smelling you, fantasizing about you, and touching myself." He kissed her again, put them in his pocket, and walked out.

"What did Chris want to talk to you about? He whipped out his best shields for that conversation. Was he reciting love sonnets at you?" Pat asked me with a smile as I grabbed a soda from the fridge and drank it quickly. I didn't want my breath to smell like semen; since pop killed the taste, it probably killed the smell as well.

"I'm bound by healer-client confidentiality," I said. It occurred to me this would probably be as good a time to tell Pat about us as any other. It depended on what he wanted to talk to me about. "What did you want to talk to me about?"

"Nothing much. Just putting him in his place. He was mooning over you again. Judging by how less than thrilled you were the last time you tangled with Mr. I'm Married, I figured getting him out of your hair might be a favor."

I laughed. "And if I don't want him out of my hair?"

"I know… But do you really want to deal with him whiny and tortured and begging you with his eyes while his mouth says no and he camps out on your sofa yet another night?"

"No. I don't want to deal with that. Before Passover I gave him a choice, either enjoy me, us, fully or stop coming around."

I felt it when Pat got what I said to him. The force of his pain rocked me back in my seat. Pat closed his eyes, inhaled deeply, and let it out slowly. I wished I hadn't said anything. He did it two more times before he looked at me again. "It would hurt you very badly if I killed him, wouldn't it?"

I realized with a jolt he wasn't joking. "Yes, it would. It would also hurt me very badly if you ended up in jail for the rest of your life. Should I have not told you?"

"No." He was quiet and angry for a long time. "I would have preferred there was nothing to tell."

"I know. I'm sorry. Will you be okay?"

"With you, yes. With him?" He shook his head and looked hard. "I don't know."

"Why him and not me?"

He didn't answer for a long time. "If he hadn't been around, I would have been enough for you." He stood up and headed to my door before I could even start to process that thought. "I'll be in the gym in half an hour, let him know."

"I will."

I went to my room and found my cell phone.

I told Pat.

A minute later it beeped at me to show me I had a text back.

How'd it go?

He tells me to tell you he'll be in the gym in 28 minutes

So much for an early night.

Don't let him hurt you too bad.

Only as much as I deserve.

That's not comforting

He won't kill me for your sake, and you can fix anything short of that.

That's not much better.

Chris wondered if it would be better to go to Pat defenses down, totally open, and just let Pat beat on him until he felt better or if he should go with every defense he could pull on, and actually fight him. More importantly once the rage was gone, what would he say to Pat?

Self-respect won over his guilt. He pulled every defense he had ever learned in a very long and successful career as a battle mage out of his bag of tricks and layered them onto himself. That didn't leave time to think of what, if anything, to say.

He could feel Pat's anger as soon as he stepped outside his shields. Pat wanted to fight, not beat on someone. He'd give Pat as good of a fight as he could. The biggest problem with that was he needed to use his weapon of choice as well. Unlike Pat, he never bothered to learn to do it in ways that didn't kill people. And killing Pat was not a good plan.

He figured he could probably blind Pat without doing any permanent damage. He also figured it wouldn't slow him down for more than a few seconds. Pat didn't need his eyes to fight.

He was out of time to plan. Pat waited silently for him. He let Chris take off his glasses and coat, but the second he stepped to the ring Pat was on him.

Chris fought as long and as hard as he could. He was certain he had managed to not only blind Pat but should have psy-vamped him hard enough to send him to the ground. Pat was pulling more energy than he could drain off. *Because he's angrier than he's ever been, and we're standing in the middle of a huge stone building.* In the end Chris curled into a ball on the floor, protected his vital organs, and endured.

It was galling. He could end the fight anytime he wanted to; he just couldn't do it and leave Pat breathing. Of course, Pat could end the fight anytime he wanted to as well, with or without Chris breathing.

Finally it was done. Pat knelt on the floor next to him, exhausted and crying. Chris slowly uncurled and mentally assessed how bad he was. He was sure his eye socket and three or four ribs were broken. His jaw, two fingers, and his right wrist were dislocated. The rest of him felt like a piece of meat beaten with a hammer to tenderize it.

"She was supposed to be mine this time," Pat finally said to him when he stopped crying.

"Nrghrc." Well, that wasn't going to work. *Can't move my jaw.* He thought at Pat by way of explanation. Pat didn't respond.

No, Ahni.

He felt defeat roll over Pat. Suddenly he knew everything Pat had ever said to him about not cheating on Althiira had been about keeping him far enough away to give Pat a decent chance at winning her first.

"Did you know before or after you slept with her?"

After

"What took you so long?"

Took me a long time to believe I could be lucky enough to have her again.

"Who else knows?"

Chuck. Dave. Don't want Autumn or Mike to know.

"That would be bad."

Yeah. I don't want her to know.

"I love Sarah as much, if not more, than I ever did Althiira. I won't do anything to risk her."

Thank you. They were both quiet for a long time. Chris hoped Pat would call for Sarah soon. He was certain he couldn't keep the pain away much longer. Once it hit, he knew he'd pass out, and he didn't want her to find him unconscious on the floor.

Can you see?

"No."

Let me fix that. Chris didn't feel like turning his head enough to see if Pat was looking around or not. He could feel the spell he had set fall away.

Can you get her here?

"How bad are you?"

I'll live, but I'm going to pass out soon.

Pat got up slowly and went to his phone. "She'll be here soon." He put his coat on and headed out of the gym.

As Pat was leaving, Chris thought he heard him say, "I had hoped if she met me first, she would have loved me."

My phone buzzed at me. You can come get him now.

Be there soon.

One minute, one and a half minutes? I don't know, but it didn't take me long to get to the gym. For one heart-stopping second I thought he was dead. He lay on his back, not moving, not breathing from what I could see, covered in blood and bruises. The first two fingers on his right hand and the hand itself were twisted in impossible positions. His left foot was pointing in the wrong direction.

Then his chest moved. My knees felt weak with relief. "You're alive." I sat on the floor next to him, surveying the damage.

Yes. I jerked when I heard his voice in my head.

"What happened?"

Can't talk. Jaw's broken or dislocated or something.

"Chris, why did you let him do this to you?"

He needed to.

"Here." I hit him with the most potent pain relief I could muster. If there had been any chance of opening his mouth, I would have tried to pour the magic hooch down his throat. As it was, that didn't look like a good idea.

That's better. Do you mind if I just pass out now?

"No." I felt my throat catch.

Are you crying?

"Yes."

How bad am I? The voice in my head sounded alarmed.

"Nothing I can't fix. I hate seeing you like this. Hating telling Pat got you in this situation. Hating…"

Shhhh… It'll be okay. It really will be. I'd certainly have wanted to do the same thing if he had won. Wake me up when it's time to go home.

"Sure." I felt him slip away from me. Then I got to work. Five and a half hours later I had him in decent enough shape to pick him up, scoot him over, and clean the blood off the floor. Then I took us home. I put him in my bed and collapsed there myself.

The sound of the door opening woke me up. My clock said it was 11:53 a.m. I got up, wrapped my robe around myself, and really hoped it wasn't Autumn looking for Chris.

I closed the door to my room behind me and found Pat on my sofa.

"Is he here?"

"Yes. Sleeping or unconscious still. You did a very thorough job."

"Good." I didn't know what to do with the immense satisfaction in his voice.

"Are you less angry?"

"Yes."

I sat down next to him. "Give me your hands." They weren't in as bad of shape as Chris'. All his fingers were still in their sockets, but that was all they had going for them. They were black and purple, with hints of green and dried blood. I held each one gently and went to work.

"You know, at this rate, I'll be able to deal with any bruise or cut in a matter of minutes," I said as I finished his first hand in less than twenty minutes. The second was quicker. "How's the rest of you?"

He took off his shirt. Chris had looked like he had been hit by a Mac truck at full speed. Pat looked like he had been hit by a Beetle at say, twenty-five miles an hour. "He fought back?"

"Yes. He did better than I thought he would. The first few seconds after he blinded me were disconcerting."

"He… wait… what?"

"I think I've got a broken rib or two."

"And nose if what I'm seeing under the swelling is right. When did he blind you? Wait. Strip off first, lie down, and tell me about it while I work on you." I got up and grabbed a few protein bars. Not my favorite breakfast but they'd do.

I bolted them down, grabbed all the ice in my freezer and my entire collection of frozen peas and corn. I covered Pat with my blanket and put the ice packs on anything I wasn't working on.

I don't like broken bones. I really don't like broken bones that have to move. Lucky for Pat, I had gotten to practice ribs on Chris last night. Having set four of his, I could do Pat's on automatic. His nose was harder. I got the swelling down; it was almost a quarter-inch too far to the left. Putting it back in place elicited a very loud "FUCK!" out of Pat.

I heard a corresponding groan out of my room. Chris was awake, probably not happy to be so.

"Do you want to be here when he comes wandering out?"

"I don't know. Why him?"

"Ask me something I can answer and not sound like a soppy idiot."

"No. Why him?"

I stopped working and looked Pat in the eyes. He looked so sad it made me want to cry. I took a deep breath. "Because it's right. It's the home I always wanted. Because being with and near him feels like what I was born to do." He nodded tiredly. When I finished up his nose, he sat up slowly. "You aren't done."

"I know. It hurts too much to lie on my back." He turned his back to me. A four inch thick purple-green bruise ran from his left shoulder to his right hip.

"How did he even do that to you?"

"I think it was his leg." The darker splotch in the middle of the bruise, about kneecap-sized, seemed to confirm that. I shook my head. The sound of my shower filled the background. I hoped Chris had the good sense to keep the water cold. He was in better shape than he had any right to be, but that didn't mean hot water on damaged tissue was a good idea.

"I'm going to be healing you two twits all damn week long," I said under my breath.

"Nah. Two, three days tops. I didn't hurt him that bad, and I know he didn't hurt me that bad."

"Four broken ribs, broken eye socket—which was not fun to fix. I still don't know if he can see properly out of that eye—dislocated jaw, two fingers, wrist, and knee. I lost count of sprains and strains. You could have hit him with a truck and done less damage to him."

"If I had hit him with a truck, I would have damaged something that matters. None of his vital organs were hurt, and he can still have kids. I think I showed remarkable restraint."

"Why? I get you being hurt. Why so angry?"

Pat shook his head. "How many times can a man steal your dream before you have the right to be angry?"

I rolled my eyes. Not that Pat didn't have a point, but I had been involved in this as well, and I found his inability to hold me responsible for my choice annoying. The water stopped. "If you want to get out of here before he comes out, now's the time."

"No. I'll be damned if I let him being around keep me from my best friend."

I smiled at him. "Lie down, let me finish up."

He settled back on the sofa. Eventually Chris came out, moving very, very slowly. His knee was back in place but not quite steady yet. His right eye was still swollen shut. I knew I had gotten the bone back together. Now it was busy hardening up. The real question was: once he got it open again would he be able to see properly out of it? I thought the answer would be yes, but there was no way to know yet. He sat down gingerly on the window seat.

"I'll make us lunch in a few minutes."

He nodded, winced, then sat quietly, watching me finish up fixing Pat.

It wasn't the single most uncomfortable meal of my life. It was definitely in the top five. They didn't talk to each other. I didn't have much to say to either of them. Pat seemed perversely pleased to see Chris couldn't use his jaw well enough to chew anything yet. I found myself thinking he had purposely taken out Chris' mouth and right hand. Pat grinned at me. I glared back at him. I came within an inch of saying, 'No problem. His hips still work, and I'm fine on top,' but decided that probably wasn't the best idea to ever cross my mind.

I must have thought it too loudly because Pat stopped eating, looked at me, and laughed. "Yes. But is he fine with you there?"

"Fine would be an understatement," Chris answered without moving his jaw. For a moment I wondered if that was going to tip us from uncomfortable into hostile. Fortunately it didn't. Pat seemed more curious than jealous. I hoped that was a good thing.

"I thought you couldn't read minds," he said to Chris.

"I thought you knew I could read hers." Still not moving his jaw but quite understandable, nonetheless. I looked at his jaw critically. I knew I had put it back in its socket, but the swelling probably made not moving it more comfortable.

"Why?"

"After Buffy, when we were on the sofa, you asked me about what she was thinking."

"What?" I looked alarmed. Memories of what I had been thinking about made me blush.

"You were thinking pretty loudly that night, too." Pat smiled at me. "I had forgotten that. If I had been less stoned, I would have asked how you knew what she was thinking."

Chris looked at Pat. I knew he said something to Pat in his mind. "Yeah, well, I can't read your minds, so stop talking in your head around me. It's annoying, and it's rude. Speak in whatever the language was before if you have to say something I can't hear but no more of these silent conversations."

There wasn't much more to say after that, but the rest of the meal was more relaxed. I checked the clock again, three minutes after one. "If I'm going to get both of you looking passable enough to eat dinner with Autumn and then do Golem, I need more sleep. I'd advise you do the same."

Pat sacked out on my sofa. Chris and I went back to bed. Shortly after three I woke up. Chris was staring at the ceiling. Usually if I woke up after him, I'd find him propped on his side watching me. Between the broken ribs, dislocated jaw, fingers, and wrist, and broken orbital bone, I guessed propped on his side just hurt too much.

"How are you feeling?"

"Like one hundred and eighty pounds of insanely pissed off warrior beat the living hell out of me."

I sat up. He was moving his jaw to speak now. That was a good sign. "Here." I hit him with some pain relief and went to work on his eye. The bone was knitting together nicely, but it would still be at least a week before it completely hardened. I got the swelling down further.

"Can you open it?"

He cracked the eye open. After seeing the horror show of Chuck's melted eyes, Chris' didn't look too bad. Of course, that was the only comparison by which Chris' eye looked good. The part I could see was a bright bloody red.

"Can you see?"

He closed his good eye. "The focus is off more than usual, and I'm looking through a red haze."

"Makes sense." I got up, found my blush, opened the compact, and showed him his eye.

"That's ugly."

"Yeah, and I can't get it full better by tonight. There's only so much your body can heal at once. The five broken bones take precedent."

"I can make sure no one sees it. Chuck'll know something's up, but my glamour is good enough none of the others will notice."

"Great." I spent another half-hour working on him. By the time I was done, he could chew and his knee would hold him without wobbling. That was as good as I could hope for in the time I had. I spent the next hour doing the same sorts of things for Pat. When they left for dinner, they were moving slowly and glamoured heavily. Part of me wanted to see how dinner went, but I didn't usually eat with them before Golem, and I wasn't about to change the pattern, especially with both of them looking like punching bags.

When I got to Golem, I was apprehensive, but the meeting went smoothly. Chuck did a good job making sure everyone else left early. By nine it was only the seven of us. Not too much planning to do tonight, there was only one square left on the map: the south side of the graveyard. Thursday would be the last night of the hunt. All of them were going to go.

When we broke off for the night, Chuck said to Chris, "Come back with me?"

"Sure." He got into his coat, and Autumn bid him a good night. Pat was already heading back to my place with me. When the four of us got outside, Chuck quietly said, "Let me get a smoke with these two."

"Fine." I wanted to be a fly on the wall of that conversation. Even if I could figure out a spell to let me listen, I was sure Chuck would have a better one up to keep me out. I headed up to my living room and began working on my homework for tomorrow.

Chuck waited until she was upstairs and the door had closed before he gave both of them cigarettes, lit them, and set a sound-dampening spell around them. The sound proofing at Sarah's left a lot to be desired, and he didn't want her hearing this.

"Is everyone friends again?"

Chris didn't know what the answer to that was. He wasn't angry at Pat. He could feel Pat hurt fiercely, but he also knew Pat had been expecting this for a while. He didn't think that made it much better, but at least it hadn't been totally out of the blue.

"We're good on my side," Chris finally said.

Pat sucked hard on the cig. "Why didn't you tell him it was her?" he asked Chuck. "When we talked back in January, I knew you knew, but I couldn't figure out why he didn't."

"I wasn't quite sure in January, but Dave was, and Dave and I decided it would be better off if she didn't remember who she was. I don't know if she's got her memory hiding in there somewhere, but we both thought getting them together would be a pretty surefire way to bring them back out again. Looks like we were wrong."

"You knew? Not just thought but knew?" Chris looked deeply angry.

"You cast a shield over her when she was fixing me. It looked too familiar. I talked to Dave about it after; he said it was her. I wasn't really convinced it was her until talking to her the day after the dance."

"You should have told me."

"Told you what? If you weren't willing to let yourself believe it, you sure as hell weren't going to take my word on it."

"You spent eight months encouraging me to start sleeping with her and don't tell me the one thing that might have made me do it?"

Chuck snorted. "Once again, if you couldn't see it for yourself, me pointing it out wasn't going to help."

Chris glared at Chuck. "You really are an asshole."

"Tell me something I don't know." Chuck nodded at both of them and exhaled. "Like, can you two still work together? I've got a lead on a ghost that might just work for our purposes; I'd like to take a stab at it Monday night."

"I'm in," Pat said.

"Where?" Chris asked.

"We're borrowing Becky's car and heading to Oil City. There's an old mansion out there that's been having ghost problems. Next question: will either of you be up for a five-mile walk on Thursday, or should I borrow her car again?"

"I will," Pat said. "Though I won't mind not having to walk it."

"Yeah. I should be able to do it as well. I won't be in fighting prime, but if we run into anything, I wouldn't be doing much fighting anyway. I'm getting closer to having the trick figured out but not there yet."

"Okay. I'll see if I can swing her car. How about you two drop the glamours and let me see what you did to each other?"

Chris let his fall first. Chuck looked him over and slipped his mind into Chris' to feel how bad he hurt. "Damn, Pat, you should have called me. We could have just gone and gotten shit-faced."

Pat let his glamour drop as well. "I'm free for the rest of tonight. If you're offering to buy, I certainly won't turn you down."

Chuck nodded at the job Chris had done on Pat. "You really are getting better at fighting, aren't you?"

"Not better enough."

"Probably just right. Any better and you might have had the power to really hurt him without the control to avoid it."

"Nah. He's still a ways away from that. He got a few lucky shots in after he took my sight away."

Chuck looked interested. "It's my only non-lethal magical attack," Chris explained. "I could have stopped your heart, melted your lungs, or blown up your brain pretty easily, but that would have been overkill."

Chuck realized, at least in part, Pat had hoped to goad Chris into doing it. "Come on, Pat. Let's go drown your sorrows. I'll see you on Thursday."

Chris headed up her stairs. Pat and Chuck walked toward town.

"A million years ago, you told me we'd get drunk and you'd tell me what was up with you and her," Pat said when he drained his third beer.

Chuck put down his shot of tequila. "You would remember that, even now."

"Yes, I would. What is it between you two?"

Chuck shot back the rest of the glass and waved for another. He shot that one back, too. "She took him away from me. Before she was there, it was just us. I was never 'the Bastard' to him, just Anthur. I was never too dark, too coarse, or too low class. I didn't have to constantly prove myself to him. Then she was there, and he was so in love with her, and she took him away." Chuck ordered a beer and sipped it. "She never much liked me. She grew up in court and knew my reputation. I fooled around with some of her friends, and back then I was stupid enough to swear undying love to get them into bed. One of them claimed I got her pregnant. Though I'm fairly sure that one wasn't mine. She told him about the parts of my life he missed by being in seminary. He started to look at me differently when he learned I had a kid I hadn't claimed. But mostly, she took his time, took his attention. He wasn't mine anymore."

Pat put his hand on Chuck's shoulder. He understood why Chuck didn't want to talk about that sober.

"You promised me you'd tell me why you wanted her, too."

"I did. Beyond the obvious, I assume."

"Beyond the fact she was pretty."

Pat snorted. "She's pretty now. She was gorgeous then. Her skin..." Pat shook his head. "The first time I went off to negotiate with her... she was just this tiny little woman, and she was up against General Qel, and she made him fold. She very calmly told him if he didn't take the deal she'd excuse herself, have me cut off his head, stick it on a pike outside his tent, and then see if his second in command would take the offer. After that, I was gone. I wanted a woman that fierce.

"Time went by, and I liked her more and more because she was that fierce, and she was kind, and she loved her men. And she was real. Do you remember how rare that was? She didn't play the games unless she made the rules. And she loved me even if she wouldn't *love* me... Fuck, I loved that, too because... because she didn't sleep with any guy who looked her way. Do you remember that look Chris would have some mornings, like he'd been fucked stupid the night before? You just had to look at her on those mornings and you'd know she was so much better than anything you ever wanted to dream about in bed. But he wouldn't talk about it, he'd just sort of smile smugly."

"You were better off with the smile. He talks a little about it now."

"Oh Lord. Good?"

"Yeah."

Pat drank more. That she was in bed with Chris now, and he was sitting in a dingy bar with Chuck hurt all the worse. "Give me a cig."

"Sure."

Pat lit up and inhaled deeply. He looked for something to say that didn't hurt. Nothing sprang to mind, and Chuck kept talking about Chris.

"I never got why he didn't talk about it before. I'd tell him about my girlfriends, and he'd just grin. Then we're here, and suddenly he's telling me way, way more than I needed to know. It was kind of a shock to find out the kid who was so innocent he couldn't figure out how it worked if she was on top is off doing stuff that doesn't show up in most porn."

Pat laughed grimly. "He was hopeless?"

"The only time he ever gave me any details before he got here, was the night after their wedding. He told me they had both ended up crying. I was the one explaining foreplay to him."

"Ouch. Amazing she ever slept with him again."

"Hey! I'd been at it for twenty years by that point. I knew what I was doing."

"Sure you did. Tell me this: if you ever had to do it without being in her mind, how good would you be?"

"Probably about as good as anyone would be who suddenly lost a sense. It'd be like trying to do it deaf, I guess."

Pat snorted. "You mean like trying to do it without your sense of touch." The memory of showing Sarah he could read minds in certain circumstances came back to Pat. He went quiet and spent a few minutes nursing his beer.

Chuck watched him. A quick probe at his mind told him there was something else. "That wasn't all of it was it?"

"No."

"Tell me?"

Pat put his beer down. "You remember the first time we lost her in the visions, back when he was wounded and..."

"Yeah. I still have nightmares about that week."

"I went into her head a few times to try to get her back, saw some of the visions. Most of them didn't make any sense to me. Fuck, we're living some of them right now. But two of them did make sense to me. I watched Chris die. Light and beautiful and consumed by his magic. Literally going out in a blaze of glory. And the one that followed it..." Pat finished his beer, thought about another, and decided not to.

"The one that followed was my death. Old, in bed, surrounded by my family. She held my hand and cried for me. There were four men with us, Chris' boys, and two women, our daughters. She wore my mark."

Chuck put his hand on Pat's shoulder. "It's never going to happen."

Pat changed his mind about the beer, ordered another, and drank a third of it straight off. "No, it's not."

Chris came up the stairs alone. I had expected to see both of them. "Where's Pat?"

"Engaging in the traditional male ritual for dealing with a broken heart. Chuck is taking him to get really, really drunk, then letting him sleep it off at his place."

"I shouldn't have told him."

"You had to sooner or later. Keeping it quiet wasn't doing him any favors."

"Telling him doesn't seem to have done him any favors, either."

"Was there ever any chance he'd be more than your friend?"

"If you hadn't been around?" Chris nodded. "I might have slept with him eventually, but no, he wasn't going to be more than my dear friend. But, if you hadn't been around, that probably would have been enough." I remembered Pat saying that and felt distressed at the truth of it. He deserved a woman who was madly in love with him.

"He's better off knowing he has to move on sooner than later. He's certainly better off without you having slept with him. That really would have broken his heart."

"I know. I still hate this." I sighed. "So, my man, what do you want to do with your broken and bruised self tonight?"

"What do I want to do? Or what am I going to do?"

"You can tell me both."

"I want to go to bed with you, do some homework, read a little, and fuck until the sky gets light. What I'm going to do is go to your medicine cabinet, pour myself a large glass of your painkilling whiskey, go to bed, and sleep for a long, long time."

"That's probably a good idea. I could use an early night, too."

I brought my bio book to bed and spent about an hour reading some, watching him sleep some, and reading some more.

After homework, I fell asleep quickly. Faster yet I was in the dream of the blue woman again. This one I knew. I'd been here before several times. Standing on a balcony, holding two small children while my two older boys held us. The fire came closer and closer while the world around me screamed in terror.

I pulled myself back out of it quickly. I didn't want to see the end of that dream. I lay in bed and tried to snuggle closer to Chris. A pained moan escaped him as I pressed close. I pulled back, turned so I was on my side, facing away from him, and rested my feet against his uninjured leg.

It took me much longer to fall asleep the second time. Like before I was among the blue-skinned people. This time I sat at a table with a man who looked much like me, the one I knew was my husband, and the dark-skinned one with the copper-colored hair. The husband talked for a long time, pacing around the room, hurt beyond words, and shocked almost to the point of panic. His world had just fallen apart, and he didn't know how to make it right again. The other three of us listened, trying to stay calm, but we were angry, too. Finally he stopped and came to sit with me. I held him close and stroked his hair. The copper-haired man said something. The shock at his words was palpable. None of us were willing to touch what he had said, yet. But soon, when we thought about it more, we'd agree to it.

After he said it, we broke apart for the night. The husband and I went to our rooms. Our youngest son was crying, and I went to get him. We settled in our bed, and I nursed the baby, leaning back against my husband, thinking about whatever the copper-haired one had said.

"I want you to be here to see him grow up." I finally knew what she was saying.

He held us close, kissed the top of my head, and petted his son. "I will."

50.

I couldn't believe I had forgotten about the dreams. Asking Chris about them made me feel uncomfortable, afraid the dreams were just my mind's way of dealing with lingering guilt about Ameena. Which meant talking to Pat alone. I didn't get a chance to until lunch on Thursday.

"Can I ask you a serious question?" I was a little nervous. The 'what's next' look in his eyes made me sad. "It's nothing bad, just weird."

"Okay. You can always ask, and I'll always try to answer."

"You all know each other from before. Do you recognize me?"

"Why are you asking now?" He looked much more disturbed than I thought this line of questioning would warrant.

"I keep having dreams. They bother me."

"Tell me about them."

"The first one was after I worked on your back the first time. I was dreaming about giving someone a drink. He was dark blue, with copper hair, and—this sounds dumb—white eyes. Or maybe really, really light gray."

"Like blind?"

"No, like the colored part of his eyes were only a little bit darker than the whites of his eyes. I was bringing him a warm drink, and we were outside of a... I guess castle is the right word. A fantasy novel castle, carved out of mountains, instead of anything built in this world. Maybe palace is better. It didn't look defensive."

Pat looked very grave. "Uh huh... Any others?"

"Yeah, that was the first one. I've had others. Looking in the mirror while another woman does my hair. That's how I know I'm very light blue with pale red, almost pink, hair though it's white in some of the dreams. A sort of robin's egg blue man with very dark, like Chris', dark red hair sitting on an ice-blue-colored throne. Four boys: I know they're my sons, the oldest two are almost men, one is a toddler, one a baby. Family stuff, dinner with the boys. Healing the man on the throne." I left out my certainty he was my husband. I wasn't too happy about the romantic content of the dreams. If I was just making it up, I didn't want anyone, even Pat, to know how far my subconscious had gone. "Arguing fiercely with a dark-blue-skinned man with dark coppery hair. Mostly just parts of a life, none of it seems vitally important, but I keep dreaming myself there.

"Then there's this one. I keep seeing it over and over. This one's important. At first it was just sound and heat. The sound of screaming and scorching heat. Then details began to form. The final version I've been seeing is the children and I. We're holding each other, standing on a balcony. The sky is on fire. That's where the heat is coming from. Like, you know how in the movies you see a meteorite and it burns?" He nodded at me. "Well, imagine one so big it blots out the entire sky. You can't see the sun, so the ground is dark, but the sky is on fire because this huge thing is burning while it comes toward us. There's screaming. So many screams. Like millions of voices all calling out at once. Everyone who can see that burning sky is pleading for salvation, and it isn't coming. The little boys in my arms are wailing. The older ones are holding me, and we're crying. But it doesn't matter because the fire is getting closer, then there's searing pain, and the stonework begins to melt, and the children are burning, and I'm burning, and then I'm awake.

"There's this: '*Ahom maun illit unc. Ergun ol wellm.*' It goes with that dream. Chris made some of the same sounds when he was out of his head, but I don't know what it means."

Pat looked seriously at me. He studied my face, almost looking inside me. "Do you like who you are?" He sounded grave and, in a strange way, betrayed.

"Yes, I do."

"Then don't tell the others about it."

"Why not?"

"Because you're either remembering these things, in which case they'll pull your brain apart trying to find out who you are and why you're here. Or you're picking the ideas out of our minds, in which case they'll go bonkers working on upping their defenses. Either way will be a bad thing."

"Don't you want to know?"

"Yes, I do. But I like you too much the way you are to see that happen to you."

"Oh."

"So, keep quiet. Don't think about it when the others are around. Especially those words. Do not think them."

"I can do that. What do they mean?"

"Lord, hear my prayer. Grant me justice."

My eyes went wide. He was more serious than I had ever seen him. "Really, don't let them know. I know they're nice and charming, but if they think you might be one of the people trying to get rid of us, they'll break you."

"You're willing to risk it?"

"I know you aren't."

"How?"

He looked into my eyes intensely. "I just know." There was a deep pain in his eyes. "Can you tell me what caused the sky to burn?"

"I'm sorry. The dream always starts with us standing on the balcony. The sky is already on fire."

"Can I try something?"

"What?"

"I'd like you to get a nap. If I could see the dream, I'd have a better idea."

"I don't always dream it."

"If you get a nap now, you will. I'll hide in the back of your mind and watch it."

"You can do that?"

"I will today."

"Okay."

It felt a little odd settling into bed with Pat next to me, especially given what I had been doing in it the night before, but I shut my eyes and the awareness of him away from me. Then I was standing on the balcony once again. Once again I held my children while our world died. When it finished, instead of jerking awake like I usually did, I found myself standing in the darkness, looking at the blue man with the copper hair and the white eyes. He was so profoundly sad. If the Golem had a face, I figured he'd have the same look as the man facing me. He walked over to me, took my face in his hands, kissed me on the forehead, and then slowly and softly on my lips.

"You were right," he whispered to me.

Then I was awake. Pat sat on the end of my bed, his head in his hands.

"What do you think?"

His head jerked up at the sound of my voice. "I think you've read too many fantasy novels. Couple that with all the weird shit going on, the bits and pieces you've heard about our world, the bits and pieces of the language you've heard from when Chris was sick, and your subconscious is creating some interesting ideas."

"Oh." That really wasn't the answer I was hoping for. "I'm not one of you?"

"No. Still, I wouldn't tell the others about this. Or think about it too loudly. You don't want Chuck trying to figure out how you got those words in your head."

"Are you okay? You seem really depressed."

He gave me a half-hearted grin. "It's hard being in someone else's dreams. It takes a while to get out of it. Also, I imagine the first time you see that dream it's much more… intense… than the later viewings."

"That's true. It's almost routine now for me."

"Exactly. It's almost time for American Lit, and I think you've got another chat with Professor Morrell to get to."

I looked at the clock. "Yes, I do. Thanks. Gotta run." I had three minutes to get across campus. I made it but only by running full out.

Pat didn't go to class. He lay back on Sarah's bed and tried to think through what he needed to do.

He had to figure out what had happened. That was their home. Althiira and her boys stood on the balcony overlooking the Yittar River as their world burst into flame.

Justice. *Oh God, she had asked for Justice!* No one ever did that unless they were insane with hate and rage. What had happened? When had it happened? It couldn't have been too long after they left because the boys all looked the same. Not more than a year or two then.

How to find out? Finding out wasn't the problem. Doing it in a way that didn't let any of the others know he had done it was.

Pat turned the problem over in his head. He could break into Sarah's mind and find the truth. But there was no way to do that without bringing Althiira back. *Oh Fuck… she asked for Justice.* Pat felt a sick fear slide through him; nothing good ever came out of asking for Justice.

No. He had to do it in a way that kept Sarah safe.

Dreams. He had hidden in her dream. Once upon a time, his father had shown him how to protect himself from dreams he didn't want. Pat could use that spell, modify it, make a stone to suggest a dream and capture it. Sarah would never know she dreamed it.

He imagined the map. There was a river behind the graveyard. Pat could get there in time to do some hunting for the stone he'd need. He'd probably have to spend most of tomorrow at it, too, but he'd find it.

Luck was with Pat. An hour of searching in the riverbed found him the stone he wanted. It was smooth and round, about the size of a silver dollar, mostly granite with a few crystals of quartz. It'd do the job nicely. He put it in his pocket and headed back to campus.

Getting through the graveyard hunt was easier than Pat had thought it would be. Nothing jumped out at them. The southern side was, for want of a better word, dead. Chuck kept watching him curiously during the three hours of conversation about what to do next that followed, but he didn't try to get into Pat's mind.

"What's up?" Chuck asked, as they walked home.

"Not sure yet. I've got an idea bubbling in the background. When I know what to do with it, I'll let you know."

"Sounds good." Chuck turned and headed down to his own home. Pat returned to his room and went through the spell in his mind.

He skipped his classes on Friday, taking the time to work on the dream catcher. He'd never made one like this before, let alone in this body. Translating the spell from one realm to another took effort and concentration, modifying it took even more. He etched a complicated design reminiscent of a spider web into the stone while focusing on what he needed to know. *What happened after they left?* With each scrape of his etching tool, Pat remembered more of the last time he saw Althiira. She walked away from the cave crying and never came back. *What had happened in the cave?*

More fine scratches in the stone. Focusing on what he was doing. Slowly building a net to catch a dream. Slowly building the spell that would ensure the dream happened. After two hours, he blew on the stone one last time, driving away the dust, satisfied the loops of the dream catcher had been properly inscribed.

During their Sabbath dinner he excused himself to use the bathroom. Pat closed the door to Sarah's room and walked over to her bed. He slid the stone under the mattress, figuring Chris would be distracted enough to not notice a tiny bit of out-of-place magic. Two nights should be long enough to get the dream he needed.

Sunday afternoon. Pat knew she'd be out for at least an hour. He slipped into her apartment and found the stone under her mattress. His mind went blank as he held the stone, hooking himself into the dream it held.

He was seeing through her eyes. Walking through the marble halls in the Palace to the rough stone basement of the castle, through the earthen tunnels under the basement to the cave. Pat saw himself through her eyes. From his own look of beaten-down weariness, he knew this had to be the last time he saw her. Watching himself from her point of view, while remembering from his own point of view what had happened was disconcerting. He thought he had smiled at her before she went in, but she remembered him looking at her with deep, tired sorrow.

Althiira walked past him into the cave. Cellin was already there, talking with Anthur about something.

"Leave." Anthur gave her a quick glare but left anyway. She walked to her husband and sat in his lap.

"More visions?" Cellin asked while caressing her hair.

"Yes." Althiira was thinking, working up the effort to say something. In the surreal geography of a dream there was no background, no setting, just the feel of Cell's arm around her, and her cheek pressed against his shoulder. "You have to stop this."

"They aren't real. It's just Mjur trying to pull you away from us."

"Yes, they are. I don't want them to be, but they are. If you go through with this... if you unmake the Presence, we will all die."

"If it frees all of our people, our children, it's a small price to pay."

"No Cell, not all of us, the seven of us. All of us. Our whole race. Our children. Our planet. Everyone dies in fire if you go through with this."

"It's not real." Cell held Althiira's face in his hands and kept his eyes focused on hers, trying to fill her with his confidence. "It can't be. Mjur knows what we want to do. It'll do anything to stop us. It's planting these visions in your head."

"Are you willing to risk that? You don't have to destroy the Presence. You don't have to go through with the Choice. We can run. Others have fled the Choice before."

"It's not because I was chosen. Even if I wasn't... this cannot continue. The Presence is eating our people. Sucking the life out of them. The Choice ends now. One thousand people every twenty years. I can save them. I have to save them."

"It's too high a price. The Presence gave us our lives. If it wants to take them back..."

"No." Cell's voice grew hard. "It's not just killing us. It's making us slaves. 'The tools of the Will of the Presence made flesh.' No more. After this, we'll be free. The tools of our own will."

Althiira was sick with her distress. "It won't work. We won't exist any longer. There will be no will, ours or Its"

He stroked her face and kissed her forehead. "The visions aren't real. Your real visions don't just come to you. You go after them. It's Mjur playing with your mind. It knows I can't do this without you."

She didn't want to say it. Pat could feel her wishing he'd change his mind, but Cell didn't. Finally she spoke. "I can't be part of this anymore."

"You'll let me die?" Cell sounded like he'd been stabbed.

"No." Her voice was anguished, her throat tight with tears. Althiira slid to the floor and knelt before him; her chin against his knees as she looked up and begged him, "Let's run. We'll take the boys and go far from here. Fairy, Hunty, or Gruthien... anywhere. I want to grow old with you and watch our children and grandchildren grow old as well."

"I can't run." Cellin slid off the chair, knelt next to her, and kissed her softly. "Someone else would have to take my place. I can't ask someone else to die for me."

"Please, run with me." She sobbed, her head pressed against his chest. "I want you. I want our lives."

He kissed her again. His voice was low, shaky with his emotions, but Pat could feel Cell's certainty in his words. "This is the right thing to do. Destroy evil. That's the whole reason I was born. It will work, and we will be fine. We'll have our lives. Nothing terrible can come out of doing what is right."

"Oh, Cell." She kissed him long and tenderly, her tears sliding down his face. "I can't do this with you. If it was just my life—If you go through with this our children will die, our people will die. I can't let that happen."

He spoke softly, his own voice on the verge of breaking: "Then you need to kill me now. I will do this. I love you. I love our children, but not more than what's right. This is right. I feel it more strongly than anything in my life. I was born for this."

Pat sat in the back of her mind, watching as she raised a hand to his head. Althiira could do it. Cellin wouldn't fight her. A soft touch, a few pulses of magic, and it would be over. Then she pulled her hand away and curled against him, crying harder. If Althiira killed him, she'd never know if she had saved their world or been the tool of Mjur. She only had so much conviction, not enough to live with herself if she took the final step.

"Please, stay with me," he whispered.

"Please, run with me," she replied.

Impasse. Slowly, she stood up and kissed him one last time. She was a few feet from the door when Cellin spoke.

"Where will you go?" He was crying now, too.

"Home."

He nodded. "Five days. This will be done in five days. I'll come for you."

She nodded. "I hope so. I'll be waiting, watching for you, on the balcony overlooking the Yittar."

"I love you."

"I know." She didn't say it back to him. She felt it and offered it to him. Althiira felt Cell's love in return. She turned and left.

There was a break in the universe. Everything before the dream sat on one side of it. Now sat on the other. Pat had helped to unmake the Presence. Hidiri was gone. The Ossolyn were dead. Sarah's dream of watching the fire come and destroy their world ran through his mind as he sat in her room and ached with the horror of it.

He'd helped kill their God, helped to kill his world. Mildred had been right. It had begged him to turn and kill Chris. It wanted revenge, and if anything ever deserved it…

Althiira wanted justice. He could be the tool of justice. Mildred wanted revenge. He could rain revenge upon them.

They lied to him because they had known he'd never go along with it. He wondered which one of them made the decision to lie to him: Chris, Chuck, Dave? It didn't matter. They had all done it. She had done it. Althiira had lied to him. The pain of that betrayal sent him running to the bathroom to throw up.

Sitting on her bathroom floor, one thought dominated his mind. Mildred hadn't gone bad. They had.

He wanted to feel Chris' skin split and bones break under his hands. Pat wanted to hear Chris scream in pain and scream along with him at the pain in his own heart. He went to the lawn near the sculpture garden and waited for Chris to come back from the library. It would be easy to get him away from everyone else. Easy to pummel him into a wet, red, pulpy mass.

What wouldn't be easy was Chuck, Autumn, and Dave. They'd be there in a minute, and they'd know something was wrong. They'd be ready to fight. He doubted they'd be dumb enough to bring Mike along. They could claim Mildred had possessed him, but that lie wouldn't hold unless Chuck was telling it. Pat stalked away from the sculpture garden before he saw Chris and let his rage make him do something stupid.

Why the hell couldn't a handful of Minions show up now? He needed to fight. He needed to destroy something and let out the rage, but all around him were happy little college students, peaceful suburbanites, and nothing even remotely worth trying to fight.

Fuck. The only person worth even trying to fight here was Mike. Which led to its own problems. Did Mike know? No. He couldn't know. Pat had been there when both of them had been told there was a new plan, but they couldn't know what it was because it was too secret. He's spent a good ten minutes trying to keep Chuck out of his mind, trying to prove he could keep the secret, but in the end he couldn't do it.

Should he tell Mike? Between the two of them they could take the other four.

Would Mike help him? He didn't know. Mike hadn't any great love of Hidiri or the Presence, and he did have a great deal of respect for Chuck and Dave. If Mike told the others he was on the warpath, that would be the end of it. He couldn't risk losing his shot at revenge.

Mildred. *You're being silly. Use the name. You want it to notice you? Use its name.*

He found a secluded bit of forest across the street from the ravine and set to calling Mildred. "Mjur. You know me. We've fought before. You knew me as Ahni Al Ath Gyr Bui. If you're out there, now's the time. Find me, and I'll bring them to you. You want your revenge? Then lead me to you, and I'll lead them to you."

For a second he thought Mildred really would take him up on his offer but nothing happened. He tried again, forcing the magic to call it, using tricks that worked with demons, claiming power over it, demanding it show itself.

Nothing.

Fuck. She'd asked for Justice, and Mjur was going to let *her* have it. That's why it wouldn't come to him now. Why it hadn't attacked her in the past.

So much for Plan A. He liked Plan B even less. He started walking to the graveyard, nonetheless.

He didn't like the odds of going after all of them at once. Unfortunately he couldn't lay in wait and pick them off one at a time. They were too connected to each other to attack any of them without the others learning what had happened.

That meant asking for a favor. He could do it. He had before. The Dark Man would likely be amenable to a deal. If it was as strong as Pat thought it was, it would be able to help him take care of this problem.

Pat stayed at the edge of the dead zone for a long time, getting a feel for the local energies and the stones around them. For thousands of feet in all directions were highly charged stones waiting for him to call upon them. If there was any better place for him to fight, he couldn't think of it.

He walked through the dead zone to the door of the broken mausoleum. The Dark Man watched him.

"You know me?"

Yes. Six years ago, you had dealings with us. It didn't so much speak as he just knew what it wanted to say to him.

"Good. You want out?"

Yes.

"Tell me your name."

Gaap.

"Soon I'll destroy your prison. I've got four people I want you to kill."

I can do that. I want to do that.

"I thought so. They're the people who put you here."

Even better.

"Do we have a deal, your freedom for four dead people?"

We have a deal.

"Wonderful."

Pat retreated to the edge of the dead zone again and thoroughly examined Chris' handiwork. It wasn't terribly sophisticated, just a series of shields blocking the magic from the area. He figured a few minutes of intense concentration would break them. The tricky part was the sanctified area right around the mausoleum. Breaking that would take some effort and pain on his part.

The last time Pat desecrated anything, it was six years ago in Manhattan and the Minion, Bruce, was winning. He didn't have the power to fight it himself then, so he called upon something that did. "Henry," what they had called it, had the power to go toe to toe with a Minion. Of course it would have, angel versus demon with two baby wizards on the side of the demon.

He'd desecrate the mausoleum the night of the attack. If he did it too far in advance, Gaap would get free on its own. That would be bad. Deals with demons never quite worked the way you wanted them to, and he wanted to make sure there would be as few opportunities for thing going wonky as possible. Getting rid of it after would be another challenge. With any luck Sarah could help him get rid of it. Banish it to where it came from or scare it into leaving them alone.

Sarah. Althiira. She had lied to him, too. Lied about what they had done and why they were doing it. And when she knew it would go bad… She had fucking walked past him and left him to help destroy their world. *Why?* He wanted to scream at her, pull her out of Sarah and shake her until she confessed. He would have followed her, gone anywhere with her, killed Cell for her if she couldn't do it for herself, and she had left him standing there. He pushed those thoughts away. If he kept thinking about it, he knew it would break him. He'd lay down and never get back up again.

Pat roamed around Reevesville for a long time. Picking up stones that caught his interest, trying to think what to do next. He wanted protection. He wanted to live through this. That meant seeing Sarah at least once before doing this. Unless he lucked out and picked one of the few nights Chris decided to stay at Writers' or Chuck's it meant seeing Chris as well.

Could he pull it off? Spend an evening with Chris? Without letting Chris know what was going on in his head? He'd have to do it. No other way to get the protection he needed. One night, the acting job of his life, and if he could pull it off…

Not if. He *had* to pull it off. Tonight.

51.

"So what's up with you? I can feel you're off, but I don't know what it is." Pat sat on my sofa looking haunted and, at the same time, relieved.

"I don't know what it is, either. Something bad is coming, soon."

"The fight?" I asked, my voice tight with fear. On Thursday they finished the hunt for the portal and found nothing. What followed was a long, frustrated, angry, and essentially useless conversation that amounted to 'We wait for Mildred to show up and try to kill us.'

Pat shook his head. "Mike doesn't feel it. He'll feel the big one, too. This one is coming on my shift, and it's personal to me. Beyond that, I don't know. I want your protection." I knew what he meant. The spell I had cast on Ari. The spell I couldn't have done for him then, but now…

"Of course. When I did it for Ari, he was naked. It was just like the walls. I wrote on him. Still want me to do it to you?"

"Yes." He was very serious. There should have been some humor or at least a little sexy banter, but he said nothing, and that scared me.

"How bad is it going to be?" I started to get a real sense his fear and sorrow.

"Bad."

"Okay. Stay dressed for a bit. I need to find what I want to write." I knew what I was looking for, but I needed to refresh it in my memory. David and Jonathan. There wasn't a specific quote I wanted, just the mindset of friends, warriors, the willingness to put your life in front of the life you love. I opened my *Tanach*. The verses flowed through my mind, wrapping me in warm, safe Hebrew. I sent a text to Chris telling him Pat would be staying over tonight. He sent me a teasing one about meeting up tomorrow afternoon. I wrapped that up quickly. The edge of Pat's fear lodged in my mind was already mucking with my concentration; I didn't need sex on top of that to distract me any further. I headed back into the living room with my quilt.

I laid it on the floor and looked up. "I know what I want to do now. Last time I did this it was not exactly sex magic but pretty close. There were two parts of it. For a long time I held him and prayed; then I began to write. So, get undressed, and I'll spoon you for a while."

He untied a shoe. I looked at the quilt on the floor. My bed would be more comfortable. I picked up the quilt. He looked at me curiously, one sock half off.

"My bed's softer. You're planning on staying over tonight?"

"Yes."

"I'll be exhausted when this is done, so all I'll want to do is sleep. Unless you think it'll bug Emily, you might as well sleep next to me."

"I don't think it will bug her. But it's not like I'll be telling her. No way to tell her what's going on. Can't tell her why I'm so tense and jumpy, either. I can't wait for this to be done. No more secrets once it's over."

I took his hand and led him to my room. He finished undressing and stood naked in front of my bed. I wanted to tell him how much I loved him, that he was my best friend, and his presence made my life better, richer, but I didn't have good words to do it. When it came down to it, I doubted right now he wanted to hear me tell him how much I loved him.

I let my touch do it instead. I lay down in my bed, and he came to lie next to me. I snuggled close against his back, wrapped an arm around his chest, scooched other arm under his neck. He laced his fingers between mine. I began to pray. Not many words. Mostly intention: begging the Lord to hold my love for this man as a shield. I could feel the energy massing around him. As it did so, he relaxed in my arms. The brittle fear around him melted slightly.

My energy, my will, and my love, all melded around him. I thanked the Lord for giving me the power to do this. For choosing me, for whatever reason, to make my will become fact. I thanked Him for keeping my friends safe. I thanked Him for my life, their lives, and that we had had the chance to do this.

I pulled back from Pat and began to write. At the crown of his head, I started the story of David and Jonathon. I didn't have the exact words, but I didn't need them. The idea of the story would do. While I wrote I kept asking, "Please, Lord, let me be Jonathon to his David. Let me put my life in front of his. Please, Lord, keep him safe from what is coming."

Down his neck to his shoulders. Focus the energy. Gather it. Make the words glow. Across his shoulders, down each arm, letters on each finger, and back up his arms. The swapping of the garments. The declaration of love. His back, buttocks, legs, and feet. Jonathon betraying his father to warn David.

"Time to roll over." Pat did. My fingers lingered on his feet, working the spell up his body. Jonathon prostrated by grief for his father's hatred. Once again, Jonathon risking his life to save David's. The letters continued to gather energy. Glow brighter. I became so focused on the spell, on the protection, on the story of David and Jonathon I lost track of where my hands were and what they were doing. By the time that happened my hands and the words didn't matter anymore, only the magic mattered, and the magic was brilliant upon his skin.

Eventually, I was at his face, exhaustedly tracing the end of the story: David's lament for his friend upon his death. I lifted my fingers from the top of his head and kissed him gently on the forehead.

I rested on my side next to him. "Do you feel bulletproof?"

He turned to face me. "As long as a bomb doesn't go off right under me, I'll be fine." His smile wasn't as sure as usual, but he was in a better place than he was when he walked in.

"Lucky for you, whatever's coming isn't likely to make bombs."

He touched my face and kissed me lightly. I could feel his sadness and regret. "What's wrong? The fear is gone, but you're still very sad."

"Same thing that's been wrong for the last week. I'm just not hiding it well now."

"Oh." I didn't know what to say to that. 'I'm sorry you weren't the guy' wasn't going to help anything.

"Do you mind if I don't grab my pants? I'd rather just fall asleep."

"I'm fine with that." I pulled the quilt over both of us. "Sleep well, Pat."

"You, too."

I woke not nearly enough hours later. Jogging flitted through my mind, and I decided to skip it. I needed the sleep and was too warm and comfortable with Pat to get up. But more sleep wouldn't come. Pat's fear and sorrow from last night wouldn't leave my mind. Eventually I noticed he wasn't sleeping, either. He quietly held me; his face nestled against my shoulder. There was still a deep sorrow to him. The more I felt it, the less I thought it was about me.

I rolled over to face him. "Why are you so sad?" He was close enough to know what I was asking.

"I don't think I can win this next one."

"You'll be fine."

He smiled at me, and the pain in that smile made my heart want to break. "If I asked you to send me off for my last fight properly, would you?"

It took me a minute to realize he was asking me to make love to him and a second to decide the answer was yes. I did love him enough to send him off properly. "This isn't going to be your last fight."

"That doesn't answer the question."

His eyes held mine while I answered. "Yes. I would." He ran his hand from my shoulder, down my arm, to my hip, and kissed me for a long time. Then he pulled back. This time his smile did break my heart.

"I don't want to pretend with you. But it's good to know you would have."

"I love you."

"I know. But not the way I love you."

"No. Not the way you love me."

He stood up and found his pants. He turned to face me, half-dressed. "Come on, let's have some breakfast. Nothing we can do about this, so we might as well get on with the day."

"Okay. You want biscuits?"

"Sure."

"You want me to stay with you today, be on hand if you need it?" I asked as I mixed up the dough.

"No!" The alarm in his voice was genuine and sent a new thrill of fear through me. "I do not want you in any more danger than is absolutely necessary."

"Fine. But I am going to be seriously annoyed if being closer could have helped."

"Yes, but I'll be too dead to care."

I whipped around to face him. "Don't joke about that!"

"It's joke or cry, and I'd rather not cry."

Pat left Sarah's home with a level of clarity he had never had before. He had, at best, a one-in-five shot of making it out of this alive. If he did make it out, he wanted Sarah as a friend and hopefully more than a friend. If he couldn't survive it, then he didn't want Chris to have her.

Pat replayed the moment where he asked Sarah to sleep with him and she said yes in his mind. She would have stabbed Chris in the back if it meant giving him the comfort to go off and die well. It left him meanly happy and quite hopeful that if Chris was out of the way, eventually she'd want him.

He spent the first hour of the morning thinking his way through the spell he wanted as his failsafe. If the fight went badly, he wanted Althiira to be able to finish it for him. She'd asked for Justice, and if he couldn't do it for her, he wanted to make sure she had the chance to get it for herself. Get it for him. Althiira was in Sarah somewhere, but she was walled off and hidden. It was time to figure out how to rip down that wall. Once Pat had it figured out, it was time to start on Plan C.

Plan C. In case he couldn't bring Althiira out of Sarah during the fight, he wanted one last back-up plan to make sure she could do it. Writing the note took less than a minute. Pat knew what he wanted to say and how to say it. The magic took longer. As he scribed each letter, Pat let the magic gather in the word; he told it how to find that wall and how to rip it down. Pat linked it to the magic of the campus and to the magic of the stones in the foundation of her house. It was harder to do that way, but if the letter had to do the job, it would be because he wasn't around to take care of it. He finished the letter, feeling it perfect and complete in his hands. When Sarah read her name, Althiira would come back.

Pat took it to the campus post office and shoved it in an oversized envelope. No way Sarah would miss it amid the junk mail. He thought about sending it to her apartment and scrapped that idea. Chris or Chuck might see it or feel it while it waited in her mailbox and dispose of it. He'd send it to her school box. She almost never checked her mail here. If it took a few weeks before she got it, then it took a few weeks. Maybe Mjur would have taken care of some or all of the job in the meantime, making it easier for her to finish it. If he did manage to survive this, Pat could get it from her box before she did.

He met Emily at lunch and debated what to do with her. Part of him wanted to take Emily home, kick Stuart out of their room, and see exactly how many orgasms he could pack into one afternoon. Part of him felt like he should break up with her. Sex won out. If by some stroke of grace he did manage to live through this, he wanted to continue seeing Emily, at least until Sarah got over Chris. Beyond that, breaking up felt too much like what you're supposed to do before you kill yourself. Even if this was going to be almost impossible, Pat wasn't willing to call it suicide.

Emily left his room three hours later with rosy cheeks and a smile, having made a date for tomorrow night. Pat knew that date wasn't going to happen. Even if everything went perfectly, he wasn't going to be going out tomorrow. If everything went perfectly he'd be with Mike and Sarah, the three of them comforting each other over the loss of their friends. Probably getting totally wasted and singing of the good times in proper Irish fashion. That would be an Oscar-worthy performance on his part.

The sun dipped below the tree line. It'd be time to head up soon. He dressed carefully. The jeans were old and comfortable. He could kick easily in them. Pat picked boots instead of sneakers. They weren't steel toed, but they'd do a better job of protecting his feet and do more damage to whomever he kicked than his Nikes. Lastly a t-shirt, any one would work for what he was going to do tonight.

The duster went over all of it. He put the black granite sphere in his pocket. Almost ready.

He dug through the top drawer of his dresser. Under the socks and underwear he found what he was looking for. The knife. It was ornate and fiddly, covered with useless curlicues and fake gems. The hairs on his arm stood up when he touched it. Memories of the fear and hate that went with the last time he used it tasted decayed and putrid in his mouth. The only reason he still had it was because an object like that is awfully hard to dispose of safely. He flicked off a flake of dried blood left over from the last time he used it and slipped it into his pocket. It didn't have a sheath because it wasn't made for fighting. The only reason to have a knife like that was to do a blood sacrifice.

All the way to the graveyard Pat envisioned the spell. He mentally walked through the words he'd use, the symbols he'd carve into his skin, and the symbols he'd draw in his blood. As he stood in front of the mausoleum, he went through it one more time quickly. Gaap strained at its bounds, eager for freedom.

Pat took off the duster and his shirt. He lifted the knife to his chest and stopped. He couldn't do it. Sarah had spent hours last night wrapping him in her love and her love of her God. He couldn't profane that by desecrating this tomb again. Pat changed plans rapidly. Putting his clothing back on, he tossed the knife aside. If he lived, he'd get it later. If he didn't, then the power of it would be gone.

Gaap screamed at him, obscene and hideous sounds echoing in his head. No matter. The holy ground should hold it in place. He sent the text message to the four of them.

911. The dead zone has fallen. I'm keeping the Dark Man pinned in. I need help.

Pat dropped the dead zone with a few carefully placed pulses of magic. It really was shoddy work on Chris' part.

The answering texts all told him they'd be there A.S.A.P. Probably ten minutes for them to run up the hill.

Good. Pat waited. Five minutes later he heard the sound of a car coming to a fast stop. Chuck must have already been on his way up for their ghost-hunting expedition when he got the text. Chuck began rebuilding the shields as soon as he was standing next to Pat. He didn't ask any questions, just got right to the magic. Dave followed three minutes later, with Chris and Autumn a minute behind him.

They didn't ask him any questions, either. Gaap's screaming was unnerving. It kept them focused on the Dark Man. That worked to Pat's advantage. They weren't even looking at him. He took two steps to the left and began to plan. He needed to knock Autumn out of the fight first. She was too dangerous. Yes, her fireball might take out Chuck and Dave if he positioned himself correctly, but it would also get him. If he landed the kick right, he'd knock her clean out, and deal with her later at his leisure.

Chris didn't fight well when he was in pain, so he was the next target. A good hard bone break should do it. From there it would take Chris at least a minute or two to decide he had to use magic to fight and another one to blow out Pat's brain. Two minutes should be plenty of time to deal with Chuck and Dave before going back to Chris.

Dave would vanish. Nothing Pat could do about that. Deal with it when it happens. Chuck would try to dominate his mind and force him to stop. All Pat had to do was hold onto his own will long enough to knock Chuck out. A good hard kick to his weak knee followed by the heel of his palm into Chuck's nose should take him out permanently.

Another hit on Chris, elbow to the temple, should keep him down long enough to find Dave. Dave had never learned to be much of a fighter, never wanted to know, and, with his vanishing skills, never needed to know. All Pat had to do was find him. One hit anywhere on Dave would do it. It wasn't an attack he used very often because it did take a lot of energy, but Dave was the only one he'd only get one shot at. Once Pat found Dave, he'd hit him hard enough to stop Dave's heart. If Dave was smart he'd run, get Mike, and come back. Dave was smart. He'd probably do that. Deal with it when or if it happens. Pat could always let Mike see the memories in his head and go from there.

One more step to the right. Pat tensed his leg and ran the fight through his mind one more time. He pulled power from the stones around him. He'd move faster and hit harder than anything they had ever seen before.

The first kick hit Autumn on the temple. She stumbled back, landing unconscious on the ground. Pat felt her skull crack and cave under his toes. With a quick lunge, he grabbed Chris' arm, giving it a good hard twist. Pat felt the first bone splinter. He snapped the other one over his knee. It shattered satisfyingly. Two down, but Dave had vanished, and Chuck was casting.

Pat could feel Chuck trying to make him stop. It wasn't working. Sarah's protection kept him safe from Chuck's mind control. Chuck blocked Pat's first kick at his bad knee. A rock hit Pat on the side of his head and sent him staggering to the side while lights danced before his eyes.

Dave had decided to stay. Pat turned to find him. Of course, he was nowhere to be seen. Another rock flew at him; he ducked it easily and focused on the area it came from. Chuck was doing something in his peripheral vision. His rattlesnake quick-kick caught Chuck on his weak knee, dropping him to the ground. Pat kicked Chuck hard in the head but didn't feel his skull crack. Chuck had time to get his defenses up.

A third rock, this time to the shoulder. Where was Dave? And then Pat caught it, a few degrees of difference in the temperature five steps in front of him. He tensed to jump, gathering the energy in his fist. One hit to kill Dave, then back to the rest of them.

The world exploded. Jagged broken rocks flew everywhere. He lay on the ground as Gaap laughed. He tried to get up but couldn't. Pat looked down at himself. A whole wall of the mausoleum had him pinned to the ground. He couldn't feel anything below his chest, but he could see it, and seeing it, he knew it was very bad.

Sarah! Pat's head fell back when he felt her hear his call. The sounds of the others fighting Gaap surrounded him. Autumn was up again, her battle screams adding to the noise. Chuck boosted Chris, getting him back up and fighting. He called to her again, quieter this time, *Sarah.*

Then Sarah was there. Her hands were golden with her magic and love. She touched him gently, saying something from far, far away. It didn't matter what the words were. She was there. He couldn't do it; he'd known that from the second he looked down and saw the wall, so she would.

Pat focused his eyes on her and set the spell. *You were right, Althiira. Finish it.*

Sounds and colors faded, just her face near his and her hands on his skin remained. Pat's eyes slid shut and everything vanished.

52.

I was finishing up my dinner when I got the text from Chris. Pat texted. He found something. We're going to check it out. Back late.

Be careful. Pat told me he feels something bad coming.

Will do. Don't wait up.

Sure. I'll just go to sleep while you rush off to mortal peril.

I got my bag packed up. Cold packs, bandages, two quarts of painkilling whiskey, and a dissection kit I had purchased online went into the bag. They weren't great tools, but if I had to cut off burned tissue again, I'd be glad to have them.

Then I waited. Five minutes became ten. Ten minutes became fifteen. I'd started and stopped reading five times in those fifteen minutes. Finally, I gave up and sat on my sofa, tense, waiting for my cell to buzz and tell me I had to go put someone back together. I urgently prayed it wasn't either of the men I loved.

Pat screamed my name. I bolted up and flung open the door. I had expected him to be on my stairs.

He wasn't. I heard him call for me again, this time softer but more urgent, and I realized the sound was inside my head. An image of where he was hit me. I ran to my bike and kicked it into motion.

The cemetery is two miles from my home. If it took me more than a minute and a half to get there, it's only because my bike didn't have enough time to get to a higher speed. Shouts, curses, words in Autumn's voice that weren't any language I had ever run into flooded the cemetery. Light flashed and reflected off the clouds like lightning.

One of those flashes showed me Pat. He was on the ground. I ran to him as fast as I could make myself go, wishing it was faster. The massive stone slab that made up a mausoleum wall had landed across him. From the chest down he was pinned under it. He wasn't making any noise. Even in the dim flickering light of the fight, he looked dangerously pale and waxy.

I knelt down beside him and started checking vitals. He was still breathing, and his heart was beating, weakly. "I'm here Pat. We're gonna get you to the hospital, and they'll get you fixed right up." I took a moment to look over the rest of him. He had blood oozing from his nose and mouth. Blood I desperately hoped came from a bitten tongue.

I began to stabilize him, using every bit of power I could muster to keep his heart beating. But it kept slowing down. Autumn showed up.

"Call 9-1-1."

"What?"

"I can't fix this! Call 9-1-1 now!"

She began to fumble for her cell phone, dropping it in her hurry. While she scrambled for it I noticed she was bleeding and bruised as well. Her clothing was ripped, and she was missing a plumb-sized patch of scalp.

Autumn picked up the phone, dialing fast. She knelt next to Pat with me and put a hand on my shoulder, offering what energy she could. It wasn't helping. He was fading fast under my hands. I couldn't hear her cell ring. She looked at the screen. "No service."

Chris and Dave staggered back toward us. Chuck limped slowly behind them. Of the five of them he seemed to be in the best shape.

"My bike's thirty feet that way." I pointed to it. "Get an ambulance here now," I ordered Chuck.

"They'll ask questions," he said calmly.

The world stopped. Pat was dying, and Chuck stood in the way of him getting the help he needed because he was afraid of answering questions.

"If there isn't an ambulance here in five minutes you'll lose your second healer in a row."

"What should I tell them?"

"I don't fucking care! Just get them here now! He's fucking dying, and you've got four minutes now."

"I don't know how to ride it."

"Learn," I hissed it at him. He walked slowly toward my bike.

"No helmet," he called back to me. I broke. I stood up from Pat, focused all the rage I could muster, and shot it at Chuck. He yelped and collapsed.

"I'll do it," Dave said. He looked like someone had taken a brick and hit him repeatedly with it in an effort to cover every inch of him in bruises. He got on my cycle, took a moment to get a feel for it, and roared off.

I knelt by Pat's head. His pulse continued to slow beneath my fingers.

"Come on Pat. I know you're in there. You called me here, and here I am. I haven't lost a patient yet. Don't you dare be the first. Stay with me." I kept babbling clichés at him as Autumn and I tried to keep him breathing and his heart beating.

I was in the middle of my litany when he opened his eyes and looked at me. He didn't speak, but once again I heard his voice in my mind. *You were right, Althiira. Finish it.*

I did speak out loud, "Don't you dare die on me. You've got plenty of time for last-minute confessions after we get you to the hospital and all put back together." I caressed his face, crying on him.

"Stay with me Pat..." His heart stopped beating. I felt for a few more seconds to make sure.

I looked over at Chris. "Help me make him live." My voice was shaky with desperation.

"I can't."

"You said anything is possible with magic."

"It is, but this is something *I* can't help you with. Can you get Claire here?"

"Fuck." The Morrells were in Pittsburgh. I looked at Autumn. "You know CPR?" Autumn nodded. "I'll do compressions. You breathe and count. Breathe on every five compressions." I knelt next to him, awkwardly bending over the mausoleum wall, and pumped his heart for him. His ribs cracked under my hands. Every five compressions, Autumn breathed.

After a minute, Autumn spelled me; she pumped, and I breathed. I could taste Pat's blood when I blew air into his lungs.

Chris touched my shoulder. "I can breathe for him next. I don't think I can pump."

He was white as a sheet, and his hand hung at a bad angle. I knew he couldn't use his right hand for anything. "You need two hands, one to hold his nose, and one to keep his airway open. Do you have enough energy to give me a boost?"

"No."

"Then just sit there and pray. If anything owes you a favor, call it in."

Autumn and I switched again. Each of us could do about a minute on the compressions. Finally, Chuck woke back up and joined us.

"What are we going to tell them happened?"

"I'm going to tell them the truth. Pat called me. I got here, and he was under a fucking stone wall."

"But..."

"But nothing. Right now I don't care if you all end up in jail. I told you to stay away from here. And look, here you are, and Pat's—" My eyes burned and my mouth wouldn't finish that sentence. "Move the fuck over," I barked at Autumn, taking over compressions. After eons of waiting, flashing lights and sirens joined us.

The medics moved us out of the way. They tried to lift the stone, but between the two of them they couldn't do it. Chuck and I offered to help, and the four of us got the stone off of

Pat. Once we moved it, I felt hope die. His pelvis was crushed flat. Fine streams of blood leaked out of his duster when they picked him up. He had bled out while we breathed for him.

"Sit tight, we'll be back in ten minutes," one of the EMTs said while he closed the door to the ambulance.

I took a deep breath, willing my voice not to break. "Ten minutes is long enough to tell me why Pat's dead."

All three of them looked battered and evasive.

"We don't really know," Autumn said. "He called us all here, told us the dead zone was down, then he turned away from us, like he was angry, and the mausoleum exploded. The wall of it caught Pat full on, and little bits and pieces got the rest of us. Before we even had time to really get back up, the Dark Man was free, and we were flinging spells as fast as possible."

"The rocks did most of the damage. The Dark Man kept us focused on fighting. I think it burned me, and it may have hurt Dave worse; he was closest to it," Chuck said. I barely heard the explanation. I looked around for something to focus on to keep myself from crying. I noticed Chris's arm again. Another job, another person to fix.

"Go find a stick," I told Chuck.

"Why?"

"Chuck, just assume for a minute I know what the fuck I'm talking about. Chris' arm is broken, bad, and he's about to slip into shock. I don't have a blanket to keep him warm with, but I can stabilize his arm so the bones don't grind against each other causing him more pain."

I turned to Chris. "Get hit with a flying rock?"

"Yes." He sounded far away and detached from reality.

Autumn gave me her sweater. I very gently wrapped it around his arm and hand. Chuck came back with two sticks. I sandwiched Chris' arm between them and used one of my shoelaces to tie it all into a bundle. I moved to his other side, holding him close, letting my heat sink into him. He was slipping away from us. I used the energy I had left to keep him here and alert.

"Autumn?" I asked.

"Cuts, bruises, some burns, and a chunk of my scalp is missing. Otherwise I'm fine."

"Chuck?"

"Same as Autumn, minus the scalp wound, plus a general numbness where the spell you threw at me hit." Chuck looked over the debris field. "We need a story."

"Car accident," I said tiredly. I was pumping as much energy as I could into keeping Chris from sliding into shock.

"In the cemetery?"

"You're the Mind Control Wizard, make them believe i!."

"I can't make it up whole cloth. It has to be at least vaguely believable."

"Car accident will work," Autumn said. "I'll make sure they think they picked us up at Becky's car. Shortly thereafter this whole thing will just fade from mind."

"Where's Mike?" I asked.

"Not here. We got here. Pat was waiting for us. Mike wasn't." Chuck concentrated for a moment. "He's in his room. Probably doing some homework."

Once again lights and sirens invaded the cemetery. The EMTs got a proper brace on Chris' arm. We rode to the hospital in silence.

Autumn and Chuck must have done a good job on the spell. The EMTs didn't ask about why I was there in perfect shape when everyone else was beat up. They did offer me a few suggestions for a towing service.

No one asked any questions.

Five minutes later, I sat in the waiting room, wondering who would come out first. Unfortunately it wasn't anyone I wanted to see. A tired and sad looking surgeon asked me, "Are you a friend of Pat Calumn?"

"Yes. I was."

He looked a little surprised to see me say 'was.' "You already know?"

"I'm the one who broke his ribs doing CPR on him. I had my finger on his pulse when his heart beat the last time. I saw his pelvis when we got the rock off of him, no one survives that." The surgeon nodded at me. "Can I see him?" I could feel him getting ready to say no. I wasn't the next of kin, and Pat didn't need to be identified, but he took pity on me.

"Yes. Come with me." He led me down a long corridor to an OR. "We'll move him soon, but you can have a few minutes with him."

"Thanks." Before I stepped in, a thought hit me. "Has anyone called his parents?"

"Yes. They'll be here by morning."

I nodded and opened the door to the OR. Pat was on the operating table. A plastic tube stuck out of his mouth, and more tubes were in his arms. They had covered him with an ugly greenish blue sheet, but that didn't do much to hide how badly broken his body was.

I touched his face, kissed his forehead, and suddenly a flash of hope hit me. I peeked under the sheet. His duster had been cut to give access to his arms, but it was still under him. I found the stone: cold, dark, and heavy. As I held it, I felt it warm against my fingers. It was dead. I collapsed onto the floor, holding the stone, whimpering.

At some point a kind woman in scrubs placed a hand on my shoulder. "Come on, dear. It's time for us to move him." She led me to a bathroom. "You might want to wash up."

I looked at her in confusion. She opened the door and pointed me toward the mirror. Pat's blood was on my lips. I looked down at the stone and my hands, and they too were covered with the blood that had seeped out of him.

The blood is the life. Pat's life on my hands, on my lips. I looked at my hands, moving the fingers slowly, watching the blood dull and dry. I didn't want to wash it off. I didn't want my last connection to him to rinse down a drain.

The blood turned faded to a rusted brown. How long for all the cells to die? Were parts of him still alive and screaming for oxygen? Was the marrow in his bones aching for fresh blood, begging for me not to give up? *Don't go there. Don't think that.*

I turned on the water and let it flow over my hands. The soap smelled like lemons. The lather turned brown and slid out of sight down the drain. I wet a paper towel and finished my face. There were ghosts of bloodstains on my skin, but it would take more scrubbing than I wanted to do in a hospital bathroom to get rid of them.

Lastly I held the stone under the water. Pat's blood rinsed off of it. I carefully dried it, making sure the paper towel didn't scratch its mirror surface. I held it to my lips and whispered to it, "I'll make sure you get back to him."

Chris' arm throbbed with each heartbeat. Electric, white pain shot through it each time he moved. Chuck stayed by him once they got to the hospital. He wanted Sarah to be there, but she wasn't. There were X-rays and papers to be signed. Awkwardly, of course Pat went for his right arm. A nurse cut him out of his shirt while another one put an IV in his left arm. A doctor explained how they needed to pin his arm back together. Chuck was there, paying attention, answering questions about Chris' allergies, and generally being helpful.

He didn't remember the operation. He remembered being wheeled into a room, looking at bright lights, then he was in a different room by himself, his mouth felt terribly dry, his arm ached, and nausea tinged everything green.

A nurse hovered in his view. "The surgery went fine. We'll get you out of here in an hour or so. Are you in pain?" He nodded; she added something to his IV. He dozed, his arm ached, his skin itched, but beyond and above that was the desire to sleep.

At some point he was in a new room, with Chuck sitting next to him. He didn't know how he had gotten from the one room to the other. He was horribly thirsty.

"Could I get some water?" he croaked.

Chuck held the cup so Chris could drink out of it. "How's your arm?"

"It hurts."

"I'll get you more pain meds." Chris nodded. He wanted to slide back into sleep again, but his arm hurt too much.

A nurse returned with Chuck and added something to his IV. "If you aren't feeling better in twenty minutes let me know. We'll up the dosage."

It didn't take twenty minutes. In five he was smiling. In seven he was giggling. "This is fucking fantastic."

"Looks like it, Chris. I want some, too."

"Not that. It failed. He tried to bring her back and failed." His head dropped back to the pillow. "She's mine, Anthur. Ahni's spell failed. He couldn't do it. He couldn't fucking do it! And it's going to work, and she's mine now. Did you feel it fail? I watched him do it, and I was so scared. For a second I knew she was going to jump up and attack us. He told her to finish it, and I was sure she was going to. That he'd pulled it off, and it was all going to fall to shit. That I'd lose her again. But it FAILED! He never muffed a spell. He barely ever tried new ones, but when he did he always nailed them. Didn't matter what it was when he put his skills to it he could do it but not this. I won, Anthur. She's mine, and she's mine, and she's MINE! After this is done, we can go home and fuck like bunnies and have a bunch of kids and get old together. It's over; she's really mine again."

"Yeah, Chris." Chuck nodded his head, looking disturbed while Chris continued to babble on. At least he was doing it in English, though his current grasp of the situation had a lot to be desired. Chuck decided there was no possible way Sarah or Autumn could be allowed to see Chris like this. He'd say something one or the other—both probably—shouldn't hear. Chuck planted a suggestion in each of the nurse's heads; Chris would get no visitors tonight. He went back to sit next to Chris and gently touched his left arm. In a few minutes the babbling wound down, and Chris was asleep again. Once Chris was breathing evenly, Chuck went to one of the nurses and asked if they could help him.

Two of them led him to the ER where they set his finger, cleaned up his cuts, and stitched three of them shut.

It was two a.m. I knew the Calumns wouldn't be getting here for at least four hours. I didn't want to go home to just come back again, but I couldn't stand sitting in the waiting room any longer.

None of the others had come to find me. I didn't know if they had gone home or if they were in rooms here somewhere getting seen to. Time to find them and lend a hand, if possible.

What would Dave do? Two o'clock, not many people wandering around a hospital not wearing scrubs. I tried to make myself feel as much like Dave as I could. Just blend into the background. No one looked at me while I walked toward the wards. I thought that was a good sign.

Through the doors, once again no one seemed to notice me. I found Autumn by accident. I walked past her room. Reading her chart told me they were keeping her for observation. Her skull hadn't cracked where the stone hit, but they didn't want to take any chances on her developing a bleed.

After her room, I went to the nurses' station. There was a whiteboard on the wall with the names of who was in what room and what had happened with them. I took a deep breath, focused on blending in, and walked to the board. B-O-Y… yep, Boyle, David. Released a few hours ago. Cuts, bruises, sprained wrist. C-U-T Cuthart, Charles. Several cuts stitched up and a broken finger set. Released ten minutes ago. M-E-T Mettinger, Christopher. Oh… That wasn't good. The break must have been awful; he'd been sent to surgery.

I headed for a map of the hospital. Surgery was a floor above me. I went up and looked for his chart. I couldn't find it. He must be in recovery or post-op. I found the map again and went looking for the recovery rooms. Once again, no chart.

Next floor up were the post- and pre-op rooms. One more set of stairs, this time I found a desk with several women in scrubs milling about. Just like the ER floor there was a whiteboard with everyone on it. I saw Chris' name. I didn't try to get near the board for more details. He had to be on this floor somewhere. I headed down the hall, checking the names on each door.

The door to room 318 had a chart with M-E-T on the label. I read through it. His ulna had been broken in six places. They had gone in and pinned it back together. The radius had a spiral fracture. They had been able to set that one without pins. The surgeon had scribbled in his notes he had never seen a break like it and couldn't understand what could have possibly done it. I tried to think my way through it, too. The best I could come up with was the rock broke the ulna; then something twisted his arm, snapping the radius.

Chris and Chuck were both sleeping in the room. Chris in the bed. Chuck sprawled out on a too small couch. No other chairs.

I eased into the bed next to Chris, careful not to lay on the IV tube. He woke and looked at me.

"I'm glad you found me," he whispered.

"How you feeling?" I whispered back.

"Pretty bad. You?"

"Trying not to think about it. I've got to hold it together for a few more hours. Pat's parents will be here then."

I cupped his face in my hand and kissed him gently, taking comfort in his presence, hoping to give him some with mine. I sensed his bones, giving his osteocytes a boost. They were already doing what they were made to do; they'd just do it a little faster and easier now.

His eyes slid shut. "I'm very tired."

"Go back to sleep. I'll stay for a while."

"How are the others?"

"They're okay. Dave was released. Autumn's sleeping a few floors down. They're keeping an eye on her to make sure the head wound wasn't serious."

"Good." His eyes drifted shut, and I closed mine as well. I may have napped or just rested. One way or another four hours passed, and it was time to go back to the waiting room. I was there for twenty minutes when I saw the Calumns walking nervously toward me.

I don't clearly remember what I said to Dan and Ellen. I'm not sure if I really said much of anything or if they read it off my face. What I do remember, in exquisite, heart-breaking detail was the look on Ellen's face and the way she fell into her husband's arms. As if the bones in her legs slowly melted.

I remember her face turned against his neck, his hand on her hair, and both of them crying quietly. Then the surgeon was there. He spoke gently while leading them away. Sometime later, they were in my apartment, and I was offering them food. They rested, made the arrangements, and asked me to clean out Pat's room. I provided as much comfort I could, but having them nearby intensified my own sorrow. Every second was a battle to maintain control of my emotions.

When they left, late that afternoon, I told them I'd be there for the funeral on Friday.

53.

They let Chris out of the hospital early Tuesday afternoon. Chuck took him home and got him into his bed.

"Would you get Sarah for me?" Chris asked.

"No."

"No?"

"No. You are stoned off your ass on pain meds, and the filter between your brain and your mouth is not working. If I go get her, you'll do something stupid like call her Althiira or ask her to marry you."

"I will not."

"Sure. Let's see if you can go five minutes without humming."

"Humming?" Chris looked perplexed; he very rarely hummed.

"Yes, when you stop paying attention to something else you start to hum. You've been doing it all day."

"Fuck. I am gone, aren't I?"

"Yes."

"What was I humming?"

"'His Name is Lancelot' most recently."

"Oh Lord." Chris spent a few minutes looking at the pictures on his wall and started to hum.

"You're doing it again," Chuck said without looking up from the book he was reading.

"Fuck. How long was that?"

"Two and a half minutes."

"Fuck."

Half an hour passed; Chuck thought Chris was asleep. He certainly looked asleep. But then, without opening his eyes, he started to speak in their old language.

"Anthur?"

"Yeah, Cell?" he answered Chris in the same language.

"How did Ahni find out?"

"I don't know. You should take a nap."

"I'm not tired."

"You're also not speaking English. The sooner you sleep and get the drugs out of your system, the sooner we can all talk about this, and the sooner you can see Sarah."

"Help me?"

"Sure." He lay his hand on Chris' arm and let the magic flow. Within a minute Chris slept again.

When the drugs had finally cleared Chris' system, one fact loomed large. Pat had known. Somehow he learned what had happened. How? What had Pat found that none of the rest of them had seen?

Chuck was still sitting next to him reading. "Can you get Autumn and Dave here without Mike?"

"Yes." Chuck called them. In a few minutes they had both entered his room.

"How did he find out?" Chris asked them.

"More importantly, how did he find out without her learning what happened?" Autumn paused, looking sick. "That's what we're not saying, right? It's really Althiira, not just someone who feels like her?"

"Yes," Chris answered. She almost flinched when he said it. "Somehow Pat found her memories."

Chuck shook his head. "I don't think they're there to be brought back. As Chris told me last night, Pat never muffed a spell. When he set his magic to something, he could do it. If he couldn't bring those memories back, if he couldn't make Althiira come out of Sarah, she's not there to come out. I think it's her soul. No memories to go with it. She was supposed to be with us last time, and now she's here with us to finish it up."

Dave laughed bitterly and leaned against the door of Chris' closet. "If it's true that would be nice, but it's not true. Pat muffed the spell. Even the great Ahni Al Ath Gyr Bui could muff a spell when he was three heartbeats away from bleeding to death. He asked her to finish it. He expected her to know immediately what was going on, where she was, and what to do about it. Not only that, he was trying to kill us; which means he knew what really happened. There's only one mind he was close enough to to get the real version and that's hers. Those memories are in there, and somehow he got wind of them."

"Were they sleeping together?" Autumn asked with real hope. "He wasn't a great empath, but that kind of intimacy would allow him to read another person quite deeply."

"And you know this how?" Chuck tried to distract attention away from Autumn's question before Chris made it horribly obvious he was sleeping with Sarah.

"The same way I know the exact same kinds of things about you," Autumn said pointedly. Chuck flinched. He hadn't thought about that night in a very long time. Dave and Chris did their best to pretend they hadn't heard. "That still doesn't answer my question. How did he find out without her knowing? Obviously she doesn't have enough of the puzzle pieces to put it together herself, but there had to be enough for him to see it, and put it together himself."

"The Golem. She told me the Golem spoke to her. That it showed her sadness, great pain, the sky on fire, and millions of voices screaming. It could have been talking to him, too," Chris said.

"No. She was the only person who's ever had any feel for that thing. If she told him what she saw or showed him, he could have understood what that meant. He knew about Althiira's visions. If she told him about what the Golem was saying…" Chuck let the idea trail off.

"He had his own problems with that, too. Remember, Mildred spoke to him. We almost lost him the first time," Dave added.

"So, if she told him about the Golem, and he put that together with his own experiences… Still doesn't tell us why he was so sure she's Althiira." Hope tinged Autumn's voice.

Chris crushed it. "It's her."

"If the memories aren't in her head… if they're from the Golem… that doesn't even make any sense. Why would the Golem be telling her about the world we came from? No. There's got to be more to it than that. They're in her head, and somehow Pat saw them," Dave said. "She's never said anything to any of you about visions?"

The others denied it.

"She told me about the Golem right after it happened, but that was months ago. She was going to go back, but I don't know if she did. She never said anything about it again," Chris told them. "If she was having visions, that's the kind of thing she would have told Pat about. He wouldn't have to see it or get any closer to her than he was. She just would have told him. Remember what we told him? That it was her fault. And right after she left, you" he looked at Autumn, "and Mike wanted her dead? He would have made her promise never to say anything about them to us because he would have considered protecting her from you the most important part of this.

"That has to be it. If he had wanted revenge more than her happiness, he would have tried to bring her out first, then planned the attack. Between the two of them they probably would have succeeded. He had to know his chances of doing it were much better with both of them. He was trying to protect her, and only when it was clear he couldn't do it alone did he call her."

"Which leaves us down one fighter and with a ticking time bomb on our hands," Chuck said. "If she ever gets a hold of those memories we're all in trouble. We don't know what triggers them or how many she's got hiding in there."

"Why are you all so scared?" Autumn wanted to know. "Yes, she'll be royally pissed if she ever remembers, but if she remembers, she'll be in the same boat we were when we first got here. She won't know how to use most of the magic she has."

Chuck held his right hand toward Autumn. There was a faint pink scar. "She doesn't need any more magic than she already has. She's already figured out how to turn the healing magic around."

"She did that to you?" Chris eyes went wide with alarm. "You said you burned yourself."

"I did. I burned myself on her. I underestimated how much energy and power she had on hand and got cocky when I took a memory away from her."

"What did you do to her?" Chris' voice was sharp and angry.

"I told her your wife and kids were dead and you thought it was your fault. Then she told me you always spoke of them as if they were still alive. I took that bit of conversation back out of her mind. It was when you were still oozing poisonous crap, and she would fall asleep if she sat down for more than a minute. I didn't think she had the energy to do anything about it. She fought me to hold the memory, but she couldn't. Then I got cocky about it, so she pinned my hand to the table and burned me. She was done before I could get a good counterattack up."

Chris looked at Chuck in horror. Autumn's look was calculating. She knew exactly how hard Chuck was. If Sarah could bite him first run out, that was extremely interesting.

"Serves you right," Dave smirked at him. "You always underestimate the ladies."

"Yeah, well, I've got no desire to underestimate that one again. Especially after last night. My hip is still numb."

"She never said anything to me about that," Chris said quietly.

"I'm not an idiot. I took that memory, too. Subtly, so she didn't notice me do it. She doesn't know the mark on my hand is from her. I'd prefer she not remember getting the drop on me and burning me with her touch."

"You fucking raped my wife's mind?" This time he wasn't quiet.

"Please, I barely copped a feel. If I had known which set of lies you had been telling her, it wouldn't have happened. This is exactly why I don't want you seeing her now. Your filters aren't working." He looked pointedly at Autumn, who was fuming.

Chris wasn't paying attention. "You went into her mind without her permission and stole her memories. That is not copping a feel! That's not some sort of minor drunken indiscretion."

Dave grabbed Autumn, all but dragging her out of the room. "They don't need an audience for this," he said quietly.

"It wasn't a big deal. Not like I stole her identity or anything. More importantly, it's not like she remembers it happening."

"That doesn't make it all right." Chris' voice rose in volume and pitch as he continued. "It's like saying roofies make it all right. You overpowered her, broke into her mind, and stole her memories. What the fuck were you thinking?"

"That you didn't want her to know they were dead. I know you've told her since, but you hadn't then. Did you want to tell her what really happened to her? Do you want her to know what you did?"

His words killed Chris' anger. "No."

"Hell, if anything will bring her out, that's probably it."

"Shit."

They were both quiet. Chris reached for the pill bottle and tried to get the top off one handed.

"Here. Let me." Chuck took the bottle from him, opened it, and handed him a Vicodin. Chris dry swallowed it and held his hand out for another. Chuck gave him one.

"I like you better when you don't tell me about doing things like that."

"I know. But you need to remember she's dangerous. We all do."

I opened the door before he could knock. Chris stood in front of me, his skin pale, eyes glassy and not focusing well. He was either in immense pain or high as a kite. "Shouldn't you still be in bed?"

"I thought you might want a friend."

"Yes. I would." He stepped into my living room and started to wrap both arms around me before he noticed the right one wasn't going to do that. I held onto him tightly for a few minutes while he swayed slightly.

"Do you want to sit down?"

"That's probably a good idea."

We snuggled on the sofa. I sat across his lap, his left arm around my shoulders, my head resting against his chest. We sat there, time passing quietly. Then he started to hum. I wasn't exactly sure of the tune. It may have been 'I'm Yours.'

"Are you humming?"

"Yes. If I stop paying attention, it happens. It's a side effect of the pain meds."

"What are you on?"

"No idea. They stop the pain. There's a few in my pocket if you want to see."

"Chuck let you out of your room in this condition?"

"He went to work."

"Oh."

"The last thing he said to me was, 'Stay put!' He's afraid I'd come over here and do something stupid."

"Like what?"

"Like tell you I love you, or how ridiculously happy I am even though I shouldn't be, or I'd start humming remarkably inappropriate show tunes, something stupid."

"Why are you happy?" My voice was flat and numb. I didn't really care what the answer was; I just wanted to hear his voice and use it to distract myself.

"I'm alive. You're alive. Chuck's alive. We made it three months longer than I thought we'd get before anyone died. I'm starting to think I might actually survive this, and beyond that I'm thinking it would be a good thing. I know I should be sad about Pat, and eventually I will be, but all I can feel right now is this insane joy of being alive."

"I remember feeling something like that when one of the guys in my unit bought it, but I can't muster much joy in being alive right now."

"I know. I don't expect you to." He pulled me closer and kissed my hair, forehead, eyelids, and lips. "God, love, you're alive. You're whole and sound and here." His hand tightened around my shoulder, and his chin rested on my head. "You're alive!" He whispered the last bit, voice soft, emotions of relief and joy intense.

"I was never in any danger, Chris." I felt that bring him up short. "What?"

He seemed like he was looking for something to say, hunting for words. "We fought it for three minutes after you got there, and yes, you were in danger."

"Oh. It felt like seconds to me."

"It wasn't." I didn't have much to say after that. He was content to sit and hold me, humming a medley of the songs he liked, occasionally kissing my forehead or stroking my shoulder.

After an hour, I heard knocking on my door. I didn't want to get it, but, for all I knew, the next crisis was starting. I opened the door. Autumn stood there, worry plastered on her face. She looked past me, saw Chris, and relaxed. She said something to me about Pat, hollow, ritually correct words with little feeling or meaning to them. I said something back to her, just as hollow and meaningless.

"I should get him home." Chris looked heartbroken at the idea of heading back to his own room with Autumn in tow.

"No need. I'm waiting for the pain meds to get out of his system so I can work on his arm. That's still a few hours off from now."

"You're sure? If you'd rather have some time off..."

"No, I'm better when I don't have to think about how sad I am."

"I could stay, too if you want company." I didn't really want Autumn in my home right now. I wanted to curl back into Chris' embrace and let the world spin around me, but I couldn't think of a good way to get rid of her.

"Sure, we're mostly just sitting here quietly."

"I'm entertaining her with a collection of badly hummed show tunes."

"Those were show tunes?"

"Very badly hummed."

"Apparently." I sighed and looked at the clock. Back home they'd know it's a *mitzvah* to bring food to those who mourn. Here, I was on my own for dinner. "Do you want to eat? I'm not very hungry myself, but it's dinner time."

"I ate before I came. That's how I noticed Chris was gone; I was bringing dinner up for him."

"I don't feel like eating," Chris said.

"When was the last time you ate anything?"

He thought about it for a minute. "I know I had dinner before the fight. After that, no clue. Time's fuzzy for me."

"That was yesterday. I'm sure they fed you in the hospital." I walked to my kitchen and took some beef barley soup out of my freezer. "I'll heat this up, and we'll eat."

Dinner passed quietly. I could feel Autumn waiting for me to finish up with Chris so she could take him home. I could feel Chris wanting her to leave him here.

After twenty minutes of her silently staring at us, I had enough of it. "Autumn, he's not going home with you. I can do a better job of keeping his pain under control with him here. I don't know how much longer it'll be before whatever's in his system wears off, and I can't start working on his arm until he's sober. And when it comes down to it, I just don't have the energy to spare to keep my emotions in check around you. Could you please go home?"

"He gets to see how you're really feeling?"

"Yes."

"But I don't?"

"My best friend died yesterday. Less than twenty-four hours ago I felt his heart beat for the last time. Today I held his parents' hands and told them he was dead. After that, I broke the news to Emily and spent an hour with her crying on me. Then I started to pack up his things." My voice broke, the memory of his rocks, heavy and dead in my hands as I put them in a box, hurt too much. Chris reached over, squeezed my hand, and I found it a little easier to continue talking, "Now I'd like the peace of spending some time without having to hold myself in check. I can do that with Chris. I'm used to having him around, but I can't do it with you here. Please, may I have some alone time?"

Autumn looked annoyed but stood up anyway. "Call me if you need anything."

"I will."

I went back to sitting in Chris' lap. He stroked my hair. "This is how you really feel?"

"No. I'm still keeping it in check."

"Okay."

More quiet time. More sitting and being held by him. "Tell me when your arm starts to hurt again."

"That was about twenty minutes ago."

I nodded at him and moved to his right side. The cast went from his bicep to his palm. I placed my fingers on his and the other hand on his shoulder. His arm was knitting up nicely; it just needed time and attention. I used the magic to make the new, soft bone calluses harden faster. A little more magic for the pain.

"I'm thinking we can cut you out of that thing in a week." I looked at him carefully. His color was better and his eyes fully alert. "Drugs out of your system?"

"Yeah."

"How's your pain level?"

"It aches but not too bad."

I hit him with another bit of pain relief. "Better?"

"Yes."

"Can we go to bed?"

"Yes."

Early the next morning I visited Professor Morrell. He looked up, surprised to see me. "I am going to have to miss our class tomorrow."

"A good reason, I hope."

"A very bad one. Pat Calumn was my best friend. His funeral is on Friday. It's too far for me to make it in one day."

"I am so sorry, Sarah. I read about that in the paper. It was a car accident, right?"

"No," I said flatly.

"Why didn't you call me?"

"It was Monday night. You and Claire were in Pittsburgh. I don't think it would have helped anyway. A mausoleum exploded, and he was crushed by one of the walls."

Morrell looked distraught. He moved around the desk and held my hand, giving me a little calming boost. "If you couldn't have kept him alive, no one else could have."

"That doesn't really help."

"I know."

He looked at me steadily. "This will come to a head soon, won't it?"

"Probably. Hopefully. We don't know. We're out of ideas on what to do next at this point, so now we're just waiting. They all think there's going to be some sort of major last battle. But if there is, the other team hasn't bothered to let us know when or where yet."

"When you go in for the last fight, I want you to call me. Even if it's just to stay at your place and put people back together when the fighting is over."

"What about Autumn?"

"That stands, we don't help her kind. But the rest of you? I'd like to be there for you even if you don't need us."

"Soon. Probably. We can all feel something coming, but I'm less sure than the others what's coming is a major fight."

Morrell thought for a moment. I could feel him working some sort of magic. "It'll be a fight. Call me when it's on. No more dead. Not if I can do anything to stop it."

"Thank you." I stood to leave.

"Sarah..."

"Yeah?"

"I really am sorry about your friend."

"Me, too." Back to my place. Before I even got up the stairs, I could feel Chris wasn't there. I debated sitting alone in my apartment and decided to head to class. I didn't think I'd get much out of it, but it would be something else to think about for a little while.

When I came back, Chris was heating more soup for us. He smiled gently while he fumbled left handed with the pot. "I thought you might want some food you didn't have to make for yourself."

"Thanks." I ate without tasting anything and returned to reading for class. He quietly kept me company, doing his own work, occasionally asked for a hit of pain relief.

That night I said to him, "You should probably go home."

"Do you want me to leave?"

"No. But... if you weren't sleeping with me, would you still be here?"

"Right now I don't care what Autumn thinks or suspects. As long as you want me here with you, I'll be here."

"Thanks." I slept very deeply, burrowed in happy dreams of time with Pat. I didn't want to leave them. When I finally did, it was time to pack to leave for the funeral.

Chris wasn't in my apartment; I wondered if he had gone to class. I couldn't remember if I had actually told him when the funeral was. I think I just assumed he'd go with me. But I didn't feel like dragging him out of class to ask him to come.

I packed quickly, shoving my things into the saddle bags. One day there, one day for the funeral, one day back. That doesn't take a lot of space. When I put them on my bike, the driveway was empty. I went back upstairs, grabbed my helmet, and found Chris, hair damp, with his backpack, leaning against the bike when I got back.

"I called Becky. She'll let us borrow her car."

I nodded at him and went to get the other helmet. I didn't speak again until we were in front of one of the old battered Victorian homes in Reevesville proper.

"Is this Chuck's house?"

"Yes."

I didn't want to be rude, but I also couldn't muster much polite chit chat. Beyond a quick introduction to Becky, I kept quiet. Chris thanked her for the use of the car, and she handed me the keys. A minute later, we were off.

Neither of us said much for the first two hours. I had memorized the trip. Had to do that because you can't easily look at a map while riding a motorcycle. Not that the first six hours are particularly difficult. Get on I-80 and go across Pennsylvania. When you hit New Jersey, it starts to get tricky.

He seemed content to just be with me. "I appreciate you can take my silence."

"You'll talk when you want to." He thought for a few miles. "There's more to it than that. I can feel your quiet is part of what's allowing you to keep the pain under control. It's part of what's keeping you functional."

"Yes."

"You'll let it go when you can. If you want me to, I'll be here to hold you through it."

"Thanks. Just gotta get through the funeral."

"Okay."

The drive didn't go especially fast or slow. Just miles and miles of farms, trees, mountains, and homes. Eventually we passed the "Welcome to New Jersey: The Garden State" sign, and he began to navigate. Telling me what exits to take and where to turn.

We crossed the bridge. "You used to be able to see the Towers from here. That's my first memory of visiting New York, my dad pointing them out to me as we drove into town."

"This is my first time here."

"When my dad was still alive, we'd come every spring and fall. Dad and Ben would meet with the restaurants that sold our meat. David and I would walk around, looking at the buildings and architecture. We'll come back and I'll show you around properly one of these days. Maybe during the summer."

"I'd like that."

Pat's parents had offered to let me stay at their house, but I didn't think I could handle their sadness on top of my own. We wound our way through New York City, looking for the hotel I had gotten a room at. It was the least expensive thing I could find within ten minutes of the Calumns' home.

Check in didn't take long. We dropped off our things, and I led Chris back out into the night. I wasn't particularly hungry, but it was dinnertime. Since I was finally in a place where I could eat kosher food without having to make it myself, I wasn't about to let that chance slide away.

As the night wore on, we lay next to each other on a lumpy mattress in a hotel room that cost more than the best room in Reevesville and was still smaller than the least desirable dorm room at Sylvianna. It was private. It was clean. And there were no weeping mothers, no distraught fathers, no mourning sisters. Just Chris and I.

I think I slept, but I don't remember dreaming or waking. Just that it went from dark to light again. I decided to go run. It beat lying in bed waiting for the hours between now and the funeral to pass. Chris slept. I wanted to leave him a note, but I didn't see a pen or any paper. I'd chance it; he was never awake before eight if no one bothered him.

No jogging clothes. *So much for that plan.*

The funeral was at ten, and I still had four hours to kill.

I ironed my dress carefully. Three hours and fifty-three minutes to go. I thought about getting a shower, but I wasn't sure if it would wake Chris up. If I had to guess, I'd say the bathroom wasn't well soundproofed.

I lay back down again, and Chris snuggled close to me. I think he half-woke up because he had to move around to find a position where his arm in the cast wasn't a problem. Once again, I may have slept or not, no memory of falling asleep or waking, but time moved oddly. Thirty minutes would go by in a few seconds. Then I'd check the clock six times in three minutes. Eventually it was late enough to poke Chris to get him up and moving.

"Do you want to get a shower?" I asked, heading to the bathroom for one of my own.

He held up his arm in its plaster cast. "Can't. I'll get a bath tonight. If you felt like giving me a hand with some hair washing later, I'd appreciate it."

"No problem."

When I came out, he was sitting on the bed reading. He had his pants on and both arms through his shirt, but he hadn't been able to button it one handed.

"Three more days," I said to him while buttoning his shirt.

"I can't wait."

Likewise, he couldn't tie his own tie. He talked me through it. After three tries, I had something that wasn't too horribly misshapen. I got into my dress quickly, and we headed out in search of breakfast before going to the church.

The entire concept of a viewing seemed obscene to me. I wanted the comfort of a simple, closed, wooden casket as opposed to the gleaming black and rosewood coffin they had put Pat in. I didn't want to walk over and lay eyes on him dead, made to look artificially alive. But his stone weighed heavily in my hand, and I had promised to give it back to him. I tried not to look at the coffin. To the left there were flowers, more pretty dead things, to the right a spread of photos of Pat, many of them heartbreaking in their joy and vitality. I looked away from them, before images of him grinning at a camera made me cry.

Each step closer to the casket made it seem another fifty feet away. The idea this walk would never end flitted through my mind. Chris squeezed my hand and whispered to me, "You don't have to do this."

I pressed the rock in my hand against him for a moment. "I have to give it back to him." My throat was tight, my composure slipping.

He took the stone from my hand. "I can do it for you."

I almost let him. To sit down and hide from Pat still forever in a box was more tempting than anything I had ever felt in my life. It wasn't like I needed closure or proof of death. If I let myself, I could still taste his blood on my lips and feel his ribs break under my hands.

I took the rock back from Chris and wrapped his arm around my shoulders. "Do it with me." He kissed my forehead and nodded.

I didn't look at Pat. When we got close enough to see, I closed my eyes. I didn't want my last image of him to be that one. Not that my real last image of him was much better, but at least it was honest.

I slid his rock into the coffin. My eyes burned, and tears seeped from under closed lids. I turned away quickly; Chris followed a minute later. I guess he said his own goodbye, but I was too wrapped up in not breaking down into keening sobs to pay much attention. Pat's sister drifted over to us and asked what I had put into the coffin. My voice cracked as I started to speak. I couldn't get my voice under control, so Chris answered for me, telling her it was Pat's favorite rock. She nodded, then gestured for us to sit near the rest of the family.

Most of the actual funeral was mercifully distant. I was too off balance to really focus on what was happening. I didn't know the prayers. I didn't know the hymns. Gentle nudges from Chris let me know when to stand, sit, or kneel.

It was abundantly clear the priest had never known Pat. His words were one long generalization about the tragedy of lost youth and the glory of the world to come. Then the surviving baby wizard, whose name I had forgotten, gave the eulogy. It wasn't the most eloquent eulogy, but it was sincere. Sincere loss felt like acid dripped onto raw skin. After a few minutes, I had to stop listening.

Numb. Just be numb. Another hour, maybe two, and I could escape to somewhere where I could really grieve.

We got a ride with Pat's family for the trip to the cemetery. I tried to introduce Chris to Pat's parents, but my voice wouldn't hold. He did it himself and told them a little about how he had known Pat. Katie asked if his arm had been broken in the same accident, and he said yes. For a moment I felt a stab of fear that we'd have to talk about what had happened, but she seemed satisfied and asked no more questions.

Bright sunshine, green grass, soft, warm late-April breezes that smelled like new flowers: I remember that very clearly.

I stood on Chris' right side, the side with the broken arm. As they lowered Pat into the ground, I couldn't keep my emotions under control any longer and began sobbing blindly. Chris moved to my other side, so he could wrap his good arm around me and hold me close to him. The tears didn't feel like they would end. Like they would swallow me whole and leave me trapped in misery if I let them. I couldn't pull myself out of it any longer.

His lips petal light against my forehead, he whispered something a bit below the point where I could make it out. Comfort spread through me. Sadness that physically and mentally ached was still there, but the hysteria I was on the verge of slipping into had fallen away.

Several deep breaths helped to fade the feeling that all of my bones had broken and ground to dust, leaving only screaming flesh begging for respite. Then, once again, we were in a car, heading back to the Calumns' apartment.

I wished we were sitting Shiva. The wake was too happy, too cheerful. People kept asking me how I knew Pat, and each time I found it more difficult to answer.

I didn't want to eat, talk, or get drunk. I wanted to sit quietly, pray, and remember, but there was nowhere to do that in the Calumns' home. Everywhere I turned there were more people. I didn't know how his parents could stand the constant rumble of voices and occasional bits of laughter that felt filthy in a house that mourned.

Chris returned with a plate covered with pieces of food. I knew I'd throw up if I tried to eat it.

"Take me home."

"Okay."

We found the Calumns. I didn't know what to say. I don't think they needed to hear any words from me. Ellen wrapped me in an embrace, and we held each other for a long time. Then we were outside in weather much too nice for a day this sad.

For a very long time she just lay on the bed. She didn't speak, cry, or move. She just lay, eyes closed, quiet, but not peaceful. Chris spooned beside her. He wanted to hold her close, but the only way to spoon up next to her left the arm he couldn't wrap around her on top.

Eventually he felt her start to shake. The walls she built to keep the pain away crumbled and long wailing sobs followed. He didn't try to calm her this time or dull the grinding broken glass pain of losing her best friend. He tried use his touch to let her know that no matter how bad it got he was there, and there was a world on the other side of the pain. Over the next two hours her sobbing slowed. She still cried, but the uncontrolled keening was over. She rolled over to face him, ready to let another person see her sorrow.

He kissed her tears. He kissed each eyelid and her forehead. He felt for her emotions as carefully as he could. He had known she didn't want anything involving any sort of emotional content over the last few days. Now he wanted to see if she was past that. He thought she could handle feeling again and decided to chance it.

Once again, he wanted to wrap his arms around her and hold her close, but the cast got in the way again. He pulled himself into a sitting position, and she straddled his lap. He wrapped his good arm around her, his hand in her hair, and kissed her gently.

"I love you." He kissed each eyelid and her lips again. He'd wanted to say that since he came out of surgery. More soft kisses, his lips wet with her tears. "I love you." His forehead rested against hers as they breathed together.

A bit of life, and if not peace, then at least not clinging to the edge of the abyss with her fingernails, was back in her eyes. He kissed her lips. This time she kissed back.

"I love you, Sarah." He cupped her face in his hand and kissed her more deeply, trying to put his feelings into his touch, force it to do what words could not.

She leaned back and watched his eyes. He knew she could read him; her walls were gone and so were his. He let his emotions flow. He loved her, and right now he was fearless. There was no reason to hide anymore, no reason to pretend she was someone else.

"I love you," he said again. "Since the moment I saw you the first time, from the second your hand touched mine." She kissed him, her mouth soft and wet. She began to undo his tie, working her fingers into the knot, pulling it out of his collar. Her hands moved faster, pushing the buttons through their holes.

She didn't bother to try to take his shirt off. It was enough to rest her hands against his chest, feel his heart beating, and smell his skin. Her lips on his, her hands on his chest, he felt himself harden in response, wanting her more than air.

He got the zipper on her dress down but couldn't undo the hook and eye with just his left hand. She reached behind herself to open the dress, pulled it over her head, and tossed it aside.

"I love you," he said while kissing her neck, sliding his mouth to her shoulder, and down to her breast. Front-clasp bra, the only one she owned he could undo one handed. He kissed her chest, each breast, and back again to her lips.

She had his belt in her hands, working the tongue through the buckle, sliding it out of the loops. It joined her dress on the floor. She slid back a few inches so she could get at his fly, then stood up, tossing her panties aside, and pulled off his pants and boxers.

She slid onto him, and his head fell back against the headboard. She was hot, tight, and still a little dry. More friction than usual and it felt fantastic. He took a deep breath, forcing himself to calm, to focus on something other than the incredible sensation in his groin. Her lips on his, her breasts against his chest, the scent of her hair: he let them fill his mind. He nuzzled against her throat and licked her ear. "I love you," he whispered it against her earlobe.

She moved against him, rising and falling in his lap. He stroked her with his left hand, rapidly realizing this was something else he didn't have the dexterity to do left handed. He pulled his hand away and ghosted it along her back and hips. "I can't do it for you left handed. Touch yourself, please, love."

She pressed her left middle finger against his lips. He got the idea, wrapping his lips around it, sucking gently. She moaned softly and began to slide against him with greater ease, her body responding to his mouth. He sucked again, nibbling the tip of that finger. Her hand dropped out of sight. While they kissed he felt the back of her hand brushing against the base of his abdomen.

She tightened against him. He knew that feeling, the way her muscles would clamp down when her orgasm was near. "I love you, Sarah." He pressed deeper into her.

She moaned, soft breathy sounds he wanted to listen to forever. Her pitch increased with each stroke. He watched her skin turn pink and her eyes lose their focus. Her hips jerked, and her body clenched around him. He let his own control drop, let the sensations overtake him, and pulled her tightly against him.

"I love you," he said as he came down, his heart rate slowing.

Her head rested against his shoulder. She was crying again. At the same time, she felt less sad to him. He stroked his fingers through her hair and kissed the top of her ear.

"I love you, Chris," she whispered into his chest. Happiness physically raced through him. He knew it was a good thing she wasn't looking at his face; he was sure he was grinning madly. Chris kissed the top of her head and ran the fingers of his left hand through her hair again. He sat there, head resting against hers, feeling her body's soft orgasmic aftershocks, replaying her words in his head. Eventually she looked up and kissed him again.

He traced his fingers over her lips. "I was wondering…" he said. She waited for him to continue and, after a little bit, gave him a nudge. "This is so inappropriate… Would you go out with me?"

"You mean to say, like a date?"

"Yeah, like a date."

She started giggling, then quickly slid into hysterical laughter. After a minute she pulled it together enough to say, "To hell with this, I'm gonna live!" and lapsed back into the giggles.

Chris wasn't sure if this was a step in the right direction or a step back. Then the reference clicked, and he knew it was a good sign and what his line was. "All that time in the ship…. I always regretted… not being with you." He joined her laughter. Reveling in the sound. He'd been missing it the last four days.

When she calmed down, she said, "You should probably use that line to motivate Autumn. She'll turn into River if you do."

"Yes, but then I'd have to sleep with her, and, well, ick." He laughed again, and she smiled at him.

"I guess that isn't the kind of promise you can welsh on."

"I'd think not."

"So, a date, huh?"

"Yes. You, me, something fun, somewhere public. I don't want to ever have to go through another night like Wednesday."

"It'll hurt her dreadfully to know."

"Yes, it will. But…" He realized what he was about to say would sound melodramatic. Given where they were and why they were there, he figured she'd forgive him for it. "It's quite possible two or three weeks is all we have left. I don't want to spend them hiding. I want to be able to touch you, hold your hand, and show the world I love you for as much time as we have left. I'm done hiding. I'm done pretending."

"In that case, how do you feel about going out and getting some dinner tonight?"

"I think that would be a very good idea. You're starting to get hungry again?"

"Yes. For the first time since Monday I want to eat something."

"Good."

"I want to go have a piece of cheesecake. It was something Pat and I were going to do together this summer." Her voice broke, and she started to wall the pain off again.

He took her hand in his and kissed the palm. "Just feel it, love. You don't have to keep pushing it away." She started crying again, and he snuggled her. His body slid from hers. A thick wetness oozed over his skin while her tears traced down his neck and chest. He could feel her crying for all the things she'd never do with Pat now. She calmed back down over the next twenty minutes and finished what she had started to say.

"Over the winter break we did that. Went and got cheesecake. We made a date to go do it again this summer. We were going to celebrate the year being done." She slid off his lap and went to the bathroom. He stood up, wiped himself off, and found his underwear and pants. At least those were two things he could put on one handed.

He was dressed, save for the buttons on his shirt, when she came out. She put on jeans and a flannel button down, then got the buttons on his shirt.

They were on the street, and he was heading toward where the car was parked when she wrapped an arm around his waist. "This way. It's close enough to walk."

"Okay." He wrapped his arm around her shoulders and shortened his steps to match hers. "Where are we going?"

"The Stage Deli." 'It's close enough to walk' meant about a mile away. She led them into a crowded restaurant with miniscule tables and even smaller spaces between those tables. He ordered a Reuben and she a piece of cheesecake. In a short time a mammoth sandwich and a slab of cheesecake large enough for three people showed up.

Sarah stared at it for a moment. Tears brimmed in her eyes again. He reached across the table to stroke her face. She looked up from the cheesecake, gave him something that could almost be called a smile, and then turned her gaze back to the dessert. She picked up her fork and speared it, said something in Hebrew, and began to chew. This time he couldn't tell if it was a prayer or not.

"What was that?"

"Until we meet again, dear friend."

54.

The sound of her engine died. She took her saddlebags off the bike, and Chris slid off as well. "I'll be back soon." Sarah nodded. She still wasn't talking much, but she was better than yesterday. He hoped she'd be better yet tomorrow.

Bruised green-violet sorrow radiated off of the Writers' House. It wasn't the pain of Mike's mourning or Dave's regret. That sorrow was Autumn's, and it had nothing to do with Pat. Chris didn't want to go in. Autumn was waiting for him. He focused more carefully, not just in there but in his room. He dragged up the steps, wanting to turn around, go to Sarah's. But this couldn't be put off forever. The door to his bedroom was already open. He stood in the doorway and dropped his backpack.

"You're fucking her, aren't you?" Autumn sat on his bed, eyes red and puffy. Even with his limited empathy he could feel her sorrow, anger, and jealousy clinging to everything like an unwholesome fog.

"Does it matter?"

"It does to me."

"For about a month now."

She stood to face him, her true face, glamours gone. She slapped him, hard. He tasted blood and tentatively licked at where his lip split.

"You owe me your life," she hissed at him.

"I owe you nothing." His voice went hard. He let the anger at her he had kept in check since finding her again free. She took a step back from him and raised her shields when she felt it. "I never did. You and Chuck brought me here against my will. You stole the death I deserved."

"That's how you see it?"

"That's what happened. You've been telling me you love me since day one, but if you had, you would have taken me home to her. If you did, you would be happy for me now she's back in my life."

Anger took over as her dominant emotion. "You don't love her. It's just sex. That's all it ever was with you two. You think I couldn't feel you up here, night after night, lusting after her. You're the one who wouldn't know love if you tripped over it. Who'd she vote for? What's her favorite book, song? How old are her brothers? How many nieces does she have? What color are her eyes? What kind of Jew is she? That's the kind of things you know about someone you love."

"McCain, and she has an amazingly descriptive way of putting her disgust at having done so. She doesn't have a favorite book, but she likes the Harry Potter series deeply, especially all the fan fic it spawned. She doesn't have a favorite song, but 'Hero's Song' and 'Human' speak deeply to her. Ben is 41, Sam is 38, and David is 36. Her nieces are Maddy, Elizabeth, and Yael. Her eyes are dark brown with a thin line of green around the edges. She's a Conservative Jew who occasionally thinks she'd like to be Orthodox." Autumn looked stunned. "And of course it's about sex. It's so ridiculously good with her I can't even begin to describe it. Good enough I'm glad I've never touched another woman because it would have been such a horrendous disappointment with someone else.

"You want to know something about love. Look at what Pat did. He loved her as she was so much he was willing to let his plan fail instead of lose her. He loved her more than revenge or justice. If you were that kind of friend to me, you'd be happy. You'd be overjoyed the person I love more than anything in the world is here with me now and loves me back."

"She doesn't love you," Autumn said coldly.

"God, Autumn, why are we even arguing this? She loves me. If you'd look through your jealousy, you'd see it."

"No, she doesn't. She doesn't know you. She loves cute, mild-mannered, somewhat tortured, romantic-hero Chris. She doesn't remember Cellin." Chris didn't know what to say to that. No idea where to even begin. Autumn kept going. "Has she even ever seen your true face? Have you told her your name? Does she know how old you are?"

"She knows how old I am. She knows who I am." He looked at her in disbelief. "Cellin wasn't some other person. Chris isn't a new identity. Autumn might be a persona you've put on like a new sweater, but Chris isn't. This is exactly who I am after what I've lived through. She knows my name. It's Christopher Luke Augustine Mettinger now, and that's what matters.

"If anyone doesn't know me, it's you. You spent two years with us before and three years this time. You never even scratched the surface of me." He turned away from her tear-stained face. He wondered if he should just order her out of his room. *No.* This was something he finally needed to finish with her.

He looked at the box where the rings hid. "She's my wife, my mate, my soul... I'm finally whole for the first time in more than twenty years, and you're angry because you aren't the one doing it. It was never going to be you. It was her from the first time I saw her, first time I touched her. Nothing was ever going to change that. She left me to die, betrayed me. That's what you keep saying, but that's not true. She left me to protect our children and our people. It hurt when she left, but it never touched my love for her. If it had worked, if we had destroyed the Presence and everything went on just like before without It, I would have gone home to her and our babies and spent the rest of my life happily twined with her. That she was right..." His eyes were bright with tears and anger.

She walked around him, forced him to look at her. "Do you think she still loves you? If she ever remembers you killed her, killed your babies, killed your world. What was it, three hundred million lives on your hands? Lives she told you *you* would end. Do you think she still loves you after that?"

"No." His voice sounded dead when he said it. That was it, the only thing he still feared. One day she would remember, and one day she would take her revenge.

"And what kind of person are you to continually hope she never remembers? What kind of love wants to deny her herself?"

"The same kind Pat had."

"Bullshit! Pat loved her the way she is and didn't want her to change. You don't want her to remember who you really are. That's not the same thing. Have you told her about the war? That you personally tortured over two thousand people to death when your daughter was killed? Have you told her why we're here? Does your Conservative Jewish girlfriend know you're here because you killed your god?"

"She knows about Iyan. No, she doesn't know why we're here."

"I could tell her."

"Do you really hate me that much?"

"I do right now."

He closed his eyes for a second and made the decision. "Then go tell her. I refuse to be blackmailed by you."

She looked like she was going to strike at him again. This time he was ready and wary, reflexes on high. "I hope she breaks your heart. Again. She didn't love you. She left you. I stayed. Everything you ever wanted, I did for you. Everything you ever needed, there I was. I left my people for you. I found you again here. I've kept you safe. She walked away from you, broke your heart, and left you to die. What do I know about love? I've been living for you since the day I first saw you. No one else can say that to you. Not Chuck, not her, not now, and not before, no one but me."

"I've never wanted anyone to live for me. Just with me."

She looked like she wanted to spit at him. Her disgust was palpable. "I'm not going to tell her. I'm going to let her stay with you. Let you 'twine yourself' with her again. One day, after you've converted and your proper Catholic family's disowned you for it, she'll remember who she is, and she'll rip your fucking heart out. When that happens, I'll laugh." Then she was gone.

Chris shoved more clothing into his backpack and put the textbooks he was using in a small pile on top of his laptop. He didn't want to be in this house a minute longer than necessary.

He jumped when Dave spoke: "You know, between Chuck and I, we can make sure she never remembers. It might be better for all of us, not just you, if that were to happen."

"She's your sister. How can you even suggest…?"

"I don't enjoy the idea. But if it's that or having her decide to kill us all… She's my sister, but if she ever remembers, then I'm just one of the guys who killed her and her children. If she never does, then she can be my friend. I don't know about you, but I prefer that ending to this story."

"You're Satan."

Dave smiled sadly, feeling exactly how tempted Chris was by the offer. "I wasn't the last time I checked."

"Entice me with the greatest treasure on Earth. Seduce me with that which I want more than my own life. No. I'm not a total bastard. If she ever remembers what happened, then we deserve what's coming. I won't let you or Chuck rape her mind to protect us from that."

"I'll respect you on that. Keep an eye on him, though. Of course, if she ever remembers, I can make sure she never finds me. He's got a much higher interest in making sure she never does."

"I'll keep that in mind."

"What happens now?"

"If I'm lucky, she'll let me move in with her, and you and Mike will have more bathroom time."

"Yes. Because your morning shower was such a pain in the ass to deal with. And if you aren't?"

"I'll be sleeping on Chuck's couch for the next few weeks. I don't want to be in the same house with Autumn anymore."

"Don't blame you." Dave's voice dropped. He was so quiet he was almost thinking the words to Chris. "We can make sure Autumn doesn't remember, either. It would take longer and be harder, but we could wipe her, leave just her human college-student self."

"No." He sighed, a thought he had been working hard not to deal with jumped on him. "With Pat gone I actually need her for the last fight."

"Fine. See you at dinner then?"

"Probably not. Hopefully not. Lunch tomorrow. I may need help moving stuff."

"I'll help you lug. Didn't I help you do this once before?"

"The way I remember it you were telling servants what boxes went where."

Dave smiled at him, remembering the day Cell Al Ath Dath Wa moved into their home. "That was a good day."

"Yes, it was."

"I'm happy you two are together again."

"Me, too."

"Well, get over there. Have her fix your face. You're a mess."

Chris was halfway down the steps when Dave said, "Chris?"

"Yeah."

"Your kids better call me Uncle Dave."

"Uncle Dave who plays hide-and-go-seek better than anyone else."

Dave chuckled. "I hadn't thought of that in a long time."

"Nor I." Chris headed down the steps and out of the Writers' House.

When he opened Sarah's door, she looked up from her biology textbook and said, "Good Lord! You were only gone for half an hour. What happened?"

"Autumn knows about us now." He slid the wedding ring off of his finger and put it in his hip pocket. "No need for this anymore."

"She hit you?" Sarah tentatively touched his split lip and the bruised skin around it.

"She was less than thrilled."

"I'll say. I suppose I should be glad she didn't burn you." She quieted and focused. The cut on his lip closed and the skin around his mouth returned to its unbruised color. "There." She kissed him. "That's better."

He held her close for a moment, resting his face against the top of her head. As much as talking with Autumn had been an exercise in futility on her part, she had brought up a few things he realized were important. He took another breath, kissed the top of her head, and moved far enough back to look her in the eye.

"She said something to me, something important. Two somethings, really." He reached under his shirt and took the moonstone off. "The first was had you ever seen my true face?" He put the stone on her table and let the spell fall from him.

For a moment she watched him, then she moved closer and let her fingers ghost along his naked face. "Would you kiss me?"

He happily obliged. After a moment, she pulled back, slightly pink and smiling. "As long as that wasn't from the stone, we're fine."

"That's a magic all its own."

"Is it horribly shallow if I say I like the way you look better with the stone?"

"No. That's what the stone does. What do I look like with it on to you?"

"Have you ever seen the Claritin commercials where they start with a low intensity faded color scheme and then turn up the colors?" He nodded. "With it on your colors are brighter, more intense. With it on your hair is so dark red, it's black in some lights. Your eyes are stony gray with little metallic flecks."

"Really?" He felt quite pleased and a bit wary to hear that.

"Yeah, why?"

"That's what I look like." He paused. "That's what I used to look like."

"Interesting. What do you think most people see?"

"Whatever combination of red hair, gray eyes, and pale skin looks most appealing to them. Those three things don't change. Everything else is fair game. Brooke and Autumn once had an argument about what color my eyes were. Brooke says almost blue. Autumn sees them as almost purple. They eventually chalked it up to how each one sees color. Good thing they never decided to compare notes on how tall I am or what my face actually looks like."

She held his face in her hands. "Your face is sharp and angular, a little on the narrow side." She stopped talking and spent a moment just looking at him. "You don't really look like James Marsters, but your face has a similar structure. It's not pretty, but I love it."

Chris smiled at her while putting the stone back on. He took her hand and led her to the sofa. When he sat down, she settled in his lap.

"What was the other thing?"

He hesitated again. Fear it would bring Althiira out warred with wanting to rip apart another wall between them. Intimacy won over fear. He kissed the top of her ear and said, "My name was Cellin Ath Dath Wa." He studied her very intently, waiting, breath held, to see if Althiira was there.

"Cellin," she said as if tasting the word. "I think I heard Chuck call you something like that." Relief washed over him as he realized it didn't trigger any memories.

"He calls me Cell."

"Cell. You looked very nervous for a second there, Cell. Want to tell me what was up?"

"It doesn't matter." She gave him a questioning look. "Just being silly and overly cautious."

"Which do you prefer I call you?"

"Chris."

She stroked his neck, her fingers traced along his collar bone. "Do you want to tell me what actually happened with Autumn?"

"I got home. She was in my room, sitting on my bed, crying. She asked if we were sleeping together. I said yes. She slapped me. We argued. She flounced out."

"Is there any hope of working out whatever it is you've got going with Autumn? Preferably without letting her beat you up. I'm comfortable with somewhat upside down gender roles, but I'm not going to play the role of the protective boyfriend and sweep in to rescue you."

He smiled dryly. "I think Autumn and I are about as done as can be now. Her last words to me were, 'One day, after you've converted and your proper Catholic family's disowned you for it, she'll rip your fucking heart out. When that happens, I'll laugh.'" He felt bad about editing the quote, but he wanted to say it to her, use it as a way to at least start the conversation about their future, even if it was much too soon to finish it.

She nodded. "Yeah. That sounds done. I was more meaning gotten to some workable compromise, not never speaking to each other again." Then what he said actually hit her. "Converted?"

"Yes." She touched his face gently; he took her hand in his and kissed her fingers. "I want to be with you for as long as I'm alive. Can I live with you? Share your home and your bed and your life?" He let her feel the question he wanted to ask, the one he wouldn't ask her until he knew he had more than two weeks of life left.

"Yes." She smiled at him. He felt her thrill at his words, thrill at the intent behind his words. He let go of her hand and cupped his hand around her cheek, drawing her face close to his. He grinned widely at her and moved the final inch to kiss her. After a few minutes, when he realized if he didn't stop now they'd never get out tonight, he pulled back from her. "Can I take you out tonight? Cook you dinner and take you to a movie or something public?"

"Yes."

He thought about it for a minute and looked at his right arm in the cast. "Ummm... I can't cut anything with my arm in a cast."

"I was wondering what you were intending to cook."

"Is there restaurant in town where you'll eat?"

She smiled at him. "Tonight I'll eat something vegetarian anywhere that serves it."

Despite what I had said to Chris about not going in as the protective boyfriend, I did want to talk to Autumn. Not so much about him. That was their business, not mine. I wanted to see if she could still work with me, and I needed to know if I had to start watching my back around her.

I knocked on her door with a sense of trepidation. Without having to try, I could feel her sorrow. She didn't reply to my knock.

"I know you're in there. Can we talk?"

She opened the door without saying anything, pointed to one of the chairs in her room, and sat down on her bed. "Talk."

"Cards on the table, can we still work together?"

She thought about it for an uncomfortably long time. I felt my defenses rise a few times during those minutes. Whatever she was fantasizing about didn't happen, eventually she answered, "Yes."

"Are you going to stick around for the last fight?"

"Yes. Morrell's bitch told me I have to be out of here after that, or she'll make sure those who remember the treaty are informed I'm here, so as soon as this is done I'm going home. But I'll stay for the last fight."

"Good." I stood up to go.

"I watched her rip his heart out and spit on it. If you do the same, I will come back and kill you slowly."

"I'll keep that in mind."

"Do you love him?"

"Yes."

"Like you loved Ari?"

"No. This is different. It's deeper... older somehow. I don't have a desire to run to another continent to give myself some breathing space." She nodded at me. "I'd appreciate it if you two managed to make some sort of peace."

"I'm not Pat. I can't sit there and be his friend and know he's fucking you. I did it for two years before. Not again. I'll stay professional, show up for the meetings, be where he needs me for the last battle, and then it's over. I don't want to see him, or smell him, or be near him."

"Okay. You won't have to see him if you don't want to. We'll get his things this afternoon."

"I'll be out after twelve until three."

"Should be plenty of time. I'm sorry you're hurting Autumn. I didn't want pain for you."

"That doesn't make it any better."

"I know. I'm still sorry."

On the way home I knocked on Allan's door. He looked curiously at me when he answered it a minute later. "Sarah?"

"Hi, Allan. My lease says I can have a roommate, and I wanted to give you a heads up that as of this afternoon I'll have one."

"Come in." I walked into his half of the house. "I thought you already had one or possibly two."

"I can see how you might have thought that."

"Who is my soon-to-be new tenant? The one with the black coat or the one with the glasses?"

That question made my throat burn and tears start. Allan looked very alarmed. "What?"

I gestured to let him know I needed a minute before I could answer. "The one with the black coat was Pat Calumn."

"Oh God. I'm sorry. I didn't realize that was him."

"No reason why you would have known." I finished pulling myself back together. "The one with the glasses is Chris Mettinger. We'll start moving him in this afternoon."

"Okay. Do you want me to add him to the lease?"

"Yes." I thought for a minute about what I was doing and then said, "with rights of survivorship."

Chris looked around his room for a few minutes. There was only one thing in it he didn't want anyone else to see. He pocketed the rings. Packing one handed was awkward and slow, but he made steady progress. He stared at the clothing in his closet and the boxes on the floor, feeling frustrated at how long it would take to remove every shirt from his closet, take them off the hangers, put them in the boxes, then lug them Sarah's, and rehang them. A clever fix came to mind when he caught a glimpse of the staff hiding behind his shirts.

He took his staff out and made sure it was thin enough to work. It would. He could hang his clothing on the staff and take it across. No need to pull his clothing off the hangers, box everything up, and put it back on the hangers. That would save time.

For right now most of his books could stay here. He'd take his textbooks and a few of the others he liked and knew she didn't have, mostly poetry. The rest could wait for him to have two working arms and a list of her collection. He was fairly certain they didn't need two copies of the *Winds of War*, let alone whatever else she already had.

He packed up his quilt, blanket, and pillows. His sheets were too small for her bed, so they could stay here as well. With his books staying behind and two-thirds of his clothing on his staff, he only needed three boxes for the rest of his stuff.

Shortly after 1:00 p.m. Dave leaned against his door. "That's less stuff than you had last time."

"I don't have to change my clothing three times a day here, and no one talks if I wear the same outfit twice in one month."

"True, I've got less stuff on this side, too." He looked at the staff balanced between Chris' desk and chair with the contents of his closet hanging off of it. "You're kidding me, right?" he said, deeply disturbed.

"It seemed like the easiest way to do it."

"Yeah, but the staff?"

"It's not a bazooka. It won't go off if you touch it wrong."

"So you say. I'm not thrilled about touching it, though."

"Don't be a wimp. It's fine." Chris stroked his finger along the wood. He had made it their freshman year when he had been feeling hopeful about ending this quickly. For more than two years now it had been sitting in his closet waiting for an opportunity to get used. Basically it was a massive energy vamp in a stick. He had it linked into a few local sources to bleed the energy off. Whack something with it and mean it and that something would very rapidly fall to the ground unable to defend itself if it was very strong and dead if it wasn't. He'd used it enough to know, at least on the Minions, it worked. Not as well as he would have hoped but not bad by any means. Then he put it aside, so it could be the ace up his sleeve.

He'd been waiting for a hand where an ace would be useful for a long damn time.

"How do you see this working?" Dave asked Chris.

"You grab one end; I'll grab the other. We'll just take it over, balance it between her desk and chair, and unpack at leisure." And that's how it worked.

"I suppose that's the easy way to do it," she said as he placed the edge of the staff on her desk.

"That was the idea," Chris answered.

"Start unpacking. The top three drawers are yours. Dave and I can get your boxes."

They left him alone to start moving his clothing into the closet. For a moment he stood there, letting the idea this was his home sink in. Then he took the first few shirts off the staff and hung them in the closet.

They returned with Mike in tow, carrying the third box. "No reason to make an extra trip for one last box," he said.

"Thanks."

"No problem. Can I use your room?" Mike asked.

"For what?"

"Mostly just storing stuff. Mine is eight by eight. That's pretty damn small."

"If you want to move the last of my stuff into yours and switch, I'm fine with that."

"Sounds good. Did you kill the magic in your room?"

"Not yet."

"Once you've got it done, I'll move in."

"Let me head over there and do it."

Chris stopped unpacking. "Back in a few minutes." He kissed Sarah and walked back to the Writers' House with Mike and Dave.

"Are you going to announce during Golem you're looking for two housemates for next year?" Chris asked Dave and Mike.

"Hadn't thought of it, but you're right, we should ask," Dave answered.

"It'll be odd to have normal housemates," Mike said.

"I doubt they'll seem normal after a few weeks living with you two."

"Yes. Because we know you were the epitome of normal before coming in contact with us," Dave said to Chris.

"A long time ago I was considered pretty normal."

"A *very* long time ago," Mike replied. "Still, new housemates could be fun. Think Harold and Josh might go for it? They both like each other, and we get along well enough with them. They'll be juniors next year…"

"Could work. You want me to ask them privately first? If they say no, go to the whole group?" Dave asked.

"Sounds good."

Chris walked into what had been his room for hopefully the last time. Killing the magic, the shields, the wards, and the traps he had set for anything silly enough to enter without his express permission took close to ten minutes. When he finished, he folded up the sheets and tucked them under his arm.

"I'd offer to pull the books out, but I can't really do that right now. If you want, I can get them in a day or so, or you can just put them in your room."

"I can get the books. What did you have in there that took that long to dismantle?" Mike questioned.

"A little of this, a little of that."

Dave shook his head. "His room made Fort Knox look undefended. Nothing was getting in there without being invited."

Mike raised an eyebrow. "Except apparently, Autumn."

"She's got an invite. For times like after the Minion with the whip got us," Chris answered.

"Ah. No more just walking into Sarah's place now," Mike said.

"You all have invites. Still, it'd be a good idea to knock anyway, if for no other reason than I don't like being walked in on when I'm having sex."

Dave laughed loudly; Mike looked shocked for a minute, then joined in. "I'll keep that in mind. I'd forgotten what a horny bastard you were when you were getting laid regularly."

Chris smirked. He was tempted to say something along the lines of when the sex is that good you always want more of it but decided with Dave right next to him that might not be a wise comment. "I'll see you at Golem," he replied, starting down the steps.

"You're not eating with us anymore?" Dave asked.

"Maybe when she does. I like your company, but the food in the cafeteria sucks. The food at her place doesn't."

He heard Mike say to Dave, "Good food, hot-and-cold-running sex, and a whole apartment to spread his stuff around. Give me that offer, and I wouldn't stay here, either."

"Even if it meant sleeping with a woman?"

"Not like I haven't done it before. Even with a woman regular sex might be better than no sex at all," Mike joked.

"Sure… You have noticed there's no shortage of women here, right?" Chris could picture the rude gesture Mike made at Dave.

"Help me move his bookcase," Mike said. Chris smiled and headed back toward Sarah's, now his, place.

She had finished putting his clothing in the closet and was looking at the boxes when he entered their bedroom. She walked up to him, wrapped her arms around him, and said, "Welcome home." He grinned, kissed her for a long time, then pulled back.

"Not quite yet." He sorted through the largest of the boxes, lifting out textbooks and miscellaneous school supplies. A minute later he found his checkbook. He wrote quickly and handed her the small rectangle of paper. "Now I'm home."

She stared at the check for a thousand dollars with her name on it. When her eyes lifted back to his, they were filled with curiosity. "What's this?"

"My half of the rent, food, utilities, gas for the bike, and whatever else goes into keeping a home for however long that lasts."

She folded up the check, put it in her pocket, and smiled at him. "I love you."

He pulled her back into another kiss. "I love you, too."

55.

"Good walk?" I asked while I passed Allan on the sidewalk. I was heading to Pat's room to pack up the last of his things.

"Yep." Every night Allan went on a walk. I knew he came back from the direction of the ravine. It hit me like a thousand pound bag of bricks. The ravine. We never checked the ravine. I didn't think it wasn't even on the map.

I knew the ravine was there. I went past it every time I went to Pat's room, every time I jogged up the hill. It surrounded three quarters of the campus. There was no way to avoid it. Yet it never moved from the back of the brain to the front of the brain.

I knew if I went back to the house to get Chris I'd forget about this. I ran to the ravine before it could slip from my mind. In the parking lot at the foot of the ravine I grabbed my cell to fire off a text, but I had no service. I thought long and hard at Chris, trying to come up with a very clear image of the ravine and let him know to come find me. *Please send him,* I prayed.

I entered the ravine. It shouldn't have been colder than the rest of the outside. It probably wasn't colder to anyone but me. But that was the point: anywhere with enough magic to mask itself the way the ravine did would feel cold to me. Really cold. Skin breaking out in goose bumps, fingernails turning blue, and shivering cold. I wanted to turn back, get a coat and maybe some long johns. Not that they'd do any good.

Once in the ravine, I couldn't believe they'd been hunting for the doorway for three years with no luck. This place pulsed with magic. The air practically sparkled. Whoever set up the cloaking had been a genius.

I walked deeper into the ravine, placing my feet carefully amid the clusters of large and small rocks, working hard to avoid slipping on patches of moss or mud or tripping on small plants. To my left and right, up the walls of the ravine, were assorted larger trees and brush. Deeper in, the small plants thinned out making walking easier. I sensed the magic had to have its source around here somewhere, but I couldn't see it yet. The temperature dropped further. Then it didn't matter. I had walked into a circle of glorious warm. It felt like stepping into a heated towel after a cold shower. It was such a delicious feeling after bone-deep shivering cold that I sighed with pleasure.

I started to really look at my surroundings. The ground was bare. No trees, no saplings, no moss, not a single weed or blade of grass. The rocks were naked. In a forest there should be plants and, at the very least, leaf debris under the trees. There should be pine cones, pine needles, and leaves underfoot. In a ravine like this, where the water rushes down during the wet season, there should be plant matter against the upstream side of each rock. But here there was just dirt and rocks.

I looked around, trying to find any reason for this dead zone. Nothing in my immediate view gave me a hint. Finally, I looked up. Instead of leaves and sky I saw something that made me shiver even in my newly found warmth.

It had to be about ten, maybe twelve, feet in the air. It was round, translucent: a drippy gray disk I doubt my eyes had anything to do with seeing. I had a feeling I could get a better sense of it from my peripheral vision than straight on. I was right. I looked to the left of it, trying not to focus on it too hard. It took about six tries to get a good feel because my eyes kept pulling toward it.

The doorway. Maybe it was my height, maybe bigger. Something sluggish and blue oozed out of it. Whatever it was collected in a sick puddle in the air about three feet above my hair. I took a deep breath and prepared myself for more cold, then walked outside of the warm, dead circle and up the side of the ravine. The portal hovered above the dead zone. The stuff that oozed out pooled on top of the area with no magic.

I went back to the no magic area to think. There was a rock that almost looked like it had been designed to sit on. I took advantage of it and looked up. The portal must have been two dimensional because, from this vantage point directly under it, all I could see was the pooling stuff.

What is the stuff? Why is it leaking? Why is this area directly below it dead? Where are the plants? All of these things passed through my mind while one of the Watchers slid out of the doorway, bounced off the warm space, and headed back toward campus without looking at me. *They can't see me here.* I didn't mind it not noticing me. By this point, I was sure all they did was watch. I still didn't like having them look at me, though.

I sat there thinking, watching the portal when a hand touched my shoulder. It's a bad idea to startle me. I jumped up, flipped him over my shoulder, and had my knife out before it occurred to me Allan wasn't a threat.

He lay panting on the ground, hands in a defensive position. I bent over him, pulled him up, begged his pardon, and babbled excuses. As I gave him a hand, I felt like a mask was ripped from his face. Allan was the brown-haired boy Chris had shown me. The beard was gone, his hair was short and graying now, but it was the same man. I stared at him, my eyes wide, not knowing what to say to him.

When he had caught his breath he said, "I was wondering if it would be you."

"Me?"

"One of your group was going to find this place eventually. The only question was which one would do it first."

"What is this place?"

"This is where it all ended the first time. Let's go home. We'll have some tea and talk. I've been watching you and the rest of them since that thing showed up outside our home." I had questions bubbling in my mind but decided to hold them until we were under the shields again. Once we were on the street, I fired off a text to Chris to get him to meet us. He sent one back saying he and Chuck would be there in a few minutes.

"Chris and Chuck are coming. They're part of this, too."

Allan nodded and opened the door to his half of the house. "Might as well wait for them to get here. Is Chris fully moved in?"

"Yes." Allan asked if we needed more furniture. I said we wouldn't mind another dresser if he had one kicking around, otherwise we'd buy one. The sound of a car stopping very quickly attracted our attention away from the half-hearted small talk. Chuck didn't bother to knock; he opened the door and walked in very quickly. Chris stayed on the other side of the doorway until Allan waved him in. He still didn't recognize Allan, and I wondered about that. Right now it could wait, we'd get to it soon enough.

"You found it?" Chuck sounded breathless.

"It's in the ravine," I answered.

"The ravine? Didn't we check the ravine, like the first week we were here?" Chris looked confused.

"No," Allan said. "You didn't. You just think you did."

"Why?" Chris asked.

"Because I'm very good at hiding things," Allan smiled grimly.

"Why hide the ravine?" Chuck wanted to know, curiosity and annoyance both audible in his tone.

"It's a long story. You should probably hear all of it."

"I've lived here all my life. Twenty-two years ago, last October, something happened. My sister used to go hiking in the ravine. It was one of her favorite places. One day she didn't come back in time for dinner. When we found her, hours after midnight, she was babbling: words, sentences, but not English. She didn't understand us or know any of our family. For three days she was like that, then, just as suddenly, she was back. Whatever had been in her left.

"Over the next few months it happened to five more people. Then it was quiet for a few months. Whatever had happened in the fall faded into the background as some sort of local oddity. It's not like things like that don't happen here on a somewhat regular basis." While Allan talked I felt Chris go cold. I squeezed his hand, knowing he could see Allan now.

Allan clutched his cup, knuckles going white. "Then it got bad. Things started coming out of the ravine. Those eyeless fuckers that stand outside the window. They began to hunt the people who had spent a few days loopy. They found them.

"After a few weeks of that, something… terrible came after my sister and the others. I was home when it happened. She was in her room, which was across the hall from mine, and something…" He just thought for a minute.

"It was beautiful. And angry. And so horribly sad. If you've ever seen pictures of an angel, you've got the idea of what it looked like. It slid through my room into hers; then she started screaming. And she kept screaming. And she didn't stop. She. Never. Stopped. She screamed until they drugged her unconscious. Whenever the drugs wore off, she'd scream again. She burned out her voice. She's in a hospital now. They keep her comatose. Every few years they try to wean her off the drugs, and every time the screaming starts again.

"Three weeks later, the same thing happened to the second person who started babbling.

"We could feel the things moving around. We knew where they came from. What we didn't know was what to do about it. Every time we got close to investigate the Doorway, we were attacked. Eventually we got enough info to come up with a rough plan. When Hank started screaming, we went for it.

"We closed the Doorway by cutting it off from the magic. Three of us vanished while doing it. We never saw Robert, Jen, or Cindy again. But no one else ended up like my sister and Hank. Ben," Allan turned to me, "your brother, John, and I cloaked the ravine. Made sure no one else would ever just wander in there. For the most part it's been quiet. Things come out of it every couple years, but they don't seem to cause any problems.

"Then you're on my front steps. Judging by the blank look you had, either the last spell we did held or you aren't very close to your brother."

"The spell held. Chris got a glimpse of you from touching my star. We tried to get Ben to tell us who you were. He still doesn't know."

Allan was quiet for a moment. "Of the six of us, he had the hardest time of it. We weren't sure if he'd make it after Jen vanished. They thought I was on the verge of breaking when my sister started to scream. Turns out none of us knew what the verge of breaking actually looked liked until we saw him realize Jennifer wasn't coming back."

"He remembers building something with you and the blonde one," I said.

"John. We needed something to hold the cloaking on the ravine. Something that would be protected. Something to do the job when we were gone. John was an art major, so for his senior project he built the statue outside, the one called 'Secrets.' We helped him and linked it to the ravine by mixing the soil from the dead area into the clay."

"So that's why…" Chris said quietly.

"Why what?" Allan asked.

"Why she's been drawn to it since day one."

"Really?" Allan looked curiously at me. I had the feeling the Golem was supposed to fly under everyone's radar.

"Yes. Because Ben helped to make it, I'd guess."

"Sounds possible. Anyway, I've been keeping an eye on things. Trying to figure out what's going on, without just barging upstairs and asking if you're the problem or the solution."

"I think we're the solution. We're trying to stop the things that keep coming through for good."

"How?"

"Massive drag-down, blow-out magical fight. Us versus them. Winner takes all," I said.

Allan looked remarkably unimpressed. "That's not much of a plan."

"Now that we know where we'll fight, we can develop a better plan," Chris responded. "But here's the gist of it. Call out Mildred." He saw Allan's bewildered look. "It's what we're calling the thing we're fighting. Then we'll make it real in this world and kill it." Allan nodded. I had a feeling he wasn't so much nodding at the idea of the plan as to the idea Chris might just be able to pull it off.

"Why are they coming?" Allan asked them.

"Because it didn't kill us," Chuck answered.

Allan was having the exact same reaction to Chuck I did. I did a very good job of not smiling as Allan said, "That's a bullshit answer if I've ever heard one. Tell me what happened, or I'll make sure you never find the ravine again."

I felt Chuck go on the offensive. He tried to make Allan think he had answered without having done it. Allan blinked slowly. Suddenly the mild, slightly defeated air he usually wore shifted to something sharp and hard. "Cut the crap. I've been at this longer than you've been wearing that body, and I've got tricks up my sleeve you've never dreamed of. Why are they hunting you?"

Chris answered instead of let Chuck try again, "Mildred was, well, angel probably is as good a term as any other. It's the right general relationship and power level. Mildred was the highest angel of the Lord. Not that that's right, but it's not wrong, either. Imagine an immensely powerful magical entity and Its most beloved right hand. It, the entity, was destroying our people. Enslaving and killing them. I was their king, and I decided it wasn't going to happen any longer. I killed It. Unfortunately I couldn't kill Mildred, and we ended up having to flee.

"Your sister's room was green with gray furniture. I'm sorry about spending some time in her body; I left as soon as I could, and I'm not the one who hurt her."

Chuck leaned forward. "Can you show me what the Angel looked like?"

Allan didn't look like he wanted Chuck in his head, but he also wanted to know what the thing that had invaded his home was. Finding out won over keeping Chuck out. I watched Chuck focus on whatever image Allan had in his head. After a minute, Chuck said, "*Nehpheem.*"

Chris looked sick. "I'm sorry. Those were particularly nasty creatures. Torment is a good description. Torment made flesh. We had good reasons for wanting them dead."

"Why my sister?"

"I didn't choose her." Chris' eyes and voice were dark. He stared at Chuck while he spoke: "I killed their leader, unmade it, took its magic and scattered it to the winds. When that was done, I was three-quarters dead, my own magic gone, and begging to be taken home to die with my family. Then I woke up in a place with trees and rocks, and you and a few others were staring at me, asking questions I didn't understand and unable to answer mine.

"Chuck found me shortly after that. Then we left, looking for bodies to call our own. I didn't know anything had followed us until I was seven. By then I was two hundred miles away."

"Why didn't they go after you? Why go after the bodies that had housed you?"

Chris and Chuck thought about it. "When did you close the door the first time?" Chris asked.

"May 2, 1987."

"My guess is they need the bodies to find us. You closed the door before any of us found a new one. I didn't have mine until...June, maybe? Chuck?"

"No idea. It was hot and the leaves were fully open, summer sometime."

"How did you close the doorway? Did you fight the Minions?" Chris questioned.

"Minions?"

"Anything that isn't Mildred get's called a 'Minion.' The thing you saw, the Nehpheem, was about as high up as a Minion could be. These days most of the things we run into are pretty low level, with the occasional mid-level thug," Chuck responded.

"What I did was go into the ravine, find the Doorway, scout out how it worked, and what was coming out of it. When the others went in to destroy the Doorway, I smoked through three packs of cigarettes while her brother tried to read his homework. I can tell you how they planned on doing it, and I can tell you what we felt when we went looking for them, but I can't tell you what actually happened."

"What was supposed to happen?" Chris wanted to know.

"The ravine was a good spot for a Doorway because it has one very powerful ley line running through it and two very close. It's filled with rocks and, half the year, water. Anything that needs to draw massive amounts of power can do so easily there. The plan was to wall off the Doorway from its power, so it would collapse.

"John's job was to reverse the flow of the ley line for as long as he could hold it. He knew he couldn't stop it or permanently reroute it, but at least for a few minutes he could disrupt it. Jen was going to build the dead zone. She succeeded. Robert and Cindy were there to fight off anything that jumped out to stop them. When we got there, John was unconscious at the foot of the ravine. Ben and I went inside to see what had happened. The Doorway was closed, stuck in the middle of the dead zone. Jen, Robert, Cindy, and anything alive in that circle was gone. When John came out of the coma, he didn't remember anything after getting to the ravine."

"Besides the Angel and the Watchers, the eyeless fuckers, did you see anything else?" Chuck asked.

"You mean when I was scouting?"

"Yeah."

"Mostly Watchers. There were things that looked like scorpions with wings standing on two legs and some sort of blue lion thing, again with wings. Actually, everything but the Watchers had wings. I'm surprised you guys don't have them."

"Who says we don't?" Chuck quipped.

I looked at Chris curiously. He thought *No* at me. Allan caught it. "Your brother over there for one."

Chuck look pleased to see Allan had caught Chris' answer and impressed he had figured out the relationship. "We didn't have wings. Most of the things we fought did. The animal types were the lower levels; the humanoid ones were the higher-ups. Mildred looked like blue and red flame made solid."

"Did you find a good way to deal with the Minions?" Chris asked.

"No. We got pretty good at running away. They succeeded, so maybe Robert and Cindy figured out how to kill them. Or maybe they just kept them busy long enough for Jen to do what she needed to. Or maybe they didn't find a way to deal with them, and that's why all three vanished. You know how to kill them?"

Chris nodded. "I know how to kill them."

"Good. Now, more importantly, can you fix my sister?"

I looked at the other two; they looked at me. "Maybe. What did Ben say?"

"Twenty-two years ago he wasn't sure there was a person still there to help; let alone that he could do it. You're a better healer than he was."

"Can you take me to her?"

"She's in an intensive care facility in Pittsburgh."

"If you're willing to ride my bike, I can get us to Pittsburgh in an hour and a half."

"How about we take my car? You and I can talk. I think those two are itching to head two doors up and talk to the others."

"Itching to get my own invisible man on the scene and see what he can tell us," Chris said.

Allan smiled. "The dark-haired one. When we get back, I definitely want to talk to him."

"His name is Dave, and he feels the same way about you," I said.

"Good."

56.

Allan was ready to get into his car and get going as fast as he could. I gave Chris a quick kiss goodbye and sent Morrell a text explaining my field trip to Pittsburgh. I got one back from him wishing me luck.

Allan drove too fast, but I had a feeling that wasn't going to be a problem. The guy who could hide the ravine wasn't likely to get pulled over for speeding.

We were a few miles onto I-79 when he asked me, "So, those two are brothers. Pat was a good friend of theirs. The blonde is something totally different. The other redhead is an employee. Dave is family to the brothers, but I don't know precisely what sort. How do you fit into this?"

"The blonde's name is Autumn. She's a fairy, and she's a friend of theirs." Allan laughed sarcastically. "Fine, she's an associate of theirs."

"Better. Don't kid yourself about her. She doesn't have friends."

"You know that just by watching her?"

"I've been watching her for almost four years. When something that distinctly not human in a human body comes strolling by my house, I pay attention. That's long enough to see she has no real affection for anyone besides your man, and he doesn't return it."

"That's why she's here. She got tangled in it for the love, lust, obsession, or whatever term you'd like to use, of him. Dave is Chris' brother-in-law. Mike, the other redhead, and Pat were his body guards. And me? Buggered if I know."

Allan didn't seem to believe that answer, so I kept talking. "He was married back there. Dave's sister. She was a healer and a seer. She didn't think what they were going to do was going to end well, so she left before it ended. Every now and again I like to think I might have been her because I've been dreaming about a life as a different person for a while now. When I asked Pat about it, my dreams didn't match with his reality. Apparently I've been making something up so I feel a little less bad about not having been his first love." Allan didn't look like he bought that either, but he didn't say anything. "Anyway, I'm here, and I'm a healer, but not a seer. I'm decent with a protection spell, so when they called Pat back, I came, too."

We drove for a few more minutes. "Tell me about your sister."

"What do you want to know?"

"What's the official diagnosis?"

"They don't have one. She's catatonic, except for the screaming. She hasn't spoken or even noticed another person in twenty-two years. They've drugged her into a coma. They make sure she gets moved around so she doesn't get bedsores. The physical therapy people come every day to exercise her so her muscles don't completely atrophy. She'll swallow if you put mush in her mouth, but she doesn't chew."

"How old is she?"

"Thirty-nine."

"Brain activity?"

"Even drugged to the hilt, her brain waves are off the charts. That's the other reason they don't have a diagnosis for her. She's a mystery, and that's why she's there. The University of Pittsburgh keeps sending students in to study her."

"What about Hank?"

"They used to study him, too. He died three years ago."

"What of?"

"Complications of MRSA. There were rumors his parents got him sick on purpose. They breathe on their own, will swallow if you give them food, and they aren't brain-dead. But they're in excruciating pain; there's no way to shut it off, no way to end it without killing them. There are no tubes to unplug, and no one at the university is willing to allow an 'accidental' overdose to happen."

"I'm sorry. I hope I can fix her."

"I hope you can, too."

"If I can't… Chris tells me he can cause an aneurism."

Allan thought about it for a moment, watching the street in front of him. "I want to see what happens if they get the Doorway closed and kill off the thing that did this. Maybe, if you can't do it, that will."

"Maybe. What happened to the Angel?"

"I don't know. It slid into my home, destroyed my sister, and slid out. I stabbed at it with my blade, but it didn't do anything. Three weeks later it found Hank and slid into his home. We got the door shut and never saw it again. Shortly after that the head of the Neuropsych Department at the University of Pittsburgh Medical School came to Reevesville General and offered April and Hank a place at their facility for as long as they needed one. My parents jumped at the chance. So did Hank's."

"Were you friends with them?"

"Not before. After weeks of sitting next to each other in the same hospital, answering the same questions over and over again, trying to find any possible link between those two, my parents and his became friends. I could have given them the real answer. They both liked to hike in the ravine, and while there they picked up something. It spent a few days hanging out, then left. That answer wasn't going to help anything. While the doctors were testing for every drug known to man and trying to come up with new ones that might possibly do what had happened to them, your brother very quietly sat in the back of the room working on a way to fix the problem. But he couldn't do it."

"Well, here's hoping I'm better at it than he is."

"You are. Here's hoping you're enough better."

He didn't say anything to me for the rest of the ride. I stared out the window, watching the sun set and the stars come out, trying to put myself in the right frame of mind to heal his sister. He drove us through Pittsburgh easily.

He pulled into a garage. "We're going to the sixth floor."

"Okay."

As hospitals went, it was fairly cheery. But it was still a hospital. The sixth floor was painted cream and beige with little hints of green to help perk things up. The nurses seemed oblivious to us. Whether they were used to Allan coming to visit so they didn't care, or they didn't see us at all, I didn't know.

He led me to room 643. Inside was a very small, very thin woman, with short white hair, and a pinched, pain-filled face. Her eyes were closed, but they fluttered like she was dreaming. I spoke quietly, which was silly. She wasn't going to wake up. "Is she dreaming?"

"Sort of. They tell me the brain waves are similar to what you'd expect for someone in REM sleep. One of the docs spent three years trying to 'wake her up.' He theorized she was dreaming and the right chemical cocktail would fix her. If such a thing exists, he couldn't find it."

"Can I touch her?"

"Sure." Allan shut the door behind us and cast a shield. Then he sat down on the small sofa, watching me.

"Hi, April. I'm Sarah. I'd like to try to help you. I hope I can. I'm going to take your hand and figure out what's wrong with you and what to do about it." I picked up her hand, holding it in mine. For a few minutes I couldn't find the problem. She was just a girl. Then I must have dug through the drugs because I was swimming in pain, fear, anguish, rage, and so many terrible feelings. I dropped her hand and stepped away before I could stop myself.

"What?" Allan asked.

"I got a quick feel for it. Give me a few minutes to get better shields in place. I want to study it, but if I feel it I'll start screaming, too, and that's not going to solve anyone's problems."

I took a few minutes to build myself an observation deck. A layer of magic to keep my mind away from the turmoil. Then I picked up her hand and went back in again. For the first few minutes all I could see was the pain. Eons of agony trapped in one girl. But as I kept at it I began to get a feel for how it worked and if not what it was, then at least how to move it.

I pulled back from her again. I wondered if Ben had been here, and if he had... "Can I borrow your car? I need to spend some time praying. There's a synagogue here I'd like to visit."

"I can drive you."

"That'll work."

We returned to his car. I gave him the directions to Temple Beth Shalom. I know he wanted to ask, but I didn't have an answer for him. Not yet. We pulled into the parking lot. "Can you tell me why you need to pray?"

"Yes. I need help."

"There's help here?"

"I hope so. Do you want to come in? Sit and pray for yourself?"

"I got out of the praying business a long time ago. There's a Starbucks a few blocks down. I'll be there."

"Okay." I walked inside wishing I knew any of the rabbis well enough to actually ask one of them my question. Instead I headed off to the *Mikvah*. I wanted the feeling of ritual purity to ask this question. I knew I could fix her. I knew how to fix her. The problem was the curse, or whatever it was, either had to die with the person it was in or move to another one. The view I had of the curse convinced me of one thing, I was not going to move it to anyone else. So, should I tell Allan I couldn't do it, or should I tell him why I wouldn't do it?

I undressed quickly and slid into the tepid water. I let it surround me, fill me, make me clean and whole. I stayed under until little lights began to flash before my eyes and came up with a gasp. Twice more I did that, begging the Lord for the peace of mind to come up with the right answer for this.

I got out, dried off, and headed to the main room. I prayed for a long time, looking for guidance as to what to tell Allan. When I was done, I was at peace with my answer, but I doubted he would be.

He looked up from his coffee when I walked in. "Ben had that same look."

I sat across from him. "I bet he did. He told you he couldn't do it, right?"

"Yeah."

"I won't do it." I felt his exhaustion, defeat, and anger rush over me. So, I kept talking. "I'd have to move it to someone else to free your sister. I can help to arrange it so she doesn't hurt anymore, but I won't give that to someone else."

"If I offered to take it from her?"

"It's not just that I don't want an innocent person—or a guilty one, for that matter—to have to endure it. I won't do it. There's a million years of anguish trapped in your sister. I will not move it to another person. I wouldn't rape you with a chainsaw if it would make her better, even if you asked for it."

He stood up slowly. I could feel he didn't like my answer, but I also had the sense he respected it. "Then we better hope killing this thing finally sets her free."

"If it doesn't..."

"I'll have a chat with Chris. Or maybe by then you'll have changed your mind."

"When we get to the car, I want you to feel the taste of it I did."

When we got there, I held the anguish in my mind for him to feel. He looked pale when he was done. "I'm sorry Allan. I'm not going to change my mind. I won't do that to another human being. Bring Hitler to your sister's room, and I won't do it to him."

57.

Chuck ran to Writers'. "She found the portal!" he yelled as he burst in. Autumn, Dave, and Mike appeared in an instant.

"What?" Dave asked.

"Chris is getting the map to show us. She saw Allan walk by the ravine. Suddenly it clicked, we hadn't checked there; the fucker wasn't even on the map, and..."

Chris came in with the map under his arm. He smoothed it open on the table. There, in the middle of the map, was a brightly glowing dot. The others drew close.

"Holy fucking Fnords! Was that always there?" Dave said as he looked at the map.

"Yeah. Just very well hidden. Allan, her brother, and another guy cloaked it." Chris was absurdly pleased to see the dot. His spell worked; he just couldn't see it through the cloaking. "Allan is interested in talking shop with you at some point," he said to Dave.

"Yeah, that sounds like a very good idea. How the hell did he pull that sort of magic?" Dave stared at the ravine on the map.

"You'll have to ask him though he says there's one major ley line in the ravine, two near it, lots of rocks, and good amounts of water seasonally."

"I will have to talk to him about it."

"Good. I don't know when he'll be back. He and Sarah are visiting his sister. That's a long story, and I'll tell you about it later, but they'll be back late tonight or tomorrow. Between now and then I want you in the ravine checking everything out. Mike, I want that square of the map blown up to three feet by three feet, and I want everything that's there on it. I want to know every stone, every tree, and every leaf of the terrain we're going to fight on. I want to know how the Door works and what's coming out of it. Autumn, tomorrow morning, on your own, I want you to take a run at it. Be bold and flashy and burn the absolute shit out of anything that jumps out at you. Then report back and tell me what came out. If the entire ravine is on fire when you're done, that's fine by me. Just make sure you come back."

"Can I wait until Sarah's back so I don't have to depend entirely on my own healing skills?"

"Sure."

"Chuck and I are going on a road trip. We were supposed to go ghost hunting the night Pat died. Time to do that now. Tomorrow I'm getting this fucking cast off one way or another. Then, with any luck, by Sunday we'll be ready to end this."

"Why Sunday?" Autumn asked.

"I don't know about you, but I want one last weekend," Chris answered.

"Amen to that," Mike said.

Chuck drove. The same contact that hooked him up with the job at Hurford's also told him about the McHale Mansion in Oil City. It had been abandoned in the late fifties. Last year a group of local teenage nitwits had wandered in. One was killed when the floor collapsed under them. The resulting ghost was new and mean. Even if they couldn't make it real, getting rid of it would be a public service.

Chris was very quiet. Chuck could tell he was already planning the fight. Trying to see it in his mind and make it happen the way he saw it.

"Get your mind back here. You need to make Mildred solid before you can fight it."

"Right. I'm trying to figure out how to fill the hole Pat left us with."

"Don't. You need to be here, now. When this is done and you know what firepower you can bring, then start thinking strategy."

Chris sighed. "I know. Okay. Any idea of the local layout here?"

"Nope. We've got to get in, scout it out, and take it down. This ghost has a reputation for being mean, but I wasn't able to find anyone who knew of it doing anything other than scaring people. No physical attacks."

"Good. I don't think there's a ghost that can scare me anymore."

"Let's hope." They drove for a few more minutes. When Chuck slowed down the car, Chris asked, "This the spot?"

"I think so." He pulled down a long, overgrown driveway toward a rotting hulk of a building. The first floor doors and windows had tape over them reading 'Condemned.'

"I think we're doing this in the open," Chris said.

"I'm fine with not going in there."

"Go find it. I'll set up the trap." It wasn't the best location for his sort of magic. He could feel two tiny, far away ley lines. The ground, a soft, deep loam, while great for farming, wasn't great for a mage with an affinity for fire or stone. He spent a few minutes continuing to look around. No neighbors. The closest building was a good four miles away. The forest was three hundred yards from the house. The house was mostly old, dry wood. The first time he did this he had wanted fire.

"Can you do double duty for me?"

"What do you want me to do?"

"There's not enough local energy here to do this, and we didn't eat properly ahead of time. If you think you can keep it in check, I'll set the house on fire and pull off of that."

"Give me a few minutes. I want to get a good feeling for how much energy it'll take to keep this thing reined in before we add a raging fire to the mix."

"Okay. Let me know when you know. Give me your keys."

Chuck tossed Chris the keys to the car. Chris pulled the car away from the house, almost to the street. When he walked back, Chuck was waiting for him. "I can do both. It's not too much of a big deal. Mostly just an obnoxious teenager with more power than any teenager should have."

"Great."

"Want me to light it for you?"

"Nah. I got this. Get far enough back not to get burned. Once I've got the circle set, chase it to me."

"Sure."

Setting the trap was easier this time. He nodded at Chuck. Soon a sulky looking ghost stared at him. He set the trap spinning and called down the fire. He hadn't done it in a long time, but it was one of his favorite tricks. He let the power gather in his hands, felt the lovely, warm glow of flames fill his mind, and shot it at the house. In a minute there was smoke. A minute after that they could see the flames spreading. He grinned and got to work, pulling energy off the fire and feeding it into the ghost.

In a matter of minutes he was sweating, and the ghost cast a shadow while the condemned building behind them roared with flames. He loved this kind of magic. It was clean and beautiful. In the end there would be nothing but light, cool ashes.

The ghost seemed intent on watching the house burn. It wasn't even paying attention to what Chris was doing to it. The flames roared, and the ghost became opaque. Chris felt it get past the point he had gotten the last one to.

He kept feeding it energy from the fire. His focus wavered for a few seconds when the house collapsed in on itself, but Chuck kept the fire away from them.

One last burst of magic flowed into the ghost while the newly fallen timbers cracked and popped as the fire found new fuel. It looked solid to him. He found a stick and poked it.

"Hey," the ghost said as it noticed him for the first time. Chris grinned at it. Its eyes went wide. It knew that grin didn't bode well for it.

It was solid. *Now what to do with it?* He let his mind go blank and slid into the trancelike state he needed to really know what was in front of him. It had human anatomy again. Beautiful. He gracefully drew a little more energy off of the burning house and carefully pulsed it into the brain of the ghost. One little burst here. One there. Another just to make sure the job was really done. It shrieked and collapsed.

Chris spent another minute staring at it, wondering what he should do with the body, but then, like the solid Minion, it vanished. He looked at the house. *Good thing it had been big.* All that was left were drifts of white ash.

Chuck walked over. "Are we going to need to set fire to fraternity row to take care of Mildred?"

"Maybe. Think we can get everyone out?"

"No."

"Probably wouldn't have worked anyway. Lots of those houses are brick. Let's go eat. I'm starving."

"Okay."

They stopped at the Perkins. The waitress was amused to see Chris order pancakes, three sides of bacon, a side of ham, hash browns, eggs, a cheeseburger, and a chocolate milkshake. Chuck decided coffee and meatloaf would do it for him.

"You know they have fried shrimp on the menu?"

"Not a big shrimp fan."

"Ahh... I thought you were ordering every un-kosher thing you could find."

"Just the ones I like."

What are you thinking of doing? Chuck asked in his head. No need for anyone else to overhear this conversation.

Don't really know yet. When Dave gets back, I'll have a better idea.

Come on, I know you're further than that.

Yeah, and you're the one who tells me to wait for all the intel before making decisions.

I don't want you to make decisions right now. I want to know what you think might work.

Okay. Rough version: use the staff to collapse the portal. See if Dave can hide this plane so whatever is still alive on the other side can't open it again and find us once more. Fight whatever comes out while drawing every bit of power I can muster to make Mildred real. When it is, you or I, whoever it's not paying attention to, will blow its mind. I'm going to have to use Autumn as a fighter, which sucks, but without Pat on my right, I don't have any other options.

Sarah?

Hopefully at home but I very much doubt it. She'll bring Morrell and Claire in for back-of-the-line healing, which, if you remember, was what we said she'd have to do if she wanted to join the fight.

Even if she didn't have a backup, I would have suggested bringing her along for this one. No reason to have her safe at home this time.

Other than I might fight better with her safe at home.

You'll have to put that aside. We'll be better off if she's there. It'll be fighting to kill this time, which means we need someone able to get to us fast.

I know. She'll be happy to be in it.

You won't.

No. But I will, as you said, get over it.

Think it'll bring out the Nehpheem again?

No. I'm pretty sure by now it's eating the higher-ups to keep going. Those things would have been on us in a heartbeat if Mildred had still had any to use when it found us again.

Yeah. That was almost fourteen years ago. The whip wielders might be the highest ones left.

I'm thinking more of the ones with swords are still hiding somewhere. At least a few of them. And a few of them is all we really need for this to get interesting. Of all the fucking bad timing for Pat to find out what happened.

Chuck shook his head. *Actually, of all the good timing. I still don't have a good feeling about this and Dave. If Dave hadn't been there, Pat would have finished us. Did you feel her protection on him? I couldn't break through it, not fast enough to have kept him from killing us. Without Dave there he would have stomped my knee, shoved my nose through my brain, kicked Autumn's skull in, and broken your neck before the mausoleum exploded. If he had done it in that order, the wall would have sailed over him.*

I know. I've been very carefully not thinking about that whole thing. One of these days I'll let myself feel it, spend an hour shaking and throwing up, and then wrap up with properly mourning him.

You miss him?

Yes. Especially now.

The food arrived, and both of them began to eat. Chris very quickly. When the waitress brought them the check, she looked at the empty plates in front of Chris with amazement.

"It was a very long day," he said by way of explanation.

"It must have been," she said as she cleared their plates. He paid, and they left.

When I got back from Pittsburgh, I found Chris and Chuck at the kitchen table, ice cream in front of them, the scent of burnt wood clinging to both of them. I grabbed a spoon and sat in Chris' lap.

"What flavor?"

"Phish Food."

"That'll do." I started to eat from his container. "I see large quantities of ice cream. What happened?"

Chris kissed me between bites of ice cream. "We went ghost hunting. I burned down a mansion, used the power to make it solid, then killed it. How about you?"

I nodded at him and ate another bite of ice cream. "I told Allan I wouldn't fix his sister."

"Wouldn't?" Chuck asked, eyebrows high.

"I can do it. Ben probably could have done it, too. But I won't. There's two ways to end it. She can die, or I can move it to someone else. I will not move it to someone else. If destroying Mildred doesn't end the curse, or whatever you want to call it, he's probably going to ask you to kill her. If you aren't willing to do it, teach me how because I will."

"I can show you how to do it."

"Good. No one should have to endure that. She's just a block of solid misery, pain beyond pain." Another bite. "Now what?"

"Sleep. Back at Writers' in the morning. Getting reports from Dave and Autumn, putting together the final plan. Then a few days off, a few days of normal, getting finals done, and some fun in. Then on Sunday, off we go."

"Sunday?"

"Yeah, why?" Chuck asked.

"Morrell and I have a running joke about the Apocalypse being scheduled for May 3. That's Sunday. He's already volunteered to help with any healing."

"Of course. Which one of you predicted the third?" Chuck took another bite of mint chocolate chip.

"He did. Why?" I reached across the table, my spoon hovering over his ice cream. He nodded to let me know it was okay to have some.

"Have to see if he's got any farseeing talent or if it was just dumb luck."

"He said it was a joke at the time."

"Let's hope it was."

"Why would we hope it was?"

Chuck answered bitterly, "Farseers mess things up. You're better off going in blind than with little bits and pieces with no context."

"It sounded like a joke when he said it; then it became a sort of code for the looming pile of shit on the horizon."

"We could always just go in on the second and take care of it like that," Chris said.

"Nah. Sunday's a good day for it. I've already got off that night."

We spent the next half-hour finishing off the ice cream. Then Chris and I went to bed, and Chuck sacked out on my sofa. When I woke up at six, I poked Chris, like he had asked me to, and we went off to Writers'.

Dave and Mike looked up from the map they were working on at the kitchen table. "Don't you two look alert and refreshed," Dave said.

"Come on, you remember how this works. We don't get to all sleep at the same time when we're on war footing. What do you have for me?"

"This." He gestured for us to come closer to the map. Mike had called up the image from Google Earth; he and Dave had carefully put each feature onto the map. The location of each rock, each tree, the dead zone, the ley line that ran through the ravine, the two nearby, notes as to what sort of energy each one carried, how each of the large stones felt were all listed.

"Did they notice you?" Chris asked Dave.

"No. They never do. What else do you need to know?"

"If you really can hide anything? Allan says they closed it once, but it's obviously been reopened from the other side. If we can get it closed again, can you hide this plane so they can't find it again to reopen the door? I want whatever's on the other side to starve to death before it can start this up again."

Dave looked thoughtful. "You want me to hide this entire plane of existence?"

Chris nodded. "Yes."

"You're kidding, right?"

"No."

"Do you have an atom bomb handy?"

"Nope. You've got to do it with the energy on hand and leave me enough to make Mildred solid so I can kill it."

"You're a fucking madman." Dave shook his head, realized Chris really meant it, and said, "First off, I am getting at least eight hours of sleep. Secondly, I'm going over to your landlord's place to have a long chat with him. I don't know if I can do it by myself. I don't know if it can be done. I'll bounce some ideas and magic around with him and see if it's even possible. I'll have an answer for you by tonight."

"Good. Now you're off duty to get as much sleep as you want. You, too, Mike. Take a break. Tonight I want you in the ravine, assuming Autumn hasn't burned it to the ground, seeing what jumps out at you."

"Okay." They both got up and headed toward their rooms.

"Why might Autumn be burning the ravine to the ground?"

"Because my assignment starts now." She came out of the kitchen, a bowl of cereal in one hand, her spoon in the other. Her hair was braided out of the way, and her clothing was much less dramatic than usual. Just a pair of sneakers, jeans, and a plain, long-sleeved t-shirt. "At least it starts when I finish breakfast. I get to go in, all on my lonesome, and see exactly how many of those bastards jump out at me. Because my fireball is an effective Minion deterrent, I have been granted permission to use it at will."

I could honestly say I had never heard that much sarcastic loathing in anyone's voice before.

Chris ignored it and explained to me, "They really hate her. Sending her in should give me a good idea of what the biggest gun Mildred has left in its arsenal is." He turned to look at Autumn, "And if you kill a bunch of them off in the process, all the better."

"All the better," Autumn said with a hard grimness in her voice.

"For the fight where my people will be in the line of fire, have you been practicing?" Chris asked.

"Got a cigarette?" Autumn responded.

He got his coat. "Yes, actually." I could see Autumn wondering why he had started to carry his own supply, look at me, and decide she didn't want to know. He stood on the other side of the room holding the pack.

"Put one between your lips."

Chris did so. "I will not be happy if you burn my face off."

"Like I care." And then from fifteen feet away she sent a tiny quarter-sized ball of fire to light the cigarette.

"That was excellent."

"Thank you. Go smoke it outside. I don't want my house smelling like cigarettes." He went outside. She finished eating her cereal. "I'll be back in an hour or so. Probably burned and hurt. Eat, grab a nap, do whatever it is you do, but be ready to heal me."

"I'll be ready. You want a prophylactic dose of pain killer?"

"No. I can do that for myself."

"I'll be waiting for you." She nodded and left out the back door.

Chris came back in a minute later. He sat next to me at the table studying the map. "Any orders for me?"

"Rest, eat, make sure you're ready anytime day or night to heal whatever might come our way. I'll be able to keep the rest of us on shifts so we all get enough down time to function. Unfortunately, I can't do that for you. You're on duty until this is done. My hope is this weekend will be free time. At least, I won't be sending anyone in harm's way after noon on Friday, but I can't guarantee any of us will actually get the weekend off."

"In that case, I'm going home to make some breakfast. I'll be back before she is."

"Good."

Chris studied the map. It was a good map. As good as a map could possibly be. That was the problem. It was a map. He couldn't go in there to scout for himself. He wanted to. Actually laying his eyes on the place he would fight had saved him on several occasions, but he was sure the moment he set foot in the ravine Mildred and whatever firepower it could bring to the party would come after him. He wasn't going to fuck this fight up by getting impatient.

Which meant waiting for others to report back.

Mike made sure the elevations were on the map as well. That helped. The bottom of the ravine was narrow, less than twenty feet. That was a good thing. Even if Mildred had hordes of Minions left, only five or six of them would be able to attack at any given time.

He tapped the map with his pen. There was a nice boulder about halfway up one side of the ravine, slightly past where the portal was. The map listed it as granite. He checked Dave's notes. They were all granite. Also a good thing. Once again he felt a stab of desire to have Pat with them. He could have left Autumn at home or sent her back to Fairy if Pat had still been there. Put him in a granite boulder-filled pit with a twenty-foot field of fight…

Stop it. Pat was gone. No use wishing for the soldier he couldn't have. No use wishing for the friend who had been on his right side at almost every battle that mattered to him. *Stop it!*

He penned Dave's name over the boulder. He'd be out of the line of fire, able to do his part. The slope was gentle enough Dave could climb out and head home as soon as he was done. In a pinch Dave was a half-decent general. There had been a few times he had been pinched enough to give Dave an army and let him have at it, but as a fighter he was useless. Well, not useless as the graveyard had proven. But if they had gotten to the point where Dave needed to fight, the battle was lost, so he might as well be out of the way, getting ready to make his life out of the view of the surviving Minions.

Because if anyone could walk away from this fight, no matter who won it, it was Dave. Except Chuck had a bad feeling about Dave. But Chuck wasn't a seer. The last absolute catastrophe Chuck had felt just fine about as they went into it. Hopefully his feelings weren't worth much.

Chris went back to studying the map. He'd put Mike behind the portal; Mike would make sure the Minions didn't have an easy line of retreat. Once the door was closed, he could go after whatever pleased him.

That left the other three of them. Chuck on his left, Autumn on his right. He and Chuck would be off to the west side, giving Autumn a fairly wide berth on the east. Mike would be in her line of fire then…

He shook his head. Mike was good enough to keep the Minions between him and her fire. He wouldn't get burned.

And Sarah would be… wherever she wanted to be. Wherever she needed to be. He circled three rocks with good line of sight and easy access to the fight. She'd start at whichever one of those three she liked.

He stared at the map, running possible fights through his head. When a soft hand touched his shoulder, he jumped slightly.

"I brought you some breakfast, too."

"There are ten biscuits there."

"Most of them are for Autumn. I thought she might be hungry when she got back. I left a bunch for Chuck as well. Talk me through what you're thinking."

He did while eating, showing her the rocks, where he hoped everyone would be, how he wanted the fight to flow: Dave's escape route.

"What are these?" She pointed at the three circled stones he hadn't mentioned.

"One of those three stones is yours."

"Good. I don't think I could have sat here, waiting for you to come back." She looked at the map for a while longer. He felt her sadness before she spoke: "You would have put Pat here," she pointed to what was now Autumn's spot, "and he could have covered your right. You'd move Autumn to fight back to back with Mike. They'd keep herding the Minions toward you and Pat."

"Chuck and Pat. I'll fight, but most of my energy will be spent making Mildred real. Chuck will be doing his best battle wizard impression, which isn't bad, and Pat would have—It doesn't matter what he would have done."

"I guess it doesn't."

I heard footsteps on the porch and looked up. Autumn was back. Her arms were burned, and she was limping.

"Let's get the burned clothing off," I said. She started to pull at the t-shirt. "Not like that. Chris, get me some scissors and my bag." He brought the bag over and headed into the kitchen for scissors. I made a mental note to add them to my pack. I didn't want to cut through her shirt with my dissection scissors. Its tiny blade would take an eon to cut through Autumn's shirt.

"You want to do this in here or in your room?"

"Here's fine."

"Okay. Drink up." I didn't hand her the bottle. Her hands and forearms had the worst of the burns. I held it for her. She leaned back and closed her eyes as the magic started to work.

"You know, that actually is pleasant."

"Good." Chris handed me the scissors. He grabbed the map and went upstairs to give us some privacy. I began to cut her out of her shirt. "No need to damage your skin worse by pulling a shirt over it. What burned you?"

"I did. Long sleeves were a bad idea. The shirt caught a few minutes in. I got done and got out. But by then..."

"By then you had first- and second-degree burns on both hands and forearms. Lucky for you I've gotten pretty handy with burns. You want another shot of the pain killer?"

"I wouldn't mind." She took another swallow. Then I got to work. Healing her took about an hour. Much easier than working with Chuck's full thickness third-degree burns. Once I got them done, I sat back for a minute to rest. "Okay, tell me about the limp."

"Right knee and ankle. I tripped over one of the rocks and landed badly."

"Got it." She'd sprained the ankle and bruised her knee. Twenty minutes later and her leg was done as well. She'd be sore for the rest of the day, but by tomorrow she'd be fully functional.

"How are you feeling?"

"Pretty good. I'd say we're even on the dress now." I laughed until I realized she was serious.

"Great. I made you some breakfast." I pointed to the biscuits on the plate. "I wasn't sure if you liked to eat after magic or not."

"I could use some food."

"There are sourdough biscuits with your name on them over there. He's going to want the update as soon as you can give it to him."

"Yes. I know. I'll get changed and join you." I went upstairs to find Chris. He was in what used to be Mike's room.

"All clear, you can go down now."

"Good." He folded up the map and headed down to wait for Autumn.

A minute later, she sat down at the table and tidily split a biscuit. "About what you were thinking. Three with swords, two with whips. If there's anything more powerful lurking around, it's waiting for you to bring it out."

"Five? You took out five of them?"

Autumn gave me a look of immense bitterness. "Their problem with me has never been about lack of power."

"It's always been about lack of control. You saw what she did to Chuck," Chris answered. "It's not enough to have massive power; you have to be able to use it without killing everyone around you. As long as it's just her and the Minions, we're fine. But it's very rarely just her and the Minions."

Autumn laughed meanly. "Sure, rarely. Just the eighteen years before I found you. But sure, me and the Minions, we're rare."

"Autumn, I don't care if you fight them every fucking day. You burned Chuck's face off, by accident. And that's not the first time you've hurt one of us. You are powerful. I've always acknowledged that, but you are dangerous because you cannot control your power. It might be fine to go off and fuck everything nearby when the fairies are in charge, it's not here. These are the people I love. I want them to come home from this fight."

"Fine. Everyone comes home. Anything else you need to know before I ask you to leave my home?"

"How'd they come out?"

"Single file, a few seconds between each one."

"Good."

"If that's everything?"

"Yes." Chris got his coat. "You're off duty until tomorrow morning. Then I want you to do exactly the same thing, preferably without burning yourself."

She flipped him a salute. "Yes, Sir!"

We headed back to my place. "Now what?"

"Now we wait. Dave will find out what he can do. Mike will take a run at them tonight. I'll send Chuck along, too. He'll make sure Mike doesn't get swamped and practice on the Minions. You'll sleep, eat, rest, and do whatever else it is you want to do. I'll stare at the map and will it to tell me how to make this work so all of my family comes home."

58.

Wednesday became Thursday. Mike and Chuck went in Wednesday night. They came out cut and bruised but in one piece. Three of the sword-wielding Minions had come out. One of the scorpion-looking ones. Now they were dead.

They were coming out solid. That bothered Chris because there really wasn't any reason for them to be solid if he wasn't along for the ride. Chuck thought Mildred might be trying to lure him into the fight sooner than he was ready. Whatever the truth was, it worked out well for us.

Dave went over to Allan's place in the middle of Wednesday afternoon. We didn't see him until dinnertime on Thursday. He looked at Chris, said, "I can do it," and headed up to his room.

Friday morning I went to see Morrell. I had been sending him text updates as to what was going on but didn't go to see him in person because I, along with the others, were officially "sick." Most of my professors seemed pretty understanding, especially since I kept emailing in my assignments.

"Good morning," I said as I entered his office.

"It really is going to be May 3."

"Looks like it. My friends are scared you're a farseer."

He laughed. "Not a chance. And even if I was I wouldn't touch the stuff. If you ask, Claire will spend hours chewing your ears off about how nothing good has ever come of prophecy. She's very vehement about it. Enough of that, what's the plan?"

"The plan is relax, rest, do whatever prep work we need to. Then Sunday night 'round about sunset, off we go to fight."

"And you are going, too?"

"I am going, too. Or, I will be if you're willing to hang out at Writers' and be our back-of-the-line healer."

"No problem."

"Would you be horribly insulted if I was to ask to move my final from Monday to Wednesday? Best-case scenario: I'll probably be pretty tired. Worst-case: I'll be dead."

"I'm fine with moving your final to Wednesday. Do you want me to intercede on your behalf for your other classes?"

"No need. I lucked out. Brit History paper isn't due 'til Wednesday. Bio's on Wednesday morning. No final for fencing. Diff Eq is Tuesday. With any luck I should be done by Wednesday evening. In addition to all the rest of this fun, Autumn's defending her senior thesis today though I'm not sure why. Chris has two ten-page papers due on Monday. He tells me he's doing as a sign of his commitment to staying alive. Dave is supposed to be taking his first final right about now. Mike has decided to blow the whole thing off. He tells me his grades are good enough he can take the hit if he somehow gets through this. As dates for the Apocalypse go, May 3 really sucks."

"It certainly could have been timed better in regards to your finals."

"To say the least."

"Anyway, off you go. Do your prep work. Write your paper. Claire and I will see you on Sunday night."

"Thank you."

Chris sat on the window seat, alternating between staring at the map and furiously typing one of his papers.

I sat next to him, staring at my Brit History assignment. Produce seven pages about any bit of British history you like. It counted for a tenth of my final grade. I currently had a B-. I debated not writing anything and taking the hit, then got started.

It went surprisingly fast. I wrote about role of the British soldier throughout the history of the British Empire. When I looked up, shocked to see not only had I finished the first draft but I had eight pages of work, it was dinnertime.

"I forgot the Sabbath."

Chris jerked at the sound of my voice, ripping himself away from his paper. "I'm sorry?"

"I forgot the Sabbath. It's Friday night, and I've got nothing ready."

"Do you think God will forgive us if we order pizza, work tonight, and take an extra-long Sabbath next week?"

"I'm willing to chance it." I stood up, ordered the pizza, then went back to my paper, rereading and messing around with it. Shortly after the pizza came, I emailed the paper off. "One final done. How close are you?"

"About a page away from done. Then all of the next one, which I am dreading: feminist literary criticism of postmodern British poetry."

"That sounds like so many shades of not fun. At least you've got something to work on. I can't do my others early. All I've got is sitting here waiting."

"You could study."

"I could study." He didn't look surprised to see me come back with my *Tanach* instead of my biology textbook.

We got to bed late. As there had been in much of the little bits and pieces of down time these last few days, there was a sort of frantic sex, making sure each minute got as much life pulled out of it as possible. After, I lay next to him and said, "Pat told me you didn't do your own protection spells before. She and Dave did them for you, so you could focus your magic on the attack."

"That's right."

"Would you like my protection?"

"Yes."

"Tomorrow I'll rest and pray. Tomorrow night, I'll do it for you."

"Thank you." He kissed me and slid into a very deep sleep. It took me longer to fall asleep, but once there I didn't dream.

The first time I cast the spell it had been a prayer written on a man I loved. The second time, I wrote it on my home. The third time I wrapped the letters around myself. The fourth didn't work. This time, the fifth, I laid my hands on this man who had become more important to me than my own life and let the magic grow and swell. This time it was sex magic and protection magic and a prayer and a hope and will and touch and faith and love made into a glowing shield to wrap around him and keep him safe from the coming fight. This time I had an idea of what precisely I was trying to protect him from; I could hold the image of the Minions in my mind and will their fight to pass him by. This time the spell closed with an orgasm so intense it made my vision gray out. When we were done, I could feel the shield, and I knew he was bulletproof.

Chris didn't want his eyes to close. She was brilliant with her magic and love, and he wanted to see it, feel it, and vanish in it. At the same time, her body sliding on his while she cast her spell felt so good his eyes tried to hide.

She moved slowly. *God and fuck it was good!* Achingly slow, soft, wet, dragging sensations made his body feel liquid. He knew this was going to take a long time. No rush here, no hurry. Let the magic gather, let it feed on the feelings, let it grow between them.

He wanted to hold her close. Wanted the slide of her whole body against his. He gripped the headboard to stop himself from grabbing her and flipping them over. The last thing he wanted to do was break her concentration.

Her fingers rested on his chest as she rose and fell against him. She looked like light made solid. *Effulgent. All I have to do is survive, and I can finish my days with this radiant creature who loves me so intensely she glows.*

Rise and fall. Her hips snug against his and then almost all the way off of him. Her breasts swayed with each thrust. He reached up to hold them. She took his hand in hers, lifted it to her lips, and sucked on his finger.

He couldn't take the teasing brush of not nearly enough of her skin any longer. This kind of sex should be close. He flipped them so he could feel all of her under him. Lips and tongues and her heart beating under his chest added to the intensity. He kept up the slow pace she had set, sinking gently into her while she wrapped him in her magic.

She whispered her prayer in Hebrew, to him, to her God. Her words tingled in his ears, making him feel connected to God in a way he hadn't since before this had begun. Making him feel he might be forgiven.

Her body pulsed around him. The extra friction tipped him from joy to ecstasy. White-hot pleasure arced through his whole body. When he could think again, he felt distilled, pure. The pain, guilt, and fear of the last twenty-three years had burned out of him.

Sunday morning Chuck came over to start getting ready. He swung by the local Dunkin' Donuts on the way. It'd be nice to get the calories in a slow, steady stream instead of eating until they wanted to burst at the end of the night.

He knocked. He wasn't used to doing that at anywhere Chris considered home, but he also didn't want to walk into anything involving either of them naked. Judging by Sarah in her bathrobe and the door to their bedroom shut, knocking had been a good idea.

He held up the box. "I brought donuts."

"Good. Get comfy. We'll be out of the shower soon."

He sat on the sofa and went after a chocolate-iced one. Fifteen minutes later, while they were still in the shower, he heard steps on the stairs. He opened the door before Mike and Dave could knock.

"Come on in. I've got donuts."

Mike looked at the box. It had thirty-six donuts in it. "You brought lots of donuts."

"I figured we'd need lots of energy, and I'm getting sick of ice cream."

"Okay." Mike took one with sprinkles. Dave grabbed a cinnamon one. "Where are our hosts?"

"In the shower."

"Remind me not to use the bathroom here," Dave said.

Chuck looked confused, but Dave just shook his head. "Where's Autumn?"

"Home. Doing whatever pre-fight communing she intends to do. I know she doesn't plan to see him until right before," Mike answered between bites.

"Okay."

Chris came out a minute later, still in his pajamas, with his hair wet. "I didn't realize you were all here."

"No need to get dressed for us. Not like any of us haven't seen you in your PJ's," Mike replied.

Chris sat at the window seat. "Toss me a Boston Cream one." Chuck sent one flying to him. He caught it deftly.

Chuck just kept staring at him. "What?" Chris finally asked.

"Your new protection spell is pretty impressive."

"Thanks," Sarah said as she came out. "I think I finally got it right."

"'Right' might be the word for it." Chuck nodded in amazement. He'd never seen Chris glow like that, not even during the height of the war when he had every protection they could think of layered on him. She picked out a jelly donut and sat on Chris' lap.

"So, now what?" she asked.

Chuck answered, "We eat. We wait. We go over the plan a few times. Eventually we retreat to our own places for last-minute prep. Then we meet up."

"Shouldn't Autumn be here for going over the plan?"

"She knows it. We know it. You know it. It's not necessary. It's just what we're going to do to kill time between now and then."

So they did. Slowly the donuts vanished, along with a huge omelet, a few pizzas, a roasted chicken, a massive salad, a loaf of French bread, and a pot of beef noodle soup. Slowly the sun crept along the sky. Finally, with an hour left to go, the group broke up.

59.

I chose my clothing carefully. I wished for my uniform; I'm used to fighting in it, but it was in a box at the farm. I slipped out of my yoga pants and changed into cargo pants. It took a few minutes to distribute the contents of my medical bag into the pockets. I wanted the most important things easiest to grab. Dissection kit went in the front pocket of the left leg, the flask of pain killer in the front pocket of the right. I skipped the cold packs; they're back-of-the-line tools. The bandages went into my hip pockets. Plastic zip cords I could use as tourniquets went in the lower left pocket. I slipped a small fire extinguisher in the bottom right pocket.

I slipped my knives into my belt and ankle sheaths. "Gun's a bad idea?"

Chris didn't answer me. He sat on the floor doing something with a candle, a knife, and three stones. He didn't hear me. A small epiphany hit. It was almost dark outside and would be darker yet by the time we got into the ravine. I strapped on my ankle holster and put the small Maglite I had for emergencies in it.

The shirt was easier to pick. Any of my t-shirts would do, so the one on the top of the pile got put on.

I kissed my star and tucked it under my shirt.

I grabbed the ponytail holders I had bought for today and pulled back my hair. Nothing left for me to do. I watched Chris wrap up his prep. He wasn't as careful about his clothing, but I don't think he expected to be hand-to-hand fighting anything. If he had to get down to physically pounding on something, the fight was pretty much lost.

He snuffed out the candles and stood up. The stones in a small semi-circle where he had been sitting glowed so strongly they hurt to look at. He tucked the knife into his belt, pocketed the stones, got the staff, laid it on the bed, and walked over to me. "Ready?"

"As I'm ever going to be. You?"

"Almost." He kissed me for a long time and held me with his chin resting on the top of my head for a longer time. I could feel his magic wrapping around me, creating a shield.

"Just a little extra protection."

"Thanks."

He picked up the staff. "Let's go."

We got to the Writers' House a minute later. Mike waited in the living room. He looked so fierce I was truly grateful he was on my side. His favorite sword was in its scabbard on his hip. The second-best one was strapped over his back. Both shimmered a delicate green I had never seen before. He had a small plain dagger tucked into his boot. Somehow, even with all the sparring, it hadn't really hit me that he used to kill people for a living. It hit me now.

I didn't see Dave until he spoke to Chris. Then he faded out of my view while I was watching him.

We heard steps on the porch: Claire and Eric. They came in and looked us all over with approval.

"Where's Autumn?" I asked.

"At the ravine. She said she'd wait for us there," Mike answered. Both Morrells looked like they expected that.

A minute later Chuck joined us. If he had any extra tools or tricks, they were well-hidden under his jeans and t-shirt. He had replaced his sneakers with boots; I had the feeling he had taped his ankle to give it a little extra stability.

I touched his shoulder. "Do you want me to help your ankle?"

"Yes."

I sank to the floor, placing my fingers on the leather of his boot. I strengthened the muscles and tendons around his ankle and gave him a little shot of preventative pain relief.

"Time to go?" Mike asked when I stood up.

"Time to go," Chris said.

It took a minute to find Autumn once we got to the ravine. She blended into the background quite well in her soft grayish-green outfit. I understood the practical value of the colors she wore. But the outfit was a long dress with short sleeves, totally impractical for walking through a forest, let alone any sort of fighting. She seemed comfortable in it. I hoped I wouldn't be healing up more burns because another of her outfits caught fire. She had two long knives, daggers really, one on each hip. I could feel they did some sort of shielding but not what precisely.

We all looked at each other and started in.

It was actually a little anticlimactic when we got there. Nothing happened. Nothing jumped out. The door was visible, but Mildred didn't come hopping out of it as soon as we got there.

Chris and Chuck walked to the dead zone and destroyed it. One minute it was there, warm and safe, and the next magic washed into the space where the vacuum had been. Still nothing happened. I felt nervous and fidgety, incapable of standing still. I picked the rock I wanted. It was about twenty feet behind the rest of them, up the side of the ravine a bit, and off to the east. It had good visibility and was large enough to provide decent cover. The others moved into their places. Then I took cover and waited, forcing my body to stay still.

Chris spoke in a voice I had never heard him use before. It was darker, harder, and much older than his usual speaking voice. I didn't know the words, but I could feel the content. He called out Mildred, commanding it to come and face them. He swung the staff through the doorway.

The sound of ripping canvas rang through the ravine when the staff cleaved the portal. The wind picked up, and the sound grew louder. Something was coming. My body knew it and wanted to run.

I didn't see Mildred emerge. One second the ravine was empty. We sat waiting, adrenaline making us shaky and tense. The next second, Mildred stood before us. Beautiful, terrible, and so horribly angry. *An angel of blue and red flame made flesh.* Had Chuck said that? Not even close. But closer than I was going to come to describing it. It felt like fire made flesh. Its rage scorched everything around it. The trees closest to Mildred smoldered, leaves sparking into flames. The stones directly beneath it began to glow dully with the heat.

I wanted to look away from Mildred. Watching it hurt, limbs snapping under the crushing weight of millions of years of sorrow, hurt. I wanted to run or cut myself and scream my pain, its pain, into the heavens.

The others were moving, attacking. Autumn screamed something, and her fire added to the glow from the burning leaves. Smaller, less terrible but still awesome, creatures filed out behind Mildred. Mike charged them, his own battle cry the near silent sound of steel slicing air. He fought two handed, sword in one hand, his knife in the other.

I scanned the fight. Dave was gone. I couldn't find him. I felt useless; I couldn't tell if he needed help if I couldn't find him. I also couldn't find the portal anymore. I knew where it should be, but it wasn't there.

The line of Minions ceased. Autumn and Mike fought the ones on the ground, twelve or so of them. She burned them. He kept both blades spinning, crazily reflecting the firelight. Slowly blue bodies fell and vanished.

It was hard to tell Chris from Chuck. Their minds were so entwined as they fought they began to blend. One would toss a spell, attract Mildred's attention, and the other would hit while it was focused on the first one. Chris would attack. Mildred would counter. Chuck would deflect. One of them was always shielding. One was always attacking.

Mike stumbled, bleeding from his right ear, two of the Minions on him. I ran to him. Autumn saw me while I was a few steps out and shifted her fire to the creatures on Mike. They retreated from him, and I pulled him away from the main fight.

"I'm fine," he gasped between fast, hard breaths.

"Really?"

"Yeah. Just stunned."

I placed a hand on his temple, feeling cracks in his skull. "You aren't fine. Hold still for a minute." I got his skull cemented back together and quickly searched his brain for bleeds. *None. Good.*

"Now you're fine." He hopped back up and ran to the nearest Minion. He neatly decapitated it before it had noticed he was near. Another saw him and looked ready to fight. It grinned at Mike as he moved closer, raised its sword in a salute, and charged.

I wanted to watch them, but Autumn was next to me, seeking aid. Her left arm was mangled, cut to the bone and spurting bright red blood. I nodded at her and got to it. It didn't have to be pretty. It didn't have to be tidy. It just had to keep her blood on the inside and her hands attached. That took longer than the work on Mike. Five minutes, eight, I didn't know. I wasn't paying attention to anything besides knitting the veins of her arm back together. I didn't want her bleeding out during the fight.

"Can you move your hand?"

She tried for a moment. "No."

"Okay. Can you fight one handed?"

"Yes."

"Give me three minutes, and if you can't move it by then, I'll finish it after."

"Okay." I went to work, reconnecting the tendons and muscles. Her arm was a mess, but she could at least flex her hand by the end of the three minutes. When she went back to the fight, there were four Minions left, and Mildred was still going strong. It was almost laughing off what Chris and Chuck were doing. They looked tired.

Autumn's fire flared behind Mildred. Another Minion went down. Soon she and Mike could turn their attention to Mildred, and that would make a difference.

Then Chuck dropped. I didn't see anything hit him. One minute he was covering Chris' attack. The next he was on the ground clutching at his leg.

I got to him a few seconds later. "What happened?"

"Don't know. I can't feel my leg, and it won't hold me."

"That's your good one, isn't it?"

"Yes."

"Come on; let me get you up and out of the way." I put an arm around him and half-dragged, half-carried him out of the line of the fight. Out of the corner of my eye I could see Autumn take his place and aim her fire at Mildred.

I got him behind the nearest boulder and tried to get a feel for what was going on. Nothing jumped out at me. I had no idea what was wrong. I took his boot off.

"Can you feel this?" I ran my finger up his foot.

"No."

Then I remembered. "Take your shield off." He quickly took the pendant out from under his shirt and handed it to me.

"Put it on you. I changed it so it'll cover both of us if you're wearing it."

"Thanks." I slid it over my head. A low, cold headache spread through me, but compared to how working with Chuck usually went, it was nothing terrible. I felt for his pulse in his ankle. "You've still got blood flow. Can you move your toes?" Nothing happened. "Foot?" Once more nothing. "Knee?" Nothing. "Hip?" There was a faint twitch as his quadriceps moved.

"Better than nothing." I put my hands on his hip, the muscles were soft, relaxed, and unresponsive. Inspiration hit. "Did you have your back turned to Mildred?"

"Yes."

I pushed him into a seated position and began feeling around his spine and pelvis. At the base of his spine, his clothing was warm and sticky. "You don't feel what I'm doing, do you?"

"Just pressure. It doesn't hurt."

"Okay. Roll on your stomach. You've got something wrong with your spine."

He rolled over. I could hear the fear in his voice. "What kind of wrong?"

"You're bleeding and you can't move most of one leg kind of wrong. I'm hoping it's just a mechanical problem. Something a little knitting will fix." I pulled his jeans down to his hips and began to feel around. Tentatively probing the wound with my fingers. Something long, thin, and hard was wedged into his low back.

I had the Maglite between my teeth and used the tweezers from the dissection kit to get it out. He cursed hotly as I eased out a two inch long splinter of stone. "Wiggle your toes."

He did. "Good. Let me fix this, and you can get back out there."

My hands were on his back, slippery with his blood, forcing the magic to do my will. Skin, muscles, tendons, and nerves all joined together again. I don't know how long it took, but he was able to stand again when I was done. I gave him back his pendant, and off he went to rejoin Chris.

He moved slowly back to the fight, his leg dragging slightly with each step. It would take more than however long I had worked on him to get him back to fully functional, but he could stand, and he could fight, and that was all that mattered.

The Minions were gone. Mike fought Mildred from behind. Autumn's yellow fire added to its red and blue flames, casting the ravine in a soft green-orange glow. She took two steps to the side so Chuck could go back to fighting with Chris.

A sound like thunder and a wave of scorching heat rolled over all of us. It knocked all of us to the ground, except Chris.

Chris stood before it, speaking again in that dark tone, bright and powerful with his magic. The rest of us were on the ground at various levels of getting back up. He jumped at Mildred, swinging the staff; it connected with a loud crystalline cracking sound, like a baseball bat hitting a glass vase. For the first time, Mildred staggered. He hit it again, and again, each time forcing it a little further backward.

Mike rolled out of the way and added his blades to the fight. His next strike drew blood. He saw that and fought faster, striking harder. One swing took off its hand.

Autumn was up again. Her flames licked at Mildred, and it screamed.

I may have been screaming, too. Anything to shut out that sound. Pain, horror, hate, and sorrow made into sound, flowing around us, echoing off of the walls of the ravine.

Chuck finally got to his feet. Somehow the others knew to step back. It didn't look like Chuck had done anything. There was no movement, no fight, and no weapon. But the screaming stopped. Mildred's eyes went blank, the heat, rage, and sorrow all dropped away. It took one step back and fell.

As soon as Mildred hit the ground, Mike was on it. In less than a minute he had its head cut off and his knife through its chest. When he pulled back, Autumn set it on fire. By the time I got there Mildred was a small charred wreck. More importantly, it was very, very dead.

For a moment we all just looked at each other, not really sure what came next. Then Mike started laughing, a high-pitched hysterical laugh, more a release of pent-up tension than anything resembling joy.

"Fucking hell, we're still alive!" He threw his head back and screamed his voice raw, "We're alive!" He continued to laugh softly.

None of the rest of us really knew what to do. We milled around looking at Mildred's corpse, almost waiting for something else to jump out and get us.

"Should we bury it?" I nudged the corpse with my foot.

"No. It won't have form for much longer. None of the Minions held their form, it won't either," Chris answered.

"What knocked us down? That didn't feel like Mildred?" Mike asked.

"Me. I made Mildred's body real in this world. That set off the shock that knocked you all down."

"That's what you were doing?" Autumn looked amazed.

He looked at her mildly, leaning against the staff. "Among other things. You know, once upon a time, I was considered something of a fierce battle mage."

"Once upon a time." Chuck laughed. "As long as your brother was right next to you to watch your flank."

He smiled at Chuck. "As long as."

"Let's go home. Eric and I can get you all fixed up. Then, I think we could all use a drink or three."

"Three?" Autumn smirked. "Try six."

"If you can take six, I'll pour them for you," Chuck said to her.

"Tonight I can. Remember, once upon a time I was considered a fierce partier." She led the way back to the Writers' House. The rest of us followed. I took one step. Chris grabbed my hand and stopped me. He pulled me against him and kissed me. The intense relief, joy, and love in his kiss made my knees go weak and my heart beat fast. The exceptionally creative and very graphic thought accompanying it made me think skipping the after party sounded like a good idea.

I heard Chuck's voice from a long way away. "Get a room."

Chris grinned against my lips. I felt him think back at Chuck, *Later.*

Back at Writers' Allan waited along with Eric and Claire. All three stood up when we walked in. Their relief we had come home and were walking under our own power was thick in the room.

I took a moment to wash Chuck's blood off my hands and explain what had happened to Eric. He took over on Chuck. I got to work on Autumn's arm. Claire made sure Mike and Chris were in one piece and fully functional.

After an hour, I stood back up and poured myself and Autumn a shot of whiskey. I handed her the glass. "Here's the final test. Can you drink it down?"

She ran her hand and all five fingers through their whole range of motion, then picked up the glass, knocking it back. "Nice work. Pour me another?"

I poured her another one. She drank that one slowly, lined up glasses for the rest of them, and poured again. She handed the drinks around, even to Claire, and raised hers. "To a nice, normal, boring rest of our lives."

We raised our glasses. "Amen," I said and drank more of mine.

Over the next hour the story of the fight got retold. Allan, Claire, and Eric asked questions, keeping them talking about each detail of the story. I listened quite intently, while healing I had missed most of what actually happened in the fight. The joy of being alive was tempered by not having Pat here to share in the celebration. I could see what he'd be doing, stretched out on the couch, drinking a beer, telling us all about how he beat the Minions into a bloody pulp.

I felt Chris' hand on my cheek. We had been reigning in the affection out of deference to Autumn, so we hadn't been touching. He leaned close and whispered to me, "I miss him, too."

"Let's go home."

"Let's." We stood up and said our goodbyes.

60.

Sarah snapped shut her Bio book and stood up. "And I'm off. Time for my last final."

"See you in a few hours." Chris stood up to kiss her.

"With any luck it'll be less."

"Good luck then." He settled back on the sofa.

She waved at Chuck; he nodded back at her and went back to his Stats book. When she left, he looked up at Chris. "You two are so cute it's disgusting."

"Get used to it. This isn't changing anytime soon." He stretched on the sofa and went back to typing the quotes he intended to use for his paper. Ten minutes passed. Chuck got through two more practice problems and looked at his brother. He enjoyed seeing him relaxed and happy. For the first time in—hell, it had to be more than eighty years—Chris looked carefree and peaceful.

"You're thinking loudly at me," Chris said without looking up.

"I was trying to remember the last time you looked like that. The best I could come up with was before you were named successor."

"Sounds about right."

"What are you going to do without some sort of looming catastrophe or massive, world-altering decisions to make?"

"Find a job I'm half decent at, be the homebody I wanted to be, focus on being a good husband and father. I'm out of the massive, world-altering decision-making business. What are you going to do?"

"Hurford's called. I've got another job set up with them."

"When?"

"Things get bad there 'round about full moon time, so I'll be going in at new moon."

"Smart. I'm coming, too."

"Yep. Maybe I'll use some of the money as a stake in a poker tournament."

"You really should. Win a few of them and you're set."

"You keep telling me that. I'm thinking start small, stay with the low-value amateurs, nothing over ten thousand. The guys who win the big pots probably have my skills and actually know how to play."

"You could go to Vegas, hang out at the low buy in tables, work your way up."

"That's an idea. I'll have enough to pay for a flight and room. Want to come, too? Bring Sarah. If the three of us are at a table, we can clean out whoever else sits down without them knowing they've been played."

"That sounds pretty close to stealing."

"Still the luck of the draw. If he gets the cards, I can't beat him."

"You'll just read the other players?" Chris didn't sound like he believed Chuck wouldn't make a guy fold if it meant a big enough pot.

"Just read them. Promise. It'll be like Blackjack. You know what everyone else has. I've got the calculations down for the odds of any given card showing up on any given round. Besides, take her to Vegas, and maybe she'll marry you."

"Maybe. We haven't talked about that yet."

"Really?"

"Really. I've been carrying these around since the day after the fight," he handed the rings over to Chuck, "and I'm thinking tonight might be a good night to see about getting them out of my pocket and onto our hands."

Chuck looked them over. "Whoever made them did a good job. That looks much closer to our mark than your tattoo."

"I'm pleased with how they turned out, too. I think the stone is especially appropriate."

Chuck rested his finger on the fire opal. "It's got a good feel to it. You can't tell when you get them online, but that one's pretty sweet."

"Pat would have approved."

"Eventually. Have you had the chance to really say goodbye to him yet?"

"Yesterday. She had a long final. I took advantage of the alone time. We should have told him… should have let him decide to join or not on his own."

"So he could have killed you then, as opposed to trying to do it now?"

Chris sighed, closed his eyes, and tried to push the oppressive guilt aside. Some things couldn't be forgiven, only endured, and that would be one of the big sins on his list for the rest of his life. He wrote for a few minutes, then asked Chuck, "Did Autumn get home okay?"

"To the best of my knowledge, yes. I dropped her off in what looked like just another random bit of forest, watched her walk in, then she vanished."

"Good. I hope she's happy back there."

They went back to studying for a few minutes. Then Chuck looked up at the clock. "I told Mike I'd help him get packed up and give him a lift to the bus station."

Chris put down his computer. "I'll give you a hand. He helped me get moved, the least I can do is give him a hand, too."

We were sitting on my sofa reading after dinner. He had a glass of wine in one hand and a book of poems in the other. I had my copy of *Monstrous Regiment* in one hand and stroked his foot with the other. I felt him watching me over the edge of the book and looked up.

"Let's get married."

The flash of romance with those words was thrilling. At the same time, lounging on the sofa was not precisely the way I had envisioned this moment. I smiled and said, "You really hate that naked finger, don't you?"

He laughed. "I'm serious. We could go get the license tomorrow and be married before I go home. I could bring you home to meet my family as my wife."

"If you think they're going to have heart failure at you living with me, what do you think is going to happen when you come home with a Jewish wife, especially since they still don't know you've got a girlfriend?"

"They'd probably be happier with me eloping than living in sin."

I smiled at him, keeping my voice light. "Tough cookies. I'm getting married to a Jew, under a Chuppa, with my family, and preferably yours, there."

"That means waiting for years."

"What's your hurry?"

He put his glass down and knelt on the floor next to me, holding both of my hands in his. His eyes held mine and his voice caressed me as he spoke: "I want to give you my life, wrap it around yours, and bind us to each other for the rest of our days. You're my soul. I know it, you know it, and I want the rest of the world to know it as well."

That was much closer to what I had been hoping for. A smile spread across my face as joy flowed through me. I looked down at my hands. He caressed my fingers with his.

"You know, there is a symbolic piece of jewelry that goes with that sort of statement. Something to show the world the girl in question is off the market."

"You're right. There is. Do you want a ring? Two rings? Six rings? Can I dress you in diamonds and rubies and gold and platinum?"

If it was possible, my smile spread wider. "How about one ring?"

"How about this ring?" From somewhere he had managed to conjure a small band of gold. He laid it on my palm. Its weight surprisingly solid for such a delicate ring. I picked it up to look at it. It was a fine filigree pattern that resembled the leaf work on his tattoo. Cupped between two of the leaves was a small oval fire opal that glowed gold and red.

"I had meant it as a wedding ring, but it will do for an engagement as well." I looked at the ring in my hand. His mark, his history, made metal and offered to me as a promise of a life together. The stone seemed to glow brighter as I held it though I could feel there wasn't any magic to it, yet. The ring and the promise it symbolized felt overwhelmingly right.

"Do you have a matching one?"

He fished a larger one out of his pocket. His didn't have a stone, but the leaf work was the same. "You don't think I'd ask you to marry me without having the rings handy?"

I took his ring out of his hand and spun it between my fingers, looking at all the sides of it. I took his left hand in mine and slipped his ring on, awash in golden satisfaction of doing something so intensely perfect. I gave him my ring. He lifted my left hand to his lips, lightly kissed my wrist, and put my ring on my finger. He held my left hand in his, palm to palm, his fingers resting on my wrist, mine on his. I felt his heart beat under my fingers and realized mine beat in synch with his.

"As long as we both shall live," I said to him, knowing those were the exact right words for this moment. I felt the magic gathering around us. I knew he had called it. I mimicked him, bringing my own magic to us. I focused it on my hand, on my life, and through my life into his. I could feel him do the same.

"As long as we both shall live," he said back.

The magic whirled around us, coalesced, binding us to each other more surely than any words or paper ever could or would.

"I love you." His eyes and lips were warm with happiness.

"I know. I love you, too. Take me to bed?"

"Yes." His entire person beamed happiness.

It finally made sense, why you'd wait for this, why you'd reserve it for only one person. Each stroke cemented us to each other. Each touch melded my life to his. Spent and twined together in our bed I knew we'd end our days together. Soul bound, life bound, magic bound, two flesh made into one soul.

I could feel joy radiating off of him like the heat from his skin. If I had to guess, I'd say I was glowing with it, too.

"I understand why you wanted this."

"Good." He rolled to his side and kissed my knee. "Worth the rush?"

"Yes." I lifted my head off of his thigh to look him in the eye. "I still want a real wedding at some point."

"So do I, but this feels immensely good."

"Yes, it does." My head sank back down to his thigh. I closed my eyes, concentrating on the feel of his leg hair against my cheek. "Forever, huh?"

"As long as we both shall live."

We didn't get out of bed much the next three days. Time got fuzzy, measured in touch, naps, and occasional meals. The fourth time his cell phone rang in what seemed to be a short span of time broke the spell.

I listened to his half of the conversation while getting us some more food. When he sat down to eat, I asked, "Was that your brother?"

"Yeah. Time for me to go… I almost said home. This is home. Go back to my parents' house."

"How long?"

"Tomorrow's the tenth. My birthday is the fifteenth. I was thinking I'd go home, tell them, and you could come for my birthday. Get to know them. Then we'd come home."

"Sounds good. Wait, it's the ninth?"

"Must be."

"Fuck." I went to my cell phone. "I had it on silent. There's twelve calls from yesterday."

"We missed your birthday, didn't we?"

"Missed the Sabbath again, too. You eat. I've got to call my brothers before they send out the Mounties to find me."

"At least we weren't working this week."

"Yeah, but it's not like we were praying, either."

"You might not have been, but I certainly remember calling out God's name a few times."

I laughed and dialed my brothers' number. For the next hour I wove creative lies to explain why I was away from my phone all day yesterday and most of today. Dave and Sam bought it. Ben laughed at me and asked if I had finally tired my new husband out.

"How do you know that?"

"I can feel you glowing from here. I'd think anyone even remotely tuned into you could do it, too."

"Wonderful."

"So, it was a happy birthday?"

"It was a happy day. I didn't realize it was my birthday until about forty-five minutes ago."

He laughed again. "Is your ring pretty?"

"Yes, it is."

"Good. Bring him home again soon."

"Will do."

Tom looked surprised to find Chris had just his backpack with him. Or maybe he was surprised to be picking him up from my place. Possibly it was that he very clearly now lived at my place. Or it could have been the very long and passionate kiss he gave me before I walked them out to the car. Whatever it was, Tom looked like he had never really seen Chris before by the time they got to the car.

Tom got in. Chris turned and kissed me one more time. "I'll see you in four days."

"Good. How do you think they'll take it?"

"Badly. I still can't convince you to marry me this weekend? We could get a license today and find someone to say the words by Sunday."

"Nope. It'll be under a Chuppa, with my family and yours there."

"Assuming they're still speaking to me."

"They will be." He gave me a long kiss and got into the car with Tom. I waved, and they drove off.

They were a few blocks down Main Street when Tom said, "You know the car isn't soundproof, right?"

"I do now."

"So, you went from 'she's not my girlfriend' to 'we're living together and engaged' in less than six months?"

"Yes."

"You need middle gears." Chris didn't respond. "You going to tell Mom and Dad?"

"I have to."

"No, you don't."

"Yes, I do. Beyond the fact lying about it would be wrong, they'll get suspicious when there's no room or board bill from the school."

"Well, that'll be a fun conversation. On the upside, I doubt anyone will care I'm getting a D in French."

"I think you can safely say I've saved you from getting chewed out about that."

They drove several more miles and got on the interstate. Tom looked over at him. "So, when?"

"When what?"

"When are you getting married?"

"Couple years. She won't marry me until I convert."

"Convert to what?"

"She's Jewish."

"Oh, God." Chris didn't have anything to say to that, either.

They drove for a few more miles in silence. Tom looked over at his hand. "I get her wearing a ring. Why are you?"

The truth really wasn't going to work for that question. "Because I'm just as much hers as she is mine. It's not a one-sided promise."

"After less than six months? Seriously, you need middle gears."

Chris thought about his relationship with Sarah from the outside. "It really does sound ridiculously stupid, doesn't it?"

"Yes. So help me out, make me see it as not stupid. If you can't do it for me, imagine how much fun Mom and Dad will be." Tom switched to his mom's voice, "'Chris,' [hug, hug] 'How was your trip? Is that a new ring?'"

"Fuck. There's no way to do this without sounding like a petulant teenager. *But we're in love!*" Tom laughed at the whiny tone Chris used for that last bit. Chris rubbed his eyebrows and shook his head. "There's nothing to say that won't sound stupid. When we celebrate our tenth anniversary, I hope you'll be there. That's probably what I'll say to them, too."

"She's not pregnant is she?"

"No! We'd be getting married a lot faster if she was pregnant. Like, yesterday, faster."

"Okay." Tom thought about it for a few more minutes. "They'll cut you off."

"I know. It's appropriate. I'm telling them I'm enough of a grown-up to stand on my own and start my own family. You can't do that if Mom and Dad are still paying for you."

"Will you drop out?"

"No. Most of the loans are already on my head anyway. I've got almost enough saved to pick up what they would have paid, and I think she can swing the rest. I will be job hunting as soon as I get back."

"Good luck."

"Thanks."

"What about her family?"

"Her brothers like me. Ben, the oldest one, is in favor of the match. Once I convert, I'm golden."

"I suppose that's one good thing. How'd you convince him?"

There was another question where the truth really wasn't a good plan. "He knows his sister has impeccable taste."

Tom snorted. "How are you going to tell them?"

"I don't suppose you'd burst into the house and tell them I'm engaged?"

"Might be fun." Tom smiled at him.

"Or I can wait for Mom to notice the new ring."

"I'll burst in. Might as well get it done fast. How long were you planning on staying after?"

"Not more than four days, possibly less if it goes very badly. She's planning on picking me up on the fifteenth."

"What's...? Oh, she's coming for your birthday party."

"That's the idea."

"So, tell me about my sister-in-law."

After Chris left, I headed across campus to go see Morrell. I wanted to know if he had any interest in keeping up the lessons over the summer. He was in his office reading something in Greek when I knocked on his door.

"Sarah. What brings you here?" He waved me in.

"I was wondering if you'd like to keep up the language lessons over the summer?"

"I would. I've enjoyed our conversations."

"So have I."

He stood up, closed the door to his office, and turned to me. He kissed me on each cheek. "It seems congratulations are in order."

"It seems they are."

"When did you two cast the binding?"

"This would be day four. He's heading home to tell his Catholic parents about us."

"Sounds like fun." This was the first time I had heard Morrell be sarcastic. He did it well, with a nicely dry flair.

"I'm not envying him tonight."

"Have they met you yet?"

"No. In a little less than a week I'll be heading over to meet them."

"I'm assuming they don't know about his magic?"

"No, they don't."

"Even better. That will be an interesting conversation for your beloved. If I had a twenty-one-year-old come home and tell me he was engaged to a woman he's been dating for less than three months, I'd want to lock him in his room and never let him out again. His best 'I'm not an idiot' argument is the kind of binding you're wearing can't be cast on a whim. It doesn't work without real attachment and commitment. *Twu wuv* won't work for that magic."

"Well, I imagine one thing might possibly horrify them worse than 'Oh, by the way, I'm living with a Jewish woman, and after I convert we're getting married,' and that would be, 'And I'm magically soul bound to her.'" Morrell nodded.

"After you bring him home, can Claire and I take you out to celebrate?"

"Yes. I'd like that very much."

W hen I got home, I found a shoe box sitting on our bed. I didn't remember it being there when I left and couldn't tell if he had magically cloaked it, or I just hadn't noticed it. I lifted the lid off and found a small bit of folded paper on top of a pile of tissue paper. Chris had written one word. *Anticipation.* Under the tissue paper lay a bottle of lube, the small, thin vibrator, and four of his ties. *Oh my.* I inhaled quickly and licked my lips. I replaced the lid, and put the box in my sock drawer.

The next few hours I spent online looking for a summer job. One looked promising. It wasn't precisely a summer job, but if it could work around school, I'd be perfect for it. Cochranton, the next town over, needed an EMT. If anyone could do the job, it was me. While getting a résumé and cover letter ready, I realized I had to physically mail the information. I looked around, saw I didn't have any stamps, and put the papers on the kitchen table with a mental note to go pick some up at the post office Monday morning.

I made myself dinner, wondering what Chris was doing. He told me he'd text when he got a chance.

I was in bed, looking at an early night when I heard my phone chirp.

Hi.

How'd it go?

'Bout as well as I expected. Not good.

Are they still speaking to you?

Yes. Yelling at me. Tom tells me to tell you thanks. He's got a free pass on his grades now.

He's welcome. That was, of course, my master plan.

Of course. Did you find my present?

Yes I did. Happily anticipating away over here.

Good. It feels very strange to be laying in my bed alone here.

I miss you, too. So, will I get to meet them? Or am I spiriting you away in the dead of night?

Nothing that dramatic. As of this point the party is still on, and you are invited.

That's good.

I can feel them debating cutting me off. Mom's afraid I'll drop out. Dad doesn't care.

Who'll win?

Dad. He's telling my mom that if I want to finish school I can enlist and do the GI Bill like my brothers.

I don't think we need to do anything that drastic. How much?

I've got 6k in the bank. I think they pay about 9k most years.

I can make up the rest.

I'll pay you back.

Ummm… weren't you intending we'd merge finances at some point?

Yes. Don't want to be a kept man.

But you'd be a cute gigolo.

Thanks. Still, I should be contributing something to this.

You are. Besides in a year you'll be working full-time, and I'll still have at least five, maybe ten, years of school left. You'll have ample time to make it up to me.

You have no idea how much I'm looking forward to doing that.

☺

Emoticons! Ohhh…

What were you intending to do with the content of that package?

My phone rang.

"No way I'm going to text that. Especially not when my brother's on a date and won't be home anytime soon."

Turned out that wasn't an early night after all.

I finished my jog by heading by the post office to see when it opened. Nine. Two hours to kill before I could send off my résumé.

Shower, breakfast, more job hunting. I checked the clock and headed off a few minutes early. I wanted to get it in the mail.

I stood outside the doors waiting for the mail ladies to let me in. I bought ten stamps, stuck one of them on the envelope, and tossed it through the slot.

I hadn't checked my mailbox at the college since before Pat died. I hadn't been very good about it to begin with, only checking mine when he checked his. In the last few weeks there just hadn't been any reason to go.

I glanced at his box, saw it was full, and walked over to tell the postal ladies his mail needed to be forwarded to his parents' house. Like any good bureaucrats they told me there was nothing they could do without word from his parents. I asked if I could send it to them. They said no.

I walked to my box, muttering under my breath, and rolling my eyes. *Idiot twits.*

It took a good minute before I remembered the combination. When I got the box open, I cleaned it out. Not too much in there. Mostly junk. Pretty much everyone who I wanted to contact me knew to send mail to my apartment. But, in between the credit card ads and the pizza coupons there was a small pink slip that meant I had a package at the desk.

Back to the mail ladies. I handed over the slip, and they fished around for a while before coming up with an oversized envelope.

I took it with curiosity. My heart stopped and then raced. I knew that angular, slanted handwriting. It was Pat's. The envelope was light in my hands and cold. I ran trembling, excitement and curiosity tingling through my skin, back to my apartment. Once inside, I tore open the envelope.

Dear Sarah,

Maybe you'll thank me for this. Maybe you'll hate me.

I love you.

I loved you then.

You were right.

There was a symbol on the page. It meant nothing to me. Just squiggles and loops. Then I felt the magic, and it did mean something. A word rang in my mind. I had heard it once before. Althiira. Pat had spoken it. He called me it. It was a name. It was my name.

Then I knew. In a rush of rage and sorrow I knew. I had been Althiira. I held my children close and burned with them when my world died. I abandoned my husband, the man I loved more than my life because I could not love him more than the three hundred million lives of our people, let alone the four lives of our children. With my last breath I called out to Mjur, "Lord, hear my prayer. Grant me Justice!"

Afterword

And with that we must leave Chris, Sarah, Chuck, and Autumn. They'll be back. Justice, the next book in the series is being written.

Sylvianna is the first of a trilogy. Justice, which picks up where Sylvianna left off, should be out by fall of 2012. One Hundred Years, the tale of how Cell and Althiira met, fell in love, and the war, will wrap up this series.

I've chosen to self publish these books for numerous reasons. (More on that can be read at my blog: www.topublishornotto.blogspot.com.) What that means as a practical matter is this: the only way anyone will learn about this book is if people who liked it spread the word. I'm guessing if you're still reading, you liked this book. So please, write a review of it, and post it anywhere that will let you post a review. If you're on Facebook or Twitter, please link to this book.

Updates, sneak peeks, links to the music in this book, recipes, and various bits of art will be going up on my website, www.kerylraist.com. Please come visit.

Thanks for reading.

Keryl Raist
Charleston, SC 2010

Made in the USA
Lexington, KY
10 August 2011